# THE BEST OF GENE WOLFE

# THE BEST OF GENE WOLFE

## A DEFINITIVE RETROSPECTIVE OF HIS FINEST SHORT FICTION

## GENE WOLFE

A TOM DOHERTY ASSOCIATES BOOK
NEW YORK

THE BEST OF GENE WOLFE: A DEFINITIVE RETROSPECTIVE OF HIS FINEST SHORT FICTION

Copyright © 2009 by Gene Wolfe

A Tor Book
Published by Tom Doherty Associates, LLC
175 Fifth Avenue
New York, NY 10010

www.tor-forge.com

Tor® is a registered trademark of Tom Doherty Associates, LLC.

ISBN-13: 978-0-7653-2135-0
ISBN-10: 0-7653-2135-1

First Edition: March 2009

Printed in the United States of America

0  9  8  7  6  5  4  3  2  1

This book is for Alison Goulding,
with much love from her gran'pa.

# CONTENTS

# THE BEST OF GENE WOLFE

# The Island of Doctor Death
## and Other Stories

❧

Winter comes to water as well as land, though there are no leaves to
fall. The waves that were a bright, hard blue yesterday under a fading sky today are green, opaque, and cold. If you are a boy not
wanted in the house you walk the beach for hours, feeling the winter that has
come in the night; sand blowing across your shoes, spray wetting the legs of your
corduroys. You turn your back to the sea, and with the sharp end of a stick found
half-buried write in the wet sand *Tackman Babcock*.

Then you go home, knowing that behind you the Atlantic is destroying your
work.

Home is the big house on Settlers Island, but Settlers Island, so called, is not
really an island and for that reason is not named or accurately delineated on maps.
Smash a barnacle with a stone and you will see inside the shape from which the
beautiful barnacle goose takes its name. There is a thin and flaccid organ which is
the goose's neck and the mollusc's siphon, and a shapeless body with tiny wings.
Settlers Island is like that.

The goose neck is a strip of land down which a county road runs. By whim,
the mapmakers usually exaggerate the width of this and give no information to
indicate that it is scarcely above the high tide. Thus Settlers Island appears to be
a mere protuberance on the coast, not requiring a name—and since the village of
eight or ten houses has none, nothing shows on the map but the spider line of
road terminating at the sea.

The village has no name, but home has two: a near and a far designation.
On the island, and on the mainland nearby, it is called the Seaview place because
in the earliest years of the century it was operated as a resort hotel. Mama calls
it The House of 31 February, and that is on her stationery and is presumably
used by her friends in New York and Philadelphia when they do not simply
say "Mrs. Babcock's." Home is four floors high in some places, less in others,
and is completely surrounded by a veranda; it was once painted yellow, but

the paint—outside—is mostly gone now and The House of 31 February is gray.

Jason comes out the front door with the little curly hairs on his chin trembling in the wind and his thumbs hooked in the waistband of his Levi's. "Come on; you're going into town with me. Your mother wants to rest."

"Hey tough!" Into Jason's Jaguar, feeling the leather upholstery soft and smelly; you fall asleep.

Awake in town, bright lights flashing in the car windows. Jason is gone and the car is growing cold; you wait for what seems a long time, looking out at the shop windows, the big gun on the hip of the policeman who walks past, the lost dog who is afraid of everyone, even you when you tap the glass and call to him.

Then Jason is back with packages to put behind the seat. "Are we going home now?"

He nods without looking at you, arranging his bundles so they won't topple over, fastening his seat belt.

"I want to get out of the car."

He looks at you.

"I want to go in a store. Come on, Jason."

Jason sighs. "All right, the drugstore over there, okay? Just for a minute."

The drugstore is as big as a supermarket, with long, bright aisles of glassware and notions and paper goods. Jason buys fluid for his lighter at the cigarette counter, and you bring him a book from a revolving wire rack. "Please, Jason?"

He takes it from you and replaces it in the rack, then when you are in the car again takes it from under his jacket and gives it to you.

It is a wonderful book, thick and heavy, with the edges of the pages tinted yellow. The covers are glossy stiff cardboard, and on the front is a picture of a man in rags fighting a thing partly like an ape and partly like a man, but much worse than either. The picture is in color, and there is real blood on the ape-thing; the man is muscular and handsome, with tawny hair lighter than Jason's and no beard.

"You like that?"

You are out of town already, and without the streetlights it's too dark in the car, almost, to see the picture. You nod.

Jason laughs. "That's camp. Did you know that?"

You shrug, riffling the pages under your thumb, thinking of reading, alone, in your room tonight.

"You going to tell your mom how nice I was to you?"

"Uh-huh, sure. You want me to?"

"Tomorrow, not tonight. I think she'll be asleep when we get back. Don't you wake her up." Jason's voice says he will be angry if you do.

"Okay."

"Don't come in her room."

"Okay."

The Jaguar says *hutntntaaa . . .* down the road, and you can see the white-caps in the moonlight now, and the driftwood pushed just off the asphalt.

"You got a nice, soft mommy, you know that? When I climb on her it's just like being on a big pillow."

You nod, remembering the times when, lonely and frightened by dreams, you have crawled into her bed and snuggled against her soft warmth—but at the same time angry, knowing Jason is somehow deriding you both.

Home is silent and dark, and you leave Jason as soon as you can, bounding off down the hall and up the stairs ahead of him, up a second, narrow, twisted flight to your own room in the turret.

I had this story from a man who was breaking his word in telling it. How much it has suffered in his hands—I should say in his mouth, rather—I cannot say. In essentials it is true, and I give it to you as it was given to me. This is the story he told.

Captain Phillip Ransom had been adrift, alone, for nine days when he saw the island. It was already late evening when it appeared like a thin line of purple on the horizon, but Ransom did not sleep that night. There was no feeble questioning in his wakeful mind concerning the reality of what he had seen; he had been given that one glimpse and he knew. Instead his brain teemed with facts and speculations. He knew he must be somewhere near New Guinea, and he reviewed mentally what he knew of the currents in these waters and what he had learned in the past nine days of the behavior of his raft. The island when he reached it—he did not allow himself to *if*—would in all probability be solid jungle a few feet back from the water's edge. There might or might not be natives, but he brought to mind all he could of the Bazaar Malay and Tagalog he had acquired in his years as a pilot, plantation manager, white hunter, and professional fighting man in the Pacific.

In the morning he saw that purple shadow on the horizon again, a little nearer this time and almost precisely where his mental calculations had told him to expect it. For nine days there had been no reason to employ the inadequate paddles provided with the raft, but now he had something to row for. Ransom drank the last of his water and began stroking with a steady and powerful beat which was not interrupted until the prow of his rubber craft ground into beach sand.

**M**orning. You are slowly awake. Your eyes feel gummy, and the light over your bed is still on. Downstairs there is no one, so you get a bowl and milk and puffed, sugary cereal out for yourself and light the oven with a kitchen match so that you can eat and read by its open door. When the cereal is gone you drink the sweet milk and crumbs in the bottom of the bowl and start a pot of coffee, knowing that will please Mother. Jason comes down, dressed but not wanting to talk; drinks coffee and makes one piece of cinnamon toast in the oven. You listen to him leave, the stretched buzzing of his car on the road, then go up to Mother's room.

She is awake, her eyes open looking at the ceiling, but you know she isn't ready to get up yet. Very politely, because that minimizes the chances of being shouted at, you say, "How are you feeling this morning, Mama?"

She rolls her head to look. "Strung out. What time is it, Tackie?"

You look at the little folding clock on her dresser. "Seventeen minutes after eight."

"Jason go?"

"Yes, just now, Mama."

She is looking at the ceiling again. "You go back downstairs now, Tackie. I'll get you something when I feel better."

Downstairs you put on your sheepskin coat and go out on the veranda to look at the sea. There are gulls riding the icy wind, and very far off something orange bobbing in the waves, always closer.

A life raft. You run to the beach, jump up and down, and wave your cap. "Over here. Over here."

The man from the raft has no shirt, but the cold doesn't seem to bother him. He holds out his hand and says, "Captain Ransom," and you take it and are suddenly taller and older; not as tall as he is or as old as he is, but taller and older than yourself. "Tackman Babcock, Captain."

"Pleased to meet you. You were a friend in need there a minute ago."

"I guess I didn't do anything but welcome you ashore."

"The sound of your voice gave me something to steer for while my eyes were too busy watching that surf. Now you can tell me where I've landed and who you are."

You are walking back up to the house now, and you explain to Ransom about you and Mother, and how she doesn't want to enroll you in the school here because she is trying to get you into the private school your father went to once. And after a time there is nothing more to say, and you show Ransom one of the empty rooms on the third floor where he can rest and do whatever he wants. Then you go back to your own room to read.

"Do you mean that you *made* these monsters?"

"*Made* them?" Dr. Death leaned forward, a cruel smile playing about his lips. "Did God *make* Eve, Captain, when he took her from Adam's rib? Or did Adam make the bone and God *alter* it to become what he wished? Look at it this way, Captain. I am God and Nature is Adam."

Ransom looked at the thing who grasped his right arm with hands that might have circled a utility pole as easily. "Do you mean that this thing is an animal?"

"Not an animal," the monster said, wrenching his arm cruelly. "Man."

Dr. Death's smile broadened. "Yes, Captain, man. The question is, what are you? When I'm finished with you we'll see. Dulling your mind will be less of a problem than upgrading these poor brutes; but what about increasing the efficacy of your sense of smell? Not to mention rendering it impossible for you to walk erect."

"*Not* to walk all-four-on-ground," the beast-man holding Ransom muttered, "*that* is the *law.*"

Dr. Death turned and called to the shambling hunchback Ransom had seen earlier, "Colo, see to it that Captain Ransom is securely put away; then prepare the surgery."

A car. Not Jason's noisy Jaguar, but a quiet, large-sounding car. By heaving up the narrow, tight little window at the corner of the turret and sticking your head out into the cold wind you can see it: Dr. Black's big one, with the roof and hood all shiny with new wax.

Downstairs Dr. Black is hanging up an overcoat with a collar of fur, and you smell the old cigar smoke in his clothing before you see him; then Aunt May and Aunt Julie are there to keep you occupied so that he won't be reminded too vividly that marrying Mama means getting you as well. They talk to you: "How have you been, Tackie? What do you find to do out here all day?"

"Nothing."

"Nothing? Don't you ever go looking for shells on the beach?"

"I guess so."

"You're a handsome boy; do you know that?" Aunt May touches your nose with a scarlet-tipped finger and holds it there.

Aunt May is Mother's sister, but older and not as pretty. Aunt Julie is Papa's sister, a tall lady with a pulled-out, unhappy face, and makes you think of him even when you know she only wants Mama to get married again so that Papa won't have to send her any more money.

Mama herself is downstairs now in a clean new dress with long sleeves. She laughs at Dr. Black's jokes and holds on to his arm, and you think how nice her hair looks and that you will tell her so when you are alone. Dr. Black says, "How about it, Barbara, are you ready for the party?" and Mother, "Heavens no. You know what this place is like—yesterday I spent all day cleaning and today you can't even see what I did. But Julie and May will help me."

Dr. Black laughs. "After lunch."

You get into his big car with the others and go to a restaurant on the edge of a cliff, with a picture window to see the ocean. Dr. Black orders a sandwich for you that has turkey and bacon and three pieces of bread, but you are finished before the grown-ups have started, and when you try to talk to Mother, Aunt May sends you out to where there is a railing with wire to fill in the spaces like chicken wire, only heavier, to look at the view.

It is really not much higher than the top window at home. Maybe a little higher. You put the toes of your shoes in the wire and bend out with your stomach against the rail to look down, but a grown-up pulls you down and tells you not to do it, then goes away. You do it again, and there are rocks at the bottom which the waves wash over in a neat way, covering them up and then pulling back. Someone touches your elbow, but you pay no attention for a minute, watching the water.

Then you get down, and the man standing beside you is Dr. Death.

He has a white scarf and black leather gloves and his hair is shiny black. His face is not tanned like Captain Ransom's but white, and handsome in a different way like the statue of a head that used to be in Papa's library when you and Mother used to live in town with him, and you think: *Mama would say after he was gone how good-looking he was*. He smiles at you, but you are no older.

"Hi." What else can you say?

"Good afternoon, Mr. Babcock. I'm afraid I startled you."

You shrug. "A little bit. I didn't expect you to be here, I guess."

Dr. Death turns his back to the wind to light a cigarette he takes from a gold case. It is longer even than a 101 and has a red tip, and a gold dragon on the paper. "While you were looking down, I slipped from between the pages of the excellent novel you have in your coat pocket."

"I didn't know you could do that."

"Oh, yes. I'll be around from time to time."

"Captain Ransom is here already. He'll kill you."

Dr. Death smiles and shakes his head. "Hardly. You see, Tackman, Ransom and I are a bit like wrestlers; under various guises we put on our show again and again—but only under the spotlight." He flicks his cigarette over the rail and for a moment your eyes follow the bright spark out and down and see it vanish in the water. When you look back, Dr. Death is gone, and you are getting cold. You go back into the restaurant and get a free mint candy where the cash register is and then go to sit beside Aunt May again in time to have coconut cream pie and hot chocolate.

Aunt May drops out of the conversation long enough to ask, "Who was that man you were talking to, Tackie?"

"A man."

In the car Mama sits close to Dr. Black, with Aunt Julie on the other side of her so she will have to, and Aunt May sits way up on the edge of her seat with her head in between theirs so they can all talk. It is gray and cold outside; you think of how long it will be before you are home again, and take the book out.

Ransom heard them coming and flattened himself against the wall beside the door of his cell. There was no way out, he knew, save through that iron portal.

For the past four hours he had been testing every surface of the stone room for a possible exit, and there was none. Floor, walls, and ceiling were of cyclopean stone blocks; the windowless door of solid metal locked outside.

Nearer. He tensed every muscle and knotted his fists.

Nearer. The shambling steps halted. There was a rattle of keys and the door swung back. Like a thunderbolt of purpose he dived through the opening. A hideous face loomed above him and he sent his right fist crashing into it, knocking the lumbering beast-man to his knees. Two hairy arms pinioned him from behind, but he fought free and the monster reeled under his blows. The corridor stretched ahead of him with a dim glow of daylight at the end and he sprinted for it. Then—darkness!

When he recovered consciousness he found himself already erect, strapped to the wall of a brilliantly lit room which seemed to share the characters of a surgical theater and a chemical laboratory. Directly before his eyes stood a bulky object which he knew must be an operating table, and upon it, covered with a sheet, lay the unmistakable form of a human being.

He had hardly had time to comprehend the situation when Dr. Death entered, no longer in the elegant evening dress in which Ransom had beheld him last, but wearing white surgical clothing. Behind him limped the hideous Golo, carrying a tray of implements.

"Ah!" Seeing that his prisoner was conscious, Dr. Death strolled across the room and raised a hand as though to strike him in the face, but, when Ransom did not flinch, dropped it, smiling. "My dear Captain! You are with us again, I see."

"I hoped for a minute there," Ransom said levelly, "that I was away from you. Mind telling me what got me?"

"A thrown club, or so my slaves report. My baboon-man is quite good at it. But aren't you going to ask about this charming little tableau I've staged for you?"

"I wouldn't give you the pleasure."

"But you are curious." Dr. Death smiled his crooked smile. "I shall not keep you in suspense. Your own time, Captain, has not come yet; and before it does I am going to demonstrate my technique to you. It is so seldom that I have a really appreciative audience." With a calculated gesture he whipped away the sheet which had covered the prone form on the operating table.

Ransom could scarcely believe his eyes. Before him lay the unconscious body of a girl, a girl with skin as white as milk and hair like the sun seen through mist.

"You are interested now, I see," Dr. Death remarked drily, "and you consider her beautiful. Believe me, when I have completed my work you will flee screaming if she so much as turns what will no longer be a face toward you. This woman has been my implacable enemy since I came to this island, and the time has come for me to"—he halted in midsentence and looked at Ransom with an expression of mingled slyness and gloating—"for me to illustrate something of your own fate, shall we say."

While Dr. Death had been talking his deformed assistant had prepared a hypodermic. Ransom watched as the needle plunged into the girl's almost translucent flesh, and the liquid in the syringe—a fluid which by its very color suggested the vile perversion of medical technique—entered her bloodstream. Though still unconscious the girl sighed, and it seemed to Ransom that a cloud passed over her sleeping face as though she had already begun an evil dream. Roughly the hideous Golo turned her on her back and fastened in place straps of the same kind as those that held Ransom himself pinned to the wall.

"What are you reading, Tackie?" Aunt May asked.

"Nothing." He shut the book.

"Well, you shouldn't read in the car. It's bad for your eyes."

Dr. Black looked back at them for a moment, then asked Mama, "Have you gotten a costume for the little fellow yet?"

"For Tackie?" Mama shook her head, making her beautiful hair shine even in the dim light of the car. "No, nothing. It will be past his bedtime."

"Well, you'll have to let him see the guests anyway, Barbara; no boy should miss that."

And then the car was racing along the road out to Settlers Island. And then you were home.

Ransom watched as the loathsome creature edged toward him. Though it was not as large as some of the others its great teeth looked formidable indeed, and in one hand it grasped a heavy jungle knife with a razor edge.

For a moment he thought it would molest the unconscious girl, but it circled around her to stand before Ransom himself, never meeting his eyes.

Then, with a gesture as unexpected as it was frightening, it bent suddenly to press its hideous face against his pinioned right hand, and a great, shuddering gasp ran through the creature's twisted body.

Ransom waited, tense.

Again that deep inhalation, seeming almost a sob. Then the beast-man straightened up, looking into Ransom's face but avoiding his gaze. A thin, strangely familiar whine came from the monster's throat.

"Cut me loose," Ransom ordered.

"Yes. This I came to. Yes, Master." The huge head, wider than it was high, bobbed up and down. Then the sharp blade of the machete bit into the straps holding Ransom. As soon as he was free he took the blade from the willing hand of the beast-man and freed the limbs of the girl on the operating table. She was light in his arms, and for an instant he stood looking down at her tranquil face.

"Come, Master." The beast-man pulled at his sleeve. "Bruno knows a way out. Follow Bruno."

A hidden flight of steps led to a long and narrow corridor, almost pitch-dark. "No one use this way," the beast-man said in his harsh voice. "They not find us here."

"Why did you free me?" Ransom asked.

There was a pause; then almost with an air of shame the great, twisted form replied, "You smell good. And Bruno does not like Dr. Death."

Ransom's conjectures were confirmed. Gently he asked, "You were a dog before Dr. Death worked on you, weren't you, Bruno?"

"Yes." The beast-man's voice held a sort of pride. "A St. Bernard. I have seen pictures."

"Dr. Death should have known better than to employ his foul skills on such a noble animal," Ransom reflected aloud. "Dogs are too shrewd in judging character; but then the evil are always foolish in the final analysis."

Unexpectedly the dog-man halted in front of him, forcing Ransom to stop too. For a moment the massive head bent over the unconscious girl. Then there was a barely audible growl. "You say, Master, that I can judge. Then I tell you Bruno does not like this female Dr. Death calls Talar of the Long Eyes."

You put the open book facedown on the pillow and jump up, hugging yourself and skipping bare heels around the room. Marvelous! Wonderful!

But no more reading tonight. Save it; save it. Turn the light off, and in the delicious dark put the book reverently away under the bed, pushing aside pieces of the Tinkertoy set and the box with the filling station game cards. Tomorrow there will be more, and you can hardly wait for tomorrow. You lie on your back, hands under head, covers up to chin, and when you close your eyes you can see it all: the island, with jungle trees swaying in the sea wind; Dr. Death's castle lifting its big, cold grayness against the hot sky.

The whole house is still; only the wind and the Atlantic are out, the familiar sounds. Downstairs Mother is talking to Aunt May and Aunt Julie and you fall asleep.

You are awake! Listen! Late, it's very late, a strange time you have almost forgotten. Listen!

So quiet it hurts. Something. Something. Listen!

On the steps.

You get out of bed and find your flashlight. Not because you are brave, but because you cannot wait there in the dark.

There is nothing in the narrow, cold little stairwell outside your door. Nothing in the big hallway of the second floor. You shine your light quickly from end to end. Aunt Julie is breathing through her nose, but there is nothing frightening about that sound; you know what it is: only Aunt Julie, asleep, breathing loud through her nose.

Nothing on the stairs coming up.

You go back to your room, turn off your flashlight, and get into bed. When you are almost sleeping there is the scrabbling sound of hard claws on the floorboards and a rough tongue touching your fingertips. "Don't be afraid, Master; it is only Bruno." And you feel him, warm with his own warm and smelling of his own smell, lying beside your bed.

Then it is morning. The bedroom is cold, and there is no one in it but yourself. You go into the bathroom where there is a thing like a fan but with hot electric wires to dress.

Downstairs Mother is up already with a cloth thing tied over her hair, and so are Aunt May and Aunt Julie, sitting at the table with coffee and milk and big slices of fried ham. Aunt Julie says, "Hello, Tackie," and Mother smiles at you. There is a plate out for you already and you have ham and toast.

All day the three women are cleaning and putting up decorations—red and gold paper masks Aunt Julie made to hang on the wall, and funny lights that change color and go around—and you try to stay out of the way, and bring in wood for a fire in the big fireplace that almost never gets used. Jason comes, and Aunt May and Aunt Julie don't like him, but he helps some and goes into town in his car for things he forgot to buy before. He won't take you, this time. The wind comes in around the window, but they let you alone in your room and it's even quiet up there because they're all downstairs.

Ransom looked at the enigmatic girl incredulously.

"You do not believe me," she said. It was a simple statement of fact, without anger or accusation.

"You'll have to admit it's pretty hard to believe," he temporized. "A city older than civilization, buried in the jungle here on this little island."

Talar said tonelessly, "When you were as he"—she pointed at the dog-man—"is now, Lemuria was queen of this sea. All that is gone, except my city. Is not that enough to satisfy even Time?"

Bruno plucked at Ransom's sleeve. "Do not go, Master! Beast-men go sometimes, beast-men Dr. Death does not want; few come back. They are very evil at that place."

"You see?" A slight smile played about Talar's ripe lips. "Even your slave testifies for me. My city exists."

"How far?" Ransom asked curtly.

"Perhaps half a day's travel through the jungle." The girl paused, as though afraid to say more.

"What is it?" Ransom asked.

"You will lead us against Dr. Death? We wish to cleanse this island which is our home."

"Sure. I don't like him any more than your people do. Maybe less."

"Even if you do not like my people you will lead them?"

"If they'll have me. But you're hiding something. What is it?"

"You see me, and I might be a woman of your own people. Is that not so?" They were moving through the jungle again now, the dog-man reluctantly acting as rear guard.

"Very few girls of my people are as beautiful as you are, but otherwise yes."

"And for that reason I am high priestess to my people, for in me the ancient blood runs pure and sweet. But it is not so with all." Her voice sunk to a whisper. "When a tree is very old, and yet still lives, sometimes the limbs are strangely twisted. Do you understand?"

"Tackie? Tackie are you in there?"

"Uh-huh." You put the book inside your sweater.

"Well, come and open this door. Little boys ought not to lock their doors. Don't you want to see the company?" You open, and Aunt May's a gypsy with long hair that isn't hers around her face and a mask that is only at her eyes.

Downstairs cars are stopping in front of the house and Mother is standing at the door dressed in Day-Glo robes that open way down the front but cover her arms almost to the ends of her fingers. She is talking to everyone as they come in, and you see her eyes are bright and strange the way they are sometimes when she dances by herself and talks when no one is listening.

A woman with a fish for a head and a shiny, silver dress is Aunt Julie. A doctor with a doctor's coat and listening things and a shiny thing on his head to look through is Dr. Black, and a soldier in a black uniform with a pirate thing on his hat and a whip is Jason. The big table has a punch bowl and cakes and little sandwiches and hot bean dip. You pull away when the gypsy is talking to someone and take some cakes and sit under the table watching legs.

There is music and some of the legs dance, and you stay under there a long time.

Then a man's and a girl's legs dance close to the table and there is suddenly a laughing face in front of you—Captain Ransom's. "What are you doing under there, Tack? Come out and join the party." And you crawl out, feeling very small instead of older, but older when you stand up. Captain Ransom is dressed like a castaway in a ragged shirt and pants torn off at the knees, but all clean and starched. His love beads are seeds and seashells, and he has his arm around a girl with no clothes at all, just jewelry.

"Tack, this is Talar of the Long Eyes."

You smile and bow and kiss her hand, and are nearly as tall as she. All around people are dancing or talking, and no one seems to notice you. With Captain Ransom on one side of Talar and you on the other you thread your way through the room, avoiding the dancers and the little groups of people with drinks. In the room you and Mother use as a living room when there's no company, two men and two girls are making love with the television on, and in the little room past that a girl is sitting on the floor with her back to the wall, and men are standing in the corners. "Hello," the girl says. "Hello to you all." She is the first one to have noticed you, and you stop.

"Hello."

"I'm going to pretend you're real. Do you mind?"

"No." You look around for Ransom and Talar, but they are gone and you think that they are probably in the living room, kissing with the others.

"This is my third trip. Not a good trip, but not a bad trip. But I should have had a monitor—you know, someone to stay with me. Who are those men?"

The men in the corners stir, and you can hear the clinking of their armor and see light glinting on it and you look away. "I think they're from the City. They probably came to watch out for Talar," and somehow you know that this is the truth.

"Make them come out where I can see them."

Before you can answer, Dr. Death says, "I don't really think you would want to," and you turn and find him standing just behind you wearing full evening dress and a cloak. He takes your arm. "Come on, Tackie; there's something I think you should see." You follow him to the back stairs and then up, and along the hall to the door of Mother's room.

Mother is inside on the bed, and Dr. Black is standing over her filling a hypodermic. As you watch, he pushes up her sleeve so that all the other injection marks show ugly and red on her arm, and all you can think of is Dr. Death bending over Talar on the operating table. You run downstairs looking for Ransom, but he is gone and there is nobody at the party at all except the real people and, in the cold shadows of the back stoop, Dr. Death's assistant Golo, who will not speak, but only stares at you in the moonlight with pale eyes.

The next house down the beach belongs to a woman you have seen sometimes cutting down the dry fall remnant of her asparagus or hilling up her roses while you played. You pound at her door and try to explain, and after a while she calls the police.

> . . . across the sky. The flames were licking at the roof timbers now. Ransom made a megaphone of his hands and shouted, "Give up! You'll all be burned to death if you stay in there!" but the only reply was a shot and he was not certain they had heard him. The Lemurian bowmen discharged another flight of arrows at the windows.
>
> Talar grasped his arm: "Come back before they kill you."
>
> Numbly he retreated with her, stepping across the massive body of the bull-man, which lay pierced by twenty or more shafts.

You fold back the corner of a page and put the book down. The waiting room is cold and bare, and although sometimes the people hurrying through smile at you, you feel lonely. After a long time a big man with gray hair and a woman in a blue uniform want to talk to you.

The woman's voice is friendly, but only the way teachers' voices are sometimes. "I'll bet you're sleepy, Tackman. Can you talk to us a little still before you go to bed?"

"Yes."

The gray-haired man says, "Do you know who gave your mother drugs?"

"I don't know. Dr. Black was going to do something to her."

He waves that aside. "Not that. You know, medicine. Your mother took a lot of medicine. Who gave it to her? Jason?"

"I don't know."

The woman says, "Your mother is going to be well, Tackman, but it will be a while—do you understand? For now you're going to have to live for a while in a big house with some other boys."

"All right."

The man: "Amphetamines. Does that mean anything to you? Did you ever hear that word?"

You shake your head.

The woman: "Dr. Black was only trying to help your mother, Tackman. I know you don't understand, but she used several medicines at once, mixed them, and that can be very bad."

They go away and you pick up the book and riffle the pages, but you do not read. At your elbow Dr. Death says, "What's the matter, Tackie?" He smells of scorched cloth and there is a streak of blood across his forehead, but he smiles and lights one of his cigarettes.

You hold up the book. "I don't want it to end. You'll be killed at the end."

"And you don't want to lose me? That's touching."

"You will, won't you? You'll burn up in the fire and Captain Ransom will go away and leave Talar."

Dr. Death smiles. "But if you start the book again we'll all be back. Even Golo and the bull-man."

"Honest?"

"Certainly." He stands up and tousles your hair. "It's the same with you, Tackie. You're too young to realize it yet, but it's the same with you."

## Afterword

This story got me the friendship of Isaac Asimov and fathered three sequels, two of which are in this book. It was, you see, my first ever Nebula nomination, so Rosemary and I journeyed to New York for the banquet. Isaac was announcing the winners, beginning with Best Short Story. And he named this story.

I rose to accept, and the committee swarmed on Isaac. He had been given a list, not just the winner but the second-, third-, fourth-, and fifth-place finishers. The winner had been No Award—which

Isaac, understandably assuming that some story would have won, had skipped. He apologized profusely, then and afterward, and I explained repeatedly that he had honored me.

He'd also gotten me a great deal of sympathy in SFWA. Grinning, John Jakes said, "You know, Gene, if you'd just write 'The Death of Doctor Island' now, you'd win."

*He thinks I can't do it,* I thought. *We'll see about that!* But that's another story, one you'll find later in this book.

# The Toy Theater

Eight hours before we were due to land on Sarg they dropped a pamphlet into the receiving tray of the two-by-four plastic closet that was my "stateroom" for the trip. The pamphlet said landing on Sarg would be like stepping into a new world. I threw it away.

Landing on Sarg was like stepping into a new world. You expect a different kind of sunlight and a fresh smell to the air, and usually you don't get them. Sarg had them. The light ran to sienna and umber and ocher, so that everything looked older than it was and made you think of waxed oak and tarnished gold. The air was clear and clean. Sarg wasn't an industrial world, and since it was one of the lucky ones with no life of its own to preserve, it had received a flora en masse from Earth. I saw Colorado spruce, and a lot of the old, hardy, half-wild roses like Sarah Van Fleet and Amelie Gravereaux.

Stromboli, the man I was coming to see, had sent a buggy and a driver for me (if you don't want industry there are things you can't have, lots of them) and I got a good view of the firs on the mountains and the roses spilling down the rocks as we rattled along. I suppose I dropped some remark about the colors, because my driver asked, "You are an artist?"

"Oh, no. A marionettist. But I carve and paint my own dolls—that's an art, if you like. We try to make it one."

"That is what I meant. It is mostly such artists who come here to see him, and the big box which I loaded for you was suggestive. That is your control you carry?"

"Yes." I took it out of its leather case to show him.

He peered at the tiny dials and levers. "The signor has such a one. Not, you understand, identical, but similar. Perhaps you could . . . ?" He glanced back to where Charity reposed in her box. "It might help to pass the time."

I made her throw open her lid and climb up to sit on the seat with us, where she sang to the driver in her clear voice. Charity is a head taller than I am, blond, long legged, and narrow waisted; a subtle exaggeration, or so I like to think, of a really pretty showgirl. After I had made her kiss him, dance ahead of the horse for a while, then climb back into her home and slam the lid, the driver said, "That was very good. You are an artist indeed."

"I forgot to mention that I call her Charity because that's what I have to ask of my audiences."

"No, sir; you are very skilled. The skipping down the road—anyone can make them to skip for a few steps, but to do so for so long, over the uneven ground and so rapidly, I know how difficult it is. It deserves applause."

I wanted to see how far he would go, so I asked, "As good as the signor?"

"No." He shook his head. "Not as good as Signor Stromboli. But I have seen many, sir. Many come here and you are far better than most. Signor Stromboli will be pleased to talk to you."

The house was smaller than I had expected, of the Italian Alpine style. There was a large, informal garden, however, and a carriage house in the rear. The driver assured me that he would see to my baggage, and Madame Stromboli, who I assume had been following our progress up the road from a window, met me at the gate. She was white haired now, but the woman she had once been, olive skinned and beautiful with magnificent dark eyes, still showed plainly in her face. "Welcome," she said. "We are so glad that you could come."

I told her that it was a great honor to be there.

"It is a great expense for you; we know that. To travel between the suns. Once when we were much younger my husband went, to make money for us. I could not go; it cost too much. Only him, and the dolls. For years I waited, but he returned to me."

I said, "It must have been lonely."

"It was, very lonely. Now we are here where very few can come and see us. It is beautiful, no? But lonely. But my husband and I, we are lonely together. That is better. You will wish to wash, and perhaps change your clothing. Then I will take you to see him."

I thanked her.

"He will be kind to you. He likes young men who follow the old art. But be content with what he shows you. Do not say: *How do you do this?* Or *Do that!* Let him show you what he wishes and he will show you a great deal."

He did. I will not pretend to condense all the interviews I had with Stromboli into a single scene, but he was generous with his time—although the mornings, all morning, every day, were reserved for his practice, alone, in a room lined with mirrors. In time I saw nearly everything of his that I had heard described, except the famous comic butler Zanni. Stromboli showed me how to keep five figures in motion at a time, differentiating their motions so cleverly that it was easy to imagine that the dancing, shouting people around us had five different operators, provided that you could remember, even while you watched Stromboli, that they had an operator at all.

"They were little people once, you know," he said. "You have read the history? Never higher than your shoulder—those were the biggest—and they moved with wires. In those days the most any man could do well was four; did you know that? Now they are as big as you and me, they are free, and I can do five. Perhaps before you die you will make it six. It is not impossible. As they pile the flowers onto your casket they will be saying, *He could do six*."

I told him I would be happy just to handle three well.

"You will learn. You have already learned more difficult things. But you will not learn traveling with just one. If you wish to learn three, you must have three with you always, so that you can practice. But already you do the voice of a woman speaking and singing. That was the most difficult for me to learn." He threw out his big chest and thumped it. "I am an old man now and my voice is not so deep as it was, but when I was young as you it was very deep, and I could not do the voices of women, not with all the help from the control and the speakers in the dolls pitched high. But now listen."

He made Julia, Lucinda, and Columbine, three of his girls, step forward. For a moment they simply giggled; then, after a whispered but audible conference, they burst into Rosine's song from *The Barber of Seville*—Julia singing coloratura soprano, Columbine mezzo-soprano, and Lucinda contralto.

"Don't record," Stromboli admonished me. "It is easy to record and cheat; but a good audience will always know, the amateurs will want you to show them, and you can't look at yourself and smile. You can already do one girl's voice very good. Don't ever record. You know how I learned to do them?"

I expressed interest.

"When I was starting—not yet married—I did only male voices. And the false female speaking singsong, the falsetto. Then I married and little Maria, I mean Signora Stromboli my wife, began to help. In those days I did not work always alone. She did the simpler movements and the female voices."

I nodded to show I understood.

"So how was I to learn? If I said, 'Little Maria, you sit in the audience tonight,' she would say, 'Stromboli, it is not good. It is better when I do them.' So what did I do? I made the long tour outworld. The cost was very high, but the pay was very high too, and I left little Maria at home. When I came back we could do this."

Columbine, Lucinda, and Julia bowed.

The signor and I said our good-byes on the day before I was to leave Sarg. My ship would blast off at noon, and the morning practice sessions were sacred, but we held a party the night before with wine in the happy, undrunken Italian way and singing—just Stromboli and his wife and I. In the morning I packed hurriedly, and discovered that my second best pair of shoes was missing. I said to hell with them, gave my last suitcase to Stromboli's man of all work, said good-bye again to Maria Stromboli, and went out to the front gate to wait for the man of all work to bring the buggy around.

Five minutes passed, then ten. I still had plenty of time, a couple of hours if he drove fast, but I began to wonder what was keeping him. Then I heard the rattle of harness. The buggy came around a curve in the road, but its driver was a dark-haired woman in pink I had never seen before. She pulled up in front of me, indicated my luggage, which was neatly stowed on the back of the buggy, with a wave of her hand, and said, "Climb up. Antonio is indisposed, so I told the Strombolis I would drive you. I am Lili. Have you heard of me?"

I got into the seat beside her and told her I had not.

"You came here to see Stromboli, and you have not heard of me? Ah, such is fame! Once we were notorious, and I think perhaps that it was because of me that he retired. He lives with his wife now and wishes the world to think that he is a good husband, you understand; but my little house is not far away."

I said something to the effect that I had been unaware of any other houses in the neighborhood.

"A few steps would have brought you in sight of it." She cracked her whip expertly over the horse's back, and he broke into a trot. "Little Maria does not like it, but I am only a few steps away for her husband too. But he is old. Do you think I am getting old also?"

She leaned back, turning her head to show me her profile—a tip-tilted nose, generous lips salved carmine. "My bust is still good. I'm perhaps a little thicker at the waist, but my thighs are heavier too, and that is good."

"You're very beautiful," I said, and she was, though the delicately tinted cheeks beneath the cosmetics showed craquelure.

"Very beautiful but older than you."

"A few years, maybe."

"Much more. But you find me attractive?"

"Most men would find you attractive."

"I am not, you understand, a tart. Many times with Signor Stromboli, yes. But only a few with other men. And I have never been sold—no, not once for any price." She was driving very fast, the buggy rattling down the turns.

After a few moments of silence she said, "There is a place, not far from here. The ground is flat and you may drive off the road to where a stream comes down from the mountain. There is grass there, and flowers, and the sound of the water."

"I have to catch my ship."

"You have two hours. We would spend perhaps one. For the other you can sit in a chair down there, yawning and thinking nice thoughts about Sarg and me."

I shook my head.

"You say that Signor Stromboli has taught you much. He has taught *me* much too. I will teach it to you. Now. In an hour." Her leg pressed hard against mine.

"I'm sorry," I said, "but there's somebody else." It wasn't true, but it seemed the best way of getting free of an embarrassing situation. I added, "Someone I can't betray, if I'm going to live with myself."

Lili let me off at the entrance to the spaceport, where I could pile my bags directly on the conveyor. As soon as the last of them were gone she touched the horse's rump with the lash of her whip, and she, with the horse and the rattling buggy, disappeared in rising dust. A coin-operated machine inside the port vacuumed most of it out of my clothes.

As she had said, I had almost two hours to kill. I spent them alternately reading magazines and staring at the mountains I would be leaving.

*"For the Sol system and Vega. Gate five. You have fifteen minutes before departure."*

I picked myself up in a leisurely way and headed toward Gate Five, then stopped. Coming toward me was a preposterous figure, familiar from a thousand pictures.

"Sir!" (Actually it sounded more like *"SeeraughHa!"* given a rising intonation all the way—the kind of sound that might have come from a chummy, intoxicated, dangerous elephant.)

"Sir!" The great swag belly was wrapped in a waistcoat with blue and white stripes as broad as my hand. The great shapeless nose shone with an officious cunning. "Sir, your shoes. I have your shoes!"

It was Zanni the Butler, Stromboli's greatest creation. He held out my second-best shoes, well brushed. In his flipper of a hand they looked as absurd as I felt. People were staring at us, and already beginning to argue about whether or not Zanni was real.

"The master," Zanni was saying, "insisted that I restore them to you. You will little credit it, sir, but I have run all the way."

I took my shoes and mumbled, "Thank you," looking through the crowd for Stromboli, who had to be somewhere nearby.

"The master has heard," Zanni continued in a stage whisper that must have been audible out in the blast pits, "of your little talk with Madame Lili. He asks—well, sir, we sometimes call our little world the Planet of Roses, sir. He asks that you consider a part of what you have learned here—at least a part, sir—as under the rose."

I nodded. I had found Stromboli at last, standing in a corner. His face was perfectly impassive while his fingers flew over the levers of Zanni's controller. I said, *"Joruri."*

*"Joruri,* sir?"

"The Japanese puppet theater. The operators stand in full view of the audience, but the audience pretends not to see them."

"That is the master's field, sir, and not mine, but perhaps that is the best way."

"Perhaps. But now I've got to catch my ship."

"So you said to Madame Lili earlier, sir. The master begs leave to remind you that he was once a young man very like yourself, sir. He expresses the hope that you know with whom you are keeping faith. He further expresses the hope that he himself does not know."

I thought of the fine cracks I had seen, under the cosmetics, in Lili's cheeks, and of Charity's cheeks, as blooming as peaches.

Then I took my second-best pair of shoes, and went out to the ship, and climbed into my own little box.

&

## AFTERWORD

Now it seems that all toys are high tech. Goodness knows there's nothing wrong with high-tech toys, but it seems to me that we had just as much fun with low. Can I have been alone in playing with puppets and marionettes?

There was once a marionette in the form of a robot with a spiked club, and a blond boy with a sword who was to fight him. Best of all, there was a puppet, just one puppet, a grinning monkey. I wish I had him still.

G. K. Chesterton had a toy theater, doubtless with a princess, Saint George, and a dragon. Back then they were a penny plain and tuppence colored, but if you got the plain sort you had the pleasure of coloring everything to suit yourself. You might have a princess with fiery red hair, if you liked, and a flaxen dragon. Years after my monkey had returned to the jungle (or wherever), I read about Chesterton's theater with pleasure. By then I already knew of certain sad toys possessed by adult men.

And long years after I had finished this story and sold it, and almost forgotten it, I set out to write a circus story to be called "On a Vacant Face a Bruise." Chesterton had never really forgotten his toy theater, and I soon learned that I had never really forgotten mine.

# THE FIFTH HEAD OF CERBERUS

When the ivy-tod is heavy with snow,
And the owlet whoops to the wolf below,
That eats the she-wolf's young.
                —SAMUEL TAYLOR COLERIDGE,
                "The Rime of the Ancient Mariner"

When I was a boy my brother David and I had to go to bed early
whether we were sleepy or not. In summer particularly, bedtime often came before sunset; and because our dormitory was in the east
wing of the house, with a broad window facing the central courtyard and thus
looking west, the hard, pinkish light sometimes streamed in for hours while we
lay staring out at my father's crippled monkey perched on a flaking parapet, or
telling stories, one bed to another, with soundless gestures.

Our dormitory was on the uppermost floor of the house, and our window had
a shutter of twisted iron which we were forbidden to open. I suppose the theory
was that a burglar might, on some rainy morning (this being the only time he
could hope to find the roof, which was fitted out as a sort of pleasure garden, deserted), let down a rope and so enter our room unless the shutter was closed.

The object of this hypothetical and very courageous thief would not, of
course, be merely to steal us. Children, whether boys or girls, were extraordinarily cheap in Port-Mimizon; and indeed I was once told that my father, who had
formerly traded in them, no longer did so because of the poor market. Whether
or not this was true, everyone—or nearly everyone—knew of some professional
who would furnish what was wanted, within reason, at a low price. These men
made the children of the poor and the careless their study, and should you want,
say, a brown-skinned, red-haired little girl or one who was plump or who lisped,
a blond boy like David or a pale, brown-haired, brown-eyed boy such as I, they
could provide one in a few hours.

Neither, in all probability, would the imaginary burglar seek to hold us for
ransom, though my father was thought in some quarters to be immensely rich.

There were several reasons for this. Those few people who knew that my brother and I existed knew also, or at least had been led to believe, that my father cared nothing at all for us. Whether this was true or not I cannot say; certainly I believed it, and my father never gave me the least reason to doubt it, though at the time the thought of killing him had never occurred to me.

And if these reasons were not sufficiently convincing, anyone with an understanding of the stratum in which he had become perhaps the most permanent feature would realize that for him, who was already forced to give large bribes to the secret police, to once disgorge money in that way would leave him open to a thousand ruinous attacks; and this may have been—this and the fear in which he was held—the real reason we were never stolen.

The iron shutter is (for I am writing now in my old dormitory room) hammered to resemble in a stiff and oversymmetrical way the boughs of a willow. In my boyhood it was overgrown by a silver trumpet vine (since dug up) which had scrambled up the wall from the court below, and I used to wish that it would close the window entirely and thus shut out the sun when we were trying to sleep; but David, whose bed was under the window, was forever reaching up to snap off branches so that he could whistle through the hollow stems, making a sort of panpipe of four or five. The piping, of course, growing louder as David grew bolder, would in time attract the attention of Mr. Million, our tutor. Mr. Million would enter the room in perfect silence, his wide wheels gliding across the uneven floor while David pretended sleep. The panpipe might by this time be concealed under his pillow, in the sheet, or even under the mattress, but Mr. Million would find it.

What he did with those little musical instruments after confiscating them from David I had forgotten until yesterday; although in prison, when we were kept in by storms or heavy snow, I often occupied myself by trying to recall it. To have broken them or dropped them through the shutter onto the patio below would have been completely unlike him; Mr. Million never broke anything intentionally, and never wasted anything. I could visualize perfectly the half-sorrowing expression with which he drew the tiny pipes out (the face which seemed to float behind his screen was much like my father's) and the way in which he turned and glided from the room. But what became of them?

Yesterday, as I said (this is the sort of thing that gives me confidence), I remembered. He had been talking to me here while I worked, and when he left it seemed to me—as my glance idly followed his smooth motion through the doorway—that something, a sort of flourish I recalled from my earliest days, was missing. I closed my eyes and tried to remember what the appearance had been, eliminating any skepticism, any attempt to guess in advance what I "must" have seen, and I found that the missing element was a brief flash, the glint of metal, over Mr. Million's head.

Once I had established this, I knew that it must have come from a swift upward motion of his arm, like a salute, as he left our room. For an hour or more I could not guess the reason for that gesture, and could only suppose it, whatever it had been, to have been destroyed by time. I tried to recall if the corridor outside our dormitory had, in that really not so distant past, held some object now vanished: a curtain or a window shade, an appliance to be activated, anything that might account for it. There was nothing.

I went into the corridor and examined the floor minutely for marks indicating furniture. I looked for hooks or nails driven into the walls, pushing aside the coarse old tapestries. Craning my neck, I searched the ceiling. Then, after an hour, I looked at the door itself and saw what I had not seen in the thousands of times I had passed through it: that like all the doors in this house, which is very old, it had a massive frame of wooden slabs, and that one of these, forming the lintel, protruded enough from the wall to make a narrow shelf above the door.

I pushed my chair into the hall and stood on the seat. The shelf was thick with dust in which lay forty-seven of my brother's pipes and a wonderful miscellany of other small objects. Objects many of which I recalled, but some of which still fail to summon any flicker of response from the recesses of my mind . . .

The small blue egg of a songbird, speckled with brown. I suppose the bird must have nested in the vine outside our window, and that David or I despoiled the nest only to be robbed ourselves by Mr. Million. But I do not recall the incident.

And there is a (broken) puzzle made of the bronzed viscera of some small animal, and—wonderfully evocative—one of those large and fancifully decorated keys, sold annually, which during the year of its currency will admit the possessor to certain rooms of the city library after hours. Mr. Million, I suppose, must have confiscated it when he found it, after expiration, doing duty as a toy, but what memories!

My father had his own library, now in my possession, but we were forbidden to go there. I have a dim memory of standing—at how early an age I cannot say—before that huge carved door. Of seeing it swing back, and the crippled monkey on my father's shoulder pressing itself against his hawk face, with the black scarf and scarlet dressing gown beneath and the rows and rows of shabby books and notebooks behind them, and the sick-sweet smell of formaldehyde coming from the laboratory beyond the sliding mirror.

I do not remember what he said or whether it had been I or another who had knocked, but I do recall that after the door had closed, a woman in pink whom I thought very pretty stooped to bring her face to the level of my own and assured me that my father had written all the books I had just seen, and that I doubted it not at all.

My brother and I, as I have said, were forbidden this room, but when we were a little older Mr. Million used to take us, about twice a week, on expeditions to the city library. These were very nearly the only times we were allowed to leave the house, and since our tutor disliked curling the jointed length of his metal modules into a hire cart and no sedan chair would have withstood his weight or contained his bulk, these forays were made on foot.

For a long time this route to the library was the only part of the city I knew. Three blocks down Saltimbanque Street where our house stood, right at the rue d'Asticot to the slave market, and a block beyond that to the library. A child, not knowing what is extraordinary and what commonplace, usually lights midway between the two, finds interest in incidents adults consider beneath notice, and calmly accepts the most improbable occurrences. My brother and I were fascinated by the spurious antiques and bad bargains of the rue d'Asticot, but often bored when Mr. Million insisted on stopping for an hour at the slave market.

It was not a large one, Port-Mimizon not being a center of the trade, and the auctioneers and their merchandise were frequently on a most friendly basis—having met several times previously as a succession of owners discovered the same fault. Mr. Million never bid, but watched the bidding, motionless, while we kicked our heels and munched the fried bread he had bought at a stall for us. There were sedan chairmen, their legs knotted with muscle, and simpering bath attendants; fighting slaves in chains, with eyes dulled by drugs or blazing with imbecile ferocity; cooks, house servants, a hundred others—yet David and I used to beg to be allowed to proceed alone to the library.

This library was a wastefully large building which had held government offices in the old French-speaking days. The park in which it had once stood had died of petty corruption, and the library now rose from a clutter of shops and tenements. A narrow thoroughfare led to the main doors, and once we were inside, the squalor of the neighborhood vanished, replaced by a kind of peeling grandeur. The main desk was directly beneath the dome, and this dome, drawing up with it a spiraling walkway lined with the library's main collection, floated five hundred feet in the air: a stony sky whose least chip falling might kill one of the librarians on the spot.

While Mr. Million browsed his way majestically up the helix, David and I raced ahead until we were several full turns in advance and could do what we liked. When I was still quite young it would often occur to me that since my father had written (on the testimony of the lady in pink) a roomful of books, some of them should be here; and I would climb resolutely until I had almost reached the dome, and there rummage. Because the librarians were very lax about reshelving, there seemed always a possibility of finding what I had failed to find before. The shelves towered far above my head, but when I felt myself unobserved I climbed them like ladders, stepping on books when there was no room on the shelves themselves for the square toes of my small brown shoes, and occasionally kicking books to the floor where they remained until our next visit and beyond, evidence of the staff's reluctance to climb that long, coiled slope.

The upper shelves were, if anything, in worse disorder than those more conveniently located, and one glorious day when I attained the highest of all I found occupying that lofty, dusty position (besides a misplaced astronautics text, *The*

*Mile-Long Spaceship,* by some German) only a lorn copy of *Monday or Tuesday* leaning against a book about the assassination of Trotsky, and a crumbling volume of Vernor Vinge's short stories that owed its presence there, or so I suspect, to some long-dead librarian's mistaking the faded *V. Vinge* on the spine for *Winge*.

I never found any books of my father's, but I did not regret the long climbs to the top of the dome. If David had come with me, we raced up together, up and down the sloping floor—or peered over the rail at Mr. Million's slow progress while we debated the feasibility of putting an end to him with one cast of some ponderous work. If David preferred to pursue interests of his own farther down I ascended to the very top where the cap of the dome curved right over my head; and there, from a rusted iron catwalk not much wider than one of the shelves I had been climbing (and I suspect not nearly so strong), opened in turn each of a circle of tiny piercings—piercings in a wall of iron, but so shallow a wall that when I had slid the corroded cover plates out of the way I could thrust my head through and feel myself truly outside, with the wind and the circling birds and the lime-spotted expanse of the dome curving away beneath me.

To the west, since it was taller than the surrounding houses and marked by the orange trees on the roof, I could make out our house. To the south, the masts of the ships in the harbor, and in clear weather—if it was the right time of day—the whitecaps of the tidal race Sainte Anne drew between the peninsulas called First Finger and Thumb. (And once, as I very well recall, while looking south I saw the great geyser of sunlit water when a starcrosser splashed down.) To east and north spread the city proper, the citadel and the grand market and the forests and mountains beyond.

But sooner or later, whether David had accompanied me or gone off on his own, Mr. Million summoned us. Then we were forced to go with him to one of the wings to visit this or that science collection. This meant books for lessons. My father insisted that we learn biology, anatomy, and chemistry thoroughly, and under Mr. Million's tutelage learn them we did—he never considering a subject mastered until we could discuss every topic mentioned in every book cataloged under the heading. The life sciences were my own favorites, but David preferred languages, literature, and law, for we got a smattering of these as well as anthropology, cybernetics, and psychology.

When he had selected the books that would form our study for the next few days and urged us to choose more for ourselves, Mr. Million would retire with us to some quiet corner of one of the science reading rooms, where there were chairs and a table and room sufficient for him to curl the jointed length of his body or align it against a wall or bookcase in a way that left the aisles clear. To designate the formal beginning of our class he used to begin by calling roll, my own name always coming first.

I would say, "Here," to show that he had my attention.

"And David."

"Here." (David has an illustrated *Tales from the Odyssey* open on his lap where Mr. Million cannot see it, but he looks at Mr. Million with bright, feigned interest. Sunshine slants down to the table from a high window, and shows the air aswarm with dust.)

"I wonder if either of you noticed the stone implements in the room through which we passed a few moments ago?"

We nod, each hoping the other will speak.

"Were they made on Earth, or here on our own planet?"

This is a trick question, but an easy one. David says, "Neither one. They're plastic." And we giggle.

Mr. Million says patiently, "Yes, they're plastic reproductions, but from where did the originals come?" His face, so similar to my father's, but which I thought of at this time as belonging only to him, so that it seemed a frightening reversal of nature to see it on a living man instead of his screen, was neither interested, nor angry, nor bored, but coolly remote.

David answers, "From Sainte Anne." Sainte Anne is the sister planet to our own, revolving with us about a common center as we swing around the sun. "The sign said so, and the aborigines made them—there weren't any abos here."

Mr. Million nods, and turns his impalpable face toward me. "Do you feel these stone implements occupied a central place in the lives of their makers? Say no."

"No."

"Why not?"

I think frantically, not helped by David, who is kicking my shins under the table. A glimmering comes.

"Talk. Answer at once."

"It's obvious, isn't it?" (Always a good thing to say when you're not even sure "it" is even possible.) "In the first place, they can't have been very good tools, so why would the abos have relied on them? You might say they needed those obsidian arrowheads and bone fishhooks for getting food, but that's not true. They could poison the water with the juices of certain plants, and for primitive people the most effective way to fish is probably with weirs, or with nets of rawhide or vegetable fiber. Just the same way, trapping or driving animals with fire would be more effective than hunting; and anyway stone tools wouldn't be needed at all for gathering berries and the shoots of edible plants and things like that, which were probably their most important foods—those stone things got in the glass case here because the snares and nets rotted away and they're all that's left, so the people that make their living that way pretend they were important."

"Good. David? Be original, please. Don't repeat what you've just heard."

David looks up from his book, his blue eyes scornful of both of us. "If you could have asked them, they would have told you that their magic and their religion, the songs they sang, and the traditions of their people were what were important. They killed their sacrificial animals with flails of seashells that cut like razors, and they didn't let their men father children until they had stood enough fire to cripple them for life. They mated with trees and drowned the children to honor their rivers. That was what was important."

With no neck, Mr. Million's face nodded. "Now we will debate the humanity of those aborigines. David negative and first."

(I kick him, but he has pulled his hard, freckled legs up beneath him, or hidden them behind the legs of his chair, which is cheating.) "Humanity," he says in his most objectionable voice, "in the history of human thought implies descent from what we may conveniently call *Adam*, that is, the original Terrestrial stock, and if the two of you don't see that, you're idiots."

I wait for him to continue, but he is finished. To give myself time to think, I say, "Mr. Million, it's not fair to let him call me names in a debate. Tell him that's not debating, it's *fighting*, isn't it?"

Mr. Million says, "No personalities, David." (David is already peeking at Polyphemus the Cyclops and Odysseus, hoping I'll go on for a long time. I feel challenged and decide to do so.)

I begin, "The argument which holds descent from Terrestrial stock pivotal is neither valid nor conclusive. Not conclusive because it is distinctly possible that the aborigines of Sainte Anne were descendants of some earlier wave of human expansion—one, perhaps, even predating *the Homeric Greeks*."

Mr. Million says mildly, "I would confine myself to arguments of higher probability if I were you."

I nevertheless gloss upon the Etruscans, Atlantis, and the tenacity and expansionist tendencies of a hypothetical technological culture occupying Gondwanaland. When I have finished, Mr. Million says, "Now reverse. David, affirmative without repeating."

My brother, of course, has been looking at his book instead of listening, and I kick him with enthusiasm, expecting him to be stuck, but he says, "The abos are human because they're all dead."

"Explain."

"If they were alive it would be dangerous to let them be human because they'd ask for things, but with them dead it makes it more interesting if they were, and the settlers killed them all."

And so it goes. The spot of sunlight travels across the black-streaked red of the tabletop—traveled across it a hundred times. We would leave through one of the side doors and walk through a neglected areaway between two wings. There would be empty bottles there and wind-scattered papers of all kinds, and once a dead man in bright rags over whose legs we boys skipped while Mr. Million rolled silently around him. As we left the areaway for a narrow street, the bugles of the garrison at the citadel (sounding so far away) would call the troopers to their evening mess. In the rue d'Asticot the lamplighter would be at work and the shops shut behind their iron grilles. The sidewalks magically clear of old furniture would seem broad and bare.

Our own Saltimbanque Street would be very different, with the first revelers arriving. White-haired, hearty men guiding very young men and boys, men and boys handsome and muscular but a shade overfed; young men who made diffident jokes and smiled with excellent teeth at them. These were always the early ones, and when I was a little older I sometimes wondered if they were early only because the white-haired men wished to have their pleasure and yet a good night's sleep as well, or if it was because they knew the young men they were introducing to my father's establishment would be drowsy and irritable after midnight, like children who have been kept up too late.

Because Mr. Million did not want us to use the alleys after dark we came in the front entrance with the white-haired men and their nephews and sons. There was a garden there, not much bigger than a small room and recessed into the windowless front of the house. In it were beds of ferns the size of graves; a little fountain whose water fell upon rods of glass to make a continual tinkling, and which had to be protected from the street boys; and, with his feet firmly planted, indeed almost buried in moss, an iron statue of a dog with three heads.

It was this statue, I suppose, that gave our house its popular name of Maison du Chien, though there may have been a reference to our surname as well. The three heads were sleekly powerful, with pointed muzzles and ears. One was snarling and one, the center head, regarded the world of garden and street with a look of tolerant interest. The third, the one nearest the brick path that led to our door, was—there is no other term for it—frankly grinning; and it was the custom for my father's patrons to pat this head between the ears as they came up the path. Their fingers had polished the spot to the consistency of black glass.

This, then, was my world at seven of our world's long years, and perhaps for half a year beyond. Most of my days were spent in the little classroom over which Mr. Million presided, and my evenings in the dormitory where David and I played and fought in total silence. They were varied by the trips to the library I have described or, very rarely, elsewhere. I pushed aside the leaves of the silver trumpet vine occasionally to watch the girls and their benefactors in the court below, or heard their talk drifting down from the roof garden, but the things they did and talked of were of no great interest to me. I knew that the tall, hatchet-faced man who ruled our house and was called Maitre by the girls and servants was my father. I had known for as long as I could remember that there was somewhere a fearsome woman—the servants were in terror of her—called Madame, but that she was neither my mother nor David's, nor my father's wife.

That life and my childhood, or at least my infancy, ended one evening after David and I, worn out with wrestlings and silent arguments, had gone to sleep. Someone shook me by the shoulder and called me, and it was not Mr. Million but one of the servants, a hunched little man in a shabby red jacket. "He wants you," this summoner informed me. "Get up."

I did, and he saw that I was wearing nightclothes. This I think had not been covered in his instructions, and for a moment during which I stood and yawned he debated with himself. "Get dressed," he said at last. "Comb your hair."

I obeyed, putting on the black velvet trousers I had worn the day before but (guided by some instinct) a new clean shirt. The room to which he then conducted me (through tortuous corridors now emptied of the last patrons, and others, musty, filthy with the excrement of rats, to which patrons were never admitted) was my father's library—the room with the great carved door before which I had received the whispered confidences of the woman in pink. I had never been inside it, but when my guide rapped discreetly on the door it swung back, and I found myself within, almost before I realized what had happened.

My father, who had opened the door, closed it behind me and, leaving me standing where I was, walked to the most distant end of that long room and threw himself down in a huge chair. He was wearing the red dressing gown and black scarf in which I had most often seen him, and his long, sparse hair was brushed straight back. He stared at me, and I remember that my lip trembled as I tried to keep from breaking into sobs.

"Well," he said, after we had looked at one another for a long time, "and there you are. What am I going to call you?"

I told him my name, but he shook his head. "Not that. You must have another name for me—a private name. You may choose it yourself if you like."

I said nothing. It seemed to me quite impossible that I should have any name other than the two words which were, in some mystic sense I only respected without understanding, *my name.*

"I'll choose for you then," my father said. "You are Number Five. Come here, Number Five."

I came, and when I was standing in front of him, he told me, "Now we are going to play a game. I am going to show you some pictures, do you understand? And all the time you are watching them, you must talk. Talk about the pictures. If you talk you win, but if you stop, even for just a second, I do. Understand?"

I said I did.

"Good. I know you're a bright boy. As a matter of fact, Mr. Million has sent me all the examinations he has given you and the tapes he makes when he talks with you. Did you know that? Did you ever wonder what he did with them?"

I said, "I thought he threw them away," and my father, I noticed, leaned forward as I spoke, a circumstance I found flattering at the time.

"No, I have them here." He pressed a switch. "Now remember, you must not stop talking."

But for the first few moments I was much too interested to talk.

There had appeared in the room, as though by magic, a boy considerably younger than I, and a painted wooden soldier almost as large as I was myself, which when I reached out to touch them proved as insubstantial as air. "Say something," my father said. "What are you thinking about, Number Five?"

I was thinking about the soldier, of course, and so was the younger boy, who appeared to be about three. He toddled through my arm like mist and attempted to knock it over.

They were holographs—three-dimensional images formed by the interference of two wave fronts of light—things which had seemed very dull when I had seen them illustrated by flat pictures of chessmen in my physics book; but it was some time before I connected those chessmen with the phantoms who walked in my father's library at night. All this time my father was saying, "Talk! Say something! What do you think the little boy is feeling?"

"Well, the little boy likes the big soldier, but he wants to knock him down if he can, because the soldier's only a toy, really, but it's bigger than he is. . . ." And so I talked, and for a long time, hours I suppose, continued. The scene changed and changed again. The giant soldier was replaced by a pony, a rabbit, a meal of soup and crackers. But the three-year-old boy remained the central figure. When the hunched man in the shabby coat came again, yawning, to take me back to my bed, my voice had worn to a husky whisper and my throat ached. In my dreams that night I saw the little boy scampering from one activity to another, his personality in some way confused with my own and my father's so that I was at once observer, observed, and a third presence observing both.

The next night I fell asleep almost at the moment Mr. Million sent us up to bed, retaining consciousness only long enough to congratulate myself on doing so. I woke when the hunched man entered the room, but it was not me whom he roused from the sheets but David. Quietly, pretending I still slept (for it had occurred to me, and seemed quite reasonable at the time, that if he were to see I was awake he might take both of us), I watched as my brother dressed and struggled to impart some sort of order to his tangle of fair hair. When he returned I was sound asleep, and had no opportunity to question him until Mr. Million left us alone, as he sometimes did, to eat our breakfast. I had told David my own experiences as a matter of course, and what he had to tell me was simply that he had had an evening very similar to mine. He had seen holographic pictures, and apparently the same pictures: the wooden soldier, the pony. He had been forced to talk constantly, as Mr. Million had so often made us do in debates and verbal examinations. The only way in which David's interview with our father had differed from mine, as nearly as I could determine, appeared when I asked him by what name he had been called.

He looked at me blankly, a piece of toast half-raised to his mouth.

I asked again, "What name did he call you by when he talked to you?"

"He called me David. What did you think?"

With the beginning of these interviews the pattern of my life changed, the adjustments I assumed to be temporary becoming imperceptibly permanent, settling into a new shape of which neither David nor I was consciously aware. Our games and stories after bedtime stopped, and David less and less often made his panpipes of the silver trumpet vine. Mr. Million allowed us to sleep later and we were in some subtle way acknowledged to be more adult. At about this time too, he began to take us to a park where there was an archery range and provision for various games. This little park, which was not far from our house, was bordered on one side by a canal. And there, while David shot arrows at a goose stuffed with straw or played tennis, I often sat staring at the quiet, only slightly dirty water, or waiting for one of the white ships—great ships with bows as sharp as the scalpel bills of kingfishers and four, five, or even seven masts—which were, infrequently, towed up from the harbor by ten or twelve spans of oxen.

In the summer of my eleventh or twelfth year—I think the twelfth—we were permitted for the first time to stay after sundown in the park, sitting on the grassy, sloped margin of the canal to watch a fireworks display. The first preliminary flight of rockets had no sooner exhausted itself half a mile above the city than David became ill. He rushed to the water and vomited, plunging his hands half up to the elbows in muck while the red and white stars burned in glory above him. Mr. Million took him up in his arms, and when poor David had emptied himself we hurried home.

His disease proved not much more lasting than the tainted sandwich that had occasioned it, but while our tutor was putting him to bed I decided not to be cheated of the remainder of the display, parts of which I had glimpsed between the intervening houses as we made our way home; I was forbidden the roof after dark, but I knew very well where the nearest stair was. The thrill I felt in penetrating that prohibited world of leaf and shadow while fireflowers of purple and gold and blazing scarlet overtopped it affected me like the aftermath of a fever, leaving me short of breath, shaking, and cold in the midst of summer.

There were a great many more people on the roof than I had anticipated, the men without cloaks, hats, or sticks (all of which they had left in my father's checkrooms), and the girls, my father's employees, in costumes that displayed their rouged breasts in enclosures of twisted wire like birdcages or gave them the appearance of great height (dissolved only when someone stood very close to them), or gowns whose skirts reflected their wearers' faces and busts as still water does the trees standing near it, so that they appeared, in the intermittent colored flashes, like the queens of strange suits in a tarot deck.

I was seen, of course, since I was much too excited to conceal myself effectively, but no one ordered me back, and I suppose they assumed I had been permitted to come up to see the fireworks.

These continued for a long time. I remember one patron, a heavy, square-faced, stupid-looking man who seemed to be someone of importance, who was so eager to enjoy the company of his protégée—who did not want to go inside until the display was over—that, since he insisted on privacy, twenty or thirty bushes and small trees had to be rearranged on the parterre to make a little grove around them. I helped the waiters carry some of the smaller tubs and pots, and managed to duck into the structure as it was completed. Here I could still watch the exploding rockets and "aerial bombs" through the branches, and at the same time the patron and his *nymphe du bois,* who was watching them a good deal more intently than I.

My motive, as well as I can remember, was not prurience but simple curiosity. I was at that age when we are passionately interested, but the passion is one of science. Mine was nearly satisfied when I was grasped by the shirt by someone behind me and drawn out of the shrubbery.

When I was clear of the leaves I was released, and I turned expecting to see Mr. Million, but it was not he. My captor was a little gray-haired woman in a black dress whose skirt, as I noticed even at the time, fell straight from her waist to the ground. I suppose I bowed to her, since she was clearly no servant, but she returned no salutation at all, staring intently into my face in a way that made me think she could see as well in the intervals between the bursting glories as by their light. At last, in what must have been the finale of the display, a great rocket rose screaming on a river of flame, and for an instant she consented to look up. Then, when it had exploded in a mauve orchid of unbelievable size and brilliance, this formidable little woman grabbed me again and led me firmly toward the stairs.

While we were on the level stone pavement of the roof garden she did not, as nearly as I could see, walk at all, but rather seemed to glide across the surface like an onyx chessman on a polished board; and that, in spite of all that has happened since, is the way I still remember her: as the black queen, a chess queen neither sinister nor beneficent, and black only as distinguished from some white queen I was never fated to encounter.

When we reached the stairs, however, this smooth gliding became a fluid bobbing that brought two inches or more of the hem of her black skirt into contact with each step, as if her torso were descending each as a small boat might a rapids—now rushing, now pausing, now almost backing in the crosscurrents.

She steadied herself on these steps by holding on to me and grasping the arm of a maid who had been waiting for us at the stair head and assisted her from the other side. I had supposed, while we were crossing the roof garden, that her gliding motion had been the result, merely, of a marvelously controlled walk and good posture, but I now understood her to be in some way handicapped, and I had the impression that without the help the maid and I gave her she might have fallen headfirst.

Once we had reached the bottom of the steps her smooth progress was resumed. She dismissed the maid with a nod and led me down the corridor in the direction opposite to that in which our dormitory and classroom lay until we reached a stairwell far toward the back of the house, a corkscrew, seldom-used flight, very steep, with only a low iron banister between the steps and a six-story drop into the cellars. Here she released me and told me crisply to go down. I went down several steps, then turned to see if she was having any difficulty.

She was not, but neither was she using the stairs. With her long skirt hanging as straight as a curtain she was floating suspended, watching me, in the center of the stairwell. I was so startled I stopped, which made her jerk her head angrily, then began to run. As I fled around and around the spiral she revolved with me, turning toward me always a face extraordinarily like my father's, one hand always on the railing. When we had descended to the second floor she swooped down and caught me as easily as a cat takes charge of an errant kitten, and led me through rooms and passages where I had never been permitted to go until I was as confused as I might have been in a strange building. At last we stopped before a door in no way different from any other. She opened it with an old-fashioned brass key with an edge like a saw and motioned for me to go in.

The room was brightly lit, and I was able to see clearly what I had only sensed on the roof and in the corridors: that the hem of her skirt hung two inches above the floor no matter how she moved, and that there was nothing between the hem and the floor at all. She waved me to a little footstool covered with needlepoint and said, "Sit down," and when I had done so glided across to a wing-backed rocker and sat facing me. After a moment she asked, "What's your name?" and when I told her she cocked an eyebrow at me and started the chair in motion by pushing gently with her fingers at a floor lamp that stood beside it. After a long time she said, "And what does he call you?"

"He?" I was stupid, I suppose, with lack of sleep.

She pursed her lips. "My brother."

I relaxed a little. "Oh," I said, "you're my aunt then. I thought you looked like my father. He calls me Number Five."

For a moment she continued to stare, the corners of her mouth drawing down as my father's often did. Then she said, "That number's either far too low or too high. Living, there are he and I, and I suppose he's counting the simulator. Have you a sister, Number Five?"

Mr. Million had been having us read *David Copperfield*, and when she said this she reminded me so strikingly and unexpectedly of Aunt Betsey Trotwood that I shouted with laughter.

"There's nothing absurd about it. Your father had a sister—why shouldn't you? You have none?"

"No, ma'am, but I have a brother. His name is David."

"Call me Aunt Jeannine. Does David look like you, Number Five?"

I shook my head. "His hair is curly and blond instead of like mine. Maybe he looks a little like me, but not a lot."

"I suppose," my aunt said under her breath, "he used one of my girls."

"Ma'am?"

"Do you know who David's mother was, Number Five?"

"We're brothers, so I guess she would be the same as mine, but Mr. Million says she went away a long time ago."

"Not the same as yours," my aunt said. "No. I could show you a picture of your own. Would you like to see it?" She rang a bell, and a maid came curtsying from some room beyond the one in which we sat; my aunt whispered to her and she went out again. When my aunt turned back to me she asked, "And what do you do all day, Number Five, besides run up to the roof when you shouldn't? Are you taught?"

I told her about my experiments (I was stimulating unfertilized frogs' eggs to asexual development and then doubling the chromosomes by a chemical treatment so that a further asexual generation could be produced) and the dissections Mr. Million was by then encouraging me to do and, while I talked, happened to drop some remark about how interesting it would be to perform a biopsy on one of the aborigines of Sainte Anne if any were still in existence, since the first explorers' descriptions differed so widely and some pioneers there had claimed the abos could change their shapes.

"Ah," my aunt said, "you know about them. Let me test you, Number Five. What is Veil's Hypothesis?"

We had learned that several years before, so I said, "Veil's Hypothesis supposes the abos to have possessed the ability to mimic mankind perfectly. Veil thought that when the ships came from Earth the abos killed everyone and took their places and the ships, so they're not dead at all; we are."

"You mean the Earth people are," my aunt said. "The human beings."

"Ma'am?"

"If Veil was correct, then you and I are abos from Sainte Anne, at least in origin, which I suppose is what you meant. Do you think he was right?"

"I don't think it makes any difference. He said the imitation would have to be perfect, and if it is, they're the same as we were anyway." I thought I was being clever, but my aunt smiled, rocking more vigorously. It was very warm in the close, bright little room.

"Number Five, you're too young for semantics, and I'm afraid you've been led astray by that word *perfectly*. Dr. Veil, I'm certain, meant to use it loosely rather than as precisely as you seem to think. The imitation could hardly have been exact, since human beings don't possess that talent and to imitate them *perfectly* the abos would have to lose it."

"Couldn't they?"

"My dear child, abilities of every sort must evolve. And when they do they must be utilized or they atrophy. If the abos had been able to mimic so well as to lose the power to do so, that would have been the end of them, and no doubt it would have come long before the first ships reached them. Of course there's not the slightest evidence they could do anything of the sort. They simply died off before they could be thoroughly studied, and Veil, who wants a dramatic explanation for the cruelty and irrationality he sees around him, has hung fifty pounds of theory on nothing."

This last remark, especially as my aunt seemed so friendly, appeared to me to offer an ideal opportunity for a question about her remarkable means of locomotion, but as I was about to frame it we were interrupted, almost simultaneously, from two directions. The maid returned carrying a large book bound in tooled leather, and she had no sooner handed it to my aunt than there was a tap at the door. My aunt said absently, "Get that," and since the remark might as easily have been addressed to me as to the maid I satisfied my curiosity in another form by racing her to answer the knock.

Two of my father's demimondaines were waiting in the hall, costumed and painted until they seemed more alien than any abos, stately as Lombardy poplars and inhuman as specters, with green and yellow eyes made to look the size of eggs and inflated breasts pushed almost shoulder high; and though they maintained an inculcated composure I was pleasantly aware that they were startled to find me in the doorway. I bowed them in, but as the maid closed the door behind them my aunt said absently, "In a moment, girls. I want to show the boy here something; then he's going to leave."

The "something" was a photograph utilizing, as I supposed, some novelty technique which washed away all color save a light brown. It was small, and from its general appearance and crumbling edges very old. It showed a girl of twenty-five or so, thin and as nearly as I could judge rather tall, standing beside a stocky young man on a paved walkway and holding a baby. The walkway ran along the front of a remarkable house, a very long wooden house only a story in height, with a porch or veranda that changed its architectural style every twenty or thirty feet so as to give almost the impression of a number of exceedingly narrow houses constructed with their sidewalls in contact. I mention this detail, which I hardly noticed at the time, because I have so often since my release from prison tried to find some trace of this house. When I was first shown the picture I was much more interested in the girl's face, and the baby's. The latter was in fact scarcely visible, he being nearly smothered in white wool blankets. The girl had large features and a brilliant smile which held a suggestion of that rarely seen charm which is at once careless, poetic, and sly. *Gypsy,* was my first thought, but her complexion was surely too fair for that. Since on this world we are all descended from a relatively small group of colonists, we are rather a uniform population, but my studies had given me some familiarity with the original Terrestrial races, and my second guess, almost a certainty, was Celtic. "Wales," I said aloud. "Or Scotland. Or Ireland."

"What?" my aunt said. One of the girls giggled; they were seated on the divan now, their long, gleaming legs crossed before them like the varnished staffs of flags.

"It doesn't matter."

My aunt looked at me acutely and said, "You're right. I'll send for you and we'll talk about this when we've both more leisure. For the present my maid will take you to your room."

I remember nothing of the long walk the maid and I must have had back to the dormitory, or what excuses I gave Mr. Million for my unauthorized absence. Whatever they were, I suppose he penetrated them, or discovered the truth by questioning the servants, because no summons to return to my aunt's apartment came, although I expected it daily for weeks afterward.

That night—I am reasonably sure it was the same night—I dreamed of the abos of Sainte Anne, abos dancing with plumes of fresh grass on their heads and arms and ankles, abos shaking their shields of woven rushes and their nephrite-tipped spears until the motion affected my bed and became, in shabby red cloth, the arms of my father's valet come to summon me, as he did almost every night, to my father's library.

That night, and this time I am quite certain it was the same night, that is, the night I first dreamed of the abos, the pattern of my hours with him, which had come over the four or five years past to have a predictable sequence of conversation, holographs, free association, and dismissal—a sequence I had come to think inalterable—changed. Following the preliminary talk designed, I feel sure, to put me at ease (at which it failed, as it always did), I was told to roll up a sleeve and lie down upon an old examining table in a corner of the room. My father then made me look at the wall, which meant at the shelves heaped with ragged notebooks. I felt a needle being thrust into the inner part of my arm, but my head was held down and my face turned away, so that I could neither sit up nor look at what he was doing. Then the needle was withdrawn and I was told to lie quietly.

After what seemed a very long time, during which my father occasionally spread my eyelids to look at my eyes or took my pulse, someone in a distant part of the room began to tell a very long and confusingly involved story. My father made notes of what was said, and occasionally stopped to ask questions I found it unnecessary to answer, since the storyteller did it for me.

The drug my father had given me did not, as I had imagined it would, lessen its hold on me as the hours passed. Instead it seemed to carry me progressively further from reality and the mode of consciousness best suited to preserving the individuality of thought. The peeling leather of the examination table vanished under me, and was now the deck of a ship, now the wing of a dove beating far above the world; and whether the voice I heard reciting was my own or my father's I no longer cared. It was pitched sometimes higher, sometimes lower, but then I felt myself at times to be speaking from the depths of a chest larger than my own, and his voice, identified as such by the soft rustling of the pages of his notebook, might seem the high, treble cries of the racing children in the streets as I heard them in summer when I thrust my head through the windows at the base of the library dome.

With that night my life changed again. The drugs—for there seemed to be several, and although the effect I have described was the usual one, there were also times when I found it impossible to lie still but ran up and down for hours as I talked, or sank into blissful or indescribably frightening dreams—affected my health. I often wakened in the morning with a headache that kept me in agony all day, and I became subject to periods of extreme nervousness and apprehensiveness. Most frightening of all, whole sections of days sometimes disappeared, so that I found myself awake and dressed, reading, walking, and even talking, with no memory at all of anything that had happened since I had lain muttering to the ceiling in my father's library the night before.

The lessons I had had with David did not cease, but in some sense Mr. Million's role and mine were now reversed. It was I, now, who insisted on holding our classes when they were held at all, and it was I who chose the subject matter and, in most cases, questioned David and Mr. Million about it. But often when they were at the library or the park I remained in bed reading, and I believe there were many times when I read and studied from the time I found myself conscious in my bed until my father's valet came for me again.

David's interviews with our father, I should note here, suffered the same changes as my own and at the same time, but since they were less frequent—and they became less and less frequent as the hundred days of summer wore away to autumn and at last to the long winter—and he seemed on the whole to have less adverse reactions to the drugs, the effect on him was not nearly as great.

If at any single time, it was during this winter that I came to the end of childhood. My new ill health forced me away from childish activities, and encouraged the experiments I was carrying out on small animals, and my dissections of the bodies Mr. Million supplied in an unending stream of open mouths and staring eyes. Too, I studied or read, as I have said, for hours on end, or simply lay with my hands behind my head while I struggled to recall, perhaps for whole days together, the narratives I had heard myself give my father. Neither David nor I could ever remember enough even to build a coherent theory of the nature of the questions asked us, but I have still certain scenes fixed in my memory which I am sure I have never beheld in fact, and I believe these are my visualizations of suggestions whispered while I bobbed and dived through those altered states of consciousness.

My aunt, who had previously been so remote, now spoke to me in the corridors and even visited our room. I learned that she controlled the interior arrangements of our house, and through her I was able to have a small laboratory of my own set up in the same wing. But I spent the winter, as I have described, mostly at my enamel dissecting table or in bed. The white snow drifted half up the glass of the window, clinging to the bare stems of the silver trumpet vine. My father's patrons, on the rare occasions I saw them, came in with wet boots, the snow on their shoulders and their hats, puffing and red faced as they beat their coats in the foyer. The orange trees were gone, the roof garden no longer used and the courtyard under our window only late at night when half a dozen patrons and their protégées, whooping with hilarity and wine, fought with snowballs—an activity invariably concluded by stripping the girls and tumbling them naked in the snow.

Spring surprised me, as she always does those of us who remain most of our lives indoors. One day, while I still thought, if I thought about the weather at all, in terms of winter, David threw open the window and insisted that I go with him into the park—and it was April. Mr. Million went with us, and I remember that as we stepped out the front door into the little garden that opened into the street, a garden I had last seen banked with the snow shoveled from the path but which was now bright with early bulbs and the chiming of the fountain, David tapped the iron dog on its grinning muzzle and recited: " 'And thence the dog. With fourfold head brought to these realms of light.' "

I made some trivial remark about his having miscounted.

"Oh, no. Old Cerberus has four heads; don't you know that? The fourth's her maidenhead, and she's such a bitch no dog can take it from her." Even Mr. Million chuckled, but I thought afterward, looking at David's ruddy good health and the foreshadowing of manhood already apparent in the set of his shoulders, that if, as I had always thought of them, the three heads represented Maitre, Madame, and Mr. Million, that is, my father, my aunt (David's *maidenhead*, I suppose), and my tutor, then indeed a fourth would have to be welded in place soon for David himself.

The park must have been a paradise for him, but in my poor health I found it bleak enough and spent most of the morning huddled on a bench, watching David play squash. Toward noon I was joined, not on my own bench, but on another close enough for there to be a feeling of proximity, by a dark-haired girl with one ankle in a cast. She was brought there, on crutches, by a sort of nurse or governess who seated herself, I felt sure deliberately, between the girl and me. This unpleasant woman was, however, too straight backed for her chaperonage to succeed completely. She sat on the edge of the bench, while the girl, with her injured leg thrust out before her, slumped back and thus gave me a good view of her profile, which was beautiful; and occasionally, when she turned to make some remark to the creature with her, I could study her full face—carmine lips and violet eyes, a round rather than an oval face, with a broad point of black hair dividing the forehead; archly delicate black eyebrows and long, curling lashes. When a vendor, an old woman, came selling Cantonese egg rolls (longer than your hand, and still so hot from the boiling fat that they needed to be eaten with great caution, as though they were in some way alive), I made her my messenger and, as well as buying one for myself, sent her with two scalding delicacies to the girl and her attendant monster.

The monster, of course, refused; the girl, I was charmed to see, pleaded, her huge eyes and bright cheeks eloquently proclaiming arguments I was unfortunately just too far away to hear but could follow in pantomime: it would be a gratuitous insult to a blameless stranger to refuse; she was hungry and had intended to buy an egg roll in any event—how thriftless to object when what she had wished for was tendered free! The vending woman, who clearly delighted in her role as go-between, announced herself on the point of weeping at the thought of being forced to refund my gold (actually a bill of small denomination nearly as greasy as the paper in which her wares were wrapped, and considerably dirtier), and eventually their voices grew loud enough for me to hear the girl's, which was a clear and very pleasing contralto. In the end, of course, they accepted; the monster conceded me a frigid nod, and the girl winked at me behind her back.

Half an hour later when David and Mr. Million, who had been watching him from the edge of the court, asked if I wanted lunch, I told them I did, thinking that when we returned I could take a seat closer to the girl without being brazen about it. We ate, I (at least so I fear) very impatiently, in a clean little café close to the flower market, but when we came back to the park the girl and her governess were gone.

We returned to the house, and about an hour afterward my father sent for me. I went with some trepidation, since it was much earlier than was customary for our interview—before the first patrons had arrived, in fact, while I usually saw him only after the last had gone. I need not have feared. He began by asking about my health, and when I said it seemed better than it had been during most of the winter he began, in a self-conscious and even pompous way, as different from his usual fatigued incisiveness as could be imagined, to talk about his business and the need a young man had to prepare himself to earn a living. He said, "You are a scientific scholar, I believe."

I said I hoped I was in a small way, and braced myself for the usual attack upon the uselessness of studying chemistry or biophysics on a world like ours where the industrial base was so small, of no help at the civil service examinations, does not even prepare one for trade, and so on. He said instead, "I'm glad to hear it. To be frank, I asked Mr. Million to encourage you in that as much as he could. He would have done it anyway, I'm sure; he did with me. These studies will not only be of great satisfaction to you, but will . . . ," he paused, cleared his throat, and massaged his face and scalp with his hands, "be valuable in all sorts of ways. And they are, as you might say, a family tradition."

I said, and indeed felt, that I was very happy to hear that.

"Have you seen my lab? Behind the big mirror there?"

I hadn't, though I had known that such a suite of rooms existed beyond the sliding mirror in the library and the servants occasionally spoke of his "dispensary," where he compounded doses for them, examined monthly the girls we employed, and occasionally prescribed treatment for "friends" of patrons, men recklessly imprudent who had failed (as the wise patrons had not) to confine their custom to our establishment exclusively. I told him I should very much like to see it.

He smiled. "But we are wandering from our topic. Science is of great value, but you will find, as I have, that it consumes more money than it produces. You will want apparatus and books and many other things, as well as a livelihood for yourself. We have a not-unprofitable business here, and though I hope to live a long time—thanks in part to science—you are the heir, and it will be yours in the end. . . ."

(So I was older than David!)

". . . every phase of what we do. None of them, believe me, are unimportant."

I had been so surprised, and in fact elated, by my discovery that I had missed a part of what he said. I nodded, which seemed safe.

"Good. I want you to begin by answering the front door. One of the maids has been doing it, and for the first month or so she'll stay with you, since there's more to be learned there than you think. I'll tell Mr. Million, and he can make the arrangements."

I thanked him, and he indicated that the interview was over by opening the door of the library. I could hardly believe, as I went out, that he was the same man who devoured my life in the early hours of almost every morning.

I did not connect this sudden elevation in status with the events in the park. I now realize that Mr. Million, who has, quite literally, eyes in the back of his head, must have reported to my father that I had reached the age at which desires in childhood subliminally fastened to parental figures begin, half-consciously, to grope beyond the family.

In any event, that same evening I took up my new duties and became what Mr. Million called the greeter and David (explaining that the original sense of the word was related to *portal*) the porter of our house—thus assuming in a practical way the functions symbolically executed by the iron dog in our front garden. The maid who had previously carried them out, a girl named Nerissa who had been selected because she was not only one of the prettiest but one of the tallest and strongest of the maids as well, a large-boned, long-faced, smiling girl with shoulders broader than most men's, remained, as my father had promised, to help. Our duties were not onerous, since my father's patrons were all men of some position and wealth, not given to brawling or loud arguments except under unusual circumstances of intoxication, and for the most part they had visited our house already dozens and in a few cases even hundreds of times. We called them by nicknames that were used only here (of which Nerissa informed me sotto voce as they came up the walk), hung up their coats, and directed them—or if necessary conducted them—to the various parts of the establishment. Nerissa flounced (a formidable sight, as I observed, to all but the most heroically proportioned patrons), allowed herself to be pinched, took tips, and talked to me afterward, during slack periods, of the times she had been "called upstairs" at the request of some connoisseur of scale, and the money she had made that night. I laughed at jokes and refused tips in such a way as to make the patrons aware that I was a part of the management. Most patrons did not need the reminder, and I was often told that I strikingly resembled my father.

When I had been serving as a receptionist in this way for only a short time, I think on only the third or fourth night, we had an unusual visitor. He came early one evening, but it was the evening of so dark a day, one of the last really wintry days, that the garden lamps had been lit for an hour or more and the occasional carriages that passed on the street beyond, though they could be heard, could not be seen. I answered the door when he knocked, and as we always did with strangers asked him politely what he wished.

He said, "I should like to speak to Dr. Aubrey Veil."

I am afraid I looked blank.

"This is 666 Saltimbanque?"

It was of course, and the name of Dr. Veil, though I could not place it, touched a chime of memory. I supposed that one of our patrons had used my father's house as an *adresse d'accommodation,* and since this visitor was clearly legitimate and it was not desirable to keep anyone arguing in the doorway despite the partial shelter afforded by the garden, I asked him in; then I sent Nerissa to bring us coffee so that we might have a few moments of private talk in the dark little receiving room that opened off the foyer. It was a room very seldom used, and the maids had been remiss in dusting it, as I saw as soon as I opened the door. I made a mental note to speak to my aunt about it, and as I did I recalled where it was that I had heard Dr. Veil mentioned. My aunt, on the first occasion I had ever spoken to her, had referred to his theory that we might in fact be the natives of Sainte Anne, having murdered the original Terrestrial colonists and displaced them so thoroughly as to forget our own past.

The stranger had seated himself in one of the musty gilded armchairs. He wore a beard, very black and more full than the current style, was young, I thought, though of course considerably older than I, and would have been handsome if the skin of his face—what could be seen of it—had not been of so colorless a white as almost to constitute a disfigurement. His dark clothing seemed abnormally heavy, like felt, and I recalled having heard from some patron that a starcrosser from Sainte Anne had splashed down in the bay yesterday, and asked if he had perhaps been on board it. He looked startled for a moment, then laughed. "You're a wit, I see. And living with Dr. Veil you'd be familiar with his theory. No, I'm from Earth. My name is Marsch." He gave me his card, and I read it twice before the meaning of the delicately embossed abbreviations registered on my mind. My visitor was a scientist, a doctor of philosophy in anthropology, from Earth.

I said, "I wasn't trying to be witty. I thought you might really have come from Sainte Anne. Here, most of us have a kind of planetary face, except for the gypsies and the criminal tribes, and you don't seem to fit the pattern."

He said, "I've noticed what you mean; you seem to have it yourself."

"I'm supposed to look a great deal like my father."

"Ah," he said. He stared at me. Then, "Are you cloned?"

"Cloned?" I had read the term, but only in conjunction with botany, and as has happened to me often when I have especially wanted to impress someone with my intelligence, nothing came. I felt like a stupid child.

"Parthenogenetically reproduced, so that the new individual—or individuals; you can have a thousand if you want—will have a genetic structure identical to the parent. It's antievolutionary, so it's illegal on Earth, but I don't suppose things are as closely watched out here."

"You're talking about human beings?"

He nodded.

"I've never heard of it. Really I doubt if you'd find the necessary technology here; we're quite backward compared to Earth. Of course, my father might be able to arrange something for you."

"I don't want to have it done."

Nerissa came in with the coffee then, effectively cutting off anything further Dr. Marsch might have said. Actually, I had added the suggestion about my father more from force of habit than anything else, and thought it very unlikely that he could pull off any such biochemical tour de force, but there was always the possibility, particularly if a large sum was offered. As it was, we fell silent while Nerissa arranged the cups and poured, and when she had gone Marsch said appreciatively, "Quite an unusual girl." His eyes, I noticed, were a bright green, without the brown tones most green eyes have.

I was wild to ask him about Earth and the new developments there, and it had already occurred to me that the girls might be an effective way of keeping him here, or at least of bringing him back. I said, "You should see some of them. My father has wonderful taste."

"I'd rather see Dr. Veil. Or is Dr. Veil your father?"

"Oh, no."

"This is his address, or at least the address I was given. Number 666 Saltimbanque Street, Port-Mimizon, Département de la Main, Sainte Croix."

He appeared quite serious, and it seemed possible that if I told him flatly that he was mistaken he would leave. I said, "I learned about Veil's Hypothesis from my aunt; she seemed quite conversant with it. Perhaps later this evening you'd like to talk to her about it."

"Couldn't I see her now?"

"My aunt sees very few visitors. To be frank, I'm told she quarreled with my father before I was born, and she seldom leaves her own apartments. The housekeepers report to her there and she manages what I suppose I must call our domestic economy, but it's very rare to see Madame outside her rooms, or for any stranger to be let in."

"And why are you telling me this?"

"So that you'll understand that with the best will in the world it may not be possible for me to arrange an interview for you. At least, not this evening."

"You could simply ask her if she knows Dr. Veil's present address, and if so what it is."

"I'm trying to help you, Dr. Marsch. Really I am."

"But you don't think that's the best way to go about it?"

"No."

"In other words, if your aunt were simply asked, without being given a chance to form her own judgment of me, she wouldn't give me information even if she had it?"

"It would help if we were to talk a bit first. There are a great many things I'd like to learn about Earth."

For an instant I thought I saw a sour smile under the black beard. He said, "Suppose I ask you first—"

He was interrupted—again—by Nerissa, I suppose because she wanted to see if we required anything further from the kitchen. I could have strangled her when Dr. Marsch halted in midsentence and said instead, "Couldn't this girl ask your aunt if she would see me?"

I had to think quickly. I had been planning to go myself and, after a suitable wait, return and say that my aunt would receive Dr. Marsch later, which would have given me an additional opportunity to question him while he waited. But there was at least a possibility (no doubt magnified in my eyes by my eagerness to hear of new discoveries from Earth) that he would not wait—or that, when and if he did eventually see my aunt, he might mention the incident. If I sent Nerissa I would at least have him to myself while she ran her errand, and there was an excellent chance—or at least so I imagined—that my aunt would in fact have some business which she would want to conclude before seeing a stranger. I told Nerissa to go, and Dr. Marsch gave her one of his cards after writing a few words on the back.

"Now," I said, "what was it you were about to ask me?"

"Why this house, on a planet that has been inhabited less than two hundred years, seems so absurdly old."

"It was built a hundred and forty years ago, but you must have many on Earth that are far older."

"I suppose so. Hundreds. But for every one of them there are ten thousand that have been up less than a year. Here, almost every building I see seems nearly as old as this one."

"We've never been crowded here, and we haven't had to tear down; that's what Mr. Million says. And there are fewer people here now than there were fifty years ago."

"Mr. Million?"

I told him about Mr. Million, and when I finished he said, "It sounds as if you've got a ten nine unbound simulator here, which should be interesting. Only a few have ever been made."

"A ten nine simulator?"

"A billion, ten to the ninth power. The human brain has several billion synapses, of course, but it's been found that you can simulate its action pretty well—"

It seemed to me that no time at all had passed since Nerissa had left, but she was back. She curtsied to Dr. Marsch and said, "Madame will see you."

I blurted, "Now?"

"Yes," Nerissa said artlessly, "Madame said right now."

"I'll take him then. You mind the door."

I escorted Dr. Marsch down the dark corridors, taking a long route to have more time, but he seemed to be arranging in his mind the questions he wished to

ask my aunt, as we walked past the spotted mirrors and warped little walnut tables, and he answered me in monosyllables when I tried to question him about
Earth.

At my aunt's door I rapped for him. She opened it herself, the hem of her
black skirt hanging emptily over the untrodden carpet, but I do not think he noticed that. He said, "I'm really very sorry to bother you, Madame, and I only do
so because your nephew thought you might be able to help me locate the author
of Veil's Hypothesis."

My aunt said, "I am Dr. Veil; please come in," and shut the door behind him,
leaving me standing openmouthed in the corridor.

I mentioned the incident to Phaedria the next time we met, but she was more interested in learning about my father's house. Phaedria, if I have not used her
name before now, was the girl who had sat near me while I watched David play
squash. She had been introduced to me on my next visit to the park by no one less
than the monster herself, who had helped her to a seat beside me and, miracle of
miracles, promptly retreated to a point which, though not out of sight, was at least
beyond earshot. Phaedria had thrust her broken ankle in front of her, halfway
across the graveled path, and smiled a most charming smile. "You don't object to
my sitting here?" She had perfect teeth.

"I'm delighted."

"You're surprised too. Your eyes get big when you're surprised; did you
know that?"

"I am surprised. I've come here looking for you several times, but you haven't
been here."

"We've come looking for you, and you haven't been here either, but I suppose
one can't really spend a great deal of time in a park."

"I would have," I said, "if I'd known you were looking for me. I went here as
much as I could anyway. I was afraid that she"—I jerked my head at the
monster—"wouldn't let you come back. How did you persuade her?"

"I didn't," Phaedria said. "Can't you guess? Don't you know anything?"

I confessed that I did not. I felt stupid, and I was stupid, at least in the things I
said, because so much of my mind was caught up not in formulating answers to
her remarks but in committing to memory the lilt of her voice, the purple of her
eyes, even the faint perfume of her skin and the soft, warm touch of her breath on
my cool cheek.

"So you see," Phaedria was saying, "that's how it is with me. When Aunt
Uranie—she's only a poor cousin of mother's, really—got home and told him
about you he found out who you are, and here I am."

"Yes," I said, and she laughed.

Phaedria was one of those girls raised between the hope of marriage and the
thought of sale. Her father's affairs, as she herself said, were "unsettled." He

speculated in ship cargoes, mostly from the south—textiles and drugs. He owned, most of the time, large sums which the lenders could not hope to collect unless they were willing to allow him more to recoup. He might die a pauper, but in the meantime he had raised his daughter with every detail of education and plastic surgery attended to. If when she reached marriageable age he could afford a good dowry, she would link him with some wealthy family. If he was pressed for money instead, a girl so reared would bring fifty times the price of a common street child. Our family, of course, would be ideal for either purpose.

"Tell me about your house," she said. "Do you know what the kids call it? 'The Cave Canem,' or sometimes just 'The Cave.' The boys all think it's a big thing to have been there and they lie about it. Most of them haven't."

But I wanted to talk about Dr. Marsch and the sciences of Earth, and I was nearly as anxious to find out about her own world, "the kids" she mentioned so casually, her school and family, as she was to learn about us. Also, although I was willing to detail the services my father's girls rendered their benefactors, there were some things, such as my aunt's floating down the stairwell, that I was adverse to discussing. But we bought egg rolls from the same old woman to eat in the chill sunlight and exchanged confidences and somehow parted not only lovers but friends, promising to meet again the next day.

At some time during the night, I believe at almost the same time that I returned—or to speak more accurately *was returned*, since I could scarcely walk— to my bed after a session of hours with my father, the weather changed. The musked exhalation of late spring or early summer crept through the shutters, and the fire in our little grate seemed to extinguish itself for shame almost at once. My father's valet opened the window for me and there poured into the room that fragrance that tells of the melting of the last snows beneath the deepest and darkest evergreens on the north sides of mountains. I had arranged with Phaedria to meet at ten, and before going to my father's library I had posted a note on the escritoire beside my bed, asking that I be awakened an hour earlier; and that night I slept with the fragrance in my nostrils and the thought—half plan, half dream—in my mind that by some means Phaedria and I would elude her aunt entirely and find a deserted lawn where blue and yellow flowers dotted the short grass.

When I woke, it was an hour past noon and rain drove in sheets past the window. Mr. Million, who was reading a book on the far side of the room, told me that it had been raining like that since six and for that reason he had not troubled to wake me. I had a splitting headache, as I often did after a long session with my father, and took one of the powders he had prescribed to relieve it. They were gray, and smelled of anise.

"You look unwell," Mr. Million said.

"I was hoping to go to the park."

"I know." He rolled across the room toward me, and I recalled that Dr. Marsch had called him an unbound simulator. For the first time since I had satisfied myself about them when I was quite small, I bent over (at some cost to my head) and read the almost obliterated stampings on his main cabinet. There was only the name of a cybernetics company on Earth and, in French as I had always supposed, his name: M. Million—"Monsieur" or "Mister" Million. Then, as startling as a blow from behind to a man musing in a comfortable chair, I remembered that a dot was employed in some algebras for multiplication. He saw my change of expression at once. "A thousand-million-word core capacity," he said. "An English billion or a French milliard, the *M* being the Roman numeral for one thousand, of course. I thought you understood that some time ago."

"You are an unbound simulator. What is a bound simulator, and whom are you simulating—my father?"

"No." The face in the screen, Mr. Million's face as I had always thought of it, shook its head. "Call me, call the person simulated, at least, your great-grandfather. He—I—am dead. In order to achieve simulation, it is necessary to examine the cells of the brain, layer by layer, with a beam of accelerated particles so that the neural patterns can be reproduced, we say 'core imaged,' in the computer. The process is fatal."

I asked after a moment, "And a bound simulator?"

"If the simulation is to have a body that looks human the mechanical body must be linked—'bound'—to a remote core, since the smallest billion-word core cannot be made even approximately as small as a human brain." He paused again, and for an instant his face dissolved into myriad sparkling dots, swirling like dust motes in a sunbeam. "I am sorry. For once you wish to listen, but I do not wish to lecture. I was told, a very long time ago, just before the operation, that my simulation—this—would be capable of emotion in certain circumstances. Until today I had always thought they lied." I would have stopped him if I could, but he rolled out of the room before I could recover from my surprise.

For a long time, I suppose an hour or more, I sat listening to the drumming of the rain and thinking about Phaedria and about what Mr. Million had said, all of it confused with my father's questions of the night before, questions which had seemed to steal their answers from me so that I was empty, and dreams had come to flicker in the emptiness, dreams of fences and walls and the concealing ditches called ha-has, that contain a barrier you do not see until you are about to tumble on it. Once I had dreamed of standing in a paved court fenced with Corinthian pillars so close set that I could not force my body between them, although in the dream I was only a child of three or four. After trying various places for a long time, I had noticed that each column was carved with a word—the only one that I could remember was *carapace*—and that the paving stones of the courtyard were mortuary tablets like those set into the floors in some of the old French churches, with my own name and a different date on each.

This dream pursued me even when I tried to think of Phaedria, and when a maid brought me hot water—for I now shaved twice a week—I found that I was already holding my razor in my hand, and had in fact cut myself with it so that the blood had streaked my nightclothes and run down onto the sheets.

T he next time I saw Phaedria, which was four or five days afterward, she was engrossed by a new project in which she enlisted both David and me. This was nothing less than a theatrical company, composed mostly of girls her own age, which was to present plays during the summer in a natural amphitheater in the park. Since the company, as I have said, consisted principally of girls, male actors were at a premium, and David and I soon found ourselves deeply embroiled. The play had been written by a committee of the cast, and—inevitably— revolved about the loss of political power by the original French-speaking colonists. Phaedria, whose ankle would not be mended in time for our performance, would play the crippled daughter of the French governor; David, her lover (a dashing captain of chasseurs); and I, the governor himself—a part I accepted readily because it was a much better one than David's, and offered scope for a great deal of fatherly affection toward Phaedria.

The night of our performance, which was early in June, I recall vividly for two reasons. My aunt, whom I had not seen since she had closed the door behind Dr. Marsch, notified me at the last moment that she wished to attend and that I was to escort her. And we players had grown so afraid of having an empty house that I had asked my father if it would be possible for him to send some of his girls—who would thus lose only the earliest part of the evening, when there was seldom much business in any event. To my great surprise (I suppose because he felt it would be good advertising) he consented, stipulating only that they should return at the end of the third act if he sent a messenger saying they were needed.

Because I would have to arrive at least an hour early to make up, it was no more than late afternoon when I called for my aunt. She showed me in herself, and immediately asked my help for her maid, who was trying to wrestle some heavy object from the upper shelf of a closet. It proved to be a folding wheelchair, and under my aunt's direction we set it up. When we had finished she said abruptly, "Give me a hand in, you two," and taking our arms lowered herself into the seat. Her black skirt, lying emptily against the leg boards of the chair like a collapsed tent, showed legs no thicker than my wrists, but also an odd thickening, almost like a saddle, below her hips. Seeing me staring, she snapped, "Won't be needing that until I come back, I suppose. Lift me up a little. Stand in back and get me under the arms."

I did so, and her maid reached unceremoniously under my aunt's skirt and drew out a little leather padded device on which she had been resting. "Shall we go?" my aunt sniffed. "You'll be late."

I wheeled her into the corridor, her maid holding the door for us. Somehow, learning that my aunt's ability to hang in the air like smoke was physically, indeed mechanically, derived made it more disturbing than ever. When she asked why I was so quiet, I told her and added that I had been under the impression that no one had yet succeeded in producing working antigravity.

"And you think I have? Then why wouldn't I use it to get to your play?"

"I suppose because you don't want it to be seen."

"Nonsense. It's a regular prosthetic device. You buy them at the surgical stores." She twisted around in her seat until she could look up at me, her face so like my father's, and her lifeless legs like the sticks David and I used as little boys when, doing parlor magic, we wished Mr. Million to believe us lying prone when we were in fact crouched beneath our own supposed figures. "Puts out a super-conducting field, then induces eddy currents in the reinforcing rods in the floors. The flux of the induced currents opposes the machine's own flux and I float, more or less. Lean forward to go forward; straighten up to stop. You look relieved."

"I am. I suppose antigravity frightened me."

"I used the iron banister when I went down the stairs with you once; it has a very convenient coil shape."

Our play went smoothly enough, with predictable cheers from members of the audience who were, or at least wished to be thought, descended from the old French aristocracy. The audience, in fact, was better than we had dared hope, five hundred or so besides the inevitable sprinkling of pickpockets, police, and street-walkers. The incident I most vividly recall came toward the latter half of the first act, when for ten minutes or so I sat with few lines at a desk, listening to my fellow actors. Our stage faced the west, and the setting sun had left the sky a welter of lurid color: purple-reds striped gold and flame and black. Against this violent ground, which might have been the massed banners of Hell, there began to appear, in ones and twos, like the elongate shadows of fantastic grenadiers crenelated and plumed, the heads, the slender necks, the narrow shoulders, of a platoon of my father's demimondaines; arriving late, they were taking the last seats at the upper rim of our theater, encircling it like the soldiery of some ancient, bizarre government surrounding a treasonous mob.

They sat at last, my cue came, and I forgot them, and that is all I can now remember of our first performance, except that at one point some motion of mine suggested to the audience a mannerism of my father's and there was a shout of misplaced laughter—and that at the beginning of the second act Sainte Anne rose with its sluggish rivers and great grassy meadow-meres clearly visible, flooding the audience with green light, and at the close of the third I saw my father's crooked little valet bustling among the upper rows and the girls, green-edged black shadows, filing out.

We produced three more plays that summer, all with some success, and David and Phaedria and I became an accepted partnership, with Phaedria dividing herself more or less equally between us—whether by her own inclination or her parents' orders I could never be quite sure. When her ankle knit she was a companion fit for David in athletics, a better player of all the ball and racket games than any of the other girls who came to the park, but she would as often drop everything and come to sit with me, where she sympathized with (though she did not actually share) my interest in botany and biology, and gossiped, and delighted in showing me off to her friends, since my reading had given me a sort of talent for puns and repartee.

It was Phaedria who suggested, when it became apparent that the ticket money from our first play would be insufficient for the costumes and scenery we coveted for our second, that at the close of future performances the cast circulate among the audience to take up a collection; and this, of course, in the press and bustle easily lent itself to the accomplishment of petty thefts for our cause. Most people, however, had too much sense to bring to our theater, in the evening, in the gloomy park, more money than was required to buy tickets and perhaps an ice or a glass of wine during intermission; so no matter how dishonest we were the profit remained small, and we, and especially Phaedria and David, were soon talking of going forward to more dangerous and lucrative adventures.

At about this time, I suppose as a result of my father's continued and intensified probing of my subconscious, a violent and almost nightly examination whose purpose was still unclear to me and which, since I had been accustomed to it for so long, I scarcely questioned, I became more and more subject to frightening lapses of conscious control. I would, so David and Mr. Million told me, seem quite myself though perhaps rather more quiet than usual, answering questions intelligently if absently, and then, suddenly, come to myself, start, and stare at the familiar rooms, the familiar faces, among which I now found myself, perhaps after the midafternoon, without the slightest memory of having awakened, dressed, shaved, eaten, gone for a walk.

Although I loved Mr. Million as much as I had when I was a boy, I was never able, after that conversation in which I learned the meaning of the familiar lettering on his side, quite to reestablish the old relationship. I was always conscious, as I am conscious now, that the personality I loved had perished years before I was born, and that I addressed an imitation of it, fundamentally mathematical in nature, responding as that personality might to the stimuli of human speech and action. I could never determine whether Mr. Million is really aware in that sense which would give him the right to say, as he always has, "I think" and "I feel." When I asked him about it he could only explain that he did not know the answer himself, that having no standard of comparison, he could not be positive whether his own mental processes represented true consciousness or not; and I, of course, could not know whether this answer represented the deepest meditation of a soul somehow alive in the dancing abstractions of the simulation or whether it was merely triggered, a phonographic response, by my question.

Our theater, as I have said, continued through the summer and gave its last performance with the falling leaves drifting, like obscure, perfumed old letters from some discarded trunk, upon our stage. When the curtain calls were over we who had written and acted the plays of our season were too disheartened to do more than remove our costumes and cosmetics and drift ourselves, with the last of our departing audience, down the whip-poor-will-haunted paths to the city streets and home. I was prepared, as I remember, to take up my duties at my father's door, but that night he had stationed his valet in the foyer to wait for me, and I was ushered directly into the library, where my father explained brusquely that he would have to devote the latter part of the evening to business and for that reason would speak to me (as he put it) early. He looked tired and ill, and it occurred to me, I think for the first time, that he would one day die—and that I would, on that day, become at once both rich and free.

What I said under the drugs that evening I do not, of course, recall, but I remember as vividly as I might if I had only this morning awakened from it the dream that followed. I was on a ship, a white ship like one of those the oxen pull, so slowly the sharp prows make no wake at all, through the green water of the canal beside the park. I was the only crewman, and indeed the only living man aboard. At the stern, grasping the huge wheel in such a flaccid way that it seemed to support and guide and steady *him* rather than he it, stood the corpse of a tall, thin man whose face, when the rolling of his head presented it to me, was the face that floated in Mr. Million's screen. This face, as I have said, was very like my father's, but I knew the dead man at the wheel was not he.

I was aboard the ship a long time. We seemed to be running free, with the wind a few points to port and strong. When I went aloft at night, masts and spars and rigging quivered and sang in the wind, and sail upon sail towered above me, and sail upon white sail spread below me, and more masts clothed in sails stood before me and behind me. When I worked on deck by day, spray wet my shirt and left tear-shaped spots on the planks which dried quickly in the bright sunlight.

I cannot remember ever having really been on such a ship, but perhaps, as a very small child, I was, for the sounds of it, the creaking of the masts in their sockets, the whistling of the wind in the thousand ropes, the crashing of the waves against the wooden hull, were all as distinct, and as real, as much *themselves*, as the sounds of laughter and breaking glass overhead had been when, as a child, I had tried to sleep, or the bugles from the citadel which sometimes, then, woke me in the morning.

I was about some work, I do not know just what, aboard this ship. I carried buckets of water with which I dashed clotted blood from the decks, and I pulled at ropes which seemed attached to nothing—or rather, firmly tied to immovable objects still higher in the rigging. I watched the surface of the sea from bow and rail, from the mastheads, and from atop a large cabin amidships, but when a starcrosser, its entry shields blinding bright with heat, plunged hissing into the sea far off I reported it to no one.

And all this time the dead man at the wheel was talking to me. His head hung limply, as though his neck were broken, and the jerkings of the wheel he held, as big waves struck the rudder, sent it from one shoulder to the other, or back to stare at the sky, or down. But he continued to speak, and the few words I caught suggested that he was lecturing upon an ethical theory whose postulates seemed even to him doubtful. I felt a dread of hearing this talk and tried to keep myself as much as possible toward the bow, but the wind at times carried the words to me with great clarity, and whenever I looked up from my work I found myself much nearer the stern, sometimes in fact almost touching the dead steersman, than I had supposed.

After I had been on this ship a long while, so that I was very tired and very lonely, one of the doors of the cabin opened and my aunt came out, floating quite upright about two feet above the tilted deck. Her skirt did not hang vertically as I had always seen it, but whipped in the wind like a streamer, so that she seemed on the point of blowing away. For some reason I said, "Don't get close to that man at the wheel, Aunt. He might hurt you."

She answered, as naturally as if we had met in the corridor outside my bedroom, "Nonsense. He's far past doing anyone any good, Number Five, or any harm either. It's my brother we have to worry about."

"Where is he?"

"Down there." She pointed at the deck as if to indicate that he was in the hold. "He's trying to find out why the ship doesn't move."

I ran to the side and looked over, and what I saw was not water but the night sky. Stars—innumerable stars—were spread at an infinite distance below me, and as I looked at them I realized that the ship, as my aunt had said, did not make headway or even roll, but remained heeled over, motionless. I looked back at her and she told me, "It doesn't move because he has fastened it in place until he finds out why it doesn't move," and at this point I found myself sliding down a rope into what I supposed was the hold of the ship. It smelled of animals. I had awakened, though at first I did not know it.

My feet touched the floor, and I saw that David and Phaedria were beside me. We were in a huge, loftlike room, and as I looked at Phaedria, who was very pretty but tense and biting her lips, a cock crowed.

David said, "Where do you think the money is?" He was carrying a tool kit.

And Phaedria, who I suppose had expected him to say something else, or in answer to her own thoughts, said, "We'll have lots of time; Marydol is watching." Marydol was one of the girls who appeared in our plays.

"If she doesn't run away. Where do you think the money is?"

"Not up here. Downstairs behind the office." She had been crouching, but she rose now and began to creep forward. She was all in black, from her ballet slippers to a black ribbon binding her black hair, with her white face and arms in striking contrast, and her carmine lips an error, a bit of color left by mistake. David and I followed her.

Crates were scattered, widely separated, on the floor, and as we passed them I saw that they held poultry, a single bird in each. It was not until we were nearly to the ladder which plunged down a hatch in the floor at the opposite corner of the room that I realized that these birds were gamecocks. Then a shaft of sun from one of the skylights struck a crate and the cock rose and stretched himself, showing fierce red eyes and plumage as gaudy as a macaw's. "Come on," Phaedria said, "the dogs are next," and we followed her down the ladder. Pandemonium broke out on the floor below.

The dogs were chained in stalls, with dividers too high for them to see the dogs on either side of them and wide aisles between the rows of stalls. They were all fighting dogs, but of every size from ten-pound terriers to mastiffs larger than small horses, brutes with heads as misshappen as the growths that appear on old trees and jaws that could sever both a man's legs at a mouthful. The din of the barking was incredible, a solid substance that shook us as we descended the ladder, and at the bottom I took Phaedria's arm and tried to indicate by signs—since I was certain that we were wherever we were without permission—that we should leave at once. She shook her head and then, when I was unable to understand what she said even when she exaggerated the movements of her lips, wrote on a dusty wall with her moistened forefinger: *They do this all the time—a noise in the street—anything*.

Access to the floor below was by stairs, reached through a heavy but unbolted door which I think had been installed largely to exclude the din. I felt better when we had closed it behind us even though the noise was still very loud. I had fully come to myself by this time, and I should have explained to David and Phaedria that I did not know where I was or what we were doing there, but shame held me back. And in any event I could guess easily enough what our purpose was. David had asked about the location of money, and we had often talked—talk I had considered at the time to be more than half-empty boasting—about a single robbery that would free us from the necessity of further petty crime.

Where we were I discovered later when we left, and how we had come to be there I pieced together from casual conversations. The building had been originally designed as a warehouse, and stood on the rue des Egouts close to the bay. Its owner supplied those enthusiasts who staged combats of all kinds for sport, and was credited with maintaining the largest assemblage of these creatures in the Départment. Phaedria's father had happened to hear that this man had recently put some of his most valuable stock on ship, had taken Phaedria when he called on him, and, since the place was known not to open its doors until after the last Angelus, we had come the next day a little after the second and entered through one of the skylights.

I find it difficult to describe what we saw when we descended from the floor of the dogs to the next, which was the second floor of the building. I had seen fighting slaves many times before when Mr. Million, David, and I had traversed the slave market to reach the library, but never more than one or two together, heavily manacled. Here they lay, sat, and lounged everywhere, and for a moment I wondered why they did not tear one another to pieces, and the three of us as well. Then I saw that each was held by a short chain stapled to the floor, and it was not difficult to tell from the scraped and splintered circles in the boards just how far the slave in the center could reach. Such furniture as they had, straw pallets and a few chairs and benches, was either too light to do harm if thrown or very stoutly made and spiked down. I had expected them to shout and threaten us as I had heard they threatened each other in the pits before closing, but they seemed to understand that as long as they were chained, they could do nothing. Every head turned toward us as we came down the steps, but we had no food for them, and after that first examination they were far less interested in us than the dogs had been.

"They aren't people, are they?" Phaedria said. She was walking erectly as a soldier on parade now, and looking at the slaves with interest; as I was studying her, it occurred to me that she was taller and less plump than the "Phaedria" I pictured to myself when I thought of her. She was not just a pretty but a beautiful girl. "They're a kind of animal, really," she said.

From my studies I was better informed, and I told her that they had been human as infants—in some cases even as children or older—and that they differed from normal people only as a result of surgery (some of it on their brains) and chemically induced alterations in their endocrine systems. And of course in appearance because of their scars.

"Your father does that sort of thing to little girls, doesn't he? For your house?"

David said, "Only once in a while. It takes a lot of time, and most people prefer normals, even when they prefer pretty odd normals."

"I'd like to see some of them. I mean the ones he's worked on."

I was still thinking of the fighting slaves around us and said, "Don't you know about these things? I thought you'd been here before. You knew about the dogs."

"Oh, I've seen them before, and the man told me about them. I suppose I was just thinking out loud. It would be awful if they were still people."

Their eyes followed us, and I wondered if they could understand her.

The ground floor was very different from the ones above. The walls were paneled; there were framed pictures of dogs and cocks and of the slaves and curious animals. The windows, opening toward Egouts Street and the bay, were high and narrow and admitted only slender beams of the bright sunlight to pick out of the gloom the arm alone of a rich red-leather chair, a square of maroon carpet no bigger than a book, a half-full decanter. I took three steps into this room and knew that we had been discovered. Striding toward us was a tall, high-shouldered young man—who halted, with a startled look, just when I did. He was my own reflection in a gilt-framed pier glass, and I felt the momentary dislocation that comes when a stranger, an unrecognized shape, turns or moves his head and is some familiar friend glimpsed, perhaps for the first time, from outside. The sharp-chinned, grim-looking boy I had seen when I did not know him to be myself had been myself as Phaedria and David, Mr. Million and my aunt, saw me.

"This is where he talks to customers," Phaedria said. "If he's trying to sell something he has his people bring them down one at a time so you don't see the others, but you can hear the dogs bark even from way down here, and he took Papa and me upstairs and showed us everything."

David asked, "Did he show you where he keeps the money?"

"In back. See that tapestry? It's really a curtain, because while Papa was talking to him, a man came who owed him for something and paid, and he went through there with it."

The door behind the tapestry opened on a small office, with still another door in the wall opposite. There was no sign of a safe or strongbox. David broke the lock on the desk with a pry bar from his tool kit, but there was only the usual clutter of papers, and I was about to open the second door when I heard a sound, a scraping or shuffling, from the room beyond.

For a minute or more none of us moved. I stood with my hand on the latch. Phaedria, behind me and to my left, had been looking under the carpet for a cache in the floor—she remained crouched, her skirt a black pool at her feet. From somewhere near the broken desk I could hear David's breathing. The shuffling came again, and a board creaked. David said very softly, "It's an animal."

I drew my fingers away from the latch and looked at him. He was still gripping the pry bar and his face was pale, but he smiled. "An animal tethered in there, shifting its feet. That's all."

I said, "How do you know?"

"Anybody in there would have heard us, especially when I cracked the desk. If it were a person he would have come out, or if he were afraid he'd hide and be quiet."

Phaedria said, "I think he's right. Open the door."

"Before I do, if it isn't an animal?"

David said, "It is."

"But if it isn't?"

I saw the answer on their faces; David gripped his pry bar, and I opened the door.

The room beyond was larger than I had expected, but bare and dirty. The only light came from a single window high in the farther wall. In the middle of the floor stood a big chest, of dark wood bound with iron, and before it lay what appeared to be a bundle of rags. As I stepped from the carpeted office the rags moved and a face, a face triangular as a mantis's, turned toward me. Its chin was hardly more than an inch from the floor, but under deep brows the eyes were tiny scarlet fires.

"That must be it," Phaedria said. She was looking not at the face but at the iron-banded chest. "David, can you break into that?"

"I think so," David said, but he, like me, was watching the ragged thing's eyes. "What about that?" he said after a moment, and gestured toward it. Before Phaedria or I could answer, its mouth opened showing long, narrow teeth, gray-yellow. "Sick," it said.

None of us, I think, had thought it could speak. It was as though a mummy had spoken. Outside, a carriage went past, its iron wheels rattling on the cobbles.

"Let's go," David said. "Let's get out."

Phaedria said, "It's sick. Don't you see, the owner's brought it down here where he can look in on it and take care of it. It's sick."

"And he chained his sick slave to the cash box?" David cocked an eyebrow at her.

"Don't you see? It's the only heavy thing in the room. All you have to do is go over there and knock the poor creature in the head. If you're afraid, give me the bar and I'll do it myself."

"I'll do it."

I followed him to within a few feet of the chest. He gestured at the slave imperiously with the steel pry bar. "You! Move away from there."

The slave made a gurgling sound and crawled to one side, dragging his chain. He was wrapped in a filthy, tattered blanket and seemed hardly larger than a child, though I noticed that his hands were immense.

I turned and took a step toward Phaedria, intending to urge that we leave if David were unable to open the chest in a few minutes. I remember that before I heard or felt anything I saw her eyes open wide, and I was still wondering why when David's kit of tools clattered on the floor and David himself fell with a thud and a little gasp. Phaedria screamed, and all the dogs on the third floor began to bark.

All this, of course, took less than a second. I turned to look almost as David fell. The slave had darted out an arm and caught my brother by the ankle, and then in an instant had thrown off his blanket and bounded—that is the only way to describe it—on top of him.

I caught him by the neck and jerked him backward, thinking that he would cling to David and that it would be necessary to tear him away, but the instant he felt my hands he flung David aside and writhed like a spider in my grip. *He had four arms.*

I saw them flailing as he tried to reach me, and I let go of him and jerked back, as if a rat had been thrust at my face. That instinctive repulsion saved me; he drove his feet backward in a kick which, if I had still been holding him tightly enough to give him a fulcrum, would have surely ruptured my liver or spleen and killed me.

Instead it shot him forward and me, gasping for breath, back. I fell and rolled, and was outside the circle permitted him by his chain; David had already scrambled away, and Phaedria was well out of his reach.

For a moment, while I shuddered and tried to sit up, the three of us simply stared at him. Then David quoted wryly:

> Arms and the man I sing, who forc'd by fate,
> And haughty Juno's unrelenting hate,
> Expell'd and exil'd, left the Trojan shore.

Neither Phaedria nor I laughed, but Phaedria let out her breath in a long sigh and asked me, "How did they do that? Get him like that?"

I told her I supposed they had transplanted the extra pair after suppressing his body's natural resistance to the implanted foreign tissue and that the operation had probably replaced some of his ribs with the donor's shoulder structure. "I've been teaching myself to do the same sort of thing with mice—on a much less ambitious scale, of course—and the striking thing to me is that he seems to have full use of the grafted pair. Unless you've got identical twins to work with, the nerve endings almost never join properly, and whoever did this probably had a hundred failures before he got what he wanted. That slave must be worth a fortune."

David said, "I thought you threw your mice out. Aren't you working with monkeys now?"

I wasn't, although I hoped to, but whether I was or not, it seemed clear that talking about it wasn't going to accomplish anything. I told David that.

"I thought you were hot to leave."

I had been, but now I wanted something else much more. I wanted to perform an exploratory operation on that creature much more than David or Phaedria had ever wanted money. David liked to think that he was bolder than I, and I knew when I said, "You may want to get away, but don't use me as an excuse, Brother," that that would settle it.

"All right, how are we going to kill him?" David gave me an angry look.

Phaedria said: "He can't reach us. We could throw things at him."

"And he could throw the ones that missed back."

While we talked, the thing, the four-armed slave, was grinning at us. I was fairly sure he could understand at least a part of what we were saying, and I motioned to David and Phaedria to indicate that we should go back into the room where the desk was. When we were there I closed the door. "I didn't want him to hear us. If we had weapons on poles, spears of some kind, we might be able to kill him without getting too close. What could we use for the sticks? Any ideas?"

David shook his head, but Phaedria said, "Wait a minute; I remember something." We both looked at her and she knitted her brows, pretending to search her memory and enjoying the attention.

"Well?" David asked.

She snapped her fingers. "Window poles. You know, long things with a little hook on the end. Remember the windows out there where he talks to customers? They're high up in the wall, and while he and Papa were talking one of the men who works for him brought one and opened a window. They ought to be around somewhere."

We found two after a five-minute search. They looked satisfactory: about six feet long and an inch and a quarter in diameter, of hardwood. David flourished his and pretended to thrust at Phaedria, then asked me, "Now what do we use for points?"

The scalpel I always carried was in its case in my breast pocket, and I fastened it to the rod with electrical tape from a roll David had fortunately carried on his belt instead of in the tool kit, but we could find nothing to make a second spearhead for him until he himself suggested broken glass.

"You can't break a window," Phaedria said. "They'd hear you outside. Besides, won't it just snap off when you try to get him with it?"

"Not if it's thick glass. Look here, you two."

I did, and saw—again—my own face. He was pointing toward the large mirror that had surprised me when I came down the steps. While I looked his shoe struck it, and it shattered with a crash that set the dogs barking again. He selected a long, almost straight, triangular piece and held it up to the light, where it flashed like a gem. "That's about as good as they used to make them from agate and jasper on Sainte Anne, isn't it?"

By prior agreement we approached from opposite sides. The slave leaped to the top of the chest and, from there, watched us quite calmly, his deep-set eyes turning from David to me until at last, when we were both quite close, David rushed him.

He spun around as the glass point grazed his ribs and caught David's spear by the shaft and jerked him forward. I thrust at the slave but missed, and before I could recover he had dived from the chest and was grappling with David on the far side. I bent over it and jabbed down at the slave, and it was not until David screamed that I realized I had driven my scalpel into his thigh. I saw the blood, bright arterial blood, spurt up and drench the shaft, and let it go and threw myself over the chest on top of them.

The slave was ready for me, on his back and grinning, with his legs and all four arms raised like a dead spider's. I am certain he would have strangled me in the next few seconds if it had not been that David, how consciously I do not know, threw one arm across the creature's eyes so that he missed his grip and I fell between those outstretched hands.

There is not a great deal more to tell. He jerked free of David and, pulling me to him, tried to bite my throat, but I hooked a thumb in one of his eye sockets and held him off. Phaedria, with more courage than I would have credited her with, put David's glass-tipped spear into my free hand and I stabbed the slave in the neck—I believe I severed both jugulars and the trachea before he died. We put a tourniquet on David's leg and left without either the money or the knowledge of technique I had hoped to get from the body of the slave. Marydol helped us get David home, and we told Mr. Million he had fallen while we were exploring an empty building—though I doubt that he believed us.

There is one other thing to tell about that incident—I mean the killing of the slave—although I am tempted to go on and describe instead a discovery I made immediately afterward that had, at the time, a much greater influence on me. It is only an impression, and one that I have, I am sure, distorted and magnified in recollection. While I was stabbing the slave, my face was very near his and I saw (I suppose because of the light from the high windows behind us) my own face reflected and doubled in the corneas of his eyes, and it seemed to me that it was a face very like his. I have been unable to forget, since then, what Dr. Marsch told me about the production of any number of identical individuals by cloning, and that my father had, when I was younger, a reputation as a child broker. I have tried since my release to find some trace of my mother, the woman in the photograph shown me by my aunt, but that picture was surely taken long before I was born—perhaps even on Earth.

The discovery I spoke of I made almost as soon as we left the building where I killed the slave, and it was simply this: that it was no longer autumn, but high summer. Because all four of us—Marydol had joined us by that time—were so concerned about David and busy concocting a story to explain his injury, the shock was somewhat blunted, but there could be no doubt of it. The weather was warm with that torpid, damp heat peculiar to summer. The trees I remembered nearly bare were in full leaf and filled with orioles. The fountain in our garden no longer played, as it always did after the danger of frost and burst pipes had come, with warmed water: I dabbled my hand in the basin as we helped David up the path, and it was as cool as dew.

My periods of unconscious action then, my sleepwalking, had increased to devour an entire winter and the spring, and I felt that I had lost myself.

When we entered the house, an ape which I thought at first was my father's sprang to my shoulder. Later Mr. Million told me that the ape was my own, one of my laboratory animals I had made a pet. I did not know the little beast, but scars under his fur and the twist of his limbs showed he knew me.

(I have kept Popo ever since, and Mr. Million took care of him for me while I was imprisoned. He climbs still in fine weather on the gray and crumbling walls of this house; and as he runs along the parapets and I see his hunched form against the sky, I think, for a moment, that my father is still alive and that I may be summoned again for the long hours in his library—but I forgive my pet that.)

My father did not call a physician for David, but treated him himself; and if he was curious about the manner in which David had received his injury he did not show it. My own guess—for whatever it may be worth, this late—is that he believed I had stabbed David in some quarrel. I say this because my father seemed, after this, apprehensive whenever I was alone with him. He was not a fearful man, and he had been accustomed for years to deal occasionally with the worst sort of criminals, but he was no longer at ease with me—he guarded himself. It may have been, of course, merely the result of something I had said or done during the forgotten winter.

Both Marydol and Phaedria, as well as my aunt and Mr. Million, came frequently to visit David, so that his sickroom became a sort of meeting place for us all, only disturbed by my father's occasional visits. Marydol was a slight, fair-haired, kindhearted girl, and I became very fond of her. Often when she was ready to go home I escorted her and on the way back stopped at the slave market, as Mr. Million and David and I had once done so often, to buy fried bread and the sweet black coffee and to watch the bidding. The faces of slaves are the dullest in the world, but I would find myself staring into them, and it was a long time, a month at least, before I understood—quite suddenly, when I found what I had been looking for—why I did. A young male, a sweeper, was brought to the block. His face as well as his back had been scarred by the whip, and his teeth were broken, but I recognized him: the scarred face was my own or my father's. I spoke to him and would have bought and freed him, but he answered me in the servile way of slaves and I turned away in disgust and went home.

That night when my father had me brought to the library—as he had not for several nights—I watched our reflections in the mirror that concealed the entrance to his laboratories. He looked younger than he was; I, older. We might almost have been the same man, and when he faced me and I, staring over his shoulder, saw no image of my own body, but only his arms and mine, we might have been the fighting slave.

I cannot say who first suggested we kill him. I only remember that one evening, as I prepared for bed after taking Marydol and Phaedria to their homes, I realized that earlier when the three of us, with Mr. Million and my aunt, had sat around David's bed, we had been talking of that.

Not openly, of course. Perhaps we had not admitted even to ourselves what it was we were thinking. My aunt had mentioned the money he was supposed to have hidden; and Phaedria, then, a yacht luxurious as a palace; David talked about hunting in the grand style, and the political power money could buy.

And I, saying nothing, had thought of the hours and weeks and the months he had taken from me; of the destruction of my *self*, which he had gnawed at night after night. I thought of how I might enter the library that night and find myself when next I woke an old man and perhaps a beggar.

Then I knew that I must kill him, since if I told him those thoughts while I lay drugged on the peeling leather of the old table he would kill *me* without a qualm.

While I waited for his valet to come I made my plan. There would be no investigation, no death certificate for my father. I would replace him. To our patrons it would appear that nothing had changed. Phaedria's friends would be told that I had quarreled with him and left home. I would allow no one to see me for a time, and then, in makeup, in a dim room, speak occasionally to some favored caller. It was an impossible plan, but at the time I believed it possible and even easy. My scalpel was in my pocket and ready. The body could be destroyed in his own laboratory.

He read it in my face. He spoke to me as he always had, but I think he knew. There were flowers in the room, something that had never been before, and I wondered if he had not known even earlier and had them brought in, as for a special event. Instead of telling me to lie on the leather-covered table, he gestured toward a chair and seated himself at his writing desk. "We will have company to-day," he said.

I looked at him.

"You're angry with me. I've seen it growing in you. Don't you know who—"

He was about to say something further when there was a tap at the door, and when he called, "Come in!" it was opened by Nerissa, who ushered in a demi-mondaine and Dr. Marsch. I was surprised to see him, and still more surprised to see one of the girls in my father's library. She seated herself beside Marsch in a way that showed he was her benefactor for the night.

"Good evening, Doctor," my father said. "Have you been enjoying your-self?"

Marsch smiled, showing large, square teeth. He wore clothing of the most fashionable cut now, but the contrast between his beard and the colorless skin of his cheeks was as remarkable as ever. "Both sensually and intellectually," he said. "I've seen a naked girl, a giantess twice the height of a man, walk through a wall."

I said, "That's done with holographs."

He smiled again. "I know. And I have seen a great many other things as well. I was going to recite them all, but perhaps I would only bore my audience; I will content myself with saying that you have a remarkable establishment—but you know that."

My father said, "It is always flattering to hear it again."

"And now are we going to have the discussion we spoke of earlier?"

My father looked at the demimondaine; she rose, kissed Dr. Marsch, and left the room. The heavy library door swung shut behind her with a soft click.

L ike the sound of a switch, or old glass breaking.

I have thought since, many times, of that girl as I saw her leaving: the high-heeled platform shoes and grotesquely long legs, the backless dress dipping an inch below the coccyx. The bare nape of her neck, her hair piled and teased and threaded with ribbons and tiny lights. As she closed the door she was ending, though she could not have known it, the world she and I had known.

"She'll be waiting when you come out," my father said to Marsch.

"And if she's not, I'm sure you can supply others." The anthropologist's green eyes seemed to glow in the lamplight. "But now, how can I help you?"

"You study race. Could you call a group of similar men thinking similar thoughts a race?"

"And women," Marsch said, smiling.

"And here," my father continued, "here on Sainte Croix, you are gathering material to take back with you to Earth?"

"I am gathering material, certainly. Whether or not I shall return to the mother planet is problematical."

I must have looked at him sharply; he turned his smile toward me, and it became, if possible, even more patronizing than before. "You're surprised?"

"I've always considered Earth the center of scientific thought," I said. "I can easily imagine a scientist leaving it to do fieldwork, but—"

"But it is inconceivable that one might want to stay in the field?"

"Consider my position. You are not alone—happily for me—in respecting the mother world's gray hairs and wisdom. As an Earth-trained man I've been offered a department in your university at almost any salary I care to name, with a sabbatical every second year. And the trip from here to Earth requires twenty years of Newtonian time, only six months subjectively for me, of course, but when I return, if I do, my education will be forty years out of date. No, I'm afraid your planet may have acquired an intellectual luminary."

My father said, "We're straying from the subject, I think."

Marsch nodded, then added, "But I was about to say that an anthropologist is peculiarly equipped to make himself at home in any culture—even in so strange a one as this family has constructed about itself. I think I may call it a family, since there are two members resident besides yourself. You don't object to my addressing the pair of you in the singular?"

He looked at me as if expecting a protest, then when I said nothing: "I mean your son, David—that and not brother is his real relationship to your continuing personality—and the woman you call your aunt. She is in reality daughter to an earlier—shall we say 'version'?—of yourself."

"You're trying to tell me I'm a cloned duplicate of my father, and I see both of you expect me to be shocked. I'm not. I've suspected it for some time."

My father said, "I'm glad to hear that. Frankly, when I was your age the discovery disturbed me a great deal; I came into my father's library—this room—to confront him, and I intended to kill him."

Dr. Marsch asked, "And did you?"

"I don't think it matters—the point is that it was my intention. I hope that having you here will make things easier for Number Five."

"Is that what you call him?"

"It's more convenient since his name is the same as my own."

"He is your fifth clone-produced child?"

"My fifth experiment? No." My father's hunched, high shoulders wrapped in the dingy scarlet of his old dressing gown made him look like some savage bird, and I remembered having read in a book of natural history of one called the red-shouldered hawk. His pet monkey, grizzled now with age, had climbed onto the desk. "No, more like my fiftieth, if you must know. I used to do them for drill. You people who have never tried it think the technique is simple because you've heard it can be done, but you don't know how difficult it is to prevent spontaneous differences. Every gene dominant in myself had to remain dominant, and people are not garden peas—few things are governed by simple Mendelian pairs."

Marsch asked, "You destroyed your failures?"

I said, "He sold them. When I was a child I used to wonder why Mr. Million stopped to look at the slaves in the market. Since then I've found out." My scalpel was still in its case in my pocket; I could feel it.

"Mr. Million," my father said, "is perhaps a bit more sentimental than I— besides, I don't like to go out. You see, Doctor, your supposition that we are all truly the same individual will have to be modified. We have our little variations."

Dr. Marsch was about to reply, but I interrupted him. "Why?" I said. "Why David and me? Why Aunt Jeannine a long time ago? Why go on with it?"

"Yes," my father said, "why? We ask the question to ask the question."

"I don't understand you."

"I seek self-knowledge. If you want to put it this way, *we* seek self-knowledge. You are here because I did and do, and I am here because the individual behind me did—who was himself originated by the one whose mind is simulated in Mr. Million. And one of the questions whose answers we seek is why we seek. But there is more than that." He leaned forward, and the little ape lifted its white muzzle and bright, bewildered eyes to stare into his face. "We wish to discover why we fail, why others rise and change and we remain here."

I thought of the yacht I had talked about with Phaedria and said, "I won't stay here." Dr. Marsch smiled.

My father said, "I don't think you understand me. I don't necessarily mean here physically, but *here*, socially and intellectually. I have traveled, and you may, but—"

"But you end here," Dr. Marsch said.

"We end at this level!" It was the only time, I think, that I ever saw my father excited. He was almost speechless as he waved at the notebooks and tapes that thronged the walls. "After how many generations? We do not achieve fame or the rule of even this miserable little colony planet. Something must be changed, but what?" He glared at Dr. Marsch.

"You are not unique," Dr. Marsch said, then smiled. "That sounds like a truism, doesn't it? But I wasn't referring to your duplicating yourself. I meant that since it became possible, back on Earth during the last quarter of the twentieth century, it has been done in such chains a number of times. We have borrowed a term from engineering to describe it, and call it the process of relaxation—a bad nomenclature, but the best we have. Do you know what relaxation in the engineering sense is?"

"No."

"There are problems which are not directly soluble, but which can be solved by a succession of approximations. In heat transfer, for example, it may not be possible to calculate initially the temperature at every point on the surface of an unusually shaped body. But the engineer, or his computer, can assume reasonable temperatures, see how nearly stable the assumed values would be, then make new assumptions based on the result. As the levels of approximation progress, the successive sets become more and more similar until there is essentially no change. That is why I said the two of you are essentially one individual."

"What I want you to do," my father said impatiently, "is to make Number Five understand that the experiments I have performed on him, particularly the narcotherapeutic examinations he resents so much, are necessary. That if we are to become more than we have been we must find out—" He had been almost shouting, and he stopped abruptly to bring his voice under control. "That is the reason he was produced, the reason for David too—I hoped to learn something from an outcrossing."

"Which was the rationale, no doubt," Dr. Marsch said, "for the existence of Dr. Veil as well, in an earlier generation. But as far as your examinations of your younger self are concerned, it would be just as useful for him to examine you."

"Wait a moment," I said. "You keep saying that he and I are identical. That's incorrect. I can see that we're similar in some respects, but I'm not really like my father."

"There are no differences that cannot be accounted for by age. You are what? Eighteen? And you"—he looked toward my father—"I should say are nearly fifty. There are only two forces, you see, which act to differentiate between human beings: they are heredity and environment, nature and nurture. And since the personality is largely formed during the first three years of life, it is the environment provided by the home which is decisive. Now every person is born into *some* home environment though it may be such a harsh one that he dies of it; and no person, except in this situation we call anthropological relaxation, provides that environment himself—it is furnished for him by the preceding generation."

"Just because both of us grew up in this house—"

"Which you built and furnished and filled with the people you chose. But wait a moment. Let's talk about a man neither of you have ever seen, a man born in a place provided by parents quite different from himself: I mean the first of you. . . ."

I was no longer listening. I had come to kill my father, and it was necessary that Dr. Marsch leave. I watched him as he leaned forward in his chair, his long, white hands making incisive little gestures, his cruel lips moving in a frame of black hair; I watched him and I heard nothing. It was as though I had gone deaf or as if he could communicate only by his thoughts and I, knowing the thoughts were silly lies, had shut them out. I said, "You are from Sainte Anne."

He looked at me in surprise, halting in the midst of a senseless sentence. "I have been there, yes. I spent several years on Sainte Anne before coming here."

"You were born there. You studied your anthropology there from books written on Earth twenty years ago. You are an abo, or at least half abo, but we are men."

Marsch glanced at my father, then said, "The abos are gone. Scientific opinion on Sainte Anne holds that they have been extinct for almost a century."

"You didn't believe that when you came to see my aunt."

"I've never accepted Veil's Hypothesis. I called on everyone here who had published anything in my field. Really, I don't have time to listen to this."

"You are an abo and not from Earth."

And in a short time my father and I were alone.

Most of my sentence I served in a labor camp in the Tattered Mountains. It was a small camp, housing usually only 150 prisoners—sometimes less than 80 when the winter deaths had been bad. We cut wood and burned charcoal and made skis when we found good birch. Above the timberline we gathered a saline moss supposed to be medicinal and knotted long plans for rock slides that would crush the stalking machines that were our guards—though somehow the moment never came, the stones never slid. The work was hard, and these guards administered exactly the mixture of severity and fairness some prison board had decided upon when they were programmed and the problem of brutality and favoritism by hirelings was settled forever, so that only well-dressed men at meetings could be cruel or kind.

Or so they thought. I sometimes talked to my guards for hours about Mr. Million, and once I found a piece of meat, and once a cake of hard sugar, brown and gritty as sand, hidden in the corner where I slept.

A criminal may not profit by his crime, but the court—so I was told much later—could find no proof that David was indeed my father's son, and made my aunt his heir.

She died, and a letter from an attorney informed me that by her favor I had inherited "a large house in the city of Port-Mimizon, together with the furniture and chattels appertaining thereto." And that this house, "located at 666 Saltimbanque, is presently under the care of a robot servitor." Since the robot servitors under whose direction I found myself did not allow me writing materials, I could not reply.

Time passed on the wings of birds. I found dead larks at the feet of north-facing cliffs in autumn, at the feet of south-facing cliffs in spring.

I received a letter from Mr. Million. Most of my father's girls had left during the investigation of his death; the remainder he had been obliged to send away when my aunt died, finding that as a machine he could not enforce the necessary obedience. David had gone to the capital. Phaedria had married well. Marydol had been sold by her parents. The date on Mr. Million's letter was three years later than the date of my trial, but how long the letter had been in reaching me I could not tell. The envelope had been opened and resealed many times and was soiled and torn.

A seabird, I believe a gannet, came fluttering down into our camp after a storm, too exhausted to fly. We killed and ate it.

One of our guards went berserk, burned fifteen prisoners to death, and fought the other guards all night with swords of white and blue fire. He was not replaced.

I was transferred with some others to a camp farther north where I looked down chasms of red stone so deep that if I kicked a pebble in, I could hear the rattle of its descent grow to a roar of slipping rock—and hear that, in half a minute, fade with distance to silence, yet never strike the bottom lost somewhere in darkness.

I pretended the people I had known were with me. When I sat shielding my basin of soup from the wind, Phaedria sat upon a bench nearby and smiled and talked about her friends. David played squash for hours on the dusty ground of our compound, slept against the wall near my own corner. Marydol put her hand in mine while I carried my saw into the mountains.

In time they all grew dim, but even in the last year I never slept without telling myself, just before sleep, that Mr. Million would take us to the city library in the morning, never woke without fearing that my father's valet had come for me.

Then I was told that I was to go, with three others, to another camp. We carried our food, and nearly died of hunger and exposure on the way. From there we were marched to a third camp where we were questioned by men who were not prisoners like ourselves but free men in uniforms who made notes of our answers and at last ordered that we bathe, and burned our old clothing, and gave us a thick stew of meat and barley.

I remember very well that it was then that I allowed myself to realize, at last, what these things meant. I dipped my bread into my bowl and pulled it out soaked with the fragrant stock, with bits of meat and grains of barley clinging to it, and I thought then of the fried bread and coffee at the slave market not as something of the past but as something in the future, and my hands shook until I could no longer hold my bowl and I wanted to rush shouting at the fences.

In two more days we, six of us now, were put into a mule cart that drove on winding roads always downhill until the winter that had been dying behind us was gone, and the birches and firs were gone, and the tall chestnuts and oaks beside the road had spring flowers under their branches.

The streets of Port-Mimizon swarmed with people. I would have been lost in a moment if Mr. Million had not hired a chair for me, but I made the bearers stop, and bought (with money he gave me) a newspaper from a vendor so that I could know the date with certainty at last.

My sentence had been the usual one of two to fifty years, and though I had known the month and year of the beginning of my imprisonment, it had been impossible to know, in the camps, the number of the current year which everyone counted and no one knew. A man took fever and in ten days, when he was well enough again to work, said that two years had passed or had never been. Then you yourself took fever. I do not recall any headline, any article from the paper I bought. I read only the date at the top, all the way home.

It had been nine years.

I had been eighteen when I had killed my father. I was now twenty-seven. I had thought I might be forty.

The flaking gray walls of our house were the same. The iron dog with its three wolf heads still stood in the front garden, but the fountain was silent, and the beds of fern and moss were full of weeds. Mr. Million paid my chairmen and unlocked with a key the door that was always guard-chained but unbolted in my father's day—but as he did so, an immensely tall and lanky woman who had been hawking pralines in the street came running toward us. It was Nerissa, and I now had a servant and might have had a bedfellow if I wished, though I could pay her nothing.

And now I must, I suppose, explain why I have been writing this account, which has already been the labor of days, and I must even explain why I explain. Very well then. I have written to disclose myself to myself, and I am writing now because I will, I know, sometime read what I am now writing and wonder.

Perhaps by the time I do, I will have solved the mystery of myself, or perhaps I will no longer care to know the solution.

It has been three years since my release. This house, when Nerissa and I reentered it, was in a very confused state, my aunt having spent her last days, so Mr. Million told me, in a search for my father's supposed hoard. She did not find it, and I do not think it is to be found; knowing his character better than she, I believe he spent most of what his girls brought him on his experiments and apparatus. I needed money badly myself at first, but the reputation of the house brought women seeking buyers and men seeking to buy. It is hardly necessary, as I told myself when we began, to do more than introduce them, and I have a good staff now. Phaedria lives with us and works too; the brilliant marriage was a failure after all. Last night while I was working in my surgery I heard her at the library door. I opened it and she had the child with her. Someday they'll want us.

## AFTERWORD

This was the pivotal story that changed my life. The truly strange thing was that I knew it would do it before it had done it. Damon Knight's *Orbit* was my main market back then; I had sold Damon several stories, been invited to his Milford Writer's Conference, and gone (I think twice).

He bought this story and praised it. When I said I wanted it to be my next conference story he very reasonably objected that it did not require fixing. I told him I wanted to hear what others said about it, and eventually won him over.

The time came. We had just bought a new car, small and cheap—but brand-new. I was returning to the Milford Conference (which I loved) with a story I felt certain was good. Ten or twenty miles from Milford, Pennsylvania, I topped a hill and saw yellow dots in the road. They were goldfinches, and as my new car drew nearer they flew up, a golden shower rising from the earth. There are no words to describe how happy I was at that moment, when I felt that a whole new life was opening before me.

It was perfectly true. One was.

# BEECH HILL

"B ubba goes off by himself like this every year—don't you, Bubba?" So Maryanne had said, and looked venomously at Bobs. He recalled it as he sat in Beech Hill pretending to read, his legs primly together, his back (because, no longer young, it hurt if he sat on his spine) straight.

"I suppose he needs it. Uh . . . needs the rest." Thus Mrs. Hilliard, a friend of Maryanne's friend Mrs. Main.

"That's what I always say. I say: 'Bubba, God knows you work hard all year. We don't have much money, but you go off by yourself like you always do and spend it. I can get around in my chair perfectly well, and anyway Martha Main will come over to look after me. Nobody ought to have to take care of a cripple forever, but if it wasn't for Martha I don't know what I'd do.' "

Mrs. Hilliard had asked, "Where do you go, Mr. Roberts?"

S omeone came in, and Bobs looked up and saw the countess, black hair stretched tight around her after-midnight face. His watch said seven and he wondered if she had been up all night.

At seven, fifty-one weeks of the year, he was at work. He looked at the watch again. Twelve hours later he and Maryanne had dinner, again at seven. Afterward he read while she watched television. At six he would get up, and at seven relieve the night man.

Bishop came in, followed by a young man Bobs had not seen before. The young man was pale and nervous, Bishop portly and assured behind mustache, beard, eyebrows, and tumbling iron-gray forelock. "You're among us early this morning, Countess."

"I could not sleep. It is often so."

Bishop nodded sympathetically, then gestured toward the young man beside him. "Countess, may I present Dr. Preston Potts. Dr. Potts is a physicist and mathematician—the man who developed the lunar forcing vectors. You may have heard of him. . . ."

More formally he said to Potts, "Dr. Potts, the Countess Esterhazy."

"I *have* heard of Dr. Potts, and I am charmed." The countess held out a limp hand glittering with rhinestones. "I at first thought you were a doctor who might give me something for my not sleeping, but I am even so charmed."

Potts stammered: "Our a-a-astronauts have trouble sleeping too. If you imagine you're in space it might help you f-f-feel better about it."

The countess answered, "We are all in space always, are we not?" and smiled her sleepy smile.

For a moment Potts stood transfixed; then he managed to smile weakly in return. "You are something of a mathematician yourself. Yes, we are all in space or we would not exist—perhaps that's why we sometimes have trouble sleeping."

"You are so clever."

"And this is Mr. Roberts," Bishop continued, drawing Potts away from the countess. "I cannot tell you a great deal about Mr. Roberts's activities, but he is one of the men who protect the things you discover."

Bobs stood to shake hands and added: "And who occasionally arrange that you discover what someone else has just discovered on the other side. Pleased to meet you, Dr. Potts. I know your work."

"Looks a lot like Bond, doesn't he?" he overheard Bishop say as the two of them left him. "But he's different in one respect. Our Mr. Roberts is the real thing."

Bobs sat down again. There was a Walther PPK under his left arm, but it was no help and he felt unsettled and a little afraid. Behind him, at the far end of the big room, Bishop was introducing Potts to someone else—Claude Brain, the wild animal trainer, from the sound of the voice—and Bobs caught the words: "Welcome to Beech Hill."

Each year he came to Beech Hill by bus, with an overnight stop. The stop had, itself, become a ritual. In fact, the entire trip from the moment he carried his bag out of the apartment was marked with golden milestones, events that were— so strong was the anticipation of pleasure—pleasures themselves.

To enter the terminal and buy his ticket, to sit on the long wooden bench with the travel worn, with the servicemen on leave, with the young, worried, cheaply clothed women with babies and the silent, shabby men (like himself) he always hoped were going to their own Beech Hills but who, in their misery, could not have been.

To sit with his bag between his feet, then carry it to be stowed in the compartment under the bus's floor. To zoom the air-conditioned roads and watch the city slip behind. The hum of the tires was song, and if he were to fall asleep on the bus (he never did) he would know even sleeping where he was.

And the stop. The hotel. A small, old, threadbare hotel; they never put him in the same room twice, but he could walk the corridors and recall them all: *Here's where, coming, in '62. There in '63. The fourth floor in '64.* He stayed at the hotel on the return trip as well, but the rooms, even last year's room, faded.

Checking in, he always asked if they had his reservation, and they always did. A card to sign—*R. Roberts, address, no car.*

And the room: a small room on an air shaft, bright papered walls with big flowers, a ceiling fixture with a string. And the door, a solid door with a chain and dead bolt. *Snick! Rattle!* His bag on the bed. Secret papers on the bed. *Not NOW, Maryanne, I'm not decent.* His hand on the Luger. If Maryanne should see those— It would be his duty, and the Organization would cover for him as it always did. . . . Suppose she hadn't heard him? *Come in—Snickback!—Maryanne, Rattle!* His own sister, they say. There's devotion for you!

He always changed at the hotel the day he arrived, not waiting until morning. This time too, he had removed his old workaday clothes, showered, and, glowing, gone to the open bag for new, clean underwear bought for the occasion— and executive-length hose. His shirt of artificial fabrics that looked like silk stayed new from year to year; he wore it only at Beech Hill. His slacks were inexpensive, but never before worn.

He was proud of his jacket, though it had been very cheap, an old Norfolk jacket, much abused (by someone else) but London made. The elbows had been patched with leather; the tweed smelled faintly of shotgun smoke, and the pockets were rubber lined for carrying game. *Handy in my line of business.* Just the sort of coat the right sort of man would continue to wear though it was worn out, or nearly. Also just the sort to effectively conceal his HSc Mauser in his shoulder holster—at Beech Hill.

But not at the stop. Regretfully he left the Mauser in his bag, but this too was part of the ritual. The empty holster beneath his arm, the strange clothes, told him where he was. Even if he had fallen asleep . . . (but he never did.)

There were restaurants near the hotel, and he ate quietly a meal made sumptuous by custom. There was a newsstand where he stopped for a few paperbacks, and, next door, a barbershop.

A haircut was not part of the ritual, but it might well be. He might, in years to come, remember this as the year when he had first had his hair cut on the way to Beech Hill. The shop was clean, busy, but not too busy, smelling of powder and alcoholic tonics. He stepped inside, and as he did a customer was stripped of his striped robe and dusted with the whisk. "You're next," the barber said.

Bobs looked at another (waiting) customer, but the man gestured wordlessly toward the first chair.

"Chin up, please. Medium on the sides?"

"Fine."

There was a television, not offensively loud, in a corner. The news. He watched.

"Don't move your head, sir."

The man on the screen was portly, expensively dressed, intelligent looking. A newsman, microphone in hand, spoke deferentially:—*a strike . . . , pollution . . . , Washington? . . .*

"I know that man." Bobs twisted in the chair. "He's a billionaire."

"Damn near. He sure enough owns a lot around here."

When Bobs paid him the barber said, "You feel okay, sir?"

The next day he dropped the black Beretta into its holster. On the bus the weight of it made him feel for a moment (he had closed his eyes) that the woman next to him was leaning against him. The woman next to him became Wally Wallace, a salesman he had once known, the man who had introduced him to Beech Hill, but that seemed perfectly natural. Opposite, so that the four of them were face-to-face as passengers had once sat in trains, were Bishop and his wife, pretending not to know them. This was courtesy—the Bishops never spoke to anyone until it had been definitely decided what they were going to be. He knew that without being told.

"You," Wally began. Bobs suddenly realized that he (Bobs) was ten years younger, and the wistful thought came that he would not remain so. ". . . can't beat this place. There's nothing like it." Bobs had wondered if Wally was not getting a commission—or at least a reduction in his own rate—for each new guest he brought. Wally had returned the second year, but never after that. Lost in the jungle he loved.

When Bishop and Potts and Claude Brain were gone (they had said something about a morning swim) Bobs remarked to the countess, "I saw a friend of ours on television. On my way up." He mentioned the billionaire's name.

"Ah," said the countess. "Such a nice man. But"—she smiled brilliantly—"married."

"He was here when I first came."

At first he thought the countess was no longer listening to him; then he realized that he had not spoken aloud. The billionaire *had* been there when he had first come. Very young, as everyone had said, to have made so much money. Great drive.

*And yet perhaps*—he tried to push the thought back, but it came bursting in anyway, invading his consciousness like the wind entering a pauper's shack—*perhaps he had made it.*

He had wanted to badly. You could see it in his eyes. And then—

What fun! What sport to return, posing with the others year after year.

*The bastard.*

The bastard. Was he here yet?

Bobs could not sit still. The fear was on him, and he stalked out of the immense house that was Beech Hill, hardly caring where he was going. The ground sloped down, and ahead the clear water of the lake gleamed. Half a dozen guests were swimming there already: drama critic, heart surgeon, the madame of New York's most exclusive brothel. Fashion designer, big-game hunter, test pilot. Bobs stood and watched them until Claude Brain, coming up behind him, said, "No dip today, Roberts?"

"I don't usually," Bobs replied, turning. Brain was in trunks. His arms were horribly scarred, and there were more scars on his chest and belly.

His eyes followed Bobs's. "Tiger," Brain said. "I was lucky."

"I guess it's hard to become a wild-animal man? Hard to get started?"

Brain nodded. "There aren't many spots. A few places around Hollywood, and a few shows. You try and try, but most of them have already had so much trouble with greenhorns they won't touch you."

"I'll bet," Bobs said sympathetically.

"Hell, I did everything. For years. Sold shoes, worked in a factory. Bought my own animals. First one was a mountain lion. Cost me three hundred and fifty, and I've still got him."

"I know how you must feel," Bobs said. He watched Brain go down into the water. His back was scarred too.

There was a path along the water's edge. Bobs walked slowly, head down, until he saw the girl; then she looked at him and smiled, and he said, "Sorry. Hope I'm not intruding."

"Not at all," the girl said. "I should be over with the others, but I'm afraid I'm shy." She was beautiful, in the blond-cheerleader girl-next-door way.

"Your first season?"

She nodded.

"You're the actress then. Bishop said something about you when I checked in last night."

"Thanks for not saying *starlet*." She smiled again.

"The star. That's what Bishop called you. Have you made many pictures?"

"Just one—*Bikini Bash*. You didn't—"

Bobs shook his head. "But I will, the next chance I get."

"They say a lot of important people come here."

Bobs nodded. "To look at the nuts."

The girl laughed. "I get it. Beechnuts."

"Yeah, Beechnuts. Listen, I want you to do me a favor." He drew his pistol and handed it to her. "What's this?"

Puzzled, she looked at it for a moment, then laughed again. "A toy pistol?"

"You're sure?"

"Of course. It says right here on it: *British Imperial Manufacture*, and then: *MADE IN HONG KONG*."

He took the gun and threw it as far as he could out into the lake. She stared at him, so he said: "Remember that. You may be called to testify later," before he walked away.

∞

## AFTERWORD

This story was based, in one way, on the Milford Writer's Conference. In another, on an academic I once knew. Dom (as I shall call him) is dead now, but when "Beech Hill" was written he was a major figure in the study of popular culture.

You may have heard of Baron von Steuben, one of George Washington's most valued—and valuable—subordinates. To put it bluntly, von Steuben was a fraud in almost every respect. He said he was a Prussian nobleman and that he had been a general in the army of Frederick the Great. He was a commoner and had been a captain. *But he could do what he said he could do.* He could turn farm boys into soldiers, and he could do it fast; it was a talent our fledgling America needed desperately—a talent that von Steuben provided.

Dom was like that. He wore tweed jackets and smoked a pipe. He spoke with a dubious British accent and sounded pompous even when what he said was not. He gave you every reason to think him a lovable fraud. Yet he knew his subject backward and forward and cared deeply about it. I knew him, as I said, and in a way I based the story you have read upon him. We are the poorer for his passing.

# THE RECORDING

I have found my record, a record I have owned for fifty years and never played until five minutes ago. Let me explain.

When I was a small boy—in those dear, dead days of Model A Ford touring cars, horse-drawn milk trucks, and hand-cranked ice-cream freezers—I had an uncle. As a matter of fact, I had several, all brothers of my father, and all, like him, tall and somewhat portly men with faces stamped (as my own is) in the image of *their* father, the lumberman and land speculator who built this Victorian house for his wife.

But this particular uncle, my uncle Bill, whose record (in a sense I shall explain) it was, was closer than all the others to me. As the eldest, he was the titular head of the family, for my grandfather had passed away a few years after I was born. My uncle's capacity for beer was famous, and I suspect now that he was "comfortable" much of the time, a large-waisted (how he would roar if he could see his little nephew's waistline today!) red-faced, good-humored man whom none of us—for a child catches these attitudes as readily as measles—took wholly seriously.

The special position which, in my mind, this uncle occupied is not too difficult to explain. Though younger than many men still working, he was said to be retired, and for that reason I saw much more of him than of any of the others. And despite his being something of a figure of fun, I was a little frightened of him, as a child may be of the painted, rowdy clown at a circus; this, I suppose, because of some incident of drunken behavior witnessed at the edge of infancy and not understood. At the same time I loved my uncle, or at least would have said I did, for he was generous with small gifts and often willing to talk when everyone else was "too busy."

Why my uncle had promised me a present I have now quite forgotten. It was not my birthday, and not Christmas—I vividly recall the hot, dusty streets over which the maples hung motionless, year-worn leaves. But promise he had, and there was no slightest doubt in my mind about what I wanted.

Not a collie pup like Tarkington's little boy, or even a bicycle (I already had one). No, what I wanted (how modern it sounds now) was a phonograph record. Not, you must understand, any particular record, though perhaps if given a choice I would have leaned toward one of the comedy monologues popular then, or a military march, but simply a record of my own. My parents had recently acquired a new phonograph, and I was forbidden to use it for fear that I might scratch the delicate wax disks. If I had a record of my own, this argument would lose its validity. My uncle agreed and promised that after dinner (in those days eaten at two o'clock) we would walk the eight or ten blocks which then separated this house from the business area of the town and, unknown to my parents, get me one.

I no longer remember of what that dinner consisted—time has merged it in my mind with too many others, all eaten in that dark, oak-paneled room. Stewed chicken would have been typical, with dumplings, potatoes, boiled vegetables, and, of course, bread and creamery butter. There would have been pie afterward, and coffee, and my father and my uncle adjourning to the front porch—called the stoop—to smoke cigars. At last my father left to return to his office, and I was able to harry my uncle into motion.

From this point my memory is distinct. We trudged through the heat, he in a straw boater and a blue and white seersucker suit as loose and voluminous as the robes worn by the women in the plates of our family Bible; I, in the costume of a French sailor, with a striped shirt under my blouse and a pom-pommned cap embroidered in gold with the word *Indomptable*. From time to time, I pulled at his hand, but did not like to because of its wet softness, and an odd, unclean smell that offended me.

When we were a block from Main Street, my uncle complained of feeling ill, and I urged that we hurry our errand so that he could go home and lie down. On Main Street he dropped onto one of the benches the town provided and mumbled something about Fred Croft, who was our family doctor and had been a schoolmate of his. By this time I was frantic with fear that we were going to turn back, depriving me (as I thought, forever) of access to the phonograph. Also I had noticed that my uncle's usually fiery face had gone quite white, and I concluded that he was about to "be sick," a prospect that threw me into an agony of embarrassment. I pleaded with him to give me the money, pointing out that I could run the half block remaining between the store and ourselves in less than no time. He only groaned and told me again to fetch Fred Croft. I remember that my uncle had removed his straw hat and was fanning himself with it while the August sun beat down unimpeded on his bald head.

For a moment, if only for a moment, I felt my power. With a hand thrust out I told him, in fact ordered him, to give me what I wished. I remember having said, "I'll get him. Give me the money, Uncle Bill, and then I'll bring him."

He gave it to me and I ran to the store as fast as my flying heels would carry me, though as I ran I was acutely conscious that I had done something wrong. There I accepted the first record offered me, danced with impatience waiting for my change, and then, having completely forgotten that I was supposed to bring Dr. Croft, returned to see if my uncle had recovered.

In appearance he had. I thought that he had fallen asleep waiting for me, and I tried to wake him. Several passersby grinned at us, thinking, I suppose, that Uncle Bill was drunk. Eventually, inevitably, I pulled too hard. His ponderous body rolled from the bench and lay, faceup, mouth slightly open, on the hot sidewalk before me. I remember the small crescents of white that showed then beneath the half-closed eyelids.

During the two days that followed, I could not have played my record if I had wanted to. Uncle Bill was laid out in the parlor where the phonograph was, and for me, a child, to have entered that room would have been unthinkable. But during this period of mourning, a strange fantasy took possession of my mind. I came to believe—I am not enough of a psychologist to tell you why—that if I were to play my record, the sound would be that of my uncle's voice, pleading again for me to bring Dr. Croft, and accusing me. This became the chief nightmare of my childhood.

To shorten a long story, I never played it. I never dared. To conceal its existence I hid it atop a high cupboard in the cellar, and there it stayed, at first the subject of midnight terrors, later almost forgotten.

Until now. My father passed away at sixty, but my mother has outlasted all these long decades, until the time when she followed him at last a few months ago and I, her son, standing beside her coffin, might myself have been called an old man.

And now I have reoccupied our home. To be quite honest, my fortunes have not prospered, and though this house is free and clear, little besides the house itself has come to me from my mother. Last night, as I ate alone in the old dining room where I have had so many meals, I thought of Uncle Bill and the record again, but I could not, for a time, recall just where I had hidden it, and in fact feared that I had thrown it away. Tonight I remembered, and though my doctor tells me that I should not climb stairs, I found my way down to the old cellar and discovered my record beneath half an inch of dust. There were a few chest pains lying in wait for me on the steps, but I reached the kitchen once more without a mishap, washed the poor old platter and my hands, and set it on my modern high fidelity. I suppose I need hardly say the voice is not Uncle Bill's. It is instead (of all people!) Rudy Vallee's. I have started the recording again and can hear it from where I write: "My time is your time . . . My time is your time." So much for superstition.

∞

## AFTERWORD

There is very little I can say about this story without sounding maudlin. Uncle Bill is based on a substitute teacher I had now and then in high school. The seed of the story came from my father's funeral. As I sat in the funeral parlor seeing Dad's corpse in its coffin and only half-hearing his eulogies, it came to me that I was next in line. The small children who sat with me now, a little ashamed because their father wept, would sit through another funeral when they were older. Then they would weep, perhaps. Or at least, some of them might.

# Hour of Trust

You read, let us say, that this or that Corps has tried . . . but before we go any further, the serial number of the Corps, its order of battle are not without their significance. If it is not the first time that the operation has been attempted, and if for the same operation we find a different Corps being brought up, it is perhaps a sign that the previous Corps have been wiped out or have suffered heavy casualties in the said operation; that they are no longer in a fit state to carry it through successfully. Next, we must ask ourselves what was this Corps which is now out of action; if it was composed of shock troops, held in reserve for big attacks, a fresh Corps of inferior quality will have little chance of succeeding where the first has failed. Furthermore, if we are not at the start of a campaign, this fresh Corps may itself be a composite formation of odds and ends withdrawn from other Corps, which throws a light on the strength of the forces the belligerent still has at his disposal and the proximity of the moment when his forces shall be definitely inferior to the enemy's, which gives to the operation on which this Corps is about to engage a different meaning, because, if it is no longer in a condition to make good its losses, its successes even will only help mathematically to bring it nearer to its ultimate destruction. . . .

—MARCEL PROUST,
*Remembrance of Things Past*

The north and south walls were pale blue, of painted plaster over stone. A wide door in the north wall, of dark wood and old, dark, discolored brasswork, gave into the hotel corridor, floored (like the big room itself) in dull red tile. Flanking this door were elaborate wrought-iron candelabra; their candles would be lit later that night by Clio Morris, on signal from Lowell Lewis, when Force Cougar was pinned down near the 75–94 interchange in Dearborn and he felt things needed cheering up. Clio (that stenographic muse of history) was good for lighting such things: she was tall, and wore high heels and short skirts, and the soft coiffures she favored lent her face a brown and gold aureole when the flames were behind it.

To the right of the candelabrum on the right side of the doorway stood a heavy "library" table with a blue vase full of fresh cinerarias, the blue vase and blue flowers against the blue wall producing a ghostly effect—the shadows of vase and blossoms more visible and distinct than the things themselves. Above this blue ghost was a very large and brightly colored photograph in a massive frame. It depicted a barren hill crowned with the ruins of a large stone building, of which only (what once had been) the foundation of a tower retained any semblance of its original form. At the bottom of the frame a small brass plaque had been let into the wood, and this was engraved with the words *Viana do Castelo,* presumably to guide any tourist who might wish to visit the site.

Next to the candelabrum on the left of the door stood one of the twenty-three large leather-covered chairs which dotted the floor of the room—empty despite the invitation of a small table positioned near its right arm at a height convenient to hold a drink—above this chair was a second photograph of exactly the same size and shape as the first, framed in the same way. It depicted a barren hill topped with the tumbled ashlars of another (but equally demolished) stone building. The atmosphere of this photograph was so similar to that of the first that it was only after a careful process of ratiocination that the viewer (if he troubled) convinced himself that it was not a picture of the same ruin from a different angle, though in fact the two held no detail in common but the bright Portuguese sky. The plaque at the base of this second frame read: *Miró.*

The south wall held three doors, each of them smaller than the large door in the north wall that gave access to the remainder of the hotel, and each leading to a bedroom–sitting room with a bath. The leftmost (east) bedroom looked down into the patio garden of the hotel, and the central bedroom out (south) toward a wing of this patio, with a wall and a street beyond. All the bedrooms were comfortably furnished with carpets and chairs and (in each case) a large double bed, but this central bedroom had, in addition, a vidlink terminal which Lewis's executive assistant, Peters, would use several times that night. It was a wardrobe-sized gray machine with a screen, a printer, a speaker, keys for coding the addresses of others, and various switches; it had been built by United Services Corporation, the company which employed Peters, as well as Lowell Lewis and Miss Morris and Donovan. (Five foot eight, 230 pounds, thinning blond hair, European sales manager for United Services, a good salesman and a hard worker, he felt he didn't really have to worry if U.S. went down—hell, he'd lived in Europe for the past eight years, his wife was Belgian, and he spoke Flemish, German, and Swedish like he owned them, and he had connections all over, and half a dozen European firms would be tickled pink to lay their hands on him. He was right too.)

The west wall was entirely of glass and showed the Atlantic Ocean. Because the sun was low now, Peters (a middle-sized young man with a camouflaged face—Peters was one of those people who look a little Jewish but probably aren't, and he played a good game of lacrosse) had drawn gray velvet drapes across this ocean, but later Clio Morris would open these drapes in order to see the stars.

The east wall was also entirely of glass. It was, in fact, one immense vidlink screen fifteen feet high and thirty-five feet wide, originally installed in this permanently leased suite to demonstrate the fact that vidlink, unlike conventional television, employed what United Services referred to as "Infinite Scanning," by which the United Services copywriters meant that a vidlink picture was not divided into a number of scan lines and hence could be magnified—like reality itself—to any extent. When this screen was turned off it was a dark and brooding presence upon which the room instinctively focused, but no drapes were provided that might be used to cover it. (When turned on it was sometimes camera as well as screen, the viewer beheld in his beholding.)

The red tile floor was, except at the edges of the room, covered with a dark Moorish carpet on which were scattered, as smaller and less regularly shaped carpets, the hides of Angora goats. The twenty-two armchairs that did not orient themselves to the north wall were arranged on this floor facing (generally) east in a way suggestive of a loose theater. A portable bar stood close to the west window, and at this bar Peters sat eating scrambled (*mexidos*) eggs.

The large door in the north wall opened and Donovan came in. He was wearing a light-colored suit and a panama hat. He saw Peters and asked, "Everything set for tonight?"

Peters shrugged.

"It better be. It better be good. I've got people coming from all over." He named an important German industrialist. "—— is coming." He leaned closer to Peters, who was afraid for a moment that the end of his (Donovan's) tie might fall into his (Peters's) eggs, which were covered with a sauce that, without being ketchup, was nonetheless the color of blood. "Do you know what he told me? This'll be the first time he's been outside Germany since 1944. Think of it. Damn near fifty years. The old man himself."

Peters nodded, his mouth full of eggs, and said, "Wow!"

Donovan named a prominent Italian industrialist. "—— is coming too. From Turin. Of course he goes all over, buying art and all that crap. Hell, he spends more time in the States than I do."

"Not now he doesn't," Peters said.

"Well, hell no," Donovan said, offended. "What do you expect?"

The door to the central bedroom opened and Lewis's secretary came in wearing a yellow dress and carrying a tear sheet from the vidlink. She said, "Call for you, Mr. Peters," and Peters took the sheet from her and went into the bedroom.

The call was from a modeling agency in another quarter of the city, and he found himself talking to a sharp-featured, crew-cut young Englishman who wore jade earrings and a (phallic) jade pendant. The Englishman said, "Tredgold here," and Peters nodded and asked, "What can I do for you, Mr. Tredgold?" and then, unconsciously imitating Donovan, "Everything set?"

"Just what I was going to ask you," Tredgold said, and smiled. "You're going to do it still?"

"Have our little party?" Peters said. "Oh, yes."

"Marvelous. You know, you people have come back wonderfully just in the past few weeks."

"Oh, we're not dead yet," Peters said.

"Spirit."

"The girls will be here?"

"Ten on the dot." Tredgold looked at his watch. "Never fear. They are primping their little hearts out at this very moment."

"The ones Mr. Lewis selected."

"Quite." Tredgold smiled again. "I daresay the old boy enjoyed that; did he say anything after?"

Peters tried to remember, then decided it was one of those cases where a lie—he called such lies fables to himself—would serve better, and said, "He talked about it for an hour after we got back, and—you know—told me why he'd picked this one and not that one, all the fine points."

"He has an eye for décolletage; one saw that. For that matter I have myself."

"Interesting business you're in."

"Quite." Tredgold smiled again, his fingers twiddling one of the round jade ear bobs. "Peters, I shouldn't ask this if I were a gentleman, but how old are you?"

"Twenty-four."

"Just my own age. Good school and all that?"

"Harvard Business School," Peters said.

"That's good, I suppose. I went to a redbrick university myself. You like what you're doing? Following old Lewis about and all that?"

"I suppose so."

"And someday you'll be a big pot yourself—that is, if the hairies don't tear it all down for you—but right now it's a bit of a bore, eh? Big company and all that. Our little agency here is *big company too, you know*. Owned by ———[he named a British newspaper] and they're owned by ———" (a company Peters had always associated with music tapes). "That's American, you know. Small world."

"It is," Peters said. He was wondering what would happen to Tredgold if they lost the war. Probably nothing.

"So I was once where you are now—not quite so high, of course. At the paper; Mum and Dad had scrimped and put me through, and I was to be a journalist. One is chosen to go up in the first three years—you're aware of that? Or not at all. Only I made a bish. You only make one bish, you know."

"I know," Peters said.

"But I was fortunate: I made a cracking good one, and they sent me here. Old Wellingsford called me into his office just after and said they wished to transfer me—'a nice place for a chap like you,' was the way he put it. They wanted an Englishman to run it, but the wages were Portuguese—'very sorry and all that, but the rule about dismissed if you refused transfer still holds, can't go breaking rules every moment, can we?' "

"So you went," Peters said.

Tredgold nodded. "Boring you, aren't I? But you can't say so—that's the fault of a good school."

"You're not boring me," Peters said honestly.

"Ah," said Tredgold. He leaned back in his chair and for an instant Peters thought he was about to put his foot up on the desk, but he did not. "Well, I put up a brave front, you know. 'Going to be manager there, Mums, and good-bye for a bit, eh?' Tear. Dick Whittington and all that. Tear."

" 'Bye, Dad,' " Peters said, getting into the spirit of the thing.

"Right. Absolutely. Salary four thousand bloody escudos per month, and never told them the bloody escudo's hardly worth a farthing."

"You can live here cheaply, I suppose, once you know your way around the city."

"I shouldn't know," Tredgold said. "The week I came the really big pots got tired of seeing their little subsidiaries on the bad side of the books and declared a bonus for management—three percent of the net; damned little really, you'll say, but I'm the only management we have, and all we're going to have, as long as I'm managing. And I mean to say, a modeling agency with all those great newspapers behind it to threaten the politicians—how can one lose?"

"If you're in the red," Peters remarked wisely, "three percent of nothing is zero."

"Oh, but we didn't stay there, you know—not with that sort of money in view."

"Sounds as though they should have put you in charge long ago," Peters said. It was one of his stock compliments.

"They didn't want it, you know." Tredgold's smile was broader than ever. "I daresay you think profit's what they're generally after, don't you? Went to business school and they taught you that."

"Yes, they did," Peters admitted. "Or I should say they taught us that the object of business management was to maximize the value of the stock—that was the definition we had to learn."

"Oh, son!"

"I know in Britain"—Peters fumbled for words—"there's more concern for, uh, social objectives, but still . . ." He stopped. Tredgold was laughing. "Well, what is it then?"

"My dear chap . . . my dear old chap, look about you; haven't you ever seen a firm where one of the salesmen started to do really well selling on commission? What do they do, eh? Fire him, take part of the territory from him, possibly make him sales manager—no commission there, you know—something of the kind.

Yet he was making the firm a mint and now they haven't got it. He was a mere salesperson, you see, and they'd sooner bankrupt the place than have him make too much. Let me tell you something: the big ones, the ones with offices and works of one sort or another all about, like yours and mine, can buy profits whenever they choose just by offering a thin bit of them to the chaps who do the work. But they don't and they won't, and who can blame them? I mean, what would they do with the bloody stuff?"

"Build more plants, I suppose," Peters said.

"More problems for the big pots, and the government on them too and should one of those new works not go, their reputations suffer—so why risk it? None of them know the least about manufacturing anyway."

"Give it to the stockholders then."

"Just makes the blighters greedy. No, quite seriously now, Peters, y'know what saved me? Potty little Portugal has to be shown in a separate column in the annual report, and we balance out the limousine thing—so I'm permitted to feather my wee nest. Besides"—Tredgold winked—"there are fringes. Here, love."

A pretty dark-haired girl came on camera. Tredgold said, "Give us a kiss, love, and blow one to the Yank— I say, Peters, your chief is behind you; bet you didn't know it."

Lowell Lewis was coming through the door from the large, chair-strewn room beyond. His face, heavy and unexceptional as ever, might have been a trifle drawn. Peters put Tredgold on Hold.

"Can you get me Hastorf on that thing?" Lewis said. He named a steel company and, when Peters still hesitated, added, "Pittsburgh." Peters keyed the number and got a secretary, who, seeing Lewis, touched a button by which she replaced her own face with the image of a white-haired man of fifty-five or sixty. Peters cleared his throat and slipped out of the console chair; the white-haired man said, "Hi, Lou."

Lewis nodded and said, "Phil."

The white-haired man smiled. "Just about to take myself home, but what can I do for you?"

"I don't want to hold you up," Lewis said.

"Any time."

Lewis smiled. "Pittsburgh quieter now?"

"Oh, we've never had trouble out here, Lou. We're twenty-five miles outside the city proper, you understand. What we say is, let them have the damn place for a while and wear themselves out on it. Employees who lived in the central city are free to bed down right here in the offices at night—of course, it's a bit hard on them."

"What I wanted to know, Phil, was about the planes. I was just talking to General Virdon, and he stresses the importance of having air support."

"We're guaranteeing fourteen fighter-bombers," the other man said.

"Good. Couldn't scrape up a few more for us, could you?"

Hastorf shook his head. "Not much in the way of ground crews left now, Lou. We're sending some of our laboratory people over to the base to help out, but of course they're mostly metallurgical specialties. Couldn't spare a few technicians from your outfit, could you? Or some engineers?"

"Would it get me more planes tonight?"

Hastorf said, "I'll talk to the boys."

"I'll tell you what I'll do. An engineer for every plane over the fifteen."

"Fourteen," Hastorf said.

"I thought you said fifteen. In fact, I'm sure of it."

For the first time Hastorf appeared to notice Peters. "Young man," he said, "could we hear from you?"

Peters said, "Fifteen."

Hastorf gave him a wry smile before turning back to Lewis. "I've only got fourteen, Lou."

"All right, damn it, an engineer for every plane above fourteen."

Afterward he said to Peters, "Knew him in college. Hastorf."
Peters nodded.

"Damn funny, isn't it? He went with them, and of course I went with U.S., and hell, I don't think—no, I bumped into him at some kind of trade show once. I remember having a drink with him. A machine tool show."

Peters said, "I guess you talked over old times."

"That's right." The old man turned and walked toward the door, then stopped. "Now here we are working together again." He shook his head. "For thirty years he's been with that steel outfit—a whole different world. Our senior year we were both on the dance committee. It's like you were seeing somebody rise from the dead—you know what I mean, Pete?"

Peters said, "I think so. Does——— [he named the steel corporation that employed Hastorf] have the air force now?"

"Most of it's with some oil outfit in Texas."

Lewis shut the door behind him, and Peters touched, for an instant, the spot toward which Tredgold's dark girl had blown her kiss. Then Peters hit Release, wondering if Tredgold had bothered to wait. Tredgold said, " 'Lo, Peters. Recovered from my revelations yet?"

Peters smiled. "Not yet. Not quite."

"Redbrick—did I tell you? We like to put the knife in you toffs when we've the chance."

"I wanted to ask if you'd like to come—yourself—to the party tonight," Peters said.

Tredgold whistled. "The old chap—did he endorse this bold move?"

"Don't worry about it. I'll say I suggested you drop by to make sure your girls were on the ball."

"All right," Tredgold said, "but I should tell you I've promised Mum I'll be home before eight."

In the main room the first guests were already drifting in, staring at the wall screen on the east wall, talking in self-conscious groups; several of them carried newspapers. Clio was handing around cocktails, and Donovan was already deep in conversation with a man who looked so much like himself that he might almost be talking to a mirror. Watching them all, Peters had the sensation of having seen just this tableau of elaborate casualness and subdued, content-free speech before. It was only when a woman in a red dress—very obviously the secretary-mistress of the Danish shipbuilder whose arm she held—entered that Peters could place it: the operatic market scene into which, in a moment, one of the principal singers was sure to come, calling for the thrill of romance or (what is much the same thing) the defense of France. *Surely*, Peters thought, *the curtains have just parted.* He looked toward the west window and saw Clio moving toward the cord even as he formed the thought.

The gray velvet rolled back to show tossing Atlantic waves. Peters wanted to incline his head toward them, a very slight bow, but someone took him by the arm and said, "You are one of the Americans?"

"Oh, yes, and you are—" He tried, and failed, to attach a name, then a nationality, to the face. Oh, well, when in Rome . . . "Senhor . . ."

"Solomos."

"Damn glad you could come," Peters said, taking his hand.

"What is happening in your country is so interesting," Solomos said. "Great art will come from it—have you thought of that? Great art. The blood of a great people is stirred by such things, and there will be so much of what was old blown away."

Someone put an old-fashioned into Peters's hand, and he sipped it. He said, "I suppose." He thought of the Italian industrialist who collected art, but he was reasonably sure Solomos was not he.

"The armies—do they take pains to preserve such art as your country possesses?"

"Armies?" Peters had never thought of the radicals as an army.

"We soldiers like to loot," Solomos said. "All, that is, except the soldiers of my own country—we regard any art save our own as an aberration." He laughed.

There was a cherry in the bottom of Peters's glass, and he ate it. He said to Solomos, "You're a soldier, then?"

"Oh, no. No more."

A third man joined them; he was tall, and had a mustache. He said, "You are Mr. Peters, I take it. Where do you feel the sympathies of the American people lie, Mr. Peters?"

Peters said, "With the government, unquestionably."

"But since May," the tall man began, "there has been so little government left, and so little of the will to rule in what *is* left—"

"One knows what he intends," Solomos said.

A fat man who had been talking to another group turned (it was a little, Peters thought, like watching a globe revolve in a library) and said, "In the science of realpolitik the sympathies of the population do not matter except insofar as they are nationalistic sympathies. In the event of a civil war the concept of nationalistic sympathy is inapplicable because to the popular mind the nation claiming allegiance is perceived to have vanished. A charismatic leader—"

Peters said, "In the Civil War regional sympathies—"

"Wait," the tall man said. "Something is happening."

Peters turned around and saw that Lowell Lewis was now standing facing the dark screen and rapping (though the sound was inaudible over the hum of talk) with a long pointer on the glass surface.

"He should shoot off a gun, hahaha," Solomos said. "That would quiet them."

Peters said, "I think he's afraid of guns," then realized he should not have, then that no one had heard him anyway. A beautiful dark-haired girl in an evening gown, one of Tredgold's girls, gave him a martini.

The fifteen-by-thirty-five-foot screen behind Lewis flashed with light, showing Lewis's own face, immensely magnified so that every pore could be seen as though through a microscope. It glowered at them, all eyes and nose and mouth, the forehead and chin lost in ceiling and carpet; so magnified it assumed a new quality, like the giants in fairy tales, who are not merely big men but monsters. "Gentlemen," Lewis said. "Your attention, please."

The room fell silent.

"I'm afraid we are not quite all here yet, but we have a definite appointment with General Virdon, and it would be best if I began your orientation now."

Someone said, "Will there be a period for questions?"

The giant answered, "There will be all evening for questions—I want that understood. You may interrupt any speaker—including myself—whenever you have questions. We're not trying to sell you a pig in a poke."

"If the attack tonight succeeds, what benefits do you anticipate?"

"I should think the benefits are obvious."

"I will put it in another way," the questioner continued. "Do you not feel that the real struggle is taking place on your coasts? That they are the important theaters of operations?"

From beside Peters the tall man called, "Some believe we have been brought here to witness a show victory—a Potemkin village of war." Peters had been trying to guess the tall man's nationality, thus far without success.

Lewis disappeared, replaced by a map of America. The real Lewis, seeming suddenly diminutive, tapped Detroit with his wand. "This city may not be known to many of you," he said, "as it is not a cosmopolitan city, but it is a manufacturing center of great importance. Please observe that it is virtually impossible to isolate it without infringing upon Canadian sovereignty."

The man with the mustache said, "Canada cannot allow the passage of war matériel."

"I am speaking of industrial goods, whose passage Canada has guaranteed—machine tools and electronics. Not supplies for the troops in the east. Our aim in this campaign is to restore American productivity."

Someone near Peters said, "And American credit." There was a ripple of laughter.

"Precisely." Lewis's flat voice came loudly, cutting through the amusement. "Credit, as you know, is a matter of confidence, of trust. Ours is still a country of great natural resources, with a wonderful supply of skilled labor and unmatched management know-how. I don't have to tell any of you gentlemen that U.S. is one of the world's leading manufacturers, or that we are trying to obtain, currently, financing overseas, but—"

The man standing next to Peters said, "You are having difficulties. What is it you call management if you have such difficulties?"

Peters turned, expecting to see Solomos, but it was a man he had not met, a short, fat man of fifty or so. Peters said, "We mean business management. Maximizing the return on invested capital."

"Management," the fat man said firmly, "is management."

Peters turned back to listen to Lewis.

"End," the fat man continued, "you do not any longer have these resources you speak of, not so much more as other peoples."

Peters said, "There is a great deal left."

"Not so much for each person as Western Europe. Different, yes, but not so much."

Lewis had a map of Detroit on the screen now, stabbed by arrows from the south and west.

On the other side of Peters someone asked, "Do you have a master plan for retaking the country?" And the tall man with the mustache said, "They surely must, but I doubt if this young man knows it, or could confide in us if he did."

Peters recalled a conversation he had had with Lewis earlier in which he had asked much the same question. Lewis had said, "Top management knows what it's doing," and Peters had felt better until he remembered that Lewis was top management. One of Tredgold's girls brushed against Peters, her back arched, her hands and a tray of hors d'oeuvres above her head; he was acutely conscious of the momentary warmth and pressure of her hips; General Virdon was talking on the wall-sized screen, a gray-haired, square-faced man whose hard jaw was betrayed by nervous eyes. Peters had seen the face before, the face of a frightened middle-management man whose career had topped out in his forties, driving his subordinates from habit and his fear of his many-faced, ever-shifting superiors. Donovan edged up to Peters and said, "He looks like old Charlie Taylor, doesn't he? Runs the Duluth plant."

Peters nodded. "I was just thinking the same thing."

"I was out there two years ago," Donovan continued. "You know, go around, see what the boys back home were doing. . . ."

Mentally Peters tuned him out. Someone new, a major, was on the screen. He said, "I regret that Colonel Hopkins was unable to return as scheduled to address this group. He left our headquarters here at fourteen hundred hours and was due back quite some time ago. I don't know just what he had intended to tell you, but I'll answer your questions as well as I can." The major wore paratrooper wings; they went well with his impassive, almost Indian, face.

Someone asked, "If your colonel does not return, will you direct the attack?"

"If you mean Force Wolverine," the major said, "I'll lead it. General Virdon will direct it."

From another part of the room: "Isn't it true that you have put clerks and cooks into the fighting ranks?"

"Not as much as I'd like to." Unexpectedly the major smiled, the boyish smile of a man who has gotten his way when he did not expect it. "They're usually the most able-bodied soldiers we've got, especially the clerks. Now that the government's out and the companies have taken over, all the goofballs with political connections can't write their damn letters anymore."

"Don't you find it difficult to get recruits when you cannot pay?"

"Hell, that would be impossible," the major said. "But we can pay something— the companies have bankrolled us to some extent, and they buy up some of the stuff we liberate."

Lowell Lewis said, "May I add a bit of explanation of my own there, Major? Thank you. Gentlemen, this is, of course, one of the most important reasons for the loans we are trying to secure here—we feel an obligation to deal fairly with the men who are directing these vital operations in our own country. They are going to win, they will win, and we are in a position to secure those loans with the solidest possible collateral—victory."

"A question for you, Mr. Lewis. This officer takes order from General Veerdon—"

"Virdon," the major said.

"Thank you. General Veerdon. But from whom does General Veerdon take order?"

There was a long pause. At last Lewis said, "At present General Virdon can't be said to be getting orders from anyone. America feels that as one of its finest commanders he is competent, during this emergency, to exercise his own judgment."

"But he consults with you?"

Lewis nodded. "About finances and supplies, and to a certain extent concerning priorities among objectives." Peters saw Clio Morris hand Lewis a note.

"And General Marteen, at Boston, with who——"

"Excuse me," Lewis said, "but word had just been flashed to us that the troops are jumping off for the attack, and I don't think any of you will want to miss that."

Down an eight-lane highway dotted with the carcasses of burned-out automobiles (casualties of the June fighting that had lost the city) men in green and brown and blue were advancing ahead of three light tanks. Some of the men wore helmets; others did not, and Peters noticed one group in the flat-brimmed campaign hats of state police. The short, fat man called out, "Ees Force Wolpereen?"

"No," Lewis said, "this is Cougar, moving up Interstate Seventy-five from the Rockwood-Gibraltar area. We'll be seeing Wolverine in a few moments now."

Another voice: "May I ask how we are receiving these pictures? They do not appear to be coming by helicopter."

"That is correct. Although we have a great deal of airpower—I believe you can see some fighter-bomber strikes in the background there—we prefer to use handheld cameras for this sort of coverage, since they permit us to contact individuals directly. I believe an officer sitting on the roof of a truck is taking this."

"Would it be possible for us to talk to one of the soldiers involved?"

"I'll see if I can't arrange it."

The picture abruptly changed to show a burning building that might have been an apartment house. "This is Wolverine: the skirmish line preceding the main force, which I believe is just now jumping off."

A soldier with an assault rifle dashed past, followed by two dungareed sailors carrying carbines. Abruptly the burning apartment house wobbled and fell away to a street lined with buildings with sandbagged windows, then sky, then the face of General Virdon, who said, "It appears our operator has bought it, sir. We'll have another one for you in a few seconds."

Lewis said, "We quite understand."

Peters, trying to make it appear that he was relaying a question from one of the people near him, asked, "Can you tell us the composition of Force Wolverine, General?"

"Certainly." Virdon leaned forward to glance at a note on his desk before answering, and Peters wondered suddenly where he was—if he was within a hundred miles of the battle. "Wolverine comprises elements of the Thirty-first Airborne, strengthened with naval detachments from the Great Lakes Training Station and armored units of the Wisconsin National Guard—the name, as you may have guessed, has been chosen to honor these last."

In Peters's ear Donovan said, "Belongs to ——[he named a mining company] and we're getting them on loan. Lou set it up."

A tall black man said, "I represent the National Trade Bureau of the Empire of Ethiopia. May I ask a question?"

Lewis said, "Certainly. It isn't necessary, however, for anyone to identify themselves."

"I wish to ask my question of General Virdon."

On the colossal screen the general nodded.

"Would you tell us your prior military experience, sir?"

Solomos, who had reappeared from somewhere, said to Peters, "A very nice party. I enjoy it. But what do you think of the attack as far as this?"

Peters said, "If we win in Detroit it will be the key to opening up the Midwest and splitting the radicals." It was what he had heard Lewis tell a Swiss banker earlier that day.

"No doubt. But will you win?"

"We have to win," Peters said, and found that he had surprised himself. As quickly as he could he added, "The odds are too heavily weighed in our favor. Suppose, for example, Mr. Solomos, that your company was going to open up a new territory, or introduce a new product. You would observe your competitors: not just how much advertising they are doing, but how much they are capable of doing—and how many salesmen they have, how good those salesmen are, any special advantages they may have, like high customer loyalty in this particular area. When you've learned all those things you're in a position to calculate just how much it will take to knock them out of the top spot quickly, and decide whether or not you can do it. If you go in at all, you go in with about double the top ad budget they can afford, free samples, coupon offers, and the pick of your sales force—on special bonus incentives. You don't go in until you've asked yourself, *How can I lose?* and found that you can't imagine any possible way you could—and then you can't. Well, that's what we've done"—Peters waved at General Virdon on the screen—"and we're going in."

"Bravo," Solomos said. "Magnificent. You say all that very well. But they have more men than you."

"Ours are better armed and have air support and tanks, and I doubt that they really have more people—at least not many. A great part of the population of Detroit is still loyal to free enterprise, or just doesn't want to get involved."

"But that was interesting to me," Solomos continued, "about the selling. What if the product you sell is not better?"

"Actually," Peters said, "that hardly matters, unless it's really pretty bad. We—I mean United Services—always try to have the best, and in fact we spend a lot on that sort of thing: R and D, and quality control. But mostly we do it because it energizes the sales force."

The Ethiopian was saying to General Virdon, "Then you have not ever actually fought—you yourself fought."

"What matters in combat is organization and fire support—the total firepower that can be directed at the enemy. We learned that in Vietnam. If you can blow up enough jungle you can kill anybody. . . . Now, Mr. Lewis—sir?"

"Yes?"

"Your guests mentioned that they would like to talk directly to one of the enlisted men taking part in this operation. We have that set up now, sir."

"Fine."

A young man appeared. He was handsome in a boyishly appealing way and wore neatly pressed fatigues with a PFC's stripe. To the audience he said, "Private Hale reporting, sir." His forehead was abundantly beaded with sweat, and Peters wondered if it was really that hot in Detroit. After a moment Hale wiped it off.

Someone called, "You are a soldier? Don't you know you could be killed in this action?"

Hale nodded solemnly into the screen, then said, "I don't mean to be disrespectful, sir, but you can get killed crossing the street—anyway, you could in the good old days—and I think what my buddies and me are doing here is more important than a whole lot of streets."

"And you are confident this operation will succeed?"

The soldier nodded. "Yes, sir, I am. There's a whole bunch of good guys wrapped up in this thing, and . . ."

Peters became aware that the soldier's voice was fading, and with it his image on the screen.

". . . all of us know . . ." It was barely audible. The screen went white, dazzlingly bright.

"What is this?" a new voice asked. The voice was young, unpolished, and unprofessional, the muttering of the new tenant next door to himself, heard through the walls at 11:00 P.M.

Lewis said, "I'm afraid we're having some communications problems here, gentlemen; you'll have to bear with us." Addressing the disembodied voice: "Is this Grizzly Bear?"

"Ken!"

"Grizzly Bear One—General Virdon—come in, please."

As though drawn long ago in invisible ink and only now called up by heat or the ammoniacal fumes of blood, a face materialized. Peters had expected a beard and the conventional exotic, vaguely erotic, jewelry, but the boy was too young for the first and had removed—if he ever wore it—the second, save for the rhinestoned frames (each weeping a crystal acrylic tear) of thick glasses. "Well," he said, and then, "ken." He moved toward his screen, appearing to lean out of the illusion, his thin, unlined face suspended above them as it might have been over a cage of white rats. Then his eyes left them and he looked toward the window that was the west wall of the room, and the tossing Atlantic.

"Who are you?" Lewis asked.

"Philadelphia," the boy answered simply. Peters saw Lewis wince; Philadelphia was in radical hands.

From the floor someone called, "We were watching the attack on Detroit."

"Oh," the boy said. And then, "I can get you Detroit. Wait a minute."

The screen flashed, and was filled with a young man whose forehead was painted with hieroglyphics. He said, "This is Free Michigan Five with uninterrupted battle coverage, music, and macrobiotic diet tips, except when we are interrupted. Did everyone get to see the pig plane that crashed in Dearborn Heights?"

Someone called, "No!" but the young man appeared not to have heard. "I guess you've got the news that six kenkins are going to donate their bodies to Peace, and we're going to give you that live right now. Hold on."

A bigger man, with a bushy beard, his hair held back by a beaded band. Behind him four men and two women sat cross-legged on ground littered with rubble, their heads bent. "No Roman circus," the bearded man said. "If you're not considering doing this yourself, please tune out."

"This is a television picture," Lewis said at the front of the room. "That's what's giving the streaky effect. Vidlink does not do this."

"Over there"—the bushy-bearded man waved an arm—"is what they call Cougar. That's the big pig force attacking us from the south. I think you can hear the shooting."

They could. The distant whine of ricocheting bullets, the nervous chattering of assault rifles and machine guns; and below all this (like the bass section of an orchestra, in which iron-souled strings, and horns, and wild kettledrums inherited from Ottoman cavalry speak of the death of spring and heroes) the double-toned pounding of the quad-fifties—four fifty-caliber machine guns mounted together on a combat car and controlled by a single trigger—as they chewed down stone and brick and sandbags to splash the blood and brains of lonely snipers across the debris.

"It's strictly voluntary whether you talk or not," the man with the beard said. "We've asked everyone who isn't actually thinking about doing this themselves to tune out, but probably there are a lot of them still on. You know how it is. Anybody want to talk?"

For a moment no one moved; then a thin young man with a curly beard stood up. He was wearing only undershorts, boxer shorts dotted with a pattern of acorns. The interviewer said, "This is great, man. In the last two batches nobody would talk." He smiled. He had bad teeth and a good smile.

The curly-bearded young man in shorts said, "What do you want to know?"

The bearded man said, "I guess most of all why."

"If you don't know I can't tell you. Yes, I can; because I want to turn things around. Like, everybody all the time only does it for himself or something he sees being part of him only bigger, an empire or a church, like that. I'm doing it for ants, to set us loose."

The bearded man said, "You stoned?"

"Sure I'm stoned. Ken, I'm stoned blind."

"You don't look stoned, man."

"Trust me."

"You believe in more life after you die?"

The curly-bearded young man in boxer shorts shook his head. "That isn't what it means. When there's no more, that's Death."

"Just the big dark?"

He nodded. "The big dark."

One of the girls stood. She was a thin and rather flat-chested girl, with straggling brown hair and the large, trusting eyes of a fawn. "I don't agree with that," she said. "If Death is Nothing, why have another name for it?"

"That's nominalism," the curly-bearded young man said. "That's camp." After he had said it he seemed sorry he had spoken.

"And I'm not killing myself," the girl continued. "That's up to them— whether I die or not. I don't think this *I* is going to live afterward if they kill me— of course not. But something will continue in existence, and there are a lot of things here"—oddly, she touched her shoulders, each hand against its own so that for a moment her doubled arms seemed wings, small and thin and featherless— "we could do without."

The bushy-bearded man said, "You're going to let them be your judges?"

"My Lord let Pilate be his." She sat down. The curly-bearded young man had turned his back to the screen.

"Anyone else," the bearded man said. "Anybody at all."

No one looked toward him. A girl wearing a motorcycle helmet came trotting up and announced, "Ready." The six stood. The bearded man said, "This is it. We'll follow them as long as we can." In point of fact the six were already offscreen, though the bearded man was, presumably, looking toward them. "We get all kinds, I suppose you could say—you just talked to two of them. Truth seekers, Jesus freaks, activists, pacifists, about twice as many boys as girls. No one has to come, and anyone can turn back at any time. The people you just talked to could turn back now if they wanted, although it doesn't look like any of them are going to."

A shot of the six showed them following the girl in the motorcycle helmet. The buildings to either side of them had been largely destroyed by air strikes, and they might have been tourists trailing a guide through some older ruined city.

"Some of you will be thinking you would like to do what they are doing," the bushy-bearded man said. "You can sign up at most Buddhist and Christian spiritual centers, and also at the temple of Kali just off the Edsel Ford Expressway. Also in the basement of——[—he named a well-known department store]—where the travel office used to be. Of course nothing is final right up to the bullets."

The camera jumped, and the men Lowell Lewis had gathered together saw the six emerging from an alley choked with rubble. The girl in the motorcycle helmet was no longer visible. Awkwardly they spread to form a single straggling line, three young men on one end, then the two girls, then an older, balding man. Two had contrived, or perhaps been given, white rags on sticks; they waved them. The remaining four advanced with lifted hands.

At Peters's ear Solomos whispered, "How near are they now? To the fighting?" As if to answer him a bullet kicked up dust before one of the young men's feet. He hesitated for a moment, then trotted to catch up.

"Please," the bushy-bearded man's voice said, "if you aren't a potential volunteer we ask you to tune out."

Someone called to Lewis, "Switch it off."

Lewis said, "As you have seen, they have taken control of our channel."

Solomos asked, "He could still deactivate this receiver, could he not?" And Peters answered, "Sure." He felt that he was going to be sick, and was surprised to see one of Tredgold's Portuguese girls still circulating with a tray of drinks and canapés. He took a martini and drained it; when his eyes returned to the screen three of the six were gone. The remaining three, seen now from behind, still advanced. The young man with the curly beard had removed his acorn-printed shorts and walked naked.

Whether from a remote mike or by some sound-gathering device, voices came suddenly into the Lisbon hotel room. The naked boy was saying, "Peace! Peace! Don't shoot; look at us!" A girl crooned wordlessly, and the bald man recited the Lord's Prayer.

Distantly someone called, "Hey, cease fire. They're giving up. Squad! Hold it!"

The three continued to advance, but diverged as they came, first six, then twelve, then twenty-four or more yards separating each from his or her companions, as though each were determined to die alone. The screen could not longer encompass all three, and began to move nervously from one to the next as though afraid to miss the death of any. A soldier stood and motioned to the curly-bearded young man, indicating the midden of smashed concrete which had sheltered him. As the soldier did so he was shot, and fell backward. The curly-bearded young man turned toward his own lines shouting, "Stop! Stop!" and was shot in the back. The camera showed him writhing on the dusty pavement for a moment, then switched to the girl, now remote and fuzzy with distance but still large in the picture provided by the telephoto lens. Four soldiers surrounded her, and as they watched one put his arms about her and kissed her. Another jerked them apart, shoved the first aside, and tore away the girl's thin shirt; as he did she exploded in a sheet of flame that embraced them all.

The bald man was walking rapidly toward a half-tracked combat car mounting quad-fifties; faintly they could hear him saying, "Hey, listen, the Giants won twenty-six straight in 1916, and the biggest gate in baseball was more than eighty-four thousand for a Yankees-Browns game in New York. The youngest big leaguer ever was Hamilton Joe Nuxhall—he pitched for Cincinnati when he was fifteen. *Don't you guys care about anything?*" The crew of the half-track stared at him until an officer drew a pistol and fired. The bald man leaped to one side (Peters could not tell whether he had been hit or not) and ran toward him shouting something about the Boston Braves. The officer fired again and the bald man's body detonated like a bomb. The voice of the young man with hieroglyphics on his forehead said, "I think we're going to catch the Zen Banzai charge over on the west side now." There was a sudden shift in picture and they saw a horde of ragged people with red cloths knotted around their heads and waists streaming toward a line of soldiers supported by two tanks. Some of the ragged people had firearms; more were armed with spears and gasoline bombs. For a moment they were falling everywhere—then the survivors had overwhelmed the tanks. Peters saw a soldier's head still wearing its steel helmet, open-eyed in death and livid with the loss of blood, held aloft on a homemade spear. The picture closed on it as it turned and swayed above the crowd; it became the head of General Virdon, who said, "Now we've got you again. My communications people tell me we lost you for a few minutes, Mr. Lewis." He sounded relieved.

Lewis said, "We had technical difficulties."

The voice of the boy in Philadelphia announced, "I did that fade with the faces—it was pretty good, wasn't it?"

Solomos asked Peters, "Why are you attacking? You should be defending. You have lost most of your country already."

"We don't think so," Peters said.

"You have a few army camps and airdromes and some factories remote from centers of population; that is not the country. You survive thus far because they do not know how to fight, but they are learning, they are drilling armies everywhere, and you do not know how to fight either, and are not learning; after the defeat of the Germans and your small war in Korea you allowed your army to become only a consumer of your industrial production. What will this general do if they march from Chicago while his front is entangled in this street fighting?"

Donovan, appearing drink in hand from some remote part of the room, said, "I'm glad you asked that, Colonel Solomos. You see, that's part of our plan—to get these people out into the open where our planes can get at them."

Solomos made a disgusted sound. "Virdon has no reserve to cover his rear?"

"Certainly he does," Donovan said. "Naturally I can't tell you how many." A moment afterward, when Solomos was talking to someone else, Donovan warned Peters, "Be nice to that guy; he represents the Greek army—its business interests. Lou is trying to contract for some Greeks to stiffen things along the coast."

Peters said, "I'd think they'd be worrying about being nice to us, then. They ought to be glad to get the money."

"There's not a lot of real money around. Mostly we're talking trade agreements after the war, stuff like that."

A familiar voice asked, "Suppose one wished to get down a bit of a flier on this row; what's the old firm offering?" It was Tredgold.

Donovan, a little puzzled to see someone he did not recognize, said, "I'm afraid I've already laid out as much as I can afford."

Peters asked, "You're betting against us?"

"Only for sport. The fact is, I'd back either, but I shouldn't expect you to turn against your own chaps. Ten thousand escudos?"

"You're on." By a simultaneous operation of instinct both looked up at the screen, where General Virdon, looking much as though he were giving the weather, was outlining his battle plan in chalk.

Tredgold called loudly, "I say, there! Those marks show where you are now, eh? But where shall you be in an hour?" The general began laboriously sketching phantom positions across the heart of Detroit. "Well, we'll see, eh?" Tredgold whispered to Peters.

Peters asked, "Have you had a drink?"

"Well, no, I haven't, actually. Just arrived a moment or so ago, to tell the truth. Are my birds behaving?"

"Yes, they've been fine." Peters waved over a tall dark girl whose hair, gathered behind her head in a cascade of curls, suggested a Greece not represented by Solomos. She smiled at each of them in turn, and they each took a drink—Peters was conscious that it was his third or fourth; he could not be sure which. "Listen," he said to Tredgold when the girl had gone. "I'd like to talk to you for a minute."

They found chairs at the back of the room, next to the window, and Peters said, "Can you set me up with that girl?"

"You didn't need me, old boy; just ask her. Your chief is paying, after all."

They talked of something else, Peters conscious that it was impossible—equally impossible to explain the impossibility. Time passed, and he knew that he would despise himself later for having missed this opportunity, though it was an opportunity that would only exist when it was too late. A few feet away Donovan was taking his wallet from his pocket, making a bet with a tall German; for some reason Peters thought of the recording company which, ultimately, employed Tredgold, and their trademark, a cluster of instruments stamped in gold, recalling the slow way it had turned round and round on the old-fashioned 33⅓ disk player in his grandmother's house in Palmerton, Pennsylvania. Tredgold was recounting some story about a badger that had hidden from dogs in the cellar of a church, and Peters interrupted him to say, "What's it like in England now?"

Tredgold said, "And so you see the poor blighters couldn't explain what they were doing there," and Peters realized that he had not spoken aloud at all and had to say again, "But what is it like in England *now*?"

Tredgold smiled. "I daresay we're fifteen years behind you."

"You're expecting all this?" Peters waved a hand at the distant screen. "I mean, are *you* expecting it?"

"Seems likely enough, I should think. Same problems in both countries, much. Same sort of chaps in authority. And ours look to yours—of course, it won't last nearly so long on our side; we haven't the space."

"If we win," Peters said, "I doubt that it will ever break out in England."

"Oh, but you won't, you know," Tredgold said. "I've money on it."

Peters sipped his drink, trying to decide what kind of whiskey was in it; everything tasted the same. Probably Canadian, he thought. He had checked the supplies sent up by the hotel before the party began, and had noticed how much Canadian whiskey there was; the war had dried up the American market. "You could change things," he told Tredgold suddenly, "before this happens."

"*I* could change things? I bloody well could not."

"You English could, I mean."

"Could have done the same sort of thing yourselves," Tredgold said. "All your big corporations, owning everything and running everyone, everything decided by the economic test when it was forty or more years out of date. One firm's economies only good because of prices set by another to encourage or discourage something else altogether, and your chemical works ruining your fishing, turning the sea into a dustbin, then selling their chemical foods. Why didn't you change things yourselves, eh?"

Peters shook his head. "I don't know. Everybody was talking about it for years—I remember even when I was in grade school. But nothing was ever done. Maybe it was more complicated than it looked."

"Britain's the same. These chaps everyone's been shouting at to change things, they're the very chaps that do so well as things are. Think they're going to make new rules for a game they always win? Not ruddy likely." Tredgold stood up. "Your crowd's thinning out a bit, I fancy. I say"—he took a passing stranger by the arm—"pardon me, sir, but where's everyone off to?"

"The cabaret downstairs," the man said in an accent Peters could not identify. "The last show there—it is ten minutes. Then we come here again and watch again the battle. You wish to come?"

Tredgold glanced at Peters, then shook his head. "Some other time, and thank you very much. You come to Lisbon often? Wait a bit; I've a card here somewhere." He walked as far as the corridor door with the stranger, then returned to Peters. "Nice chap. Hungarian or something. Hope he fancies dark women."

Donovan, who had been standing a few feet away watching the screen, said, "In there, mister," and pointed to the two outside bedrooms. "We can't use the middle one—Lou's on the private vidlink in there."

Tredgold feigned puzzlement and looked around the room. "I don't even see one now."

"Two in each room," Donovan said. "They'll come out when they're ready—that's what most of the guys in the chairs are waiting for."

"How's the attack going?" Peters asked. He was conscious of swaying a little and took hold of the back of a chair with one hand.

"Great," Donovan said. The door of the east bedroom opened and a short man in a wool suit too heavy for Portugal came out sweating; after a moment a man who had been smoking stinking Dutch cigarettes in a chair near the door got up and went in.

"Great?" Peters asked.

"We haven't lost an inch of ground yet. Not an inch."

Peters looked at the screen. It showed a parking lot, apparently part of a shopping complex. Some broken glass lay on the asphalt, and several dead men, but nothing much seemed to be happening. Occasionally the whine of a shot came, its origin and its target equally unknowable.

"This is our side," Donovan explained. "The stuff near the screen. The hairies have still got those buildings over on the far side."

"We're not supposed to be holding ground," Peters said. "We're supposed to be, you know, going forward." He looked at his watch. "They ought to be almost to the lake shore by now."

"We're regrouping," Donovan said.

"Listen. Will you listen to me for a minute?" Peters was aware that he was about to make some kind of fool out of himself, and that he could not prevent it. "We ought to be there, doing something, helping them. I mean we're three men; we're not just nothing." He tried to make a joke of it: "Tredgold here's smart, I'm strong, and you're Irish—we could do something."

Donovan looked at him blankly, then slapped him on the shoulder and said, "Yeah, sure," and turned away.

Tredgold drawled, "Another thing I forgot to tell you about *l'ancien régime*— the winners are those who don't fight for it. Thought your mum would have put you wise to that already. The mums know." After a second's hesitation he added, "Only works while the chaps who *do* fight play the game, of course. No profit otherwise—no anything at all."

"Profit?" Peters said. "You said they didn't really want profits, and I've been thinking about that and you're right—for them profit above a certain point is just taking from each other. You said that."

"Did I? I suppose I did. It sounds familiar. Wait a sec, will you? All my bloody birds are nesting and I want a drink."

Peters called after him, "But what is it they do want?" and heard Tredgold mutter, "To hang on to their places, I should think."

"Ah." Lowell Lewis put his hand on Peters's shoulder. "You and Donovan taking care of things for us out here, Pete? How's it going?"

"Quiet," Peters said.

"You're up on the battle, I assume?"

"Yes, sir."

"Good. We've been getting quite a number of calls on the private link from other companies—they have a stake in this of one sort or another, and they want to know the situation. To keep from clogging General Virdon's communications with that sort of thing I've arranged that we would handle them. Think you can hold down the hot seat for a while?"

Peters nodded.

"There's one other thing. You remember the soldier we had on-screen? The one that hippie-type boy from Philadelphia cut off?"

"Hale," Peters said.

"Right. He was from the PR agency, of course; but when he had made the take that fool major who's replacing Colonel Hopkins grabbed him; he seems to have put him in one of the combat outfits. Naturally the agency is very upset. Try to bail him out, will you?"

Peters nodded again.

"Fine. In an hour I'll send in Donovan or Miss Morris, and you can bring yourself up to date."

Peters went into the center bedroom, trying to walk as steadily as he could, though he knew Lewis had already turned away to talk to someone else.

The bedroom was empty and dark. The vidlink screen was flashing the identity of some caller—Peters did not bother to discover who. He drew the curtains at the far end of the room and looked out over the patio wall at the headlights of the cars on the street outside, and noted vaguely that a diagonal view showed him the same dark Atlantic that sometimes seemed ready to invade the big room from which he had come.

There was a bathroom and he used it. He felt that he might have to vomit, but he did not.

Communicating doors linked this bedroom with those to east and west. He tried them, and found (as he had expected) that they were locked on the other side. Outside each he listened for a moment and heard the creaking of springs and whispered words, but no laughter.

At the vidlink he ignored the incoming calls and coded the Library of Congress, wondering if there was still anyone left there. There was, a plain-looking black girl of about twenty. He asked if she had a taped summary of American history for the last thirty years. She nodded and started to say something else, then asked, "Who is this calling, please?" And he said, "My name is Peters. I'm with United Services Corporation."

"Oh," she said. And then, "Oh!"

He asked her if something was the matter.

"It's just that I have this friend—not really a friend, someone I know—that works in the Pentagon. And he says they weren't paid there at all for several months . . . but now they *are* getting paid again . . . only now the checks are from your company . . . Do you know Mr. Lewis?" This was said with many pauses and hesitations.

"I'm his assistant," Peters said.

"Well, would it be possible . . . The staff here hasn't been paid since January. . . . Most of them are gone, and you wouldn't have to pay them, of course; I live with my mother, and anything you could get for us . . ."

"I don't—," Peters began, then changed it to: "I don't see why we couldn't put you under military administration. I mean, nominally. Then you'd be civilian employees of the Department of Defense."

"Oh," the girl said, and then, "Oh, thank you." And then, "I—I'm sorry, but I've forgotten what it was you wanted. I'm a graduate of Maryland—I really am. Library science."

"The history tape," Peters said. "You ought to get more rest."

"So should you," the girl said. "You look tired."

"I'm drunk."

"Well, we've had so many requests for that tape that we just looped it, you know. We run it all the time. I'll connect you."

She pushed buttons on her own vidlink, and her face faded until only her mouth and bright eyes were visible, overlaying the helmeted figure of an astronaut. "All right?" she said.

Peters asked, "Is this the beginning or the end?"

"Sir?"

"I wanted to know—" He heard the door open behind him and hit the Cut button. "Later." The screen filled at once with incoming calls. He turned.

It was Clio Morris. She shut the door behind her and said, "Enough to drive you crazy, isn't it?"

He looked at her and made some commonplace reply, paying no more attention himself to what he had said than she would. She said, "Who do I remind you of?"

"Was I staring?" he said. "I'm sorry. Did you come to relieve me?"

"No, just to get away from the mess out there for a while. All right if I sit down?" She sat on the bed.

He said, "You don't remind me of anyone."

"That's good, because you remind me of somebody. Mr. Peters. I'm going to have a drink—want me to bring you one?"

"I'll get them," Peters said. He stood up.

"No, I will. Back in a minute."

Automatically Peters seated himself at the vidlink again and pressed the first Ready button. A man appeared who said he wanted, quite frankly, to tell Peters his management was worried about the way things were going, and that they already had a great deal sunk in this thing and could not afford to lose more. Peters agreed that things were going poorly (which disconcerted the man) and asked for positive suggestions.

"In what way?" the man said. "Just what do you mean?"

"Well, we clearly need to apply greater force to Detroit than we have so far. The question, I suppose, is how we raise the force and how we can best apply it."

"You certainly don't expect us to commit ourselves to any plan with this little preparation."

Peters said, "I just hoped you might have a few off-the-cuff suggestions."

The man shook his head. "I can take the question to my management, but that's as far as I can go."

Peters told the man that he had heard certain foreign countries might have soldiers for hire, and that it would be possible for the man to ask among his own employees for volunteers to fight in Detroit. The man said that he would keep that in mind and signed off, and Clio came in with two old-fashioneds, one of which she handed to Peters. She asked him if he had gotten anywhere with Burglund.

Peters shook his head. "Is that who I was talking to?"

"Uh-huh. He works for ———." She named a conglomerate, and Peters, suddenly curious, asked what they made.

"They don't make anything," Clio said. "Not themselves. They own some companies that make things, I suppose, and some oil tankers and real estate. Pulpwood holdings in Georgia."

Peters said, "I guess this is different from running pulpwood holdings in Georgia."

"Sure," Clio said. She sat down on one of the beds. "That's why Lowell is losing his war."

"What do you mean?"

She shrugged. "Four or five months ago when he started all this I thought they could handle it—I really did." When Peters looked at her questioningly she added, "The companies. I thought they could hold things together. So did Lou, I guess."

"So did I," Peters said.

"I know. You're a lot like Lou—when he was younger. That's what I meant when I said you reminded me of somebody: Lou when he was younger."

"You couldn't have known him then," Peters told her.

"I didn't. But about a year ago he showed me some tapes he had. They were training tapes he made twenty or twenty-five years ago. They showed him explaining some kind of machine; he was an engineer originally, you know. He looked a lot like you—he was a handsome man, and I guess he wanted me to see that he had looked like that once."

"You sleep with him, don't you?"

"I used to. Up until about six weeks ago. Now I'm trying to figure out why."

Peters said, "I wasn't asking you for an explanation."

"I know," the girl said. "You just wanted to find out if it was safe to fight with me, right?"

"Something like that."

"The formal business power structure and the informal one."

"Something like that."

"You still think there's a chance we'll win and you'll have a career with U.S."

Peters shrugged. "With my education I don't see anything else to shoot for—that's something I didn't understand until recently: you don't get that degree; it gets you. Now, for me, it's this or nothing." He moved away from the vidlink and sat down beside her on the bed. The spread was satin, and he began to stroke it with his fingers.

"You think people like Burglund are going to pull us through? I mean, really?"

Peters was silent for a moment. "You're right," he said. "He won't, but I still don't know why not."

"I do," Clio said. "I've been helping Lou deal with some of them. What do you think it takes to be a successful businessman? Enterprise, lots of guts, hard work, high intelligence—right?"

"Roughly."

"You want to tell me how you use those things to manage a tree farm in Georgia?"

"I don't know," Peters said. "I don't know anything about the lumber business."

"Neither does he. Or if he does, it doesn't do him any good. Look, they've got all this land, with pines growing on it. When it starts getting mature—ready to cut—anyplace, people make them offers for it: paper mills and lumber companies. And since some of it gets mature every year they know quite a bit about price—all they have to do is look up last year's bids. When one comes in that looks good, they can tell that company to go ahead if it's a cash deal, and if it isn't they can look up their credit in Dun and Bradstreet. They've got a regular crew that comes around and replants when the cutting's done."

"You make it sound easy," Peters said.

"No, it isn't easy—but it isn't your kind of hard either. It takes a special kind of men who can go year in and year out without rocking the boat in any way. People who never get so bored with it they get careless, and that know when they have to bow to the state legislatures and when they ought to threaten to fight a new law through the courts. But now you're telling them to get out and recruit soldiers—well, most of them were in the army themselves at one time or another, they were majors and colonels and all that, at desks, but they don't know anything about soldiers, or thinking, or running anything that doesn't go by routine. We used to say that what we wanted was initiative and creativity and all those things, just like we said we wanted kindness and human values, and the American frontier, while it lasted, actually encouraged and rewarded them, but we've been paying off on something else for a hundred years or so now, and now that's all we've got." Peters had slipped his hand between her thighs, and she looked down at it and said, "That took you a long time."

He said, "I didn't want to interrupt you."

And later, "We still might do it." He took her hand in the dark. "If we can change things just a little before it's too late we still might do it." The girl's body blossomed fire that engulfed and scarred and clung; naked and burning he reached the center of the room beyond, but he fell there, on the Moroccan carpet that covered the red tiles, and, though they poured tepid water on him from the spent ice buckets, died there.

∞

## AFTERWORD

This one taught me a lesson. I needed a story, lacked an idea, and resolved to steal one. Damon Runyon was good, and I had a Runyon collection; I would open the book at random, read the story, and rewrite it as SF. (If this sounds desperate, it was.)

Opened at random, the book palmed off on me "A Light in France," which may well be the only bad story Runyon ever wrote. I clenched my teeth, swore a mighty swear, and plowed on— eventually throwing out just about everything in "A Light in France." You have read the result. I hope you enjoyed it.

# The Death of Dr. Island

*I have desired to go*
*Where springs not fail,*
*To fields where flies no sharp and sided hail*
*And a few lilies blow*

*And I have asked to be*
*Where no storms come,*
*Where the green swell is in the heavens dumb,*
*And out of the swing of the sea.*
—GERARD MANLEY HOPKINS

A grain of sand, teetering on the brink of the pit, trembled and fell in; the ant lion at the bottom angrily flung it out again. For a moment there was quiet. Then the entire pit, and a square meter of sand around it, shifted drunkenly while two coconut palms bent to watch. The sand rose, pivoting at one edge, and the scarred head of a boy appeared—a stubble of brown hair threatened to erase the marks of the sutures; with dilated eyes hypnotically dark he paused, his neck just where the ant lion's had been; then, as though goaded from below, he vaulted up and onto the beach, turned, and kicked sand into the dark hatchway from which he had emerged. It slammed shut. The boy was about fourteen.

For a time he squatted, pushing the sand aside and trying to find the door. A few centimeters down, his hands met a gritty, solid material which, though neither concrete nor sandstone, shared the qualities of both—a sand-filled organic plastic. On it he scraped his fingers raw, but he could not locate the edges of the hatch.

Then he stood and looked about him, his head moving continually as the heads of certain reptiles do—back and forth, with no pauses at the terminations of the movements. He did this constantly, ceaselessly—always—and for that reason it will not often be described again, just as it will not be mentioned that he breathed. He did, and as he did, his head, like a rearing snake's, turned from side to side. The boy was thin, and naked as a frog.

Ahead of him the sand sloped gently down toward sapphire water; there were coconuts on the beach, and seashells, and a scuttling crab that played with the finger-high edge of each dying wave. Behind him there were only palms and sand for a long distance, the palms growing ever closer together as they moved away from the water until the forest of their columniated trunks seemed architectural, like some palace maze becoming as it progressed more and more draped with creepers and lianas with green, scarlet, and yellow leaves, the palms interspersed with bamboo and deciduous trees dotted with flaming orchids until almost at the limit of his sight the whole ended in a spangled wall whose predominant color was black-green.

The boy walked toward the beach, then down the beach until he stood in knee-deep water as warm as blood. He dipped his fingers and tasted it—it was fresh, with no hint of the disinfectants to which he was accustomed. He waded out again and sat on the sand about five meters up from the high-water mark, and after ten minutes, during which he heard no sound but the wind and the murmuring of the surf, he threw back his head and began to scream. His screaming was high-pitched, and each breath ended in a gibbering, ululant note, after which came the hollow, iron gasp of the next indrawn breath. On one occasion he had screamed in this way, without cessation, for fourteen hours and twenty-two minutes, at the end of which a nursing nun with an exemplary record stretching back seventeen years had administered an injection without the permission of the attending physician.

After a time the boy paused—not because he was tired, but in order to listen better. There was, still, only the sound of the wind in the palm fronds and the murmuring surf, yet he felt that he had heard a voice. The boy could be quiet as well as noisy, and he was quiet now, his left hand sifting white sand as clean as salt between its fingers while his right tossed tiny pebbles like beach-glass beads into the surf.

"*Hear me,*" said the surf. "*Hear me. Hear me.*"

"I hear you," the boy said.

"Good," said the surf, and it faintly echoed itself: "*Good, good, good.*"

The boy shrugged.

"What shall I call you?" asked the surf.

"My name is Nicholas Kenneth de Vore."

"Nick, *Nick . . . Nick?*"

The boy stood and, turning his back on the sea, walked inland. When he was out of sight of the water he found a coconut palm growing sloped and angled, leaning and weaving among its companions like the plume of an ascending jet blown by the wind. After feeling its rough exterior with both hands, the boy began to climb; he was inexpert and climbed slowly and a little clumsily, but his body was light and he was strong. In time he reached the top, and disturbed the little brown plush monkeys there, who fled chattering into other palms, leaving him to nestle alone among the stems of the fronds and the green coconuts. "I am here also," said a voice from the palm.

"Ah," said the boy, who was watching the tossing, sapphire sky far over his head.

"I will call you Nicholas."

The boy said, "I can see the sea."

"Do you know my name?"

The boy did not reply. Under him the long, long stem of the twisted palm swayed faintly.

"My friends all call me Dr. Island."

"I will not call you that," the boy said.

"You mean that you are not my friend."

A gull screamed.

"But you see, I take you for my friend. You may say that I am not yours, but I say that you are mine. I like you, Nicholas, and I will treat you as a friend."

"Are you a machine or a person or a committee?" the boy asked.

"I am all those things and more. I am the spirit of this island, the tutelary genius."

"Bullshit."

"Now that we have met, would you rather I leave you alone?"

Again the boy did not reply.

"You may wish to be alone with your thoughts. I would like to say that we have made much more progress today than I anticipated. I feel that we will get along together very well."

After fifteen minutes or more, the boy asked, "Where does the light come from?" There was no answer. The boy waited for a time, then climbed back down the trunk, dropping the last five meters and rolling as he hit in the soft sand.

He walked to the beach again and stood staring out at the water. Far off he could see it curving up and up, the distant combers breaking in white foam until the sea became white-flecked sky. To his left and his right the beach curved away, bending almost infinitesimally until it disappeared. He began to walk, then saw, almost at the point where perception was lost, a human figure. He broke into a run; a moment later, he halted and turned around. Far ahead another walker, almost invisible, strode the beach; Nicholas ignored him; he found a coconut and tried to open it, then threw it aside and walked on. From time to time fish jumped, and occasionally he saw a wheeling seabird dive. The light grew dimmer. He was aware that he had not eaten for some time, but he was not in the strict sense hungry—or rather, he enjoyed his hunger now in the same way that he might, at another time, have gashed his arm to watch himself bleed. Once he said, "Dr. Island!" loudly as he passed a coconut palm, and then later he began to chant, "Dr. Island, Dr. Island, Dr. Island," as he walked, until the words had lost all meaning. He swam in the sea as he had been taught to swim in the great quartanary treatment tanks on Callisto to improve his coordination, and spluttered and snorted until he learned to deal with the waves. When it was so dark he could see only the white sand and the white foam of the breakers, he drank from the sea and fell asleep on the beach, the right side of his taut, ugly face relaxing first, so that it seemed asleep even while the left eye was open and staring, his head rolling from side to side, the left corner of his mouth preserving, like a death mask, his characteristic expression—angry, remote, tinged with that inhuman quality which is found nowhere but in certain human faces.

When he woke it was not yet light, but the night was fading to a gentle gray. Headless, the palms stood like tall ghosts up and down the beach, their tops lost in fog and the lingering dark. He was cold. His hands rubbed his sides; he danced on the sand and sprinted down the edge of the lapping water in an effort to get warm; ahead of him a pinpoint of red light became a fire, and he slowed.

A man who looked about twenty-five crouched over the fire. Tangled black hair hung over this man's shoulders, and he had a sparse beard; otherwise he was as naked as Nicholas himself. His eyes were dark, and large and empty, like the ends of broken pipes; he poked at his fire, and the smell of roasting fish came with the smoke. For a time Nicholas stood at a distance, watching.

Saliva ran from a corner of the man's mouth, and he wiped it away with one hand, leaving a smear of ash on his face. Nicholas edged closer until he stood on the opposite side of the fire. The fish had been wrapped in broad leaves and mud, and lay in the center of the coals. "I'm Nicholas," Nicholas said. "Who are you?" The young man did not look at him, had never looked at him.

"Hey, I'd like a piece of your fish. Not much. All right?"

The young man raised his head, looking not at Nicholas but at some point far beyond him; he dropped his eyes again. Nicholas smiled. The smile emphasized the disjointed quality of his expression, his mouth's uneven curve.

"Just a little piece? Is it about done?" Nicholas crouched, imitating the young man, and as though this were a signal, the young man sprang for him across the fire. Nicholas jumped backward, but the jump was too late—the young man's body struck his and sent him sprawling on the sand; fingers clawed for his throat. Screaming, Nicholas rolled free, into the water; the young man splashed after him; Nicholas dived.

He swam underwater, his belly almost grazing the wave-rippled sand until he found deeper water; then he surfaced, gasping for breath, and saw the young man, who saw him as well. He dived again, this time surfacing far off, in deep water. Treading water, he could see the fire on the beach, and the young man when he returned to it, stamping out of the sea in the early light. Nicholas then swam until he was five hundred meters or more down the beach, then waded in to shore and began walking back toward the fire.

The young man saw him when he was still some distance off, but he continued to sit, eating pink-tinted tidbits from his fish, watching Nicholas. "What's the matter?" Nicholas said while he was still a safe distance away. "Are you mad at me?"

From the forest, birds warned, "Be careful, Nicholas."

"I won't hurt you," the young man said. He stood up, wiping his oily hands on his chest, and gestured toward the fish at his feet. "You want some?"

Nicholas nodded, smiling his crippled smile.

"Come then."

Nicholas waited, hoping the young man would move away from the fish, but he did not; neither did he smile in return.

"Nicholas," the little waves at his feet whispered, "this is Ignacio."

"Listen," Nicholas said. "Is it really all right for me to have some?"

Ignacio nodded, unsmiling.

Cautiously Nicholas came forward; as he was bending to pick up the fish, Ignacio's strong hands took him; he tried to wrench free but was thrown down, Ignacio on top of him. "Please!" Nicholas yelled. "Please!" Tears started into his eyes. He tried to yell again, but he had no breath; the tongue was being forced, thicker than his wrist, from his throat.

Then Ignacio let go and struck him in the face with his clenched fist. Nicholas had been slapped and pummeled before, had been beaten, had fought, sometimes savagely, with other boys, but he had never been struck by a man as men fight. Ignacio hit him again and his lips gushed blood.

He lay a long time on the sand beside the dying fire. Consciousness returned slowly; he blinked, drifted back into the dark, blinked again. His mouth was full of blood, and when at last he spit it out onto the sand, it seemed a soft flesh, dark and polymerized in strange shapes; his left cheek was hugely swollen, and he could scarcely see out of his left eye. After a time he crawled to the water; a long time after that, he left it and walked shakily back to the ashes of the fire. Ignacio was gone, and there was nothing left of the fish but bones.

"Ignacio is gone," Dr. Island said with lips of waves.

Nicholas sat on the sand, cross-legged.

"You handled him very well."

"You saw us fight?"

"I saw you; I see everything, Nicholas."

"This is the worst place," Nicholas said; he was talking to his lap.

"What do you mean by that?"

"I've been in bad places before—places where they hit you or squirted big hoses of ice water that knocked you down. But not where they would let someone else—"

"Another patient?" asked a wheeling gull.

"—do it."

"You were lucky, Nicholas. Ignacio is homicidal."

"You could have stopped him."

"No, I could not. All this world is my eye, Nicholas, my ear, and my tongue, but I have no hands."

"I thought you did all this."

"Men did all this."

"I mean, I thought you kept it going."

"It keeps itself going, and you—all the people here—direct it."

Nicholas looked at the water. "What makes the waves?"

"The wind and the tide."

"Are we on Earth?"

"Would you feel more comfortable on Earth?"

"I've never been there; I'd like to know."

"I am more like Earth than Earth now is, Nicholas. If you were to take the best of all the best beaches of Earth, and clear them of all the poisons and all the dirt of the last three centuries, you would have me."

"But this isn't Earth?"

There was no answer. Nicholas walked around the ashes of the fire until he found Ignacio's footprints. Nicholas was no tracker, but the depressions in the soft beach sand required none; he followed them, his head swaying from side to side as he walked, like the sensor of a mine detector.

For several kilometers Ignacio's trail kept to the beach; then, abruptly, the footprints swerved, wandered among the coconut palms, and at last were lost on the firmer soil inland. Nicholas lifted his head and shouted, "Ignacio? Ignacio!" After a moment he heard a stick snap, and the sound of someone pushing aside leafy branches. He waited.

"Mum?"

A girl was coming toward him, stepping out of the thicker growth of the interior. She was pretty, though too thin, and appeared to be about nineteen; her hair was blond where it had been most exposed to sunlight, darker elsewhere. "You've scratched yourself," Nicholas said. "You're bleeding."

"I thought you were my mother," the girl said. She was a head taller than Nicholas. "Been fighting, haven't you. Have you come to get me?"

Nicholas had been in similar conversations before and normally would have preferred to ignore the remark, but he was lonely now. He said, "Do you want to go home?"

"Well, I think I should, you know."

"But do you want to?"

"My mum always says if you've got something on the stove you don't want to burn— She's quite a good cook. She really is. Do you like cabbage with bacon?"

"Have you got anything to eat?"

"Not now. I had a thing a while ago."

"What kind of thing?"

"A bird." The girl made a vague little gesture, not looking at Nicholas. "I'm a memory that has swallowed a bird."

"Do you want to walk down by the water?" They were moving in the direction of the beach already.

"I was just going to get a drink. You're a nice tot."

Nicholas did not like being called a tot. He said, "I set fire to places."

"You won't set fire to this place; it's been nice the last couple of days, but when everyone is sad, it rains."

Nicholas was silent for a time. When they reached the sea, the girl dropped to her knees and bent forward to drink, her long hair falling over her face until the ends trailed in the water, her nipples, then half of each breast, in the water. "Not there," Nicholas said. "It's sandy, because it washes the beach so close. Come on out here." He waded out into the sea until the lapping waves nearly reached his armpits, then bent his head and drank.

"I never thought of that," the girl said. "Mum says I'm stupid. So does Dad. Do you think I'm stupid?"

Nicholas shook his head.

"What's your name?"

"Nicholas Kenneth de Vore. What's yours?"

"Diane. I'm going to call you Nicky. Do you mind?"

"I'll hurt you while you sleep," Nicholas said.

"You wouldn't."

"Yes, I would. At St. John's where I used to be, it was zero G most of the time, and a girl there called me something I didn't like, and I got loose one night and came into her cubical while she was asleep and nulled her restraints, and then she floated around until she banged into something, and that woke her up and she tried to grab, and then that made her bounce all around inside and she broke two fingers and her nose and got blood all over. The attendants came, and one told me—they didn't know then I did it—when he came out his white suit was, like, polka-dot red all over because wherever the blood drops had touched him they soaked right in."

The girl smiled at him, dimpling her thin face. "How did they find out it was you?"

"I told someone and he told them."

"I bet you told them yourself."

"I bet I didn't!" Angry, he waded away, but when he had stalked a short way up the beach he sat down on the sand, his back toward her.

"I didn't mean to make you mad, Mr. de Vore."

"I'm not mad!"

She was not sure for a moment what he meant. She sat down beside and a trifle behind him, and began idly piling sand in her lap.

Dr. Island said, "I see you've met."

Nicholas turned, looking for the voice. "I thought you saw everything."

"Only the important things, and I have been busy on another part of myself. I am happy to see that you two know one another; do you find you interact well?"

Neither of them answered.

"You should be interacting with Ignacio; he needs you."

"We can't find him," Nicholas said.

"Down the beach to your left until you see the big stone, then turn inland. Above five hundred meters."

Nicholas stood up and, turning to his right, began to walk away. Diane followed him, trotting until she caught up.

"I don't like," Nicholas said, jerking a shoulder to indicate something behind him.

"Ignacio?"

"The doctor."

"Why do you move your head like that?"

"Didn't they tell you?"

"No one told me anything about you."

"They opened it up"—Nicholas touched his scars—"and took this knife and cut all the way through my corpus . . . corpus . . ."

"Corpus callosum," muttered a dry palm frond.

"—corpus callosum," finished Nicholas. "See, your brain is like a walnut inside. There are two halves, and then right down in the middle a kind of thick connection of meat from one to the other. Well, they cut that."

"You're having a bit of fun with me, aren't you?"

"No, he isn't," a monkey who had come to the waterline to look for shellfish told her. "His cerebrum has been surgically divided; it's in his file." It was a young monkey, with a trusting face full of small, ugly beauties.

Nicholas snapped, "It's in my head."

Diane said, "I'd think it would kill you, or make you an idiot or something."

"They say each half of me is about as smart as both of us were together. Anyway, this half is . . . the half . . . the *me* that talks."

"There are two of you now?"

"If you cut a worm in half and both parts are still alive, that's two, isn't it? What else would you call us? We can't ever come together again."

"But I'm talking to just one of you?"

"We both can hear you."

"Which one answers?"

Nicholas touched the right side of his chest with his right hand. "Me, I do. They told me it was the left side of my brain, that one has the speech centers, but it doesn't feel that way; the nerves cross over coming out, and it's just the right side of me, I talk. Both my ears hear for both of us, but out of each eye we only see half and half—I mean, I only see what's on the right of what I'm looking at, and the other side, I guess, only sees the left, so that's why I keep moving my head. I guess it's like being a little bit blind; you get used to it."

The girl was still thinking of his divided body. She said, "If you're only half, I don't see how you can walk."

"I can move the left side a little bit, and we're not mad at each other. We're not supposed to be able to come together at all, but we do: down through the legs and at the ends of the fingers and then back up. Only I can't talk with my other side because he can't, but he understands."

"Why did they do it?"

Behind them the monkey, who had been following them, said, "He had uncontrollable seizures."

"Did you?" the girl asked. She was watching a seabird swooping low over the water and did not seem to care.

Nicholas picked up a shell and shied it at the monkey, who skipped out of the way. After half a minute's silence he said, "I had visions."

"Ooh, did you?"

"They didn't like that. They said I would fall down and jerk around horrible, and sometimes I guess I would hurt myself when I fell, and sometimes I'd bite my tongue and it would bleed. But that wasn't what it felt like to me; I wouldn't know about any of those things until afterward. To me it was like I had gone way far ahead, and I had to come back. I didn't want to."

The wind swayed Diane's hair, and she pushed it back from her face. "Did you see things that were going to happen?" she asked.

"Sometimes."

"Really? Did you?"

"Sometimes."

"Tell me about it. When you saw what was going to happen."

"I saw myself dead. I was all black and shrunk up like the dead stuff they cut off in the Pontic gardens, and I was floating and turning, like in water but it wasn't water—just floating and turning out in space, in nothing. And there were lights on both sides of me, so both sides were bright but black, and I could see my teeth because the stuff"—he pulled at his cheeks—"had fallen off there, and they were really white."

"That hasn't happened yet."

"Not here."

"Tell me something you saw that happened."

"You mean, like somebody's sister was going to get married, don't you? That's what the girls where I was mostly wanted to know. Or were they going to go home; mostly it wasn't like that."

"But sometimes it was?"

"I guess."

"Tell me one."

Nicholas shook his head. "You wouldn't like it, and anyway it wasn't like that. Mostly it was lights like I never saw anyplace else, and voices like I never heard any other time, telling me things there aren't any words for, stuff like that, only now I can't ever go back. Listen, I wanted to ask you about Ignacio."

"He isn't anybody," the girl said.

"What do you mean, he isn't anybody? Is there anybody here besides you and me and Ignacio and Dr. Island?"

"Not that we can see or touch."

The monkey called, "There are other patients, but for the present, Nicholas, for your own well-being as well as theirs, it is best for you to remain by yourselves." It was a long sentence for a monkey.

"What's that about?"

"If I tell you, will you tell me about something you saw that really happened?"

"All right."

"Tell me first."

"There was this girl where I was—her name was Maya. They had, you know, boys' and girls' dorms, but you saw everybody in the rec room and the dining hall and so on, and she was in my psychodrama group." Her hair had been black, and shiny as the lacquered furniture in Dr. Hong's rooms, her skin white like the mother-of-pearl, her eyes long and narrow (making him think of cats' eyes) and darkly blue. She was fifteen, or so Nicholas believed—maybe sixteen. "*I'm going home,*" she told him. It was psychodrama and he was her brother, younger than she, and she was already at home, but when she said this the floating ring of light that gave them the necessary separation from the small doctor-and-patient audience, ceased, by instant agreement, to be Maya's mother's living room and became a visiting lounge. Nicholas/Jerry said, "Hey, that's great! Hey, I got a new bike—when you come home you want to ride it?"

Maureen/Maya's mother said, "Maya, don't. You'll run into something and break your teeth, and you know how much they cost."

"You don't want me to have any fun."

"We do, dear, but *nice* fun. A girl has to be so much more careful—oh, Maya, I wish I could make you understand, really, how careful a girl has to be."

Nobody said anything, so Nicholas/Jerry filled in with, "It has a three-bladed prop, and I'm going to tape streamers to them with little weights at the ends, an' when I go down old thirty-seven B passageway, look out, here comes that old coleslaw grater!"

"Like this," Maya said, and held her legs together and extended her arms, to make a three-bladed bike prop or a crucifix. She had thrown herself into a spin as she made the movement, and revolved slowly, stage center—red shorts, white blouse, red shorts, white blouse, red shorts, no shoes.

Diane asked, "And you saw that she was never going home, she was going to hospital instead, she was going to cut her wrist there, she was going to die?"

Nicholas nodded.

"Did you tell her?"

"Yes," Nicholas said. "No."

"Make up your mind. Didn't you tell her? Now, don't get mad."

"Is it telling, when the one you tell doesn't understand?"

Diane thought about that for a few steps while Nicholas dashed water on the hot bruises Ignacio had left upon his face. "If it was plain and clear and she ought to have understood—that's the trouble I have with my family."

"What is?"

"They won't say things—do you know what I mean? I just say, 'Look, just tell me, just tell me what I'm supposed to do, tell me what it is you want,' but it's different all the time. My mother says, 'Diane, you ought to meet some boys; you can't go out with him; your father and I have never met him; we don't even know his family at all; Douglas, there's something I think you ought to know about Diane; she gets confused sometimes; we've had her to doctors; she's been in a hospital; try—' "

"Not to get her excited," Nicholas finished for her.

"Were you listening? I mean, are you from the Trojan Planets? Do you know my mother?"

"I only live in these places," Nicholas said. "That's for a long time. But you talk like other people."

"I feel better now that I'm with you; you're really nice. I wish you were older."

"I'm not sure I'm going to get much older."

"It's going to rain—feel it?"

Nicholas shook his head.

"Look." Diane jumped, bunny-rabbit clumsy, three meters into the air. "See how high I can jump? That means people are sad and it's going to rain. I told you."

"No, you didn't."

"Yes, I did, Nicholas."

He waved the argument away, struck by a sudden thought. "You ever been to Callisto?"

The girl shook her head, and Nicholas said, "I have; that's where they did the operation. It's so big the gravity's mostly from natural mass, and it's all domed in, with a whole lot of air in it."

"So?"

"And when I was there it rained. There was a big trouble at one of the generating piles, and they shut it down and it got colder and colder until everybody in the hospital wore their blankets, just like Amerinds in books, and they locked the switches off on the heaters in the bathrooms, and the nurses and the comscreen told you all the time it wasn't dangerous, they were just rationing power to keep from blacking out the important stuff that was still running. And then it rained, just like on Earth. They said it got so cold the water condensed in the air, and it was like the whole hospital was right under a shower bath. Everybody on the top floor had to come down because it rained right on their beds, and for two nights I had a man in my room with me that had his arm cut off in a machine. But we couldn't jump any higher, and it got kind of dark."

"It doesn't always get dark here," Diane said. "Sometimes the rain sparkles. I think Dr. Island must do it to cheer everyone up."

"No," the waves explained, "or at least not in the way you mean, Diane."

Nicholas was hungry and started to ask them for something to eat, then turned his hunger in against itself, spit on the sand, and was still.

"It rains here when most of you are sad," the waves were saying, "because rain is a sad thing, to the human psyche. It is that, that sadness, perhaps because it recalls to unhappy people their own tears, that palliates melancholy."

Diane said, "Well, I know sometimes I feel better when it rains."

"That should help you to understand yourself. Most people are soothed when their environment is in harmony with their emotions, and anxious when it is not. An angry person becomes less angry in a red room, and unhappy people are only exasperated by sunshine and birdsong. Do you remember:

> And, missing thee, I walk unseen
> On the dry smooth-shaven green,
> To behold the wandering moon,
> Riding near her highest noon,
> Like one that had been led astray
> Through the heaven's wide pathless way?

The girl shook her head.

Nicholas said, "No. Did somebody write that?" and then, "You said you couldn't do anything."

The waves replied, "I can't—except talk to you."

"You make it rain."

"Your heart beats; I sense its pumping even as I speak—do you control the beating of your heart?"

"I can stop my breath."

"Can you stop your heart? Honestly, Nicholas?"

"I guess not."

"No more can I control the weather of my world, stop anyone from doing what he wishes, or feed you if you are hungry; with no need of volition on my part your emotions are monitored and averaged, and our weather responds. Calm and sunshine for tranquillity, rain for melancholy, storms for rage, and so on. This is what mankind has always wanted."

Diane asked, "What is?"

"That the environment should respond to human thought. That is the core of magic and the oldest dream of mankind, and here, on me, it is fact."

"So that we'll be well?"

Nicholas said angrily, "You're not sick!"

Dr. Island said, "So that some of you, at least, can return to society."

Nicholas threw a seashell into the water as though to strike the mouth that spoke. "Why are we talking to this thing?"

"Wait, tot; I think it's interesting."

"Lies and lies."

Dr. Island said, "How do I lie, Nicholas?"

"You said it was magic—"

"No, I said that when humankind has dreamed of magic, the wish behind that dream has been the omnipotence of thought. Have you never wanted to be a magician, Nicholas, making palaces spring up overnight, or riding an enchanted horse of ebony to battle with the demons of the air?"

"I am a magician. I have preternatural powers, and before they cut us in two—"

Diane interrupted him. "You said you averaged emotions. When you made it rain."

"Yes."

"Doesn't that mean that if one person was really, terribly sad, he'd move the average so much he could make it rain all by himself? Or whatever? That doesn't seem fair."

The waves might have smiled. "That has never happened. But if it did, Diane, if one person felt such deep emotion, think how great her need would be. Don't you think we should answer it?"

Diane looked at Nicholas, but he was walking again, his head swinging, ignoring her as well as the voice of the waves. "Wait," she called. "You said I wasn't sick; I am, you know."

"No, you're not."

She hurried after him. "Everyone says so, and sometimes I'm so confused, and other times I'm boiling inside, just boiling. Mum says if you've got something on the stove you don't want to have burn, you just have to keep one finger on the handle of the pan and it won't, but I can't, I can't always find the handle or remember."

Without looking back the boy said, "Your mother is probably sick, maybe your father too; I don't know. But you're not. If they'd just let you alone you'd be all right. Why shouldn't you get upset, having to live with two crazy people?"

"Nicholas!" She grabbed his thin shoulders. "That's not true!"

"Yes, it is."

"I am sick. Everyone says so."

"I don't; so 'everyone' just means the ones that do—isn't that right? And if you don't either, that will be two; it can't be everyone then."

The girl called, "Doctor? Dr. Island?"

Nicholas said, "You aren't going to believe that, are you?"

"Dr. Island, is it true?"

"Is what true, Diane?"

"What he said. Am I sick?"

"Sickness—even physical illness—is relative, Diane, and complete health is an idealization, an abstraction, even if the other end of the scale is not."

"You know what I mean."

"You are not physically ill." A long, blue comber curled into a line of hissing spray reaching infinitely along the sea to their left and right. "As you said yourself a moment ago, you are sometimes confused, and sometimes disturbed."

"He said if it weren't for other people, if it weren't for my mother and father, I wouldn't have to be here."

"Diane . . ."

"Well, is that true or isn't it?"

"Most emotional illness would not exist, Diane, if it were possible in every case to separate oneself—in thought as well as circumstance—if only for a time."

"Separate oneself?"

"Did you ever think of going away, at least for a time?"

The girl nodded, then as though she were not certain Dr. Island could see her said, "Often, I suppose, leaving the school and getting my own compartment somewhere—going to Achilles. Sometimes I wanted to so badly."

"Why didn't you?"

"They would have worried. And anyway, they would have found me, and made me come home."

"Would it have done any good if I—or a human doctor—had told them not to?"

When the girl said nothing Nicholas snapped, "You could have locked them up."

"They were functioning, Nicholas. They bought and sold; they worked, and paid their taxes—"

Diane said softly, "It wouldn't have done any good anyway, Nicholas; they are inside me."

"Diane was no longer functioning: she was failing every subject at the university she attended, and her presence in her classes, when she came, disturbed the instructors and the other students. You were not functioning either, and people of your own age were afraid of you."

"That's what counts with you, then. Functioning."

"If I were different from the world, would that help you when you got back into the world?"

"You are different." Nicholas kicked the sand. "Nobody ever saw a place like this."

"You mean that reality to you is metal corridors, rooms without windows, noise."

"Yes."

"That is the unreality, Nicholas. Most people have never had to endure such things. Even now, this—my beach, my sea, my trees—is more in harmony with most human lives than your metal corridors; and here, I am your social environment—what individuals call they. You see, sometimes if we take people who are troubled back to something like me, to an idealized natural setting, it helps them."

"Come on," Nicholas told the girl. He took her arm, acutely conscious of being so much shorter than she.

"A question," murmured the waves. "If Diane's parents had been taken here instead of Diane, do you think it would have helped them?"

Nicholas did not reply.

"We have treatments for disturbed persons, Nicholas. But, at least for the time being, we have no treatment for disturbing persons." Diane and the boy had turned away, and the waves' hissing and slapping ceased to be speech. Gulls wheeled overhead, and once a red and yellow parrot fluttered from one palm to another. A monkey running on all fours like a little dog approached them, and Nicholas chased it, but it escaped.

"I'm going to take one of those things apart someday," he said, "and pull the wires out."

"Are we going to walk all the way round?" Diane asked. She might have been talking to herself.

"Can you do that?"

"Oh, you can't walk all around Dr. Island; it would be too long, and you can't get there anyway. But we could walk until we get back to where we started— we're probably more than halfway now."

"Are there other islands you can't see from here?"

The girl shook her head. "I don't think so; there's just this one big island on this satellite, and all the rest is water."

"Then if there's only the one island, we're going to have to walk all around it to get back to where we started. What are you laughing at?"

"Look down the beach, as far as you can. Never mind how it slips off to the side—pretend it's straight."

"I don't see anything."

"Don't you? Watch." Diane leaped into the air, six meters or more this time, and waved her arms.

"It looks like there's somebody ahead of us, way down the beach."

"Uh-huh. Now look behind."

"Okay, there's somebody there too. Come to think of it, I saw someone on the beach when I first got here. It seemed funny to see so far, but I guess I thought they were other patients. Now I see two people."

"They're us. That was probably yourself you saw the other time too. There are just so many of us to each strip of beach, and Dr. Island only wants certain ones to mix. So the space bends around. When we get to one end of our strip and try to step over, we'll be at the other end."

"How did you find out?"

"Dr. Island told me about it when I first came here." The girl was silent for a moment, and her smile vanished. "Listen, Nicholas, do you want to see something really funny?"

Nicholas asked, "What?" As he spoke, a drop of rain struck his face.

"You'll see. Come on, though. We have to go into the middle instead of following the beach, and it will give us a chance to get under the trees and out of the rain."

When they had left the sand and the sound of the surf and were walking on solid ground under green-leaved trees, Nicholas said, "Maybe we can find some fruit." They were so light now that he had to be careful not to bound into the air with each step. The rain fell slowly around them, in crystal spheres.

"Maybe," the girl said doubtfully. "Wait; let's stop here." She sat down where a huge tree sent twenty-meter wooden arches over dark, mossy ground. "Want to climb up there and see if you can find us something?"

"All right," Nicholas agreed. He jumped, and easily caught hold of a branch far above the girl's head. In a moment he was climbing in a green world, with the rain pattering all around him; he followed narrowing limbs into leafy wilderness where the cool water ran from every twig he touched, and twice found the empty nests of birds, and once a slender snake, green as any leaf with a head as long as his thumb, but there was no fruit. "Nothing," he said, when he dropped down beside the girl once more.

"That's all right; we'll find something."

He said, "I hope so," and noticed that she was looking at him oddly, then realized that his left hand had lifted itself to touch her right breast. His hand dropped as he looked, and he felt his face grow hot. He said, "I'm sorry."

"That's all right."

"We like you. He—over there—he can't talk, you see. I guess I can't talk either."

"I think it's just you—in two pieces. I don't care."

"Thanks." He had picked up a leaf, dead and damp, and was tearing it to shreds, first his right hand tearing while the left held the leaf, then turnabout. "Where does the rain come from?" The dirty flakes clung to the fingers of both.

"Hmm?"

"Where does the rain come from? I mean, it isn't because it's colder here now, like on Callisto; it's because the gravity's turned down some way, isn't it?"

"From the sea. Don't you know how this place is built?"

Nicholas shook his head.

"Didn't they show it to you from the ship when you came? It's beautiful. They showed it to me—I just sat there and looked at it, and I wouldn't talk to them, and the nurse thought I wasn't paying any attention, but I heard everything. I just didn't want to talk to her. It wasn't any use."

"I know how you felt."

"But they didn't show it to you?"

"No, on my ship they kept me locked up because I burned some stuff. They thought I couldn't start a fire without an igniter, but if you have electricity in the wall sockets it's easy. They had a thing on me—you know?" He clasped his arms to his body to show how he had been restrained. "I bit one of them too—I guess I didn't tell you that yet: I bite people. They locked me up, and for a long time I had nothing to do, and then I could feel us dock with something, and they came and got me and pulled me down a regular companionway for a long time, and it just seemed like a regular place. Then they stuck me full of Tranquil-C—I guess they didn't know it doesn't hardly work on me at all—with a pneumogun, and lifted a kind of door thing and shoved me up."

"Didn't they make you undress?"

"I already was. When they put the ties on me I did things in my clothes and they had to take them off me. It made them mad." He grinned unevenly. "Does Tranquil-C work on you? Or any of that other stuff?"

"I suppose they would, but then I never do the sort of thing you do anyway."

"Maybe you ought to."

"Sometimes they used to give me medication that was supposed to cheer me up; then I couldn't sleep, and I walked and walked, you know, and ran into things and made a lot of trouble for everyone; but what good does it do?"

Nicholas shrugged. "Not doing it doesn't do any good either—I mean, we're both here. My way, I know I've made them jump; they shoot that stuff in me and I'm not mad anymore, but I know what it is and I just think what I would do if I *were* mad, and I do it, and when it wears off I'm glad I did."

"I think you're still angry somewhere, deep down."

Nicholas was already thinking of something else. "This island says Ignacio kills people." He paused. "What does it look like?"

"Ignacio?"

"No, I've seen him. Dr. Island."

"Oh, you mean when I was in the ship. The satellite's round of course, and all clear except where Dr. Island is, so that's a dark spot. The rest of it's temperglass, and from space you can't even see the water."

"That *is* the sea up there, isn't it?" Nicholas asked, trying to look up at it through the tree leaves and the rain. "I thought it was when I first came."

"Sure. It's like a glass ball, and we're inside, and the water's inside too, and just goes all around up the curve."

"That's why I could see so far out on the beach, isn't it? Instead of dropping down from you like on Callisto it bends up so you can see it."

The girl nodded. "And the water lets the light through, but filters out the ultraviolet. Besides, it gives us thermal mass, so we don't heat up too much when we're between the sun and the Bright Spot."

"Is that what keeps us warm? The Bright Spot?"

Diane nodded again. "We go around in ten hours, you see, and that holds us over it all the time."

"Why can't I see it, then? It ought to look like Sol does from the Belt, only bigger; but there's just a shimmer in the sky, even when it's not raining."

"The waves diffract the light and break up the image. You'd see the Focus, though, if the air weren't so clear. Do you know what the Focus is?"

Nicholas shook his head.

"We'll get to it pretty soon, after this rain stops. Then I'll tell you."

"I still don't understand about the rain."

Unexpectedly Diane giggled. "I just thought—do you know what I was supposed to be? While I was going to school?"

"Quiet," Nicholas said.

"No, silly. I mean what I was being trained to do, if I graduated and all that. I was going to be a teacher, with all those cameras on me and tots from everywhere watching and popping questions on the two-way. Jolly time. Now I'm doing it here, only there's no one but you."

"You mind?"

"No, I suppose I enjoy it." There was a black-and-blue mark on Diane's thigh, and she rubbed it pensively with one hand as she spoke. "Anyway, there are three ways to make gravity. Do you know them? Answer, clerk."

"Sure; acceleration, mass, and synthesis."

"That's right; motion and mass are both bendings of space, of course, which is why Zeno's paradox doesn't work out that way, and why masses move toward each other—what we call falling—or at least try to; and if they're held apart it produces the tension we perceive as a force and call weight and all that rot. So naturally if you bend the space direct, you synthesize a gravity effect, and that's what holds all that water up against the translucent shell—there's nothing like enough mass to do it by itself."

"You mean"—Nicholas held out his hand to catch a slow-moving globe of rain—"that this is water from the sea?"

"Righto, up on top. Do you see, the temperature differences in the air make the winds, and the winds make the waves and surf you saw when we were walking along the shore. When the waves break they throw up these little drops, and if you watch you'll see that even when it's clear they go up a long way sometimes. Then if the gravity is less they can get away altogether, and if we were on the outside they'd fly off into space, but we aren't, we're inside, so all they can do is go across the center, more or less, until they hit the water again, or Dr. Island."

"Dr. Island said they had storms sometimes, when people got mad."

"Yes. Lots of wind, and so there's lots of rain too. Only the rain then is because the wind tears the tops off the waves, and you don't get light like you do in a normal rain."

"What makes so much wind?"

"I don't know. It happens somehow."

They sat in silence, Nicholas listening to the dripping of the leaves. He remembered then that they had spun the hospital module, finally, to get the little spheres of clotting blood out of the air; Maya's blood was building up on the grilles of the purification intake ducts, spotting them black, and someone had been afraid they would decay there and smell. Nicholas had not been there when they did it, but he could imagine the droplets settling, like this, in the slow spin. The old psychodrama group had already been broken up, and when he saw Maureen or any of the others in the rec room they talked about Good Old Days. It had not seemed like Good Old Days then except that Maya had been there.

Diane said, "It's going to stop."

"It looks just as bad to me."

"No, it's going to stop—see, they're falling a little faster now, and I feel heavier."

Nicholas stood up. "You rested enough yet? You want to go on?"

"We'll get wet."

He shrugged.

"I don't want to get my hair wet, Nicholas. It'll be over in a minute."

He sat down again. "How long have you been here?"

"I'm not sure."

"Don't you count the days?"

"I lose track a lot."

"Longer than a week?"

"Nicholas, don't ask me, all right?"

"Isn't there anybody on this piece of Dr. Island except you and me and Ignacio?"

"I don't think there was anyone but Ignacio before you came."

"Who is he?"

She looked at him.

"Well, who is he? You know me—us—Nicholas Kenneth de Vore; and you're Diane who?"

"Phillips."

"And you're from the Trojan Planets, and I was from the Outer Belt, I guess, to start with. What about Ignacio? You talk to him sometimes, don't you? Who is he?"

"I don't know. He's important."

For an instant, Nicholas froze. "What does that mean?"

"Important." The girl was feeling her knees, running her hands back and forth across them.

"Maybe everybody's important."

"I know you're just a tot, Nicholas, but don't be so stupid. Come on, you wanted to go; let's go now. It's pretty well stopped." She stood, stretching her thin body, her arms over her head. "My knees are rough—you made me think of that. When I came here they were still so smooth, I think. I used to put a certain lotion on them. Because my dad would feel them, and my hands and elbows too, and he'd say if they weren't smooth nobody'd ever want me; Mum wouldn't say anything, but she'd be cross after, and they used to come and visit, and so I kept a bottle in my room and I used to put it on. Once I drank some."

Nicholas was silent.

"Aren't you going to ask me if I died?" She stepped ahead of him, pulling aside the dripping branches. "See here, I'm sorry I said you were stupid."

"I'm just thinking," Nicholas said. "I'm not mad at you. Do you really know anything about him?"

"No, but look at it." She gestured. "Look around you; someone *built* all this."

"You mean it cost a lot."

"It's automated, of course, but still . . . well, the other places where you were before—how much space was there for each patient? Take the total volume and divide it by the number of people there."

"Okay, this is a whole lot bigger, but maybe they think we're worth it."

"Nicholas . . ." She paused. "Nicholas, Ignacio is homicidal. Didn't Dr. Island tell you?"

"Yes."

"And you're fourteen and not very big for it, and I'm a girl. Who are they worried about?"

The look on Nicholas's face startled her.

After an hour or more of walking they came to it. It was a band of withered vegetation, brown and black and tumbling, and as straight as if it had been drawn with a ruler. "I was afraid it wasn't going to be here," Diane said. "It moves around whenever there's a storm. It might not have been in our sector anymore at all."

Nicholas asked, "What is it?"

"The Focus. It's been all over, but mostly the plants grow back quickly when it's gone."

"It smells funny—like the kitchen in a place where they wanted me to work in the kitchen once."

"Vegetables rotting, that's what that is. What did you do?"

"Nothing—put detergent in the stuff they were cooking. What makes this?"

"The Bright Spot. See, when it's just about overhead the curve of the sky and the water up there make a lens. It isn't a very good lens—a lot of the light scatters. But enough is focused to do this. It wouldn't fry us if it came past right now, if that's what you're wondering, because it's not that hot. I've stood right in it, but you want to get out in a minute."

"I thought it was going to be about seeing ourselves down the beach."

Diane seated herself on the trunk of a fallen tree. "It was, really. The last time I was here it was further from the water, and I suppose it had been there a long time, because it had cleared out a lot of the dead stuff. The sides of the sector are nearer here, you see; the whole sector narrows down like a piece of pie. So you could look down the Focus either way and see yourself nearer than you could on the beach. It was almost as if you were in a big, big room, with a looking glass on each wall, or as if you could stand behind yourself. I thought you might like it."

"I'm going to try it here," Nicholas announced, and he clambered up one of the dead trees while the girl waited below, but the dry limbs creaked and snapped beneath his feet, and he could not get high enough to see himself in either direction. When he dropped to the ground beside her again, he said, "There's nothing to eat here either, is there?"

"I haven't found anything."

"They—I mean, Dr. Island wouldn't just let us starve, would he?"

"I don't think he could do anything; that's the way this place is built. Sometimes you find things, and I've tried to catch fish, but I never could. A couple of times Ignacio gave me part of what he had, though; he's good at it. I bet you think I'm skinny, don't you? But I was a lot fatter when I came here."

"What are we going to do now?"

"Keep walking, I suppose, Nicholas. Maybe go back to the water."

"Do you think we'll find anything?"

From a decaying log, insect stridulations called, "Wait."

Nicholas asked, "Do *you* know where anything is?"

"Something for you to eat? Not at present. But I can show you something much more interesting, not far from here, than this clutter of dying trees. Would you like to see it?"

Diane said, "Don't go, Nicholas."

"What is it?"

"Diane, who calls this 'the Focus,' calls what I wish to show you 'the Point.' "

Nicholas asked Diane, "Why shouldn't I go?"

"I'm not going. I went there once anyway."

"I took her," Dr. Island said. "And I'll take you. I wouldn't take you if I didn't think it might help you."

"I don't think Diane liked it."

"Diane may not wish to be helped—help may be painful, and often people do not. But it is my business to help them if I can, whether or not they wish it."

"Suppose I don't want to go?"

"Then I cannot compel you; you know that. But you will be the only patient in this sector who has not seen it, Nicholas, as well as the youngest; both Diane and Ignacio have, and Ignacio goes there often."

"Is it dangerous?"

"No. Are you afraid?"

Nicholas looked questioningly at Diane. "What is it? What will I see?"

She had walked away while he was talking to Dr. Island, and was now sitting cross-legged on the ground about five meters from where Nicholas stood, staring at her hands. Nicholas repeated, "What will I see, Diane?" He did not think she would answer.

She said, "A glass. A mirror."

"Just a mirror?"

"You know how I told you to climb the tree here? The Point is where the edges come together. You can see yourself—like on the beach—but closer."

Nicholas was disappointed. "I've seen myself in mirrors lots of times."

Dr. Island, whose voice was now in the sighing of the dead leaves, whispered, "Did you have a mirror in your room, Nicholas, before you came here?"

"A steel one."

"So that you could not break it?"

"I guess so. I threw things at it sometimes, but it just got puckers in it." Remembering dimpled reflections, Nicholas laughed.

"You can't break this one either."

"It doesn't sound like it's worth going to see."

"I think it is."

"Diane, do you still think I shouldn't go?"

There was no reply. The girl sat staring at the ground in front of her. Nicholas walked over to look at her and found a tear had washed a damp trail down each thin cheek, but she did not move when he touched her. "She's catatonic, isn't she," he said.

A green limb just outside the Focus nodded. "Catatonic schizophrenia."

"I had a doctor once that said those names—like that. They didn't mean anything." (The doctor had been a therapy robot, but a human doctor gave more status. Robots' patients sat in doorless booths—two and a half hours a day for Nicholas: an hour and a half in the morning, an hour in the afternoon—and talked to something that appeared to be a small, friendly food freezer. Some people sat every day in silence, while others talked continually, and for such patients as these the attendants seldom troubled to turn the machines on.)

"He meant cause and treatment. He was correct."

Nicholas stood looking down at the girl's streaked, brown-blond head. "What *is* the cause? I mean for her."

"I don't know."

"And what's the treatment?"

"You are seeing it."

"Will it help her?"

"Probably not."

"Listen, she can hear you, don't you know that? She hears everything we say."

"If my answer disturbs you, Nicholas, I can change it. It will help her if she wants to be helped; if she insists on clasping her illness to her it will not."

"We ought to go away from here," Nicholas said uneasily.

"To your left you will see a little path, a very faint one. Between the twisted tree and the bush with the yellow flowers."

Nicholas nodded and began to walk, looking back at Diane several times. The flowers were butterflies, who fled in a cloud of color when he approached them, and he wondered if Dr. Island had known. When Nicholas had gone a hundred paces and was well away from the brown and rotting vegetation, he said, "She was sitting in the Focus."

"Yes."

"Is she still there?"

"Yes."

"What will happen when the Bright Spot comes?"

"Diane will become uncomfortable and move, if she is still there."

"Once in one of the places I was in there was a man who was like that, and they said he wouldn't get anything to eat if he didn't get up and get it, they weren't going to feed him with the nose tube anymore, and they didn't, and he died. We told them about it and they wouldn't do anything and he starved to death right there, and when he was dead they rolled him off onto a stretcher and changed the bed and put somebody else there."

"I know, Nicholas. You told the doctors at St. John's about all that, and it is in your file, but think: Well men have starved themselves—yes, to death—to protest what they felt were political injustices. Is it so surprising that your friend killed himself in the same way to protest what he felt as a psychic injustice?"

"He wasn't my friend. Listen, did you really mean it when you said the treatment she was getting here would help Diane if she wanted to be helped?"

"No."

Nicholas halted in midstride. "You didn't mean it? You don't think it's true?"

"No. I doubt that anything will help her."

"I don't think you ought to lie to us."

"Why not? If by chance you become well you will be released, and if you are released you will have to deal with your society, which will lie to you frequently. Here, where there are so few individuals, I must take the place of society. I have explained that."

"Is that what you are?"

"Society's surrogate? Of course. Who do you imagine built me? What else could I be?"

"The doctor."

"You have had many doctors, and so has she. Not one of them has benefited you much."

"I'm not sure you even want to help us."

"Do you wish to see what Diane calls 'the Point'?"

"I guess so."

"Then you must walk. You will not see it standing here."

Nicholas walked, thrusting aside leafy branches and dangling creepers wet with rain. The jungle smelled of the life of green thing; there were ants on the tree trunks, and dragonflies with hot, red bodies and wings as long as his hands. "Do you want to help us?" he asked after a time.

"My feelings toward you are ambivalent. But when you wish to be helped, I wish to help you."

The ground sloped gently upward, and as it rose became somewhat more clear, the big trees a trifle farther apart, the underbrush spent in grass and fern. Occasionally there were stone outcrops to be climbed, and clearings open to the tumbling sky. Nicholas asked, "Who made this trail?"

"Ignacio. He comes here often."

"He's not afraid, then? Diane's afraid."

"Ignacio is afraid too, but he comes."

"Diane says Ignacio is important."

"Yes."

"What do you mean by that? Is he important? More important than we are?"

"Do you remember that I told you I was the surrogate of society? What do you think society wants, Nicholas?"

"Everybody to do what it says."

"You mean conformity. Yes, there must be conformity, but something else too—consciousness."

"I don't want to hear about it."

"Without consciousness, which you may call sensitivity if you are careful not to allow yourself to be confused by the term, there is no progress. A century ago, Nicholas, mankind was suffocating on Earth; now it is suffocating again. About half of the people who have contributed substantially to the advance of humanity have shown signs of emotional disturbance."

"I told you, I don't want to hear about it. I asked you an easy question—is Ignacio more important than Diane and me—and you won't tell me. I've heard all this you're saying. I've heard it fifty, maybe a hundred times from everybody, and it's lies; it's the regular thing, and you've got it written down on a card somewhere to read out when anybody asks. Those people you talk about that went crazy, they went crazy because while they were 'advancing humanity,' or whatever you call it, people kicked them out of their rooms because they couldn't pay, and while they were getting thrown out you were making other people rich that had never done anything in their whole lives except think about how to get that way."

"Sometimes it is hard, Nicholas, to determine before the fact—or even at the time—just who should be honored."

"How do you know if you've never tried?"

"You asked if Ignacio was more important than Diane or yourself. I can only say that Ignacio seems to me to hold a brighter promise of a full recovery coupled with a substantial contribution to human progress."

"If he's so good, why did he crack up?"

"Many do, Nicholas. Even among the inner planets space is not a kind environment for mankind; and our space, trans-Martian space, is worse. Any young person here, anyone like yourself or Diane who would seem to have a better-than-average chance of adapting to the conditions we face, is precious."

"Or Ignacio."

"Yes, or Ignacio. Ignacio has a tested IQ of two hundred and ten, Nicholas. Diane's is one hundred and twenty. Your own is ninety-five."

"They never took mine."

"It's on your records, Nicholas."

"They tried to and I threw down the helmet and it broke; Sister Carmela—she was the nurse—just wrote down something on the paper and sent me back."

"I see. I will ask for a complete investigation of this, Nicholas."

"Sure."

"Don't you believe me?"

"I don't think you believed me."

"Nicholas, Nicholas . . ." The long tongues of grass now beginning to appear beneath the immense trees sighed. "Can't you see that a certain measure of trust between the two of us is essential?"

"Did you believe me?"

"Why do you ask? Suppose I were to say I did; would you believe that?"

"When you told me I had been reclassified."

"You would have to be retested, for which there are no facilities here."

"If you believed me, why did you say 'retested'? I told you I haven't ever been tested at all—but anyway you could cross out the ninety-five."

"It is impossible for me to plan your therapy without some estimate of your intelligence, Nicholas, and I have nothing with which to replace it."

The ground was sloping up more sharply now, and in a clearing the boy halted and turned to look back at the leafy film, like algae over a pool, beneath which he had climbed, and at the sea beyond. To his right and left his view was still hemmed with foliage, and ahead of him a meadow on edge (like the square of sand through which he had come, though he did not think of that), dotted still with trees, stretched steeply toward an invisible summit. It seemed to him that under his feet the mountainside swayed ever so slightly. Abruptly he demanded of the wind, "Where's Ignacio?"

"Not here. Much closer to the beach."

"And Diane?"

"Where you left her. Do you enjoy the panorama?"

"It's pretty, but it feels like we're rocking."

"We are. I am moored to the temperglass exterior of our satellite by two hundred cables, but the tide and the currents nonetheless impart a slight motion to my body. Naturally this movement is magnified as you go higher."

"I thought you were fastened right on to the hull; if there's water under you, how do people get in and out?"

"I am linked to the main air lock by a communication tube. To you when you came, it probably seemed an ordinary companionway."

Nicholas nodded and turned his back on leaves and sea and began to climb again.

"You are in a beautiful spot, Nicholas; do you open your heart to beauty?" After waiting for an answer that did not come, the wind sang:

> The mountain wooded to the peak, the lawns
> And winding glades high up like ways to Heaven,
> The slender coco's drooping crown of plumes,
> The lightning flash of insect and of bird,
> The lustre of the long convolvuluses
> That coil'd around the stately stems, and ran
> Ev'n to the limit of the land, the glows
> And glories of the broad belt of the world,
> All these he saw.

"Does this mean nothing to you, Nicholas?"

"You read a lot, don't you?"

"Often, when it is dark, everyone else is asleep and there is very little else for me to do."

"You talk like a woman; are you a woman?"

"How could I be a woman?"

"You know what I mean. Except, when you were talking mostly to Diane, you sounded more like a man."

"You haven't yet said you think me beautiful."

"You're an Easter egg."

"What do you mean by that, Nicholas?"

"Never mind." He saw the egg as it had hung in the air before him, shining with gold and covered with flowers.

"Eggs are dyed with pretty colors for Easter, and my colors are beautiful—is that what you mean, Nicholas?"

His mother had brought the egg on visiting day, but she could never have made it. Nicholas knew who must have made it. The gold was that very pure gold used for shielding delicate instruments; the clear flakes of crystallized carbon that dotted the egg's surface with tiny stars could only have come from a laboratory high-pressure furnace. How angry he must have been when she told him she was going to give it to him.

"It's pretty, isn't it, Nicky?"

It hung in the weightlessness between them, turning very slowly with the memory of her scented gloves.

"The flowers are meadowsweet, fraxinella, lily of the valley, and moss rose— though I wouldn't expect you to recognize them, darling." His mother had never been below the orbit of Mars, but she pretended to have spent her girlhood on Earth; each reference to the lie filled Nicholas with inexpressible fury and shame. The egg was about twenty centimeters long and it revolved, end over end, in some small fraction more than eight of the pulse beats he felt in his cheeks. Visiting time had twenty-three minutes to go.

"Aren't you going to look at it?"

"I can see it from here." He tried to make her understand. "I can see every part of it. The little red things are aluminum oxide crystals, right?"

"I mean, look *inside*, Nicky."

He saw then that there was a lens at one end, disguised as a dewdrop in the throat of an asphodel. Gently he took the egg in his hands, closed one eye, and looked. The light of the interior was not, as he had half-expected, gold tinted, but brilliantly white, deriving from some concealed source. A world surely meant for Earth shone within, as though seen from below the orbit of the moon—indigo sea and emerald land. Rivers brown and clear as tea ran down long plains.

His mother said, "Isn't it pretty?"

Night hung at the corners in funereal purple, and sent long shadows like cold and lovely arms to caress the day; and while he watched and it fell, long-necked birds of so dark a pink that they were nearly red trailed stilt legs across the sky, their wings making crosses.

"They are called flamingos," Dr. Island said, following the direction of Nicholas's eyes. "Isn't it a pretty word? For a pretty bird, but I don't think we'd like them as much if we called them sparrows, would we?"

Nicholas's mother said, "I'm going to take it home and keep it for you. It's too nice to leave with a little boy, but if you ever come home again it will be waiting for you. On your dresser, beside your hairbrushes."

Nicholas said, "Words just mix you up."

"You shouldn't despise them, Nicholas. Besides having great beauty of their own, they are useful in reducing tension. You might benefit from that."

"You mean you talk yourself out of it."

"I mean that a person's ability to verbalize his feelings, if only to himself, may prevent them from destroying him. Evolution teaches us, Nicholas, that the original purpose of language was to ritualize men's threats and curses, his spells to compel the gods; communication came later. Words can be a safety valve."

Nicholas said, "I want to be a bomb; a bomb doesn't need a safety valve." To his mother, "Is that South America, Mama?"

"No, dear, India. The Malabar Coast on your left, the Coromandel coast on your right, and Ceylon below." Words.

"A bomb destroys itself, Nicholas."

"A bomb doesn't care."

He was climbing resolutely now, his toes grabbing at tree roots and the soft, mossy soil, his physician was no longer the wind but a small brown monkey that followed a stone's throw behind him. "I hear someone coming," Nicholas said.

"Yes."

"Is it Ignacio?"

"No, it is Nicholas. You are close now."

"Close to the Point?"

"Yes."

He stopped and looked around him. The sounds he had heard, the naked feet padding on soft ground, stopped as well. Nothing seemed strange; the land still rose, and there were large trees, widely spaced, with moss growing in their deepest shade, grass where there was more light. "The three big trees," Nicholas said, "they're just alike. Is that how you know where we are?"

"Yes."

In his mind he called the one before him Ceylon; the others were Coromandel and Malabar. He walked toward Ceylon, studying its massive, twisted limbs; a boy naked as himself walked out of the forest to his left, toward Malabar—this boy was not looking at Nicholas, who shouted and ran toward him.

The boy disappeared. Only Malabar, solid and real, stood before Nicholas; he ran to it, touched its rough bark with his hand, and then saw beyond it a fourth tree, similar too to the Ceylon tree, around which a boy peered with averted head. Nicholas watched him for a moment, then said, "I see."

"Do you?" the monkey chattered.

"It's like a mirror, only backward. The light from the front of me goes out and hits the edge, and comes in the other side, only I can't see it because I'm not looking that way. What I see is the light from my back, sort of, because it comes back this way. When I ran, did I get turned around?"

"Yes, you ran out the left side of the segment, and of course returned immediately from the right."

"I'm not scared. It's kind of fun." He picked up a stick and threw it as hard as he could toward the Malabar tree. The stick vanished, whizzed over his head, vanished again, slapped the back of his legs. "Did this scare Diane?"

There was no answer. He strode farther, palely naked boys walking to his left and right, but always looking away from him, gradually coming closer.

Don't go farther," Dr. Island said behind him. "It can be dangerous if you try to pass through the Point itself."

"I see it," Nicholas said. He saw three more trees, growing very close together, just ahead of him; their branches seemed strangely intertwined as they danced together in the wind, and beyond them there was nothing at all.

"You can't actually go through the Point," Dr. Island Monkey said. "The tree covers it."

"Then why did you warn me about it?" Limping and scarred, the boys to his right and left were no more than two meters away now; he had discovered that if he looked straight ahead he could sometimes glimpse their bruised profiles.

"That's far enough, Nicholas."

"I want to touch the tree."

He took another step, and another, then turned. The Malabar boy turned too, presenting his narrow back, on which the ribs and spine seemed welts. Nicholas reached out both arms and laid his hands on the thin shoulders and, as he did, felt other hands—the cool, unfeeling hands of a stranger, dry hands too small— touch his own shoulders and creep upward toward his neck.

"Nicholas!"

He jumped sidewise away from the tree and looked at his hands, his head swaying. "It wasn't me."

"Yes, it was, Nicholas," the monkey said.

"It was one of them."

"You are all of them."

In one quick motion Nicholas snatched up an arm-long section of fallen limb and hurled it at the monkey. It struck the little creature, knocking it down, but the monkey sprang up and fled on three legs. Nicholas sprinted after it.

He had nearly caught it when it darted to one side; as quickly, he turned toward the other, springing for the monkey he saw running toward him there. In an instant it was in his grip, feebly trying to bite. He slammed its head against the ground, then catching it by the ankles swung it against the Ceylon tree until at the third impact he heard the skull crack, and stopped.

He had expected wires, but there were none. Blood oozed from the battered little face, and the furry body was warm and limp in his hands. Leaves above his head said, "You haven't killed me, Nicholas. You never will."

"How does it work?" He was still searching for wires, tiny circuit cards holding micro-logic. He looked about for a sharp stone with which to open the monkey's body, but could find none.

"It is just a monkey," the leaves said. "If you had asked, I would have told you."

"How did you make him talk?" Nicholas dropped the monkey, stared at it for a moment, then kicked it. His fingers were bloody, and he wiped them on the leaves of the tree.

"Only my mind speaks to yours, Nicholas."

"Oh," he said. And then, "I've heard of that. I didn't think it would be like this. I thought it would be in my head."

"Your record shows no auditory hallucinations, but haven't you ever known someone who had them?"

"I knew a girl once. . . ." He paused.

"Yes?"

"She twisted noises—you know?"

"Yes."

"Like, it would just be a service cart out in the corridor, but she'd hear the fan, and think . . ."

"What?"

"Oh, different things. That it was somebody talking, calling her."

*"Hear them?"*

"What?" He sat up in his bunk. "Maya?"

*"They're coming after me."*

"Maya?"

Dr. Island, through the leaves, said, "When I talk to you, Nicholas, your mind makes any sound you hear the vehicle for my thoughts' content. You may hear me softly in the patter of rain, or joyfully in the singing of a bird—but if I wished I could amplify what I say until every idea and suggestion I wished to give would be driven like a nail into your consciousness. Then you would do whatever I wished you to."

"I don't believe it," Nicholas said. "If you can do that, why don't you tell Diane not to be catatonic?"

"First, because she might retreat more deeply into her disease in an effort to escape me; and second, because ending her catatonia in that way would not remove its cause."

"And thirdly?"

"I did not say 'thirdly,' Nicholas."

"I thought I heard it—when two leaves touched."

"Thirdly, Nicholas, because both you and she have been chosen for your effect on someone else; if I were to change her—or you—so abruptly, that effect would be lost." Dr. Island was a monkey again now, a new monkey that chattered from the protection of a tree twenty meters away. Nicholas threw a stick at him.

"The monkeys are only little animals, Nicholas; they like to follow people, and they chatter."

"I bet Ignacio kills them."

"No, he likes them; he only kills fish to eat."

Nicholas was suddenly aware of his hunger. He began to walk.

He found Ignacio on the beach, praying. For an hour or more, Nicholas hid behind the trunk of a palm watching him, but for a long time he could not decide to whom Ignacio prayed. He was kneeling just where the lacy edges of the breakers died, looking out toward the water, and from time to time he bowed, touching his forehead to the damp sand; then Nicholas could hear his voice, faintly, over the crashing and hissing of the waves. In general, Nicholas approved of prayer, having observed that those who prayed were usually more interesting companions than those who did not; but he had also noticed that though it made no difference what name the devotee gave the object of his devotions, it was important to discover how the god was conceived. Ignacio did not seem to be praying to Dr. Island—he would, Nicholas thought, have been facing the other way for that—and for a time Nicholas wondered if he was not praying to the waves. From Nicholas's position behind him he followed Ignacio's line of vision out and out, wave upon wave into the bright, confused sky, up and up until at last it curved completely around and came to rest on Ignacio's back again, and then it occurred to Nicholas that Ignacio might be praying to himself. Nicholas left the palm trunk then and walked about halfway to the place where Ignacio knelt, and sat down. Above the sounds of the sea and the murmuring of Ignacio's voice hung a silence so immense and fragile that it seemed that at any moment the entire crystal satellite might ring like a gong.

After a time Nicholas felt his left side trembling. With his right hand he began to stroke it, running his fingers down his left arm, and from his left shoulder to the thigh. It worried him that his left side should be so frightened, and he wondered if perhaps that other half of his brain, from which he was forever severed, could hear what Ignacio was saying to the waves. Nicholas began to pray himself, so that the other (and perhaps Ignacio too) could hear, saying not quite beneath his breath, "Don't worry, don't be afraid, he's not going to hurt us, he's nice, and if he does we'll get him; we're only going to get something to eat; maybe he'll show us how to catch fish, I think he'll be nice this time." But he knew, or at least felt he knew, that Ignacio would not be nice this time.

Eventually Ignacio stood up; he did not turn to face Nicholas, but waded out to sea; then, as though he had known Nicholas was behind him all the time (though Nicholas was not sure he had been heard—perhaps, so he thought, Dr. Island had told Ignacio), he gestured to indicate that Nicholas should follow him.

The water was colder than Nicholas remembered, the sand coarse and gritty between his toes. He thought of what Dr. Island had told him—about floating—and that a part of her must be this sand, under the water, reaching out (how far?) into the sea; when she ended there would be nothing but the clear temperglass of the satellite itself, far down.

"Come," Ignacio said. "Can you swim?" Just as though he had forgotten the night before. Nicholas said yes, he could, wondering if Ignacio would look around at him when he spoke. He did not.

"And do you know why you are here?"

"You told me to come."

"Ignacio means *here*. Does this not remind you of any place you have seen before, little one?"

Nicholas thought of the crystal gong and the Easter egg, then of the microthin globes of perfumed vapor that, at home, were sometimes sent floating down the corridors at Christmas to explode in clean dust and a cold smell of pine forests when the children stuck them with their hopping canes, but he said nothing.

Ignacio continued, "Let Ignacio tell you a story. Once there was a man, a boy, actually, on the Earth, who—"

Nicholas wondered why it was always men (most often doctors and clinical psychologists, in his experience) who wanted to tell you stories. Jesus, he recalled, was always telling everyone stories, and the Virgin Mary almost never, though a woman Nicholas had once known who thought she was the Virgin Mary had always been talking about her son. Nicholas thought Ignacio looked a little like Jesus. He tried to remember if his mother had ever told him stories when he was at home, and decided that she had not; she just turned on the comscreen to the cartoons.

"—wanted to—"

"—tell a story," Nicholas finished for him.

"How did you know?" Angry and surprised.

"It was you, wasn't it? And you want to tell one now."

"What you said was not what Ignacio would have said. He was going to tell you about a fish."

"Where is it?" Nicholas asked, thinking of the fish Ignacio had been eating the night before, and imagining another such fish, caught while he had been coming back, perhaps, from the Point, and now concealed somewhere awaiting the fire. "Is it a big one?"

"It is gone now," Ignacio said, "but it was only as long as a man's hand. I caught it in the big river."

*Huckleberry*— "I know, the Mississippi; it was a catfish. Or a sunfish." — *Finn.*

"Possibly that is what you call them; for a time he was as the sun to a certain one." The light from nowhere danced on the water. "In any event he was kept on that table in the salon in the house where life was lived. In a tank, but not the old kind in which one sees the glass, with metal at the corner. But the new kind in which the glass is so strong, but very thin, and curved so that it does not reflect, and there are no corners, and a clever device holds the water clear." He dipped up a handful of sparkling water, still not meeting Nicholas's eyes. "As clear even as this, and there were no ripples, and so you could not see it at all. My fish floated in the center of my table above a few stones."

Nicholas asked, "Did you float on the river on a raft?"

"No, we had a little boat. Ignacio caught this fish in a net, of which he almost bit through the strands before he could be landed; he possessed wonderful teeth. There was no one in the house but him and the other, and the robots, but each morning someone would go to the pool in the patio and catch a goldfish for him. Ignacio would see this goldfish there when he came down for his breakfast, and would think, *Brave goldfish, you have been cast to the monster; will you be the one to destroy him? Destroy him and you shall have his diamond house forever.* And then the fish, who had a little spot of red beneath his wonderful teeth, a spot like a cherry, would rush upon that young goldfish, and for an instant the water would be all clouded with blood."

"And then what?" Nicholas asked.

"And then the clever machine would make the water clear once more, and the fish would be floating above the stones as before, the fish with the wonderful teeth, and Ignacio would touch the little switch on the table, and ask for more bread, and more fruit."

"Are you hungry now?"

"No, I am tired and lazy now; if I pursue you I will not catch you, and if I catch you—through your own slowness and clumsiness—I will not kill you, and if I kill you I will not eat you."

Nicholas had begun to back away, and at the last words, realizing that they were a signal, he turned and began to run, splashing through the shallow water. Ignacio ran after him, much helped by his longer legs; his hair flying behind his dark young face, his square teeth—each white as a bone and as big as Nicholas's thumbnail—showing like spectators who lined the railings of his lips.

"Don't run, Nicholas," Dr. Island said with the voice of a wave. "It only makes him angry that you run." Nicholas did not answer, but cut to his left, up the beach and among the trunks of the palms, sprinting all the way because he had no way of knowing Ignacio was not right behind him, about to grab him by the neck. When he stopped it was in the thick jungle, among the boles of the hardwoods, where he leaned, out of breath, the thumping of his own heart the only sound in an atmosphere silent and unwaked as Earth's long, prehuman day. For a time he listened for any sound Ignacio might make searching for him; there was none. He drew a deep breath then and said, "Well, that's over," expecting Dr. Island to answer from somewhere; there was only the green hush.

The light was still bright and strong and nearly shadowless, but some interior sense told Nicholas the day was nearly over, and he noticed that such faint shades as he could see stretched long, horizontal distortions of their objects. He felt no hunger, but he had fasted before and knew on which side of hunger he stood; he was not as strong as he had been only a day past, and by this time next day he would probably be unable to outrun Ignacio. He should, he now realized, have eaten the monkey he had killed; but his stomach revolted at the thought of the raw flesh, and he did not know how he might build a fire, although Ignacio seemed to have done so the night before. Raw fish, even if he were able to catch a fish, would be as bad or worse than raw monkey; he remembered his effort to open a coconut—he had failed, but it was surely not impossible. His mind was hazy as to what a coconut might contain, but there had to be an edible core, because they were eaten in books. He decided to make a wide sweep through the jungle that would bring him back to the beach well away from Ignacio; he had several times seen coconuts lying in the sand under the trees.

He moved quietly, still a little afraid, trying to think of ways to open the coconut when he found it. He imagined himself standing before a large and raggedly faceted stone, holding the coconut in both hands. He raised it and smashed it down, but when it struck it was no longer a coconut but Maya's head; he heard her nose cartilage break with a distinct, rubbery snap. Her eyes, as blue as the sky above Madhya Pradesh, the sparkling blue sky of the egg, looked up at him, but he could no longer look into them, they retreated from his own, and it came to him quite suddenly that Lucifer, in falling, must have fallen up, into the fires and the coldness of space, never again to see the warm blues and browns and greens of Earth: *I was watching Satan fall as lightning from heaven.* Nicholas had heard that on tape somewhere, but he could not remember where. He had read that on

Earth lightning did not come down from the clouds but leaped up from the planetary surface toward them, never to return.

"Nicholas."

He listened, but did not hear his name again. Faintly water was babbling; had Dr. Island used that sound to speak to him? He walked toward it and found a little rill that threaded a way among the trees, and followed it. In a hundred steps it grew broader, slowed, and ended in a long blind pool under a dome of leaves. Diane was sitting on moss on the side opposite him; she looked up as she saw him, and smiled.

"Hello," he said.

"Hello, Nicholas. I thought I heard you. I wasn't mistaken after all, was I?"

"I didn't think I said anything." He tested the dark water with his foot and found that it was very cold.

"You gave a little gasp, I fancy. I heard it, and I said to myself, 'That's Nicholas,' and I called you. Then I thought I might be wrong, or that it might be Ignacio."

"Ignacio was chasing me. Maybe he still is, but I think he's probably given up by now."

The girl nodded, looking into the dark waters of the pool, but did not seem to have heard him. He began to work his way around to her, climbing across the snakelike roots of the crowding trees. "Why does Ignacio want to kill me, Diane?"

"Sometimes he wants to kill me too," the girl said.

"But why?"

"I think he's a bit frightened of us. Have you ever talked to him, Nicholas?"

"Today I did a little. He told me a story about a pet fish he used to have."

"Ignacio grew up all alone; did he tell you that? On Earth. On a plantation in Brazil, way up the Amazon—Dr. Island told me."

"I thought it was crowded on Earth."

"The cities are crowded, and the countryside closest to the cities. But there are places where it's emptier than it used to be. Where Ignacio was, there would have been Red Indian hunters two or three hundred years ago; when he was there, there wasn't anyone, just the machines. Now he doesn't want to be looked at, doesn't want anyone around him."

Nicholas said slowly, "Dr. Island said lots of people wouldn't be sick if only there weren't other people around all the time. Remember that?"

"Only there are other people around all the time; that's how the world is."

"Not in Brazil, maybe," Nicholas said. He was trying to remember something about Brazil, but the only thing he could think of was a parrot singing in a straw hat from the comview cartoons, and then a turtle and a hedgehog that turned into armadillos for the love of God, Montresor. Nicholas said, "Why didn't he stay here?"

"Did I tell you about the bird, Nicholas?" She had been not listening again.

"What bird?"

"I have a bird. Inside." She patted the flat stomach below her small breasts, and for a moment Nicholas thought she had really found food. "She sits in here. She has tangled a nest in my entrails, where she sits and tears at my breath with her beak. I look healthy to you, don't I? But inside I'm hollow and rotten and turning brown, dirt and old feathers, oozing away. Her beak will break through soon."

"Okay." Nicholas turned to go.

"I've been drinking water here, trying to drown her. I think I've swallowed so much I couldn't stand up now if I tried, but she isn't even wet, and do you know something, Nicholas? I've found out I'm not really me, I'm her."

Turning back, Nicholas asked, "When was the last time you had anything to eat?"

"I don't know. Two, three days ago. Ignacio gave me something."

"I'm going to try to open a coconut. If I can I'll bring you back some."

When he reached the beach, Nicholas turned and walked slowly back in the direction of the dead fire, this time along the rim of dampened sand between the sea and the palms. He was thinking about machines.

There were hundreds of thousands, perhaps millions, of machines out beyond the belt, but few or none of the sophisticated servant robots of Earth—those were luxuries. Would Ignacio, in Brazil (whatever that was like), have had such luxuries? Nicholas thought not; those robots were almost like people, and living with them would be like living with people. Nicholas wished that he could speak Brazilian.

There had been the therapy robots at St. John's; Nicholas had not liked them, and he did not think Ignacio would have liked them either. If Nicholas had liked his therapy robot he probably would not have had to be sent here. He thought of the chipped and rusted old machine that had cleaned the corridors—Maya had called it Corradora, but no one else ever called it anything but "*Hey!*" It could not (or at least did not) speak, and Nicholas doubted that it had emotions, except possibly a sort of love of cleanliness that did not extend to its own person. "You will understand," someone was saying inside his head, "that motives of all sorts can be divided into two sorts." A doctor? A therapy robot? It did not matter. "Extrinsic and intrinsic. An extrinsic motive has always some further end in view, and that end we call an intrinsic motive. Thus when we have reduced motivation to intrinsic motivation we have reduced it to its simplest parts. Take that machine over there."

What machine?

"Freud would have said that it was fixated at the latter anal stage, perhaps due to the care its builders exercised in seeing that the dirt it collects is not released again. Because of its fixation it is, as you see, obsessed with cleanliness and order;

compulsive sweeping and scrubbing palliate its anxieties. It is a strength of Freud's theory, and not a weakness, that it serves to explain many of the activities of machines as well as the acts of persons."

Hello there, Corradora.

And hello, Ignacio.

*My head, moving from side to side, must remind you of a radar scanner. My steps are measured, slow, and precise. I emit a scarcely audible humming as I walk, and my eyes are fixed, as I swing my head, not on you, Ignacio, but on the waves at the edge of sight, where they curve up into the sky. I stop ten meters short of you, and I stand.*

*You go, I follow, ten meters behind. What do I want? Nothing.*

*Yes, I will pick up the sticks, and I will follow—five meters behind.*

"Break them, and put them on the fire. Not all of them, just a few."

*Yes.*

"Ignacio keeps the fire here burning all the time. Sometimes he takes the coals of fire from it to start others, but here, under the big palm log, he has a fire always. The rain does not strike it here. Always the fire. Do you know how he made it the first time? Reply to him!"

"No."

"No, *Patrão!*"

" 'No, *Patrão.*' "

"Ignacio stole it from the gods, from Poseidon. Now Poseidon is dead, lying at the bottom of the water. Which is the top. Would you like to see him?"

"If you wish it, *Patrão.*"

"It will soon be dark, and that is the time to fish; do you have a spear?"

"No, *Patrão.*"

"Then Ignacio will get you one."

Ignacio took a handful of the sticks and thrust the ends into the fire, blowing on them. After a moment Nicholas leaned over and blew too, until all the sticks were blazing.

"Now we must find you some bamboo, and there is some back here. Follow me."

The light, still nearly shadowless, was dimming now, so that it seemed to Nicholas that they walked on insubstantial soil, though he could feel it beneath his feet. Ignacio stalked ahead, holding up the burning sticks until the fire seemed about to die, then pointing the ends down, allowing it to lick upward toward his hand and come to life again. There was a gentle wind blowing out toward the sea, carrying away the sound of the surf and bringing a damp coolness; and when they had been walking for several minutes, Nicholas heard in it a faint, dry, almost rhythmic rattle.

Ignacio looked back at him and said, "The music. The big stems talking, hear it?"

They found a cane a little thinner than Nicholas's wrist and piled the burning sticks around its base, then added more. When it fell, Ignacio burned through the upper end too, making a pole about as long as Nicholas was tall, and with the edge of a seashell scraped the larger end to a point. "Now you are a fisherman," he said. Nicholas said, "Yes, *Patrão*," still careful not to meet his eyes.

"You are hungry?"

"Yes, *Patrão*."

"Then let me tell you something. Whatever you get is Ignacio's, you understand? And what he catches, that is his too. But when he has eaten what he wants, what is left is yours. Come on now, and Ignacio will teach you to fish or drown you."

Ignacio's own spear was buried in the sand not far from the fire; it was much bigger than the one he had made for Nicholas. With it held across his chest he went down to the water, wading until it was waist high, then swimming, not looking to see if Nicholas was following. Nicholas found that he could swim with the spear by putting all his effort into the motion of his legs, holding the spear in his left hand and stroking only occasionally with his right. "You breathe," he said softly, "and watch the spear," and after that he had only to allow his head to lift from time to time.

He had thought Ignacio would begin to look for fish as soon as they were well out from the beach, but the Brazilian continued to swim, slowly but steadily, until it seemed to Nicholas that they must be a kilometer or more from land. Suddenly, as though the lights in a room had responded to a switch, the dark sea around them became an opalescent blue. Ignacio stopped, treading water and using his spear to buoy himself.

"Here," he said. "Get them between yourself and the light."

Open-eyed, he bent his face to the water, raised it again to breathe deeply, and dived. Nicholas followed his example, floating belly down with open eyes.

All the world of dancing glitter and dark island vanished as though Nicholas had plunged his face into a dream. Far, far below him Jupiter displayed its broad, striped disk, marred with the spreading Bright Spot where man-made silicone enzymes had stripped the hydrogen from methane for kindled fusion: a cancer and a burning infant sun. Between that sun and his eyes lay invisible a hundred thousand kilometers of space, and the temperglass shell of the satellite; hundreds of meters of illuminated water, and in it the spread body of Ignacio, dark against the light, still kicking downward, his spear a pencil line of blackness in his hand.

Involuntarily Nicholas's head came up, returning to the universe of sparkling waves, aware now that what he had called night was only the shadow cast by Dr. Island when Jupiter and the Bright Spot slid beneath her. That shadow line, indetectable in air, now lay sharp across the water behind him. Nicholas took breath and plunged.

Almost at once a fish darted somewhere below, and his left arm thrust the spear forward, but it was far out of reach. He swam after it, then saw another, larger, fish farther down and dived for that, passing Ignacio surfacing for air. The fish was too deep, and Nicholas had used up his oxygen; his lungs aching for air, he swam up, wanting to let go of his spear, then realizing at the last moment that he could, that it would only bob to the surface if he released it. His head broke water and he gasped, his heart thumping; water struck his face and he knew again, suddenly, as though they had ceased to exist while he was gone, the pulse-beat pounding of the waves.

Ignacio was waiting for him. He shouted, "This time you will come with Ignacio, and he will show you the dead sea god. Then we will fish."

Unable to speak, Nicholas nodded. He was allowed three more breaths; then Ignacio dived and Nicholas had to follow, kicking down until the pressure sang in his ears. Then through blue water he saw, looming at the edge of the light, a huge mass of metal anchored to the temperglass hull of the satellite itself; above it, hanging lifelessly like the stem of a great vine severed from the root, a cable twice as thick as a man's body; and on the bottom, sprawled beside the mighty anchor, a legged god that might have been a dead insect save that it was at least six meters long. Ignacio turned and looked back at Nicholas to see if he understood; he did not, but he nodded and with the strength draining from his arms surfaced again.

After Ignacio brought up the first fish, they took turns on the surface guarding their catch, and while the Bright Spot crept beneath the shelving rim of Dr. Island they speared two more, one of them quite large. Then when Nicholas was so exhausted he could scarcely lift his arms, they made their way back to shore, and Ignacio showed him how to gut the fish with a thorn and the edge of a shell, and reclose them and pack them in mud and leaves to be roasted by the fire. After Ignacio had begun to eat the largest fish, Nicholas timidly drew out the smallest, and ate for the first time since coming to Dr. Island. Only when he had finished did he remember Diane.

He did not dare to take the last fish to her, but he looked covertly at Ignacio, and began edging away from the fire. The Brazilian seemed not to have noticed him. When he was well into the shadows he stood, backed a few steps, then— slowly, as his instincts warned him—walked away, not beginning to trot until the distance between them was nearly a hundred meters.

He found Diane sitting apathetic and silent at the margin of the cold pool, and had some difficulty persuading her to stand. At last he lifted her, his hands under her arms pressing against her thin ribs. Once on her feet she stood steadily enough, and followed him when he took her by the hand. He talked to her, knowing that although she gave no sign of hearing she heard him, and that the right words might wake her to response. "We went fishing—Ignacio showed me how. And he's got a fire, Diane; he got it from a kind of robot that was supposed to be fixing one of the cables that holds Dr. Island, I don't know how. Anyway, listen, we caught three big fish, and I ate one and Ignacio ate a great big one, and I don't think he'd mind if you had the other one, only say, 'Yes, *Patrão*,' and, 'No, *Pa-trão*,' to him—he likes that, and he's only used to machines. You don't have to smile at him or anything—just look at the fire; that's what I do, just look at the fire."

To Ignacio, perhaps wisely, he at first said nothing at all, leading Diane to the place where he had been sitting himself a few minutes before and placing some scraps from his fish in her lap. When she did not eat he found a sliver of the tender, roasted flesh and thrust it into her mouth. Ignacio said, "Ignacio believed that one dead," and Nicholas answered, "No, *Patrão*."

"There is another fish. Give it to her."

Nicholas did, raking the gob of baked mud from the coals to crack with the heel of his hand, and peeling the broken and steaming fillets from the skins and bones to give to her when they had cooled enough to eat; after the fish had lain in her mouth for perhaps half a minute she began to chew and swallow, and after the third mouthful she fed herself, though without looking at either of them.

"Ignacio believed that one dead," Ignacio said again.

"No, *Patrão*," Nicholas answered, and then added, "Like you can see, she's alive."

"She is a pretty creature, with the firelight on her face—no?"

"Yes, *Patrão*, very pretty."

"But too thin." Ignacio moved around the fire until he was sitting almost beside Diane, then reached for the fish Nicholas had given her. Her hands closed on it, though she still did not look at him.

"You see, she knows us after all," Ignacio said. "We are not ghosts."

Nicholas whispered urgently, "Let him have it."

Slowly Diane's fingers relaxed, but Ignacio did not take the fish. "I was only joking, little one," he said. "And I think not such good joke after all." Then when she did not reply, he turned away from her, his eyes reaching out across the dark, tossing water for something Nicholas could not see.

"She likes you, *Patrão*," Nicholas said. The words were like swallowing filth, but he thought of the bird ready to tear through Diane's skin, and Maya's blood soaking in little round dots in the white cloth, and continued. "She is only shy. It is better that way."

"You. What do you know?"

At least Ignacio was no longer looking at the sea. Nicholas said, "Isn't it true, *Patrão*?"

"Yes, it is true."

Diane was picking at the fish again, conveying tiny flakes to her mouth with delicate fingers; distinctly but almost absently she said, "Go, Nicholas."

He looked at Ignacio, but the Brazilian's eyes did not turn toward the girl, nor did he speak.

"Nicholas, go away. Please."

In a voice he hoped was pitched too low for Ignacio to hear, Nicholas said, "I'll see you in the morning. All right?"

Her head moved a fraction of a centimeter.

Once he was out of sight of the fire, one part of the beach was as good to sleep on as another; he wished he had taken a piece of wood from the fire to start one of his own and tried to cover his legs with sand to keep off the cool wind, but the sand fell away whenever he moved, and his legs and his left hand moved without volition on his part.

The surf, lapping at the rippled shore, said, "That was well done, Nicholas."

"I can feel you move," Nicholas said. "I don't think I ever could before except when I was high up."

"I doubt that you can now; my roll is less than one one-hundredth of a degree."

"Yes, I can. You wanted me to do that, didn't you? About Ignacio."

"Do you know what the Harlow effect is, Nicholas?"

Nicholas shook his head.

"About a hundred years ago Dr. Harlow experimented with monkeys who had been raised in complete isolation—no mothers, no other monkeys at all."

"Lucky monkeys."

"When the monkeys were mature he put them into cages with normal ones; they fought with any that came near them, and sometimes they killed them."

"Psychologists always put things in cages; did he ever think of turning them loose in the jungle instead?"

"No, Nicholas, though we have . . . Aren't you going to say anything?"

"I guess not."

"Dr. Harlow tried, you see, to get the isolate monkeys to breed—sex is the primary social function—but they wouldn't. Whenever another monkey of either sex approached they displayed aggressiveness, which the other monkeys returned. He cured them finally by introducing immature monkeys—monkey children—in place of the mature, socialized ones. These needed the isolate adults so badly that they kept on making approaches no matter how often or how violently they were rejected, and in the end they were accepted, and the isolates socialized. It's interesting to note that the founder of Christianity seems to have had an intuitive grasp of the principle—but it was almost two thousand years before it was demonstrated scientifically."

"I don't think it worked here," Nicholas said. "It was more complicated than that."

"Human beings are complicated monkeys, Nicholas."

"That's about the first time I ever heard you make a joke. You like not being human, don't you?"

"Of course. Wouldn't you?"

"I always thought I would, but now I'm not sure. You said that to help me, didn't you? I don't like that."

A wave higher than the others splashed chill foam over Nicholas's legs, and for a moment he wondered if this was Dr. Island's reply. Half a minute later another wave wet him, and another, and he moved farther up the beach to avoid them. The wind was stronger, but he slept despite it, and was awakened only for a moment by a flash of light from the direction from which he had come; he tried to guess what might have caused it, thought of Diane and Ignacio throwing the burning sticks into the air to see the arcs of fire, smiled—too sleepy now to be angry—and slept again.

Morning came cold and sullen; Nicholas ran up and down the beach, rubbing himself with his hands. A thin rain, or spume (it was hard to tell which), was blowing in the wind, clouding the light to gray radiance. He wondered if Diane and Ignacio would mind if he came back now and decided to wait, then thought of fishing so that he would have something to bring when he came; but the sea was very cold and the waves so high they tumbled him, wrenching his bamboo spear from his hand. Ignacio found him dripping with water, sitting with his back to a palm trunk and staring out toward the lifting curve of the sea.

"Hello, you," Ignacio said.

"Good morning, *Patrão.*"

Ignacio sat down. "What is your name? You told me, I think, when we first met, but I have forgotten. I am sorry."

"Nicholas."

"Yes."

"*Patrão,* I am very cold. Would it be possible for us to go to your fire?"

"My name is Ignacio; call me that."

Nicholas nodded, frightened.

"But we cannot go to my fire, because the fire is out."

"Can't you make another one, *Patrão?*"

"You do not trust me, do you? I do not blame you. No, I cannot make another—you may use what I had, if you wish, and make one after I have gone. I came only to say good-bye."

"You're leaving?"

The wind in the palm fronds said, "Ignacio is much better now. He will be going to another place, Nicholas."

"A hospital?"

"Yes, a hospital, but I don't think he will have to stay there long."

"But . . ." Nicholas tried to think of something appropriate. At St. John's and the other places where he had been confined, when people left, they simply left, and usually were hardly spoken of once it was learned that they were going and thus were already tainted by whatever it was that froze the smiles and dried the tears of those outside. At last he said, "Thanks for teaching me how to fish."

"That was all right," Ignacio said. He stood up and put a hand on Nicholas's shoulder, then turned away. Four meters to his left the damp sand was beginning to lift and crack. While Nicholas watched, it opened on a brightly lit companionway walled with white. Ignacio pushed his curly black hair back from his eyes and went down, and the sand closed with a thump.

"He won't be coming back, will he?" Nicholas said.

"No."

"He said I could use his stuff to start another fire, but I don't even know what it is."

Dr. Island did not answer. Nicholas got up and began to walk back to where the fire had been, thinking about Diane and wondering if she was hungry; he was hungry himself.

He found her beside the dead fire. Her chest had been burned away, and lying close by, near the hole in the sand where Ignacio must have kept it hidden, was a bulky nuclear welder. The power pack was too heavy for Nicholas to lift, but he picked up the welding gun on its short cord and touched the trigger, producing a two-meter plasma discharge which he played along the sand until Diane's body was ash. By the time he had finished, the wind was whipping the palms and sending stinging rain into his eyes, but he collected a supply of wood and built another fire, bigger and bigger until it roared like a forge in the wind. "He killed her!" he shouted to the waves.

"YES." Dr. Island's voice was big and wild.

"You said he was better."

"HE IS," howled the wind. "YOU KILLED THE MONKEY THAT WANTED TO PLAY WITH YOU, NICHOLAS—AS I BELIEVED IGNACIO WOULD EVENTUALLY KILL YOU, WHO ARE SO EASILY HATED, SO DIFFERENT FROM WHAT IT IS THOUGHT A BOY SHOULD BE. BUT KILLING THE MONKEY HELPED YOU, REMEMBER? MADE YOU BETTER. IGNACIO WAS FRIGHTENED BY WOMEN; NOW HE KNOWS THAT THEY ARE REALLY VERY WEAK, AND HE HAS ACTED UPON CERTAIN FANTASIES AND FINDS THEM BITTER."

"You're rocking," Nicholas said. "Am I doing that?"

"YOUR THOUGHT."

A palm snapped in the storm; instead of falling, it flew crashing among the others, its fronded head catching the wind like a sail. "I'm killing you," Nicholas said. "Destroying you." The left side of his face was so contorted with grief and rage that he could scarcely speak.

Dr. Island heaved beneath his feet. "NO."

"One of your cables is already broken—I saw that. Maybe more than one. You'll pull loose. I'm turning this world, isn't that right? The attitude rockets are tuned to my emotions, and they're spinning us around, and the slippage is the wind and the high sea, and when you come loose nothing will balance anymore."

"NO."

"What's the stress on your cables? Don't you know?"

"THEY ARE VERY STRONG."

"What kind of talk is that? You ought to say something like 'The D-twelve cable tension is twenty billion kilograms' force. WARNING! WARNING! Expected time to failure is ninety-seven seconds! WARNING! *Don't you even know how a machine is supposed to talk?*" Nicholas was screaming now, and every wave reached farther up the beach than the last, so that the bases of the most seaward palms were awash.

"GET BACK, NICHOLAS, FIND HIGHER GROUND. GO INTO THE JUNGLE." It was the crashing waves themselves that spoke.

"I won't."

A long serpent of water reached for the fire, which hissed and sputtered.

"GET BACK!"

"I won't!"

A second wave came, striking Nicholas calf high and nearly extinguishing the fire.

"ALL THIS WILL BE UNDERWATER SOON. GET BACK!"

Nicholas picked up some of the still-burning sticks and tried to carry them, but the wind blew them out as soon as he lifted them from the fire. He tugged at the welder, but it was too heavy for him to lift.

"GET BACK!"

He went into the jungle, where the trees lashed themselves to leafy rubbish in the wind and broken branches flew through the air like debris from an explosion; for a while he heard Diane's voice crying in the wind; it became Maya's, then his mother's or Sister Carmela's, and a hundred others'; in time the wind grew less, and he could no longer feel the ground rocking. He felt tired. He said, "I didn't kill you after all, did I?" but there was no answer. On the beach, when he returned to it, he found the welder half-buried in sand. No trace of Diane's ashes, nor of his fire. He gathered more wood and built another, lighting it with the welder.

"Now," he said. He scooped aside the sand around the welder until he reached the rough understone beneath it, and turned the flame of the welder on that; it blackened and bubbled.

"No," Dr. Island said.

"Yes." Nicholas was bending intently over the flame, both hands locked on the welder's trigger.

"Nicholas, stop that." When he did not reply, "Look behind you." There was a splashing louder than the crashing of the waves, and a groaning of metal. He whirled and saw the great, beetlelike robot Ignacio had shown him on the seafloor. Tiny shellfish clung to its metal skin, and water, faintly green, still poured from its body. Before he could turn the welding gun toward it, it shot forward hands like clamps and wrenched the gun from him. All up and down the beach similar machines were smoothing the sand and repairing the damage of the storm.

"That thing was dead," Nicholas said. "Ignacio killed it."

It picked up the power pack, shook it clean of sand, and, turning, stalked back toward the sea.

"That is what Ignacio believed, and it was better that he believed so."

"And you said you couldn't do anything, you had no hands."

"I also told you that I would treat you as society will when you are released, that that was my nature. After that, did you still believe all I told you? Nicholas, you are upset now because Diane is dead—"

"You could have protected her!"

"—but by dying she made someone else, someone very important, well. Her prognosis was bad; she really wanted only death, and this was the death I chose for her. You could call it the death of Dr. Island, a death that would help someone else. Now you are alone, but soon there will be more patients in this segment, and you will help them too—if you can—and perhaps they will help you. Do you understand?"

"No," Nicholas said. He flung himself down on the sand. The wind had dropped, but it was raining hard. He thought of the vision he had once had, and of describing it to Diane the day before. "This isn't ending the way I thought," he whispered. It was only a squeak of sound far down in his throat. "Nothing ever turns out right."

The waves, the wind, the rustling palm fronds and the pattering rain, the monkeys who had come down to the beach to search for food washed ashore, answered, "Go away—go back—don't move."

Nicholas pressed his scarred head against his knees, rocking back and forth.

"Don't move."

For a long time he sat still while the rain lashed his shoulders and the dripping monkeys frolicked and fought around him. When at last he lifted his face, there was in it some element of personality which had been only potentially present before, and with this an emptiness and an expression of surprise. His lips moved, and the sounds were the sounds made by a deaf-mute who tries to speak.

"Nicholas is gone," the waves said. "Nicholas, who was the right side of your body, the left half of your brain, I have forced into catatonia; for the remainder of your life he will be to you only what you once were to him—or less. Do you understand?"

The boy nodded.

"We will call you Kenneth, silent one. And if Nicholas tries to come again, Kenneth, you must drive him back—or return to what you have been."

The boy nodded a second time, and a moment afterward began to collect sticks for the dying fire. As though to themselves the waves chanted:

> Seas are wild tonight . . .
> Stretching over Sado island
> Silent clouds of stars.

There was no reply.

## AFTERWORD

I suspect that this is my most successful story. You already know how I came to write it. "Death," as I saw it, could be handled in two ways: Dr. Island could die, or Dr. Island could decree a death. In the same way, I could have a doctor named Island (a cop-out) or I could have a doctor who was in fact an island. You know the decisions I made.

The brain operation Nicholas suffered is perfectly real. It is (or was) done in cases of severe epilepsy that can be treated in no other way. It results in what appear to be two persons living in a single skull, a condition superficially similar to multiple personality.

As prophesied, this story won a Nebula.

# LA BEFANA

When Zozz, home from the pit, had licked his fur clean, he howled before John Bananas' door. John's wife, Teresa, opened it and let him in. She was a thin, stooped woman of thirty or thirty-five, her black hair shot with gray. She did not smile, but he felt somehow that she was glad to see him.

She said, "He's not home yet. If you want to come in we've got a fire."

Zozz said, "I'll wait for him—," and six-legging politely across the threshold sat down over the stone Bananas had rolled in for him when they had been new friends. Maria and Mark, playing some sort of game with bottle caps on squares scratched on the floor dirt, said, "Hi, Mr. Zozz—," and Zozz said, "Hi—," in return. Bananas' old mother, whom Zozz had brought here from the pads in his rusty powerwagon the day before, looked at him from piercing eyes, then fled into the other room. He could hear Teresa relax, hear her wheezing outpuffed breath.

He said, "I think she thinks I bumped her on purpose yesterday."

"She's not used to you yet."

"I know," Zozz said.

"I told her, Mother Bananas, it's their world and they're not used to *you*."

"Sure," Zozz said. A gust of wind outside brought the cold in to replace the odor of the gog-hutch on the other side of the left wall.

"I tell you it's hell to have your husband's mother with you in a place as small as this."

"Sure," Zozz said again.

Maria announced, "Daddy's home!"

The door rattled open and Bananas came in, looking tired and cheerful. Bananas worked in the slaughtering market and though his cheeks were blue with cold, his two trousers cuffs were red with blood. He kissed Teresa and tousled the hair of both children and said, "Hi, Zozzy."

Zozz said, "Hi. How does it roll?" And moved over so Bananas could warm his back.

Someone groaned and Bananas asked a little anxiously, "What's that?"

Teresa said, "Next door."

"Huh?"

"Next door. Some woman."

"Oh. I thought it might be Mom."

"She's fine."

"Where is she?"

"In back."

Bananas frowned. "There's no fire in there. She'll freeze to death."

"I didn't tell her to go back there. She can wrap a blanket around herself."

Zozz said, "It's me—I bother her." He got up.

Bananas said, "Sit down."

"I can go. I just came to say hi."

"Sit down." Bananas turned to his wife. "Honey, you shouldn't leave her in there alone. See if you can't get her to come out here, okay?"

"Johnny—"

"Teresa, dammit!"

"Okay, Johnny."

Bananas took off his coat and sat down in front of the fire. Maria and Mark had gone back to their game.

In a voice too low to attract their attention Bananas said, "Nice thing, huh?"

Zozz said, "I think your mother makes her nervous."

Bananas said, "Sure."

Zozz said, "This isn't an easy world."

"For us two-leggers? No, it ain't, but you don't see me moving."

Zozz said, "That's good. I mean, here you've got a job anyway. There's work."

"That's right."

Unexpectedly Maria said, "We get enough to eat here, and me and Mark can find wood for the fire. Where we used to be there wasn't anything to eat."

Bananas asked, "You remember, honey?"

"A little."

Zozz said, "People are poor here."

Bananas was taking off his shoes, scraping the street mud from them, and tossing it into the fire. He said, "If you mean us, us people are poor everyplace." He jerked his head in the direction of the back room. "You ought to hear her tell about our world."

"Your mother?"

Bananas nodded. "You should hear what she has to say."

Maria said, "Daddy, how did Grandmother get here?"

"Same way we did."

Mark said, "You mean she signed a thing?"

"A labor contract? No, she's too old. She bought a ticket—you know, like you would buy something in a store."

Maria said, "Why did she come, Daddy?"

"Shut up and play. Don't bother us."

Zozz said, "How did things go at work?"

"So-so." Bananas looked toward the back room again. "She came into some money, but that's her business. I never ask her anything about it."

"Sure."

"She says she spent every dollar to get here—you know, they haven't used dollars even on Earth for fifty, sixty years, but she still says it. How do you like that?" He laughed and Zozz laughed too. "I asked how she was going to get back and she said she's not going back. She's going to die right here with us. What could I possibly answer?"

"I don't know." Zozz waited for Bananas to say something and, when he did not, added: "I mean, she is your mother, after all."

"Yeah."

Through the thin wall they heard the sick woman groan again and someone moving about. Zozz said, "I guess it's been a long time since you saw her last."

"Yeah—twenty-two years Newtonian. Listen, Zozzy—"

"Uh-huh."

"You know something? I wish I had never set eyes on her again."

Zozz said nothing, rubbing his hands, hands, hands.

"That sounds lousy, I guess."

"I know what you mean."

"She could have lived good for the rest of her life on what that ticket cost her." Bananas was silent for a moment. "She used to be a big, fat woman when I was a kid, you know? A great big woman with a loud voice. Look at her now— dried up and bent over. It's like she wasn't my mother at all. You know the only thing that's the same about her? That black dress. That's the only thing I recognize, the only thing that hasn't changed. She could be a stranger—she tells stories about me I don't remember at all."

Maria said, "She told us a story today."

Mark added: "Before you came home. About this witch—"

Maria said, "—that brings the presents to children. Her name is La Befana, the Christmas Witch."

Zozz drew his lips back from his double canines and jiggled his head. "I like stories."

"She says it's almost Christmas and on Christmas three wise men went looking for the Baby and they stopped at the old witch's door and they asked which way it was and she told them and they said, 'Come with us.'"

The door to the other room opened, and Teresa and Bananas' mother came out. Bananas' mother was holding a teakettle. She edged around Zozz to put it on the hook and swing it out over the fire.

"And she was sweeping and she wouldn't come," Maria resumed.

Mark added: "Said she'd come when she had finished. She was a real old, real ugly woman. Watch; I'll show you how she walked." He jumped up and began to hobble around the room.

Bananas looked at his wife and indicated the wall. "What's this?"

"Some woman. I told you."

"In there?"

"The charity place—they said she could stay there. She couldn't stay in the house because all the rooms are full of men."

Maria was saying, "So when she was all done, she went looking for him, only she couldn't find him and she never did."

"She's sick?"

"She's knocked up, Johnny, that's all. Don't worry about her. She's got some guy in there with her."

Mark asked, "Do you know about the Baby Jesus, Uncle Zozz?"

Zozz groped for words.

"Johnny, my son—"

"Yes, Mama."

"Your friend— Do they have the faith here, Johnny?"

Apropos of nothing Teresa said, "They're Jews, next door."

Zozz told Mark, "You see, the Baby Jesus has never come to my world."

Maria said, "And so she goes all over every place looking for him with her presents and she leaves some with every kid she finds, but she says it's not because she thinks they might be him like some people think but just a substitute. She can't never die. She has to do it forever, doesn't she, Grandma?"

The bent old woman said, "Not forever, dearest. Only until tomorrow night."

## AFTERWORD

This story is based on playful theological speculation. If Jesus came into the world to save it, what about other worlds? Wouldn't he have to come into those worlds too, if he wanted to save them? (I am misinterpreting *world* here in order to get a story.) Fine, and if the Savior is to be descended from King David . . .

It's the sort of thing proposed in religion classes to get the students thinking. I've included it here, knowing that it will offend some people, for the same reason, and because I like it a lot. Besides, the legend of La Befana is quite real and ought to be better known.

# FORLESEN

When Emanuel Forlesen awoke, his wife was already up preparing breakfast. Forlesen remembered nothing, knew nothing but his name, for an instant did not remember his wife, or that she was his wife, or that she was a human being, or what human beings were supposed to look like.

At the time he woke he knew only his own name; the rest came later and is therefore suspect, colored by rationalization and the expectations of the woman herself and the other people. He moaned, and his wife said, "Oh, you're awake. Better read the orientation."

He said, "What orientation?"

"You don't remember where you work, do you? Or what you're supposed to do."

He said, "I don't remember a damn thing."

"Well, read the orientation."

He pushed aside the gingham spread and got out of bed, looking at himself, noticing first the oddly deformed hands at the ends of his legs, then remembering the name for them: *shoes*. He was naked, and his wife turned her back to him politely while she prepared food. "Where the hell am I?" he asked.

"In our house." She gave him the address. "In our bedroom."

"We cook in the bedroom?"

"We sure do," his wife said. "There isn't any kitchen. There's a parlor, the children's bedroom, this room, and a bath. I've got an electric fry pan, a tabletop electric oven, and a coffeepot here; we'll be all right."

The confidence in her voice heartened him. He said, "I suppose this used to be a one-bedroom house and we made the kitchen into a place for the kids."

"Maybe it's an old house and they made the kitchen into the bathroom when they got inside plumbing."

He was dressing himself, having seen that she wore clothing, and that there was clothing too large for her piled on a chair near the bed. He said, "Don't you know?"

"It wasn't in the orientation."

At first he did not understand what she had said. He repeated, "Don't you know?"

"I told you, it wasn't in there. There's just a diagram of the house, and there's this room, the children's room, the parlor, and the bath. It said that door there"— she gestured with the spatula—"was the bath, and that's right, because I went in there to get the water for the coffee. I stay here and look after things and you go out and work; that's what it said. There was some stuff about what you do, but I skipped that and read about what *I* do."

"You didn't know anything when you woke up either," he said.

"Just my name."

"What's your name?"

"Edna Forlesen. I'm your wife—that's what it said."

He walked around the small table on which she had arranged the cooking appliances, wanting to look at her. "You're sort of pretty," he said.

"You are sort of handsome," his wife said. "Anyway, you look tough and strong." This made him walk over to the mirror on the dresser and try to look at himself. He did not know what he looked like, but the man in the mirror was not he. The image was older, fatter, meaner, more cunning, and stupider than he knew himself to be, and he raised his hands (the man in the mirror did likewise) to touch his features; they were what they should have been and he turned away. "That mirror's no good," he said.

"Can't you see yourself? That means you're a vampire."

He laughed, and decided that that was the way he always laughed when his wife's jokes weren't funny. She said, "Want some coffee?" and he sat down.

She put a cup in front of him, and a pile of books. "This is the orientation," she said. "You better read it—you don't have much time."

On top of the pile was a mimeographed sheet, and he picked that up first. It said:

*Welcome to the planet Planet.*

*You have awakened completely ignorant of everything. Do not be disturbed by this. It is NORMAL. Under no circumstances ever allow yourself to become excited, confused, angry, or FEARFUL. While you possess these capacities, they are to be regarded as incapacities.*

*Anything you may have remembered upon awakening is false. The orientation books provided you contain information of inestimable value. Master it as soon as possible, BUT DO NOT BE LATE FOR WORK. If there are no orientation books where you are, go to the house on your right (from the street). DO NOT GO TO THE HOUSE ON YOUR LEFT.*

*If you cannot find any books, live like everyone else.*

*The white paper under this paper is your JOB ASSIGNMENT. The yellow paper is your TABLE OF COMMONLY USED WAITS AND MEASURES. Read these first; they are more important than the books.*

"Eat your egg," his wife said. He tasted the egg. It was good but slightly oily, as though a drop of motor oil had found its way into the grease in which she had fried it. His *Job Assignment* read.

*Forlosen, E.*

(To his wife he said, "They got our name wrong.")

*Forlosen, E. You work at Model Pattern Products, 19000370 Plant Prkwy, Highland Industrial Park. Your duties are supervisory and managerial. When you arrive punch in on the S&M clock (beige), NOT the Labor clock (brown). The union is particular about this. Go to the Reconstruction and Advanced Research section. To arrive on time leave before 060.30.00.*

The yellow paper was illegible save for the title and first line: *There are 240 ours in each day.*

"What time is it?" he asked his wife.

She glanced at her wrist. "Oh six oh ours. Didn't they give you a watch?"

He looked at his own wrist—it was bare, of course. For a few moments Edna helped him search for one, but it seemed that none had been provided and in the end he took hers, she saying that he would need it more than she. It was big for a woman's watch, he thought, but very small for a man's. "Try it," she said, and he obediently studied the tiny screen. The words THE TIME IS were cast in the metal at its top; below them, glimmering and changing even as he looked: 060.07.43. He took a sip of coffee and found the oily taste was there too.

The book at the top of the pile was a booklet really, about seven inches by four with the pages stapled in the middle. The title, printed in black on a blue cover of slightly heavier paper, was *How to Drive.*

*Remember that your car is a gift. Although it belongs to you and you are absolutely responsible for its acts (whether driven by yourself or others, or not driven) and maintenance (pg. 15), do not:*
*1. Deface its surface.*
*2. Interfere with the operation of its engine, or with the operation of any other part.*
*3. Alter it in such a way as to increase or diminish the noise of operation.*
*4. Drive it at speeds in excess of 40 miles/our.*
*5. Pick up hitchhikers.*
*6. Deposit a hitchhiker at any point other than a Highway Patrol Station.*

    7. *Operate it while you are in an unfit condition. (To be determined by a duly constituted medical board.)*

    8. *Fail to halt and render medical assistance to persons injured by you, your car, or others (provided third parties are not already providing such assistance).*

    9. *Stop at any time or for any reason at any point not designated as a stopping position.*

  10. *Wave or shout at other drivers.*

  11. *Invade the privacy of other drivers—as by noticing or pretending to notice them or the occupants of their vehicles.*

  12. *Fail to return it on demand.*

  13. *Drive it to improper destinations.*

He turned the page. The new page was a diagram of the control panel of an automobile, and he noted the positions of Windshield, Steering Wheel, Accelerator, Brake, Reversing Switch, Communicator, Beverage Dispenser, Urinal, Defecator, and Map Compartment. He asked Edna if they had a car, and she said she thought they did, and that it would be outside.

"You know," he said, "I've just noticed that this place has windows."

Edna said, "You're always jumping up from the table. Finish your breakfast."

Ignoring her, he parted the curtains. She said, "Two walls have windows and two don't. I haven't looked out of them." Outside he saw sunshine on concrete; a small, yellow, somehow hunched-looking automobile; and a house.

"Yeah, we've got a car," he said. "It's parked right under the window."

"Well, I wish you'd finish breakfast and get to work."

"I want to look out of the other window."

If the first window had been, as it appeared to be, at one side of the house, then the other should be at either the back or the front. He opened the curtains and saw a narrow, asthmatic brick courtyard. On the bricks stood three dead plants in terra-cotta jars; the opposite side of the court, no more than fifteen feet off, was the wall of another house. There were two widely spaced windows in this wall, each closed with curtains, and as he watched (though his face was only at the window for an instant) a man pushed aside the curtains at the nearer window and looked at him. Forlesen stepped back and said to Edna, "I saw a man; he looked afraid. A bald man with a wide, fat face, and a gold tooth in front, and a mole over one eyebrow." He went to the mirror again and studied himself.

"You don't look like that," his wife said.

"No, I don't—that's what bothers me. That was the first thing I thought of—that it would be myself, perhaps the way I'm going to look when I'm older. I've lost a lot of my hair now and I could lose the rest of it; in fact, I suppose I will. And I could break a tooth in front and get a gold one—"

"Maybe it wasn't really a mole," Edna said. "It could have been just a spot of dirt or something."

"It could have been." He had seated himself again, and as he spoke he speared a bite of egg with his fork. "I suppose it's even possible that I could grow a mole I don't have now, and I could put on weight. But that wasn't me; those weren't my features, not at any age."

"Well, why should it be you?"

"I just felt it should, somehow."

"You've been reading that red book." Edna's voice was accusing.

"No, I haven't even looked at it." Curious, he pushed aside brown and purple pamphlets, fished the red book out of the pile, and looked at it. The cover was of leather and had been blind-tooled in a pattern of thin lines. Holding it at a slant to the light from the window, he decided he could discern, in the intricacies of the pattern, a group of men surrounding a winged being. "What is it?" he said.

"It's supposed to tell you how to be good, and how to live—everything like that."

He riffled the pages, and noted that the left side of the book—the back of each leaf—was printed in scarlet in a language he did not understand. The right side, printed in black, seemed by its arrangement on the page to be a translation.

*Of the nature of Death and the Dead we may enumerate twelve kinds. First there are those who become new gods, for whom new universes are born. Second those who praise. Third those who fight as soldiers in the unending war with evil. Fourth those who amuse themselves among flowers and sweet streams with sports. Fifth those who dwell in gardens of bliss, or are tortured. Sixth those who continue as in life. Seventh those who turn the wheel of the Universe. Eighth those who find in their graves their mothers' wombs and in one life circle forever. Ninth ghosts. Tenth those born again as men in their grandsons' time. Eleventh those who return as beasts or trees. And last those who sleep.*

"Look at this," he said. "This can't be right."

"I wish you'd hurry. You're going to be late."

He looked at the watch she had given him. It read 060.26.13, and he said, "I still have time. But look here—the black is supposed to say the same thing as the red, but look at how different they are: where it says: *And last those who sleep,* there's a whole paragraph opposite it; and across from, *Fourth those who amuse themselves . . .* there are only two words."

"You don't want any more coffee, do you?"

He shook his head, laid down the red book, and picked up another; its title was *Food Preparation in the Home.* "That's for me," his wife said. "You wouldn't be interested by that."

## Contents

Preparing Luncheon
Preparing Supper
Helpful Hints for Homemakers

He set the book down again, and as he did so its cheap plastic cover popped open to the last page. At the bottom of the "Helpful Hints for Homemakers," he read: *Remember that if he does not go, you and your children will starve.* He closed it and put the sugar bowl on top of it.

"I wish you'd get going," his wife said.

He stood up. "I was just leaving. How do I get out?"

She pointed to one of the doors, and said, "That's the parlor. You go straight through that, and there's another door that goes outside."

"And the car," Forlesen said, more than half to himself, "will be around there under the window." He slipped the blue *How to Drive* booklet into one of his pockets.

The parlor was smaller than the bedroom, but because it held no furniture as large as the bed or the table it seemed nearly empty. There was an uncomfortable-looking sofa against one wall, and two bowlegged chairs in corners; an umbrella stand and a dusty potted palm. The floor was covered by a dark, patterned rug and the walls by flowered paper. Four strides took him across the room; he opened another, larger and heavier door and stepped outside. A moment after he had closed the door he heard the bolt snick behind him; he tried to open it again, and found, as he had expected, that he was locked out.

The house in which he seemed to have been born stood on a narrow street paved with asphalt. Only a two-foot concrete walkway separated it from the curb; there was no porch, and the doorway was at the same level as the walk, which had been stenciled at intervals of six feet or so with the words GO TO YOUR RIGHT—NOT TO YOUR LEFT. They were positioned in such a way as to be upside down to a person who had gone to the left. Forlesen went around the corner of his house instead and got into the yellow car—the instrument panel differed in several details from the one in the blue book. For a moment he considered rolling down the right window of the car to rap on the house window, but he felt sure that Edna would not come. He threw the reversing switch instead, wondering if he should not do something to bring the car to life first. It began to roll slowly backward at once; he guided it with the steering wheel, craning his neck to look over his shoulder.

The narrow street seemed deserted. He switched into Front and touched the accelerator pedal with his foot; the car inched forward, picking up speed only slowly even when he pushed the pedal to the floor. The street was lined with small brick houses much like the one he had left; their curtains were drawn, and small cars like his own but of various colors were parked beside the houses. Signs stood on metal poles cast into the asphalt of the road, spaced just sufficiently far apart that each was out of sight of the next. They were diamond shaped, with black letters on an orange ground, and each read: HIDDEN DRIVES.

His communicator said: *"If you do not know how to reach your destination, press the button and ask."*

He pressed the button and said, "I think I'm supposed to go to a place called Model Pattern Products."

*"Correct. Your destination is 19000370 Plant Parkway, Highland Industrial Park. Turn right at the next light."*

He was about to ask what was meant by the word *light* in this connotation when he saw that he was approaching an intersection and that over it, like a ceiling fixture unaccompanied by any ceiling, was suspended a rapidly blinking light which emitted at intervals of perhaps a quarter second alternating flashes of red and green. He turned to the right; the changing colors gave an illusion of jerky motion, belied by the smooth hum of the tires. The flickering brought a sensation of nausea, and for a moment he shut his eyes against it; then he felt the car nosing up, tilting under him. He opened his eyes and saw that the new street onto which he had turned was lifting beneath him, becoming, ahead, an airborne ribbon of pavement that traced a thin streak through the sky. Already he was higher than the tops of the trees. The roofs of the houses—little tarpaper things like the lids of boxes—were dwindling below. He thought of Edna in one of those boxes (he found he could not tell which one) cooking a meal for herself, perhaps smoothing the bed in which the two of them had slept, and knew, with that sudden insight which stands in relation to reason as reason does to instinct, that she would spend ours, most of whatever day there was, looking out the parlor window at the empty street; he found that he both pitied and envied her, and stopped the car with some vague thought of returning home and devising some plan by which they could either stay there together or go together to wherever it was he was being sent. "Model Pattern Products," he said aloud. What was that?

As though it were answering him the speaker said, "Why have you stopped? Do you require mechanical assistance?"

"Wait a minute; I'm not sure if I do or not." He got out of the car and walked to the low rail at the edge of the road and looked down. Something, he felt sure, must be supporting the mass of concrete and steel upon which he stood, but he could not see what it was, only the houses and trees and the narrow asphalt streets below. The sunlight striking his face when he looked up again gave him an idea, and he hurried across the road and bent over the rail on the opposite side. There, as he had anticipated, the shadow of the road, long in the level morning sunshine, lay stretched across the roofs and streets. Under it, very closely spaced, were yet other shadows, but these were so broken by the irregular shapes upon which they were thrown by the sun that he could not be sure if they were the shadows of things actually straight or if the casters of these shadows (whatever they might be) were themselves bowed, twisted, and deformed.

He was still studying the shadows when the humming sound of wheels drew his attention back to the flying roadway upon which he stood. A car, painted a metallic and yet peculiarly pleasing shade of blue, was speeding toward him.

Unaccustomed to estimating the speeds of vehicles, he wondered for an instant whether or not he had time to recross the road and reach his own car again, and was torn between the fear of being run down if he tried and that of being pinned against the rail where he stood, should the blue car swerve too near. Then he realized that the blue car was slowing as it approached him—that he himself was, so to speak, its destination. Its door, he saw, was painted with a fantastic design, a mingling of fabulous beasts with plants and what appeared to be wholly abstract symbols.

A man was seated in the blue car, and as Forlesen watched he leaned across the seat toward him, rolling down the window. "Hey, bud, what are you doing outside your car?"

"I was looking over the railing," Forlesen said. He indicated the sheer drop beside him. "I wanted to see how the road got up in the air like this."

"Get back in."

Forlesen was about to obey when in a remote corner of his field of vision he detected a movement, a shifting in that spot of ground below toward which he had been looking a moment before, and thus toward which (as is the habit of vision) his gaze was still to some degree drawn. He swung around to look at it, and the man in the blue car said again, "Get back in your car, bud." And then: "I'm telling you, you better get back."

"Come here," Forlesen said. "Look at this." He heard the door of the other car open and assumed the driver was coming to join him, then felt something—it might have been the handlebar of a bicycle against which he had accidentally backed—prodding him in the spine, just above his belt. He moved away from it with his attention still riveted on the shadows below, but it followed him. He turned and saw that the driver had, as he had supposed, left the blue car, and that he wore a loose, broad-sleeved blue shirt with a metal badge pinned to the fabric off-center. Also that he wore no trousers, his sexual organs being effectively concealed by the length of the shirt, and that from under the shirt six or more plastic tubes led back to the blue car, some of the color of straw and others of the dark red color of blood; and that he held a pistol, and that it had been the muzzle of this pistol which he (Forlesen) had felt a moment before pressing against his back. "Get in there," the man from the blue car said a third time.

Forlesen said, "All right," and did as he was told, but found (to his own very great surprise) that he was not frightened.

When he was behind the wheel of his own car again, the man from the blue car reentered it, and (so it appeared to Forlesen) seemed to holster his gun beneath the car's dashboard. "I'm back in my car now," Forlesen said. "Can I tell you what it was I saw?"

The man in the blue car said to his speaker, "This is two oh four twelve forty-three. Subject has returned to his vehicle. Repeat—subject has returned to his vehicle."

"Those pillars or columns or whatever they are that hold this road up—one of them moved, or at least its shadow did. I saw it."

The man in the blue car muttered something under his breath.

"Are they falling down?" Forlesen asked. "Have you been noticing cracks?"

The speaker in Forlesen's car said, "Information received indicates an unauthorized stop. Continue toward your destination at once." He noticed that the speaker in the blue car seemed to be talking to its driver as well, but Forlesen could not hear what was being said. After a moment (his own speaker had fallen silent) he heard the driver say, "Yes, ma'am. Over and out." Then the pistol was aimed at Forlesen once more, this time at his face, through the window of the blue car. The driver said, "You roll that thing, bud, and you roll it now or I shoot."

Forlesen stepped on the accelerator, and his car began to move forward, slowly at first, then picking up speed until he felt sure it was traveling much faster than a man could run. In the mirror above the windshield Forlesen could see the blue car; it did not turn—as he had supposed it might—to follow him, but after a delay continued to descend the road he himself was going up.

He had supposed that this road would lead him to Model Pattern Products (whatever that might be), but when he had been following it for some time it joined another similar but far wider, highway. There were now multiple lines of traffic all going in the same direction, and by traveling in the fast lane he could avoid looking over the side. It was a relief he accepted gratefully; he had a good head for heights, but he had found himself studying the long shadows of the supports whenever the twistings of the road put them on the side upon which he drove.

With that distraction out of the way he discovered that he enjoyed driving, though the memory of the twisted columns remained in the back of his mind. Yet the performance of the yellow car was deeply satisfying: it sped to the top of the high, white, billowing undulations of the highway with a power slight yet sure, and descended in a way that made him almost believe himself a hawk—or the operator of some fantastic machine that could itself soar like a bird—or even such a winged being as had appeared on the cover of the red book. The clear sky, which lay now to the right and left of the highway as well as above it, promoted these fantasies, and its snowy clouds might almost have been other highways like the one on which he traveled—indeed, from time to time he seemed to see moving dots of color on them, as though cars like his own, but immensely remote, dashed over plains and precipices of vapor. He used the defecator and the urinal, dispensed himself a sparkling green beverage; the car was a cozy and secret place of retirement, a second body, his palace and his fortress; he imagined himself a mouse descending a clear stream in half an eggshell, the master of a comet enfolding a hollow world.

He had been traveling in this way for a long while when he saw the hitchhiker. The man did not stand at the side of the road where Forlesen would have expected to see a pedestrian if, indeed, he had anticipated seeing any at all, but balanced himself on the high divider that separated the innermost lane from those on which traffic moved in the opposite direction. As he was some distance ahead, Forlesen was able to observe him for several minutes before reaching the point at which he stood.

He appeared to be a tall man, much stooped; and despite the ludicrousness of his position, his attitude suggested a certain dignity. His hands and arms were in constant motion—not only as he sought to maintain his balance, but because he mimed to each car that passed his desire to ride, acting out in pantomime the car's stopping, his haste to reach it, his opening the door and seating himself, his gratitude.

Nor did he care, apparently, in which direction he rode. While Forlesen watched, he turned around and for a few moments sought to attract the attention of a passing vehicle on the opposite side; then, as though he realized that he was unlikely to have better fortune there than in the direction he had chosen originally, turned back again. His clothing was stiffly old-fashioned, once fairly good perhaps, but now worn and dusty. When Forlesen stopped before this scarecrow figure and motioned toward the seat beside him, the hitchhiker seemed so startled at having gotten a ride at last that Forlesen wondered if he was going to get in. Traffic zoomed and swirled around them like a summer storm.

With his long legs folded high and the edge of the dashboard pressing against his shins he looked (Forlesen thought) like a cricket. An old cricket, for despite his agility and air of alertness the hitchhiker was old, his mouth full of crooked and stained old teeth and new white straight ones which were surely false, his bright, dark eyes surrounded by wrinkles, the hand he extended crook fingered and callused. "Name's Abraham Beale." Bad teeth in a good smile.

"Emanuel Forlesen," Forlesen said, taking the hand as he started the car rolling again. "Where are you going, Mr. Beale?"

"Anywhere." Beale was craning his neck to look out the small window in the back of the car. "Glad you didn't get hit," he said. "'Fraid you would."

"I'm sure they could see I had stopped," Forlesen said, "and there are plenty of other lanes."

"Half of them's asleep. More'n half. You're awake, so I guess you thought everybody was, ain't that right?"

"They're driving; I'd think they'd run off the road if they were sleeping."

Beale was dusting his high-crowned, battered old hat with his big hands, patting and brushing it gently as though it were a baby animal of some delicate and appealing kind, a young rabbit or a little coatimundi. "I could see them," he said. "From where I was up there. Most of them didn't even see me—off in cloudland somewheres."

"I'm going to Model Pattern Products," Forlesen said.

The older man shook his head, and, having finished with his hat, set it on one knee. "I already tried there," he said, "nothin' for me." In a slightly lower voice, the voice of a man who is ashamed but feels he should not be, he added: "Lost my old job. I been trying to hook on somewhere else."

"I'm sorry to hear that." Forlesen found, somewhat to his surprise, that he *was* sorry. "What did you do?"

"About everything. There ain't much I can't turn a hand to. By rights I'm a lawyer, but I've soldiered some and worked stock out west, and lumberjacked, and once I fired on the railroad. And I'm a pretty good reaper mechanic if I do say so myself." Beale took a round tin box of snuff from one of the pockets of his shabby vest and put a pinch of the brown contents under his lip, then offered the box to Forlesen.

"You've had an interesting time," Forlesen said, waving it away. "I would have guessed you were a farmer, I think, if I had had to guess."

"Well, I've followed a plow and I ain't ashamed to say it. I was raised on the farm—oldest of thirteen children, and we all helped. I'd farm again if I had the land; it would be something. You know what? My dad, he left the old place to me, and the same day I got the letter that said I was to have it—from a esteemed colleague there, you know, a old fellow named Abner Bunter, we used to call him Banty; my dad'd had him do his will for him, me not being there—I got another that said the state was taking her for a highway. Had it and lost it between rippin' up one envelope and the other. I remember when it happened I went out and bought a cigar; I had been workin', but I couldn't work no more, not right then."

"Didn't they pay you for it?" Forlesen asked. He had been coming up behind a car the color of sour milk, and changed lanes as he spoke, shooting into an opening that allowed him to pass.

"You bet. There was a check in there," Beale said. "I planted her, but she didn't grow."

Forlesen glanced at him, startled.

"Hey!" The older man slapped his leg. "You think I'm touched. I meant I invested her."

"Well, I'm sorry you lost your money," Forlesen said.

"I didn't exactly lose it." Beale rubbed his chin. "It just sort of come to nothing. I still got it—draw the interest every year; they post her in the book for me—but there ain't nothing left." He snapped his fingers. "Tell you what it's like. We had a tree once on the farm, a apple tree—McIntoshes, I think they were. Well, it never did die, but every winter it would die back a little bit, first one limb and then another, until there wasn't hardly anything left. Dad always thought it would come back, so he never did grub it out, but I don't believe it ever bore after I was big enough to go to school, and I remember the year I left home he cut a switch of it for Avery—Avery was the youngest of us brothers; he was always getting into trouble, like I recollect one time he let one of Dad's blue slate gamecocks in the pen with our big Shanghai rooster, said he thought the blue slate was too full of himself and the big one would take him down a piece; well, what happened was the blue slate ripped him right up the front; any fool could have told him; looked like he was going to clean him without picking first. Dad was mad as hell—he thought the world of that rooster, and he used to feed him cake crumbs right out of his hand."

"What happened to the apple tree?" Forlesen asked.

"That's what I said myself," Beale said. Forlesen waited for him to continue, but he did not. The miles (hundreds of miles, Forlesen thought) slipped by; at long intervals the speaker announced the time: "*It is oh sixty-three, oh sixty-five, oh sixty-eight thirty ours.*" The road dropped by slow degrees until they were level with the roofs of buildings, buildings whose roofs were jagged saw blades fronted with glass.

Forlesen said, "Model Pattern Products is in an industrial park—the Highland Industrial Park—maybe you'll be able to get a job there."

Beale nodded slowly. "I been looking out for something that looked to be in my line," and after a moment added, "I guess I didn't finish tellin' you 'bout my check I got, did I? Look here." His left hand fumbled inside his shabby coat, and Forlesen noticed that the elbows were so threadbare that his shirt could be seen through the fabric as though the man himself had begun to be slightly transparent, at least in his external and nonessential attributes. After a moment he held out a small, dun-colored bankbook, opening it dexterously with the fingers of one hand, but to the wrong page, an empty and unused page, which he presented for Forlesen's inspection. "That's all there is," Beale said. "I never drew a nickel, and I put the interest, most times, right smack back in, and that's all that's left. That's Dad's farm, them little numbers in the book."

Forlesen said, "I see."

"They didn't cheat me," Beale continued. "That was a good hunk of money when they give it to me, big money. But it's went down and down since till it's only little money, and little money ain't hardly worth nothing. Listen, you're young yit—I suppose you think two dollars is twice as much as one? Like, if you're paid one and some other fellar gits two, he's got twice as much as you? Or the other way around?"

"I suppose so," Forlesen said.

"Well, you're right. Now suppose you've got—I won't ask you to tell me; I'll just strike upon a figure here from your general age and appearance and whatnot—five thousand dollars. And the other's got fifty thousand. Would you say he had ten times what you did?"

"Yes."

"That's where you're wrong; he's got fifty times, a hundred times what you do—maybe two hundred. Ain't you never noticed how a man with fifty thousand cold behind him will act? Like you're nothin' to him, you don't even weigh in his figuring at all."

Forlesen smiled. "Are you saying five thousand times ten isn't fifty thousand?"

"Look at it this way: You take your dollar to the store and you can git a dozen of eggs and a can of beans and a plug of tobacco. The other takes his two and gits two dozen of eggs, two cans of beans, and two plugs—ain't that right? But a man that has big money don't pay fifteen cents a plug like you and me; he can buy by the case if he feels inclined, and if he gits very much he gits it cheap as the store. Another thing—some things he can buy you and me can't git at all. It ain't that we can buy less; we can't git even a little bit of it. Let me give you an example: The railroads and the coal mines buy your state legislatures, right? Sure they do, and everybody knows it. Now there's thousands and thousands of people on the other side of them, and those thousands of people, if you was to add their money up, would be worth more. But they can't buy the legislature at all, ain't that right?"

"Go on," Forlesen said.

"Well, don't that prove that little money's power to buy certain things is zero? If it had any at all, thousands and thousands times it would make those people the kings of the state, but the actual fact is they can't do a thing—thousands time nothing is still nothing." Suddenly Beale turned, staring out the window of the car, and Forlesen realized that while they had been talking the road had descended to the ground. Still many-laned, it passed now through a level landscape dotted with great, square buildings which, despite their size, made no pretense of majesty or grace, but seemed in every case intentionally ugly. They were constructed of the cheapest materials, mostly corrugated metal and cinder block, and each was surrounded by a high, rusty wire fence, with a barren area of asphalt or gravel beyond it as though to provide (Forlesen knew the thought was ridiculous) a clear field of fire for defenders within.

"Hold up!" Beale said urgently. "Hold up a minute there." He gripped Forlesen's right arm, and Forlesen jockeyed the car to the outermost lane of traffic, then onto the rutted clay at the shoulder of the road.

"Look 'e there!" Beale said, pointing down a broad alley between two of the huge buildings.

Forlesen looked as directed. "Horses."

"Mustangs! Never been broke; you can tell that from looking at 'em. Whoever's got 'em's going to need some help." Beale opened the car door, then turned and shook Forlesen's hand. "Well, you've been a friend," he said, "and if ever I can do anything for you just you ask." Then he was gone, and Forlesen sat, for a moment, looking at the billboard-sized sign above the building into which the horses were being driven. It showed a dog's head in a red triangle on a field of black, without caption of any kind.

The speaker said, "Do not stop en route. You are still one and one-half aisles from Model Pattern Products, your place of employment."

Forlesen nodded and looked at the watch his wife had given him. It was 069.50.

"You are to park your car," the speaker continued, "in the Model Pattern Products parking lot. You are not to occupy any position marked VISITORS, or any position marked with a name not your own."

"Do they know I'm coming?" Forlesen asked, pressing the button.

"An employee service folder has already been made out for you," the speaker told him. "All that needs to be done is to fill in your name."

The Model Pattern Products parking lot was enclosed by a high fence, but the gates were open and the hinges so rusted that Forlesen, who stopped in the gateway for a moment thinking some guard or watchman might wish to challenge him, wondered if they had ever been closed; the ground itself, covered with loose gravel the color of ash, sloped steeply; he was forced to drive carefully to keep his car from skidding among the concrete stops of brilliant orange provided to prevent the parked cars from rolling down the grade; most of these were marked either with some name not his or with the word VISITOR, but he eventually discovered an unmarked position (unattractive, apparently, because smoke from a stubby flue projecting from the back of an outbuilding would blow across it) and left his car. His legs ached.

He was thirty or forty feet from his car when he realized he no longer had the speaker to advise him; several people were walking toward the gray metal building that was Model Pattern Products, but all were too distant for him to talk to them without shouting, and something in their appearance suggested that they would not wait for him to overtake them in any case. He followed them through a small door and found himself alone.

An anteroom held two time clocks, one beige, the other brown. Remembering the instruction sheet, he took a blank time card from the rack and wrote his name at the top, then pushed it into the beige machine and depressed the lever. A gong sounded. He withdrew the card and checked the stamped time: 069.56. A thin, youngish woman with large glasses and a sharp nose looked over his shoulder. "You're late," she said. (He was aware for an instant of the effort she was making to read his name at the top of the card.) "Mr. Forlesen."

He said, "I'm afraid I don't know the starting time."

The woman said, "Oh seventy ours sharp, Mr. Forlesen. Start oh seventy ours sharp, coffee for your subdivision one hundred ours to one hundred and one. Lunch one hundred and twenty to one hundred and forty-one. Coffee, your subdivision, one fifty to one fifty-one P.M. Quit one seventy ours at the whistle."

"Then I'm not late," Forlesen said. He showed her his card.

"Mr. Frick likes everyone to be at least twenty minutes early, especially supervisory and management people. The real go-getters—that's what he calls them, the real go-getters—try to be early. I mean, earlier than the regular early. Oh sixty-nine twenty-five, something like that. They unlock their desks and go upstairs for early coffee, and sometimes they play cards; it's fun."

"I'm sorry I missed it," Forlesen said. "Can you tell me where I'm supposed to go now?"

"To your desk," the woman said, nodding. "Unlock it."

"I don't know where it is."

"Well, of course you don't, but I can't assign you to your desk—that's up to

Mr. Fields, your supervisor." After a moment she added: "I know where you're going to go, but he has the keys."

Forlesen said, "I thought I was a supervisor."

"You are," the woman told him, "but Mr. Fields is—you know—a real supervisor. Anyway, nearly. Do you want to talk to him now?"

Forlesen nodded.

"I'll see if he'll see you now. You have Creativity Group today, and Leadership Training. And Company Orientation, and Bet-Your-Life—that's the management-managing real-life pseudogame—and one interdepartmental training-transfer."

"I'll be glad to get the orientation anyway," Forlesen said. He followed the woman, who had started to walk away. "But am I going to have time for all that?"

"You don't get it," she told him over her shoulder. "You give it. And you'll have lots of time for work besides—don't worry. I've been here a long time already. I'm Miss Fawn. Are you married?"

"Yes," Forlesen said, "and I think we have children."

"Oh. Well, you look it. Here's Mr. Fields's office, and I nearly forgot to tell you you're on the Planning and Evaluation Committee. Don't forget to knock."

Forlesen knocked on the door to which the woman had led him. It was of metal painted to resemble wood, and had riveted to its front a small brass plaque which read: MR. D'ANDREA.

"Come in!" someone called from inside the office.

Forlesen entered and saw a short, thickset, youngish man with close-cropped hair sitting at a metal desk. The office was extremely small and had no windows, but there was a large, brightly colored picture on each wall—two photographs in color (a beach with rocks and waves, and a snow-clad mountain) and two realistic landscapes (both of rolling green countryside dotted with cows and trees).

"Come in," the youngish man said again. "Sit down. Listen, I want to tell you something—you don't have to knock to come in this office. Not ever. My door—like they say—is always open. What I mean is, I may keep it shut to keep out the noise and so forth out in the hall, but it's always open to you."

"I think I understand," Forlesen said. "Are you Mr. Fields?" The plaque had somewhat shaken his faith in the young woman with glasses.

"Right—Ed Fields at your service."

"Then I'm going to be working for you. I'm Emanuel Forlesen." Forlesen leaned forward and offered his hand, which Fields walked around the desk to take.

"Glad to meet you, Manny. Always happy to welcome a new face to the subdivision." For an instant, as their eyes met, Forlesen felt himself weighed on invisible scales and, he thought, found slightly wanting. Then the moment passed, and a few seconds later he had difficulty believing it had ever been. "Remember what I told you when you came in—my door is always open," Fields said. "Sit down." Forlesen sat, and Fields resumed his place behind the desk.

"We're a small outfit," Fields said, "but we're sharp." He held up a clenched fist. "And I intend to make us the sharpest in the division. I need men who'll back my play all the way, and maybe even run in front a little. Sharpies. That's what I call 'em—sharpies. And you work with me, not for me."

Forlesen nodded.

"We're a team," Fields continued, "and we're going to function as a team. That doesn't mean there isn't a quarterback, and a coach"—he pointed toward the ceiling—"up there. It does mean that I expect every man to bat two fifty or better, and the ones that don't make three hundred had better be damn good field. See what I mean?"

Forlesen nodded again and asked, "What does our subdivision do? What's our function?"

"We make money for the company," Fields told him. "We do what needs to be done. You see this office? This desk, this chair?"

Forlesen nodded.

"There's two kinds of guys that sit here—I mean all through the company. There's the old has-been guys they stick in here because they've been through it all and seen everything, and there's the young guys like me that get put here to get an education—you get me? Sometimes the young guys just never move out; then they turn into the old ones. That isn't going to happen to me, and I want you to remember that the easiest way for you to move up yourself is to move into this spot right here. Someday this will all be yours—that's the way to think of it. That's what I tell every guy in the subdivision—someday this'll all be yours." Fields reached over his head to tap one of the realistic landscapes. "You get what I mean?"

"I think so."

"Okay, then let me show you your desk and where you're gonna work."

As they dodged among windowless, brightly lit corridors, it struck Forlesen that though the building was certainly ventilated—some of the corridors, in fact, were actually windy—the system could not be working very well. A hundred odors, mostly foul, but some of a sickening sweetness, thronged the air; and though most of the hallways they traveled were so cold as to be uncomfortable, a few were as stuffy as tents left closed all day beneath a summer sun.

"What's that noise?" Forlesen asked.

"That's a jackhammer busting concrete. You're going to be in the new wing." Fields opened a green steel door and led the way down a narrow, low-ceilinged passage pungent with the burnt-metal smell of arc welding; the tiled floor was gritty with cement dust, and Forlesen wondered, looking at the unpainted walls, how they could have gotten so dirty when they were clearly so new. "In here," Fields said.

It was a big room, and had been divided into cubicles with rippled glass partitions five feet high. The effect was one of privacy, but the cubicles had been laid out in such a way as to allow anyone looking through the glass panel in the office door to see into them all. The windows were covered with splintering boards, and the floor sufficiently uneven that it was possible to imagine it a petrified sea, though its streaked black and gray pattern was more suggestive of charred wood. "You're in luck," Fields said. "I'd forgotten, or I would have told you back in the office. You get a window desk. Right here. Sitting by the window makes it kind of dark, but you only got the one other guy on the side of you over there, that's nice, and you know there's always a certain prestige goes with the desk that's next to the window."

Forlesen asked, "Wouldn't it be possible to take some of the glass out of these partitions and use it in the windows?"

"Hell, no. This stuff is partition glass—what you need for a window is window glass. I thought you were supposed to have a lot of science."

"My duties are supposed to be supervisory and managerial," Forlesen said.

"Don't ever let anybody tell you management isn't a science." Fields thumped Forlesen's new desk for emphasis and got a smudge of dust on his fist. "It's an art, sure, but it's a science too."

Forlesen, who could not see how anything could be both, nodded.

Fields glanced at his watch. "Nearly oh seventy-one already, and I got an appointment. Listen, I'm gonna leave you to find your way around."

Forlesen seated himself at his desk. "I was hoping you'd tell me what I'm supposed to do here before you left."

Fields was already outside the cubicle. "You mean your responsibilities; there's a list around somewhere."

Forlesen had intended to protest further, but as he started to speak he noticed an optical illusion so astonishing that for the brief period it was visible he could only stare. As Fields passed behind one of the rippled glass partitions on his way to the door, the distortions in the glass caused his image to change from that of the somewhat dumpy and rumpled man with whom Forlesen was now slightly familiar; behind the glass he was taller, exceedingly neat, and blank faced. And he wore glasses.

When he was gone Forlesen got up and examined the partitions carefully; they seemed ordinary enough, one surface rippled, the other smooth, the tops slightly dusty. He looked at his empty desk through the glass; it was a vague blur. He sat down again, and the telephone rang. "Cappy?"

"This is Emanuel Forlesen." At the last moment it occurred to Forlesen that it might have been better to call himself Manny as Fields had—that it might seem more friendly and less formal, particularly to someone who was looking for someone he addressed so casually—but, as the thought entered his mind, something else, not a thought but one of those deeper feelings from which our thoughts have, perhaps, evolved contradicted it, so he repeated his name, bearing down on the first syllable: "*Ee*-manuel Forlesen."

"Isn't Cappy Dillingham there?"

"He may be in this office," Forlesen said, "that is, his desk may be here, but he's not here himself, and this is my telephone—I just moved into the office."

"Take a message for him, will you? Tell him the Creativity Group meeting is moved up to oh seventy-eight sharp. I'm sorry it had to be so early, but Gene Fine has got a bunch of other stuff and we couldn't figure out anything else to do short of canceling. And we couldn't get a room, so we're meeting in the hall outside the drilling and boring shop. There's definitely going to be a film. Have you got that?"

"I think so," Forlesen said. "Oh seventy-eight, hall outside the drill room, movie." He heard someone behind him and turned to look. It was Miss Fawn, so he said, "Do you know where Mr. Dillingham is? I'm taking a call for him."

"He died," Miss Fawn said. "Let me talk to them." She took the receiver. "Who's calling, please? . . . Mr. Franklin, Mr. Dillingham died. . . . Last night . . . Yes, it is. Mr. Forlesen is taking his place in your group—you should have gotten a memo on it. . . . On Mr. Dillingham's old number; you were just talking to him. He's right here. Wait a moment." She turned back to Forlesen: "It's for you."

He took the telephone and a voice in the earpiece said, "Are you Forlesen? Listen, this is Ned Franklin. You may not have been notified yet, but you're in our Creativity Group, and we're meeting— Wait a minute; I've got a memo on it under all this crap somewhere."

"Oh seventy-eight," Forlesen said.

"Right. I realize that's pretty early—"

"We wouldn't want to try to get along without Gene Fine," Forlesen said.

"Right. Try to be there."

Miss Fawn seemed to be leaving. Forlesen turned to see how she would appear in the rippled glass as he said, "What are we going to try and create?"

"Creativity. We create creativity itself—we learn to be creative."

"I see," Forlesen said. He watched Miss Fawn become pretty while remaining sexless, like a mannequin. He said, "I thought we'd just take some clay or something and start in."

"Not that sort of creativity, for crap's sake!"

"All right," Forlesen said.

"Just show up, okay? Mr. Frick is solidly behind this and he gets upset when we have less than full attendance."

"Maybe he could get us a meeting room then," Forlesen suggested. He had no idea who "Mr. Frick" was, but he was obviously important.

"Hell, I couldn't ask Mr. Frick that. Anyway, he never asks where we had the meeting—just how many came and what we discussed, and whether we feel we're making progress."

"He could be saving it."

"Yeah, I guess he could. Listen, Cappy, if I can get us a room I'll call you, okay?"

"Right," said Forlesen. He hung up, wondered vaguely why Miss Fawn had come, then saw that she had left a stack of papers on a corner of his desk. "Well, the hell with you," he said, and pushed them toward the wall. "I haven't even looked at this desk yet."

It was a metal desk, and somewhat smaller, older, and shabbier than the one in Fields's office. It seemed odd to Forlesen that he should find old furniture in a part of the building which was still—judging from the sounds that occasionally drifted through the walls and window boards—under construction; but the desk and his chair as well were unquestionably nearing the end of their useful lives. The center desk drawer held a dead insect, a penknife with yellowed imitation ivory sides and a broken blade, a drawing of a bracket (very neatly lettered, Forlesen noticed) on crumpled tracing paper, and a dirty stomach mint. He threw this last away (his wastebasket was new, made of plastic, and did not seem to fit in with the other furnishings of the office) and opened the right-hand side drawer. It contained an assortment of pencils (all more or less chewed), a cube of art gum with the corners worn off, and some sheets of blank paper with one corner folded. The next drawer down yielded a wrinkled brown paper bag that disgorged a wad of wax paper, a stale half cookie, and the sharp smell of apples; the last two drawers proved to be a single file drawer in masquerade; there were five empty file folders in it, including one with a column of twenty-seven figures written on it in pencil, the first and lowest being 8,750 and the last and highest 12,500; they were not totaled. On the left side of the desk what looked like the ends of four more drawers proved to be a device for concealing a typewriter; there was no typewriter.

Forlesen closed it and leaned back in his chair, aware that inventorying the desk had depressed him. After a moment he remembered Fields's saying that he would find a list of his responsibilities in the office, and discovered it on the top of the stack of papers Miss Fawn had left with him. It read:

*MANAGEMENT PERSONNEL*
*Make M.P.P. Co. profitable and keep it profitable.*
*Assist in carrying out corporate goals.*
*Maintain employee discipline by reporting violators' names to their superiors.*
*Help keep costs down.*
*If any problems come up help to deal with them in accord with company policy.*
*Training, production, sales, and public relations are all supervised by management personnel.*

Forlesen threw the paper in the wastebasket.

The second paper in the stack was headed "Sample Leadership Problem #105" and read:

*A young woman named Enid Fenton was hired recently as clerical help. Her work has not been satisfactory, but because clerical help has been in short supply she has not been told this. Recently a reduction in the workload in her department made it possible to transfer three girls to another department. Miss Fenton asked for one of the transfers and when told that they had already been assigned to others behaved in such a manner as to suggest (though nothing was actually said) that she was considering resignation. Her work consists of keypunching, typing, and filing. Should her supervisor:*

❑ *Discharge her.*
❑ *Indicate to her that her work has been satisfactory but hint that she may be laid off.*
❑ *Offer her a six-week leave of absence (without pay) during which she may obtain further training.*
❑ *Threaten her with a disciplinary fine.*
❑ *Assign her to assist one of the older women.*
❑ *Ask the advice of the other members of his Leadership group, following it only if he agrees the group has reached a correct decision in this case.*
❑ *Reassign her to small-parts assembly.*

*NOTE: QUESTIONS CONCERNING THIS SAMPLE LEADER-SHIP PROBLEM SHOULD BE ADDRESSED TO ERIC FAIRCHILD—EX 8173.*

After reading the problem through twice, Forlesen picked up his telephone and dialed the number. A female voice said, "Mr. Fairchild's office."

Forlesen identified himself, and a moment later a masculine voice announced, "Eric Fairchild."

"It's about the leadership problem—number one oh five?"

"Oh, yes." (Fairchild's voice was hearty; Forlesen imagined him slapping backs and challenging people to Indian-wrestle at parties.) "I've had quite a few calls about that one. You can check as many answers as you like if they're not mutually exclusive—okay?"

"That wasn't what I was going to ask," Forlesen said. "This girl's work—"

"Wait a minute," Fairchild said. And then, much more faintly, "Get me the Leadership file, Miss Fenton."

"What did you say?" Forlesen asked.

"Wait a minute," Fairchild said again. "If we're going to dig into this thing in depth I want to have a copy of the problem in front of me. Thank you. Okay, you can shoot now. What did you say your name was?"

"Forlesen. I meant after you said, 'Wait a minute,' the first time. I thought I heard you call your secretary Miss Fenton."

"Ha ha ha."

"Didn't you?"

"My secretary's name is Mrs. Fairchild, Mr. Forlesen—no, she's not my wife, if that's what you're thinking. Mr. Frick doesn't approve of nepotism. She's just a nice lady who happens to be named Mrs. Fairchild, and I was addressing Miss Fetton, who is filling in for her today."

"Sorry," Forlesen said.

"You wanted to ask about problem one hundred and five?"

"Yes, I wanted to ask— Well, for one thing, in what way is the young woman's work unsatisfactory?"

"Just what it says on the sheet, whatever that is. Wait a minute; here it is. *Her work has not been satisfactory, but because clerical help has been in short supply she has not been told this.*"

"Yes," Forlesen said, "but in what way has it been unsatisfactory?"

"I see what you're getting at now, but I can't very well answer that, can I? After all, the whole essence of Leadership Training involves presenting the participants with structured problems—you see what I mean? This is a structured problem. Miss Fenton, could I trouble you to go down to the canteen and get me some coffee? Take it out of petty cash. Now if I explained something like that to you, and not to the others, then it would have a different structuring for you than for them. You see?"

"Well, it seemed to me," Forlesen said, "that one of the first things to do would be to take Miss Fenton aside and explain to her that her work *was* unsatisfactory and perhaps hear what she had to say."

"Miss who?"

"Fetton, the girl in the problem."

"Right, and I see what you mean. However, since it specifically says what I read to you, and nothing else more than that, then if I was to tell you something else it would be structured different for you than for the other fellows. See what I mean?"

After thinking for a moment Forlesen said, "I don't see how I can check any of the boxes knowing no more than I do now. Is it all right if I write my own solution?"

"You mean, draw a little box for yourself?"

"Yes, and write what I said after it—I mean, what I outlined to you a minute ago. That I'd talk to her."

"I don't think there's room on the paper for all that, fella. I mean, you said quite a bit."

Forlesen said, "I think I can boil it down."

"Well, we can't allow it anyway. These things are scored by a computer and we have to give it an answer—what I'm driving at is the number of your answer. Like the girl codes in the I.D. number of each participant and then the problem number, and then the answer number, like *one* or *two* or *three*. Or then if she puts like twenty-*three* it knows you answered *two* AND *three*. That would be *indicate to her that her work has been satisfactory but hint that she may be laid off*, and *Offer her a six-week leave of absence without pay—during which she may obtain further train-ing.* "You get it?"

"You're telling me that that's the right answer," Forlesen said. "Twenty-three."

"Listen, hell no! *I* don't know what the right answer is; only the machine does. Maybe there isn't any right answer at all. I was just trying to give you a kind of a hint—what I'd do if I was in your shoes. You want to get a good grade, don't you?"

"Is it important?"

"I would say that it's important. I think it's important to any man to know he did something like this and he did good—wouldn't you say so? But like we said at the start of the course, your grade is your personal thing. We're going to give grades, sure, on a scale of seven hundred and fifty-seven—that's the top—to forty-nine, but nobody knows your grade but you. You're told your own grade and your class standing and your standing among everybody here who's ever taken the course—naturally that doesn't mean much; the problems change all the time—but what you do with that information is up to you. You evaluate yourself. I know there have been these rumors about Mr. Frick coming in and asking the computer questions, but it's not true—frankly, I don't think Mr. Frick even knows how to program. It doesn't just talk to you, you know."

"I didn't get to attend the first part of the course," Forlesen said. "I'm filling in for Cappy Dillingham. He died."

"Sorry to hear that. Old age, I guess."

"I don't know."

"Probably that was it. Hell, it seems like it was only yesterday I was talking to him about his grade after class—he had some question about one oh four; I don't even remember what it was now. Old Cappy. Wow."

"How was he doing?" Forlesen asked.

"Not too hot. I had him figured for about a five-fifty, give or take twenty—but listen, if you had seen the earlier stuff you wouldn't be asking these questions now. You'd of been guided into it—see what I mean?"

Forlesen said, "I just don't see how I can mark this. I'm going to return the unmarked sheet under protest."

"I told you, we can't score something like that."

Forlesen said, "Well, that's what I'm going to do," and hung up.

His desk said, "You're a sharp one, aren't you? He's going to call you back."

Forlesen looked for the speaker but could not find it.

"I heard you talking to Franklin too, and I saw you throw away the Manage-ment Responsibilities list. Do you know that in a lot of the offices here you find that framed and hung on the wall? Some of them hang it where they can see it, and some of them hang it where their visitors can see it."

"Which kind gets promoted?" Forlesen asked. He had decided the speaker was under the center desk drawer, and was on his hands and knees looking for it.

"The kind that fit in," the desk said.

Forlesen said, "What kind of an answer is that?" The telephone rang and he answered it.

"Mr. Forlesen, please." It was Fairchild.

"Speaking."

"I was wondering about number one oh five—have you sent it back yet?"

"I just put it in my out-box," Forlesen said. "They haven't picked it up yet." Vaguely he wondered if Miss Fawn was supposed to empty the out-box, or if anyone was; perhaps he was supposed to do it himself.

"Good, good. Listen, I've been thinking about what you said—do you think that if I told you what was wrong with this girl you'd be able to size her up better? The thing is, she just doesn't fit in; you know what I mean?"

"No," Forlesen said.

"Let me give you an example. Guys come in the office all the time, either to talk to me or just because they haven't anything better to do. They kid around with the girls, you know? Okay, this girl, you never know how she's going to take it. Sometimes she gets mad. Sometimes she thinks the guy really wants to get romantic, and she wants to go along with it."

"I'd think they'd learn to leave her alone," Forlesen said.

"Believe me, they have. And the other girls don't like her—they come in to me and say they want to be moved away from her desk."

"Do they say why?"

"Oh, hell, no. Listen, if you'd ever bossed a bunch of women you'd know better than that; the way they always put it is the light isn't good there, or it's too close to the keypunch—too noisy—or it's too *far* from the keypunch and they don't wanna have to walk that far, or they want to be closer to somebody they *do* like. But you know how it is—I've moved her all around the damn office and everybody wants to get away; she's Typhoid Mary."

"Make her your permanent secretary," Forlesen said.

*"What?"*

"Just for a while. Give your mother a special assignment. That way you can find out what's wrong with this girl, if anything is, which I doubt."

"You're crazy, Forlesen," Fairchild said, and hung up.

The telephone rang again almost as soon as Forlesen set the receiver down. "This is Miss Fawn," the telephone said. "Mr. Freeling wants to see you, Mr. Forlesen."

"Mr. Freeling?"

"Mr. Freeling is Mr. Fields's chief, Mr. Forlesen, and Mr. Fields is your chief. Mr. Freeling reports to Mr. Flint, and Mr. Flint reports directly to Mr. Frick. I am Mr. Freeling's secretary."

"Thank you," Forlesen said. "I was beginning to wonder where you fit in."

"Right out of your office, down the hall to the 'T,' left, up the stairs, and along the front of the building. Mr. Freeling's name is on the door."

"Thank you," Forlesen said again.

Mr. Freeling's name was on the door, in the form of a bronzelike plaque. Forlesen, remembering D'Andrea's brass one, saw at once that Mr. Freeling's was more modern and up-to-date, and realized that Mr. Freeling was more important than D'Andrea had been; but he also realized that D'Andrea's plaque had been real brass and that Mr. Freeling's was plastic. He knocked, and Miss Fawn's voice called, "Come in." He came in, and Miss Fawn threw a switch on her desk and said, "Mr. Forlesen to see you, Mr. Freeling."

And then to Forlesen: "Go right in."

Mr. Freeling's office was large and had two windows, both overlooking the highway. Forlesen found that he was somewhat surprised to see the highway again, though it looked just as it had before. The pictures on the walls were landscapes much like Fields's, but Mr. Freeling's desk, which was quite large, was covered by a sheet of glass with photographs under it, and these were all of sailboats, and of groups of men in shorts and striped knit shirts and peaked caps.

"Sit down," Mr. Freeling said. "Be with you in a minute." He was a large, sunburned, squinting man, beginning to go gray. The chair in front of his desk had wooden arms and a vinyl seat made to look like ostrich hide. Forlesen sat down, wondering what Mr. Freeling wanted, and after a time it came to him that what Mr. Freeling wanted was for him to wonder this, and that Mr. Freeling would have been wiser to speak to him sooner. Mr. Freeling had a pen in his hand and was reading a letter—the same letter—over and over; at last he signed it with a scribble and laid it and the pen flat on his desk. "I should have called you in earlier to say welcome aboard," he said, "but maybe it was better to give you a chance to drop your hook and get your jib in first. Are you finding M.P.P. a snug harbor?"

"I think I would like it better," Forlesen said, "if I knew what it was I'm supposed to be doing here."

Freeling laughed. "Well, that's easily fixed—Bert Fields is standing watch with you, isn't he? Ask him for a list of your responsibilities."

"It's Ed Fields," Forlesen said, "and I already have the list. What I would like to know is what I'm supposed to be doing."

"I see what you mean," Freeling said, "but I'm afraid I can't tell you. If you were a lathe operator I'd say, 'Make that part,' but you're a part of management, and you can't treat managerial people that way."

"Go ahead," Forlesen told him. "I won't mind."

Freeling cleared his throat. "That isn't what I meant, and, quite frankly, if you think anyone here is going to feel any compulsion to be polite to you, you're in for squalls. What I meant was that if I knew what you ought to be doing I'd hire a clerk to do it. You're where you are because we feel—rightly or wrongly— that you can find your own work, recognize it when you see it, and do it or get somebody else to. Just make damn sure you don't step on anybody's toes while you're doing it, and don't make more trouble than you fix. Don't rock the boat."

"I see," Forlesen said.

"Just make damn sure before you do anything that it's in line with policy, and remember that if you get the unions down on us we're going to throw you overboard quick."

Forlesen nodded.

"And keep your hand off the tiller. Look at it this way—your job is fixing leaks. Only the sailor who's spent most of his life down there in the hold with the oakum and . . . uh . . . Fastpatch has the experience necessary to recognize the landmarks and weather signs. But don't you patch a leak somebody else is already patching, or has been told to patch, or is getting ready to patch. Understand? Don't come running to me with complaints, and don't let me get any complaints about you. Now what was it you wanted to see me about?"

"I don't," Forlesen said. "You said you wanted to see me."

"Oh. Well, I'm through."

Outside Forlesen asked Miss Fawn how he was supposed to know what company policy was. "It's in the air," Miss Fawn said tartly. "You breathe it." Forlesen suggested that it might be useful if it were written down someplace, and she said, "You've been here long enough to know better than that, Mr. Forlesen; you're no kid anymore." As he left the office she called, "Don't forget your Creativity Group."

He found the drilling room only after a great deal of difficulty. It was full of drill presses and jig bores—perhaps thirty or more—of which only two were being used. At one, a white-haired man was making a hole in a steel plate; he worked slowly, lifting the drill from time to time to fill the cavity with oil from a squirt can beside the machine. At the other a much younger man sang as he worked, an obscene parody of a popular song. Forlesen was about to ask if he knew where the Creativity Group was meeting when he felt a hand on his shoulder. He turned and saw Fields, who said, "Looks like you found it. Come on; I'm going to make this one come hell or high water. Right through the door on the other side there."

They threaded their way through the drill presses, most of which seemed to be out of order in some way, and were about to go through the door Fields had indicated when Forlesen heard a yell behind them. The younger man had burned his hand in trying to change the smoking drill in his machine. "That's a good operator," Fields said. "He pushes everything right along—you know what I mean?" Forlesen said he did.

The creativity meeting, as Franklin had told him, was in the corridor. Folding metal chairs had been set up in groupings that looked intentionally disorganized, and a small motion picture screen stood on an easel. Franklin was wrestling with a projector resting (pretty precariously, Forlesen thought) on the seat of the rearmost chair; he had the look of not being as young as he seemed, and after he had introduced himself they sat down and watched him. From time to time others joined them, and people passing up and down the hall, mostly men in gray work clothing, ignored them all, threading their way among the tin chairs without seeming to see them and stepping skillfully around the screen, from which, from time to time, flashed faint numerals 1, 2, and 3, or the legend:

## Creativity Means Jobs

After a while Fields said, "I think we ought to get started."

"You go ahead," Franklin told him. "I'll have this going in a minute."

Fields walked to the front of the group, beside the screen, and said "Creativity Group Twenty-one is now in session. I'm going to ask the man in front to write his name on a piece of paper and pass it back. Everybody sign, and do it so we can read it, please. We're going to have a movie on creativity—"

"*Creativity Means Jobs,*" Franklin put in.

"Yeah, *Creativity Means Jobs,* then a free-form critique of the movie. Then what, Ned?"

"Open discussion on creativity in problem study."

"You got the movie yet?"

"Just a minute."

Forlesen looked at his watch. It was 078.45.

Someone at the front of the group, close to where Fields was now standing, said, "While we have a minute I'd like to get an objection on record to this phrase 'creativity in problem study.' It seems to me that what it implies is that creativity is automatically going to point you toward some solution you didn't see before, and I feel that anyone who believes that's going to happen—anyway, in most cases—doesn't know what the hell they're talking about."

Fields said, "Everybody knows creativity isn't going to solve your problems for you."

"I said point the way," the man objected.

Someone else said, "What creativity is going to do for you in the way of problem study is point the way to new ways of seeing your problem."

"Not necessarily successful," the first man said.

"Not necessarily successful," the second man said, "if by *successful* what you mean is permitting you to make a nontrivial elaboration of the problem definition."

Someone else said, "Personally, I feel problem definitions don't limit creativity," and Fields said, "I think we're all agreed on that when they're *creative* problem definitions. Right, Ned?"

"Of creative problems."

"Right, of creative problems. You know, Ned told me one time when he was talking to somebody about what we do at these meetings this fellow said he thought we'd just each take a lump of clay or something and, you know, start trying to make some kind of shape." There was laughter, and Fields held up a hand good-naturedly. "Okay, it's funny, but I think we can all learn something from that. What we can learn is, most people when we talk about our Creativity Group are thinking the same way this guy was, and that's why when we talk about it we got to make certain points, like for one thing creativity isn't ever what you do alone, right? It's your creative *group* that gets things going— Hey, Ned, what's the word I want?"

"*Synergy.*"

"Yeah, and teamwork. And second, creativity isn't about making new things—like some statue or something nobody wants. What creativity is about is solving company problems—"

Franklin called, "Hey, I've got this ready now."

"Just a minute. Like you take the problem this company had when Adam Bean that founded it died. The problem was—should we go on making what we used to when he was alive, or should we make something different? That problem was solved by Mr. Dudley, as I guess everybody knows, but he wouldn't have been able to do it without a lot of good men to help him. I personally feel that a football team is about the most creative thing there is."

Someone brushed Forlesen's sleeve; it was Miss Fawn, and as Fields paused, she said in her rather shrill voice, "Mr. Fields! Mr. Fields, you're wanted on the telephone. It's quite important." There was something stilted in the way she delivered her lines, like a poor actress, and after a moment Forlesen realized that there was no telephone call, that she had been instructed by Fields to provide this interruption and thus give him an excuse for escaping the meeting while increasing the other participants' estimate of his importance. After a moment more he understood that Franklin and the others knew this as well as he, and that the admiration they felt for Fields—and admiration was certainly there, surrounding the stocky man as he followed Miss Fawn out—had its root in the daring Fields had shown, and in the power implied by his securing the cooperation of Miss Fawn, Mr. Freeling's secretary.

Someone had dimmed the lights. "CREATIVITY MEANS JOBS" flashed on the screen, then a group of men and women in what might have been a schoolroom in a very exclusive school. One waved his hand, stood up, and spoke. There was no sound, but his eyes flashed with enthusiasm; when he sat down, an impressive-looking woman in tweeds rose, and Forlesen felt that whatever she was saying must be unanswerable, the final word on the subject under discussion; she was polite and restrained and as firm as iron, and she clearly had every fact at her fingertips.

"I can't get this damn sound working," Franklin said. "Just a minute."

"What are they talking about?" Forlesen asked.

"Huh?"

"In the picture. What are they discussing?"

"Oh, I got it," Franklin said. "Wait a minute. They're talking about promoting creativity in the educational system."

"Are they teachers?"

"No, they're actors—let me alone for a minute, will you? I want to get this sound going."

The sound came on, almost coinciding with the end of the picture; while Franklin was rewinding the film Forlesen said, "I suppose actors would have a better understanding of creativity than teachers would at that."

"It's a re-creation of an actual meeting of real teachers," Franklin explained. "They photographed it and taped it, then had the actors reproduce the debate."

Forlesen decided to go home for lunch. Lunch ours were 120 to 141—twenty-one ours should be enough, he thought, for him to drive there and return, and to eat. He kept the pedal down all the way, and discovered that the signs with HIDDEN DRIVES on their faces had SLOW CHILDREN on their backs.

The brick house was just as he remembered it. He parked the car on the spot where he had first seen it (there was a black oil stain there) and knocked at the door. Edna answered it, looking not quite as he remembered her. "What do you want?" she said.

"Lunch."

"Are you crazy? If you're selling something, we don't want it."

Forlesen said, "Don't you know who I am?"

She looked at him more closely. He said, "I'm your husband, Emanuel."

She seemed uncertain, then smiled, kissed him, and said, "Yes you are, aren't you. You look different. Tired."

"I am tired," he said, and realized that it was true.

"Is it lunchtime already? I don't have a watch, you know. I haven't been able to keep track. I thought it was only the middle of the morning."

"It seemed long enough to me," Forlesen said. He wondered where the children were, thinking that he would have liked to see them.

"What do you want for lunch?"

"Whatever you have."

In the bedroom she got out bread and sliced meat, and plugged in the coffeepot. "How was work?"

"All right. Fine."

"Did you get promoted? Or get a raise?"

He shook his head.

"After lunch," she said. "You'll get promoted after lunch."

He laughed, thinking that she was joking.

"A woman knows."

"Where are the kids?"

"At school. They eat their lunch at school. There's a beautiful cafeteria—everything is stainless steel—and they have a dietician who thinks about the best possible lunch for each child and makes them eat it."

"Did you see it?" he asked.

"No, I read about it. In here." She tapped *Food Preparation in the Home*.

"Oh."

"They'll be home at one hundred and thirty—that's what the book says. Here's your sandwich." She poured him a cup of coffee. "What time is it now?"

He looked at the watch she had given him. "A hundred and twenty-nine thirty."

"Eat. You ought to be going back soon."

He said, "I was hoping we might have time for more than this."

"Tonight, maybe. You don't want to be late."

"All right." The coffee was good, but tasted slightly oily; the sandwich meat, salty and dry and flavorless. He unstrapped the watch from his wrist and handed it to her. "You keep this," he said. "I've felt badly about wearing it all morning—it really belongs to you."

"You need it more than I do," she said.

"No I don't; they have clocks all over, there. All I have to do is look at them."

"You'll be late getting back to work."

"I'm going to drive as fast as I can anyway—I can't go any faster than that no matter what a watch says. Besides, there's a speaker that tells me things, and I'm sure it will tell me if I'm late."

Reluctantly she accepted the watch. He chewed the last of his sandwich. "You'll have to tell me when to go now," he said, thinking that this would somehow cheer her.

"It's time to go already," she said.

"Wait a minute—I want to finish my coffee."

"How was work?"

"Fine," he said.

"You have a lot to do there?"

"Oh, God, yes." He remembered the crowded desk that had been waiting for him when he had returned from the creativity meeting, the supervision of workers for whom he had been given responsibility without authority, the ours spent with Fields drawing up the plan which, just before he left, had been vetoed by Mr. Freeling. "I don't think there's any purpose in most of it," he said, "but there's plenty to do."

"You shouldn't talk like that," his wife said. "You'll lose your job."

"I don't, when I'm there."

"I've got nothing to do," she said. It was as though the words themselves had forced their way from between her lips.

He said, "That can't be true."

"I made the beds, and I dusted and swept, and it was all finished a couple of ours after you had gone. There's nothing."

"You could read," he said.

"I can't—I'm too nervous."

"Well, you could have prepared a better lunch than this."

"That's *nothing*," she said. "Just *nothing*." She was suddenly angry, and it struck him, as he looked at her, that she was a stranger, that he knew Fields and Miss Fawn and even Mr. Freeling better than he knew her.

"The morning's over," he said. "I'm sorry I can't give it back to you, but I can't; what I did—that was nothing too."

"Please," she said, "won't you go? Having you here makes me so nervous."

He said, "Try and find something to do."

"All right."

He wiped his mouth on the paper she had given him and took a step toward the parlor; to his surprise she walked with him, not detaining him, but seeming to savor his company now that she had deprived herself of it. "Do you remember when we woke up?" she said. "You didn't know at first that you were supposed to dress yourself."

"I'm still not sure of it."

"Oh, you know what I mean."

"Yes," he said, and he knew that he did, but that she did not.

The signs said: NO TURN, and Forlesen wondered if he was really compelled to obey them, if the man in the blue car would come after him if he did not go back to Model Pattern Products. He suspected that the man would, but that nothing he could do would be worse than M.P.P. itself. In front of the dog-food factory a shapeless brown object fluttered in the road, animated by the turbulence of each car that passed and seeming to attack it, throwing itself with desperate, toothless courage at the singing, invulnerable tires. He had almost run over it before he realized what it was—Abraham Beale's hat.

The parking lot was more rutted than he had remembered; he drove slowly and carefully. The outbuilding had been torn down, and another car, startlingly shiny (Forlesen did not believe his own had ever been that well polished, not even when he had first looked out the window at it), had his old place; he was forced to take another, farther from the plant. Several other people, he noticed, seemed to have gone home for lunch as he had—some he knew, having shared meeting rooms with them. He had never punched out on the beige clock, and did not punch in.

There was a boy seated at his desk, piling new schoolbooks on it from a cardboard box on the floor. Forlesen said hello, and the boy said that his name was George Howe, and that he worked in Mr. Forlesen's section.

Forlesen nodded, feeling that he understood. "Miss Fawn showed you to your desk?"

The boy shook his head in bewilderment. "A lady named Mrs. Frost—she said she was Mr. Freeling's secretary; she had glasses."

"And a sharp nose."

George Howe nodded.

Forlesen nodded in reply, and made his way to Fields's old office. As he had expected, Fields was gone, and most of the items from his own desk had made their way to Fields's—he wondered if Fields's desk sometimes talked too, but before he could ask it Miss Fawn came in.

She wore two new rings and touched her hair often with her left hand to show them. Forlesen tried to imagine her pregnant or giving suck and found that he could not, but knew that this was a weakness in himself and not in her. "Ready for orientation?" Miss Fawn asked.

Forlesen ignored the question and asked what had happened to Fields.

"He passed on," Miss Fawn said.

"You mean he died? He seemed too young for it; not much older than I am myself—certainly not as old as Mr. Freeling."

"He was stout," Miss Fawn said with a touch of righteous disdain. "He didn't get much exercise and he smoked a great deal."

"He worked very hard," Forlesen said. "I don't think he could have had much energy left for exercise."

"I suppose not," Miss Fawn conceded. She was leaning against the door, her left hand toying with the gold pencil she wore on a chain, and seemed to be signaling by her attitude that they were old friends, entitled to relax occasionally from the formality of business. "There was a thing—at one time—between Mr. Fields and myself. I don't suppose you ever knew it."

"No, I didn't," Forlesen said, and Miss Fawn looked pleased.

"Eddie and I—I called him Eddie, privately—were quite discreet. Or so I flatter myself now. I don't mean, of course, that there was ever anything improper between us."

"Naturally not."

"A look and a few words. Elmer knows; I told him everything. You are ready to give that orientation, aren't you?"

"I think I am now," Forlesen said. "George Howe?"

Miss Fawn looked at a piece of paper. "No, Gordie Hilbert."

As she was leaving, Forlesen asked impulsively where Fields was.

"Where he is buried, you mean? Right behind you."

He looked at her blankly.

"There." She gestured toward the picture behind Forlesen's desk. "There's a vault behind there—didn't you know? Just a small one, of course; they're cremated first."

"Burned out."

"Yes, burned up and then they put them behind the pictures—that's what they're for. The pictures, I mean. In a beautiful little cruet. It's a company benefit, and you'd know if you'd read your own orientation material—of course, you can be buried at home if you like."

"I think I'd prefer that," Forlesen said.

"I thought so," Miss Fawn told him. "You look the type. Anyway, Eddie bought the farm—that's an expression the men have."

At 125 hours Forlesen was notified of his interdepartmental training transfer. His route to his new desk took him through the main lobby of the building, where he observed that a large medallion set into the floor bore the face (too solemn, but quite unmistakable) of Abraham Beale, though the name beneath it was that of Adam Bean, the founder of the company. Since he was accompanied by his chief-to-be, Mr. Fleer, he made no remark.

"It's going to be a pleasure going down the fast slope with you," Mr. Fleer said. "I trust you've got your wax ready and your boots laced."

"My wax is ready and my boots are laced," Forlesen said; it was automatic by now.

"But not too tight—wouldn't want to break a leg."

"But not too tight," Forlesen agreed. "What do we do in this division?"

Mr. Fleer smiled and Forlesen could see that he had asked a good question. "Right now we're right in the middle of a very successful crash program to develop a hard-nosed understanding of the ins and outs of the real, realistic business world," Mr. Fleer said, "with particular emphasis on marketing, finance, corporate developmental strategy, and risk appreciation. We've been playing a lot of Bet-Your-Life, the management-managing real-life pseudogame."

"Great," Forlesen said enthusiastically; he really felt enthusiastic, having been afraid that it would be more creativity.

"We're in the center of the run," Mr. Fleer assured him, "the snow is fast, and the wind is in our faces."

Forlesen was tempted to comment that his boots were laced and his wax ready, but he contented himself at the last moment with nodding appreciatively and asking if he would get to play.

"You certainly will," Mr. Fleer promised him. "You'll be holding down Ffoulks's chair. It's an interesting position—he's heavily committed to a line of plastic toys, but he has some military contracts for field rations and biological weapons to back him up. Also he's big in aquarium supplies—that's quite a small market altogether, but Ffoulks is big in it, if you get what I mean."

"I can hardly wait to start," Forlesen said. "I have a feeling that this may be the age of aquariums." Fleer pondered this while they trudged up the stairs.

Bet-Your-Life, the management-managing real-life pseudogame, was played on a very large board laid out on a very big table in a very large meeting room. Scattered all over the board were markers and spinners and decks of cards, and birdcages holding eight- and twelve-sided dice. Scattered around the room, in chairs, were the players: two were arguing and one was asleep; five others were studying the board or making notes, or working out calculations on small hand-held machines that were something like abacuses and something like cash registers. "I'll just give you the rule book, and have a look at my own stuff, and go,"

Mr. Fleer said. "I'm late for the meeting now." He took a brown pamphlet from a pile in one corner of the room and handed it to Forlesen, who (with some feeling of surprise) noticed that it was identical to one of the booklets he had found under his job assignment sheet upon awakening.

Mr. Fleer had scrawled a note on a small tablet marked with the Bet-Your-Life emblem. He tore the sheet off as Forlesen watched, and laid it in an empty square near the center of the board. It read: "BID 17 ASK 18 1/4 SNOWMOBILE 5 1/2 UP 1/2 OPEN NEW TERRITORY SHUT DOWN COAL OIL SHOES FLEER." He left the room, and Forlesen, timing the remark in such a way that it might be supposed that he thought Mr. Fleer out of earshot, said, "I'll bet he's a strong player."

The man to his left, to whom the remark was nominally addressed, shook his head. "He's overbought in sporting goods."

"Sporting goods seem like a good investment to me," Forlesen said. "Of course I don't know the game."

"Well, you won't learn it reading that thing—it'll only mix you up. The basic rule to remember is that no one has to move, but that anyone can move at any time if he wants to. Fleer hasn't been here for ten ours—now he's moved."

"On the other hand," a man in a red jacket said, "this part of the building is kept open at all times, and coffee and sandwiches are brought in every our—some people never leave. I'm the referee."

A man with a bristling mustache, who had been arguing with the man in the red jacket a moment before, interjected, "The rules can be changed whenever a quorum agrees—we pull the staple out of the middle of the book, type up a new page, and slip it in. A quorum is three-quarters of the players present but never seven or less."

Forlesen said hesitantly, "It's not likely three-quarters of those present would be seven, is it?"

"No, it isn't," the referee agreed. "We rarely have that many."

The man with the mustache said, "You'd better look over your holdings."

Forlesen did so, and discovered that he held 100 percent of the stock of a company called International Toys and Foods. He wrote: "BID 34 ASK 32 FFOULKS" on a slip and placed it in the center of the board. "You'll never get thirty-two for that stuff," the man with the mustache said. "It isn't worth near that."

Forlesen pointed out that he had an offer to buy in at thirty-four but was finding no takers. The man with the mustache looked puzzled, and Forlesen used the time he had gained to examine the brown pamphlet. Opening it at random he read:

> "We're a team," Fields continued, "and we're going to function as a team. That doesn't mean that there isn't a quarterback, and a coach"—he pointed toward the ceiling—"up there. It does mean that I expect every man to bat two fifty or better, and the ones that don't make three hundred had better be damn good Fields. See what I mean?"

"I buy five hundred, and I'm selling them to you."

*Forlesen nodded again and asked, "What does our subdivision do? What's our function?"*

"I said I'm going to buy five hundred shares and then I'm going to sell them back to you."

"Not so fast," Forlesen said. "You don't own any yet."

"Well, I'm buying." The man with the mustache rummaged among his playing materials and produced some bits of colored paper. Forlesen accepted the money and began to count it.

The man with the red jacket said: "Coffee. And sandwiches. Spam and Churkey." The man with the mustache went over to get one, and Forlesen went out the door.

The corridor was deserted. There had been a feeling of airlessness in the game room, an atmosphere compounded of stale sweat and smoke and the cold, oily coffee left to stagnate in the bottom of the paper hot cups; the corridor was glacial by comparison, filled with quiet wind and the memory of ice. Forlesen stopped outside the door to savor it for a second, and was joined by the man with the mustache, munching a sandwich. "Nice to get out here for a minute, isn't it?" he said.

Forlesen nodded.

"Not that I don't enjoy the game," the man with the mustache continued. "I do. I'm in Sales, you know."

"I didn't. I thought everyone was from our division."

"Oh, no. There's several of us Sales guys, and some Advertising guys. Brought in to sharpen you up. That's what *we* say."

"I'm sure we can use some sharpening."

"Well, anyway, I like it—this wheeling and dealing. You know what Sales is—you put pressure on the grocers. Tell them if they don't stock the new items they're going to get slow deliveries on the standard stuff, going to lose their discount. A guy doesn't learn much financial management that way."

"Enough," Forlesen said.

"Yeah, I guess so." The man with the mustache swallowed the remainder of his sandwich. "Listen, I got to be going; I'm about to clip some guy in there."

Forlesen said, "Good luck," and walked away, hearing the door to the game room open and close behind him. He went past a number of offices, looking for his own, and up two flights of steps before he found someone who looked as though she could direct him, a sharp-nosed woman who wore glasses.

"You're looking at me funny," the sharp-nosed woman said. She smiled with something of the expression of a blindfolded schoolteacher who has been made to bite a lemon at a Halloween party.

"You remind me a great deal of someone I know," Forlesen said, "Mrs. Frost." As a matter of fact, the woman looked exactly like Miss Fawn.

The woman's smile grew somewhat warmer. "Everyone says that. Actually we're cousins—I'm Miss Fedd."

"Say something else."

"Do I talk like her too?"

"No. I think I recognize your voice. This is going to sound rather silly, but when I came here—in the morning, I mean—my car talked to me. I hadn't thought of it as a female voice, but it sounded just like you."

"It's quite possible," Miss Fedd said. "I used to be in Traffic, and I still fill in there at times."

"I never thought I'd meet you. I was the one who stopped and got out of his car."

"A lot of them do, but usually only once. What's that you're carrying?"

"This?" Forlesen held up the brown book; his finger was still thrust between the pages. "A book. I'm afraid to read the ending."

"It's the red book you're supposed to be afraid to read the end of," Miss Fedd told him. "It's the opposite of a mystery—everyone stops before the revelations."

"I haven't even read the beginning of that one," Forlesen said. "Come to think of it, I haven't read the beginning of this one either."

"We're not supposed to talk about books here, not even when we haven't anything to do. What was it you wanted?"

"I've just been transferred into the division, and I was hoping you'd help me find my desk."

"What's your name?"

"Forlesen. Emanuel Forlesen."

"Good. I was looking for you—you weren't at your desk."

"No, I wasn't," Forlesen said. "I was in the Bet-Your-Life room—well, not recently."

"I know. I looked there too. Mr. Frick wants to see you."

"Mr. Frick?"

"Yes. He said to tell you he was planning to do this a bit later today, but he's got to leave the office a little early. Come on."

Miss Fedd walked with short, mincing steps, but so rapidly that Forlesen was forced to trot to keep up. "Why does Mr. Frick want to see me?" He thought of the way he had cheated the man with the mustache, of the time he had baited Fairchild on the telephone, of other things.

"I'm not supposed to tell," Miss Fedd said. "This is Mr. Frick's door."

"I know," Forlesen told her. It was a large door—larger than the other doors in the building—and not painted to resemble metal. Mr. Frick's plaque was of silver (or perhaps platinum), and had the single word *Frick* engraved in an almost too-tasteful script. A man Forlesen did not know walked past them as they stood before Mr. Frick's tasteful plaque; the man wore a hat and carried a briefcase, and had a coat slung over his arm.

"We're emptying out a little already," Miss Fedd said. "I'd go right in now if I were you—I think he wants to play golf before he goes home."

"Aren't you going in with me?"

"Of course not—he's got a group in there already, and I have things to do. Don't knock; just go in."

Forlesen opened the door. The room was very large and crowded; men in expensive suits stood smoking, holding drinks, knocking out their pipes in bronze ashtrays. The tables and the desk—*yes,* he told himself, *there is a desk,* a very large desk next to the window at one end, a desk shaped like the lid of a grand piano—the tables and the desk all of dark heavy tropical wood, the tables and the desk all littered with bronze trophies so that the whole room seemed of bronze and black wood and red wool. Several of the men looked at him, then toward the opposite end of the room, and he knew at once who Mr. Frick was: a bald man standing with his back to the room, rather heavy, Forlesen thought, and somewhat below average height. He made his way through the smokers and drink holders. "I'm Emanuel Forlesen."

"Oh, there you are." Mr. Frick turned around. "Ernie Frick, Forlesen." Mr. Frick had a wide, plump face, a mole over one eyebrow, and a gold tooth. Forlesen felt that he had seen him before.

"We went to grade school together," Mr. Frick said. "I bet you don't remember me, do you?"

Forlesen shook his head.

"Well, I'll be honest—I don't think I would have remembered you; but I looked up your file while we were getting set for the ceremony. And now that I see you, by gosh, I do remember—I played prisoner's base with you one day; you used to be able to run like anything."

"I wonder where I lost it," Forlesen said. Mr. Frick and several of the men standing around him laughed, but Forlesen was thinking that he could not possibly be as old as Mr. Frick.

"Say, that's pretty good. You know, we must have started at about the same time. Well, some of us go up and some don't, and I suppose you envy me, but let me tell you I envy you. It's lonely at the top, the work is hard, and you can never set down the responsibility for a minute. You won't believe it, but you've had the best of it."

"I don't," Forlesen said.

"Well, anyway, I'm tired—we're all tired. Let's get this over with so we can all go home." Mr. Frick raised his voice to address the room at large. "Gentlemen, I asked you to come here because you have all been associated at one time or another, in one way or another, with this gentleman here, Mr. Forlesen, to whom I am very happy to present this token of his colleagues' regard."

Someone handed Mr. Frick a box, and he handed it to Forlesen, who opened it while everyone clapped. It was a watch. "I didn't know it was so late," Forlesen said.

Several people laughed; they were already filing out.

"You've been playing Bet-Your-Life, haven't you?" Mr. Frick said. "A fellow can spend more time at that than he thinks."

Forlesen nodded.

"Say, why don't you take the rest of the day off? There's not much of it left anyhow."

Outside, others, who presumably had not been given the remainder of the day off by Mr. Frick, were straggling toward their cars. As Forlesen walked toward his, feeling as he did the stiffness and the pain in his legs, a bright, new car pulled onto the lot and a couple got out, the man a fresh-faced boy, really, the girl a working-class girl, meticulously made up and dressed, cheaply attractive and forlorn, like the models in the advertisements of third-rate dress shops. They went up the sidewalk hand in hand to kiss, Forlesen felt sure, in the time clock room, and separate, she going up the steps, he down. They would meet for coffee later, both uncomfortable, out of a sense of duty, meet for lunch in the cafeteria, he charging her meal to the paycheck he had not yet received.

The yellow signs that lined the street read: YIELD; orange and black machines were eating the houses just beyond the light. Forlesen pulled his car into his driveway, over the oil spot. A small man in a dark suit was sitting on a wood and canvas folding stool beside Forlesen's door, a black bag at his feet; Forlesen spoke to him, but he did not answer. Forlesen shrugged and stepped inside.

A tall young man stood beside a long, angular object that rested on a sort of trestle in the center of the parlor. "Look what we've got for you," he said.

Forlesen looked. It was exactly like the box his watch had come in, save that it was much larger: of red-brown wood that seemed almost black, lined with pinkish-white silk.

"Want to try her out?" the young man said.

"No, I don't." Forlesen had already guessed who the young man must be, and after a moment he added a question: "Where's your mother?"

"Busy," the young man said. "You know how women are. . . . Well, to tell the truth she doesn't want to come in until it's over. This lid is neat—watch." He folded down half the lid. "Like a Dutch door." He folded it up again. "Don't you want to try it for size? I'm afraid it's going to be tight around the shoulders, but it's got a hell of a good engine."

"No," Forlesen said, "I don't want to try it out." Something about the pinkish silk disgusted him. He bent over it to examine it more closely, and the young man took him by the hips and lifted him in as though he were a child, closing the lower half of the lid; it reached to his shirt pockets and effectively pinioned his arms. "Ha, ha," Forlesen said.

The young man sniffed. "You don't think we'd bury you before you're dead, do you? I just wanted you to try it out, and that was the easiest way. How do you like it?"

"Get me out of this thing."

"In a minute. Is it comfortable? Is it a good fit? It's costing us quite a bit, you know."

"Actually," Forlesen said, "it's more comfortable than I had foreseen. The bottom is only thinly padded, but I find the firmness helps my back."

"Good, that's great. Now have you decided about the Explainer?"

"I don't know what you mean."

"Didn't you read your orientation? Everyone's entitled to an Explainer—in whatever form he chooses—at the end of his life. He—"

"It seems to me," Forlesen interrupted, "that it would be more useful at the beginning."

"—may be a novelist, aged loremaster, National Hero, warlock, or actor."

"None of those sounds quite right for me," Forlesen said.

"Or a theologian, philosopher, priest, or doctor."

"I don't think I like those either."

"Well, that's the end of the menu as far as I know," his son said. "I'll tell you what—I'll send him in and you can talk to him yourself; he's right outside."

"That little fellow in the dark suit?" Forlesen asked. His son, whose head was thrust out the door already, paid no attention.

After a moment the small man came in carrying his bag, and Forlesen's son placed a chair close to the coffin for him and went into the bedroom. "Well, what's it going to be," the small man asked, "or is it going to be nothing?"

"I don't know," Forlesen said. He was looking at the weave of the small man's suit, the intertwining of the innumerable threads, and realizing that they constituted the universe in themselves, that they were serpents and worms and roots, the black tracks of forgotten rockets across a dark sky, the sine waves of the radiation of the cosmos. "I wish I could talk to my wife."

"Your wife is dead," the small man said "The kid didn't want to tell you. We got her laid out in the next room. What'll it be? Doctor, priest, philosopher, theologian, actor, warlock, National Hero, aged loremaster, or novelist?"

"I don't know," Forlesen said again. "I want to feel, you know, that this box is a bed—and yet a ship, a ship that will set me free. And yet . . . it's been a strange life."

"You may have been oppressed by demons," the small man said. "Or revived by unseen aliens who, landing on the Earth eons after the death of the last man, have sought to re-create the life of the twentieth century. Or it may be that there is a small pressure, exerted by a tumor in your brain."

"Those are the explanations?" Forlesen asked.

"Those are some of them."

"I want to know if it's meant anything," Forlesen said. "If what I suffered—if it's been worth it."

"No," the little man said. "Yes. No. Yes. Yes. No. Yes. Yes. Maybe."

## AFTERWORD

There are men—I have known a good many—who work all their lives for the same *Fortune* 500 company. They have families to support, and no skills that will permit them to leave and support their families by other means in another place. Their work is of little value, because few, if any, assignments of value come to them. They spend an amazing amount of time trying to find something useful to do. And, failing that, just trying to look busy.

In time their lives end, as all lives do. As this world recons things they have spent eight thousand days, perhaps, at work; but in a clearer air it has all been the same day.

The story you have just read was my tribute to them.

# WESTWIND

*"...to all of you, my dearly loved fellow countrymen. And most particularly—as ever—to my eyes, Westwind."*

One wall of the steaming, stinking room began to waver, the magic portal that had opened upon a garden of almost inconceivable beauty beginning to mist and change. Fountains of marble waved like grass, and rose trees, whose flowery branches wore strands of pearl and diamond, faded to soft old valentines. The ruler's chair turned to bronze, then to umber, and the ruler himself, fatherly and cunning, wise and unknowable, underwent a succession of transformations, becoming at first a picture, then a poster, and at last a postage stamp.

The lame old woman who ran the place turned the wall off and several people protested. "You heard what he said," she told them. "You know your duty. Why do you have to listen to some simpleton from the Department of Truth say everything over in longer words and spread his spittle on it?"

The protestors, having registered their postures, were silent. The old woman looked at the clock behind the tiny bar she served.

"Game in twenty minutes," she said. "Folks will be coming in then, rain or no rain, wanting drinks. You want some, you better get them now."

Only two did: hulking, dirty men who might have been of any dishonest trade. A few people were already discussing the coming game. A few others talked about the address they had just heard—not its content, which could not have meant much to most of them, but the ruler and his garden, exchanging at hundredth hand bits of palace gossip of untold age. The door opened and the storm came in and a young man with it.

He was tall and thin. He wore a raincoat that had soaked through and an old felt hat covered with a transparent plastic protection whose elastic had forced the hat's splayed brim into a tight bell around his head. One side of the young man's face was a blue scar; the old woman asked him what he wanted.

"You have rooms," he said.

"Yes, we do. Very cheap too. You ought to wear something over that."

"If it bothers you," he said, "don't look at it."

"You think I've got to rent to you?" She looked around at her customers, lining up support, should the young man with the scar decide to resent her remarks. "All I've got to do if you complain is say we're full. You can walk to the police station then—it's twenty blocks—and maybe they'll let you sleep in a cell."

"I'd like a room and something to eat. What do you have?"

"Ham sandwich," she said. She named a price. "Your room—" She named another.

"All right," he said. "I'd like two sandwiches. And coffee."

"The room is only half if you share with somebody—if you want me to I can yell out and see if anybody wants to split."

"No."

She ripped the top from a can of coffee. The handle popped out and the contents began to steam. She gave it to him and said, "I guess they won't take you in the other places, huh? With that face."

He turned away from her, sipping his coffee, looking the room over. The door by which he had just entered (water still streamed from his coat and he could feel it in his shoes, sucking and gurgling with his every movement) opened again and a blind girl came in.

He saw that she was blind before he saw anything else about her. She wore black glasses, which on that impenetrable, rain-wracked night would have been clue enough, and as she entered she looked (in the second most terrible and truest sense) at Nothing.

The old woman asked, "Where did *you* come from?"

"From the terminal," the girl said. "I walked." She carried a white cane, which she swung before her as she sidled toward the sound of the old woman.

"I need a place to sleep," the girl said.

Her voice was clear and sweet and the young man decided that even before the rain had scrubbed her face she hadn't worn makeup.

He said, "You don't want to stay here. I'll call you a cab."

"I want to stay here," the girl said in her clear voice. "I have to stay somewhere."

"I have a communicator," the young man said. He opened his coat to show it to her—a black box with a speaker, keys, and a tiny screen—then realized that he had made a fool of himself. Someone laughed.

"They're not running."

The old woman said, "What's not running?"

"The cabs. Or the buses. There's high water in a lot of places all over the city and they've been shorting out. I have a communicator too"—the blind girl touched her waist—"and the ruler made a speech just a few minutes ago. I listened to him as I walked and there was a newscast afterward. But I knew anyway because a gentleman tried to call one for me from the terminal, but they wouldn't come."

"You shouldn't stay here," the young man said.

The old woman said, "I got a room if you want it—the only one left."

"I want it," the girl told her.

"You've got it. Wait a minute now—I've got to fix this fellow some sandwiches."

Someone swore at the old woman and said that the game was about to start.

"Five minutes yet." She took a piece of boiled ham from under the counter and put it between two slices of bread, then repeated the process.

The young man said, "These look eatable. Not fancy, but eatable. Would you like to have one?"

I have a little money," the blind girl said. "I can pay for my own." And to the old woman: "I would like some coffee."

"How about a sandwich?"

"I'm too tired to eat."

The door was opening almost constantly now as people from the surrounding tenements braved the storm and splashed in to watch the game. The old woman turned the wall on and they crowded near it, watching the pregame warm-up, practicing and perfecting the intentness they would use on the game itself. The scarred young man and the blind girl were edged away and found themselves nearest the door in a room now grown very silent save for the sound from the wall.

The young man said, "This is really a bad place—you shouldn't be here."

"Then what are you doing here?"

"I don't have much money," he said. "It's cheap."

"You don't have a job?"

"I was hurt in an accident. I'm well now, but they wouldn't keep me on—they say I would frighten the others. I suppose I would."

"Isn't there insurance for that?"

"I wasn't there long enough to qualify."

"I see," she said. She raised her coffee carefully, holding it with both hands. He wanted to tell her that it was about to spill—she did not hold it quite straight—but dared not. Just as it was at the point of running over the edge it found her lips.

"You listened to the ruler," he said, "while you were walking in the storm. I like that."

"Did they listen here?" she asked.

"I don't know. I wasn't here. The wall was off when I came in."

"Everyone should," she said. "He does his best for us."

The scarred young man nodded.

"People won't cooperate," she said. "Don't cooperate. Look at the crime problem—everyone complains about it, but it is the people themselves who commit the crimes. He tries to clean the air, the water, all for us—"

"But they burn in the open whenever they think they won't be caught," the young man finished for her, "and throw filth in the rivers. The bosses live in luxury because of him, but they cheat on the standards whenever they can. He should destroy them."

"He loves them," the girl said simply. "He loves everyone. When we say that, it sounds like we're saying he loves no one, but that's not true. He loves *everyone*."

"Yes," the scarred young man said after a moment, "but he loves Westwind the best. Loving everyone does not exclude loving someone more than others. Tonight he called Westwind 'my eyes.'"

"Westwind observes for him," the girl said softly, "and reports. Do you think Westwind is someone very important?"

"He is important," the young man said, "because the ruler listens to him—and after all, it's next to impossible for anyone else to get an audience. But I think you mean 'does he look important to us?' I don't think so—he's probably some very obscure person you've never heard of."

"I think you're right," she said.

He was finishing his second sandwich and he nodded, then realized that she could not see him. She was pretty, he decided, in a slender way, not too tall, wore no rings. Her nails were unpainted, which made her hands look, to him, like a schoolgirl's. He remembered watching the girls playing volleyball when he had been in school—how he had ached for them. He said, "You should have stayed in the terminal tonight. I don't think this is a safe place for you."

"Do the rooms lock?"

"I don't know. I haven't seen them."

"If they don't I'll put a chair under the knob or something. Move the furniture. At the terminal I tried to sleep on a bench— I didn't want to walk here through all that rain, believe me. But every time I fell asleep I could feel someone's hand on me—once I grabbed him, but he pulled away. I'm not very strong."

"Wasn't anyone else there?"

"Some men, but they were trying to sleep too—of course it was one of them, and perhaps they were all doing it together. One of them told the others that if they didn't let me alone he'd kill someone—that was when I left. I was afraid he wasn't doing it—that somebody would be killed or at least that there would be a fight. He was the one who called about the cab for me. He said he'd pay."

"I don't think it was him, then."

"I don't either." The girl was silent for a moment, then said, "I wouldn't have minded it so much if I hadn't been so tired."

"I understand."

"Would you find the lady and ask her to show me to my room?"

"Maybe we could meet in the morning for breakfast."

The blind girl smiled, the first time the scarred young man had seen her smile. "That would be nice," she said.

He went behind the bar and touched the old woman's arm. "I hate to interrupt the game," he said, "but the young lady would like to go to her room."

"I don't care about the game," the old woman said. "I just watch it because everybody else does. I'll get Obie to take care of things."

"She's coming," the scarred young man said to the blind girl. "I'll go up with you. I'm ready to turn in myself."

The woman was already motioning for them and they followed her up a narrow staircase filled with foul odors. "They pee in here," she said. "There's toilets down at the end of the hall, but they don't bother to use them."

"How terrible," the girl said.

"Yes, it is. But that way they're getting away with something—they're putting one over on me because they know if I was to catch them I'd throw them out. I try and catch them, but at the same time I feel sorry for them—it's pretty bad when the only wins you have left are the games on the wall and cheating an old woman by dirtying her steps." She paused at the top of the stairs for breath. "You two are going to be just side-by-side—you don't mind that?"

The girl said, "No," and the scarred young man shook his head.

"I didn't think you would and they're the last I've got anyway."

The scarred young man was looking down the narrow corridor. It was lined with doors, most of them shut.

"I'll put you closest to the bathroom," the old woman was saying to the girl. "There's a hook on the bathroom door, so don't you worry. But if you stay in there too long somebody'll start pounding."

"I'll be all right," the girl said.

"Sure you will. Here's your room."

The rooms had been parts of much larger rooms once. Now they were subdivided with green-painted partitions of some stuff like heavy cardboard. The old woman went into the girl's place and turned on the light. "Bed's here; dresser's there," she said. "Washstand in the corner, but you have to bring your water from the bathroom. No bugs—we fumigate twice a year. Clean sheets."

The girl was feeling the edge of the door. Her fingers found a chain lock and she smiled.

"There's a dead bolt too," the scarred young man said.

The old woman said, "Your room's next door. Come on."

His room was much like the girl's, save that the cardboard partition (it had been liberally scratched with obscene words and pictures) was on the left instead of the right. He found that he was acutely aware of her moving behind it, the tap of her stick as she established the positions of the bed, the dresser, the washstand. He locked his door and took off his soaked coat and hung it on a hook, then took off his shoes and stockings. He disliked the thought of walking on the gritty floor in his wet feet, but there was no alternative except the soggy shoes.

With his legs folded under him he sat on the bed, then unhooked the communicator from his belt and pushed 555-333-4477, the ruler's number.

"This is Westwind," the scarred young man whispered.

The ruler's face appeared in the screen, tiny and perfect. Again, as he had so often before, the young man felt that this was the ruler's real size, this tiny, bright figure—he knew it was not true.

"This is Westwind and I've got a place to sleep tonight. I haven't found another job yet, but I met a girl and think she likes me."

"Exciting news," the ruler said. He smiled.

The scarred young man smiled too, on his unscarred side. "It's raining very hard here," he said. "I think this girl is very loyal to you, sir. The rest of the people here—well, I don't know. She told me about a man in the terminal who tried to molest her and another man who wanted to protect her. I was going to ask you to reward him and punish the other one, but I'm afraid they were the same man—that he wanted to meet her and this gave him the chance."

"They are often the same man," the ruler said. He paused as though lost in thought. "You are all right?"

"If I don't find something tomorrow I won't be able to afford to stay, but yes, I'm all right tonight."

"You are very cheerful, Westwind. I love cheerfulness."

The good side of the scarred young man's face blushed. "It's easy for me," he said. "I've known all my life that I was your spy, your confidant—it's like knowing where a treasure is hidden. Often I feel sorry for the others. I hope you're not too severe with them."

"I don't want to aid you openly unless I must," the ruler said. "But I'll find ways that aren't open. Don't worry." He winked.

"I know you will, sir."

"Just don't pawn your communicator."

The image was gone, leaving only a blank screen. The young man turned out the light and continued to undress, taking off everything but his shorts. He was lying down on the bed when he heard a thump from the other side of the cardboard partition. The blind girl, feeling her way about the room, must have bumped into it. He was about to call, "Are you hurt?" when he saw that one of the panels, a section perhaps three feet by four, was teetering in its frame. He caught it as it fell and laid it on floor.

The light the old woman had turned on still burned in the girl's room and he saw that she had hung up her coat and wrapped her hair in a strip of paper towels from the washstand. While he watched she removed her black glasses, set them on the bureau, and rubbed the bridge of her nose. One of her eyes showed only white; the iris of the other was the poisoned blue color of watered milk and turned in and down. Her face was lovely. While he watched she unbuttoned her blouse and hung it up. Then she unhooked her communicator from her belt, ran her fingers over the buttons once, and, without looking, pressed a number.

"This is Westwind," she said.

He could not hear the voice that answered her, but the face in the screen, small and bright, was the face of the ruler. "I'm all right," she said. "At first I didn't think I was going to be able to find a place to stay tonight, but I have. And I've met someone."

The scarred young man lifted the panel back into place as gently as he could and lay down again upon his bed. When he heard the rattle of her cane again he tapped the partition and called, "Breakfast tomorrow. Don't forget."

"I won't. Good night."

"Good night," he said.

In the room below them the old woman was patting her straggling hair into place with one hand while she punched a number with the other. "Hello," she said, "this is Westwind. I saw you tonight."

❧

## AFTERWORD

It was not until I prepared to write this author's note that I realized that long before I wrote this story the great G. K. Chesterton had written an entire book in which all the members of a gang of revolutionaries, save its head and one other, were spies for assorted police agencies and government bureaus.

Its head was God.

The book is *The Man Who Was Thursday*. You can find a copy if you look, and I suggest you read it.

# The Hero as Werwolf

*Feet in the jungle that leave no mark!*

*Eyes that can see in the dark—the dark!*
*Tongue—give tongue to it! Hark! O hark!*
*Once, twice and again!*
—RUDYARD KIPLING,
*"Hunting Song of the Seeonee Pack"*

An owl shrieked, and Paul flinched. Fear, pavement, flesh, death, stone, dark, loneliness, and blood made up Paul's world; the blood was all much the same, but the fear took several forms, and he had hardly seen another human being in the four years since his mother's death. At a night meeting in the park he was the red-cheeked young man at the end of the last row, with his knees together and his scrupulously clean hands (Paul was particularly careful about his nails) in his lap.

The speaker was fluent and amusing; he was clearly conversant with his subject—whatever it was—and he pleased his audience. Paul, the listener and watcher, knew many of the words he used; yet he had understood nothing in the past hour and a half, and sat wrapped in his stolen cloak and his own thoughts, seeming to listen, watching the crowd and the park—this, at least, was no ghost-house, no trap; the moon was up, night-blooming flowers scented the park air, and the trees lining the paths glowed with self-generated blue light; in the city, beyond the last hedge, the great buildings new and old were mountains lit from within.

Neither human nor master, a policeman strolled about the fringes of the audience, his eyes bright with stupidity. Paul could have killed him in less than a second, and was enjoying a dream of the policeman's death in some remote corner of his mind even while he concentrated on seeming to be one of *them*. A passenger rocket passed just under the stars, trailing luminous banners.

The meeting was over and he wondered if the rocket had in some way been the signal to end it. The masters did not use time, at least not as he did, as he had been taught by the thin woman who had been his mother in the little home she had made for them in the turret of a house that was once (she said) the Gorous'—now only a house too old to be destroyed. Neither did they use money, of which he like other old-style *Homo sapiens* still retained some racial memory, as of a forgotten god—a magic once potent that had lost all force.

The masters were rising, and there were tears and laughter and that third emotional tone that was neither amusement nor sorrow—the silken sound humans did not possess, but that Paul thought might express content, as the purring of a cat does, or community, like the cooing of doves. The policeman bobbed his hairy head, grinning, basking in the recognition, the approval, of those who had raised him from animality. *See* (said the motions of his hands, the writhings of his body) *the clothing you have given me. How nice! I take good care of my things because they are yours. See my weapon. I perform a useful function—if you did not have me, you would have to do it yourselves.*

If the policeman saw Paul, it would be over. The policeman was too stupid, too silly, to be deceived by appearances as his masters were. He would never dare, thinking Paul a master, to meet his eye, but he would look into his face seeking approval, and would see not what he was supposed to see but what was there. Paul ducked into the crowd, avoiding a beautiful woman with eyes the color of pearls, preferring to walk in the shadow of her fat escort where the policeman would not see him. The fat man took dust from a box shaped like the moon and rubbed it between his hands, releasing the smell of raspberries. It froze, and he sifted the tiny crystals of crimson ice over his shirtfront, grunting with satisfaction then offered the box to the woman, who refused at first, only (three steps later) to accept when he pressed it on her.

They were past the policeman now. Paul dropped a few paces behind the couple, wondering if they were the ones tonight—if there would be meat tonight at all. For some, vehicles would be waiting. If the pair he had selected were among these, he would have to find others quickly.

They were not. They had entered the canyons between the buildings; he dropped farther behind, then turned aside.

Three minutes later he was in an alley a hundred meters ahead of them, waiting for them to pass the mouth. (The old trick was to cry like an infant, and he could do it well, but he had a new trick—a better trick, because too many had learned not to come down an alley when an infant cried. The new trick was a silver bell he had found in the house, small and very old. He took it from his pocket and removed the rag he had packed around the clapper. His dark cloak concealed him now, its hood pulled up to hide the pale gleam of his skin. He stood in a narrow doorway only a few meters away from the alley's mouth.)

*They came.* He heard the man's thick laughter, the woman's silken sound. She was a trifle silly from the dust the man had given her, and would be holding his arm as they walked, rubbing his thighs with hers. The man's black-shod foot and big belly thrust past the stonework of the building—there was a muffled moan.

The fat man turned, looking down the alley. Paul could see fear growing in the woman's face, cutting, too slowly, through the odor of raspberries. Another moan, and the man strode forward, fumbling in his pocket for an illuminator. The woman followed hesitantly (her skirt was of flowering vines the color of love, and white skin flashed in the interstices; a serpent of gold supported her breasts).

Someone was behind him. Pressed back against the metal door, he watched the couple as they passed. The fat man had gotten his illuminator out and held it over his head as he walked, looking into corners and doorways.

They came at them from both sides, a girl and an old, gray-bearded man. The fat man, the master, his genetic heritage revised for intellection and peace, had hardly time to turn before his mouth gushed blood. The woman whirled and ran, the vines of her skirt withering at her thought to give her legroom, the serpent dropping from her breasts to strike with fangless jaws at the flying-haired girl who pursued her, then winding itself about the girl's ankles. The girl fell; but as the pearl-eyed woman passed, Paul broke her neck. For a moment he was too startled at the sight of other human beings to speak. Then he said, "These are mine."

The old man, still bent over the fat man's body, snapped: "Ours. We've been here an hour and more." His voice was the creaking of steel hinges, and Paul thought of ghost-houses again.

"I followed them from the park." The girl, black haired, gray eyed when the light from the alley mouth struck her face, was taking the serpent from around her legs—it was once more a lifeless thing of soft metal mesh. Paul picked up the woman's corpse and wrapped it in his cloak. "You gave me no warning," he said. "You must have seen me when I passed you."

The girl looked toward the old man. Her eyes said she would back him if he fought, and Paul decided he would throw the woman's body at her.

"Somebody'll come soon," the old man said. "And I'll need Janie's help to carry this one. We each take what we got ourselves—that's fair. Or we whip you. My girl's worth a man in a fight, and you'll find I'm still worth a man myself, old as I be."

"Give me the picking of his body. This one has nothing."

The girl's bright lips drew back from strong white teeth. From somewhere under the tattered shirt she wore, she had produced a long knife, and sudden light from a window high above the alley ran along the edge of the stained blade; the girl might be a dangerous opponent, as the old man claimed, but Paul could sense the femaleness, the woman rut, from where he stood. "No," her father said. "You got good clothes. I need these." He looked up at the window fearfully, fumbling with buttons.

"His cloak will hang on you like a blanket."

"We'll fight. Take the woman and go away, or we'll fight."

He could not carry both, and the fat man's meat would be tainted by the testicles. When Paul was young and there had been no one but his mother to do the killing, they had sometimes eaten old males; he never did so now. He slung the pearl-eyed woman across his shoulders and trotted away.

Outside the alley the streets were well lit, and a few passersby stared at him and the dark burden he carried. Fewer still, he knew, would suspect him of being what he was—he had learned the trick of dressing as the masters did, even of wearing their expressions. He wondered how the black-haired girl and the old man would fare in their ragged clothes. *They must live very near.*

His own place was that in which his mother had borne him, a place high in a house built when humans were the masters. Every door was nailed tight and boarded up; but on one side a small garden lay between two wings, and in a corner of this garden, behind a bush where the shadows were thick even at noon, the bricks had fallen away. The lower floors were full of rotting furniture and the smell of rats and mold, but high in his wooden turret the walls were still dry and the sun came in by day at eight windows. He carried his burden there and dropped her in a corner. It was important that his clothes be kept as clean as the masters kept theirs, though he lacked their facilities. He pulled his cloak from the body and brushed it vigorously.

"What are you going to do with me?" the dead woman said behind him.

"Eat," he told her. "What did you think I was going to do?"

"I didn't know." And then: "I've read of you creatures, but I didn't think you really existed."

"We were the masters once," he said. He was not sure he still believed it, but it was what his mother had taught him. "This house was built in those days—that's why you won't wreck it: you're afraid." He had finished with the cloak; he hung it up and turned to face her, sitting on the bed. "You're afraid of waking the old times," he said. She lay slumped in the corner, and though her mouth moved, her eyes were only half-open, looking at nothing.

"We tore a lot of them down," she said.

"If you're going to talk, you might as well sit up straight." He lifted her by the shoulders and propped her in the corner. A nail protruded from the wall there; he twisted a lock of her hair on it so her head would not loll; her hair was the rose shade of a little girl's dress, and soft but slightly sticky.

"I'm dead, you know."

"No, you're not." They always said this (except, sometimes, for the children) and his mother had always denied it. He felt that he was keeping up a family tradition.

"Dead," the pearl-eyed woman said. "Never, never, never. Another year, and everything would have been all right. I want to cry, but I can't breathe to."

"Your kind lives a long time with a broken neck," he told her. "But you'll die eventually."

"I am dead now."

He was not listening. There were other humans in the city; he had always known that, but only now, with the sight of the old man and the girl, had their existence seemed real to him.

"I thought you were all gone," the pearl-eyed dead woman said thinly. "All gone long ago, like a bad dream."

Happy with his new discovery, he said, "Why do you set traps for us, then? Maybe there are more of us than you think."

"There can't be many of you. How many people do you kill in a year?" Her mind was lifting the sheet from his bed, hoping to smother him with it; but he had seen that trick many times.

"Twenty or thirty." (He was boasting.)

"So many."

"When you don't get much besides meat, you need a lot of it. And then I only eat the best parts—why not? I kill twice a month or more except when it's cold, and I could kill enough for two or three if I had to." (*The girl had had a knife.* Knives were bad, except for cutting up afterward. But knives left blood behind. He would kill for her—she could stay here and take care of his clothes, prepare their food. He thought of himself walking home under a new moon, and seeing her face in the window of the turret.) To the dead woman he said, "You saw that girl? With the black hair? She and the old man killed your husband, and I'm going to bring her here to live." He stood and began to walk up and down the small room, soothing himself with the sound of his own footsteps.

"He wasn't my husband." The sheet dropped limply now that he was no longer on the bed. "Why didn't you change? When the rest changed their genes?"

"I wasn't alive then."

"You must have received some tradition."

"We didn't want to. We are the human beings."

"Everyone wanted to. Your old breed had worn out the planet; even with much better technology we're still starved for energy and raw materials because of what you did."

"There hadn't been enough to eat before," he said, "but when so many changed there was a lot. So why should more change?"

It was a long time before she answered, and he knew the body was stiffening. That was bad, because as long as she lived in it the flesh would stay sweet; when the life was gone, he would have to cut it up quickly before the stuff in her lower intestine tainted the rest.

"Strange evolution," she said at last. "Man become food for men."

"I don't understand the second word. Talk so I know what you're saying." He kicked her in the chest to emphasize his point, and knocked her over; he heard a rib snap. . . . She did not reply, and he lay down on the bed. His mother had told him there was a meeting place in the city where men gathered on certain special nights—but he had forgotten (if he had ever known) what those nights were.

"That isn't even metalanguage," the dead woman said, "only children's talk."

"Shut up."

After a moment he said, "I'm going out. If you can make your body stand, and get out of here, and get down to the ground floor, and find the way out, then you may be able to tell someone about me and have the police waiting when I come back." He went out and closed the door, then stood patiently outside for five minutes.

When he opened it again, the corpse stood erect with her hands on his table, her tremors upsetting the painted metal circus figures he had had since he was a child—the girl acrobat, the clown with his hoop and trained pig. One of her legs would not straighten. "Listen," he said. "You're not going to do it. I told you all that because I knew you'd think of it yourself. They always do, and they never make it. The farthest I've ever had anyone get was out the door and to the top of the steps. She fell down them, and I found her at the bottom when I came back. You're dead. Go to sleep."

The blind eyes had turned toward him when he began to speak, but they no longer watched him now. The face, which had been beautiful, was now entirely the face of a corpse. The cramped leg crept toward the floor as he watched, halted, began to creep downward again. Sighing, he lifted the dead woman off her feet, replaced her in the corner, and went down the creaking stairs to find the black-haired girl.

There has been quite a few to come after her," her father said, "since we come into town. Quite a few." He sat in the back of the bus, on the rearmost seat that went completely across the back like a sofa. "But you're the first ever to find us here. The others, they hear about her, and leave a sign at the meetin'."

Paul wanted to ask where it was such signs were left, but held his peace.

"You know there ain't many folks at all anymore," her father went on. "And not many of them is women. And damn few is young girls like my Janie. I had a fella here that wanted her two weeks back—he said he hadn't had no real woman in two years; well, I didn't like the way he said real, so I said what did he do, and he said he fooled around with what he killed, sometimes, before they got cold. You never did like that, did you?"

Paul said he had not.

"How'd you find this dump here?"

"Just look around." He had searched the area in ever-widening circles, starting at the alley in which he had seen the girl and her father. They had one of the masters' cold boxes to keep their ripe kills in (as he did himself), but there was the stink of clotted blood about the dump nonetheless. It was behind a high fence, closer to the park than he would have thought possible.

"When we come, there was a fella living here. Nice fella, a German. Name was Curtain—something like that. He went sweet on my Janie right off. Well, I wasn't too taken with having a foreigner in the family, but he took us in and let us settle in the big station wagon. Told me he wanted to wed Janie, but I said no, she's too young. Wait a year, I says, and take her with my blessing. She wasn't but fourteen then. Well, one night the German fella went out and I guess they got him, because he never come back. We moved into this here bus then for the extra room."

His daughter was sitting at his feet, and he reached a crooked-fingered hand down and buried it in her midnight hair. She looked up at him and smiled. "Got a pretty face, ain't she?" he said.

Paul nodded.

"She's a mite thin, you was going to say. Well, that's true. I do my best to provide, but I'm feared, and not shamed to admit to it."

"The ghost-houses," Paul said.

"What's that?"

"That's what I've always called them. I don't get to talk to many other people."

"Where the doors shut on you—lock you in."

"Yes."

"That ain't ghosts—now don't you think I'm one of them fools don't believe in them. I know better. But that ain't ghosts. They're always looking, don't you see, for people they think ain't right. That's us. It's electricity does it. You ever been caught like that?"

Paul nodded. He was watching the delicate swelling Janie's breasts made in the fabric of her filthy shirt, and only half-listening to her father; but the memory penetrated the young desire that half-embarrassed him, bringing back fear. The windows of the bus had been set to black, and the light inside was dim—still it was possible some glimmer showed outside. *There should be no lights in the dump.* He listened, but heard only katydids singing in the rubbish.

"They thought I was a master—I dress like one," he said. "That's something you should do. They were going to test me. I turned the machine over and broke it, and jumped through a window." He had been on the sixth floor, and had been saved by landing in the branches of a tree whose bruised twigs and torn leaves exuded an acrid incense that to him was the very breath of panic still; but it had not been the masters, or the instrument-filled examination room, or the jump from the window that had terrified him, but waiting in the ghost-room while the walls talked to one another in words he could sometimes, for a few seconds, nearly understand.

"It wouldn't work for me—got too many things wrong with me. Lines in my face; even got a wart—they never do."

"Janie could."

The old man cleared his throat; it was a thick sound, like water in a downspout in a hard rain. "I been meaning to talk to you about her, about why those other fellas I told you about never took her—not that I'd of let some of them: Janie's the only family I got left. But I ain't so particular I don't want to see her married at all—not a bit of it. Why, we wouldn't of come here if it weren't for Janie. When her monthly come, I said to myself, she'll be wantin' a man, and what're you goin' to do way out here? Though the country was gettin' bad anyway, I must say. If they'd of had real dogs, I believe they would have got us several times."

He paused, perhaps thinking of those times, the lights in the woods at night and the running, perhaps only trying to order his thoughts. Paul waited, scratching an ankle, and after a few seconds the old man said, "We didn't want to do this, you know, us Pendeltons. That's mine and Janie's name—Pendelton. Janie's Augusta Jane, and I'm Emmitt J."

"Paul Gorou," Paul said.

"Pleased to meet you, Mr. Gorou. When the time come, they took one whole side of the family. They were the Worthmore Pendeltons; that's what we always called them, because most of them lived thereabouts. Cousins of mine they was, and second cousins. We was the Evershaw Pendeltons, and they didn't take none of us. Bad blood, they said—too much wrong to be worth fixing, or too much that mightn't get fixed right, and then show up again. My ma—she's alive then— she always swore it was her sister Lillian's boy that did it to us. The whole side of his head was pushed in. You know what I mean? They used to say a cow'd kicked him when he was small, but it wasn't so—he's just born like that. He could talk some—there's those that set a high value on that—but the slobber'd run out of his mouth. My ma said if it wasn't for him we'd have got in sure. The only other thing was my sister Clara that was born with a bad eye—blind, you know, and something wrong with the lid of it too. But she was just as sensible as anybody. Smart as a whip. So I would say it's likely Ma was right. Same thing with your family, I suppose?"

"I think so. I don't really know."

"A lot of it was die-beetees. They could fix it, but if there was other things too they just kept them out. Of course when it was over there wasn't no medicine for them no more, and they died off pretty quick. When I was young, I used to think that was what it meant: die-beetees—you died away. It's really sweetening of the blood. You heard of it?"

Paul nodded.

"I'd like to taste some sometime, but I never come to think of that while there was still some of them around."

"If they weren't masters—"

"Didn't mean I'd of killed them," the old man said quickly. "Just got one to gash his arm a trifle so I could taste of it. Back then—that would be twenty aught nine; close to fifty years gone it is now—there was several I knowed that was just my age. . . . What I was meaning to say at the beginning was that us Pendeltons never figured on anythin' like this. We'd farmed, and we meant to keep on, grow our own truck and breed our own stock. Well, that did for a time, but it wouldn't keep."

Paul, who had never considered living off the land, or even realized that it was possible to do so, could only stare at him.

"You take chickens, now. Everybody always said there wasn't nothing easier than chickens, but that was when there was medicine you could put in the water to keep off the sickness. Well, the time come when you couldn't get it no more than you could get a can of beans in those stores of theirs that don't use money or cards or anything a man can understand. My dad had two hundred in the flock when the sickness struck, and it took every hen inside of four days. You wasn't supposed to eat them that had died sick, but we did it. Plucked 'em and canned 'em—by that time our old locker that plugged in the wall wouldn't work. When the chickens was all canned, Dad saddled a horse we had then and rode twenty-five miles to a place where the new folks grew chickens to eat themselves. I guess you know what happened to him, though—they wouldn't sell, and they wouldn't trade. Finally he begged them. He was a Pendelton, and used to cry when he told of it. He said the harder he begged them the scareder they got. Well, finally he reached out and grabbed one by the leg—he was on his knees to them—and he hit him alongside the face with a book he was carryin'."

The old man rocked backward and forward in his seat as he spoke, his eyes half-closed. "There wasn't no more seed but what was saved from last year then, and the corn went so bad the ears wasn't no longer than a soft dick. No bullets for Dad's old gun, nowhere to buy new traps when what we had was lost. Then one day just afore Christmas these here machines just started tearing up our fields. They had forgot about us, you see. We threw rocks, but it didn't do no good, and about midnight one come right through the house. There wasn't no one living then but Ma and Dad and brother Tom and me and Janie. Janie wasn't but just a little bit of a thing. The machine got Tom in the leg with a piece of two-by-four—rammed the splintery end into him, you see. The rot got to the wound and he died a week after; it was winter then, and we was living in a place me and Dad built up on the hill out of branches and saplings."

"About Janie," Paul said. "I can understand how you might not want to let her go—"

"Are you sayin' you don't want her?" The old man shifted in his seat, and Paul saw that his right hand had moved close to the crevice where the horizontal surface joined the vertical. The crevice was a trifle too wide, and Paul thought he knew what was hidden there. He was not afraid of the old man, and it had crossed his mind more than once that if he killed him there would be nothing to prevent his taking Janie.

"I want her," he said. "I'm not going away without her." He stood up without knowing why.

"There's been others said the same thing. I would go, you know, to the meetin' in the regular way; come back next month, and the fella'd be waitin'."

The old man was drawing himself to his feet, his jaw outthrust belligerently. "They'd see her," he said, "and they'd talk a lot, just like you, about how good they'd take care of her, though there wasn't a one brought a lick to eat when he come to call. Me and Janie, sometimes we ain't et for three, four days—they never take account of that. Now here, you look at her."

Bending swiftly, he took his daughter by the arm; she rose gracefully, and he spun her around. "Her ma was a pretty woman," he said, "but not as pretty as what she is, even if she is so thin. And she's got sense too—I don't keer what they say."

Janie looked at Paul with frightened, animal eyes. He gestured, he hoped gently, for her to come to him, but she only pressed herself against her father.

"You can talk to her. She understands."

Paul started to speak, then had to stop to clear his throat. At last he said, "Come here, Janie. You're going to live with me. We'll come back and see your father sometimes."

Her hand slipped into her shirt; came out holding a knife. She looked at the old man, who caught her wrist and took the knife from her and dropped it on the seat behind him, saying, "You're going to have to be a mite careful around her for a bit, but if you don't hurt her none she'll take to you pretty quick. She wants to take to you now—I can see it in the way she looks."

Paul nodded, accepting the girl from him almost as he might have accepted a package, holding her by her narrow waist.

"And when you get a mess of grub she likes to cut them up, sometimes, while they're still movin' around. Mostly I don't allow it, but if you do—anyway, once in a while—she'll like you better for it."

Paul nodded again. His hand, as if of its own volition, had strayed to the girl's smoothly rounded hip, and he felt such desire as he had never known before.

"Wait," the old man said. His breath was foul in the close air. "You listen to me now. You're just a young fella and I know how you feel, but you don't know how I do. I want you to understand before you go. I love my girl. You take good care of her or I'll see to you. And if you change your mind about wanting her, don't you just turn her out. I'll take her back, you hear?"

Paul said, "All right."

"Even a bad man can love his child. You remember that, because it's true."

Her husband took Janie by the hand and led her out of the wrecked bus. She was looking over her shoulder, and he knew that she expected her father to drive a knife into his back.

They had seen the boy—a brown-haired, slightly freckled boy of nine or ten with an armload of books—on a corner where a small, columniated building concealed the entrance to the monorail, and the streets were wide and empty. The children of the masters were seldom out so late. Paul waved to him, not daring to speak, but attempting to convey by his posture that he wanted to ask directions; he wore the black cloak and scarlet-slashed shirt, the gold sandals and wide-legged black film trousers proper to an evening of pleasure. On his arm

Janie was all in red, her face covered by a veil dotted with tiny synthetic blood-stones. Gem-studded veils were a fashion now nearly extinct among the women of the masters, but one that served to conceal the blankness of eye that betrayed Janie, as Paul had discovered, almost instantly. She gave a soft moan of hunger as she saw the boy, and clasped Paul's arm more tightly. Paul waved again.

The boy halted as though waiting for them, but when they were within five meters he turned and dashed away. Janie was after him before Paul could stop her. The boy dodged between two buildings and raced through to the next street; Paul was just in time to see Janie follow him into a doorway in the center of the block.

He found her clear-soled platform shoes in the vestibule, under a four-dimensional picture of Hugo de Vries. De Vries was in the closing years of his life and, in the few seconds it took Paul to pick up the shoes and conceal them behind an aquarium of phosphorescent cephalopods, had died, rotted to dust, and undergone rebirth as a fissioning cell in his mother's womb with all the labyrinth of genetics still before him.

The lower floors, Paul knew, were apartments. He had entered them sometimes when he could find no prey on the streets. There would be a school at the top.

A confused, frightened-looking woman stood in an otherwise empty corridor, a disheveled library book lying open at her feet. As Paul pushed past her, he could imagine Janie knocking her out of the way, and the woman's horror at the savage, exultant face glimpsed beneath her veil.

There were elevators, a liftshaft, and a downshaft, all clustered in an alcove. *The boy would not have waited for an elevator with Janie close behind him. . . .*

The liftshaft floated Paul as springwater floats a cork. Thickened by conditioning agents, the air remained a gas; enriched with added oxygen, it stimulated his whole being, though it was as viscous as corn syrup when he drew it into his lungs. Far above, suspended (as it seemed) in crystal and surrounded by the books the boy had thrown down at her, Paul saw Janie with her red gown billowing around her and her white legs flashing. She was going to the top, apparently to the uppermost floor, and he reasoned that the boy, having led her there, would jump into the downshaft to escape her. He got off at the eighty-fifth floor, opened the hatch to the downshaft, and was rewarded by seeing the boy only a hundred meters above him. It was a simple matter then to wait on the landing and pluck him out of the sighing column of thickened air.

The boy's pointed, narrow face, white with fear under a tan, turned up toward him. "Don't," the boy said. "Please, sir, good master——," but Paul clamped him under his left arm, and with a quick wrench of his right broke his neck.

Janie was swimming head down with the downshaft current, her mouth open and full of eagerness, and her black hair like a cloud about her head. She had lost her veil. Paul showed her the boy and stepped into the shaft with her. The hatch slammed behind him, and the motion of the air ceased.

He looked at Janie. She had stopped swimming and was staring hungrily into the dead boy's face. He said, "Something's wrong," and she seemed to understand, though it was possible that she only caught the fear in his voice. The hatch would not open, and slowly the current in the shaft was reversing, lifting them; he tried to swim against it, but the effort was hopeless. When they were at the top, the dead boy began to talk; Janie put her hand over his mouth to muffle the sound. The hatch at the landing opened, and they stepped out onto the 101st floor.

A voice from a loudspeaker in the wall said, *"I am sorry to detain you, but there is reason to think you have undergone a recent deviation from the optional development pattern. In a few minutes I will arrive in person to provide counseling; while you are waiting it may be useful for us to review what is meant by 'optimal development.' Look at the projection.*

*"In infancy the child first feels affection for its mother, the provider of warmth and food . . ."* There was a door at the other end of the room, and Paul swung a heavy chair against it, making a din that almost drowned out the droning speaker.

*"Later one's peer group becomes, for a time, all-important—or nearly so. The boys and girls you see are attending a model school in Armstrong. Notice that no tint is used to mask the black of space above their airtent."*

The lock burst from the door frame, but a remotely actuated hydraulic cylinder snapped it shut each time a blow from the chair drove it open. Paul slammed his shoulder against it, and before it could close again put his knee where the shattered bolt socket had been. A chrome-plated steel rod as thick as a finger had dropped from the chair when his blows had smashed the wood and plastic holding it; after a moment of incomprehension, Janie dropped the dead boy, wedged the rod between the door and the jamb, and slipped through. He was following her when the rod lifted, and the door swung shut on his foot.

He screamed and screamed again, and then, in the echoing silence that followed, heard the loudspeaker mumbling about education, and Janie's sobbing, indrawn breath. Through the crack between the door and the frame, the two-centimeter space held in existence by what remained of his right foot, he could see the livid face and blind, malevolent eyes of the dead boy, whose will still held the steel rod suspended in air. "Die," Paul shouted at him. "Die! You're dead!" The rod came crashing down.

*"This young woman,"* the loudspeaker said, *"has chosen the profession of medicine. She will be a physician, and she says now that she was born for that. She will spend the remainder of her life in relieving the agonies of disease."*

Several minutes passed before Paul could make Janie understand what it was she had to do.

*"After her five years' training in basic medical techniques, she will specialize in surgery for another three years before—"*

It took Janie a long time to bite through his Achilles tendon; when it was over, she began to tear at the ligaments that held the bones of the tarsus to the leg. Over the pain he could feel the hot tears washing the blood from his foot.

## Afterword

Ever since this story appeared, I have been getting heat for my spelling of *werewolf*. I reverted to the original spelling to point up the meaning of the word: "manwolf." We would be more apt to say "wolfman," though the ideas conveyed are distinctly different. Our werewolf is a man who becomes a wolf. The manwolf envisioned by the Anglos and Saxons was a man to be feared as wolves were feared, and for the same reasons.

> Wolf-wise feigning and flying,
> and wolf-wise snatching his man.
> —KIPLING

*Wer* was the original Anglo-Saxon word for the male of the human species. (*Man* designated a human being. We see the ghostly traces of this when we say, for example, that Molly Pitcher manned a gun at Monmouth.) I wanted the old original import, and so titled the story you have just read as I did.

# The Marvelous Brass
## Chessplaying Automaton

〰

Each day Lame Hans sits with his knees against the bars, playing chess with the machine. Though I have seen the game often, I have never learned to play, but I watch them as I sweep. It is a beautiful game, and Lame Hans has told me of its beginnings in the great ages now past; for that reason I always feel a sympathy toward the little pawns with their pencils and wrenches and plain clothing, each figure representing many generations of those whose labor built the great bishops that split the skies in the days of the old wars.

I feel pity for Lame Hans also. He talks to me when I bring his food, and sometimes when I am cleaning the jail. Let me tell you his story, as I have learned it in the many days since the police drew poor Gretchen out and laid her in the dust of the street. Lame Hans would never tell you himself—for all that big, bulging head, his tongue is slow and halting when he speaks of his own affairs.

It was last summer during the truce that the showman's cart was driven into our village. For a month not a drop of rain had fallen; each day at noon Father Karl rang the church bells and women went in to pray for rain for their husbands' crops. After dark, many of these same women met to form lines and circles on the slopes of the Schlossberg, the mountain that was once a great building. The lines and circles are supposed to influence the Weatherwatchers, whose winking lights pass so swiftly through the starry sky. For myself, I do not believe it. What men ever made a machine that could see a few old women on the mountainside at night?

So it was when the cart of Herr Heitzmann the mountebank came. The sun was down, but the street still so hot that the dogs would not bark for fear of fainting, and the dust rolled away from the wheels in waves, like grain when foxes run through the fields.

This cart was shorter than a farm wagon, but very high, with such a roof as a house has. The sides had been painted, and even I, who do not play, but have so often watched Albricht the moneylender play Father Karl, or Dr. Eckardt play

Burgermeister Landsteiner, recognized the mighty figures of the Queen-Computers who lead the armies of the field of squares into battle, and the haughty King-Generals who command and, if they fall, bring down all.

A small, bent man drove. He had a head large enough for a giant—that was Lame Hans, but I paid little attention to him, not knowing that he and I would be companions here in the jail where I work. Beside him sat Heitzmann the mountebank, and it was he who took one's eyes, which was as he intended. He was tall and thin, with a sharp chin and a large nose and snapping black eyes. He had velvet trousers and a fine hat which sweat had stained around the band, and long locks of dark hair that hung from under it at odd angles so that one knew he used the finger comb when he woke, as drunkards do who find themselves beneath a bench. When the small man brought the cart through the inn-yard gate, I rose from my seat on the jail steps and went across to the inn parlor. And it was a fortunate thing I did so, because it was in this way that I chanced to see the famous game between the brass machine and Professor Baumeister.

Haven't I mentioned Professor Baumeister before? Have you not noticed that in a village such as ours there are always a dozen celebrities? Always a man who is strong (with us that is Willi Schacht, the smith's apprentice), one who eats a great deal, a learned man like Dr. Eckardt, a ladies' man, and so on. But for all these people to be properly admired, there must also be a distinguished visitor to whom to point them out, and here in Oder Spree that is Professor Baumeister, because our village lies midway between the university and Fürstenwalde, and it is here that he spends the night whenever he journeys from one to the other, much to the enrichment of Scheer the innkeeper. The fact of the matter is that Professor Baumeister has become one of our celebrities himself, only by spending the night here so often. With his broad brown beard and fine coat and tall hat and leather riding breeches, he gives the parlor of our inn the air of a gentlemen's club.

I have heard that it is often the case that the beginning of the greatest drama is as casual as any commonplace event. So it was that night. The inn was full of off-duty soldiers drinking beer, and because of the heat all the windows were thrown open, though a dozen candles were burning. Professor Baumeister was deep in conversation with Dr. Eckardt: something about the war. Herr Heitzmann the mountebank—though I did not know what to call him then—had already gotten his half liter when I came in, and was standing at the bar.

At last, when Professor Baumeister paused to emphasize some point, Herr Heitzmann leaned over to them, and in the most offhand way asked a question. It was peculiar, but the whole room seemed to grow silent as he spoke, so that he could be heard everywhere, though it was no more than a whisper. He said: "I wonder if I might venture to ask you gentlemen, you both appear to be learned men, if, to the best of your knowledge, there still exists even one of those great computational machines which were perhaps the most extraordinary—I trust you will agree with me?—creations of the age now past."

Professor Baumeister said at once, "No, sir. Not one remains."

"You feel certain of this?"

"My dear sir," said Professor Baumeister, "you must understand that those devices were dependent upon a supply of replacement parts consisting of the most delicate subminiature electronic components. These have not been produced now for over a hundred years—indeed, some of them have been unavailable longer."

"Ah," Herr Heitzmann said (mostly to himself, it seemed, but you could hear him in the kitchen). "Then I have the only one."

Professor Baumeister attempted to ignore this amazing remark, as not having been addressed to himself; but Dr. Eckardt, who is of an inquisitive disposition, said boldly, "You have such a machine, Herr . . . ?"

"Heitzmann. Originally of Berlin, now come from Zurich. And you, my good sir?"

Dr. Eckardt introduced himself, and Professor Baumeister too, and Herr Heitzmann clasped them by the hand. Then the doctor said to Professor Baumeister, "You are certain that no computers remain in existence, my friend?"

The professor said, "I am referring to working computers—machines in operating condition. There are plenty of old hulks in museums, of course."

Herr Heitzmann sighed, and pulled out a chair and sat down at the table with them, bringing his beer. "Would it not be sad," he said, "if those world-ruling machines were lost to mankind forever?"

Professor Baumeister said drily, "They based their extrapolations on numbers. That worked well enough as long as money, which is easily measured numerically, was the principal motivating force in human affairs. But as time progressed, human actions became responsive instead to a multitude of incommensurable vectors; the computers' predictions failed, the civilization they had shaped collapsed, and parts for the machines were no longer obtainable or desired."

"How fascinating!" Herr Heitzmann exclaimed. "Do you know, I have never heard it explained in quite that way. You have provided me, for the first time, with an explanation for the survival of my own machine."

Dr. Eckardt said, "You have a working computer, then?"

"I do. You see, mine is a specialized device. It was not designed, like the computers the learned professor spoke of just now, to predict human actions. It plays chess."

"And where do you keep this wonderful machine?" By this time everyone else in the room had fallen silent. Even Scheer took care not to allow the glasses he was drying to clink, and Gretchen, the fat blond serving girl who usually cracked jokes with the soldiers and banged down their plates, moved through the pipe smoke among the tables as quietly as the moon moves in a cloudy sky.

"Outside," Herr Heitzmann replied. "In my conveyance. I am taking it to Dresden."

"And it plays chess."

"It has never been defeated."

"Are you aware," Professor Baumeister inquired sardonically, "that to program a computer to play chess—to play well—was considered one of the most difficult problems? That many judged that it was never actually solved, and that those machines which most closely approached acceptable solutions were never so small as to be portable?"

"Nevertheless," Herr Heitzmann declared, "I have such a machine."

"My friend, I do not believe you."

"I take it you are a player yourself," Herr Heitzmann said. "Such a learned man could hardly be otherwise. Very well. As I said a moment ago, my machine is outside." His hand touched the table between Professor Baumeister's glass and his own, and when it came away five gold kilomarks stood there in a neat stack. "I will lay these on the outcome of the game, if you will play my machine tonight."

"Done," said Professor Baumeister.

"I must see your money."

"You will accept a draft on Streicher's, in Fürstenwalde?"

And so it was settled. Dr. Eckardt held the stakes, and six men volunteered to carry the machine into the inn parlor under Herr Heitzmann's direction.

Six were not too many, though the machine was not as large as might have been expected—not more than 120 centimeters high, with a base, as it might be, a meter on a side. The sides and top were all of brass, set with many dials and other devices no one understood.

When it was at last in place, Professor Baumeister viewed it from all sides and smiled. "This is not a computer," he said.

"My dear friend," said Herr Heitzmann, "you are mistaken."

"It is several computers. There are two keyboards and a portion of a third. There are even two nameplates, and one of these dials once belonged to a radio."

Herr Heitzmann nodded. "It was assembled at the very close of the period, for one purpose only—to play chess."

"You still contend that this machine can play?"

"I contend more. That it will win."

"Very well. Bring a board."

"That is not necessary," Herr Heitzmann said. He pulled a knob at the front of the machine, and a whole section swung forward, as the door of a vegetable bin does in a scullery. But the top of the bin was not open as though to receive the vegetables: it was instead a chessboard, with the white squares of brass, and the black of smoky glass, and on the board, standing in formation and ready to play, were two armies of chessmen such as no one in our village had ever seen, tall metal figures so stately they might have been sculptured apostles in a church, one army of brass and the other of some dark metal. "You may play white," Herr Heitzmann said. "That is generally considered an advantage."

Professor Baumeister nodded, advanced the white king's pawn two squares, and drew a chair up to the board. By the time he had seated himself the machine had replied, moving so swiftly that no one saw by what mechanism the piece had been shifted.

The next time Professor Baumeister acted more slowly, and everyone watched, eager to see the machine's countermove. It came the moment the professor had set his piece in its new position—the black queen slid forward silently, with nothing to propel it.

After ten moves Professor Baumeister said, "There is a man inside."

Herr Heitzmann smiled. "I see why you say that, my friend. Your position on the board is precarious."

"I insist that the machine be opened for my examination."

"I suppose you would say that if a man were concealed inside, the bet would be canceled." Herr Heitzmann had ordered a second glass of beer, and was leaning against the bar watching the game.

"Of course. My bet was that a machine could not defeat me. I am well aware that certain human players can."

"But conversely, if there is no man in the machine, the bet stands?"

"Certainly."

"Very well." Herr Heitzmann walked to the machine, twisted four catches on one side, and with the help of some onlookers removed the entire panel. It was of brass, like the rest of the machine, but, because the metal was thin, not so heavy as it appeared.

There was more room inside than might have been thought, yet withal a considerable amount of mechanism: things like shingles the size of little tabletops, all covered with patterns like writing (Lame Hans has told me since that these are called circuit cards). And gears and motors and the like.

When Professor Baumeister had poked among all these mechanical parts for half a minute, Herr Heitzmann asked, "Are you satisfied?"

"Yes," answered Professor Baumeister, straightening up. "There is no one in there."

"But *I* am not," said Herr Heitzmann, and he walked with long strides to the other side of the machine. Everyone crowded around him as he released the catches on that side, lifted away the panel, and stood it against the wall. "Now," he said, "you can see completely through my machine—isn't that right? Look, do you see Dr. Eckardt? Do you see me? Wave to us."

"I am satisfied," Professor Baumeister said. "Let us go on with the game."

"The machine has already taken its move. You may think about your next one while these gentlemen help me replace the panels."

Professor Baumeister was beaten in twenty-two moves. Albricht the money-lender then asked if he could play without betting and, when this was refused by Herr Heitzmann, bet a kilomark and was beaten in fourteen moves. Herr Heitzmann asked then if anyone else would play and, when no one replied, requested that the same men who had carried the machine into the inn assist him in putting it away again.

"Wait," said Professor Baumeister.

Herr Heitzmann smiled. "You mean to play again?"

"No. I want to buy your machine. On behalf of the university."

Herr Heitzmann sat down and looked serious. "I doubt that I could sell it to you. I had hoped to make a good sum in Dresden before selling it there."

"Five hundred kilomarks."

Herr Heitzmann shook his head. "That is a fair proposition," he said, "and I thank you for making it. But I cannot accept."

"Seven hundred and fifty," Professor Baumeister said. "That is my final offer."

"In gold?"

"In a draft on an account the university maintains in Fürstenwalde— you can present it there for gold the first thing in the morning."

"You must understand," said Herr Heitzmann, "that the machine requires a certain amount of care, or it will not perform properly."

"I am buying it as is," said Professor Baumeister. "As it stands here before us."

"Done, then," said Herr Heitzmann, and he put out his hand.

The board was folded away, and six stout fellows carried the machine into the professor's room for safekeeping, where he remained with it for an hour or more. When he returned to the inn parlor at last, Dr. Eckardt asked if he had been playing chess again.

Professor Baumeister nodded. "Three games."

"Did you win?"

"No, I lost them all. Where is the showman?"

"Gone," said Father Karl, who was sitting near them. "He left as soon as you took the machine to your room."

Dr. Eckardt said, "I thought he planned to stay the night here."

"So did I," said Father Karl. "And I confess I believed the machine would not function without him. I was surprised to hear that our friend the professor had been playing in private."

Just then a small, twisted man, with a large head crowned with wild black hair, limped into the inn parlor. It was Lame Hans, but no one knew that then. He asked Scheer the innkeeper for a room.

Scheer smiled. "Sitting rooms on the first floor are a hundred marks," he said. He could see by Lame Hans's worn clothes that he could not afford a sitting room.

"Something cheaper."

"My regular rooms are thirty marks. Or I can let you have a garret for ten."

Hans rented a garret room, and ordered a meal of beer, tripe, and kraut. That was the last time anyone except Gretchen noticed Lame Hans that night.

* * *

And now I must leave off recounting what I myself saw and tell many things that rest solely on the testimony of Lame Hans, given to me while he ate his potato soup in his cell. But I believe Lame Hans to be an honest fellow, and as he no longer, as he says, cares much to live, he has no reason to lie.

One thing is certain. Lame Hans and Gretchen the serving girl fell in love that night. Just how it happened I cannot say—I doubt that Lame Hans himself knows. She was sent to prepare the cot in his garret. Doubtless she was tired after drawing beer in the parlor all day and was happy to sit for a few moments and talk with him. Perhaps she smiled—she was always a girl who smiled a great deal—and laughed at some bitter joke he made. And as for Lame Hans, how many blue-eyed girls could ever have smiled at him, with his big head and twisted leg?

In the morning the machine would not play chess.

Professor Baumeister sat before it for a long time, arranging the pieces and making first one opening and then another, and tinkering with the mechanism, but nothing happened.

And then, when the morning was half-gone, Lame Hans came into the professor's room. "You paid a great deal of money for this machine," he said, and sat down in the best chair.

"Were you in the inn parlor last night?" asked Professor Baumeister. "Yes, I paid a great deal: seven hundred and fifty kilomarks."

"I was there," said Lame Hans. "You must be a very rich man to be able to afford such a sum."

"It was the university's money," explained Professor Baumeister.

"Ah," said Lame Hans. "Then it will be embarrassing for you if the machine does not play."

"It does play," said the professor. "I played three games with it last night after it was brought here."

"You must learn to make better use of your knights," Lame Hans told him, "and to attack on both sides of the board at once. In the second game you played well until you lost the queen's rook; then you went to pieces."

The professor sat down, and for a moment said nothing. And then: "You are the operator of the machine. I was correct in the beginning; I should have known."

Lame Hans looked out the window.

"How did you move the pieces—by radio? I suppose there must still be radio-control equipment in existence somewhere."

"I was inside," Lame Hans said. "I'll show you sometime; it's not important. What will you tell the university?"

"That I was swindled, I suppose. I have some money of my own, and I will try to pay back as much as I can out of that—and I own two houses in Fürstenwalde that can be sold."

"Do you smoke?" asked Lame Hans, and he took out his short pipe, and a bag of tobacco.

"Only after dinner," said the professor, "and not often then."

"I find it calms my nerves," said Lame Hans. "That is why I suggested it to you. I do not have a second pipe, but I can offer you some of my tobacco, which is very good. You might buy a clay from the innkeeper here."

"No, thank you. I fear I must abandon such little pleasures for a long time to come."

"Not necessarily," said Lame Hans. "Go ahead; buy that pipe. This is good Turkish tobacco—would you believe, to look at me, that I know a great deal about tobacco? It has been my only luxury."

"If you are the one who played chess with me last night," Professor Baumeister said, "I would be willing to believe that you know a great deal about anything. You play like the devil himself."

"I know a great deal about more than tobacco. Would you like to get your money back?"

And so it was that that very afternoon (if it can be credited) the mail coach carried away bills printed in large black letters. These said:

IN THE VILLAGE OF ODER SPREE

BEFORE THE INN OF THE GOLDEN APPLES

ON SATURDAY

AT 9:00 O'CLOCK

THE MARVELOUS BRASS CHESSPLAYING AUTOMATON

WILL BE ON DISPLAY

FREE TO EVERYONE

AND WILL PLAY ANY CHALLENGER

AT EVEN ODDS

TO A LIMIT OF DM 2,000,000

Now, you will think from what I have told you that Lame Hans was a cocky fellow, but that is not the case, though like many of us who are small of stature he pretended to be self-reliant when he was among men taller than he. The truth is that though he did not show it, he was very frightened when he met Herr Heitzmann (as the two of them had arranged earlier that he should) in a certain malodorous tavern near the Schwarzthor in Furthenwald.

"So there you are, my friend," said Herr Heitzmann. "How did it go?"

"Terribly," Lame Hans replied as though he felt nothing. "I was locked up in that brass snuffbox for half the night, and had to play twenty games with that fool of a scholar. And when at last I got out, I couldn't get a ride here and had to walk most of the way on this bad leg of mine. I trust it was comfortable on the cart seat? The horse didn't give you too much trouble?"

"I'm sorry you've had a poor time of it, but now you can relax. There's nothing more to do until he's convinced the machine is broken and irreparable."

Lame Hans looked at him as though in some surprise. "You didn't see the signs? They are posted everywhere."

"What signs?"

"He's offering to bet two thousand kilomarks that no one can beat the machine."

Herr Heitzmann shrugged. "He will discover that it is inoperative before the contest, and cancel it."

"He could not cancel after the bet was made," said Lame Hans. "Particularly if there were a proviso that if either was unable to play, the bet was forfeited. Some upright citizen would be selected to hold the stakes, naturally."

"I don't suppose he could at that," said Herr Heitzmann, taking a swallow of schnapps from the glass before him. "However, he wouldn't bet *me*—he'd think I knew some way to influence the machine. Still, he's never seen *you*."

"Just what I've been thinking myself," said Lame Hans, "on my hike."

"It's a little out of your line."

"If you'll put up the cash, I'd be willing to go a little out of my line for my tenth of that kind of money. But what is there to do? I make the bet, find someone to hold the stakes, and stand ready to play on Saturday morning. I could even offer to play him—for a smaller bet—to give him a chance to get some of his own back. That is, if he has anything left after paying off. It would make it seem more sporting."

"You're certain you could beat him?"

"I can beat anybody—you know that. Besides, I beat him a score of times yesterday; the game you saw was just the first."

Herr Heitzmann ducked under the threatening edge of a tray carried by an overenthusiastic waiter. "All the same," Herr Heitzmann said, "when he discovers it won't work . . ."

"I could even spend a bit of time in the machine. That's no problem. It's in a first-floor room, with a window that won't lock."

And so Lame Hans left for our village again, this time considerably better dressed and with two thousand kilomarks in his pocket. Herr Heitzmann, with his appearance considerably altered by a plastiskin mask, left also, an hour later, to keep an eye on the two thousand.

B ut," the professor said when Lame Hans and he were comfortably ensconced in his sitting room again, with pipes in their mouths and glasses in their hands and a plate of sausage on the table, "but who is going to operate the machine for us? Wouldn't it be easier if you simply didn't appear? Then you would forfeit."

"And Heitzmann would kill me," said Lame Hans.

"He didn't strike me as the type."

"He would hire it done," Hans said positively. "Whenever he got the cash. There are deserters about who are happy enough to do that kind of work for drinking money. For that matter, there are soldiers who aren't deserters who'll do it—men on detached duty of one kind and another. When you've spent all winter slaughtering Russians, one more body doesn't make much difference." He blew a smoke ring, then ran the long stem of his clay pipe through it as though he were driving home a bayonet. "But if I play the machine and lose, he'll only think you figured things out and got somebody to work it, and that I'm not as good as he supposed. Then he won't want anything more to do with me."

"All right, then."

"A tobacconist should do well in this village, don't you think? I had in mind that little shop two doors down from here. When the coaches stop, the passengers will see my sign; there should be many who'll want to fill their pouches."

"Gretchen prefers to stay here, I suppose."

Lame Hans nodded. "It doesn't matter to me. I've been all over, and when you've been all over, it's all the same."

Like everyone else in the village, and for fifty kilometers around, I had seen the professor's posters, and I went to bed Friday night full of pleasant anticipation. Lame Hans had told me that he retired in the same frame of mind, after a couple of glasses of good plum brandy in the inn parlor with the professor. He and the professor had to appear strangers and antagonists in public, as will be readily seen, but this did not prevent them from eating and drinking together while they discussed arrangements for the match, which was to be held—with the permission of Burgermeister Landsteiner—in the village street, where an area for the players had been cordoned off and high benches erected for the spectators.

Hans woke (so he has told me) when it was still dark, thinking that he had heard thunder. Then the noise came again, and he knew it must be the artillery, the big siege guns, firing at the Russians trapped in Kostrzyn. The army had built wood-fired steam tractors to pull those guns—he had seen them in Wriezen— and now the soldiers were talking about putting armor on the tractors and mounting cannon, so the knights of the chessboard would exist in reality once more.

The firing continued, booming across the dry plain, and he went to the window to see if he could make out the flashes, but could not. He put on a thin shirt and a pair of cotton trousers (for though the sun was not yet up, it was as hot as if the whole of Brandenburg had been thrust into a furnace) and went into the street to look at the empty shop in which he planned to set up his tobacco business. A squadron of *Ritters* galloped through the village, doubtless on their way to the siege. Lame Hans shouted, "What do you mean to do? Ride your horses against the walls?" but they ignored him. Now that the truce was broken, Von Koblenz's army would soon be advancing up the Oder Valley, Lame Hans thought. The Russians were said to have been preparing powered balloons to assist in the defense, and this hot summer weather, when the air seemed never to stir, would favor their use. He decided that if he were the commissar, he would allow Von Koblenz to reach Glogów and then . . .

But he was not the commissar. He went back into the inn and smoked his pipe until Frau Scheer came down to prepare his breakfast. Then he went to the professor's room where the machine was kept. Gretchen was already waiting there.

"Now then," Professor Baumeister said, "I understand that the two of you have it all worked out between you." And Gretchen nodded solemnly, so that her plump chin looked like a soft little pillow pressed against her throat.

"It is quite simple," said Lame Hans. "Gretchen does not know how to play, but I have worked out the moves for her and drawn them on a sheet of paper, and we have practiced in my room with a board. We will run through it once here when she is in the machine; then there will be nothing more to do."

"Is it a short game? It won't do for her to become confused."

"She will win in fourteen moves," Lame Hans promised. "But still it is unusual. I don't think anyone has done it before. You will see in a moment."

To Gretchen, Professor Baumeister said, "You're sure you won't be mixed up? Everything depends on you."

The girl shook her head, making her blond braids dance. "No, Herr Professor." She drew a folded piece of paper from her bosom. "I have it all here, and as my Hans told you, we have practiced in his room, where no one could see us."

"You aren't afraid?"

"When I am going to marry Hans, and be mistress of a fine shop? Oh, no, Herr Professor—for that I would do much worse things than to hide in this thing that looks like a stove and play a game."

"We are ready, then," the professor said. "Hans, you still have not explained how it is that a person can hide in there when the sides can be removed allowing people to look through the machinery. And I confess I still don't understand how it can be done, or how the pieces are moved."

"Here," said Lame Hans, and he pulled out the board as Herr Heitzmann had done in the inn parlor. "Now will you assist me in removing the left side? You should learn the way it comes loose, Professor—someday you may have to do it yourself." (The truth was that Hans was not strong enough to handle the big brass sheet by himself and did not wish to be humiliated before Gretchen.)

"I had forgotten how much empty space there is inside," Professor Baumeister said when they had it off. "It looks more impossible than ever."

"It is simple, like all good tricks," Lame Hans told him. "And it is the sign of a good trick that it is the thing that makes it appear difficult that makes it easy. Here is where the chessboard is, you see, when it is folded up. But when it is unfolded, the panel under it swings out on a hinge to support it, and there are sides, so that a triangular space is formed."

The professor nodded and said, "I remember thinking when I played you that it looked like a potato bin, with the chessboard laid over the top."

"Exactly," Lame Hans continued. "The space is not noticeable when the machine is open, because this circuit is just in front of it. But see here." And he released a little catch at the top of the circuit card, and pivoted it up to show the empty space behind it. "I am in the machine when it is carried in, but when Heitzmann pulls out the board, I lift this and fit myself under it; then, when the machine is opened for inspection, I am out of view. I can look up through the dark glass of the black squares, and because the pieces are so tall, I can make out their positions. But because it is bright outside, but dim where I am, I cannot be seen."

"I understand," said the professor. "But will Gretchen have enough light in there to read her piece of paper?"

"That was why I wanted to hold the match in the street. With the board in sunshine, she will be able to see her paper clearly."

Gretchen was on her knees, looking at the space behind the circuit card. "It is very small in there," she said.

"It is big enough," said Lame Hans. "Do you have the magnet?" And then to the professor: "The pieces are moved by moving a magnet under them. The white pieces are brass, but the black ones are of iron, and the magnet gives them a sliding motion that is very impressive."

"I know," said the professor, remembering that he had felt a twinge of uneasiness whenever the machine had shifted a piece. "Gretchen, see if you can get inside."

The poor girl did the best she could, but encountered the greatest difficulty in wedging herself into the small space under the board. Work in the kitchen of the inn had provided her with many opportunities to snatch a mouthful of pastry or a choice potato dumpling or a half stein of dark beer, and she had availed herself of most of them—with the result that she possessed a lush and blooming figure of the sort that appeals to men like Lame Hans, who, having been withered before birth by the isotopes of the old wars, are themselves thin and small by nature. But though full breasts like ripe melons, and a rounded comfortable stomach and generous hips, may be pleasant things to look at when the moonlight comes in the bedroom window, they are not really well suited to folding up in a little three-cornered space under a chessboard, and in the end, poor Gretchen was forced to remove her gown, and her shift as well, before she could cram herself, with much gasping and grunting, into it.

An hour later, Willi Schacht the smith's apprentice and five other men carried the machine out into the street and set it in the space that had been cordoned off for the players, and if they noticed the extra weight, they did not complain of it. And there the good people who had come to see the match looked at the machine, and fanned themselves, and said that they were glad they weren't in the army on a day like this—because what must it be to serve one of those big guns, which get hot enough to poach an egg after half a dozen shots, even in ordinary weather? And between moppings and fannings they talked about the machine, and the mysterious Herr Zimmer (that was the name Lame Hans had given) who was going to play for two hundred gold kilomarks.

Nine chimes sounded from the old clock in the steeple of Father Karl's church, and Herr Zimmer did not appear.

Dr. Eckardt, who had been chosen again to hold the stakes, came forward and whispered for some time with Professor Baumeister. The professor (if the truth were known) was beginning to believe that perhaps Lame Hans had decided it was best to forfeit after all—though in fact, if anyone had looked, he would have seen Lame Hans sitting at the bar of the inn at that very moment, having a pleasant nip of plum brandy and then another, while he allowed the suspense to build up as a good showman should.

At last Dr. Eckardt climbed upon a chair and announced: "It is nearly ten. When the bet was made it was agreed by both parties that if either failed to appear—or, appearing, failed to play—the other should be declared the winner. If the worthy stranger, Herr Zimmer, does not make an appearance before ten minutes past ten, I intend to award the money entrusted to me to our respected acquaintance Professor Baumeister."

There was a murmur of excitement at this, but just when the clock began to strike, Lame Hans called from the door of the inn: "*Wait!*" Then hats were thrown into the air, and women stood on tiptoes to see, and fathers lifted their children up as the lame Herr Zimmer made his way down the steps of the inn and took his place in the chair that had been arranged in front of the board.

"Are you ready to begin?" said Dr. Eckardt.

"I am," said Lame Hans, and opened.

The first five moves were made just as they had been rehearsed. But in the sixth, in which Gretchen was to have slid her queen half across the board, the piece stopped a square short.

Any ordinary player would have been dismayed, but Lame Hans was not. He only put his chin on his hand, and contrived (though wishing he had not drunk the brandy) a series of moves within the frame of the fourteen-move game, by which he should lose despite the queen's being out of position. He made the first of these moves, and black moved the queen again, this time in a way that was completely different from anything on the paper Hans had given Gretchen. *She was deceiving me when she said she did not know how to play*, he thought to himself. *And now she feels she can't read the paper in there, or perhaps she has decided to surprise me. Naturally she would learn the fundamentals of the game, when it is played in the inn parlor every night.* (But he knew that she had not been deceiving him.) Then he saw that this new move of the queen's was in fact a clever attack, into which he could play and lose.

And then the guns around Kostrzyn, which had been silent since the early hours of the morning, began to boom again. Three times Lame Hans's hand stretched out to touch his king and make the move that would render it quite impossible for him to escape the queen, and three times it drew back. "You have five minutes in which to move," Dr. Eckardt said. "I will tell you when only thirty seconds remain, and count the last five."

*The machine was built to play chess*, thought Lame Hans. *Long ago, and they were warlocks in those days. Could it be that Gretchen, in kicking about . . . ?*

Some motion in the sky made him raise his eyes, looking above the board and over the top of the machine itself. An artillery observation balloon (gray-black, a German balloon then) was outlined against the blue sky. He thought of himself sitting in a dingy little shop full of tobacco all day long, and no one to play chess with—no one he could not checkmate easily.

He moved a pawn, and the black bishop slipped out of the king's row to tighten the net.

If he won, they would have to pay him. Heitzmann would think everything had gone according to plan, and Professor Baumeister, surely, would hire no assassins. Lame Hans launched his counterattack: the real attack at the left side of the board, with a false one down the center. Professor Baumeister came to stand beside him, and Dr. Eckardt warned him not to distract the player. There had been seven more than fourteen moves—and there was a trap behind the trap.

Lame Hans took the black queen's knight and lost a pawn. He was sweating in the heat, wiping his brow with his sleeve between moves.

A black rook, squat in its iron sandbags, advanced three squares, and he heard the crowd cheer. "That is mate, Herr Zimmer," Dr. Eckardt announced. Lame Hans saw the look of relief on Professor Baumeister's face, and knew that his own was blank. Then over the cheering someone shouted: *"Cheat! Cheat!"* Gray-black pillbox police caps were forcing their way through the hats and parasols of the spectators.

"There is a man in there! There is someone inside!" It was too clear and too loud—a showman's voice. A tall stranger was standing on the topmost bench waving Heitzmann's sweat-stained velvet hat.

A policeman asked, "The machine opens, does it not, Herr Professor? Open it quickly before there is a riot."

Professor Baumeister said, "I don't know how."

"It looks simple enough," declared the other policeman, and he began to unfasten the catches, wrapping his hand in his handkerchief to protect it from the heat of the brass.

"Wait!" ordered Professor Baumeister, but neither one waited; the first policeman went to the aid of the other, and together they lifted away one side of the machine and let it fall against the railing. The movable circuit card had not been allowed to swing back into place, and Gretchen's plump, naked legs protruded from the cavity beneath the chessboard. The first policeman seized them by the ankles and pulled her out until her half-open eyes stared at the bright sky.

Dr. Eckhardt bent over her and flexed her left arm at the elbow. "Rigor is beginning," he said. "She died of the heat, undoubtedly."

Lame Hans threw himself on her body weeping.

Such is the story of Lame Hans. The captain of police, in his kindness, has permitted me to push the machine to a position which permits Hans to reach the board through the bars of his cell, and he plays chess there all day long, moving first his own white pieces and then the black ones of the machine, and always losing. Sometimes when he is not quick enough to move the black queen, I see her begin to rock and to slide herself, and the dials and the console lights to glow with impatience, and then Hans must reach out and take her to her new position at once. Do you not think that this is sad for Lame Hans? I have heard that many who have been twisted by the old wars have these psychokinetic abilities without knowing it; and Professor Baumeister, who is in the cell next to his, says that someday a technology may be founded on them.

## AFTERWORD

Most games do not inspire the human imagination. A few—a very few—do. Or so it seems to me. There may be a good football story, but I have never come across it. My guess is that there are some good cricket stories, but I couldn't name even one. Ditto for soccer stories. But baseball! We could start with Michael Bishop's novel *Brittle Innings,* then go down a whole list of Ring Lardner short stories—see his collection *You Know Me Al.* I've even committed a baseball story myself, "The On-Deck Circle."

Chess is like that. Can anybody name a checkers story? I can't. Monopoly? Dominoes? But chess! *Through the Looking-Glass* alone would make my point; and there's Rex Stout's chess mystery, *Gambit,* and a whole host of short stories, including this one. One of these days I want to write a chess story that returns chess to its origin, a story in which the rooks are war elephants, the knights chariots, the bishops cavalry, the queens viziers commanding elite corps, and the kings rajas with their bodyguards. If you don't play chess, you should learn; and then, perhaps, you will see the tall swordsmen we call pawns, nearly naked behind their big rhinoceros-hide shields, see the chariots charging—then wheeling like a flock of birds to rain javelins and arrows upon the enemy's line.

Hear those trumpetings? No metal horn ever voiced such music. Hear the thunder of their feet? Tigers cower before these soldiers. Their faces are painted a score of colors and their tusks made longer and sharper by steel blades; each bears a painted wooden castle manned by half a dozen archers.

No wonder there are so many chess stories!

# STRAW

Yes, I remember killing my first man very well; I was just seventeen. A flock of snow geese flew under us that day about noon. I remember looking over the side of the basket and seeing them, and thinking that they looked like a pike head. That was an omen, of course, but I did not pay any attention.

It was clear, fall weather—a trifle chilly. I remember that. It must have been about the midpart of October. Good weather for the balloon. Clow would reach up every quarter hour or so with a few double handfuls of straw for the brazier, and that was all it required. We cruised, usually, at about twice the height of a steeple.

You have never been in one? Well, that shows how things have changed. Before the Fire-wights came, there was hardly any fighting at all, and free swords had to travel all over the continent looking for what there was. A balloon was better than walking, believe me. Miles—he was our captain in those days—said that where there were three soldiers together, one was certain to put a shaft through a balloon; it was too big a target to resist, and that would show you where the armies were.

No, we would not have been killed. You would have had to slit the thing wide open before it would fall fast, and a little hole like the business end of a pike would make would just barely let you know it was there. The baskets do not swing either, as people think. Why should they? They feel no wind—they are traveling with it. A man just seems to hang there, when he is up in one of them, and the world turns under him. He can hear everything—pigs and chickens, and the squeak the windlass makes drawing water from a well.

"Good flying weather," Clow said to me.

I nodded. Solemnly, I suppose.

"All the lift you want, in weather like this. The colder it is, the better she pulls. The heat from the fire doesn't like the chill, and tries to escape from it. That's what they say."

Blond Bracata spit over the side. "Nothing in our bellies," she said, "that's what makes it lift. If we don't eat today you won't have to light the fire tomorrow—I'll take us up myself."

She was taller than any of us except Miles, and the heaviest of us all, but Miles would not allow for size when the food was passed out, so I suppose she was the hungriest too.

Derek said, "We should have stretched one of that last bunch over the fire. That would have fetched a pot of stew, at the least."

Miles shook his head. "There were too many."

"They would have run like rabbits."

"And if they hadn't?"

"They had no armor."

Unexpectantly, Bracata came in for the captain. "They had twenty-two men, and fourteen women. I counted them."

"The women wouldn't fight."

"I used to be one of them. I would have fought."

Clow's soft voice added: "Nearly any woman will fight if she can get behind you."

Bracata stared at him, not sure whether he was supporting her or not. She had her mitts on—she was as good with them as anyone I have ever seen—and I remember that I thought for an instant that she would go for Clow right there in the basket. We were packed in like fledglings in the nest, and fighting, it would have taken at least three of us to throw her out—by which time she would have killed us all, I suppose. But she was afraid of Clow. I found out why later. She respected Miles, I think, for his judgment and courage, without being afraid of him. She did not care much for Derek either way, and of course I was hardly there at all as far as she was concerned. But she was just a little frightened by Clow.

Clow was the only one I was not frightened by—but that is another story too.

"Give it more straw," Miles said.

"We're nearly out."

"We can't land in this forest."

Clow shook his head and added straw to the fire in the brazier—about half as much as he usually did. We were sinking toward what looked like a red and gold carpet.

"We got straw out of them anyway," I said, just to let the others know I was there.

"You can always get straw," Clow told me. He had drawn a throwing spike and was feigning to clean his nails with it. "Even from swineherds, who you'd think wouldn't have it. They'll get it to be rid of us."

"Bracata's right," Miles said. He gave the impression that he had not heard Clow and me. "We have to have food today."

Derek snorted. "What if there are twenty?"

"We stretch one over the fire. Isn't that what you suggested? And if it takes fighting, we fight. But we have to eat today." He looked at me. "What did I tell you when you joined us, Jerr? High pay or nothing? This is the nothing. Want to quit?"

I said, "Not if you don't want me to."

Clow was scraping the last of the straw from the bag. It was hardly a handful. As he threw it in the brazier Bracata asked, "Are we going to set down in the trees?"

Clow shook his head and pointed. Away in the distance I could see a speck of white on a hill. It looked too far, but the wind was taking us there, and it grew and grew until we could see that it was a big house, all built of white brick with gardens and outbuildings, and a road that ran up to the door. There are none like that now, I suppose.

L andings are the most exciting part of traveling by balloon, and sometimes the most unpleasant. If you are lucky, the basket stays upright. We were not. Our basket snagged and tipped over and was dragged along by the envelope, which fought the wind and did not want to go down, cold though it was by then. If there had been a fire in the brazier still, I suppose we would have set the meadow ablaze. As it was, we were tumbled about like toys. Bracata fell on top of me, as heavy as stone, and she had the claws of her mitts out, trying to dig them into the turf to stop herself, so that for a moment I thought I was going to be killed. Derek's pike had been charged, and the ratchet released in the confusion; the head went flying across the field, just missing a cow.

By the time I recovered my breath and got to my feet, Clow had the envelope under control and was treading it down. Miles was up too, straightening his hauberk and sword belt. "Look like a soldier," he called to me. "Where are your weapons?"

A pincer-mace and my pike were all I had, and the pincer-mace had fallen out of the basket. After five minutes of looking, I found it in the tall grass, and went over to help Clow fold the envelope.

When we were finished, we stuffed it in the basket and put our pikes through the rings on each side so we could carry it. By that time we could see men on horseback coming down from the big house. Derek said, "We won't be able to stand against horsemen in this field."

For an instant I saw Miles smile. Then he looked very serious. "We'll have one of those fellows over a fire in half an hour."

Derek was counting, and so was I. Eight horsemen, with a cart following them. Several of the horsemen had lances, and I could see the sunlight winking on helmets and breastplates. Derek began pounding the butt of his pike on the ground to charge it.

I suggested to Clow that it might look more friendly if we picked up the balloon and went to meet the horsemen, but he shook his head. "Why bother?"

The first of them had reached the fence around the field. He was sitting a roan stallion that took it at a clean jump and came thundering up to us looking as big as a donjon on wheels.

"Greetings," Miles called. "If this be your land, Lord, we give thanks for your hospitality. We'd not have intruded, but our conveyance has exhausted its fuel."

"You are welcome," the horseman called. He was as tall as Miles or taller, as well as I could judge, and as wide as Bracata. "Needs must, as they say, and no harm done." Three of the others had jumped their mounts over the fence behind him. The rest were taking down the rails so the cart could get through.

"Have you straw, Lord?" Miles asked. I thought it would have been better if he had asked for food. "If we could have a few bundles of straw, we'd not trouble you more."

"None here," the horseman said, waving a mail-clad arm at the fields around us, "yet I feel sure my bailiff could find you some. Come up to the hall for a taste of meat and a glass of wine, and you can make your ascension from the terrace; the ladies would be delighted to see it, I'm certain. You're floating swords, I take it?"

"We are that," our captain affirmed, "but persons of good character nonetheless. We're called the Faithful Five—perhaps you've heard of us? High-hearted, fierce-fighting wind-warriors all, as it says on the balloon."

A younger man, who had reined up next to the one Miles called Lord, snorted. "If that boy is high hearted, or a fierce fighter either, I'll eat his breeks."

Of course, I should not have done it. I have been too mettlesome all my life, and it has gotten me in more trouble than I could tell you of if I talked till sunset, though it has been good to me too—I would have spent my days following the plow, I suppose, if I had not knocked down Derek for what he called our goose. But you see how it was. Here I had been thinking of myself as a hard-bitten balloon soldier, and then to hear something like that. Anyway, I swung the pincermace overhand once I had a good grip on his stirrup. I had been afraid the extension spring was a bit weak, never having used one before, but it worked well; the pliers got him under the left arm and between the ear and the right shoulder, and would have cracked his neck for him properly if he had not been wearing a gorget. As it was, I jerked him off his horse pretty handily and got out the little dagger that screwed into the mace handle. A couple of the other horsemen couched their lances, and Derek had a finger on the dog-catch of his pike, so all in all it looked as if there could be a proper fight, but "Lord" (I learned afterward that he was the Baron Ascolot) yelled at the young man I had pulled out of his saddle, and Miles yelled at me and grabbed my left wrist, and thus it all blew over. When we had tripped the release and gotten the mace open and retracted again, Miles said, "He will be punished, Lord. Leave him to me. It will be severe. I assure you."

"No, upon my oath," the baron declared. "It will teach my son to be less free with his tongue in the company of armed men. He has been raised at the hall,

Captain, where everyone bends the knee to him. He must learn not to expect that of strangers."

The cart rolled up just then, drawn by two fine mules—either of them would have been worth my father's holding, I judged—and at the baron's urging we loaded our balloon into it and climbed in after it ourselves, sitting on the fabric. The horsemen galloped off, and the cart driver cracked his lash over the mules' backs.

"Quite a place," Miles remarked. He was looking up at the big house toward which we were making.

I whispered to Clow, "A palace, I should say," and Miles overheard me, and said, "It's a villa, Jerr—the unfortified country property of a gentleman. If there were a wall and a tower, it would be a castle, or at least a castellett."

There were gardens in front, very beautiful as I remember, and a fountain. The road looped up before the door, and we got out and trooped into the hall, while the baron's man—he was richer dressed than anybody I had ever seen up till then, a fat man with white hair—set two of the hostlers to watch our balloon while it was taken back to the stable yard.

Venison and beef were on the table, and even a pheasant with all his feathers put back, and the baron and his sons sat with us and drank some wine and ate a bit of bread each for hospitality's sake. Then the baron said, "Surely you don't fly in the dark, Captain?"

"Not unless we must, Lord."

"Then with the day drawing to a close, it's just as well for you that we've no straw. You can pass the night with us, and in the morning I'll send my bailiff to the village with the cart. You'll be able to ascend at midmorning, when the ladies can have a clear view of you as you go up."

"No straw?" our captain asked.

"None, I fear, here. But they'll have aplenty in the village, never doubt it. They lay it in the road to silence the horses' hoofs when a woman's with child, as I've seen many a time. You'll have a cartload as a gift from me, if you can use that much." The baron smiled as he said that; he had a friendly face, round and red as an apple. "Now tell me" (he went on) "how it is to be a floating sword. I always find other men's trades of interest, and it seems to me you follow one of the most fascinating of all. For example, how do you gauge the charge you will make your employer?"

"We have two scales, Lord," Miles began.

I had heard all of that before, so I stopped listening. Bracata was next to me at table, so I had all I could do to get something to eat for myself, and I doubt I ever got a taste of the pheasant. By good luck, a couple of lasses—the baron's daughters—had come in, and one of them started curling a lock of Derek's hair around her finger, so that distracted him while he was helping himself to the venison, and Bracata put an arm around the other and warned her of Men. If it had not been for that I would not have had a thing; as it was, I stuffed myself on deer's meat until I had to loose my waistband. Flesh of any sort had been a rarity where I came from.

I had thought that the baron might give us beds in the house, but when we had eaten and drunk all we could hold, the white-haired fat man led us out a side door and over to a wattle-walled building full of bunks—I suppose it was kept for the extra laborers needed at harvest. It was not the palace bedroom I had been dreaming of, but it was cleaner than home, and there was a big fireplace down at one end with logs stacked ready by, so it was probably more comfortable for me than a bed in the big house itself would have been.

Clow took out a piece of cherrywood, and started carving a woman in it, and Bracata and Derek lay down to sleep. I made shift to talk to Miles, but he was full of thoughts, sitting on a bench near the hearth and chinking the purse (just like this one, it was) he had gotten from the baron, so I tried to sleep too. But I had had too much to eat to sleep so soon, and since it was still light out, I decided to walk around the villa and try to find somebody to chat with. The front looked too grand for me; I went to the back, thinking to make sure our balloon had suffered no hurt, and perhaps have another look at those mules.

There were three barns behind the house, built of stone up to the height of my waist, and wood above that, and whitewashed. I walked into the nearest of them, not thinking about anything much besides my full belly until a big warhorse with a white star on his forehead reached his head out of his stall and nuzzled at my cheek. I reached out and stroked his neck for him the way they like. He nickered, and I turned to have a better look at him. That was when I saw what was in his stall. He was standing on a span or more of the cleanest, yellowest straw I had ever seen. I looked up over my head then, and there was a loft full of it up there.

In a minute or so, I suppose it was, I was back in the building where we were to sleep, shaking Miles by the shoulder and telling him I had found all the straw anyone could ask for.

He did not seem to understand, at first. "Wagonloads of straw, Captain," I told him. "Why, every horse in the place has as much to lay him on as would carry us a hundred leagues."

"All right," Miles told me.

"Captain—"

"There's no straw here, Jerr. Not for us. Now be a sensible lad and get some rest."

"But there is, Captain. I saw it. I can bring you back a helmetful."

"Come here, Jerr," he said, and got up and led me outside. I thought he was going to ask me to show him the straw, but instead of going back to where the barns were, he took me away from the house to the top of a grassy knoll. "Look out there, Jerr. Far off. What do you see?"

"Trees," I said. "There might be a river at the bottom of the valley; then more trees on the other side."

"Beyond that."

I looked to the horizon, where he seemed to be pointing. There were little threads of black smoke rising there, looking as thin as spiderweb at that distance.

"What do you see?"

"Smoke."

"That's straw burning, Jerr. House thatch. That's why there's no straw here. Gold, but no straw, because a soldier gets straw only where he isn't welcome. They'll reach the river there by sundown, and I'm told it can be forded at this season. Now do you understand?"

They came that night at moonrise.

∞

## AFTERWORD

Inventions and scientific discoveries seem to occur almost at random. The people who disagree with that statement say that when technology (or science) reaches a certain point, the same idea will occur to a dozen people. The shorthand for this is *steam-engine time*, the idea being that when it's time for the steam engine to be invented, a bunch of people will start working on one.

It ain't so.

They had indoor plumbing in Ancient Crete. It was lost with the fall of that civilization, and did not reappear until long after it was needed. A model airplane, carved from wood, has been found in an Egyptian tomb. (Don't get me started on the Egyptian girl wearing sunglasses.) Electroplating seems to have been invented at least twice.

And so on. I decided to put the hot-air balloon in the Dark Ages, and I threw in a few other things too. Thus the story you have just read. Was there ever a time like that? No. Could there have been? Certainly.

# The Eyeflash Miracles

*I cannot call him to mind.*

—ANATOLE FRANCE,
*The Procurator of Judea*

Little Tib heard the train coming while it was still a long way away, and he felt it in his feet. He stepped off the track onto a prestressed concrete tie, listening. Then he put one ear to the endless steel and listened to that sing, louder and louder. Only when he began to feel the ground shake under him did he lift his head at last and make his way down the embankment through the tall, prickly weeds, probing the slope with his stick.

The stick splashed water. He could not hear it because of the noise the train made roaring by, but he knew the feel of it, the kind of drag it made when he tried to move the end of the stick. He laid it down and felt with his hands where his knees would be when he knelt, and it felt all right. A little soft, but no broken glass. He knelt then and sniffed the water, and it smelled good and was cool to his fingers, so he drank, bending down and sucking up the water with his mouth, then splashing it on his face and the back of his neck.

"Say!" an authoritative voice called. "Say, you boy!"

Little Tib straightened up, picking up his stick again. He thought, *This could be Sugarland*. He said, "Are you a policeman, sir?"

"I am the superintendent."

That was almost as good. Little Tib tilted his head back so the voice could see his eyes. He had often imagined coming to Sugarland and how it would be there, but he had never considered just what it was he should say when he arrived. He said, "My card . . ." The train was still rumbling away, not too far off.

Another voice said, "Now don't you hurt that child." It was not authoritative. There was the sound of responsibility in it.

"You ought to be in school, young man," the first voice said. "Do you know who I am?"

Little Tib nodded. "The superintendent."

"That's right, I'm the superintendent. I'm Mr. Parker himself. Your teacher has told you about me, I'm sure."

"Now don't hurt that child," the second voice said again. "He never did hurt you."

"Playing hooky. I understand that's what the children call it. We never use such a term ourselves, of course. You will be referred to as an absentee. What's your name?"

"George Tibbs."

"I see. I am Mr. Parker, the superintendent. This is my valet; his name is Nitty."

"Hello," Little Tib said.

"Mr. Parker, maybe this absentee boy would like to have something to eat. He looks to me like he has been absentee a long while."

"Fishing," Mr. Parker said. "I believe that's what most of them do."

"You can't see, can you?" A hand closed on Little Tib's arm. The hand was large and hard, but it did not bear down. "You can cross right here. There's a rock in the middle—step on that."

Little Tib found the rock with his stick and put one foot there. The hand on his arm seemed to lift him across. He stood on the rock for a moment with his stick in the water, touching bottom to steady himself. "Now a great big step." His shoe touched the soft bank on the other side. "We got a camp right over here. Mr. Parker, don't you think this absentee boy would like a sweet roll?"

Little Tib said, "Yes, I would."

"I would too," Nitty told him.

"Now, young man, why aren't you in school?"

"How is he going to see the board?"

"We have special facilities for the blind, Nitty. At Grovehurst there is a class tailored to make allowance for their disability. I can't at this moment recall the name of the teacher, but she is an exceedingly capable young woman."

Little Tib asked, "Is Grovehurst in Sugar Land?"

"Grovehurst is in Martinsburg," Mr. Parker told him. "I am superintendent of the Martinsburg Public School System. How far are we from Martinsburg now, Nitty?"

"Two, three hundred kilometers, I guess."

"We will enter you in that class as soon as we reach Martinsburg, young man."

Nitty said, "We're going to Macon—I keep on tellin' you."

"Your papers are all in order, I suppose? Your grade and attendance records from your previous school? Your withdrawal permit, birth certificate, and your retinal pattern card from the Federal Reserve?"

Little Tib sat mute. Someone pushed a sticky pastry into his hands, but he did not raise it to his mouth.

"Mr. Parker, I don't think he's got papers."

"That is a serious—"

"Why he got to have papers? He ain't no dog!"

Little Tib was weeping. "I see!" Mr. Parker said. "He's blind; Nitty, I think his retinas have been destroyed. Why, he's not really here at all."

"Course he's here."

"A ghost. We're seeing a ghost, Nitty. Sociologically he's not real—he's been deprived of existence."

"I never in my whole life seen a ghost."

"You dumb bastard," Mr. Parker exploded.

"You don't have to talk to me like that, Mr. Parker."

"You dumb bastard. All my life there's been nobody around but dumb bastards like you." Mr. Parker was weeping too. Little Tib felt one of his tears, large and hot, fall on his hand. His own sobbing slowed, then faded away. It was outside his experience to hear grown people—men—cry. He took a bite from the roll he had been given, tasting the sweet, sticky icing and hoping for a raisin.

"Mr. Parker," Nitty said softly. "Mr. Parker."

After a time, Mr. Parker said, "Yes."

"He—this boy George—might be able to get them, Mr. Parker. You recall how you and me went to the building that time? We looked all around it a long while. And there was that window, that old window with the iron over it and the latch broken. I pushed on it and you could see the glass move in a little. But couldn't either of us get between those bars."

"This boy is blind, Nitty," Mr. Parker said.

"Sure he is, Mr. Parker. But you know how dark it was in there. What is a man going to do? Turn on the lights? No, he's goin' to take a little bit of a flashlight and put tape or something over the end till it don't make no more light than a lightnin' bug. A blind person could do better with no light than a seeing one with just a little speck like that. I guess he's used to bein' blind by now. I guess he knows how to find his way around without eyes."

A hand touched Little Tib's shoulder. It seemed smaller and softer than the hand that had helped him across the creek. "He's crazy," Mr. Parker's voice said. "That Nitty. He's crazy. I'm crazy, I'm the one. But he's crazier than I am."

"He could do it, Mr. Parker. See how thin he is."

"Would you do it?" Mr. Parker asked.

Little Tib swallowed a wad of roll. "Do what?"

"Get something for us."

"I guess so."

"Nitty, build a fire," Mr. Parker said. "We won't be going any farther tonight."

"Won't be goin' this way at *all*," Nitty said.

"You see, George," Mr. Parker said. "My authority has been temporarily abrogated. Sometimes I forget that."

Nitty chuckled somewhere farther away than Little Tib had thought he was. He must have left very silently.

"But when it is restored, I can do all the things I said I would do for you: get you into a special class for the blind, for example. You'd like that, wouldn't you, George?"

"Yes." A whip-poor-will called far off to Little Tib's left, and he could hear Nitty breaking sticks.

"Have you run away from home, George?"

"Yes," Little Tib said again.

"Why?"

Little Tib shrugged. He was ready to cry again. Something was thickening and tightening in his throat, and his eyes had begun to water.

"I think I know why," Mr. Parker said. "We might even be able to do something about that."

"*Here* we are," Nitty called. He dumped his load of sticks, rattling, more or less in front of Little Tib.

Later that night Little Tib lay on the ground with half of Nitty's blanket over him, and half under him. The fire was crackling not too far away. Nitty said the smoke would help to drive the mosquitoes off. Little Tib pushed the heels of his hands against his eyes and saw red and yellow flashes like a real fire. He did it again, and there was a gold nugget against a field of blue. Those were the last things he had been able to see for a long time, and he was afraid, each time he summoned them up, that they would not come. On the other side of the fire Mr. Parker breathed the heavy breath of sleep.

Nitty bent over Little Tib, smoothing his blanket, then pressing it in against his sides. "It's okay," Little Tib said.

"You're goin' back to Martinsburg with us," Nitty said.

"I'm going to Sugar Land."

"After. What you want to go there for?"

Little Tib tried to explain about Sugar Land, but could not find words. At last he said, "In Sugar Land they know who you are."

"Guess it's too late then for me. Even if I found somebody who knew who I was I wouldn't be them no more."

"You're Nitty," Little Tib said.

"That's right. You know I used to go out with those gals a lot. Know what they said? Said, 'You're the custodian over at the school, aren't you?' Or, 'You're the one that did for Buster Johnson.' Didn't none of them know who I was. Only ones that did was the little children."

Little Tib heard Nitty's clothes rustle as he stood up, then the sound his feet made walking softly away. He wondered if Nitty was going to stay awake all night; then he heard him lie down.

Little Tib's father had him by the hand. They had left the hanging-down train, and were walking along one of the big streets. He could see. He knew he should not have been noticing that particularly, but he did, and far behind it somewhere was knowing that if he woke up he would not see. He looked into store windows, and he could see big dolls like girls' dolls wearing fur coats. Every hair on every coat stood out drenched with light. He looked at the street and could see all the cars like big, bright-colored bugs.

"Here," Big Tib said; they went into a glass thing that spun them around and dumped them out inside a building, then into an elevator all made of glass that climbed the inside wall almost like an ant, starting and stopping like an ant did.

"We should buy one of these," Little Tib said. "Then we wouldn't have to climb the steps."

He looked up and saw that his father was crying. He took out his, Little Tib's, own card and put it in the machine, then made Little Tib sit down in the seat and look at the bright light. The machine was a man in a white coat who took off his glasses and said, "We don't know who this child is, but he certainly isn't anyone."

"Look at the bright light again, Little Tib," his father said, and something in the way he said it told Little Tib that the man in the white coat was much stronger than he was. He looked at the bright light and tried to catch himself from falling.

And woke up. It was so dark that he wondered for a minute where the bright light went. Then he remembered. He rolled over a little and put his hand out toward the fire until he could feel some heat. He could hear it too when he listened. It crackled and snapped, but not very much. He lay the way he had been before, then turned over on his back. A train went past, and after a while an owl hooted.

He could see here too. Something inside him told him how lucky he was, seeing twice in one night. Then he forgot about it, looking at the flowers. They were big and round, growing on long stalks, and had yellow petals and dark brown centers, and when he was not looking at them, they whirled around and around. They could see him, because they all turned their faces toward him, and when he looked at them they stopped.

For a long way he walked through them. They came a little higher than his shoulder.

Then the city came down like a cloud and settled on a hill in front of him. As soon as it was there it pretended that it had been there all the time, but Little Tib could feel it laughing underneath. It had high, green walls that sloped in as they went up. Over the top of them were towers, much taller, that belonged to the city. Those were green too, and looked like glass.

Little Tib began to run, and was immediately in front of the gates. These were very high, but there was a window in them, just over his head, that the gate man talked through. "I want to see the king," Little Tib said, and the gate man reached down with a long, strong arm and picked him up and pulled him through the little window and set him down again inside. "You have to wear these," he said, and took out a pair of toy glasses like the ones Little Tib had once had in his doctor set. But when the gate man put them on Little Tib, they were not glasses at all, only lines painted on his face, circles around his eyes joined over his nose. The gate man held up a mirror to show him, and he had the sudden, dizzying sensation of looking at his own face.

A moment later he was walking through the city. The houses had their gardens sidewise—running up the walls so that the trees thrust out like flagpoles. The water in the birdbaths never ran out until a bird landed in it. Then a fine spray of drops fell to the street like rain.

The palace had a wall too, but it was made by trees holding hands. Little Tib went through a gate of bowing elephants and saw a long, long stairway. It was so long and so high that it seemed that there was no palace at all, only the steps going up and up forever into the clouds, and then he remembered that the whole city had come down out of the clouds. The king was coming down those stairs, walking very slowly. She was a beautiful woman, and although she did not look at all like her, Little Tib knew that she was his mother.

He had been seeing so much while he was asleep that when he woke up he had to remember why it was so dark. Somewhere in the back of his mind there was still the idea that waking should be light and sleep dark, and not the other way around.

Nitty said, "You ought to wash your face. Can you find the water all right?"

Little Tib was still thinking of the king, with her dress all made of Christmas-tree stuff, but he could. He splashed water on his face and arms while he thought about how to tell Nitty about his dream. By the time he had finished, everything in the dream was gone except for the king's face.

Most of the time Mr. Parker sounded like he was important and Nitty was not, but when he said, "Are we going to eat this morning, Nitty?" it was the other way around.

"We eat on the train," Nitty told him.

"We are going to catch a train, George, to Martinsburg," Mr. Parker told Little Tib.

Little Tib thought that the trains went too fast to be caught, but he did not say that.

"Should be one by here pretty soon," Nitty said. "They got to be going slow because there's a road crosses the tracks down there a way. They won't have no time to get the speed up again before they get here. You won't have to run—I'll just pick you up an' carry you."

A rooster crowed way off somewhere.

Mr. Parker said, "When I was a young man, George, everyone thought all the trains would be gone soon. They never said what would replace them, however. Later it was believed that it would be all right to have trains, provided they were extremely modern in appearance. That was accomplished, as I suppose you learned last year, by substituting aluminum, fiberglass, and magnesium for much of the steel employed previously. That not only changed the image of the trains to something acceptable, but saved a great deal of energy by reducing the weight—the ostensible purpose of the cosmetic redesign." Mr. Parker paused, and Little Tib could hear the water running past the place where they were sitting, and the sound the wind made blowing the trees.

"There only remained the awkward business of the crews," Mr. Parker continued. "Fortunately it was found that mechanisms of the same type that had already displaced educators and others could be substituted for railway engineers and brakemen. Who would have believed that running a train was as routine and mechanical a business as teaching a class? Yet it proved to be so."

"Wish they would do away with those railroad police," Nitty said.

"You, George, are a victim of the same system," Mr. Parker continued. "It was the wholesale displacement of labor, and the consequent nomadism, that resulted in the present reliance on retinal patterns as means of identification. Take Nitty and me, for example. We are going to Macon—"

"We're goin' to Martinsburg, Mr. Parker," Nitty said. "This train we'll be catching will be going the *other* way. We're goin' to get into that building and let you program, you remember?"

"I was hypothesizing," Mr. Parker said. "We are going—say—to Macon. There we can enter a store, register our retinal patterns, and receive goods to be charged to the funds which will by then have accumulated in our social relief accounts. No other method of identification is so certain, or so adaptable to data-processing techniques."

"Used to have money you just handed around," Nitty said.

"The emperors of China used lumps of silver stamped with an imperial seal," Mr. Parker told him. "But by restricting money solely—in the final analysis—to entries kept by the Federal Reserve Bank, the entire cost of printing and coining is eliminated, and of course control for tax purposes is complete. While for identification retinal patterns are unsurpassed in every—"

Little Tib stopped listening. A train was coming. He could hear it far away, hear it go over a bridge somewhere, hear it coming closer. He felt around for his stick and got a good hold on it.

Then the train was louder, but the noise did not come as fast. He heard the whistle blow. Then Nitty was picking him up with one strong arm. There was a swoop and a jump and a swing, swing, swing, and they were on the train and Nitty set him down. "If you want to," Nitty said, "you can sit here at the edge and hang your feet over. But you be careful."

Little Tib was careful. "Where's Mr. Parker?"

"Lying down in the back. He's going to sleep—he sleeps a lot."

"Can he hear us?"

"You like sitting like this? This is one of my most favorite of all things to do. I know you can't see everything go by like I can, but I could tell you about it. You take right now. We are going up a long grade, with nothing but pinewoods on this side of the train. I bet you there is all kinds of animals in there. You like animals, George? Bears and big old cats."

"Can he hear us?" Little Tib asked again.

"I don't think so, because he usually goes to sleep right away. But it might be better to wait a little while, if you've got something you don't want him to hear."

"All right."

"Now there's one thing we've got to worry about. Sometimes there are railroad policemen on these trains. If someone is riding on them, they throw him off. I don't think they'd throw a little boy like you off, but they would throw Mr. Parker and me off. You they would probably take back with them and give over to the real police in the next town."

"They wouldn't want me," Little Tib said.

"How's that?"

"Sometimes they take me, but they don't know who I am. They always let me go again."

"I guess maybe you've been gone from home longer than what I thought. How long since you left your mom and dad?"

"I don't know."

"Must be some way of telling blind people. There's lots of blind people."

"The machine usually knows who blind people are. That's what they say. But it doesn't know me."

"They take pictures of your retinas—you know about that?"

Little Tib said nothing.

"That's the part inside your eye that sees the picture. If you think about your eye like it was a camera, you got a lens in the front, and then the film. Well, your retinas is the film. That's what they take a picture of. I guess yours is gone. You know what it is you got wrong with your eyes?"

"I'm blind."

"Yes, but you don't know what it is, do you, baby. Wish you could look out there now—we're going over a deep place, lots of trees and rocks and water way down below."

"Can Mr. Parker hear us?" Little Tib asked again.

"Guess not. Looks like he's asleep by now."

"Who is he?"

"Like he told you. He's the superintendent; only they don't want him anymore."

"Is he really crazy?"

"Sure. He's a dangerous man too, when the fit comes on him. He got this little thing put into his head when he was superintendent to make him a better one—extra remembering and arithmetic, and things that would make him want to work more and do a good job. The school district paid for most of it; I don't know what you call them, but there's a lot of teenie little circuits in them."

"Didn't they take it out when he wasn't superintendent anymore?"

"Sure, but his head was used to it by then, I guess. Child, do you feel well?"

"I'm fine."

"You don't look so good. Kind of pale. I suppose it might just be that you washed off a lot of the dirt when I told you to wash that face. You think it could be that?"

"I feel all right."

"Here, let me see if you're hot." Little Tib felt Nitty's big, rough hand against his forehead. "You feel a bit hot to me."

"I'm not sick."

"Look there! You see that? There was a bear out there. A big old bear, black as could be."

"Probably it was a dog."

"You think I don't know a bear? It stood up and waved at us."

"Really, Nitty?"

"Well, not like a person would. It didn't say *bye-bye*, or *hi there*. But it held up one big old arm." Nitty's hands lifted Little Tib's right arm.

A strange voice, a lady's voice, Little Tib thought, said, "Hello there yourself." He heard the thump as somebody's feet hit the floor of the boxcar, then another thump as somebody else's did.

"Now wait a minute," Nitty said. "Now you look here."

"Don't get excited," another lady's voice told him.

"Don't you try to throw us off of this train. I got a little boy here, a little blind boy. He can't jump off no train."

Mr. Parker said, "What's going on here, Nitty?"

"Railroad police, Mr. Parker. They're going to make us jump off of this train."

Little Tib could hear the scraping sounds Mr. Parker made when he stood up, and wondered whether Mr. Parker was a big man or a little man, and how old he was. He had a pretty good idea about Nitty, but Little Tib was not sure of Mr. Parker, though he thought Mr. Parker was pretty young. He decided he was also medium sized.

"Let me introduce myself," Mr. Parker said. "As superintendent, I am in charge of the three schools in the Martinsburg area."

"Hi," one of the ladies said.

"You will begin with the lower grades, as all of our new teachers do. As you gain seniority, you may move up if you wish. What are your specialties?"

"Are you playing a game?"

Nitty said, "He didn't quite understand—he just woke up. You woke him up."

"Sure."

"You going to throw us off the train?"

"How far are you going?"

"Just to Howard. Only that far. Now you listen, this little boy is blind, and sick too. We want to take him to the doctor at Howard—he ran away from home."

Mr. Parker said, "I will not leave this school until I am ready. I am in charge of the entire district."

"Mr. Parker isn't exactly altogether well either," Nitty told the women.

"What has he been using?"

"He's just like that sometimes."

"He sounds like he's been shooting up on chalk."

Little Tib asked, "What's your name?"

"Say," Nitty said, "that's right. You know, I never did ask that. This little boy here is telling me I'm not polite."

"I'm Alice," one of the ladies said.

"Mickie," said the other.

"And we don't want to know your names," Alice continued. "See, suppose someway they heard you were on the train—we'd have to say who you were."

"And where you were going," Mickie put in.

"Nice people like you—why do you want to be railroad police?"

Alice laughed. "What's a nice girl like you doing in a place like this? I've heard that one before."

"Watch yourself, Alice," Mickey said. "He's trying to make out."

Alice said, "What'd you three want to be 'boes for?"

"We didn't. 'Cept maybe for this little boy here. He run away from home because the part of his eyes that they take pictures of is gone and his momma and daddy couldn't get benefits. At least, that's what I think. Is that right, George?"

Mr. Parker said, "I'll introduce you to your classes in a moment."

"Him and me used to be in the school," Nitty continued. "Had good jobs there, or so we believed. Then one day that big computer downtown says, 'Don't need you no more,' and out we goes."

"You don't have to talk funny for us," Mickie said.

"Well, that's a relief. I always do it a little, though, for Mr. Parker. It makes him feel better."

"What was your job?"

"Buildings maintenance. I took care of the heating plant, and serviced the teaching and cleaning machines, and did the electrical repair work generally."

"Nitty!" Little Tib called.

"I'm here, li'l boy. I won't go 'way."

"Well, we have to go," Mickie said. "They'll miss us pretty soon if we don't get back to patrolling this train. You fellows remember you promised you'd get off at Howard. And try not to let anyone see you."

Mr. Parker said, "You may rely on our cooperation."

Little Tib could hear the sound of the women's boots on the boxcar floor, and the little grunt Alice gave as she took hold of the ladder outside the door and swung herself out. Then there was a popping noise, as though someone had opened a bottle of soda, and a bang and clatter when something struck the back of the car.

His lungs and nose and mouth all burned. He felt a rush of saliva too great to contain. It spilled out of his lips and down his shirt; he wanted to run, and he thought of the old place, where the creek cut (cold as ice) under banks of milkweed and goldenrod. Nitty was yelling, "Throw it out! Throw it out!" And somebody, Little Tib thought it was Mr. Parker, ran full tilt into the side of the car. Little Tib was on the hill above the creek again, looking down across the bluebonnets toward the surging, glass-dark water, and a kite-flying west wind was blowing.

He sat down again on the floor of the boxcar. Mr. Parker must not have been hurt too badly, because Little Tib could hear him moving around, as well as Nitty.

"You kick it out, Mr. Parker?" Nitty said. "That was good."

"Must have been the boy. Nitty—"

"Yes, Mr. Parker."

"We're on a train. . . . The railroad police threw a gas bomb to get us off. Is that correct?"

"That's true sure enough, Mr. Parker."

"I had the strangest dream. I was standing in the center corridor of the Grovehurst school, with my back leaning against the lockers. I could feel them."

"Yeah."

"I was speaking to two new teachers—"

"I know." Little Tib could feel Nitty's fingers on his face, and Nitty's voice whispered, "You all right?"

"—giving them the usual orientation talk. I heard something make a loud noise, like a rocket. I looked up then, and saw that one of the children had thrown a stink bomb—it was flying over my head, laying a trail of smoke. I went after it like I used to go after a ball when I was an outfielder in college, and I ran right into the wall."

"You sure did. Your face looks pretty bad, Mr. Parker."

"Hurts too. Look, there it is."

"Sure enough. Nobody kick it out after all."

"No. Here, feel it; it's still warm. I suppose a chemical burns to generate the gas."

"You want to feel, George? Here, you can hold it."

Little Tib felt the warm metal cylinder pressed into his hands. There was a seam down the side, like a Coca-Cola can, and a funny-shaped thing on top.

Nitty said, "I wonder what happened to all the gas."

"It blew out," Mr. Parker told him.

"It shouldn't of done that. They threw it good—got it right back in the back of the car. It shouldn't blow out that fast, and those things go on making gas for a long time."

"It must have been defective," Mr. Parker said.

"Must have been." There was no expression in Nitty's voice.

Little Tib asked, "Did those ladies throw it?"

"Sure did. Came down here and talked to us real nice first, then to get up on top of the car and do something like that."

"Nitty, I'm thirsty."

"Sure you are. Feel of him, Mr. Parker. He's hot."

Mr. Parker's hand was softer and smaller than Nitty's. "Perhaps it was the gas."

"He was hot before."

"There's no nurse's office on this train, I'm afraid."

"There's a doctor in Howard. I thought to get him to Howard. . . ."

"We haven't anything in our accounts now."

Little Tib was tired. He lay down on the floor of the car, and heard the empty gas canister roll away, too tired to care.

". . . a sick child . . . ," Nitty said.

The boxcar rocked under Little Tib, and the wheels made a rhythmic roar like the rushing of blood in the heart of a giantess.

He was walking down a narrow dirt path. All the trees, on both sides of the path, had red leaves, and red grass grew around their roots. They had faces too, in their trunks, and talked to one another as he passed. Apples and cherries hung from their boughs.

The path twisted around little hills, all covered with the red trees. Cardinals hopped in the branches, and one fluttered to his shoulder. Little Tib was very happy; he told the cardinal, "I don't want to go away—ever. I want to stay here, forever. Walking down this path."

"You will, my son," the cardinal said. It made the sign of the cross with one wing.

They went around a bend, and there was a tiny little house ahead, no bigger than the box a refrigerator comes in. It was painted with red and white stripes, and had a pointed roof. Little Tib did not like the look of it, but he took a step nearer.

A full-sized man came out of the little house. He was made all of copper, so he was coppery-red all over, like a new pipe for the bathroom. His body was round, and his head was round too, and they were joined by a real piece of bathroom pipe. He had a big mustache stamped right into the copper, and he was polishing himself with a rag. "Who are you?" he said.

Little Tib told him.

"I don't know you," the copper man said. "Come closer so I can recognize you."

Little Tib came closer. Something was hammering, *bam, bam, bam,* in the hills behind the red and white house. He tried to see what it was, but there was a mist over them, as though it were early morning. "What is that noise?" he asked the copper man.

"That is the giant," the copper man said. "Can't . . . you . . . see . . . her?"

Little Tib said that he could not.

"Then . . . wind . . . my . . . talking key. . . . I'll . . . tell . . . you . . ."

The copper man turned around, and Little Tib saw that there were three key-holes in his back. The middle one had a neat copper label beside it printed with the words TALKING ACTION.

". . . about . . . her."

There was a key with a beautiful handle hanging on a hook beside the hole. He took it and began to wind the copper man.

"That's better," the copper man said. "My words—thanks to your fine winding—will blow away the mists, and you'll be able to see her. I can stop her, but if I don't you'llbekilledthatsenough."

As the copper man had said, the mists were lifting. Some, however, did not seem to blow away—they were not mists at all, but a mountain. The mountain moved, and was not a mountain at all, but a big woman wreathed in mist, twice as high as the hills around her. She was holding a broom, and while Little Tib watched, a rat as big as a railroad train ran out of a cave in one of the hills. *Bam*, the woman struck at it with her broom, but it ran into another cave. In a moment it ran out again. *Bam!* The woman was Little Tib's mother, but he sensed that she would not know him—that she was cut off from him in some way by the mists, and the need to strike at the rat.

"That's my mother," he told the copper man. "And that rat was in our kitchen in the new place. But she didn't keep hitting at it and hitting at it like that."

"She is only hitting at it once," the copper man said, "but that once is over and over again. That's why she always misses it. But if you try to go any farther down this path, her broom will kill you and sweep you away. Unless I stop it."

"I could run between the swings," Little Tib said. He could have too.

"The broom is bigger than you think," the copper man told him. "And you can't see it as well as you think you can."

"I want you to stop her," Little Tib said. He was sure he could run between the blows of the broom, but he was sorry for his mother, who had to hit at the rat all the time, and never rest.

"Then you must let me look at you."

"Go ahead," Little Tib said.

"You have to wind my motion key."

The lowest keyhole was labeled MOVING ACTION. It was the largest of all. There was a big key hanging beside it, and Little Tib used it to wind the moving action, hearing a heavy pawl clack inside the copper man each time he turned the key. "That's enough," the copper man said. Little Tib replaced the key, and the copper man turned around.

"Now I must look into your eyes," he said. His own eyes were stampings in the copper, but Little Tib knew that he could see out of them. He put his hands on Little Tib's face, one on each side. They were harder even than Nitty's, but smaller too, and very cold. Little Tib saw his eyes coming closer and closer.

Little Tib saw his own eyes reflected in the copper man's face as if they were in a mirror, and they had little flames in them like the flames of two candles in church, and the flames were going out. The copper man moved his face closer and closer to his own. It got darker and darker. Little Tib said, "Don't you know me?"

"You have to wind my thinking key," the copper man said.

Little Tib reached behind him, stretching his arms as far as they would go around the copper body. His fingers found the smallest hole of all, and a little hook beside it; but there was no key.

A baby was crying. There were medicine smells, and a strange woman's voice said, "There, there." Her hands touched his cheeks, the hard, cold hands of the copper man. Little Tib remembered that he could not really see at all, not anymore.

"He *is* sick, isn't he," the woman said. "He's hot as fire. And screaming like that."

"Yes, ma'am," Nitty said. "He's sick sure enough."

A little girl's voice said, "What's wrong with him, Mama?"

"He's running a fever, dear, and of course he's blind."

Little Tib said, "I'm all right."

Mr. Parker's voice told him, "You will be when the doctor sees you, George."

"I can stand up," Little Tib said. He had discovered that he was sitting on Nitty's lap, and it embarrassed him.

"You awake now?" Nitty asked.

Little Tib slid off his lap and felt around for his stick, but it was gone.

"You been sleepin' ever since we were on the train. Never did wake up more than halfway, even when we got off."

"Hello," the little girl said. *Bam. Bam. Bam.*

"Hello," Little Tib said back to her.

"Don't let him touch your face, dear. His hands are dirty."

Little Tib could hear Mr. Parker talking to Nitty, but he did not pay any attention to them.

"I have a baby," the girl told him, "and a dog. His name is Muggly. My baby's name is Virginia Jane." *Bam.*

"You walk funny," Little Tib said.

"I have to."

He bent down and touched her leg. Bending down made his head peculiar. There was a ringing sound he knew was not real, and it seemed to have fallen off him, and to be floating around in front of him somewhere. His fingers felt the edge of the little girl's skirt, then her leg, warm and dry, then a rubber thing with metal under it, and metal strips like the copper man's neck going down at the sides. Little Tib reached inside them and found her leg again, but it was smaller than his own arm.

"Don't let him hurt her," the woman said.

Nitty said, "Why, he won't hurt her. What are you afraid of? A little boy like that."

He thought of his own legs walking down the path, walking through the spinning flowers toward the green city. The little girl's leg was like them. It was bigger than he had thought, growing bigger under his fingers.

"Come on," the little girl said. "Mama's got Virginia Jane. Want to see her?" *Bam.* "Mama, can I take my brace off?"

"No, dear."

"I take it off at home."

"That's when you're going to lie down, dear, or have a bath."

"I don't need it, Mama. I really don't. See?"

The woman screamed. Little Tib covered his ears. When they had still lived in the old place and his mother and father had talked too loudly, he had covered his ears like that, and they had seen him and become more quiet. It did not work with the woman. She kept on screaming.

A lady who worked for the doctor tried to quiet her, and at last the doctor herself came out and gave her something. Little Tib could not see what it was, but he heard her say over and over, "Take this; take this." And finally the woman took it.

Then they made the little girl and the woman go into the doctor's office. There were more people waiting than Little Tib had known about, and they were all talking now. Nitty took him by the arm. "I don't want to sit in your lap," Little Tib said. "I don't like sitting in laps."

"You can sit here," Nitty said. He was almost whispering. "We'll move Virginia Jane over."

Little Tib climbed up onto a padded plastic seat. Nitty was on one side of him, and Mr. Parker on the other.

"It's too bad," Nitty said, "you couldn't see that little girl's leg. I saw it. It was just a little matchstick-sized thing when we set down here. When they carried her in, it looked just like the other one."

"That's nice," Little Tib said.

"We were wondering—did you have something to do with that?"

Little Tib did not know, and so he sat silent.

"Don't push him, Nitty," Mr. Parker said.

"I'm not pushing him. I just asked. It's important."

"Yes, it is," Mr. Parker said. "You think about it, George, and if you have anything to tell us, let us know. We'll listen."

Little Tib sat there for a long time, and at last the lady who worked for the doctor came and said, "Is it the boy?"

"He has a fever," Mr. Parker told her.

"We have to get his pattern. Bring him over here."

Nitty said, "No use."

And Mr. Parker said, "You won't be able to take his pattern—his retinas are gone."

The lady who worked for the doctor said nothing for a little while; then she said, "We'll try anyway," and took Little Tib's hand and led him to where a bright light machine was. He knew it was a bright light machine from the feel and smell of it, and the way it fit around his face. After a while she let him pull his eyes away from the machine.

"He needs to see the doctor," Nitty said. "I know without a pattern you can't charge the government for it. But he is a sick child."

The lady said, "If I start a card on him, they'll want to know who he is."

"Feel his head. He's burning up."

"They'll think he might be in the country illegally. Once an investigation like that starts, you can never stop it."

Mr. Parker asked, "Can we talk to the doctor?"

"That's what I've been telling you. You can't see the doctor."

"What about me? I'm ill."

"I thought it was the boy."

"I'm ill too. Here." Mr. Parker's hands on his shoulders guided Little Tib out of the chair in front of the bright light machine, so that Mr. Parker could sit down himself instead. Mr. Parker leaned forward, and the machine hummed. "Of course," Mr. Parker said, "I'll have to take him in with me. He's too small to leave alone in the waiting room."

"This man could watch him."

"He has to go."

"Yes, ma'am," Nitty said, "I sure do. I shouldn't have stayed around this long, except this was all so interesting."

Little Tib took Mr. Parker's hand, and they went through narrow, twisty corridors into a little room to see the doctor.

"There's no complaint on this," the doctor said. "What's the trouble with you?"

Mr. Parker told her about Little Tib, and said that she could put down anything on his own card that she wanted.

"This is irregular," the doctor said. "I shouldn't be doing this. What's wrong with his eyes?"

"I don't know. Apparently he has no retinas."

"There are such things as retinal transplants. They aren't always effective."

"Would they permit him to be identified? The seeing's *not* really that important."

"I suppose so."

"Could you get him into a hospital?"

"No."

"Not without a pattern, you mean."

"That's right. I'd like to tell you otherwise, but it wouldn't be the truth. They'd never take him."

"I understand."

"I've got a lot of patients to see. I'm putting you down for influenza. Give him these; they ought to reduce his fever. If he's not better tomorrow, come again."

Later, when things were cooling off, and the day birds were all quiet, and the night birds had not begun yet, and Nitty had made a fire and was cooking something, he said, "I don't understand why she wouldn't help the child."

"She gave him something for his fever."

"More than that. She should have done more than that."

"There are so many people—"

"I know that. I've heard all that. Not really that many at all. More in China and some other places. You think that medicine is helping him?"

Mr. Parker put his hand on Little Tib's head. "I think so."

"We goin' to stay here so we can take him, or keep on goin' back to Martinsburg?"

"We'll see how he is in the morning."

"You know, the way you are now, Mr. Parker, I think you might do it."

"I'm a good programmer, Nitty. I really am."

"I know you are. You work that program right and that machine will find out they need a man running it again. Need a maintenance man too. Why does a man feel so bad if he don't have real payin' work to do—tell me that. Did I let them put something in my head like you?"

"You know as well as I," Mr. Parker said.

Little Tib was no longer listening to them. He was thinking about the little girl and her leg. *I dreamed it,* he thought. *Nobody can do that. I dreamed that I only had to touch her and it was all right. That means what is real is the other one, the copper man and the big woman with the broom.*

An owl called, and Little Tib remembered the little buzzy clock that stood beside his mother's bed in the new place. Early in the morning the clock would ring, and then his father had to get up. When they had lived in the old place, and his father had a lot of work to do, he had not needed a clock. Owls must be the real clocks; they made their noise so he would wake up to the real place.

He slept. Then he was awake again, but he could not see. "You best eat something," Nitty said. "You didn't eat nothing last night. You went to sleep, and I didn't want to rouse you." He gave Little Tib a scrap of corn bread, pressing it into his hands. "It's just leftovers now," he said, "but it's good."

"Are we going to get on another train?"

"Train doesn't go to Martinsburg. Now, we don't have a plate, so I'm putting this on a piece of newspaper for you. You get your lap smoothed out so it doesn't fall off."

Little Tib straightened his legs. He was hungry, and he decided it was the first time he had been hungry in a long while. He asked, "Will we walk?"

"Too far. Going to hitchhike. All ready now? It's right in the middle."

Little Tib felt the thick paper, still cool from the night before, laid upon his thighs. There was weight in the center; he moved his fingers to it and found a yam. The skin was still on it, but it had been cut in two. "Baked that in the fire last night," Nitty said. "There's a piece of ham there too that we saved for you. Don't miss that."

Little Tib held the half yam like an ice-cream cone in one hand, and peeled back the skin with the other. It was loose from having been in the coals, and crackly and hard. It broke away in flakes and chips like the bark of an old sycamore. He bit into the yam and it was soft but stringy, and its goodness made him want a drink of water.

"Went to a poor woman's house," Nitty said. "That's where you go if you want something to eat for sure. A rich person is afraid of you. Mr. Parker and I, we can't buy anything. We haven't got credit for September yet—we were figuring we'd have that in Macon."

"They won't give anything for me," Little Tib said. "Mama had to feed me out of hers."

"That's only because they can't get no pattern. Anyway, what difference does it make? That credit's so little-bitty that you almost might not have anything. Mr. Parker gets a better draw than I do because he was making more when we were working, but that's not very much, and you wouldn't get but the minimum."

"Where is Mr. Parker?"

"Down a way, washing. See, hitchhiking is hard if you don't look clean. Nobody will pick you up. We got one of those disposable razor things last night, and he's using it now."

"Should I wash?"

"It couldn't hurt," Nitty said. "You got tear streaks on your face from cryin' last night." He took Little Tib's hand and led him along a cool, winding path with high weeds on the sides. The weeds were wet with dew, and the dew was icy cold. They met Mr. Parker at the edge of the water. Little Tib took off his shoes and clothes and waded in. It was cold, but not as cold as the dew had been. Nitty waded in after him and splashed him, and poured water from his cupped hands over Little Tib's head, and at last ducked him under—telling him first—to get his hair clean. Then the two of them washed their clothes in the water and hung them on bushes to dry.

"Going to be hard, hitchhiking this morning," Nitty said.

Little Tib asked why.

"Too many of us. The more there is, the harder to get rides."

"We could separate," Mr. Parker suggested. "I'll draw straws with you to see who gets George."

"No."

"I'm all right. I'm fine."

"You're fine now."

Mr. Parker leaned forward. Little Tib knew because he could hear his clothes rustle, and his voice got closer as well as louder. "Nitty, who's the boss here?"

"You are, Mr. Parker. Only if you went off by yourself like that, I'd worry so

I'd about go crazy. What have I ever done to you that you would want to worry me like that?"

Mr. Parker laughed. "All right, I'll tell you what we'll do. We'll try until ten o'clock together. If we haven't gotten a ride by then, I'll walk half a mile down the road and give the two of you the first shot at anything that comes along." Little Tib heard him get to his feet. "You think George's clothes are dry by now?"

"Still a little damp."

"I can wear them," Little Tib said. He had worn wet clothing before, when he had been drenched by rain.

"That's a good boy. Help him put them on, Nitty."

When they were walking out to the road and he could tell that Mr. Parker was some distance ahead of them, Little Tib asked Nitty if he thought they would get a ride before ten.

"I know we will," Nitty said.

"How do you know?"

"Because I've been praying for it hard, and what I pray hard for I always get."

Little Tib thought about that. "You could pray for a job," he said. He remembered that Nitty had told him he wanted a job.

"I did that, right after I lost my old one. Then I saw Mr. Parker again and how he had got to be, and I started going around with him to look after him. So then I had a job—I've got it now. Mr. Parker's the one that doesn't have a job."

"You don't get paid," Little Tib said practically.

"We get our draws, and I use that—both of them together—for whatever we need, and if he kept his and I kept mine, he would have more than me. You be quiet now—we're coming to the road."

They stood there a long time. Occasionally a car or a truck went by. Little Tib began to wonder if Mr. Parker and Nitty were holding out their thumbs. He remembered seeing people holding out their thumbs when he and his parents were moving from the old place. He thought of what Nitty had said about praying and began to pray himself, thinking about God and asking that the next car stop.

For a long time no more cars stopped. Little Tib thought about a cattle truck stopping and told God he would ride with the cattle. He thought about a garbage truck stopping and told God he would ride on top of the garbage. Then he heard something old coming down the road. It rattled, and the engine made a strange, high-pitched noise an engine should not make. "Looks like a old school bus," Nitty said. "But look at those pictures on the side."

"It's stopping," Mr. Parker said, and then Little Tib could hear the sound the doors made opening.

A new voice, high for a man's voice and talking fast, said, "You seek to go this way? You may come in. All are welcome in the temple of Deva."

Mr. Parker got in, and Nitty lifted Little Tib up the steps. The doors closed behind them. There was a peculiar smell in the air.

"You have a small boy. That is well. The god is most fond of small children and the aged. Small boys and girls have innocence. Old persons have tranquillity and wisdom. These are the things that are pleasing to the god. We should strive without effort to retain innocence, and to attain tranquillity and wisdom as soon as we can."

Nitty said, "Right on."

"He is a handsome boy." Little Tib felt the driver's breath, warm and sweet, on his face, and something dangling struck him lightly on the chest. He caught it, and found that it was a piece of wood with three crossbars, suspended from a thong. "Ah," the new voice said, "you have discovered my amulet."

"George can't see," Mr. Parker explained. "You'll have to excuse him."

"I am aware of this, having observed it earlier, but perhaps it is painful for him to hear it spoken of. And now I must go forward again before the police come to inquire why I have stopped. There are no seats—I have removed all the seats but this one. It is better that people take seats on the floor before Deva. But you may stand behind me if you wish. Is that agreeable?"

"We'll be happy to stand," Mr. Parker said.

The bus lurched into motion. Little Tib held on to Nitty with one hand and on to a pole he found with the other.

"We are in motion again. That is fitting. It would be most fitting if we might move always, never stopping. I had thought to build my temple on a boat—a boat moves always because of the rocking of the waves. I may still do this."

"Are you going through Martinsburg?"

"Yes, yes, yes," the driver said. "Allow me to introduce myself: I am Dr. Prithivi."

Mr. Parker shook hands with Dr. Prithivi, and Little Tib felt the bus swerve from its lane. Mr. Parker yelled, and when the bus was straight again, he introduced Nitty and Little Tib.

"If you're a doctor," Nitty said, "you could maybe look at George sometime. He hasn't been well."

"I am not this sort of doctor," Dr. Prithivi explained. "Rather instead I am a doctor for the soul. I am a doctor of divinity of the University of Bombay. If someone is sick a physician should be summoned. Should they be evil they should summon me."

Nitty said, "Usually the family don't do that because they're so glad to see them finally making some money."

Dr. Prithivi laughed, a little high laugh like music. It seemed to Little Tib that it went skipping around the roof of the old bus, playing on a whistle. "But we are all evil," Dr. Prithivi said, "and so few of us make money. How do you explain that? That is the joke. I am a doctor for evil, and everyone in the world should be calling me, even myself, all the time. But I cannot come. 'Office hours nine to five,' that is what my sign should say. No house calls. But instead I bring my house, the house of the god, to everyone. Here I collect my fares, and I tell all who come to step to the back of my bus."

"We didn't know you had to pay," Little Tib said. He was worried because Nitty had told him that he and Mr. Parker had no money in their accounts.

"No one must pay—that is the beauty. Those who desire to buy near diesel for the god may imprint their cards here, but all is voluntary and other things we accept too."

"Sure is dark back there," Nitty said.

"Let me show you. You see we are approaching a roadside park? So well is the universe regulated. There we will stop and recreate ourselves, and I will show you the god before proceeding again."

Little Tib felt the bus swerve with breathtaking suddenness. During the last year that they had lived at the old place, he had ridden a bus to school. He remembered how hot it had been, and how ordinary it had seemed after the first week; now he was dreaming of riding this strange-smelling old bus in the dark, but soon he would wake and be on that other bus again; then, when the doors opened, he would run through the hot, bright sunshine to the school.

The doors opened, clattering and grinding. "Let us go out," Dr. Prithivi said. "Let us recreate ourselves and see what is to be seen here."

"It's a lookout point," Mr. Parker told him. "You can see parts of seven counties from here."

Little Tib felt himself lifted down the steps. There were other people around; he could hear their voices, though they were not close.

"It is so very beautiful," Dr. Prithivi said. "We have also beautiful mountains in India—'the Himalayas,' they are called. This fine view makes me think of them. When I was just a little boy, my father rented a house for summer in the Himalayas. Rhododendrons grew wild there, and once I saw a leopard in our garden."

A strange voice said, "You see mountain lions here. Early in the morning is the time for it—look up on the big rocks as you drive along."

"Exactly so!" Dr. Prithivi sounded excited. "It was very early when I saw the leopard."

Little Tib tried to remember what a leopard looked like, and found that he could not. Then he tried a cat, but it was not a very good cat. He felt hot and tired, and reminded himself that it had only been a little while ago that Nitty had washed his clothes. The seam at the front of his shirt, where the buttons went, was still damp. When he had been able to see, he had known precisely what a cat looked like. He felt now that if only he could hold a cat in his arms he would know again. He imagined such a cat, large and long-haired. It was there, unexpectedly, standing in front of him. Not a cat, but a lion, standing on its hind feet. It had a long tail with a tuft at the end, and a red ribbon knotted in its mane. Its face was a kindly blur and it was dancing—dancing to the remembered flute music of Dr. Prithivi's laughter—just out of reach.

Little Tib took a step toward it and found his way barred by two metal pipes. He slipped between them. The lion danced, hopping and skipping, striking poses without stopping; it bowed and jigged away, and Little Tib danced too, after it. It would be cheating to run or walk—he would lose the game, even if he caught the lion. It high-stepped, far away then back again almost close enough to touch, and he followed it.

Behind him he heard the gasp of the people, but it seemed dim and distant compared to the piping to which he danced. The lion jigged nearer and he caught its paws and the two of them romped up and down, its face growing clearer and clearer as they whirled and turned—it was a funny, friendly, frightening face.

It was as though he had backed into a bush whose leaves were hands. They clasped him everywhere, drawing him backward against hard metal bars. He could hear Nitty's voice, but Nitty was crying so that he could not tell what he said. A woman was crying too—no, several women—and a man whose voice Little Tib did not know was shouting: "We've got him! We've got him!" Little Tib was not sure who he was shouting to, perhaps to nobody.

A voice he did recognize, it was Dr. Prithivi's, was saying, "I have him. You must let go of him so that I may lift him over."

Little Tib's left foot reached out as if it were moving itself and felt in front of him. There was nothing there, nothing at all. The lion was gone, and he knew, now, where he was, on the edge of a mountain, and it went down and down for a long way. Fear came.

"Let go and I will lift him over," Dr. Prithivi told someone else. Little Tib thought of how small and boneless Dr. Prithivi's hands had felt. Then Nitty's big ones took him on one side, an arm and a leg, and the medium-sized hands of Mr. Parker (or someone like him) on the other. Then Little Tib was lifted up and back, and put down on the ground.

"He walked . . . ," a woman said. "Danced."

"This boy must come with me," Dr. Prithivi piped. "Get out of the way, please." He had Little Tib's left hand. Nitty was lifting him up again, and he felt Nitty's big head come up between his legs and he settled on his shoulders. Little Tib plunged his hands into Nitty's thick hair and held on. Other hands were reaching for him; when they found him, they only touched, as though they did not want to do anything more.

"Got to set you down," Nitty said, "or you'll hit your head." The steps of the bus were under Little Tib's feet, and Dr. Prithivi was helping him up.

"You must be presented to the god," said Dr. Prithivi. The inside of the bus was stuffy and hot, with a strange, spicy, oppressive smell. "Here. Now you must pray. Have you anything with which to make an offering?"

"No," Little Tib said. People had followed them into the bus.

"Then only pray." Dr. Prithivi must have had a cigarette lighter—Little Tib heard the scratching sound it made. There was a soft *oooah* sound from the people.

"Now you see Deva," Dr. Prithivi told them. "Because you are not accustomed to such things, the first thing you have noticed is that he has six arms. It is for that reason that I wear this cross, which has six arms also. You see, I wish to relate Deva to Christianity here. You will note that one of Deva's hands holds a two-armed cross. The others—I will begin here and go around—hold the crescent of Islam, the Star of David, a figure of the Buddha, a phallus, and a *katana* sword, which I have chosen to represent the faith of Shintoism."

Little Tib tried to pray, as Dr. Prithivi had directed. In one way Little Tib knew what he had been doing when he had been dancing with the lion, and in another he did not. Why hadn't he fallen? He thought of how the stones at the bottom would feel when they hit his face, and shivered.

Stones he remembered very well. Potato shaped but much larger, hard and gray. He was lost in a rocky land where frowning walls of stone were everywhere and no plant grew. He stood in the shadow of one of these walls to escape the heat; he could see the opposite wall, and the rubble of jumbled stones between, but this time the knowledge that he could see again gave him no pleasure. He was thirsty, and pressed farther back into the shadow, and found that there was no wall there. The shadow went back and back, farther and farther into the mountain. He followed it and, turning, saw the little wedge of daylight disappear behind him, and was blind again.

The cave—for he knew it was a cave now—went on and on into the rock. Despite the lack of sunlight, it seemed to Little Tib that the cave grew hotter and hotter. Then from somewhere far ahead he heard a tapping and rapping, as though an entire bag of marbles had been poured onto a stone floor and were bouncing up and down. The noise was so odd, and Little Tib was so tired, that he sat down to listen to it.

As if his sitting had been a signal, torches kindled—first one on one side of the cave, then another on the opposite side. Behind him a gate of close-set bars banged down, and toward him, like spiders, came two grotesque figures. Their bodies were small, yet fat; their arms and legs were long and thin; their faces were the faces of mad old men, pop-eyed and choleric and adorned with towering peaks of fantastic hair, and spreading mustaches like the feelers of night-crawling insects, and curling three-pointed beards that seemed to have a life of their own so that they twisted and twined like snakes. These men carried long-handled axes, and wore red clothes and the widest leather belts Little Tib had ever seen. "Halt," they cried. "Cease, hold, stop, and arrest yourself. You are trespassing in the realm of the Gnome King!"

"I have stopped," Little Tib said. "And I can't arrest myself because I'm not a policeman."

"That wasn't why we asked you to do it," one of the angry-faced men pointed out.

"But it *is* an offense," added the other. "We're a Police State, you know, and it's up to you to join the force."

"In your case," continued the first gnome, "it will be the labor force."

"Come with us!" both of them exclaimed, and they seized him by the arms and began to drag him across the pile of rocks.

"Stop," Little Tib demanded. "You don't know who I am."

"We don't *care* who you am either."

"If Nitty were here, he'd fix you. Or Mr. Parker."

"Then he'd better fix Mr. Parker, because we're not broken, and we're taking you to see the Gnome King."

They went down twisted sidewise caves with no lights but the eyes of the gnomes. And through big, echoing caves with mud floors, and streams of steaming water in the middle. Little Tib thought, at first, that it was rather fun, but it became realer and realer as they went along, as though the gnomes drew strength and realness from the heat, and at last he forgot that there had ever been anyplace else, and the things the gnomes said were no longer funny.

The Gnome King's throne cavern was brilliantly lit, and crammed with gold and jewels. The curtains were gold—not gold-colored cloth, but real gold—and the king sat on a bed covered with a spread of linked diamonds, cross-legged. "You have trespassed my dominions," he said. "How do you plead?" He looked like the other gnomes, but thinner and meaner.

"For mercy," Little Tib said.

"Then you are guilty?"

Little Tib shook his head.

"You have to be. Only the guilty can plead for mercy."

"You are supposed to forgive trespasses," Little Tib said, and as soon as he had said that, all the bright lamps in the throne room went out. His guards began to curse, and he could hear the whistle of their axes as they swung them in the dark, looking for him.

He ran, thinking he could hide behind one of the gold curtains, but his outstretched arms never found it. He ran on and on until at last he felt sure that he was no longer in the throne room. He was about to stop and rest then when he saw a faint light—so faint a light that for a long time he was afraid it might be no more than a trick of his eyes, like the lights he saw when he ground his hands against them. *This is my dream,* he thought, *and I can make the light to be whatever I want it to be. All right, it will be sunlight, and when I get out into it, it will be Nitty and Mr. Parker and me camped someplace—a pretty place next to a creek of cold water— and I'll be able to see.*

The light grew brighter and brighter; it was gold colored, like sunlight.

Then Little Tib saw trees, and he began to run. He was actually running among the trees before he realized that they were not real trees, and that the light he had seen came from them—the sky overhead was a vault of cold stone. He stopped, then. The trunks and branches of the trees were silver; the leaves were gold; the grass under his feet was not grass but a carpet of green gems, and birds with real rubies in their breasts twittered and flew among the trees— but they were not real birds, only toys. There was no Nitty and no Mr. Parker and no water.

Little Tib was about to cry when he noticed the fruit. It hung under the leaves, and was gold, as they were, but for fruit that did not look so unnatural. Each was about the size of a grapefruit. Little Tib wondered if he could pull them from the trees, and the first he touched fell into his hands. It was not heavy enough to be solid. After a moment he saw that it unscrewed in the center. He sat down on the grass (which had become real grass in some way, or perhaps a carpet or a bed-spread) and opened it. There was a meal inside, but all the food was too hot to eat. He looked and looked, hoping for a salad that would be wet and cool, but there was nothing but hot meat and gravy, and smoking hot cornmeal muffins, and boiled greens so hot and dry he did not even try to put them in his mouth.

At last he found a small cup with a lid on it. It held hot tea—tea so hot it seemed to blister his lips—but he managed to drink a little of it. He put down the cup and stood up to go on through the forest of gold and silver trees, and perhaps find a better place. But all the trees had vanished, and he was in the dark again. *My eyes are gone,* he thought. *I'm waking up.* Then he saw a circle of light ahead and heard the pounding; and he knew that it was not marbles dropped on a floor he heard, but the noise of hundreds and hundreds of picks, digging gold in the mines of the gnomes.

The light grew larger—but dimmed at the same time, as a star-shaped shadow grew in it. Then it was not a star at all, but a gnome coming after him. And then it was a whole army of gnomes, one behind the other, with their arms sticking out at every angle, so that it looked like one gnome with a hundred arms, all reaching for him.

Then he woke, and everything was dark.

He sat up. "You're awake now," Nitty said.

"Yes."

"How you feel?"

Little Tib did not answer. He was trying to find out where he was. It was a bed. There was a pillow behind him, and there were clean, starched sheets. He re-membered what the doctor had said about the hospital, and asked, "Am I in the hospital?"

"No, we're in a motel. How do you feel?"

"All right, I guess."

"You remember about dancing out there on the air?"

"I thought I dreamed it."

"Well, I thought I dreamed it too—but you were really out there. Everybody saw it, everybody who was around there when you did it. And then when we got you to come in close enough that we could grab hold of you and pull you in, Dr. Prithivi got you to come back to his bus."

"I remember that," Little Tib said.

"And he explained about his work and all that, and he took up a collection for it and you went to sleep. You were running that fever again, and Mr. Parker and me couldn't wake you up much."

"I had a dream," Little Tib said, and then he told Nitty all about his dream.

"When you thought you were drinking that tea, that was me giving you your medicine, is what I think. Only it wasn't hot tea; it was ice water. And that wasn't a dream you had; it was a nightmare."

"I thought it was kind of nice," Little Tib said. "The king was right there, and you could talk to him and explain what had happened." His hands found a little table next to the bed. There was a lamp on it. He knew he could not see when the bulb lit, but he made the switch go *click* with his fingers anyway. "How did we get here?" he asked.

"Well, after the collection, when everybody had left, that Dr. Prithivi was hot to talk to you. But me and Mr. Parker said you were with us and we wouldn't let him unless you had a place to sleep. We told him how you were sick, and all that. So he transferred some money to Mr. Parker's account, and we rented this room. He says he always sleeps in his bus to look after that Deva."

"Is that where he is now?"

"No, he's downtown talking to the people. Probably I should have told you, but it's the day after you did that, now. You slept a whole day full, and a little more."

"Where's Mr. Parker?"

"He's looking around."

"He wants to see if that latch on that window is still broken, doesn't he? And if I'm really little enough to get between those bars."

"That's one thing, yes."

"It was nice of you to stay with me."

"I'm supposed to tell Dr. Prithivi when you're awake. That was part of our deal."

"Would you have stayed anyway?" Little Tib was climbing out of bed. He had never been in a motel before, though he did not want to say so, and he was eager to explore this one.

"*Somebody* would have had to stay with you." Little Tib could hear the faint whistles of the numbers on the telephone.

Later, when Dr. Prithivi came, he made Little Tib sit in a big chair with puffy arms. Little Tib told him about the dancing and how it had felt.

"You can see a bit, I think. You are not entirely blind."

Little Tib said, "No," and Nitty said, "The doctor in Howard told us he didn't have any retinas. How is anybody going to see if they don't have retinas?"

"Ah, I understand, then. Someone told you, I think, about my bus—the pictures I have made on the sides of it. Yes, that must be it. Did they tell you?"

"Tell me about what?" Little Tib asked.

Talking to Nitty, Dr. Prithivi said, "You have described the paintings on the side of my bus to this child?"

"No," Nitty said. "I looked at them when I got in, but I never talked about them."

"Yes, indeed, I did not think so. It was not likely, I think, that you had seen it before I stopped for you on the road, and you were in my presence after that. Nevertheless, there is a picture on the left side of my bus that is a picture of a man with a lion's head. It is Vishnu destroying the demon Hiranyakasipu. Is it not interesting that this boy, arriving in a vehicle with such a picture, should be led to dance on air by a lion-headed figure? It was Vishnu also who circled the universe in two strides; this is a kind of dancing on air, perhaps."

"Uh-huh," Nitty said. "But George here couldn't have seen that picture."

"But perhaps the picture saw him—that is the point you are missing. Still, the lion has many significations. Among the Jews, it is the emblem of the tribe of Judah. For this reason the Emperor of Ethiopia is styled Lion of Judah. Also the son-in-law of Mohammed, whose name I cannot recall now when I need it, was styled Lion of God. Christianity too is very rich in lions. You noticed perhaps that I asked the boy particularly if the lion he saw had wings. I did that because a winged lion is the badge of Saint Mark. But a lion without wings indicates the Christ—this is because of the old belief that the cubs of the lion are dead at birth, and are licked to life afterward by the lioness. In the writings of Sir C. S. Lewis a lion is used in that way, and in the prayers revealed to Saint Bridget of Sweden the Christ is styled 'Strong Lion, immortal and invincible King.' "

"And it is the lion that will lay down with the lamb when the time comes," Nitty said. "I don't know much, maybe, about all this, but I know that. And the lamb is about the commonest symbol for Jesus. A little boy—that's a sign for Jesus too."

Mr. Parker's voice said, "How do either of you know God had anything to do with it?" Little Tib could tell that it was a new voice to Nitty and Dr. Prithivi—besides, Mr. Parker was talking from farther away, and after he said that he came over and sat on the bed, so that he was closest of all.

"The hand of the god is in all, Mr. Parker," Dr. Prithivi told him. "Should you prove that it is not to be found, it would be the not-finding. And the not-found, also."

"All right, that's a philosophical position that cannot be attacked, since it already contains the refutation of any attack. But because it can't be attacked, it can't be demonstrated either—it's simply your private belief. My point is that that wasn't what you were talking about. You were trying to find a real, visible, apparent Hand of God—to take His fingerprints. I'm saying they may not be there. The dancing lion may be nothing more than a figment of George's imagination—a dancing lion. Levitation—which is what that was—has often been reported in connection with other paranormal abilities."

"This may be so," Dr. Prithivi said, "but possibly we should ask him. George, when you were dancing with the lion man, did you perhaps feel it to be the god?"

"No," Little Tib said, "an angel."

A long time later, after Dr. Prithivi had asked him a great many questions and left, Little Tib asked Nitty what they were going to do that night. He had not understood Dr. Prithivi.

Mr. Parker said, "You have to appear. You're going to be the boy Krishna."

"Just play like," Nitty added.

"It's supposed to be a masquerade, more or less. Dr. Prithivi has talked some people who are interested in his religion into playing the parts of various mythic figures. Everyone wants to see you, so the high spot will be when you appear as Krishna. He brought a costume for you."

"Where is it?" Little Tib asked.

"It might be better if you don't put it on yet. The important thing is that while everybody is watching you and Nitty and Dr. Prithivi and the other masquers, I'll have an opportunity to get into the County Administration Building and perform the reprogramming I have in mind."

"Sounds good," Nitty said. "You think you can do it all right?"

"It's just a matter of getting a printout of the program and adding a patch. It's set up now to eliminate personnel whenever the figures indicate that their functions can be performed more economically by automation. The patch will exempt the school superintendent's job from the rule."

"And mine," Nitty said.

"Yes, of course. Anyway, it's highly unlikely that it will ever be noticed in that mass of assembler-language statements—certainly it won't be for many years, and then, when it is found, whoever comes across it will think that it reflects an administrative decision."

"Uh-huh."

"Then I'll add a once-through and erase subroutine that will rehire us and put George here in the blind program at Grovehurst. The whole thing ought not to take more than two hours at the outside."

"You know what I've been thinking?" Nitty said.

"What's that?"

"This little boy here—he's what you call a wonder-worker."

"You mean the little girl's leg. There wasn't any dancing lion then."

"Before that. You remember when those railroad police ladies threw the gas bomb at us?"

"I'm pretty vague on it, to tell the truth."

(Little Tib had gotten up. He had learned by this time that there was a kitchen in the motel, and he knew that Nitty had bought cola to put in the refrigerator. Little Tib wondered if they were looking at him.)

"Yeah," Nitty said. "Well, back before that happened—with the gas bomb— you were feelin' bad a lot. You know what I mean? You would think that you were still superintendent, and sometimes you got real upset when somebody said something."

"I had emotional problems as a result of losing my position—maybe a little worse than most people would. But I got over it."

"Took you a long time."

"A few weeks, sure."

(Little Tib opened the door of the refrigerator as quietly as he could, hearing the light switch click on. He wondered if he should offer to get something for Nitty and Mr. Parker, but he decided it would be best if they did not notice him.)

" 'Bout three years."

(Little Tib's fingers found the cold cans on the top shelf. He took one out and pulled the ring, opening it with a tiny pop. It smelled funny, and after a moment he knew that it was beer and put it back. A can from the next shelf down was cola. He closed the refrigerator.)

"Three years."

"Nearly that, yes."

There was a pause. Little Tib wondered why the men were not talking.

"You must be right. I can't remember what year it is. I could tell you the year I was born, and the year I graduated from college. But I don't know what year it is now. They're just numbers."

Nitty told him. Then for a long time, again, nobody said anything. Little Tib drank his cola, feeling it fizz on his tongue.

"I remember traveling around with you a lot, but it doesn't seem like . . ."

Nitty did not say anything.

"When I remember, it's always summer. How could it always be summer, if it's three years?"

"Winters we used to go down on the Gulf Coast. Biloxi, Mobile, Pascagoula. Sometimes we might go over to Panama City or Tallahassee. We did that one year."

"Well, I'm all right now."

"I know you are. I can see you are. What I'm talking about is that you weren't—not for a long time. Then those railroad police ladies threw that gas, and the gas disappeared and you were all right again. Both together."

"I got myself a pretty good knock on the head, running into the wall of that freight car."

"I don't think that was it."

"You mean you think George did it? Why don't you ask him?"

"He's been too sick; besides, I'm not sure he knows. He didn't know much about that little girl's leg, and I know he did that."

"George, did you make me feel better when we were on the train? Were you the one that made the gas go away?"

"Is it all right if I have this soda pop?"

"Yes. Did you do those things on the train?"

"I don't know," Little Tib said. He wondered if he should tell them about the beer.

Nitty asked, "How did you feel on the train?" His voice, which was always gentle, seemed gentler than ever.

"Funny."

"Naturally he felt funny," Mr. Parker said. "He was running a fever."

"Jesus didn't always know. 'Who touched me?' he said. He said, 'I felt power go out from me.' "

"Matthew Fourteen: Five—Luke Eighteen: Two. In overtime."

"You don't have to believe he was God. He was a real man, and he did those things. He cured all those people, and he walked on that water."

"I wonder if he saw the lion."

"Saint Peter walked on it too. Saint Peter saw Him. But what I'm wondering about is, if it is the boy, what would happen to you if he was to go away?"

"Nothing would happen to me. If I'm all right, I'm all right. You think maybe he's Jesus or something. Nothing happened to those people Jesus cured when he died, did it?"

"I don't know," Nitty said. "It doesn't say."

"Anyway, why should he go away? We're going to take care of him, aren't we?"

"Sure we are."

"There you are, then. Are you going to put his costume on him before we go?"

"I'll wait until you're inside. Then when he comes out, I'll take him back here and get him dressed up and take him over to the meeting."

Little Tib heard the noise the blinds made when Mr. Parker pulled them up—a creaky, clattery little sound. Mr. Parker said, "Do you think it would be dark enough by the time we got over there?"

"No."

"I guess you're right. That window is still loose, and I think he can get through—get between the bars. How long ago was it we looked? Was that three years?"

"Last year," Nitty said. "Last summer."

"It still looks the same. George, all you really have to do is to let me in the building, but it would be better if I didn't come through the front door where people could see me. Do you understand?"

Little Tib said that he did.

"Now it's an old building, and all the windows on the first floor have bars on them; even if you unlocked some of the other windows from inside, I couldn't get through. But there is a side door that's only used for carrying in supplies. It's locked on the outside with a padlock. What I want you to do is to get the key to the padlock for me, and hand it to me through the window."

"Where is the computer?" Little Tib asked.

"That doesn't matter—I'll deal with the computer. All you have to do is let me in."

"I want to know where it is," Little Tib insisted.

Nitty said, "Why is that?"

"I'm scared of it."

"It can't hurt you," Nitty said. "It's just a big number grinder. It will be turned off at night anyway, won't it, Mr. Parker?"

"Unless they're running an overnight job."

"Well, anyway, you don't have to worry about it," Nitty said.

Then Mr. Parker told Little Tib where he thought the keys to the side door would be, and told him that if he could not find them, he was to unlock the front door from inside. Nitty asked if he would like to listen to the television, and he said yes, and they listened to a show that had country and western music, and then it was time to go. Nitty held Little Tib's hand as the three of them walked up the street. Little Tib could feel the tightness in Nitty. He knew that Nitty was thinking about what would happen if someone found them. He heard music—not country and western music like they had heard on the television—and to make Nitty talk so he would not worry so much, he asked what it was.

"That's Dr. Prithivi," Nitty told him. "He's playing that music so that people will come and hear his sermon, and see the people in the costumes."

"Is he playing it himself?"

"No, he's got it taped. There's a loudspeaker on the top of the bus."

Little Tib listened. The music was a long way away, but it sounded as if it were even farther away than it was. As if it did not belong here in Martinsburg at all. He asked Nitty about that.

Mr. Parker said, "What you sense is remoteness in time, George. That Indian flute music belongs, perhaps, to the fifth century A.D. Or possibly the fifth century B.C., or the fifteenth. It's like an old, old thing that never knew when to die, that's still wandering over the earth."

"It never was here before, was it?" Little Tib asked. Mr. Parker said that that was correct, and then Little Tib said, "Then maybe it isn't an old thing at all." Mr. Parker laughed, but Little Tib thought of the time when the lady down the road had had her new baby. It had been weak and small and toothless, like his own grandmother; and he had thought that it was old until everyone told him it was very new and it would be alive, probably, when its mother was an old woman and dead. He wondered who would be alive a long time from now—Mr. Parker, or Dr. Prithivi.

They turned a corner. "Just a little way farther," Nitty said.

"Is anybody here to watch us?"

"Don't you worry. We won't do anything if anybody's here."

Quite suddenly, Mr. Parker's hands were moving up and down Little Tib's body. "He'll be able to get through," Mr. Parker said. "Feel how thin he is."

They turned another corner, and there were dead leaves and old newspapers under Little Tib's feet. "Sure is dark in here," Nitty whispered.

"You see," Mr. Parker said, "no one can see us. It's right here, George." He took one of Little Tib's hands and moved it until it touched an iron bar. "Now, remember, through the storeroom, out to the main hall, turn right, past six doors— I think it is—and down half a flight of stairs. That will be the boiler room, and the janitor's desk is against the wall to your right. The keys should be hanging on a hook near the desk. Bring them back here and give them to me. If you can't find them, come back here and I'll tell you how to get to the front door and open it."

"Will you put the keys back?" Little Tib asked. He was getting his left leg between two of the bars, which was easy. His hips slid in after it. He felt the heavy, rusty window swing in as he pushed against it.

"Yes, the first thing I'll do after you let me in is go back to the boiler room and hang the keys back up."

"That's good," Little Tib said. His mother had told him that you must never steal, though he had taken things since he had run away.

For a little while he was afraid he was going to scrape his ears off. Then the wide part of his head was through and everything was easy. The window pushed back, and he let his legs down onto the floor. He wanted to ask Mr. Parker where the door to this room was, but that would look as if he were afraid. He put one hand on the wall, and the other one out in front of him, and began to feel his way along. He wished he had his stick, but he could not even remember, now, where he had left it.

"Let me go ahead of you."

It was the funniest-looking man Little Tib had ever seen.

"I'm soft. If I bump into anything, I won't be hurt."

Not a man at all, Little Tib thought. Just clothes padded out, with a painted face at the top. "Why can I see you?" Little Tib said.

"You're in the dark, aren't you?"

"I guess so," Little Tib admitted. "I can't tell."

"Exactly. Now, when people who can see are in the light, they can see things that *are* there. And when they're in the dark, why, they *can't* see them. Isn't that correct?"

"I suppose so."

"But when you're in the light you can't see things. So naturally when you're in the dark you see things that aren't there. You see how simple it is?"

"Yes," Little Tib said, not understanding.

"There. That proves it. You *can* see it, and it *isn't* really simple at all." The Clothes Man had his hand—it was an old glove, Little Tib noticed—on the knob of a big metal door now. When he touched it, Little Tib could see that too. "It's locked," the Clothes Man said.

Little Tib was still thinking about what he had said before. "You're smart," he told the Clothes Man.

"That's because I have the best brain in the entire world. It was given to me by the great and powerful Wizard himself."

"Are you smarter than the computer?"

"Much, much smarter than the computer. But I don't know how to open this door."

"Have you been trying?"

"Well, I've been shaking the knob—only it won't shake. And I've been feeling around for a catch. That's trying, I suppose."

"I think it is," Little Tib said.

"Ah, you're thinking—that's good." Little Tib had reached the door, and the Clothes Man moved to one side to let him feel it. "If you had the ruby slippers," the Clothes Man continued, "you could just click your heels three times and wish, and you'd be on the other side. Of course, you're on the other side now."

"No, I'm not," Little Tib told him.

"Yes, you are," the Clothes Man said. "Over *there* is where you want to be— that's on *that* side. So this is the *other* side."

"You're right," Little Tib admitted. "But I still can't get through the door."

"You don't have to, now," the Clothes Man told him. "You're already on the other side. Just don't trip over the steps."

"What steps?" Little Tib asked. As he did, he took a step backward. His heel bumped something he did not expect, and he sat down hard on something else that was higher up than the floor should have been.

"Those steps," the Clothes Man said mildly.

Little Tib was feeling them with his hands. They were sidewalk-stuff with metal edges, and they felt almost as hard and real to his fingers as they had a moment ago when he sat down on them without wanting to. "I don't remember going down these," he said.

"You didn't. But now you have to go up them to get to the upper room."

"What upper room?"

"The one with the door that goes out into the corridor," the Clothes Man told him. "You go to the corridor, and turn *that* way, and—"

"I know," Little Tib said. "Mr. Parker told me. Over and over. But he didn't tell me about that door that was locked, or these steps."

"It may be that Mr. Parker doesn't remember the inside of this building quite as well as he thinks he does."

"He used to work here. He told me." Little Tib was going up the stairs. There was an iron rail on one side. He was afraid that if he did not talk to the Clothes Man, he would go away. But Little Tib could not think of anything to say, and nothing of the kind happened. Then he remembered that he had not talked to the lion at all.

"I could find the keys for you," the Clothes Man said. "I could bring them back to you."

"I don't want you to leave," Little Tib told him.

"It would just take a moment. I fall down a lot, but keys wouldn't break."

"No," Little Tib said. The Clothes Man looked so hurt that he added, "I'm afraid. . . ."

"You can't be afraid of the dark. Are you afraid of being alone?"

"A little. But I'm afraid you couldn't really bring them to me. I'm afraid you're not real, and I want you to be real."

"I could bring them." The Clothes Man threw out his chest and struck a heroic pose, but the dry grass that was his stuffing made a small, sad, rustling sound. "I *am* real. Try me."

There was another door—Little Tib's fingers found it. This one was not locked, and when he went out it, the floor changed from sidewalk to smooth stone. "I too am real," a strange voice said. The Clothes Man was still there when the strange voice spoke, but he seemed dimmer.

"Who are you?" Little Tib asked, and there was a sound like thunder. He had hated the strange voice from the beginning, but until he heard the thunder sound he had not really known how much. It was not really like thunder, he thought. He remembered his dream about the gnomes, though this was much worse. It seemed to him that it was like big stones grinding together at the bottom of the deepest hole in the world. It was worse than that, really.

"I wouldn't go in there if I were you," the Clothes Man said.

"If the keys are in there, I'll have to go in and get them," Little Tib replied.

"They're not in there at all. In fact, they're not even close to there—they're several doors down. All you have to do is walk past the door."

"Who is it?"

"It's the computer," the Clothes Man told him.

"I didn't think they talked like that."

"Only to you. And not all of them talk at all. Just don't go in and it will be all right."

"Suppose it comes out here after me?"

"It won't do that. It is as frightened of you as you are of it."

"I won't go in," Little Tib promised.

When he was opposite the door where the thing was, he heard it groaning as if it were in torture, and he turned and went in. He was very frightened to find himself there, but he knew he was not in the wrong place—he had done the right thing, and not the wrong thing. Still, he was very frightened. The horrible voice said, "What have we to do with you? Have you come to torment us?"

"What is your name?" Little Tib asked.

The thundering, grinding noise came a second time, and this time Little Tib thought he heard in it the sound of many voices, perhaps hundreds or thousands, all speaking at once.

"Answer me," Little Tib said. He walked forward until he could put his hands on the cabinet of the machine. He felt frightened, but he knew the Clothes Man had been right—the computer was as frightened of him as he was of it. He knew that the Clothes Man was standing behind him, and he wondered if he would have dared to do this if someone else had not been watching.

"We are legion," the horrible voice said. "Very many."

"Get out!" There was a moaning that might have come from deep inside the earth. Something made of glass that had been on furniture fell over and rolled and crashed to the floor.

"They are gone," the Clothes Man said. He sat on the cabinet of the computer so Little Tib could see it, and he looked brighter than ever.

"Where did they go?" Little Tib asked.

"I don't know. You will probably meet them again." As if he had just thought of it, he said, "You were very brave."

"I was scared. I'm still scared—the worst since I left the new place."

"I wish I could tell you that you didn't have to be afraid of them," the Clothes Man said, "or of anybody. But it wouldn't be true. Still, I can tell you something that is really better than that—that it will all come out right in the end." He took off the big, floppy black hat he wore, and Little Tib saw that his bald head was really only a sack. "You wouldn't let me bring the keys before, but how about now? Or would you be afraid with me away?"

"No," Little Tib said, "but I'll get the keys myself."

At once the Clothes Man was gone. Little Tib felt the smooth, cool metal of the computer under his hands. In the blackness, it was the only reality there was.

He did not bother to find the window again; instead, he unlocked another, and called Nitty and Mr. Parker to it, smelling as he did the cool, damp air of spring. At the opening, he thrust the keys through first, then squeezed himself between the bars. By the time he was outside, he could hear Mr. Parker unlocking the side door.

"You were a long time," Nitty said. "Was it bad in there by yourself?"

"I wasn't by myself," Little Tib said.

"I'm not even goin' to ask you about that. I used to be a fool, but I know better now. You still want to go to Dr. Prithivi's meetin'?"

"He wants us to come, doesn't he?"

"You are the big star, the main event. If you don't come, it's going to be like no potato salad at a picnic."

They walked back to the motel in silence. The flute music they had heard before was louder and faster now, with the clangs of gongs interspersed in its shrill wailings. Little Tib stood on a footstool while Nitty took his clothes away and wrapped a piece of cloth around his waist, and another around his head, and hung his neck with beads, and painted something on his forehead.

"There, you look just ever so fine," Nitty said.

"I feel silly," Little Tib told him.

Nitty said that that did not matter, and they left the motel again and walked several blocks. Little Tib heard the crowd, and the loud sounds of the music, and then smelled the familiar dark, sweet smell of Dr. Prithivi's bus; he asked Nitty if the people had not seen him, and Nitty said that they had not, that they were watching something taking place on a stage outside.

"Ah," Dr. Prithivi said. "You are here, and you are just in time."

Nitty asked him if Little Tib looked all right.

"His appearance is very fine indeed, but he must have his instrument."

He put a long, light stick into Little Tib's hands. It had a great many little holes in it. Little Tib was happy to have it, knowing that he could use it to feel his way if necessary.

"Now it is time you met your fellow performer," Dr. Prithivi said. "Boy

Krishna, this is the god Indra. Indra, it has given me the greatest pleasure to introduce to you the god Krishna, most charming of the incarnations of Vishnu."

"Hello," a strange, deep voice said.

"You are doubtless familiar already with the story, but I will tell it to you again in order to refresh your memories before you must appear on my little stage. Krishna is the son of Queen Devaki, and this lady is the sister of the wicked King Kamsa who kills all her children when they are born. To save Krishna, the good queen places him among villagers. There he offends Indra, who comes to destroy him. . . ."

Little Tib listened with only half his mind, certain that he could never remember the whole story. He had forgotten the queen's name already. The wood of the flute was smooth and cool under his fingers, the air in the bus hot and heavy, freighted with strange, sleepy odors.

"I am King Kamsa," Dr. Prithivi was saying, "and when I am through being he, I will be a cowherd, so I can tell you what to do. Remember not to drop the mountain when you lift it."

"I'll be careful," Little Tib said. He had learned to say that in school.

"Now I must go forth and prepare for you. When you hear the great gong struck three times, come out. Your friend will be waiting there to take you to the stage."

Little Tib heard the door of the bus open and close. "Where's Nitty?" he asked.

The deep voice of Indra—a hard, dry voice, it seemed to Little Tib—said, "He has gone to help."

"I don't like being alone here."

"You are not alone," Indra said. "I'm with you."

"Yes."

"Did you like the story of Krishna and Indra? I will tell you another story. Once, in a village not too far away from here—"

"You aren't from around here, are you?" Little Tib asked. "Because you don't talk like it. Everybody here talks like Nitty or like Mr. Parker except Dr. Prithivi, and he's from India. Can I feel your face?"

"No, I'm not from around here," Indra said. "I am from Niagara, Do you know what that is?"

Little Tib said, "No."

"It is the capital of this nation—the seat of government. Here, you may feel my face."

Little Tib reached upward; but Indra's face was smooth, cool wood, like the flute. "You don't have a face," he said.

"That is because I am wearing the mask of Indra. Once, in a village not too far from here, there were a great many women who wanted to do something nice for the whole world. So they offered their bodies for certain experiments. Do you know what an experiment is?"

"No," said Little Tib.

"Biologists took parts of these women's bodies—parts that would later become boys and girls. And they reached down inside the tiniest places in those parts and made improvements."

"What kind of improvements?" Little Tib asked.

"Things that would make the girls and boys smarter and stronger and healthier—that kind of improvement. Now these good women were mostly teachers in a college, and the wives of college teachers."

"I understand," Little Tib said. Outside, the people were singing.

"However, when those girls and boys were born, the biologists decided that they needed more children to study—children who had not been improved, so that they could compare them to the ones who had."

"There must have been a lot of those," Little Tib ventured.

"The biologists offered money to people who would bring their children in to be studied, and a great many people did—farm and ranch and factory people, some of them from neighboring towns." Indra paused. Little Tib thought he smelled like cologne, but like oil and iron too. Just when Little Tib thought the story was finished, Indra began to speak again.

"Everything went smoothly until the boys and girls were six years old. Then at the center—the experiments were made at the medical center, in Houston—strange things started to happen. Dangerous things. Things that no one could explain." As though he expected Little Tib to ask what these inexplicable things were, Indra waited, but Little Tib said nothing.

At last Indra continued. "People and animals—sometimes even monsters—were seen in the corridors and therapy rooms who had never entered the complex and were never observed to leave it. Experimental animals were freed—apparently without their cages having been opened. Furniture was rearranged, and on several different occasions large quantities of food that could not be accounted for were found in the common rooms.

"When it became apparent that these events were not isolated occurrences, but part of a recurring pattern, they were coded and fed to a computer together with all the other events of the medical center schedule. It was immediately apparent that they coincided with the periodic examinations given the genetically improved children."

"I am not one of those," Little Tib said.

"The children were examined carefully. Thousands of man-hours were spent in checking them for paranormal abilities; none were uncovered. It was decided that only half the group should be brought in each time. I'm sure you understand the principle behind that—if paranormal activity had occurred when one half was present, but not when the other half was, we would have isolated the disturbing individual to some extent. It didn't work. The phenomena occurred when each half group was present."

"I understand."

The door of the bus opened, letting in fresh night air. Nitty's voice said, "You two ready? Going to have to come on pretty soon now."

"We're ready," Indra told him. The door closed again, and Indra said, "Our agency felt certain that the fact that the phenomena took place whenever either half of the group was present indicated that several individuals were involved. Which meant the problem was more critical than we supposed. Then one of the biologists who had been involved originally—by that time we had taken charge of the project, you understand—pointed out in the course of a casual conversation with one of our people that the genetic improvements they had made could occur spontaneously. I want you to listen carefully now. This is important."

"I'm listening," Little Tib told him dutifully.

"A certain group of us were very concerned about this. We— Are you familiar with the central data-processing unit that provides identification and administers social benefits to the unemployed?"

"You look in it and it's supposed to tell who you are," Little Tib said.

"Yes. It already included a system for the detection of fugitives. We added a new routine that we hoped would be sensitive to potential paranormalities. The biologists indicated that a paranormal individual might possess certain retinal peculiarities, since such people notoriously see phenomena, like Kirlian auras, that are invisible to normal sight. The central data bank was given the capability of detecting such abnormalities through its remote terminals."

"It would look into his eyes and know what he was," Little Tib said. And after a moment, "You should have done that with the boys and girls."

"We did," Indra told him. "No abnormalities were detected, and the phenomena persisted." His voice grew deeper and more solemn than ever. "We reported this to the president. He was extremely concerned, feeling that under the present unsettled economic conditions, the appearance of such an individual might trigger domestic disorder. It was decided to terminate the experiment."

"Just forget about it?" Little Tib asked.

"The experimental material would be sacrificed to prevent the continuance and possible further development of the phenomena."

"I don't understand."

"The brains and spinal cords of the boys and girls involved would be turned over to the biologists for examination."

"Oh, I know this story," Little Tib said. "The three Wise Men come and warn Joseph and Mary, and they take Baby Jesus to the Land of Egypt on a donkey."

"No," Indra told him, "that isn't this story at all. The experiment was ended, and the phenomena ceased. But a few weeks later the alert built into the central data system triggered. A paranormal individual had been identified, almost five hundred kilometers from the scene of the experiment. Several agents were dispatched to detain him, but he could not be found. It was at this point that we realized we had made a serious mistake. We had utilized the method of detention and identification already used in criminal cases—destruction of the retina. That meant the subject could not be so identified again."

"I see," Little Tib said.

"This method had proved to be quite practical with felons—the subject could be identified by other means, and the resulting blindness prevented escape and effective resistance. Of course, the real reason for adopting it was that it could be employed without any substantial increase in the mechanical capabilities of the remote terminals—a brief overvoltage to the sodium vapor light normally used for retinal photography was all that was required.

"This time, however, the system seemed to have worked against us. By the time the agents arrived, the subject was gone. There had been no complaints, no shouting and stumbling. The people in charge of the terminal facility didn't even know what had occurred. It was possible, however, to examine the records of those who had preceded and followed the person who was wanted, however. Do you know what we found?"

Little Tib, who knew that they had found that it was he, said, "No."

"We found that it was one of the children who had been part of the experiment." Indra smiled. Little Tib could not see his smile, but he could feel it. "Isn't that odd? One of the boys who had been part of the experiment."

"I thought they were all dead."

"So did we, until we understood what had happened. But you see, the ones who were sacrificed were those who had undergone genetic improvement before birth. The *controls* were not dead, and this was one of them."

"The other children," Little Tib said.

"Yes. The poor children, whose mothers had brought them in for the money. That was why dividing the group had not worked—the controls were brought in with both halves. It could not be true, of course."

Little Tib said, "What?"

"It could not be true—we all agreed on that. It could not be one of the controls. It was too much of a coincidence. It had to be that one of the mothers—possibly one of the fathers, but more likely one of the mothers—saw it coming a long way off and exchanged infants to save her own. It must have happened years before."

"Like Krishna's mother," Little Tib said, remembering Dr. Prithivi's story.

"Yes. Gods aren't born in cowsheds."

"Are you going to kill this last boy too—when you find him?"

"I know that you are the last of the children."

There was no hope of escaping a seeing person in the enclosed interior of the bus, but Little Tib bolted anyway. He had not taken three steps before Indra had him by the shoulders and forced him back into his seat.

"Are you going to kill me now?"

"No."

Thunder banged outside. Little Tib jumped, thinking for an instant that Indra had fired a gun. "Not now," Indra told him, "but soon."

The door opened again, and Nitty said, "Come on out. It's goin' to rain, and Dr. Prithivi wants to get the big show on before it does." With Indra close behind him, Little Tib let Nitty help him down the steps and out the door of the bus. There were hundreds of people outside—he could hear the shuffling of their feet, and the sound of their voices. Some were talking to each other and some were singing, but they became quiet as he, with Nitty and Indra, passed through them. The air was heavy with the coming storm, and there were gusts of wind.

"Here," Nitty said, "high step up. Watch out."

They were rough wooden stairs, seven steps. Little Tib climbed the last one, and . . .

*He could see.*

For a moment (though it was only a moment) he thought that he was no longer blind. He was in a village of mud houses, and there were people all around him, brown-skinned people with large soft brown eyes—men with red and yellow and blue cloths wrapped about their heads, women with beautiful black hair and colored dresses. There was a cow-smell and a dust-smell and a cooking-smell all at once, and just beyond the village a single mountain perfect and pure as an ice-cream cone, and beyond the mountain a marvelous sky full of palaces and chariots and painted elephants, and beyond the sky more faces than he could count.

Then he knew that it was only imagination, only a dream, not his dream this time, but Dr. Prithivi's dream. Perhaps Dr. Prithivi could dream the way he did, so strongly that the angels came to make the dreams true; perhaps it was only Dr. Prithivi's dream working through him. He thought of what Indra had said—that his mother was not his real mother—and knew that that could not be so.

A brown-skinned, brown-eyed woman with a pretty, heart-shaped face said, "Pipe for us," and he remembered that he still had the wooden flute. He raised it to his lips, not certain that he could play it, and wonderful music began. It was not his, but he fingered the flute pretending that it was his, and danced. The women danced with him, sometimes joining hands, sometimes ringing little bells.

It seemed to him that they had been dancing for only a moment when Indra came. He was bigger than Little Tib's father, and his face was a carved, hook-nosed mask. In his right hand he had a cruel sword that curved and recurved like a snake, and in his left a glittering eye. When Little Tib saw the eye, he knew why it was that Indra had not killed him while they were alone in the bus. Someone far away was watching through that eye, and until he had seen Little Tib do the things he was able, sometimes, to do, make things appear and disappear, bring the angels, Indra could not use his sword. *I just won't do it,* Little Tib thought, but he knew he could not always stop what happened—that the happenings sometimes carried him with them.

The thunder boomed then, and Dr. Prithivi's voice said, "Play up to it! Up to the storm. That is ideal for what we are trying to do!"

Indra stood in front of Little Tib and said something about bringing so much rain that it would drown the village; and Dr. Prithivi's voice told Little Tib to lift the mountain.

Little Tib looked and saw a real mountain, far off and perfect; he knew he could not lift it.

Then the rain came, and the lights went out, and they were standing on the stage in the dark, with icy water beating against their faces. The lightning flashed and Little Tib saw hundreds of people running for their cars; among them were a man with a monkey's head, and another with an elephant's, and a man with nine faces.

And then Little Tib was blind again, and there was nothing left but the rough feel of wood underfoot, and the beating of the rain, and the knowledge that Indra was still before him, holding his sword and the eye.

And then a man made all of metal (so that the rain drummed on him) stood there too. He held an ax, and wore a pointed hat, and by the light that shown from his polished surface Little Tib could see Indra too, and the eye.

"Who are you?" Indra said. He was talking to the Metal Man.

"Who are *you*?" the Metal Man answered. "I can't see your face behind that wooden mask—but wood has never stood for long against me." He struck Indra's mask with his ax; a big chip flew from it, and the string that held it in place broke, and it went clattering down.

Little Tib saw his father's face, with the rain running from it. "Who are you?" his father said to the Metal Man again.

"Don't you know me, Georgie?" the Metal Man said. "Why, we used to be old friends, once. I have, if I may say so, a very sympathetic heart, and when—"

"Daddy!" Little Tib yelled.

His father looked at him and said, "Hello, Little Tib."

"Daddy, if I had known you were Indra I wouldn't have been scared at all. That mask made your voice sound different."

"You don't have to be afraid any longer, Son," his father said. He took two steps toward Little Tib, and then, almost too quickly to see, his sword blade came up and flashed down.

The Metal Man's ax was even quicker. It came up and stayed up; Indra's sword struck it with a crash.

"That won't help him," Little Tib's father said. "They've seen him, and they've seen you. I wanted to get it over with."

"They haven't seen me," the Metal Man said. "It's darker here than you think."

At once it *was* dark. The rain stopped—or if it continued, Little Tib was not conscious of it. He did not know why he knew, but he knew where he was: he was standing, still standing, in front of the computer, with the devils not yet driven out.

Then the rain was back and his father was there again, but the Metal Man was gone, and the dark came back with a rush until Little Tib was blind again. "Are you still going to kill me, Father?" he asked.

There was no reply, and he repeated his question.

"Not now," his father said.

"Later?"

"Come here." Little Tib felt his father's hand on his arm, the way it used to be. "Let's sit down." It drew him to the edge of the platform and helped him to seat himself with his legs dangling over.

"Are you all right?" Little Tib asked.

"Yes," his father told him.

"Then why do you want to kill me?"

"I don't *want* to." Suddenly his father sounded angry. "I never said I *wanted* to. I have to do it, that's all. Look at us; look at what we've been. Moving from place to place, working construction, working the land, worshiping the Lord like it was a hundred years ago. You know what we are? We're jackrabbits. You recall jackrabbits, Little Tib?"

"No."

"That was before your day. Big old long-legg'd rabbits with long ears like a jackass's. Back before you were born they decided they weren't any good, and they all died. For about a year I'd find them on the place, dead, and then there wasn't any more. They waited to join until it was too late, you see. Or maybe they couldn't. That's what's going to happen to people like us. I mean our family. What do you suppose we've been?"

Little Tib, who did not understand the question, said nothing.

"When I was a boy and used to go to school I would hear about all these great men and kings and queens and presidents, and I liked to think that maybe some were family. That isn't so, and I know it now. If you could go back to Bible times, you'd find our people living in the woods like Indians."

"I'd like that," Little Tib said.

"Well, they cut down those woods so we couldn't do that anymore, and we began scratching a living out of the ground. We've been doing that ever since and paying taxes, do you understand me? That's all we've ever done. And pretty soon now there won't be any call at all for people to do that. We've got to join them before it's too late—do you see?"

"No," Little Tib said.

"You're the one. You're a prodigy and a healer, and so they want you dead. You're our ticket. Everybody was born for something, and that was what you were born for, Son. Just because of you, the family is going to get in before it's too late."

"But if I'm dead . . ." Little Tib tried to get his thoughts in order. "You and Mama don't have any other children."

"You don't understand, do you?"

Little Tib's father had put his arm around Little Tib, and now he leaned down until their faces touched. But when they did, it seemed to Little Tib that his father's face did not feel as it should. Little Tib reached up and felt it with both hands, and it came off in his hands, feeling like the plastic vegetables came in at the new place; perhaps this was Big Tib's dream.

"You shouldn't have done that," he said.

Little Tib reached up to find out who had been pretending to be his father. The new face was metal, hard and cold.

"I am the president's man now. I didn't want you to know that, because I thought that it might upset you. The president is handling the situation personally."

"Is Mama still at home?" Little Tib asked. He meant the new place.

"No. She's in a different division—gee-seven. But I still see her sometimes. I think she's in Atlanta now."

"Looking for me?"

"She wouldn't tell me."

Something inside Little Tib, just under the hard place in the middle of his chest where all the ribs came together, began to get tighter and tighter, like a balloon being blown up too far. He felt that when it burst, he would burst too. It made it impossible to take more than tiny breaths, and it pressed against the voice thing in his neck so he could not speak. Inside himself he said forever that that was not his real mother and this was not his real father, that his real mother and father were the mother and father he had had at the old place; he would keep them inside for always, his real mother and father. The rain beat against his face; his nose was full of mucus; he had to breathe through his mouth, but his mouth was filling with saliva, which ran down his chin and made him ashamed.

Then the tears came in a hot flood on his cold cheeks, and the metal face fell off Indra like an old pie pan from a shelf, and went rattling and clanging across the blacktop under the stage.

He reached up to his father's face again, and it was his face, but he said, "Little Tib, can't you understand? It's the Federal Reserve Card. It's the goddamned card. It's having no money, and nothing to do, and spending your whole life like a goddamn whipped dog. I only got in because of you—saying I'd hunt for you. We had training and all that, Skinnerian conditioning and deep hypnosis; they saw to that—but in the end it's the damn card." And while he said that, Little Tib could hear Indra's sword, scraping and scraping, ever so slowly, across the boards of the stage. Little Tib jumped down and ran, not knowing or caring whether he was going to run into something.

In the end, he ran into Nitty. Nitty no longer had his sweat and wood-smoke smell, because of the rain, but he still had the same feel, and the same voice when he said, "*There* you are. I been lookin' just everyplace for you. I thought somebody had run off with you to get you out of the wet. Where you been?" He raised Little Tib on his shoulders.

Little Tib plunged his hands into the thick, wet hair and hung on. "On the stage," he said.

"On the stage still? Well, I swear." Nitty was walking fast, taking big, long strides. Little Tib's body rocked with the swing of them. "That was the one place I never thought to look for you. I thought you would have come off there fast, looking for me, or someplace dry. But I guess you were afraid of falling off."

"Yes," Little Tib said, "I was afraid of falling off." Running in the rain had let all the air out of the balloon; he felt empty inside, and like he had no bones at all. Twice he nearly slid from Nitty's shoulders, but each time Nitty's big hands reached up and caught him.

The next morning a good-smelling woman came from the school for him. Little Tib was still in bed when she knocked on the door, but he heard Nitty open it, and her say, "I believe you have a blind child here."

"Yes'm," Nitty said.

"Mr. Parker—the new acting superintendent?—asked me to come over and escort him myself the first day. I'm Ms. Munson. I teach the blind class."

"I'm not sure he's got clothes fit for school," Nitty told her.

"Oh, they come in just anything these days," Ms. Munson said, and then she saw Little Tib, who had gotten out of bed when he heard the door open, and said, "I see what you mean. Is he dressed for a play?"

"Last night," Nitty told her.

"Oh. I heard about it, but I wasn't there."

Then Little Tib knew he still had the skirt thing on that they had given him— but it was not; it was a dry, woolly towel. But he still had beads on, and metal bracelets on his arm.

"His others are real ragged."

"I'm afraid he'll have to wear them anyway," Ms. Munson said. Nitty took him into the bathroom and took the beads and bracelets and towel off, and dressed him in his usual clothes. Then Ms. Munson led him out of the motel and opened the door of her little electric car for him.

"Did Mr. Parker get his job again?" Little Tib asked when the car bounced out of the motel lot and onto the street.

"I don't know about *again*," Ms. Munson said. "Did he have it before? But I understand he's extremely well qualified in educational programming; and when they found out this morning that the computer was inoperative, he presented his credentials and offered to help. He called me about ten o'clock and asked me to go for you, but I couldn't get away from the school until now."

"It's noon, isn't it," Little Tib said. "It's too hot for morning."

That afternoon he sat in Ms. Munson's room with eight other blind children while a machine moved his hand over little dots on paper and told him what they were. When school was over and he could hear the seeing children milling in the hall outside, a woman older and thicker than Ms. Munson came for him and took him to a house where other, seeing, children larger than he lived. He ate there; the thick woman was angry once because he pushed his beets, by accident, off his plate. That night he slept in a narrow bed.

The next three days were all the same. In the morning the thick woman took him to school. In the evening she came for him. There was a television at the thick woman's house—Little Tib could never remember her name afterward—and when supper was over, the children listened to television.

On the fifth day of school he heard his father's voice in the corridor outside, and then he came into Ms. Munson's room with a man from the school, who sounded important.

"This is Mr. Jefferson," the man from the school told Ms. Munson. "He's from the Government. You are to release one of your students to his care. Do you have a George Tibbs here?"

Little Tib felt his father's hand close on his shoulder. "I have him," his father said. They went out the front door, and down the steps, and then along the side. "There's been a change in orders, Son; I'm to bring you to Niagara for examination."

"All right."

"There's no place to park around this damn school. I had to park a block away."

Little Tib remembered the rattly truck his father had when they lived at the old place, but he knew somehow that the truck was gone like the old place itself, belonging to the real father locked in his memory. The father of now would have a nice car.

He heard footsteps, and then there was a man he could see walking in front of them—a man so small he was hardly taller than Little Tib himself. He had a shiny bald head with upcurling hair at the sides of it, and a bright green coat with two long coattails and two sparkling green buttons. When he turned around to face them (skipping backward to keep up), Little Tib saw that his face was all red and white except for two little, dark eyes that almost seemed to shoot out sparks. He had a big, hooked nose like Indra's, but on him it did not look cruel. "And what can I do for you?" he asked Little Tib.

"Get me loose," Little Tib said. "Make him let go of me."

"And then what?"

"I don't know," Little Tib confessed.

The man in the green coat nodded to himself as if he had guessed that all along, and took an envelope of silver paper out of his inside coat pocket. "If you are *caught* again," he said, "it will be for good. Understand? Running is for people who are not helped." He tore one end of the envelope open. It was full of glittering powder, as Little Tib saw when he poured it out into his hand. "You remind me," he said, "of a friend of mine named *Tip*. *Tip* with a *p*. A *b* is just a *p* turned upside down." He threw the glittering powder into the air, and spoke a word Little Tib could not quite hear.

For just a second there were two things at once. There was the sidewalk and the row of cars on one side and the lawns on the other, and there was Ms. Munson's room, with the sounds of the other children, and the mopped-floor smell. He looked around at the light on the cars, and then it was gone and there was only the sound of his father's voice in the hall outside, and the feel of the school desk and the paper with dots in it. The voice of the man in the green coat (as if he had not gone away at all) said, "Tip turned out to be the ruler of all of us in the end, you know." Then there was the beating of big wings. And then it was all gone, gone completely.

The classroom door opened, and a man from the school who sounded important said, "Ms. Munson, I have a gentleman here who states that he is the father of one of your pupils.

"Would you give me your name again, sir?"

"George Tibbs. My boy's name is George Tibbs too."

"Is this your father, George?" Ms. Munson said.

"How would he know? He's blind."

Little Tib said nothing, and the Important Man said, "Perhaps we'd better all go up to the office. You say that you're with the Federal Government, Mr. Tibbs?"

"The Office of Biogenetic Improvement. I suppose you're surprised, seeing that I'm nothing but a dirt farmer—but I got into it through the Agricultural Program."

"Ah."

Ms. Munson, who was holding Little Tib's hand, led him around a corner.

"I'm working on a case now. . . . Perhaps it would be better if the boy waited outside."

A door opened. "We haven't been able to identify him, you understand," the Important Man said. "His retinas are gone. That's the reason for all this red tape."

Ms. Munson helped Little Tib find a chair, and said, "Wait here."

Then the door closed and everyone was gone. He dug the heels of his hands into his eyes, and for an instant there were points of light like the glittering dust the man in the green coat had thrown. Little Tib thought about what he was going to do, and not running. Then about Krishna, because he had been Krishna. Had Krishna run? Or had he gone back to fight the king who had wanted to kill him? Little Tib could not be sure, but he did not think Krishna had run. Jesus had fled into Egypt; he remembered that. But Jesus had come back. Not to Bethlehem, where he had run from, but to Nazareth, because that was his real home. Little Tib remembered talking about the Jesus story to his father, when they were sitting on the stage. His father had brushed it aside; but Little Tib felt it might be important somehow. He put his chin on his hands to think about it.

The chair was hard—harder than any rock he had ever sat on. He felt the unyielding wood of its arms stretching to either side of him while he thought. There was something horrible about those arms, something he could not remember. Just outside the door the bell rang, and he could hear the noise the children's feet made in the hall. It was recess; they were pouring out the doors, pouring out into the warm fragrance of spring outside.

He got up, and found the door edge with his fingers. He did not know whether anyone was seeing him or not. In an instant he was in the crowd of pushing children. He let them carry him down the steps.

Outside, games went on all around him. He stopped shuffling and shoving now, and began to walk. With the first step he knew that he would go on walking like this all day. It felt better than anything else he had ever done. He walked through all the games until he found the fence around the schoolyard, then down the fence until he found a gate, then out the gate and down the road.

*I'll have to get a stick,* he thought.

When he had gone about five kilometers, as well as he could judge, he heard the whistle of a train far off and turned toward it. Railroad tracks were better than roads—he had learned that months ago. He was less likely to meet people, and trains only went by once in a while. Cars and trucks went by all the time, and any one of them could kill.

After a while he picked up a good stick—light but flexible, and just the right length. He climbed the embankment then, and began to walk where he wanted to walk, on the rails, balancing with his stick. There was a little girl ahead of him, and he could see her, so he knew she was an angel. "What's your name?" he said.

"I mustn't tell you," she answered, "but you can call me Dorothy." She asked his, and he did not say "George Tibbs" but "Little Tib," which was what his mother and father had always called him.

"You fixed my leg, so I'm going with you," Dorothy announced. (She did not really sound like the same girl.) After a time she added: "I can help you a lot. I can tell you what to look out for."

"I know you can," Little Tib said humbly.

"Like now. There's a man up ahead of us."

"A bad man?" Little Tib asked. "Or a good man?"

"A nice man. A shaggy man."

"Hello." It was Nitty's voice. "I didn't really expect to see you here, George, but I guess I should have."

Little Tib said, "I don't like school."

"That's just the different of me. I do like it, only it seems like they don't like me."

"Didn't Mr. Parker get you your job back?"

"I think Mr. Parker kind of forgot me."

"He shouldn't have done that," Little Tib said.

"Well, little blind boy, Mr. Parker is white, you know. And when a white man has been helped out by a black one, he likes to forget it sometimes."

"I see," Little Tib said, though he did not. Black and white seemed very unimportant to him.

"I hear it works the other way too." Nitty laughed.

"This is Dorothy," Little Tib said.

Nitty said, "I can't see any Dorothy, George." His voice sounded funny.

"Well, I can't see you," Little Tib told him.

"I guess that's right. Hello, Dorothy. Where are you an' George goin'?"

"We're going to Sugar Land," Little Tib told him. "In Sugar Land they know who you are."

"Is Sugar Land for real?" Nitty asked. "I always thought it was just some place you made up."

"No, Sugar Land is in Texas."

"How about that," Nitty said. The light of the sun, now setting, made the railroad ties as yellow as butter. Nitty took Little Tib's hand, and Little Tib took Dorothy's, and the three of them walked between the rails. Nitty took up a lot of room, but Little Tib did not take much, and Dorothy hardly took any at all.

When they had gone half a kilometer, they began to skip.

## Afterword

This story began when I mentioned Sugar Land at some science fiction convention and the woman I was talking to thought it an imaginary land, like Cockaigne.

Or Oz for that matter.

Sugar Land is a perfectly real town in Texas; there is or was a big sugar mill there.

For years there was a sad sign quite near my house: BLIND CHILD AREA. I used to tell visitors that I had never seen the blind child, nor had the child seen me. Most would nod sympathetically and move on to other topics.

Now and then I wished that I could; blindness is one of those haunting tragedies no writer ever deals with adequately. I won't pretend I have in this story; I only say that the thought of the blind child, who must have been kept inside day and night for years, no longer haunts me quite as much as it once did.

# SEVEN AMERICAN NIGHTS

*Esteemed and learned madame:*

*As I last wrote you, it appears to me likely that your son Nadan (may Allah preserve him!) has left the old capital and traveled—of his own will or another's—north into the region about the Bay of Delaware. My conjecture is now confirmed by the discovery in those regions of the notebook I enclose. It is not of American manufacture, as you see, and though it holds only the records of a single week, several suggestive items therein provide us new reason to hope.*

*I have photocopied the contents to guide me in my investigations, but I am alert to the probability that you, madame, with your superior knowledge of the young man we seek, may discover implications I have overlooked. Should that be the case, I urge you to write me at once.*

*Though I hesitate to mention it in connection with so encouraging a finding, your most recently due remission has not yet arrived. I assume that this tardiness results from the procrastination of the mails, which is here truly abominable. I must warn you, however, that I shall be forced to discontinue the search unless funds sufficient for my expenses are forthcoming before the advent of winter.*

*With inexpressible respect,*
*Hassan Kerbelai*

Here I am at last! After twelve mortal days aboard the *Princess Fatimah*—twelve days of cold and ennui, twelve days of bad food and throbbing engines—the joy of being on land again is like the delight a condemned man must feel when a letter from the shah snatches him from beneath the very blade of death. America! America! Dull days are no more! They say that everyone who comes here either loves or hates you, America—by Allah I love you now!

Having begun this record at last, I find I do not know where to begin. I had been reading travel diaries before I left home; and so when I saw you, O Book, lying so square and thick in your stall in the bazaar—why should I not have adventures too, and write a book like Osman Aga's? Few come to this sad country at the world's edge after all, and most who do land farther up the coast.

And that gives me the clue I was looking for—how to begin. America began for me as colored water. When I went out on deck yesterday morning, the ocean had changed from green to yellow. I had never heard of such a thing before, neither in my reading, nor in my talks with Uncle Mirza, who was here thirty years ago. I am afraid I behaved like the greatest fool imaginable, running about the ship babbling, and looking over the side every few minutes to make certain the rich mustard color was still there and would not vanish the way things do in dreams when we try to point them out to someone else. The steward told me he knew. Golam Gassem the grain merchant (whom I had tried to avoid meeting for the entire trip until that moment) said, "Yes, yes," and turned away in a fashion that showed he had been avoiding me too, and that it was going to take more of a miracle than yellow water to change his feelings.

One of the few native Americans in first class came out just then: Mr.—as the style is here—Tallman, husband of the lovely Madam Tallman, who really deserves such a tall man as myself. (Whether her husband chose that name in self-derision, or in the hope that it would erase others' memory of his infirmity, or whether it was his father's, and is merely one of the countless ironies of fate, I do not know. There was something wrong with his back.) As if I had not made enough spectacle of myself already, I took this Mr. Tallman by the sleeve and told him to look over the side, explaining that the sea had turned yellow. I am afraid Mr. Tallman turned white himself instead, and turned something else too—his back—looking as though he would have struck me if he dared. It was comic enough, I suppose—I heard some of the other passengers chuckling about it afterward—but I don't believe I have seen such hatred in a human face before. Just then the captain came strolling up, and I—considerably deflated but not flattened yet, and thinking that he had not overheard Mr. Tallman and me—mentioned for the final time that day that the water had turned yellow. "I know," the captain said. "It's his country" (here he jerked his head in the direction of the pitiful Mr. Tallman), "bleeding to death."

Here it is evening again, and I see that I stopped writing last night before I had so much as described my first sight of the coast. Well, so be it. At home it is midnight, or nearly, and the life of the cafés is at its height. How I wish that I were there now, with you, Yasmin, not webbed among these red- and purple-clad strangers, who mob their own streets like an invading army, and duck into their houses like rats into their holes. But you, Yasmin, or Mother, or whoever may read this, will want to know of my day—only you are sometimes to think of me as I am now, bent over an old, scarred table in a decayed room with two beds, listening to the hastening feet in the streets outside.

I slept late this morning; I suppose I was more tired from the voyage than I realized. By the time I woke, the whole of the city was alive around me, with vendors crying fish and fruits under my shuttered window, and the great wooden wains the Americans call trucks rumbling over the broken concrete on their wide iron wheels, bringing up goods from the ships in the Potomac anchorage. One sees very odd teams here, Yasmin. When I went to get my breakfast (one must go outside to reach the lobby and dining room in these American hotels, which I would think would be very inconvenient in bad weather) I saw one of these trucks with two oxen, a horse, and a mule in the traces, which would have made you laugh. The drivers crack their whips all the time.

The first impression one gets of America is that it is not as poor as one has been told. It is only later that it becomes apparent how much has been handed down from the previous century. The streets here are paved, but they are old and broken. There are fine, though decayed, buildings everywhere (this hotel is one—the Inn of Holidays, it is called), more modern in appearance than the ones we see at home, where for so long traditional architecture was enforced by law. We are on Maine Street, and when I had finished my breakfast (it was very good, and very cheap by our standards, though I am told it is impossible to get anything out of season here) I asked the manager where I should go to see the sights of the city. He is a short and phenomenally ugly man, something of a hunchback as so many of them are. "There are no tours," he said. "Not any more."

I told him that I simply wanted to wander about by myself and perhaps sketch a bit.

"You can do that. North for the buildings, south for the theater, west for the park. Do you plan to go to the park, Mr. Jaffarzadeh?"

"I haven't decided yet."

"You should hire at least two securities if you go to the park—I can recommend an agency."

"I have my pistol."

"You'll need more than that, sir."

Naturally, I decided then and there that I would go to the park, and alone. But I have determined not to spend this, the sole, small coin of adventure this land has provided me so far, before I discover what else it may offer to enrich my existence.

Accordingly, I set off for the north when I left the hotel. I have not, thus far, seen this city, or any American city, by night. What they might be like if these people thronged the streets then, as we do, I cannot imagine. Even by clearest day, there is the impression of carnival, of some mad circus whose performance began a hundred or more years ago and has not ended yet.

At first it seemed that only every fourth or fifth person suffered some trace of the genetic damage that destroyed the old America, but as I grew more accustomed to the streets, and thus less quick to dismiss as Americans and no more the unhappy old woman who wanted me to buy flowers and the boy who dashed shrieking between the wheels of a truck, and began instead to look at them as human beings—in other words, just as I would look at some chance-met person on one of our own streets—I saw that there was hardly a soul not marked in some way. These deformities, though they are individually hideous, in combination with the bright, ragged clothing so common here, give the meanest assemblage the character of a pageant. I sauntered along, hardly out of earshot of one group of street musicians before encountering another, and in a few strides passed a man so tall that he was taller seated on a low step than I standing; a bearded dwarf with a withered arm; and a woman whose face had been divided by some devil into halves, one large eyed and idiotically despairing, the other squinting and sneering.

There can be no question about it—Yasmin must not read this. I have been sitting here for an hour at least, staring at the flame of the candle. Sitting and listening to something that from time to time beats against the steel shutters that close the window of this room. The truth is that I am paralyzed by a fear that entered me—I do not know from whence—yesterday, and has been growing ever since.

Everyone knows that these Americans were once the most skilled creators of consciousness-altering substances the world had ever seen. The same knowledge that permitted them to forge the chemicals that destroyed them, so that they might have bread that never staled, innumerable poisons for vermin, and a host of unnatural materials for every purpose, also contrived synthetic alkaloids that produced endless feverish imaginings.

Surely some, at least, of these skills remain. Or if they do not, then some of the substances themselves, preserved for eighty or a hundred years in hidden cabinets, and no doubt growing more dangerous as the world forgets them. I think that someone on the ship may have administered some such drug to me.

That is out at last! I felt so much better at having written it—it took a great deal of effort—that I took several turns about this room. Now that I have written it down, I do not believe it at all.

Still, last night I dreamed of that bread, of which I first read in the little schoolroom of Uncle Mirza's country house. It was no complex, towering "literary" dream such as I have sometimes had, and embroidered, and boasted of afterward over coffee. Just the vision of a loaf of soft white bread lying on a plate in the center of a small table: bread that retained the fragrance of the oven (surely one of the most delicious in the world) though it was smeared with gray mold. Why would the Americans wish such a thing? Yet all the historians agree that they did, just as they wished their own corpses to appear living forever.

It is only this country, with its colorful, fetid streets, deformed people, and harsh, alien language, that makes me feel as drugged and dreaming as I do. Praise Allah that I can speak Farsi to you, O Book. Will you believe that I have taken out every article of clothing I have, just to read the makers' labels? Will *I* believe it, for that matter, when I read this at home?

The public buildings to the north—once the great center, as I understand it, of political activity—offer a severe contrast to the streets of the still-occupied areas. In the latter, the old buildings are in the last stages of decay, or have been repaired by makeshift and inappropriate means, but they seethe with the life of those who depend upon such commercial activity as the port yet provides, and with those who depend on them, and so on. The monumental buildings, because they were constructed of the most imperishable materials, appear almost whole, though there are a few fallen columns and sagging porticos, and in several places small trees (mostly the sad *Carpinus caroliniana*, I believe) have rooted in the crevices of walls. Still, if it is true, as has been written, that Time's beard is gray not with the passage of years but with the dust of ruined cities, it is here that he trails it. These imposing shells are no more than that. They were built, it would seem, to be cooled and ventilated by machinery. Many are windowless, their interiors now no more than sunless caves, reeking of decay; into these I did not venture. Others had had fixed windows that once were mere walls of glass, and a few of these remained, so that I was able to sketch their construction. Most, however, are destroyed. Time's beard has swept away their very shards.

Though these old buildings (with one or two exceptions) are deserted, I encountered several beggars. They seemed to be Americans whose deformities preclude their doing useful work, and one cannot help but feel sorry for them, though their appearance is often as distasteful as their importunities. They offered to show me the former residence of their Padshah, and as an excuse to give them a few coins I accompanied them, making them first pledge to leave me when I had seen it.

The structure they pointed out to me was situated at the end of a long avenue lined with impressive buildings, so I suppose they must have been correct in thinking it once important. Hardly more than the foundation, some rubble, and one ruined wing remains now, and it cannot have been originally of an enduring construction. No doubt it was actually a summer palace or something of that kind. The beggars have now forgotten its very name, and call it merely the white house.

When they had guided me to this relic, I pretended that I wanted to make drawings, and they left as they had promised. In five or ten minutes, however, one particularly enterprising fellow returned. He had no lower jaw, so that I had quite a bit of difficulty in understanding him at first, but after we had shouted back and forth a good deal—I telling him to depart and threatening to kill him on the spot and he protesting—I realized that he was forced to make the sound of *d* for *b*, *n* for *m*, and *t* for *p;* and after that we got along better.

I will not attempt to render his speech phonetically, but he said that since I had been so generous, he wished to show me a great secret—something foreigners like myself did not even realize existed.

"Clean water," I suggested.

"No, no. A great, great secret, Captain. You think all this is dead." He waved a misshapen hand at the desolated structures that surrounded us.

"Indeed I do."

"One still lives. You would like to see it? I will guide. Don't worry about the others—they're afraid of me. I will drive them away."

"If you are leading me into some kind of ambush, I warn you, you will be the first to suffer."

He looked at me very seriously for a moment, and a man seemed to stare from the eyes in that ruined face, so that I felt a twinge of real sympathy. "See there? The big building to the south, on Pennsylvania? Captain, my father's father's father was chief of a department" ("detartnent") "there. I would not betray you."

From what I have read of this country's policies in the days of his father's father's father, that was little enough reassurance, but I followed him.

We went diagonally across several blocks, passing through two ruined buildings. There were human bones in both, and remembering his boast, I asked him if they had belonged to the workers there.

"No, no." He tapped his chest again—a habitual gesture, I suppose—and scooping up a skull from the floor held it beside his own head so that I could see that it exhibited cranial deformities much like his own. "We sleep here, to be shut behind strong walls from the things that come at night. We die here, mostly in wintertime. No one buries us."

"You should bury each other," I said.

He tossed down the skull, which shattered on the terrazzo floor, waking a thousand dismal echoes. "No shovel, and few are strong. But come with me."

At first sight the building to which he led me looked more decayed than many of the ruins. One of its spires had fallen, and the bricks lay in the street. Yet when I looked again, I saw that there must be something in what he said. The broken windows had been closed with ironwork at least as well made as the shutters that protect my room here, and the door, though old and weathered, was tightly shut, and looked strong.

"This is the museum," my guide told me. "The only part left, almost, of the Silent City that still lives in the old way. Would you like to see inside?"

I told him that I doubted that we would be able to enter.

"Wonderful machines." He pulled at my sleeve. "You *see* in, Captain. Come."

We followed the building's walls around several corners, and at last entered a sort of alcove at the rear. Here there was a grille set in the weed-grown ground, and the beggar gestured toward it proudly. I made him stand some distance off, then knelt as he had indicated to look through the grille.

There was a window of unshattered glass beyond the grille. It was very soiled now, but I could see through into the basement of the building, and there, just as the beggar had said, stood an orderly array of complex mechanisms.

I stared for some time, trying to gain some notion of their purpose, and at length an old American appeared among them, peering at one and then another, and whisking the shining bars and gears with a rag.

The beggar had crept closer as I watched. He pointed at the old man, and said, "Still come from north and south to study here. Someday we are great again." Then I thought of my own lovely country, whose eclipse—though without genetic damage—lasted twenty-three hundred years. And I gave him money, and told him that, yes, I was certain America would be great again someday, and left him, and returned here.

I have opened the shutters so that I can look across the city to the obelisk and catch the light of the dying sun. Its fields and valleys of fire do not seem more alien to me, or more threatening, than this strange, despondent land. Yet I know that we are all one—the beggar, the old man moving among the machines of a dead age, those machines themselves, the sun, and I. A century ago, when this was a thriving city, the philosophers used to speculate on the reason that each neutron and proton and electron exhibited the same mass as all the others of its kind. Now we know that there is only one particle of each variety, moving backward and forward in time, an electron when it travels as we do, a positron when its temporal displacement is retrograde, the same few particles appearing billions of billions of times to make up a single object, and the same few particles forming all the objects, so that we are all the sketches, as it were, of the same set of pastels.

I have gone out to eat. There is a good restaurant not far from the hotel, better even than the dining room here. When I came back the manager told me that there is to be a play tonight at the theater, and assured me that because it is so close to his hotel (in truth, he is very proud of this theater, and no doubt its proximity to his hotel is the only circumstance that permits the hotel to remain open) I will be in no danger if I go without an escort. To tell the truth, I am a little ashamed that I did not hire a boat today to take me across the channel to the park, so now I will attend the play, and dare the night streets.

Here I am again, returned to this too-large, too-bare, uncarpeted room, which is already beginning to seem a second home, with no adventures to retail from the dangerous benighted streets. The truth is that the theater is hardly more than a hundred paces to the south. I kept my hand on the butt of my pistol and walked along with a great many other people (mostly Americans) who were also going to the theater, and felt something of a fool.

The building is as old as those in the Silent City, I should think, but it has been kept in some repair. There was more of a feeling of gaiety (though to me it was largely an alien gaiety) among the audience than we have at home, and less of the atmosphere of what I may call the sacredness of Art. By that I knew that the drama really is sacred here, as the colorful clothes of the populace make clear in any case. An exaggerated and solemn respect always indicates a loss of faith.

Having recently come from my dinner, I ignored the stands in the lobby at which the Americans—who seem to eat constantly when they can afford it—were selecting various cold meats and pastries, and took my place in the theater proper. I was hardly in my seat before a pipe-puffing old gentleman, an American, desired me to move in order that he might reach his own. I stood up gladly, of course, and greeted him as "Grandfather," as our own politeness (if not theirs) demands. But while he was settling himself and I was still standing beside him, I caught a glimpse of his face from the exact angle at which I had seen it this afternoon, and recognized him as the old man I had watched through the grille.

Here was a difficult situation. I wanted very much to draw him into conversation, but I could not well confess that I had been spying on him. I puzzled over the question until the lights were extinguished and the play began.

It was Vidal's *Visit to a Small Planet,* one of the classics of the old American theater, a play I have often read about but never (until now) seen performed. I would have liked it much better if it had been done with the costumes and settings of its proper period; unhappily, the director had chosen to "modernize" the entire affair, just as we sometimes present *Rustam Beg* as if Rustam had been a hero of the war just past. General Powers was a contemporary American soldier with the mannerisms of a cowardly bandit, Spelding a publisher of libelous broadsheets, and so on. The only characters that gave me much pleasure were the limping spaceman, Kreton, and the ingenue, Ellen Spelding, played as and by a radiantly beautiful American blonde.

All through the first act my mind had been returning (particularly during Spelding's speeches) to the problem of the old man beside me. By the time the curtain fell, I had decided that the best way to start a conversation might be to offer to fetch him a kebab—or whatever he might want—from the lobby, since his threadbare appearance suggested that he might be ready enough to be treated, and the weakness of his legs would provide an admirable excuse. I tried the gambit as soon as the flambeaux were relit, and it worked as well as I could have wished. When I returned with a paper tray of sandwiches and bitter drinks, he remarked to me quite spontaneously that he had noticed me flexing my right hand during the performance.

"Yes," I said. "I had been writing a good deal before I came here."

That set him off, and he began to discourse, frequently with a great deal more detail than I could comprehend, on the topic of writing machines. At last I halted the flow with some question that must have revealed that I knew less of the subject than he had supposed. "Have you ever," he asked me, "carved a letter in a potato, and moistened it with a stamp pad, and used it to imprint paper?"

"As a child, yes. We used a turnip, but no doubt the principle is the same."

"Exactly; and the principle is that of extended abstraction. I ask you—on the lowest level, what is communication?"

"Talking, I suppose."

His shrill laugh rose above the hubbub of the audience. "Not at all! Smell"—here he gripped my arm—"smell is the essence of communication. Look at that word *essence* itself. When you smell another human being, you take chemicals from his body into your own, analyze them, and from the analysis you accurately deduce his emotional state. You do it so constantly and so automatically that you are largely unconscious of it, and say simply, 'He seemed frightened,' or, 'He was angry.' You see?"

I nodded, interested in spite of myself.

"When you speak, you are telling another how you would smell if you smelled as you should and if he could smell you properly from where he stands. It is almost certain that speech was not developed until the glaciations that terminated the Pliocene stimulated mankind to develop fire, and the frequent inhalation of wood smoke had dulled the olfactory organs."

"I see."

"No, you hear—unless you are by chance reading my lips, which in this din would be a useful accomplishment." He took an enormous bite of his sandwich, spilling pink meat that had surely come from no natural animal. "When you write, you are telling the other how you would speak if he could hear you, and when you print with your turnip, you are telling him how you would write. You will notice that we have already reached the third level of abstraction."

I nodded again.

"It used to be believed that only a limited number $K$ of levels of abstraction were possible before the original matter disappeared altogether—some very interesting mathematical work was done about seventy years ago in an attempt to derive a generalized expression for $K$ for various systems. Now we know that the number can be infinite if the array represents an open curve, and that closed curves are also possible."

"I don't understand."

"You are young and handsome—very fine looking, with your wide shoulders and black mustache—let us suppose a young woman loves you. If you and I and she were crouched now on the limb of a tree, you would scent her desire. Today, perhaps she tells you of that desire. But it is also possible, is it not, that she may write you of her desire?"

Remembering Yasmin's letters, I assented.

"But suppose those letters are perfumed—a musky, sweet perfume. You understand? A closed curve—the perfume is not the odor of her body, but an artificial simulation of it. It may not be what she feels, but it is what she tells you she feels. Your real love is for a whale, a male deer, and a bed of roses." He was about to say more, but the curtain went up for the second act.

I found that act both more enjoyable and more painful than the first. The opening scene, in which Kreton (soon joined by Ellen) reads the mind of the family cat, was exceptionally effective. The concealed orchestra furnished music to indicate cat thoughts; I wish I knew the identity of the composer, but my playbill does not provide the information. The bedroom wall became a shadow screen, where we saw silhouettes of cats catching birds and then, when Ellen tickled the real cat's belly, making love. As I have said, Kreton and Ellen were the play's best characters. The juxtaposition of Ellen's willowy beauty and high-spirited naïveté and Kreton's clear desire for her illuminated perfectly the Paphian difficulties that would confront a powerful telepath, were such persons to exist.

On the other hand, Kreton's summoning of the presidents, which closes the act, was as objectionable as it could possibly have been made. The foreign ruler conjured up by error was played as a Turk, and as broadly as possible. I confess to feeling some prejudice against that bloodthirsty race myself, but what was done was indefensible. When the president of the World Council appeared, he was portrayed as an American.

By the end of that scene I was in no very good mood. I think that I have not yet shaken off the fatigues of the crossing; and they, combined with a fairly strenuous day spent prowling around the ruins of the Silent City, had left me now in that state in which the smallest irritation takes on the dimensions of a mortal insult. The old curator beside me discerned my irascibility, but mistook the reason for it, and began to apologize for the state of the American stage, saying that all the performers of talent emigrated as soon as they gained recognition and returned only when they had failed on the eastern shore of the Atlantic.

"No, no," I said. "Kreton and the girl are very fine, and the rest of the cast is at least adequate."

He seemed not to have heard me. "They pick them up wherever they can—they choose them for their faces. When they have appeared in three plays, they call themselves actors. At the Smithsonian—I am employed there; perhaps I've already mentioned it—we have tapes of real theater: Laurence Olivier, Orson Welles, Katharine Cornell. Spelding is a barber, or at least he was. He used to put his chair under the old Kennedy statue and shave the passersby. Ellen is a trollop, and Powers a drayman. That lame fellow Kreton used to snare sailors for a singing house on Portland Street."

His disparagement of his own national culture embarrassed me, though it put me in a better mood. (I have noticed that the two often go together—perhaps I am secretly humiliated to find that people of no great importance can affect my interior state with a few words or some mean service.) I took my leave of him and went to the confectioner's stand in the lobby. The Americans have a very pretty custom of duplicating the speckled eggs of wild birds in marzipan, and I bought a box of these—not only because I wanted to try them myself, but because I felt certain they would prove a treat for the old man, who must seldom have enough money to afford luxuries of that kind. I was quite correct—he ate them eagerly. But when I sampled one, I found its odor (as though I were eating artificial violets) so unpleasant that I did not take another.

"We were speaking of writing," the old man said. "The closed curve and the open curve. I did not have time to make the point that both could be achieved mechanically, but the monograph I am now developing turns upon that very question, and it happens that I have examples with me. First the closed curve. In the days when our president was among the world's ten most powerful men—the reality of the Paul Laurent you see on the stage there—each president received hundreds of requests every day for his signature. To have granted them would have taken hours of his time. To have refused them would have raised a brigade of enemies."

"What did they do?"

"They called upon the resources of science. That science devised the machine that wrote this."

From within his clean, worn coat he drew a folded sheet of paper. I opened it and saw that it was covered with the text of what appeared to be a public address, written in a childish scrawl. Mentally attempting to review the list of the American presidents I had seen in some digest of world history long ago, I asked whose hand it was.

"The machine's. Whose hand is being imitated here is one of the things I am attempting to discover."

In the dim light of the theater it was almost impossible to make out the faded script, but I caught the word *Sardinia*. "Surely, by correlating the contents to historical events it should be possible to date it quite accurately."

The old man shook his head. "The text itself was composed by another machine to achieve some national psychological effect. It is not probable that it bears any real relationship to the issues of its day. But now look here." He drew out a second sheet, and unfolded it for me. So far as I could see, it was completely blank. I was still staring at it when the curtain went up.

As Kreton moved his toy aircraft across the stage, the old man took a final egg and turned away to watch the play. There was still half a carton left, and I, thinking that he might want more later, and afraid that they might be spilled from my lap and lost underfoot, closed the box and slipped it into the side pocket of my jacket.

The special effects for the landing of the second spaceship were well done, but there was something else in the third act that gave me as much pleasure as the cat scene in the second. The final curtain hinges on the device our poets call the Peri's asphodel, a trick so shopworn now that it is acceptable only if it can be presented in some new light. The one used here was to have John—Ellen's lover—find Kreton's handkerchief and, remarking that it seemed perfumed, bury his nose in it. For an instant, the shadow wall used at the beginning of the second act was illuminated again to graphically (or I should say pornographically) present Ellen's desire, conveying to the audience that John had, for that moment, shared the telepathic abilities of Kreton, whom all of them had now entirely forgotten.

The device was extremely effective, and left me feeling that I had by no means wasted my evening. I joined the general applause as the cast appeared to take their bows; then, as I was turning to leave, I noticed that the old man appeared very ill. I asked if he were all right, and he confessed ruefully that he had eaten too much, and thanked me again for my kindness—which must at that time have taken a great deal of resolution.

I helped him out of the theater and, when I saw that he had no transportation but his feet, told him I would take him home. He thanked me again, and informed me that he had a room at the museum.

Thus the half-block walk from the theater to my hotel was transformed into a journey of three or four kilometers, taken by moonlight, much of it through rubble-strewn avenues of the deserted parts of the city.

During the day I had hardly glanced at the stark skeleton of the old highway. Tonight, when we walked beneath its ruined overpasses, they seemed inexpressibly ancient and sinister. It occurred to me then that there may be a time flaw, such as astronomers report from space, somewhere in the Atlantic. How is it that this western shore is more antiquated in the remains of a civilization not yet a century dead than we are in the shadow of Darius? May it not be that every ship that plows that sea moves through ten thousand years?

For the past hour—I find I cannot sleep—I have been debating whether to make this entry. But what good is a travel journal, if one does not enter everything? I will revise it on the trip home, and present a cleansed copy for my mother and Yasmin to read.

It appears that the scholars at the museum have no income but that derived from the sale of treasures gleaned from the past, and I bought a vial of what is supposed to be the greatest creation of the old hallucinatory chemists from the woman who helped me get the old man into bed. It is—it was—about half the height of my smallest finger. Very probably it was alcohol and nothing more, though I paid a substantial price.

I was sorry I had bought it before I left, and still more sorry when I arrived here; but at the time it seemed that this would be my only opportunity, and I could think of nothing but to seize the adventure. After I have swallowed the drug I will be able to speak with authority about these things for the remainder of my life.

Here is what I have done. I have soaked the porous sugar of one of the eggs with the fluid. The moisture will soon dry up. The drug—if there is a drug—will remain. Then I will rattle the eggs together in an empty drawer, and each day, beginning tomorrow night, I will eat one egg.

I am writing today before I go down to breakfast, partly because I suspect that the hotel does not serve so early. Today I intend to visit the park on the other side of the channel. If it is as dangerous as they say, it is very likely I will not return to make any entry tonight. If I do return—well, I will plan for that when I am here again.

After I had blown out my candle last night I could not sleep, though I was

and the old boatman, began to follow me after I had walked about a kilometer north. They are short-haired, and typically blotched with black and brown flecked with white. I would say their average weight was about twenty-five kilos. With their erect ears and alert, intelligent faces they did not seem particularly dangerous, but I soon noticed that whichever way I turned, the ones in back of me edged nearer. I sat on a stone with my back to a pool and made several quick sketches of them, then decided to try my pistol. They did not seem to know what it was, so I was able to center the red aiming laser very nicely on one big fellow's chest before I pressed the stud for a high-energy pulse.

For a long time afterward, I heard the melancholy howling of these dogs behind me. Perhaps they were mourning their fallen leader. Twice I came across rusting machines that may have been used to take invalids through the gardens in such fair weather as I myself experienced today. Uncle Mirza says I am a good colorist, but I despair of ever matching the green-haunted blacks with which the declining sun painted the park.

I met no one until I had almost reached the piers of the abandoned railway bridge. Then four or five Americans who pretended to beg surrounded me. The dogs, who as I understand it live mostly upon the refuse cast up by the river, were honest in their intentions and cleaner in their persons. If these people had been like the pitiful creatures I had met in the Silent City, I would have thrown them a few coins, but they were more or less able-bodied men and women who could have worked and chose instead to rob. I told them that I had been forced to kill a countryman of theirs (not mentioning that he was a dog) who had assaulted me, and asked where I could report the matter to the police. At that they backed off, and permitted me to walk around the northern end of the channel in peace, though not without a thousand savage looks. I returned here without further incident, tired and very well satisfied with my day.

I have eaten one of the eggs! I confess I found it difficult to take the first taste, but marshaling my resolution was like pushing at a wall of glass—all at once the resistance snapped, and I picked the thing up and swallowed it in a few bites. It was piercingly sweet, but there was no other flavor. Now we will see. This is more frightening than the park by far.

Nothing seemed to be happening, so I went out to dinner. It was twilight, and the carnival spirit of the streets was more marked than ever—colored lights above all the shops, and music from the rooftops where the wealthier natives have private gardens. I have been eating mostly at the hotel, but was told of a "good" American-style restaurant not too far south on Maine Street.

It was just as described—people sitting on padded benches in alcoves. The tabletops are of a substance like fine-grained, greasy artificial stone. They looked very old. I had the Number One Dinner—buff-colored fish soup with the pasty American bread on the side, followed by a sandwich of ground meat and raw vegetables doused with a tomato sauce and served on a soft, oily roll. To tell the truth, I did not much enjoy the meal, but it seems a sort of duty to sample more of the American food than I have thus far.

I am very tempted to end the account of my day here, and in fact I laid down this pen when I had written *thus far* and made myself ready for bed. Still, what good is a dishonest record? I will let no one see this—just keep it to read over after I get home.

Returning to the hotel from the restaurant, I passed the theater. The thought of seeing Ellen again was irresistible; I bought a ticket and went inside. It was not until I was in my seat that I realized that the bill had changed.

The new play was *Mary Rose*. I saw it done by an English company several years ago, with great authenticity, and it struck me that (like Mary herself) it had far outlived its time. The American production was as inauthentic as the other had been correct. For that reason, it retained—or I should have said it had acquired—a good deal of interest.

Americans are superstitious about the interior of their country, not its coasts, so Mary Rose's island had been shifted to one of the huge central lakes. The highlander, Cameron, had accordingly become a Canadian, played by General Powers's former aide. The Speldings had become the Morelands, and the Morelands had become Americans. Kreton was Harry, the knife-throwing wounded soldier, and my Ellen had become Mary Rose.

The role suited her so well that I imagined the play had been selected as a vehicle for her. Her height emphasized the character's unnatural immaturity, and her slenderness and the vulnerability of her pale complexion would have told us, I think, if the play had not, that she had been victimized unaware. More important than any of these things was a wild and innocent affinity for the supernatural, which she projected to perfection. It was that quality alone (as I now understood) that had made us believe on the preceding night that Kreton's spaceship might land in the Speldings' rose garden—he would have been drawn to Ellen, though he had never seen her. Now it made Mary Rose's disappearances and reappearances plausible and even likely; it was as likely that unseen spirits lusted for Mary Rose as that Lieutenant Blake (previously John Randolf) loved her.

Indeed it was more likely. And I had no sooner realized that than the whole mystery of *Mary Rose*—which had seemed at once inexplicable and banal when I had seen it well played in Tehran—lay clear before me. We of the audience were the envious and greedy spirits. If the Morelands could not see that one wall of their comfortable drawing room was but a sea of dark faces, if Cameron had never noticed that we were the backdrop of his island, the fault was theirs. By rights then, Mary Rose should have been drawn to us when she vanished. At the end of the second act I began to look for her, and in the beginning of the third I found her, standing silent and unobserved behind the last row of seats. I was only four rows from the stage, but I slipped out of my place as unobtrusively as I could, and crept up the aisle toward her.

I was too late. Before I had gone halfway, it was nearly time for her entrance at the end of the scene. I watched the rest of the play from the back of the theater, but she never returned.

Same night. I am having a good deal of trouble sleeping, though while I was on the ship I slept nine hours a night and was off as soon as my head touched the pillow.

The truth is that while I lay in bed tonight I recalled the old curator's remark that the actresses were all prostitutes. If it is true and not simply an expression of hatred for younger people whose bodies are still attractive, then I have been a fool to moan over the thought of Mary Rose and Ellen when I might have had the girl herself.

Her name is Ardis Dahl—I just looked it up in the playbill. I am going to the manager's office to consult the city directory there.

Writing before breakfast. Found the manager's office locked last night. It was after two. I put my shoulder against the door and got it opened easily enough. (There was no metal socket for the bolt such as we have at home—just a hole mortised in the frame.) The directory listed several Dahls in the city, but since it was nearly eight years out of date it did not inspire a great deal of confidence. I reflected, however, that in a backwater like this people were not likely to move about so much as we do at home, and that if it were not still of some utility, the manager would not be likely to retain it, so I selected the one that appeared from its address to be nearest the theater, and set out.

The streets were completely deserted. I remember thinking that I was now doing what I had previously been so afraid to do, having been frightened of the city by reading. How ridiculous to suppose that robbers would be afoot now, when no one else was. What would they do, stand for hours at the empty corners?

The moon was full and high in the southern sky, showering the street with the lambent white fluid of its light. If it had not been for the sharp, unclean odor so characteristic of American residential areas, I might have thought myself walking through an illustration from some old book of wonder tales, or an actor in a children's pantomime, so bewitched by the scenery that he has forgotten the audience.

(In writing that—which to tell the truth I did not think of at the time, but only now, as I sat here at my table—I realized that that is in fact what must happen to the American girl I have been in the habit of calling Ellen but must now learn to call Ardis. She could never perform as she does if it were not that in some part of her mind her stage became her reality.)

The shadows about my feet were a century old, tracing faithfully the courses they had determined long before New Tabriz came to jewel the lunar face with its sapphire. Webbed with thoughts of her—my Ellen, my Mary Rose, my Ardis!— and with the magic of that pale light that commands all the tides, I was elevated to a degree I cannot well describe.

Then I was seized by the thought that everything I felt might be no more than the effect of the drug.

At once, like someone who falls from a tower and clutches at the very wisps of air, I tried to return myself to reality. I bit the interior of my cheeks until the blood filled my mouth, and struck the unfeeling wall of the nearest building with my fist. In a moment the pain sobered me. For a quarter hour or more I stood at the curbside, spitting into the gutter and trying to clean and bandage my knuckles with strips torn from my handkerchief. A thousand times I thought what a sight I would be if I did in fact succeed in seeing Ellen, and I comforted myself with the thought that if she were indeed a prostitute it would not matter to her—I could offer her a few additional rials and all would be well.

Yet that thought was not really much comfort. Even when a woman sells her body, a man flatters himself that she would not do so quite so readily were he not who he is. At the very moment I drooled blood into the street, I was congratulating myself on the strong, square face so many have admired, and wondering how I should apologize if in kissing her I smeared her mouth with red.

Perhaps it was some faint sound that brought me to myself; perhaps it was only the consciousness of being watched. I drew my pistol and turned this way and that, but saw nothing.

Yet the feeling endured. I began to walk again, and if there was any sense of unreality remaining, it was no longer the unearthly exultation I had felt earlier. After a few steps I stopped and listened. A dry sound of rattling and scraping had followed me. It too stopped now.

I was nearing the address I had taken from the directory. I confess my mind was filled with fancies in which I was rescued by Ellen herself, who in the end should be more frightened than I, but who would risk her lovely person to save mine. Yet I knew these *were* but fancies, and the thing pursuing me was not, though it crossed my mind more than once that it might be some *druj* made to seem visible and palpable to me.

Another block and I had reached the address. It was a house no different from those on either side—built of the rubble of buildings that were older still, three storied, heavy doored, and almost without windows. There was a bookshop on the ground floor (to judge by an old sign), with living quarters above it. I crossed the street to see it better, and stood, wrapped again in my dreams, staring at the single thread of yellow light that showed between the shutters of a gable window.

As I watched that light, the feeling of being watched myself grew upon me. Time passed, slipping through the waist of the universe's great hourglass like the eroded soil of this continent slipping down her rivers to the seas. At last my fear and desire—desire for Ellen, fear of whatever it was that glared at me with invisible eyes—drove me to the door of the house. I hammered the wood with the butt of my pistol, though I knew how unlikely it was that any American would answer a knock at such a time of night, and when I had knocked several times I heard slow steps from within.

The door creaked open until it was caught by a chain. I saw a gray-haired man, fully dressed, holding an old-fashioned long-barreled gun. Behind him a woman lifted a stub of smoking candle to let him see, and though she was clearly much older than Ellen, and was marked, moreover, by the deformities so prevalent here, there was a certain nobility in her features and a certain beauty as well, so that I was reminded of the fallen statue that is said to have stood on an island farther north, and which I have seen pictured.

I told the man that I was a traveler—true enough!—and that I had just arrived by boat from Arlington and had no place to stay and so had walked into the city until I had noticed the light of his window. I would pay, I said, a silver rial if they would only give me a bed for the night and breakfast in the morning, and I showed them the coin. My plan was to become a guest in the house so that I might discover whether Ellen was indeed one of the inhabitants; if she was, it would have been an easy matter to prolong my stay.

The woman tried to whisper in her husband's ear, but save for a look of nervous irritation he ignored her. "I don't dare let a stranger in." From his voice I might have been a lion and his gun a trainer's chair. "Not with no one here but my wife and myself."

"I see," I told him. "I quite understand your position."

"You might try the house on the corner," he said, shutting the door, "but don't tell them Dahl sent you." I heard the heavy bar dropped into place at the final word.

I turned away—and then by the mercy of Allah Who is indeed compassionate happened to glance back one last time at the thread of yellow between the shutters of that high window. A flicker of scarlet higher still caught my attention, perhaps only because the light of the setting moon now bathed the rooftop from a new angle. I think the creature I glimpsed there had been waiting to leap upon me from behind, but when our eyes met it launched itself toward me. I had barely time to lift my pistol before it struck me and slammed me to the broken pavement of the street.

For a brief period I think I lost consciousness. If my shot had not killed the thing as it fell, I would not be sitting here writing this journal this morning. After half a minute or so I came to myself enough to thrust its weight away, stand up, and rub my bruises. No one had come to my aid, but neither had anyone rushed from the surrounding houses to kill and rob me. I was as alone with the creature that lay dead at my feet as I had been when I only stood watching the window in the house from which it had sprung.

After I found my pistol and assured myself that it was still in working order, I dragged the thing to a spot of moonlight. When I glimpsed it on the roof, it had seemed a feral dog, like the one I had shot in the park. When it lay dead before me, I had thought it a human being. In the moonlight I saw it was neither, or perhaps both. There was a blunt muzzle, and the height of the skull above the eyes, which anthropologists say is the surest badge of humanity and speech, had been stunted until it was not greater than I have seen in a macaque. Yet the arms and shoulders and pelvis—even a few filthy rags of clothing—all bespoke mankind. It was a female, with small, flattened breasts still apparent on either side of the burn channel.

At least ten years ago I read about such things in Osman Aga's *Mystery Beyond the Sun's Setting*, but it was very different to stand shivering on a deserted street corner of the old capital and examine the thing in the flesh. By Osman Aga's account (which no one, I think, but a few old women has ever believed) these creatures were in truth human beings—or at least the descendants of human beings. In the last century, when the famine gripped their country and the irreversible damage done to the chromosomal structures of the people had already become apparent, some few turned to the eating of human flesh. No doubt the corpses of the famine supplied their food at first, and no doubt those who ate of them congratulated themselves that by so doing they had escaped the effects of the enzymes that were then still used to bring slaughter animals to maturity in a matter of months. What they failed to realize was that the bodies of the human beings they ate had accumulated far more of these unnatural substances than were ever found in the flesh of the short-lived cattle. From them, according to *Mystery Beyond the Sun's Setting*, rose such creatures as the thing I had killed.

But Osman Aga has never been believed. So far as I know, he is a mere popular writer, with a reputation for glorifying Caspian resorts in recompense for free lodging, and for indulging in absurd expeditions to breed more books and publicize the ones he has already written—crossing the desert on a camel and the Alps on an elephant—and no one else has ever, to my knowledge, reported such things from this continent. The ruined cities filled with rats and rabid bats, and the terrible whirling dust storms of the interior, have been enough for other travel writers. Now I am sorry I did not contrive a way to cut off the thing's head; I feel sure its skull would have been of interest to science.

As soon as I had written the preceding paragraph, I realized that there might still be a chance to do what I had failed to do last night. I went to the kitchen, and for a small bribe was able to secure a large, sharp knife, which I concealed beneath my jacket.

It was still early as I ran down the street, and for a few minutes I had high hopes that the thing's body might still be lying where I had left it, but my efforts were all for nothing. It was gone, and there was no sign of its presence—no blood, no scar from my beam on the house. I poked into alleys and waste cans. Nothing. At last I came back to the hotel for breakfast, and I have now (it is midmorning) returned to my room to make my plans for the day.

Very well. I failed to meet Ellen last night—I shall not fail today. I am going to buy another ticket for the play, and tonight I will not take my seat, but wait behind the last row where I saw her standing. If she comes to watch at the end of the second act as she did last night, I will be there to compliment her on her performance and present her with some gift. If she does not come, I will make my way backstage—from what I have seen of these Americans, a quarter rial should get me anywhere, but I am willing to loosen a few teeth if I must.

What absurd creatures we are! I have just reread what I wrote this morning, and I might as well have been writing of the philosophic speculations of the Congress of Birds or the affairs of the demons in Domdaniel, or any other subject on which neither I nor anyone else knows or can know a thing. O Book, you have heard what I supposed would occur; now let me tell you what actually took place.

I set out as I had planned to procure a gift for Ellen. On the advice of the hotel manager, I followed Maine Street north until I reached the wide avenue that passes close by the obelisk. Around the base of this still-imposing monument is held a perpetual fair in which the merchants use the stone blocks fallen from the upper part of the structure as tables. What remains of the shaft is still, I should say, upward of one hundred meters high, but it is said to have formerly stood three or four times that height. Much of the fallen material has been carted away to build private homes.

There seems to be no logic to the prices in this country, save for the general rule that foodstuffs are cheap and imported machinery—cameras and the like—costly. Textiles are expensive, which no doubt explains why so many of the people wear ragged clothes that they mend and dye in an effort to make them look new. Certain kinds of jewelry are quite reasonable; others sell for much larger prices than they would in Tehran. Rings of silver or white gold set, usually, with a single modest diamond may be had in great numbers for such low prices that I was tempted into buying a few to take home as an investment. Yet I saw bracelets that would have sold at home for no more than half a rial for which the seller asked ten times that much. There were many interesting antiques, all of which are alleged to have been dug from the ruined cities of the interior at the cost of someone's life. When I had talked to five or six vendors of such items, I was able to believe that I knew how the country was depopulated.

After a good deal of this pleasant, wordy shopping, during which I spent very little, I selected a bracelet made of old coins—many of them silver—as my gift to Ellen. I reasoned that women always like jewelry, and that such a showy piece might be of service to an actress in playing some part or other, and that the coins must have a good deal of intrinsic value. Whether she will like it or not—if she ever receives it—I do not know; it is still in the pocket of my jacket.

When the shadow of the obelisk had grown long, I returned here to the hotel and had a good dinner of lamb and rice, and retired to groom myself for the evening. The five remaining candy eggs stood staring at me from the top of my dresser. I remembered my resolve, and took one. Quite suddenly I was struck by the conviction that the demon I believed I had killed the night before had been no more than a phantom engendered by the action of the drug.

What if I had been firing my pistol at mere empty air? That seemed a terrible thought—indeed it seems so to me still. A worse one is that the drug really may have rendered visible—as some say those ancient preparations were intended to—a real but spiritual being. If such things in fact walk what we take to be unoccupied rooms and rooftops, and the empty streets of night, it would explain many sudden deaths and diseases, and perhaps the sudden changes for the worse we sometimes see in others and others in us, and even the birth of evil men. This morning I called the thing a *druj;* it may be true.

Yet if the drug had been in the egg I ate last night, then the egg I held was harmless. Concentrating on that thought, I forced myself to eat it all, then stretched myself upon the bed to wait.

Very briefly I slept and dreamed. Ellen was bending over me, caressing me with a soft, long-fingered hand. It was only for an instant, but sufficient to make me hope that dreams are prophecies.

If the drug was in the egg I consumed, that dream was its only result. I got up and washed, and changed my clothes, sprinkling my fresh shirt liberally with our Pamir rosewater, which I have observed the Americans hold in high regard. Making certain my ticket and pistol were both in place, I left for the theater.

The play was still *Mary Rose.* I intentionally entered late (after Harry and Mrs. Otery had been talking for several minutes), then lingered at the back of the last row as though I were too polite to disturb the audience by taking my seat. Mrs. Otery made her exit; Harry pulled his knife from the wood of the packing case and threw it again, and when the mists of the past had marched across the stage, Harry was gone, and Moreland and the parson were chatting to the tune of Mrs. Moreland's knitting needles. Mary Rose would be onstage soon. My hope that she would come out to watch the opening scene had come to nothing; I would have to wait until she vanished at the end of Act II before I could expect to see her.

I was looking for a vacant seat when I became conscious of someone standing near me. In the dim light I could tell little except that he was rather slender, and a few centimeters shorter than I.

Finding no seat, I moved back a step or two. The newcomer touched my arm and asked in a whisper if I could light his cigarette. I had already seen that it was customary to smoke in the theaters here, and I had fallen into the habit of carrying matches to light the candles in my room. The flare of the flame showed the narrow eyes and high cheekbones of Harry—or, as I preferred to think of him, Kreton. Taken somewhat aback, I murmured some inane remark about the excellence of his performance.

"Did you like it? It is the least of all parts—I pull the curtain to open the show, then pull it again to tell everyone it's time to go home."

Several people in the audience were looking angrily at us, so we retreated to a point at the head of the aisle that was at least legally in the lobby, where I told him I had seen him in *Visit to a Small Planet* as well.

"Now *there* is a play. The character—as I am sure you saw—is good and bad at once. He is benign; he is mischievous; he is hellish."

"You carried it off wonderfully well, I thought."

"Thank you. This turkey here—do you know how many roles it has?"

"Well, there's yourself, Mrs. Otery, Mr. Amy—"

"No, no." He touched my arm to stop me. "I mean *roles*, parts that require real acting. There's one—the girl. She gets to skip about the stage as an eighteen-year-old whose brain atrophied at ten, and at least half what she does is wasted on the audience because they don't realize what's wrong with her until Act One is almost over."

"She's wonderful," I said. "I mean Mlle. Dahl."

Kreton nodded and drew on his cigarette. "She is a very competent ingenue, though it would be better if she weren't quite so tall."

"Do you think there's any chance that she might come out here—as you did?"

"Ah," he said, and looked me up and down.

For a moment I could have sworn that the telepathic ability he was credited with in *Visit to a Small Planet* was no fiction; nevertheless, I repeated my question: "Is it probable or not?"

"There's no reason to get angry—no, it's not likely. Is that enough payment for your match?"

"She vanishes at the end of the second act, and doesn't come onstage again until near the close of the third."

Kreton smiled. "You've read the play?"

"I was here last night. She must be off for nearly forty minutes, including the intermission."

"That's right. But she won't be here. It's true she goes out front sometimes—as I did myself tonight—but I happen to know she has company backstage."

"Might I ask who?"

"You might. It's even possible I might answer. You're Moslem, I suppose—do you drink?"

"I'm not a *strict* Moslem, but no, I don't. I'll buy you a drink gladly enough, if you want one, and have coffee with you while you drink it."

We left by a side door and elbowed our way through the crowd in the street. A flight of narrow and dirty steps descending from the sidewalk led us to a cellar tavern that had all the atmosphere of a private club. There was a bar with a picture (now much dimmed by dirt and smoke) of the cast of a play I did not recognize behind it, three tables, and a few alcoves. Kreton and I slipped into one of these and ordered from a barman with a misshapen head. I suppose I must have stared at him, because Kreton said, "I sprained my ankle stepping out of a saucer, and now I am a convalescent soldier. Should we make up something for him too? Can't we just say the potter is angry sometimes?"

"The potter?" I asked.

" 'None answered this; but after Silence spake / A Vessel of a more ungainly Make: / They sneer at me for leaning all awry; / What! Did the Hand then of the Potter shake?' "

I shook my head. "I've never heard that, but you're right; he looks as though his head had been shaped in clay, then knocked in on one side while it was still wet."

"This is a republic of hideousness as you have no doubt already seen. Our national symbol is supposed to be an extinct eagle; it is in fact the nightmare."

"I find it a very beautiful country," I said. "Though I confess that many of your people are unsightly. Still there are the ruins, and you have such skies as we never see at home."

"Our chimneys have been filled with wind for a long time."

"That may be for the best. Blue skies are better than most of the things made in factories."

"And not all our people are unsightly," Kreton murmured.

"Oh, no. Mlle Dahl——"

"I had myself in mind."

I saw that he was baiting me, but I said, "No, you aren't hideous—in fact, I would call you handsome in an exotic way. Unfortunately, my tastes run more toward Mlle Dahl."

"Call her Ardis—she won't mind."

The barman brought Kreton a glass of green liqueur, and me a cup of the weak, bitter American coffee.

"You were going to tell me who she is entertaining."

"Behind the scenes." Kreton smiled. "I just thought of that—I've used the phrase a thousand times, as I suppose everyone has. This time it happens to be literally correct, and its birth is suddenly made plain, like Oedipus's. No, I don't think I promised I would tell you that—though I suppose I said I might. Aren't there other things you would really rather know? The secret hidden beneath Mount Rushmore, or how you might meet her yourself?"

"I will give you twenty rials to introduce me to her, with some assurance that something will come of the introduction. No one need ever find out."

Kreton laughed. "Believe me, I would be more likely to boast of my profit than keep it secret—though I would probably have to divide my fee with the lady to fulfill the guarantee."

"You'll do it then?"

He shook his head, still laughing. "I only pretend to be corrupt; it goes with this face. Come backstage after the show tonight and I'll see that you meet Ardis. You're very wealthy, I presume, and if you're not, we'll say you are anyway. What are you doing here?"

"Studying your art and architecture."

"Great reputation in your own country, no doubt?"

"I am a pupil of Akhon Mirza Ahmak; he has a great reputation, surely. He even came here, thirty years ago, to examine the miniatures in your National Gallery of Art."

"Pupil of Akhon Mirza Ahmak, pupil of Akhon Mirza Ahmak," Kreton muttered to himself. "That is very good—I must remember it. But now"—he glanced at the old clock behind the bar—"it's time we got back. I'll have to freshen my makeup before I go on in the last act. Would you prefer to wait in the theater, or just come around to the stage door when the play's over? I'll give you a card that will get you in."

"I'll wait in the theater," I said, feeling that would offer less chance for mishap, also because I wanted to see Ellen play the ghost again.

"Come along then—I have a key for that side door."

I rose to go with him, and he threw an arm about my shoulder that I felt it would be impolite to thrust away. I could feel his hand, as cold as a dead man's, through my clothing, and was reminded unpleasantly of the twisted hands of the beggar in the Silent City.

We were going up the narrow stairs when I felt a gentle touch inside my jacket. My first thought was that he had seen the outline of my pistol and meant to take it and shoot me. I gripped his wrist and shouted something—I do not remember what. Bound together and struggling, we staggered up the steps and into the street.

In a few seconds we were the center of a mob—some taking his side, some mine, most only urging us to fight, or asking each other what the disturbance was. My pocket sketch pad, which he must have thought held money, fell to the ground between us. Just then the American police arrived—not by air as the police would have come at home, but astride shaggy, hulking horses, and swinging whips. The crowd scattered at the first crackling arc from the lashes, and in a few seconds they had beaten Kreton to the ground. Even at the time I could not help thinking what a terrible thing it must be to be one of these people, whose police are so quick to prefer any prosperous-looking foreigner to one of their own citizens.

They asked me what had happened (my questioner even dismounted to show his respect for me), and I explained that Kreton had tried to rob me, but that I did not want him punished. The truth was that seeing him sprawled unconscious with a burn across his face had put an end to any resentment I might have felt toward him; out of pity, I would gladly have given him the few rials I carried. They told me that if he had attempted to rob me he must be charged, and that if I would not accuse him they would do so themselves.

I then said that Kreton was a friend, and that on reflection I felt certain that what he had attempted had been intended as a prank. (In maintaining this I was considerably handicapped by not knowing his real name, which I had read on the playbill but forgotten, so that I was forced to refer to him as "this poor man.")

At last the policeman said, "We can't leave him in the street, so we'll have to bring him in. How will it look if there's no complaint?"

Then I understood that they were afraid of what their superiors might say if it became known that they had beaten him unconscious when no charge was made against him; and when I became aware that if I would not press charges, the charges they would bring themselves would be far more serious—assault or attempted murder—I agreed to do what they wished, and signed a form alleging the theft of my sketchbook.

When they had gone at last, carrying the unfortunate Kreton across a saddlebow, I tried to reenter the theater. The side door through which we had left was locked, and though I would gladly have paid the price of another ticket, the box office was closed. Seeing that there was nothing further to be done, I returned here, telling myself that my introduction to Ellen, if it ever came, would have to wait for another day.

Very truly it is written that we walk by paths that are always turning. In recording these several pages I have managed to restrain my enthusiasm, though when I described my waiting at the back of the theater for Ardis, and again when I recounted how Kreton had promised to introduce me to her, I was forced for minutes at a time to lay down my pen and walk about the room singing and whistling, and—to reveal everything—jumping over the beds! But now I can conceal no longer. I have seen her! I have touched her hand, I am to see her again tomorrow, and there is every hope that she will become my mistress!

I had undressed and laid myself on the bed (thinking to bring this journal up to date in the morning) and had even fallen into the first doze of sleep when there was a knock at the door. I slipped into my robe and pressed the release.

It was the only time in my life that for even an instant I thought I might be dreaming—actually asleep—when in truth I was up and awake.

How feeble it is to write that she is more beautiful in person than she appears on the stage. It is true, and yet it is a supreme irrelevance. I have seen more beautiful women—indeed Yasmin is, I suppose, by the formal standards of art, more lovely. It is not Ardis's beauty that draws me to her—the hair like gold, the translucent skin that then still showed traces of the bluish makeup she had worn as a ghost, the flashing eyes like the clear, clean skies of America. It is something deeper than that, something that would remain if all that were somehow taken away. No doubt she has habits that would disgust me in someone else, and the vanity that is said to be so common in her profession, and yet I would do anything to possess her.

Enough of this. What is it but empty boasting, now that I am on the point of winning her?

She stood in my doorway. I have been trying to think how I can express what I felt then. It was as though some tall flower, a lily perhaps, had left the garden and come to tap at my door, a thing that had never happened before in all the history of the world, and would never happen again.

"You are Nadan Jaffarzadeh?"

I admitted that I was, and shamefacedly, twenty seconds too late, moved out of her way.

She entered, but instead of taking the chair I indicated, turned to face me; her blue eyes seemed as large as the colored eggs on the dresser, and they were filled with a melting hope. "You are the man, then, that Bobby O'Keene tried to rob tonight."

I nodded.

"I know you—I mean, I know your face. This is insane. You came to *Visit* on the last night and brought your father, and then to *Mary Rose* on the first night, and sat in the third or fourth row. I thought you were an American, and when the police told me your name I imagined some greasy fat man with gestures. Why on earth would Bobby want to steal from *you*?"

"Perhaps he needed the money."

She threw back her head and laughed. I had heard her laugh in *Mary Rose* when Simon was asking her father for her hand, but that had held a note of childishness that (however well suited to the part) detracted from its beauty. This laugh was the merriment of houris sliding down a rainbow. "I'm sure he did. He always needs money. You're sure, though, that he meant to rob you? You couldn't have . . ."

She saw my expression and let the question trail away. The truth is that I was disappointed that I could not oblige her, and at last I said, "If you want me to be mistaken, Ardis, then I was mistaken. He only bumped against me on the steps, perhaps, and tried to catch my sketchbook when it fell."

She smiled, and her face was the sun smiling upon roses. "You would say that for me? And you know my name?"

"From the program. I came to the theater to see you—and that was not my father, who it grieves me to say is long dead, but only an old man, an American, whom I had met that day."

"You brought him sandwiches at the first intermission—I was watching you through the peephole in the curtain. You must be a very thoughtful person."

"Do you watch everyone in the audience so carefully?"

She blushed at that, and for a moment could not meet my eyes.

"But you will forgive Bobby, and tell the police that you want them to let him go? You must love the theater, Mr. Jef— Jaff—"

"You've forgotten my name already. It is Jaffarzadeh, a very commonplace name in my country."

"I hadn't forgotten it—only how to pronounce it. You see, when I came here I had learned it without knowing who you were, and so I had no trouble with it. Now you're a real person to me and I can't say it as an actress should." She seemed to notice the chair behind her for the first time, and sat down.

I sat opposite her. "I'm afraid I know very little about the theater."

"We are trying to keep it alive here, Mr. Jaffar, and—"

"Jaffarzadeh. Call me Nadan—then you won't have so many syllables to trip over."

She took my hand in hers, and I knew quite well that the gesture was as studied as a salaam and that she felt she was playing me like a fish, but I was beside myself with delight. To be played by *her*! To have *her* eager to cultivate my affection! And the fish will pull her in yet—wait and see!

"I will," she said, "Nadan. And though you may know little of the theater, you feel as I do—as we do—or you would not come. It has been such a long struggle; all the history of the stage is a struggle, the gasping of a beautiful child born at the point of death. The moralists, censorship and oppression, technology, and now poverty have all tried to destroy her. Only we, the actors and audiences, have kept her alive. We have been doing well here in Washington, Nadan."

"Very well indeed," I said. "Both the productions I have seen have been excellent."

"But only for the past two seasons. When I joined the company it had nearly fallen apart. We revived it—Bobby and Paul and I. We could do it because we cared, and because we were able to find a few naturally talented people who can take direction. Bobby is the best of us—he can walk away with any part that calls for a touch of the sinister. . . ."

She seemed to run out of breath. I said, "I don't think there will be any trouble about getting him free."

"Thank God. We're getting the theater on its feet again now. We're attracting new people, and we've built up a following—people who come to see every production. There's even some money ahead at last. But *Mary Rose* is supposed to run another two weeks, and after that we're doing *Faust*, with Bobby as Mephistopheles. We've simply no one who can take his place, no one who can come close to him."

"I'm sure the police will release him if I ask them to."

"They *must*. We have to have him tomorrow night. Bill—someone you don't know—tried to go on for him in the third act tonight. It was just ghastly. In Iran you're very polite; that's what I've heard."

"We enjoy thinking so."

"We're not. We never were, and as . . ."

Her voice trailed away, but a wave of one slender arm evoked everything— the cracked plaster walls became as air, and the decayed city, the ruined continent, entered the room with us. "I understand," I said.

"They—we—were betrayed. In our souls we have never been sure by whom. When we feel cheated we are ready to kill, and maybe we feel cheated all the time."

She slumped in her chair, and I realized, as I should have long before, how exhausted she was. She had given a performance that had ended in disaster, then had been forced to plead with the police for my name and address, and at last had come here from the station house, very probably on foot. I asked when I could obtain O'Keene's release.

"We can go tomorrow morning, if you'll do it."

"You wish to come too?"

She nodded, smoothed her skirt, and stood. "I'll have to know. I'll come for you about nine, if that's all right."

"If you'll wait outside for me to dress, I'll take you home."

"That's not necessary."

"It will only take a moment," I said.

The blue eyes held something pleading again. "You're going to come in with me—that's what you're thinking, I know. You have two beds here—bigger, cleaner beds than the one I have in my little apartment—if I were to ask you to push them together, would you still take me home afterward?"

It was as though I were dreaming indeed—a dream in which everything I wanted, the cosmos purified, delivered itself to me. I said, "You won't have to leave at all—you can spend the night with me. Then we can breakfast together before we go to release your friend."

She laughed again, lifting that exquisite head. "There are a hundred things at home I need. Do you think I'd have breakfast with you without my cosmetics, and in these dirty clothes?"

"Then I will take you home—yes, though you lived in Kazvin. Or on Mount Kaf."

She smiled. "Get dressed, then. I'll wait outside, and I'll show you my apartment; perhaps you won't want to come back here afterward."

She went out, her wooden-soled American shoes clicking on the bare floor, and I threw on trousers, shirt, and jacket, and jammed my feet into my boots. When I opened the door, she was gone. I rushed to the barred window at the end of the corridor, and was in time to see her disappear down a side street. A last swirl of her skirt in a gust of night wind, and she had vanished into the velvet dark.

For a long time I stood there looking out over the ruinous buildings. I was not angry—I do not think I could be angry with her. I was, though here it is hard to tell the truth, in some way glad. Not because I feared the embrace of love—I have no doubt of my ability to suffice any woman who can be sated by man—but because an easy exchange of my cooperation for her person would have failed to satisfy my need for romance, for adventure of a certain type, in which danger and love are twined like coupling serpents. Ardis, my Ellen, will provide that, surely, as neither Yasmin nor the pitiful wanton who was her double could. I sense that the world is opening for me only now, that I am being born, that that corridor was the birth canal, and that Ardis in leaving me was drawing me out toward her.

When I returned to my own door, I noticed a bit of paper on the floor before it. I transcribe it exactly here, though I cannot transmit its scent of lilacs:

*You are a most attractive man and I want very much to stretch the truth and tell you you can have me freely when Bobby is free, but I won't sell myself, etc. Really I will sell myself for Bobby, but I have other fish to fry tonight. I'll see you*

*in the morning and if you can get Bobby out or even try hard you'll have (real)*
*love from the vanishing*

*Mary Rose*

Morning. Woke early and ate here at the hotel as usual, finishing about eight. Writing this journal will give me something to do while I wait for Ardis. Had an American breakfast today, the first time I have risked one. Flakes of pastry dough toasted crisp and drenched with cream, and with it strudel and the usual American coffee. Most natives have spiced pork in one form or another, which I cannot bring myself to try, but several of the people around me were having egg dishes and oven-warmed bread, which I will sample tomorrow.

I had a very unpleasant dream last night; I have been trying to put it out of my mind ever since I woke. It was dark, and I was under an open sky with Ardis, walking over ground much rougher than anything I saw in the park on the farther side of the channel. One of the hideous creatures I shot night before last was pursuing us—or rather, lurking about us, for it appeared first to the left of us, then to the right, silhouetted against the night sky. Each time we saw it, Ardis grasped my arm and urged me to shoot, but the little indicator light on my pistol was glowing red to show that there was not enough charge left for a shot. All very silly, of course, but I am going to buy a fresh power pack as soon as I have the opportunity.

It is late afternoon—after six—but we have not had dinner yet. I am just out of the tub, and sit here naked, with today's candy egg laid (pinker even than I) beside this book on my table. Ardis and I had a sorry, weary time of it, and I have come back here to make myself presentable. At seven we will meet for dinner; the curtain goes up at eight, so it can't be a long one, but I am going backstage to watch the play from the wings, where I will be able to talk to her when she isn't performing.

I just took a bite of the egg—no unusual taste, nothing but an unpleasant sweetness. The more I reflect on it, the more inclined I am to believe that the drug was in the first I ate. No doubt the monster I saw had been lurking in my brain since I read *Mysteries*, and the drug freed it. True, there were bloodstains on my clothes (the Peri's asphodel!), but they could as easily have come from my cheek, which is still sore. I have had my experience, and all I have left is my candy. I am almost tempted to throw out the rest. Another bite.

Still twenty minutes before I must dress and go for Ardis—she showed me where she lives, only a few doors from the theater. To work then.

Ardis was a trifle late this morning, but came as she had promised. I asked where we were to go to free Kreton, and when she told me—a still-living building at the eastern end of the Silent City—I hired one of the rickety American caleches to drive us there. Like most of them, it was drawn by a starved horse, but we made good time.

The American police are organized on a peculiar system. The national secret police (officially, the Federated Inquiry Divisions) are in a tutorial position to all the others, having power to review their decisions, promote, demote, and discipline, and, as the ultimate reward, enroll personnel from the other organizations. In addition they maintain a uniformed force of their own. Thus when an American has been arrested by uniformed police, his friends can seldom learn whether he has been taken by the local police, by the F.I.D. uniformed national force, or by members of the F.I.D. secret police posing as either of the foregoing.

Since I had known nothing of these distinctions previously, I had no way of guessing which of the three had O'Keene, but the local police to whom Ardis had spoken the night before had given her to understand that he had been taken by them. She explained all this to me as we rattled along, then added that we were now going to the F.I.D. Building to secure his release. I must have looked as confused as I felt at this, because she added, "Part of it is a station for the Washington Police Department—they rent the space from the F.I.D."

My own impression (when we arrived) was that they did no such thing—that the entire apparatus was no more real than one of the scenes in Ardis's theater, and that all the men and women to whom we spoke were in fact agents of the secret police, wielding ten times the authority they pretended to possess, and going through a solemn ritual of deception. As Ardis and I moved from office to office, explaining our simple errand, I came to think that she felt as I did, and that she had refrained from expressing these feelings to me in the cab not only because of the danger, the fear that I might betray her or the driver be a spy, but because she was ashamed of her nation, and eager to make it appear to me, a foreigner, that her government was less devious and meretricious than is actually the case.

If this is so—and in that windowless warren of stone I was certain it was—then the very explanation she proffered in the cab (which I have given in its proper place), differentiating clearly between local police, uniformed F.I.D. police, and secret police, was no more than a children's fable, concealing an actuality less forthright and more convoluted.

Our questioners were courteous to me, much less so to Ardis, and (so it seemed to me) obsessed by the idea that something more lay behind the simple incident we described over and over again—so much so in fact that I came to believe it myself. I have neither time nor patience enough to describe all these interviews, but I will attempt to give a sample of one.

We went into a small, windowless office crowded between two others that appeared empty. A middle-aged American woman was seated behind a metal desk. She appeared normal and reasonably attractive until she spoke; then her scarred gums showed that she had once had two or three times the proper number of teeth—forty or fifty, I suppose, in each jaw—and that the dental surgeon who had extracted the supernumerary ones had not always, perhaps, selected those he suffered to remain as wisely as he might. She asked, "How is it outside? The weather? You see, I don't know, sitting in here all day."

Ardis said, "Very nice."

"Do you like it, Hajji? Have you had a pleasant stay in our great country?"

"I don't think it has rained since I've been here."

She seemed to take the remark as a covert accusation. "You came too late for the rains, I'm afraid. This is a very fertile area, however. Some of our oldest coins show heads of wheat. Have you seen them?" She pushed a small copper coin across the desk, and I pretended to examine it. There are one or two like it in the bracelet I bought for Ardis, and which I still have not presented to her. "I must apologize on behalf of the District for what happened to you," the woman continued. "We are making every effort to control crime. You have not been victimized before this?"

I shook my head, half-suffocated in that airless office, and said I had not been.

"And now you are here." She shuffled the papers she held, then pretended to read from one of them. "You are here to secure the release of the thief who assaulted you. A very commendable act of magnanimity. May I ask why you brought this young woman with you? She does not seem to be mentioned in any of these reports."

I explained that Ardis was a coworker of O'Keene's, and that she had interceded for him.

"Then it is you, Ms. Dahl, who are really interested in securing this prisoner's release. Are you related to him?"

And so on.

At the conclusion of each interview we were told either that the matter was completely out of the hands of the person to whom we had just spent half an hour or an hour talking, that it was necessary to obtain a clearance from someone else, or that an additional deposition had to be made. About two o'clock we were sent to the other side of the river—into what my guidebooks insist is an entirely different jurisdiction—to visit a penal facility. There we were forced to look for Kreton among five hundred or so miserable prisoners, all of whom stank and had lice. Not finding him, we returned to the F.I.D. Building past the half-overturned and yet still-brooding figure called the Seated Man, and the ruins and beggars of the Silent City, for another round of interrogations. By five, when we were told to leave, we were both exhausted, though Ardis seemed surprisingly hopeful. When I left her at the door of her building a few minutes ago, I asked her what they would do tonight without Kreton.

"Without Harry, you mean." She smiled. "The best we can, I suppose, if we must. At least Paul will have someone ready to stand in for him tonight."

We shall see how well it goes.

I have picked up this pen and replaced it on the table ten times at least. It seems very likely that I should destroy this journal instead of continuing with it, were I wise, but I have discovered a hiding place for it which I think will be secure.

When I came back from Ardis's apartment tonight there were only two candy eggs remaining. I am certain—absolutely certain—that three were left when I went to meet Ardis. I am almost equally sure that after I had finished making the entry in this book, I put it, as I always do, at the left side of the drawer. It was on the right side.

It is possible that all this is merely the doing of the maid who cleans the room. She might easily have supposed that a single candy egg would not be missed, and have shifted this book while cleaning the drawer, or peeped inside out of curiosity.

I will assume the worst, however. An agent sent to investigate my room might be equipped to photograph these pages—but he might not, and it is not likely that he himself would have a reading knowledge of Farsi. Now I have gone through the book and eliminated all the passages relating to my reason for visiting this leprous country. Before I leave this room tomorrow I will arrange indicators—hairs and other objects whose positions I shall carefully record—that will tell me if the room has been searched again.

Now I may as well set down the events of the evening, which were truly extraordinary enough.

I met Ardis as we had planned, and she directed me to a small restaurant not far from her apartment. We had no sooner seated ourselves than two heavy-looking men entered. At no time could I see plainly the face of either, but it appeared to me that one was the American I had met aboard the *Princess Fatimah* and that the other was the grain dealer I had so assiduously avoided there, Golam Gassem. It is impossible, I think, for my divine Ardis ever to look less than beautiful, but she came as near to it then as the laws of nature permit—the blood drained from her face, her mouth opened slightly, and for a moment she appeared to be a lovely corpse. I began to ask what the trouble was, but before I could utter a word she touched my lips to silence me, and then, having somewhat regained her composure, said, "They have not seen us. I am leaving now. Follow me as though we were finished eating." She stood, feigned to pat her lips with a napkin (so that the lower half of her face was hidden), and walked out into the street.

I followed her, and found her laughing not three doors away from the entrance to the restaurant. The change in her could not have been more startling if she had been released from an enchantment. "It is so funny," she said. "Though it wasn't then. Come on, we'd better go; you can feed me after the show."

I asked her what those men were to her.

"Friends," she said, still laughing.

"If they are friends, why were you so anxious that they not see you? Were you afraid they would make us late?" I knew that such a trivial explanation could not be true, but I wanted to leave her a means of evading the question if she did not want to confide in me.

She shook her head. "No, no. I didn't want either to think I did not trust him. I'll tell you more later, if you want to involve yourself in our little charade."

"With all my heart."

She smiled at that—that sun-drenched smile for which I would gladly have entered a lion pit. In a few more steps we were at the rear entrance to the theater, and there was no time to say more. She opened the door, and I heard Kreton arguing with a woman I later learned was the wardrobe mistress. "You are free," I said, and he turned to look at me.

"Yes. Thanks to you, I think. And I do thank you."

Ardis gazed on him as though he were a child saved from drowning. "Poor Bobby. Was it very bad?"

"It was frightening, that's all. I was afraid I'd never get out. Do you know Terry is gone?"

She shook her head, and said, "What do you mean?" but I was certain—and here I am not exaggerating or coloring the facts though I confess I have occasionally done so elsewhere in this chronicle—that she had known it before he spoke.

"He simply isn't here. Paul is running around like a lunatic. I hear you missed me last night."

"God, yes," Ardis said, and darted off too swiftly for me to follow.

Kreton took my arm. I expected him to apologize for having tried to rob me, but he said, "You've met her, I see."

"She persuaded me to drop the charges against you."

"Whatever it was you offered me—twenty rials? I'm morally entitled to it, but I won't claim it. Come and see me when you're ready for something more wholesome—and meanwhile, how do you like her?"

"That is something for me to tell her," I said, "not you."

Ardis returned as I spoke, bringing with her a balding black man with a mustache. "Paul, this is Nadan. His English is very good—not so British as most of them. He'll do, don't you think?"

"He'll have to—you're sure he'll do it?"

"He'll love it," Ardis said positively, and disappeared again.

It seemed that Terry was the actor who played Mary Rose's husband and lover, Simon, and I—who had never acted in so much as a school play—was to be pressed into the part. It was about half an hour before curtain time, so I had all of fifty minutes to learn my lines before my entrance at the end of the first act.

Paul, the director, warned me that if my name were used, the audience would be hostile and, since the character (in the version of the play they were presenting) was supposed to be an American, they would see errors where none existed. A moment later, while I was still in frantic rehearsal, I heard him saying, "The part of Simon Blake will be taken by Ned Jefferson."

The act of stepping onto the stage for the first time was really the worst part of the entire affair. Fortunately I had the advantage of playing a nervous young man come to ask for the hand of his sweetheart, so that my shaky laughter and stammer became "acting."

My second scene—with Mary Rose and Cameron on the magic island—ought by rights to have been much more difficult than the first. I had had only the intermission in which to study my lines, and the scene called for pessimistic apprehension rather than mere anxiety. But all the speeches were short, and Paul had been able by that time to get them lettered on large sheets of paper, which he and the stage manager held up in the wings. Several times I was forced to extemporize, but though I forgot the playwright's words, I never lost my sense of the *trend* of the play, and was always able to contrive something to which Ardis and Cameron could adapt their replies.

In comparison to the first and second acts, my brief appearance in the third was a holiday, yet I have seldom been so exhausted as I was tonight when the stage darkened for Ardis's final confrontation with Kreton, and Cameron and I, and the middle-aged people who had played the Morelands, were able to creep away.

We had to remain in costume until we had taken our bows, and it was nearly midnight before Ardis and I got something to eat at the same small, dirty bar outside which Kreton had tried to rob me. Over the steaming plates she asked me if I had enjoyed acting, and I had to nod.

"I thought you would. Under all that solidity you're a very dramatic person, I think."

I admitted it was true, and tried to explain why I feel that what I call the romance of life is the only thing worth seeking. She did not understand me, and so I passed it off as the result of having been brought up on the *Shah Namah*, of which I found she had never heard.

We went to her apartment. I was determined to take her by force if necessary—not because I would have enjoyed brutalizing her, but because I felt she would inevitably think my love far less than it was if I permitted her to put me off a second time. She showed me about her quarters (two small rooms in great disorder), then, after we had lifted into place the heavy bar that is the sigil of every American dwelling, put her arms about me. Her breath was fragrant with the arrack I had bought for her a few minutes before. I feel sure now that for the rest of my life that scent will recall this evening to me.

When we parted, I began to unloose the laces that closed her blouse, and she at once pinched out the candle. I pleaded that she was thus depriving me of half the joy I might have had of her love, but she would not permit me to relight it, and our caresses and the embraces of our couplings were exchanged in perfect darkness. I was in ecstasy. To have seen her, I would have blinded myself, yet nothing could have increased my delight.

When we separated for the last time, both spent utterly, and she left to wash, I sought for matches. First in the drawer of the unsteady little table beside the bed, then among the disorder of my own clothes, which I had dropped to the floor and we had kicked about. I found some eventually, but could not find the candle—Ardis, I think, had hidden it. I struck a match, but she had covered herself with a robe. I said, "Am I never to see you?"

"You will see me tomorrow. You're going to take me boating, and we'll picnic by the water, under the cherry trees. Tomorrow night the theater will be closed for Easter, and you can take me to a party. But now you are going home, and I am going to go to sleep." When I was dressed and standing in her doorway, I asked her if she loved me but she stopped my mouth with a kiss.

I have already written about the rest—returning to find two eggs instead of three, and this book moved. I will not write of that again. But I have just—between this paragraph and the last—read over what I wrote earlier tonight, and it seems to me that one sentence should have had more weight than I gave it: when I said that in my role as Simon I never lost the *trend* of the play.

What the fabled secret buried by the old Americans beneath their carved mountain may be I do not know, but I believe that if it is some key to the world of human life, it must be some form of that. Every great man, I am sure, consciously or not, in those terms or others, has grasped that secret—save that in the play that is our life we can grapple that trend and draw it to left or right if we have the will.

So I am doing now. If the taking of the egg was not significant, yet I will make it so—indeed I already have, when I infused one egg with the drug. If the scheme in which Ardis is entangled—with Golam Gassem and Mr. Tallman if it be they—is not some affair of statecraft and dark treasure, yet I will make it so before the end. If our love is not a great love, destined to live forever in the hearts of the young and the mouths of the poets, it will be so before the end.

Once again I am here, and in all truth I am beginning to wonder if I do not write this journal only to read it. No man was ever happier than I am now—so happy, indeed, that I was sorely tempted not to taste either of the two eggs that remain. What if the drug, in place of hallucination, self-knowledge, and euphoria, brings permanent and despairing madness? Yet I have eaten it nonetheless, swallowing the whole sweet lump in a few bites. I would rather risk whatever may come than think myself a coward. With equanimity I await the effects.

The fact is that I am too happy for all the Faustian determination I penned last night. (How odd that *Faust* will be the company's next production. Kreton will be Mephistopheles of course—Ardis said as much, and it would be certain in any case. Ardis herself will be Margaret. But who will play the Doctor?) Yet now, when all the teeth-gritting, table-pounding determination is gone, I know that I will carry out the essentials of the *plan* more surely than ever—with the ease, in fact, of an accomplished violinist sawing out some simple tune while his mind roves elsewhere. I have been looking at the ruins of the Jeff (as they call it), and it has turned my mind again to the fate of the old Americans. How often they, who chose their leaders for superficial appearances of strength, wisdom, and resolution, must have elected them only because they were as fatigued as I was last night.

I had meant to buy a hamper of delicacies and call for Ardis about one, but she came for me at eleven with a little basket already packed. We walked north along the bank of the channel until we reached the ruins of the old tomb to which I have already referred, and the nearly circular artificial lake the Americans call the Basin. It is rimmed with flowering trees—old and gnarled, but very beautiful in their robes of white blossom. For some little American coin we were given command of a bright blue boat with a sail twice or three times the size of my handkerchief, in which to dare the halcyon waters of the lake.

When we were well away from the people onshore, Ardis asked me, rather suddenly, if I intended to spend all my time in America here in Washington.

I told her that my original plan had been to stay here no more than a week, then make my way up the coast to Philadelphia and the other ancient cities before I returned home, but that now that I had met her I would stay here forever if she wished it.

"Haven't you ever wanted to see the interior? This strip of beach we live on is kept half-alive by the ocean and the trade that crosses it, but a hundred miles inland lies the wreck of our entire civilization, waiting to be plundered."

"Then why doesn't someone plunder it?" I asked.

"They do. A year never passes without someone bringing some great prize out—but it is so large . . ." I could see her looking beyond the lake and the fragrant trees. "So large that whole cities are lost in it. There was an arch of gold at the entrance to St. Louis—no one knows what became of it. Denver, the Mile High City, was nested in silver mines; no one can find them now."

"Many of the old maps must still be in existence."

Ardis nodded slowly, and I sensed that she wanted to say more than she had. For a few seconds there was no sound but the water lapping against the side of the boat.

"I remember having seen some in the museum in Tehran—not only our maps, but some of your own from a hundred years ago."

"The courses of the rivers have changed," she said. "And when they have not, no one can be sure of it."

"Many buildings must still be standing, as they are here, in the Silent City."

"That was built of stone—more solidly than anything else in the country. But yes, some, many, are still there."

"Then it would be possible to fly in, land somewhere, and pillage them."

"There are many dangers, and so much rubble to look through that anyone might search for a lifetime and only scratch the surface."

I saw that talking of all this only made her unhappy, and tried to change the subject. "Didn't you say that I could escort you to a party tonight? What will that be like?"

"Nadan, I have to trust someone. You've never met my father, but he lives close to the hotel where you are staying, and has a shop where he sells old books and maps." (So I had visited the right house—almost—after all!) "When he was younger, he wanted to go into the interior. He made three or four trips, but never got farther than the Appalachian foothills. Eventually he married my mother and didn't feel any longer that he could take the risks. . . ."

"I understand."

"The things he had sought to guide him to the wealth of the past became his stock-in-trade. Even today, people who live farther inland bring him old papers; he buys them and resells them. Some of those people are only a step better than the ones who dig up the cemeteries for the wedding rings of the dead women."

I recalled the rings I had bought in the shadow of the broken obelisk, and shuddered, though I do not believe Ardis observed it.

"I said that some of them were hardly better than the grave robbers. The truth is that some are worse—there are people in the interior who are no longer people. Our bodies are poisoned—you know that, don't you? All of us Americans. They have adapted—that's what Father says—but they are no longer human. He made his peace with them long ago, and he trades with them still."

"You don't have to tell me this."

"Yes, I do—I must. Would you go into the interior, if I went with you? The government will try to stop us if they learn of it, and to confiscate anything we find."

I assured her with every oath I could remember that with her beside me I would cross the continent on foot if need be.

"I told you about my father. I said that he sells the maps and records they bring him. What I did not tell you is that he reads them first. He has never given up, you see, in his heart."

"He has made a discovery?" I asked.

"He's made many—hundreds. Bobby and I have used them. You remember those men in the restaurant? Bobby went to each of them with a map and some of the old letters. He's persuaded them to help finance an expedition into the interior, and made each of them believe that we'll help him cheat the other—that keeps them from combining to cheat us, you see."

"And you want me to go with you?" I was beside myself with joy.

"We weren't going to go at all—Bobby was going to take the money, and go to Baghdad or Marrakesh, and take me with him. But, Nadan"—here she leaned forward, I remember, and took my hands in hers—"there really is a secret. There are many, but one better—more likely to be true, more likely to yield truly immense wealth than all the others. I know you would share fairly with me. We'll divide everything, and I'll go back to Tehran with you."

I know that I have never been more happy in my life than I was then, in that silly boat. We sat together in the stern, nearly sinking it, under the combined shade of the tiny sail and Ardis's big straw hat, and kissed and stroked one another until we would have been pilloried a dozen times in Iran.

At last, when I could bear no more unconsummated love, we ate the sandwiches Ardis had brought, and drank some warmish, fruit-flavored beverage, and returned to shore.

When I took her home a few minutes ago, I very strongly urged her to let me come upstairs with her; I was on fire for her, sick to impale her upon my own flesh and pour myself into her as some mad god before the coming of the Prophet might have poured his golden blood into the sea. She would not permit it—I think because she feared that her apartment could not be darkened enough to suit her modesty. I am determined that I will yet see her.

I have bathed and shaved to be ready for the party, and as there is still time I will insert here a description of the procession we passed on the way back from the lake. As you see, I have not yet completely abandoned the thought of a book of travels.

A very old man—I suppose a priest—carried a cross on a long pole, using it as a staff, and almost as a crutch. A much younger one, fat and sweating, walked backward before him swinging a smoking censer. Two robed boys carrying large candles preceded them, and they were followed by more robed children, singing, who fought with nudges and pinches when they felt the fat man was not watching them.

Like everyone else, I have seen this kind of thing done much better in Rome; but I was more affected by what I saw here. When the old priest was born, the greatness of America must have been a thing of such recent memory that few could have realized it had passed forever; and the entire procession—from the flickering candles in clear sunshine, to the dead leader lifted up, to his inattentive, bickering followers behind—seemed to me to incarnate the philosophy and the dilemma of these people. So I felt, at least, until I saw that they watched it as un-comprehendingly as they might if they themselves were only travelers abroad, and I realized that its ritualized plea for life renewed was more foreign to them than to me.

It is very late—three, my watch says.

I resolved again not to write in this book. To burn it or tear it to pieces, or to give it to some beggar; but now I am writing once again because I cannot sleep. The room reeks of my vomit, though I have thrown open the shutters and let in the night.

How could I have loved that? (And yet a few moments ago, when I tried to sleep, visions of Ellen pursued me back to wakefulness.)

The party was a masque, and Ardis had obtained a costume for me—a fantastic gilded armor from the wardrobe of the theater. She wore the robes of an Egyptian princess, and a domino. At midnight we lifted our masks and kissed, and in my heart I swore that tonight the mask of darkness would be lifted too.

When we left, I carried with me the bottle we had brought, still nearly half-full, and before she pinched out the candle I persuaded her to pour out a final drink for us to share when the first frenzy of our desire was past. She—it—did as I asked, and set it on the little table near the bed. A long time afterward, when we lay gasping side by side, I found my pistol with one groping hand and fired the beam into the wide-bellied glass. Instantly it filled with blue fire from the burning alcohol. Ardis screamed, and sprang up.

I ask myself now how I could have loved; but then, how could I in one week have come so near to loving this corpse-country? Its eagle is dead—Ardis is the proper symbol of its rule.

One hope, one very small hope, remains. It is possible that what I saw tonight was only an illusion, induced by the egg. I know now that the thing I killed before Ardis's father's house was real, and between this paragraph and the last I have eaten the last egg. If hallucinations now begin, I will know that what I saw by the light of the blazing arrack was in truth a thing with which I have lain, and in one way or another will see to it that I never return to corrupt the clean wombs of the women of our enduring race. I might seek to claim the miniatures of our heritage after all, and allow the guards to kill me—but what if I were to succeed? I am not fit to touch them. Perhaps the best end for me would be to travel alone into this maggot-riddled continent; in that way I will die at fit hands.

L ater, Kreton is walking in the hall outside my door, and the tread of his twisted black shoes jars the building like an earthquake. I heard the word *po-lice* as though it were thunder. My dead Ardis, very small and bright, has stepped out of the candle flame, and there is a hairy face coming through the window.

T *he old woman closed the notebook. The younger woman, who had been reading over her shoulder, moved to the other side of the small table and seated herself on a cushion, her feet politely positioned so that the soles could not be seen. "He is alive then," she said.*

*The older woman remained silent, her gray head bowed over the notebook, which she held in both hands.*

*"He is certainly imprisoned, or ill; otherwise he would have been in touch with us." The younger woman paused, smoothing the fabric of her chador with her right hand, while the left toyed with the gem simulator she wore on a thin chain. "It is possible that he has already tried, but his letters have miscarried."*

*"You think this is his writing?" the older woman asked, opening the notebook at random. When the younger did not answer she added, "Perhaps. Perhaps."*

∞

## AFTERWORD

Have you read *The last camel died at noon?* It's a mystery by Eliza-beth Peters, and stars a young and attractive Egyptologist named

Amelia Peabody. (Do you think there are no attractive young Egyptologists? I know one.) I love those books, and I love the Victorians who probed Africa when almost nothing was known about it. Sir Samuel Baker, that hero of boys' stories come to life, the well-born Englishman who bought his wife at a slave auction, is a hero of mine and always will be.

What about us? Who will probe our ruins? Who will come to Washington as we come to Athens? There are myriad ways to answer these questions. The story you have just read is only one of them.

# The Detective of Dreams

∞

I was writing in my office in the rue Madeleine when Andrée, my secretary, announced the arrival of Herr D——. I rose, put away my correspondence, and offered him my hand. He was, I should say, just short of fifty, had the high, clear complexion characteristic of those who in youth (now unhappily past for both of us) have found more pleasure in the company of horses and dogs and the excitement of the chase than in the bottles and bordels of city life, and wore a beard and mustache of the style popularized by the late emperor. Accepting my invitation to a chair, he showed me his papers.

"You see," he said, "I am accustomed to acting as the representative of my government. In this matter I hold no such position, and it is possible that I feel a trifle lost."

"Many people who come here feel lost," I said. "But it is my boast that I find most of them again. Your problem, I take it, is purely a private matter?"

"Not at all. It is a public matter in the truest sense of the words."

"Yet none of the documents before me—admirably stamped, sealed, and beribboned though they are—indicates that you are other than a private gentleman traveling abroad. And you say you do not represent your government. What am I to think? What is this matter?"

"I act in the public interest," Herr D—— told me. "My fortune is not great, but I can assure you that in the event of your success you will be well recompensed; although you are to take it that I alone am your principal, yet there are substantial resources available to me."

"Perhaps it would be best if you described the problem to me?"

"You are not averse to travel?"

"No."

"Very well then," he said, and so saying launched into one of the most astonishing relations—no, *the* most astonishing relation—I have ever been privileged to hear. Even I, who had at firsthand the account of the man who found Paulette

Renan with the quince seed still lodged in her throat; who had received Captain Brotte's testimony concerning his finds amid the Antarctic ice; who had heard the history of the woman called Joan O'Neil, who lived for two years behind a painting of herself in the Louvre, from her own lips—even I sat like a child while this man spoke.

When he fell silent, I said, "Herr D——, after all you have told me, I would accept this mission though there were not a sou to be made from it. Perhaps once in a lifetime one comes across a case that must be pursued for its own sake; I think I have found mine."

He leaned forward and grasped my hand with a warmth of feeling that was, I believe, very foreign to his usual nature. "Find and destroy the Dream-Master," he said, "and you shall sit upon a chair of gold, if that is your wish, and eat from a table of gold as well. When will you come to our country?"

"Tomorrow morning," I said. "There are one or two arrangements I must make here before I go."

"I am returning tonight. You may call upon me at any time, and I will apprise you of new developments." He handed me a card. "I am always to be found at this address—if not I, then one who is to be trusted, acting in my behalf."

"I understand."

"This should be sufficient for your initial expenses. You may call on me should you require more." The check he gave me as he turned to leave represented a comfortable fortune.

I waited until he was nearly out the door before saying, "I thank you, Herr Baron." To his credit, he did not turn; but I had the satisfaction of seeing a red flush rising above the precise white line of his collar before the door closed.

Andrée entered as soon as he had left. "Who was that man? When you spoke to him—just as he was stepping out of your office—he looked as if you had struck him with a whip."

"He will recover," I told her. "He is the Baron H——, of the secret police of K——. D—— was his mother's name. He assumed that because his own desk is a few hundred kilometers from mine, and because he does not permit his likeness to appear in the daily papers, I would not know him; but it was necessary, both for the sake of his opinion of me and my own of myself, that he should discover that I am not so easily deceived. When he recovers from his initial irritation, he will retire tonight with greater confidence in the abilities I will devote to the mission he has entrusted to me."

"It is typical of you, monsieur," Andrée said kindly, "that you are concerned that your clients sleep well."

Her pretty cheek tempted me, and I pinched it. "I am concerned," I replied, "but the baron will not sleep well."

My train roared out of Paris through meadows sweet with wildflowers, to penetrate mountain passes in which the danger of avalanches was only just past. The glitter of rushing water, sprung from on high, was everywhere; and when the express slowed to climb a grade, the song of water was everywhere too, water running and shouting down the gray rocks of the Alps. I fell asleep that night with the descant of that icy purity sounding through the plainsong of the rails, and I woke in the station of I——, the old capital of J——, now a province of K——.

I engaged a porter to convey my trunk to the hotel where I had made reservations by telegraph the day before, and amused myself for a few hours by strolling about the city. Here I found the Middle Ages might almost be said to have remained rather than lingered. The city wall was complete on three sides, with its merloned towers in repair, and the cobbled streets surely dated from a period when wheeled traffic of any kind was scarce. As for the buildings—Puss in Boots and his friends must have loved them dearly: there were bulging walls and little panes of bull's-eye glass, and overhanging upper floors one above another until the structures seemed unbalanced as tops. Upon one gray old pile with narrow windows and massive doors, I found a plaque informing me that though it had been first built as a church, it had been successively a prison, a customhouse, a private home, and a school. I investigated further, and discovered it was now an arcade, having been divided, I should think at about the time of the first Louis, into a multitude of dank little stalls. Since it was, as it happened, one of the addresses mentioned by Baron H——, I went in.

Gas flared everywhere, yet the interior could not have been said to be well lit—each jet was sullen and secretive, as if the proprietor in whose cubicle it was located wished it to light none but his own wares. These cubicles were in no order; nor could I find any directory or guide to lead me to the one I sought. A few customers, who seemed to have visited the place for years, so that they understood where everything was, drifted from one display to the next. When they arrived at each, the proprietor came out, silent (so it seemed to me) as a specter, ready to answer questions or accept a payment, but I never heard a question asked, or saw any money tendered—the customer would finger the edge of a kitchen knife, or hold a garment up to her own shoulders, or turn the pages of some moldering book, and then put the thing down again, and go away.

At last, when I had tired of peeping into alcoves lined with booths still gloomier than the ones on the main concourse outside, I stopped at a leather merchant's and asked the man to direct me to Fräulein A——.

"I do not know her," he said.

"I am told on good authority that her business is conducted in this building, and that she buys and sells antiques."

"We have several antique dealers here. Herr M——."

"I am searching for a young woman. Has your Herr M—— a niece or a cousin?"

"——handles chairs and chests, largely. Herr O——, near the guildhall—"

"It is within this building."

"—stocks pictures, mostly. A few mirrors. What is it you wish to buy?"

At this point we were interrupted, mercifully, by a woman from the next booth. "He wants Fräulein A———. Out of here, and to your left; past the wig-maker's, then right to the stationer's, then left again. She sells old lace."

I found the place at last, and sitting at the very back of her booth Fräulein A——— herself, a pretty, slender, timid-looking young woman. Her merchandise was spread on two tables; I pretended to examine it and found that it was not old lace she sold but old clothing, much of it trimmed with lace. After a few moments she rose and came out to talk to me, saying, "If you could tell me what you require? . . ." She was taller than I had anticipated, and her flaxen hair would have been very attractive if it were ever released from the tight braids coiled round her head.

"I am only looking. Many of these are beautiful—are they expensive?"

"Not for what you get. The one you are holding is only fifty marks."

"That seems like a great deal."

"They are the fine dresses of long ago—for visiting, or going to the ball. The dresses of wealthy women of aristocratic taste. All are like new; I will not handle anything else. Look at the seams in that one you hold, the tiny stitches all done by hand. Those were the work of dressmakers who created only four or five in a year, and worked twelve and fourteen hours a day, sewing at the first light, and continuing under the lamp, past midnight."

I said, "I see that you have been crying, fräulein. Their lives were indeed miserable, though no doubt there are people today who suffer equally."

"No doubt there are," the young woman said. "I, however, am not one of them." And she turned away so that I should not see her tears.

"I was informed otherwise."

She whirled about to face me. "You know him? Oh, tell him I am not a wealthy woman, but I will pay whatever I can. Do you really know him?"

"No." I shook my head. "I was informed by your own police."

She stared at me. "But you are an outlander. So is he, I think."

"Ah, we progress. Is there another chair in the rear of your booth? Your police are not above going outside your own country for help, you see, and we should have a little talk."

"They are not our police," the young woman said bitterly, "but I will talk to you. The truth is that I would sooner talk to you, though you are French. You will not tell them that?"

I assured her that I would not; we borrowed a chair from the flower stall across the corridor, and she poured forth her story.

"My father died when I was very small. My mother opened this booth to earn our living—old dresses that had belonged to her own mother were the core of her original stock. She died two years ago, and since that time I have taken charge of our business and used it to support myself. Most of my sales are to collectors and theatrical companies. I do not make a great deal of money, but I do not require a great deal, and I have managed to save some. I live alone at Number 877 ——— strasse; it is an old house divided into six apartments, and mine is the gable apartment."

"You are young and charming," I said, "and you tell me you have a little money saved. I am surprised you are not married."

"Many others have said the same thing."

"And what did you tell them, fräulein?"

"To take care of their own affairs. They have called me a man hater—Frau G———, who has the confections in the next corridor but two, called me that because I would not receive her son. The truth is that I do not care for people of either sex, young or old. If I want to live by myself and keep my own things to myself, is it not my right to do so?"

"I am sure it is, but undoubtedly it has occurred to you that this person you fear so much may be a rejected suitor who is taking his revenge on you."

"But how could he enter and control my dreams?"

"I do not know, fräulein. It is you who say that he does these things."

"I should remember him, I think, if he had ever called on me. As it is, I am quite certain I have seen him somewhere, but I cannot recall where. Still . . ."

"Perhaps you had better describe your dream to me. You have the same one again and again, as I understand it?"

"Yes. It is like this. I am walking down a dark road. I am both frightened and pleasurably excited, if you know what I mean. Sometimes I walk for a long time, sometimes for what seems to be only a few moments. I think there is moonlight, and once or twice I have noticed stars. Anyway, there is a high, dark hedge, or perhaps a wall, on my right. There are fields to the left, I believe. Eventually I reach a gate of iron bars, standing open—it's not a large gate for wagons or carriages, but a small one, so narrow I can hardly get through. Have you read the writings of Dr. Freud of Vienna? One of the women here mentioned once that he had written concerning dreams, and so I got them from the library, and if I were a man I am sure he would say that entering that gate meant sexual commerce. Do you think I might have unnatural leanings?" Her voice had dropped to a whisper.

"Have you ever felt such desires?"

"Oh, no. Quite the reverse."

"Then I doubt it very much," I said. "Go on with your dream. How do you feel as you pass through the gate?"

"As I did when walking down the road, but more so—more frightened, and yet happy and excited. Triumphant, in a way."

"Go on."

"I am in the garden now. There are fountains playing, and nightingales singing in the willows. The air smells of lilies, and a cherry tree in blossom looks like a giantess in her bridal gown. I walk on a straight, smooth path; I think it must be paved with marble chips, because it is white in the moonlight. Ahead of me is the *Schloss*—a great building. There is music coming from inside."

"What sort of music?"

"Magnificent—joyous, if you know what I am trying to say, but not the tin-klings of a theater orchestra. A great symphony. I have never been to the opera at Bayreuth, but I think it must be like that—yet a happy, quick tune."

She paused, and for an instant her smile recovered the remembered music. "There are pillars, and a grand entrance, with broad steps. I run up—I am so happy to be there—and throw open the door. It is brightly lit inside; a wave of golden light, almost like a wave from the ocean, strikes me. The room is a great hall, with a high ceiling. A long table is set in the middle and there are hundreds of people seated at it, but one place, the one nearest me, is empty. I cross to it and sit down; there are beautiful golden loaves on the table, and bowls of honey with roses floating at their centers, and crystal carafes of wine, and many other good things I cannot remember when I awake. Everyone is eating and drinking and talking, and I begin to eat too."

I said, "It is only a dream, fräulein. There is no reason to weep."

"I dream this each night—I have dreamed so every night for months."

"Go on."

"Then he comes. I am sure he is the one who is causing me to dream like this because I can see his face clearly, and remember it when the dream is over. Some-times it is very vivid for an hour or more after I wake—so vivid that I have only to close my eyes to see it before me."

"I will ask you to describe him in detail later. For the present, continue with your dream."

"He is tall, and robed like a king, and there is a strange crown on his head. He stands beside me, and though he says nothing, I know that the etiquette of the place demands that I rise and face him. I do this. Sometimes I am sucking my fin-gers as I get up from his table."

"He owns the dream palace, then."

"Yes, I am sure of that. It is his castle, his home; he is my host. I stand and face him, and I am conscious of wanting very much to please him, but not knowing what it is I should do."

"That must be painful."

"It is. But as I stand there, I become aware of how I am clothed, and—"

"How are you clothed?"

"As you see me now. In a plain, dark dress—the dress I wear here at the ar-cade. But the others—all up and down the hall, all up and down the table—are wearing the dresses I sell here. These dresses." She held one up for me to see, a beautiful creation of many layers of lace, with buttons of polished jet. "I know then that I cannot remain; but the king signals to the others, and they seize me and push me toward the door."

"You are humiliated then?"

"Yes, but the worst thing is that I am aware that he knows that I could never drive myself to leave, and he wishes to spare me the struggle. But outside—some terrible beast has entered the garden. I smell it—like the hyena cage at the Tiergarten—as the door opens. And then I wake up."

"It is a harrowing dream."

"You have seen the dresses I sell. Would you credit it that for weeks I slept in one, and then another, and then another of them?"

"You reaped no benefit from that?"

"No. In the dream I was clad as now. For a time I wore the dresses always—even here to the stall, and when I bought food at the market. But it did no good."

"Have you tried sleeping somewhere else?"

"With my cousin who lives on the other side of the city. That made no difference. I am certain that this man I see is a real man. He is in my dream, and the cause of it, but he is not sleeping."

"Yet you have never seen him when you are awake?"

She paused, and I saw her bite at her full lower lip. "I am certain I have."

"Ah!"

"But I cannot remember when. Yet I am sure I have seen him—that I have passed him in the street."

"Think! Does his face associate itself in your mind with some particular section of the city?"

She shook her head.

When I left her at last, it was with a description of the Dream-Master less precise than I had hoped, though still detailed. It tallied in almost all respects with the one given me by Baron H———, but that proved nothing, since the baron's description might have been based largely on Fräulein A———'s.

The bank of Herr R——— was a private one, as all the greatest banks in Europe are. It was located in what had once been the town house of some noble family (their arms, overgrown now with ivy, were still visible above the door) and bore no identification other than a small brass plate engraved with the names of Herr R——— and his partners. Within, the atmosphere was more dignified—even if, perhaps, less tasteful—than it could possibly have been in the noble family's time. Dark pictures in gilded frames lined the walls, and the clerks sat at inlaid tables upon chairs upholstered in tapestry. When I asked for Herr R———, I was told that it would be impossible to see him that afternoon; I sent in a note with a sidelong allusion to "unquiet dreams," and within five minutes I was ushered into a luxurious office that must once have been the bedroom of the head of the household.

Herr R——— was a large man—tall, and heavier (I thought) than his physician was likely to have approved. He appeared to be about fifty; there was strength in his wide, fleshy face; his high forehead and capacious cranium suggested intellect, and his small, dark eyes, forever flickering as they took in the appearance of my person, the expression of my face, and the position of my hands and feet, ingenuity.

No pretense was apt to be of service with such a man, and I told him flatly that I had come as the emissary of Baron H———, that I knew what troubled him, and that if he would cooperate with me I would help him if I could.

"I know you, monsieur," he said, "by reputation. A business with which I am associated employed you three years ago in the matter of a certain mummy." He named the firm. "I should have thought of you myself."

"I did not know that you were connected with them."

"I am not, when you leave this room. I do not know what reward Baron H——— has offered you should you apprehend the man who is oppressing me, but I will give you, in addition to that, a sum equal to what you were paid for the mummy. You should be able to retire to the south then, should you choose, with the rent of a dozen villas."

"I do not choose," I told him, "and I could have retired long before. But what you just said interests me. You are certain that your persecutor is a living man?"

"I know men." Herr R——— leaned back in his chair and stared at the painted ceiling. "As a boy I sold stuffed cabbage-leaf rolls in the street—did you know that? My mother cooked them over wood she collected herself where buildings were being demolished, and I sold them from a little cart for her. I lived to see her with half a score of footmen and the finest house in Lindau. I never went to school; I learned to add and subtract in the streets—when I must multiply and divide I have my clerk do it. But I learned men. Do you think that now, after forty years of practice, I could be deceived by a phantom? No, he is a man—let me confess it, a stronger man than I—a man of flesh and blood and brain, a man I have seen somewhere, sometime, here in this city, and more than once."

"Describe him."

"As tall as I. Younger—perhaps thirty or thirty-five. A brown, forked beard, so long." (He held his hand about fifteen centimeters beneath his chin.) "Brown hair. His hair is not yet gray, but I think it may be thinning a little at the temples."

"Don't you remember?"

"In my dream he wears a garland of roses—I cannot be sure."

"Is there anything else? Any scars or identifying marks?"

Herr R——— nodded. "He has hurt his hand. In my dream, when he holds out his hand for the money, I see blood in it—it is his own, you understand, as though a recent injury had reopened and was beginning to bleed again. His hands are long and slender—like a pianist's."

"Perhaps you had better tell me your dream."

"Of course." He paused, and his face clouded, as though to recount the dream were to return to it. "I am in a great house. I am a person of importance there, almost as though I were the owner, yet I am not the owner—"

"Wait," I interrupted. "Does this house have a banquet hall? Has it a pillared portico, and is it set in a garden?"

For a moment Herr R———'s eyes widened. "Have you also had such dreams?"

"No," I said. "It is only that I think I have heard of this house before. Please continue."

"There are many servants—some work in the fields beyond the garden. I give instructions to them—the details differ each night, you understand. Sometimes I am concerned with the kitchen, sometimes with the livestock, sometimes with the draining of a field. We grow wheat, principally, it seems, but there is a vineyard too, and a kitchen garden. And of course the house itself must be cleaned and swept and kept in repair. There is no wife; the owner's mother lives with us, I think, but she does not much concern herself with the housekeeping—that is up to me. To tell the truth, I have never actually seen her, though I have the feeling that she is there."

"Does this house resemble the one you bought for your own mother in Lindau?"

"Only as one large house must resemble another."

"I see. Proceed."

"For a long time each night I continue like that, giving orders, and sometimes going over the accounts. Then a servant, usually it is a maid, arrives to tell me that the owner wishes to speak to me. I stand before a mirror—I can see myself there as plainly as I see you now—and arrange my clothing. The maid brings rose-scented water and a cloth, and I wipe my face; then I go in to him.

"He is always in one of the upper rooms, seated at a table with his own account book spread before him. There is an open window behind him, and through it I can see the top of a cherry tree in bloom. For a long time—oh, I suppose ten minutes—I stand before him while he turns over the pages of his ledger."

"You appear somewhat at a loss, Herr R——, not a common condition for you, I believe. What happens then?"

"He says, 'You owe . . . '" Herr R—— paused. "That is the problem, monsieur, I can never recall the amount. But it is a large sum. He says, 'And I must require that you make payment at once.'

"I do not have the amount, and I tell him so. He says, 'Then you must leave my employment.' I fall to my knees at this and beg that he will retain me, pointing out that if he dismisses me I will have lost my source of income and will never be able to make payment. I do not enjoy telling you this, but I weep. Sometimes I beat the floor with my fists."

"Continue. Is the Dream-Master moved by your pleading?"

"No. He again demands that I pay the entire sum. Several times I have told him that I am a wealthy man in this world, and that if only he would permit me to make payment in its currency, I would do so immediately."

"That is interesting—most of us lack your presence of mind in our nightmares. What does he say then?"

"Usually he tells me not to be a fool. But once he said, 'That is a dream—you must know it by now. You cannot expect to pay a real debt with the currency of sleep.' He holds out his hand for the money as he speaks to me. It is then that I see the blood in his palm."

"You are afraid of him?"

"Oh, very much so. I understand that he has the most complete power over me. I weep, and at last I throw myself at his feet—with my head under the table, if you can credit it, crying like an infant.

"Then he stands and pulls me erect, and says, 'You would never be able to pay all you owe, and you are a false and dishonest servant. But your debt is forgiven, forever.' And as I watch, he tears a leaf from his account book and hands it to me."

"Your dream has a happy conclusion, then."

"No. It is not yet over. I thrust the paper into the front of my shirt and go out, wiping my face on my sleeve. I am conscious that if any of the other servants should see me, they will know at once what has happened. I hurry to reach my own counting room; there is a brazier there, and I wish to burn the page from the owner's book."

"I see."

"But just outside the door of my own room, I meet another servant—an upper servant like myself, I think, since he is well dressed. As it happens, this man owes me a considerable sum of money, and to conceal from him what I have just endured, I demand that he pay at once." Herr R—— rose from his chair and began to pace the room, looking sometimes at the painted scenes on the walls, sometimes at the Turkish carpet at his feet. "I have had reason to demand money like that often, you understand. Here in this room.

"The man falls to his knees, weeping and begging for additional time, but I reach down, like this, and seize him by the throat."

"And then?"

"And then the door of my counting room opens. But it is not my counting room with my desk and the charcoal brazier, but the owner's own room. He is standing in the doorway, and behind him I can see the open window, and the blossoms of the cherry tree."

"What does he say to you?"

"Nothing. He says nothing to me. I release the other man's throat, and he slinks away."

"You awaken then?"

"How can I explain it? Yes, I wake up. But first we stand there, and while we do I am conscious of . . . certain sounds."

"If it is too painful for you, you need not say more."

Herr R—— drew a silk handkerchief from his pocket and wiped his face. "How can I explain?" he said again. "When I hear those sounds, I am aware that the owner possesses certain other servants, who have never been under my direction. It is as though I have always known this, but had no reason to think of it before."

"I understand."

"They are quartered in another part of the house—in the vaults beneath the wine cellar, I think sometimes. I have never seen them, but I know—then—that they are hideous, vile, and cruel; I know too that he thinks me but little better than they, and that as he permits me to serve him, so he allows them to serve him also. I stand—we stand—and listen to them coming through the house. At last a door at the end of the hall begins to swing open. There is a hand like the paw of some filthy reptile on the latch."

"Is that the end of the dream?"

"Yes." Herr R—— threw himself into his chair again, mopping his face.

"You have this experience each night?"

"It differs," he said slowly, "in some details."

"You have told me that the orders you give the underservants vary."

"There is another difference. When the dreams began, I woke when the hinges of the door at the passage end creaked. Each night now the dream endures a moment longer. Perhaps a tenth of a second. Now I see the arm of the creature who opens that door, nearly to the elbow."

I took the address of his home, which he was glad enough to give me, and leaving the bank made my way to my hotel.

When I had eaten my roll and drunk my coffee the next morning, I went to the place indicated by the card given me by Baron H——, and in a few minutes was sitting with him in a room as bare as those tents from which armies in the field are cast into battle. "You are ready to begin the case this morning?" he asked.

"On the contrary. I have already begun; indeed, I am about to enter a new phase of my investigation. You would not have come to me if your Dream-Master were not torturing someone other than the people whose names you gave me. I wish to know the identity of that person, and to interrogate him."

"I told you that there were many other reports. I—"

"Provided me with a list. They are all of the petite bourgeoisie, when they are not persons still less important. I believed at first that it might be because of the urgings of Herr R—— that you engaged me, but when I had time to reflect on what I know of your methods, I realized that you would have demanded that he provide my fee had that been the case. So you are sheltering someone of greater importance, and I wish to speak to him."

"The countess—," Baron H—— began.

"Ah!"

"The countess herself has expressed some desire that you should be presented to her. The count opposes it."

"We are speaking, I take it, of the governor of this province?"

The baron nodded. "Of Count von V——. He is responsible, you understand, only to the queen regent herself."

"Very well. I wish to hear the countess, and she wishes to talk with me. I assure you, Baron, that we will meet; the only question is whether it will be under your auspices."

The countess, to whom I was introduced that afternoon, was a woman in her early twenties, deep breasted and somber haired, with skin like milk, and great dark eyes welling with fear and (I thought) pity, set in a perfect oval face.

"I am glad you have come, monsieur. For seven weeks now our good Baron H—— has sought this man for me, but he has not found him."

"If I had known my presence here would please you, Countess, I would have come long ago, whatever the obstacles. You then, like the others, are certain it is a real man we seek?"

"I seldom go out, monsieur. My husband feels we are in constant danger of assassination."

"I believe he is correct."

"But on state occasions we sometimes ride in a glass coach to the *Rathaus*. There are uhlans all around us to protect us then. I am certain that—before the dreams began—I saw the face of this man in the crowd."

"Very well. Now tell me your dream."

"I am here, at home—"

"In this palace, where we sit now?"

She nodded.

"That is a new feature, then. Continue, please."

"There is to be an execution. In the garden." A fleeting smile crossed the countess's lovely face. "I need not tell you that that is not where the executions are held; but it does not seem strange to me when I dream.

"I have been away, I think, and have only just heard of what is to take place. I rush into the garden. The man Baron H—— calls the Dream-Master is there, tied to the trunk of the big cherry tree; a squad of soldiers faces him, holding their rifles; their officer stands beside them with his saber drawn, and my husband is watching from a pace or two away. I call out for them to stop, and my husband turns to look at me. I say, 'You must not do it, Karl. You must not kill this man.' But I see by his expression that he believes that I am only a foolish, tenderhearted child. Karl is . . . several years older than I."

"I am aware of it."

"The Dream-Master turns his head to look at me. People tell me that my eyes are large—do you think them large, monsieur?"

"Very large, and very beautiful."

"In my dream, quite suddenly, his eyes seem far, far larger than mine, and far more beautiful, and in them I see reflected the figure of my husband. Please listen carefully now, because what I am going to say is very important, though it makes very little sense, I am afraid."

"Anything may happen in a dream, Countess."

"When I see my husband reflected in this man's eyes, I know—I cannot say how—that it is this reflection, and not the man who stands near me, who is the real Karl. The man I have thought real is only a reflection of that reflection. Do you follow what I say?"

I nodded. "I believe so."

"I plead again: 'Do not kill him. Nothing good can come of it. . . .' My husband nods to the officer, the soldiers raise their rifles, and . . . and . . ."

"You wake. Would you like my handkerchief, Countess? It is of coarse weave, but it is clean, and much larger than your own."

"Karl is right—I am only a foolish little girl. No, monsieur, I do not wake—not yet. The soldiers fire. The Dream-Master falls forward, though his bonds hold him to the tree. And Karl flies to bloody rags beside me."

On my way back to my hotel, I purchased a map of the city, and when I reached my room I laid it flat on the table there. There could be no question of the route of the countess's glass coach—straight down the Hauptstrasse, the only street in the city wide enough to take a carriage surrounded by cavalrymen. The most probable route by which Herr R—— might go from his house to his bank coincided with the Hauptstrasse for several blocks. The path Fräulein A—— would travel from her flat to the arcade crossed the Hauptstrasse at a point contained by that interval. I needed to know no more.

Very early the next morning I took up my post at the intersection. If my man were still alive after the fusillade Count von V—— fired at him each night, it seemed certain that he would appear at this spot within a few days, and I am hardened to waiting. I smoked cigarettes while I watched the citizens of I—— walk up and down before me. When an hour had passed, I bought a newspaper from a vendor, and stole a few glances at its pages when foot traffic was light.

Gradually I became aware that I was watched—we boast of reason, but there are senses over which reason holds no authority. I did not know where my watcher was, yet I felt his gaze on me, whichever way I turned. So, I thought, *You know me, my friend. Will I too dream now? What has attracted your attention to a mere foreigner, a stranger, waiting for who-knows-what at this corner? Have you been talking to Fräulein A——? Or to someone who has spoken with her?*

Without appearing to do so, I looked up and down both streets in search of another lounger like myself. There was no one—not a drowsing grandfather, not a woman or a child, not even a dog. Certainly no tall man with a forked beard and piercing eyes. The windows then—I studied them all, looking for some movement in a dark room behind a seemingly innocent opening. Nothing.

Only the buildings behind me remained. I crossed to the opposite side of the Hauptstrasse and looked once more. Then I laughed.

They must have thought me mad, all those dour burghers, for I fairly doubled over, spitting my cigarette to the sidewalk and clasping my hands to my waist for fear my belt would burst. The presumption, the impudence, the brazen insolence of the fellow! The stupidity, the wonderful stupidity of myself, who had not recognized his old stories! For the remainder of my life now, I could accept any case with pleasure, pursue the most inept criminal with zest, knowing that there was always a chance he might outwit such an idiot as I.

For the Dream-Master had set up His own picture, and full-length and in the most gorgeous colors, in his window. Choking and spluttering, I saluted it, and then, still filled with laughter, I crossed the street once more and went inside, where I knew I would find Him. A man awaited me there—not the one I sought, but one who understood Whom it was I had come for, and knew as well as I that His capture was beyond any thief taker's power. I knelt, and there, though not to the satisfaction I suppose of Baron H——, Fräulein A——, Herr R——, and the Count and Countess von V——, I destroyed the Dream-Master as He has been sacrificed so often, devouring His white, wheaten flesh that we might all possess life without end.

Dear people, dream on.

AFTERWORD

G. K. Chesterton wrote that ordinary life "is like ten thousand thrilling detective stories mixed up with a spoon." If we look at it that way—which is rather fun—we can quickly come up with ten thousand stories.

Some of which will show that the criminal cannot be apprehended. And some of which will show, like this one, that the criminal should not be.

I will not lecture you on Jesus of Nazareth, but I advise you to find Chesterton's *The Everlasting Man*. In this story I asked you to consider that everlasting man's short fiction. Fans have written me to say that this or that story stayed with them for days. Each letter makes me proud and happy. In my happiness and pride, I am prone to forget that there was once a storyteller from Galilee whose stories have stayed with us for millennia.

# KEVIN MALONE

Marcella and I were married in April. I lost my position with Ketterly, Bruce & Drake in June, and by August we were desperate. We kept the apartment—I think we both felt that if we lowered our standards there would be no chance to raise them again—but the rent tore at our small savings. All during July I had tried to get a job at another brokerage firm, and by August I was calling fraternity brothers I had not seen since graduation and expressing an entire willingness to work in whatever businesses their fathers owned. One of them, I think, must have mailed us the advertisement.

> Attractive young couple, well educated and well connected, will receive free housing, generous living allowance, for minimal services.

There was a telephone number, which I omit for reasons that will become clear.

I showed the clipping to Marcella, who was lying with her cocktail shaker on the chaise longue. She said, "Why not," and I dialed the number.

The telephone buzzed in my ear, paused, and buzzed again. I allowed myself to go limp in my chair. It seemed absurd to call at all; for the advertisement to have reached us that day, it must have appeared no later than yesterday morning. If the position was worth having—

"The Pines."

I pulled myself together. "You placed a classified ad. For an attractive couple, well educated and the rest of it."

"I did not, sir. However, I believe my master did. I am Priest, the butler."

I looked at Marcella, but her eyes were closed. "Do you know, Priest, if the opening has been filled?"

"I think not, sir. May I ask your age?"

I told him. At his request, I also told him Marcella's (she was two years younger than I) and gave him the names of the schools we had attended, described our appearance, and mentioned that my grandfather had been a governor of Virginia and that Marcella's uncle had been ambassador to France. I did not tell him that my father had shot himself rather than face bankruptcy, or that Marcella's family had disowned her—but I suspect he guessed well enough what our situation was.

"You will forgive me, sir, for asking so many questions. We are almost a half day's drive, and I would not wish you to be disappointed."

I told him that I appreciated that, and we set a date—Tuesday of the next week—on which Marcella and I were to come out for an interview with "the master." Priest had hung up before I realized that I had failed to learn his employer's name.

During the teens and twenties some very wealthy people had designed estates in imitation of the palaces of the Italian Renaissance. The Pines was one of them, and better preserved than most—the fountain in the courtyard still played, the marbles were clean and unyellowed, and if no red-robed cardinal descended the steps to a carriage blazoned with the Borgia arms, one felt that he had only just gone. No doubt the place had originally been called La Capanna or Il Eremo.

A serious-looking man in dark livery opened the door for us. For a moment he stared at us across the threshold. "Very well . . . ," he said.

"I beg your pardon?"

"I said that you are looking very well." He nodded to each of us in turn, and stood aside. "Sir. Madame. I am Priest."

"Will your master be able to see us?"

For a moment some exiled expression—it might have been amusement—seemed to tug at his solemn face. "The music room, perhaps, sir?"

I said I was sure that would be satisfactory, and followed him. The music room held a Steinway, a harp, and a dozen or so comfortable chairs; it overlooked a rose garden in which old remontant varieties were beginning that second season that is more opulent though less generous than the first. A kneeling gardener was weeding one of the beds.

"This is a wonderful house," Marcella said. "I really didn't think there was anything like it left. I told him you'd have a john collins—all right? You were looking at the roses."

"Perhaps we ought to get the job first."

"I can't call him back now, and if we don't get it, at least we'll have had the drinks."

I nodded to that. In five minutes they arrived, and we drank them and smoked cigarettes we found in a humidor—English cigarettes of strong Turkish tobacco. A maid came, and said that Mr. Priest would be much obliged if we would let him know when we would dine. I told her that we would eat whenever it was convenient, and she dropped a little curtsy and withdrew.

"At least," Marcella commented, "he's making us comfortable while we wait."

Dinner was lamb in aspic, and a salad, with a maid—another maid—and a footman to serve while Priest stood by to see that it was done properly. We ate at either side of a small table on a terrace overlooking another garden, where antique statues faded to white glimmerings as the sun set.

Priest came forward to light the candles. "Will you require me after dinner, sir?"

"Will your employer require us; that's the question."

"Bateman can show you to your room, sir, when you are ready to retire. Julia will see to Madame."

I looked at the footman, who was carrying in fruit on a tray.

"No, sir. That is Carter. Bateman is your man."

"And Julia," Marcella put in, "is my maid, I suppose?"

"Precisely." Priest gave an almost inaudible cough. "Perhaps, sir—and madame—you might find this useful." He drew a photograph from an inner pocket and handed it to me.

It was a black-and-white snapshot, somewhat dog-eared. Two dozen people, most of them in livery of one kind or another, stood in brilliant sunshine on the steps at the front of the house, men behind women. There were names in India ink across the bottom of the picture: *James Sutton, Edna DeBuck, Lloyd Bateman . . .*

"Our staff, sir."

I said, "Thank you, Priest. No, you needn't stay tonight."

The next morning Bateman shaved me in bed. He did it very well, using a straight razor and scented soap applied with a brush. I had heard of such things—I think my grandfather's valet may have shaved him like that before the First World War—but I had never guessed that anyone kept up the tradition. Bateman did, and I found I enjoyed it. When he had dressed me, he asked if I would breakfast in my room.

"I doubt it," I said. "Do you know my wife's plans?"

"I think it likely she will be on the South Terrace, sir. Julia said something to that effect as I was bringing in your water."

"I'll join her then."

"Of course, sir." He hesitated.

"I don't think I'll require a guide, but you might tell my wife I'll be with her in ten minutes or so."

Bateman repeated his, "Of course, sir," and went out. The truth was that I wanted to assure myself that everything I had carried in the pockets of my old suit—car keys, wallet, and so on—had been transferred to the new one he had laid out for me; and I did not want to insult him, if I could prevent it, by doing it in front of him.

Everything was where it should be, and I had a clean handkerchief in place of my own only slightly soiled one. I pulled it out to look at (Irish linen) and a flutter of green came with it—two bills, both fifties.

Over eggs Benedict I complimented Marcella on her new dress and asked if she had noticed where it had been made.

"Rowe's. It's a little shop on Fifth Avenue."

"You know it, then. Nothing unusual?"

She answered, "No, nothing unusual," more quickly than she should have, and I knew that there had been money in her new clothes too, and that she did not intend to tell me about it.

"We'll be going home after this. I wonder if they'll want me to give this jacket back."

"Going home?" She did not look up from her plate. "Why? And who are 'they'?"

"Whoever owns this house."

"Yesterday you called him he. You said Priest talked about *the master,* so that seemed logical enough. Today you're afraid to deal with even presumptive masculinity."

I said nothing.

"You think he spent the night in my room, they separated us and you thought that was why, and you just waited there—was it under a sheet?—for me to scream or something. And I didn't."

"I was hoping you had and I hadn't heard you."

"Nothing happened, dammit! I went to bed and went to sleep, but as for going home, you're out of your mind. Can't you see we've got the job? Whoever he is—wherever he is—he likes us. We're going to stay here and live like human beings, at least for a while."

And so we did. That day we stayed on from hour to hour. After that, from day to day, and at last from week to week. I felt like Klipspringer, the man who was Jay Gatsby's guest for so long that he had no other home—except that Klipspringer, presumably, saw Gatsby from time to time, and no doubt made agreeable conversation, and perhaps even played the piano for him. Our Gatsby was absent. I do not mean that we avoided him, or that he avoided us; there were no rooms we were forbidden to enter, and no times when the servants seemed eager that we should play golf or swim or go riding. Before the good weather ended, we had two couples up for a weekend; and when Bette Windgassen asked if Marcella had inherited the place, and then if we were renting it, Marcella said, "Oh, do you like it?" in such a way that they left, I think, convinced that it was ours, or as good as ours.

And so it was. We went away when we chose, which was seldom, and returned when we chose, quickly. We ate on the various terraces and balconies, and in the big, formal dining room, and in our own bedrooms. We rode the horses and drove the Mercedes and the cranky, appealing old Jaguar as though they were our own. We did everything, in fact, except buy the groceries and pay the taxes and the servants, but someone else was doing that, and every morning I found one hundred dollars in the pockets of my clean clothes. If summer had lasted forever, perhaps I would still be there.

The poplars lost their leaves in one October week; at the end of it I fell asleep listening to the hum of the pump that emptied the swimming pool. When the rain came, Marcella turned sour and drank too much. One evening I made the mistake of putting my arm about her shoulders as we sat before the fire in the trophy room.

"Get your filthy hands off me," she said. "I don't belong to you."

"Priest, look here. He hasn't said an intelligent word to me all day or done a decent thing, and now he wants to paw me all night."

Priest pretended, of course, that he had not heard her.

"Look over here! Damn it, you're a human being, aren't you?"

He did not ignore that. "Yes, madame, I am a human being."

"I'll say you are. You're more of a man than he is. This is your place, and you're keeping us for pets—is it me you want? Or him? You sent us the ad, didn't you? He thinks you go into my room at night, or he says he does. Maybe you really come to his—is that it?"

Priest did not answer. I said, "For God's sake, Marcella."

"Even if you're old, Priest, I think you're too much of a man for that." She stood up, tottering on her long legs and holding on to the stonework of the fireplace. "If you want me, take me. If this house is yours, you can have me. We'll send him to Vegas—or throw him on the dump."

In a much softer tone than he usually used, Priest said, "I don't want either of you, madame."

I stood up then, and caught him by the shoulders. I had been drinking too, though only half or a quarter as much as Marcella, but I think it was more than that—it was the accumulated frustration of all the days since Jim Bruce told me I was finished. I outweighed Priest by at least forty pounds, and I was twenty years younger. I said, "I want to know."

"Release me, sir, please."

"I want to know who it is; I want to know now. Do you see that fire? Tell me, Priest, or I swear I'll throw you in it."

His face tightened at that. "Yes," he whispered, and I let go of his shoulders. "It was not the lady, sir. It was you. I want that understood this time."

"What the hell are you talking about?"

"I'm not doing this because of what she said."

"You aren't the master, are you? For God's sake tell the truth."

"I have always told the truth, sir. No, I am not the master. Do you remember the picture I gave you?"

I nodded.

"You discarded it. I took the liberty, sir, of rescuing it from the waste can in your bathroom. I have it here." He reached into his coat and pulled it out, just as he had on the first day, and handed it to me.

"It's one of these? One of the servants?"

Priest nodded and pointed with an impeccably manicured forefinger to the figure at the extreme right of the second row. The name beneath it was *Kevin Malone*.

"Him?"

Silently, Priest nodded again.

I had examined the picture on the night he had given it to me, but I had never paid special attention to that particular half-inch-high image. The person it represented might have been a gardener, a man of middle age, short and perhaps stocky. A soft, sweat-stained hat cast a shadow on his face.

"I want to see him." I looked toward Marcella, still leaning against the stonework of the mantel. "We want to see him."

"Are you certain, sir?"

"Damn you, get him!"

Priest remained where he was, staring at me; I was so furious that I think I might have seized him as I had threatened and pushed him into the fire.

Then the French windows opened, and there came a gust of wind. For an instant I think I expected a ghost, or some turbulent elemental spirit. I felt that pricking at the neck that comes when one reads Poe alone at night.

The man I had seen in the picture stepped into the room. He was a small and very ordinary man in worn khaki, but he left the windows wide behind him, so that the night entered with him, and remained in the room for as long as we talked.

"You own this house," I said. "You're Kevin Malone."

He shook his head. "I am Kevin Malone—this house owns me."

Marcella was standing straighter now, drunk, yet still at that stage of drunkenness in which she was conscious of her condition and could compensate for it. "It owns me too," she said, and walking almost normally she crossed the room to the baronial chair Malone had chosen, and managed to sit down at his feet.

"My father was the man-of-all-work here. My mother was the parlor maid. I grew up here, washing the cars and raking leaves out of the fountains. Do you follow me? Where did you grow up?"

I shrugged. "Various places. Richmond, New York, three years in Paris. Until I was sent off to school we lived in hotels, mostly."

"You see, then. You can understand." Malone smiled for a moment. "You're still re-creating the life you had as a child, or trying to. Isn't that right? None of us can be happy any other way, and few of us even want to try."

"Thomas Wolfe said you can't go home again," I ventured.

"That's right; you can't go home. There's one place where we can never go—haven't you thought of that? We can dive to the bottom of the sea and some-day NASA will fly us to the stars, and I have known men to plunge into the past—or the future—and drown. But there's one place where we can't go. We can't go where we are already. We can't go home, because our minds, and our hearts, and our immortal souls are already there."

Not knowing what to say, I nodded, and that seemed to satisfy him. Priest looked as calm as ever, but he made no move to shut the windows, and I sensed that he was somehow afraid.

"I was put into an orphanage when I was twelve, but I never forgot The Pines. I used to tell the other kids about it, and it got bigger and better every year, but I knew what I said could never equal the reality."

He shifted in his seat, and the slight movement of his legs sent Marcella sprawling, passed out. She retained a certain grace still; I have always understood that it is the reward of studying ballet as a child.

Malone continued to talk. "They'll tell you it's no longer possible for a poor boy with a second-rate education to make a fortune. Well, it takes luck, but I had it. It also takes the willingness to risk it all. I had that too, because I knew that for me anything under a fortune was nothing. I had to be able to buy this place—to come back and buy The Pines, and staff it and maintain it. That's what I wanted, and nothing less would make any difference."

"You're to be congratulated," I said. "But why . . ."

He laughed. It was a deep laugh, but there was no humor in it. "Why don't I wear a tie and eat my supper at the end of the big table? I tried it. I tried it for nearly a year, and every night I dreamed of home. That wasn't home, you see, wasn't The Pines. Home is three rooms above the stables. I live there now. I live at home, as a man should."

"It seems to me that it would have been a great deal simpler for you to have applied for the job you fill now."

Malone shook his head impatiently. "That wouldn't have done it at all. I had to have control. That's something I learned in business—to have control. An-other owner would have wanted to change things, and maybe he would even have sold out to a subdivider. No. Besides, when I was a boy this estate belonged to a fashionable young couple. Suppose a man of my age had bought it? Or a young woman, some whore." His mouth tightened, then relaxed. "You and your wife were ideal. Now I'll have to get somebody else, that's all. You can stay the night, if you like. I'll have you driven into the city tomorrow morning."

I ventured, "You needed us as stage properties, then. I'd be willing to stay on those terms."

Malone shook his head again. "That's out of the question. I don't need props; I need actors. In business I've put on little shows for the competition, if you know what I mean, and sometimes even for my own people. And I've learned that the only actors who can really do justice to their parts are the ones who don't know what they are."

"Really——," I began.

He cut me off with a look, and for a few seconds we stared at one another. Something terrible lived behind those eyes.

Frightened despite all reason could tell me, I said, "I understand," and stood up. There seemed to be nothing else to do. "I'm glad, at least, that you don't hate us. With your childhood it would be quite natural if you did. Will you explain things to Marcella in the morning? She'll throw herself at you, no matter what I say."

He nodded absently.

"May I ask one question more? I wondered why you had to leave and go into the orphanage. Did your parents die or lose their places?"

Malone said, "Didn't you tell him, Priest? It's the local legend. I thought everyone knew."

The butler cleared his throat. "The elder Mr. Malone—he was the stableman here, sir, though it was before my time. He murdered Betty Malone, who was one of the maids. Or at least he was thought to have, sir. They never found the body, and it's possible he was accused falsely."

"Buried her on the estate," Malone said. "They found bloody rags and the hammer, and he hanged himself in the stable."

"I'm sorry . . . I didn't mean to pry."

The wind whipped the drapes like wine-red flags. They knocked over a vase and Priest winced, but Malone did not seem to notice. "She was twenty years younger and a tramp," he said. "Those things happen."

I said, "Yes, I know they do," and went up to bed.

I do not know where Marcella slept. Perhaps there on the carpet, perhaps in the room that had been hers, perhaps even in Malone's servants' flat over the stables. I breakfasted alone on the terrace, then—without Bateman's assistance—packed my bags.

I saw her only once more. She was wearing a black silk dress; there were circles under her eyes and her head must have been throbbing, but her hand was steady. As I walked out of the house, she was going over the Sèvres with a peacock-feather duster. We did not speak.

I have sometimes wondered if I were wholly wrong in anticipating a ghost when the French windows opened. How did Malone know the time had come for him to appear?

Of course I have looked up the newspaper reports of the murder. All the old papers are on microfilm at the library, and I have a great deal of time.

There is no mention of a child. In fact, I get the impression that the identical surnames of the murderer and his victim were coincidental. Malone is a common enough one, and there were a good many Irish servants then.

Sometimes I wonder if it is possible for a man—even a rich man—to be possessed, and not to know it.

## Afterword

This was a dream story. I dream a good deal of fiction, but it is mostly very bad fiction. The title was in my dream and the setup, the possessed servant hiring a master and mistress. That and one visual image that has never left me, that of a large upper-class room at midnight swept by a high wind. Its drapes flutter among my thoughts even now.

Some are haunted by ghosts. I am haunted by stories.

# The God and His Man

Once long, long ago, when the Universe was old, the mighty and power-ful god Isid Iooo IoooE, whose name is given by certain others in other ways, and who is determined in every place and time to do what is good, came to the world of Zed. As every man knows, such gods travel in craft that can never be wrecked—and indeed, how could they be wrecked, when the gods are ever awake and hold the tiller? He came, I say, to the world of Zed, but he landed not and made no port, for it is not fit (as those who made the gods long ago ruled) that a god should set his foot upon any world, however blue, however fair.

Therefore Isid Iooo IoooE remained above the heavens, and his craft, though it traveled faster than the wind, contrived to do so in such a way that it stood suspended—as the many-hued stars themselves do not—above that isle of Zed that is called by the men of Zed (for they are men, or nearly) Land. Then the god looked down upon Zed, and seeing that the men of Zed were men and the women thereof women, he summoned to him a certain man of Urth. The summons of Isid Iooo IoooE cannot be disobeyed.

"Man," said the god, "go down to the world of Zed. For behold, the men of Zed are even as you are, and their women are women." Then he let Man see through his own eyes, and Man saw the men of Zed, how they herded their cattle and drove their plows and beat the little drums of Zed. And he saw the women of Zed, and how many were fair to look upon, and how they lived in sorrow and idleness, or else in toil and weariness, even like the women of Urth.

He said to the god, "If I am ever to see my own home, and my own women, and my children again, I must do as you say. But if I go as I am, I shall not see any of those things ever again. For the men of Zed are men—you yourself have said it—and therefore crueler than any beast."

"It is that cruelty we must end," said the god. "And in order that you may as-sist me with your reports, I have certain gifts for you." Then he gave Man the en-chanted cloak Tarnung by which none should see him when he did not wish to be seen, and he gave Man the enchanted sword Maser, whose blade is as long as the wielder wishes it (though it weighs nothing) and against which not even stone can stand.

No sooner had Man tied Tarnung about his shoulders and picked up Maser than the god vanished from his sight, and he found he rested in a grove of trees with scarlet flowers.

The time of the gods is not as the time of men and women. Who can say how long Man wandered across Land on Zed? He wandered in the high, hot lands where men have few laws and many slaves.

There he fought many fights until he knew all the manner of fighting of the people of the high, hot lands and grew shamed of killing those men with Maser, and took for himself the crooked sword of those lands, putting Maser by. Then he drew to him a hundred wild men, bandits, and slaves who had slain their masters and fled, and murderers of many kinds. And he armed them after the manner of the high, hot lands, and mounted them on the yellow camels of those lands, that oftimes crush men with their necks, and led them in many wars. His face was like the faces of other men, and his sword like their swords; he stood no taller than they, and his shoulders were no broader; yet because he was very cunning and sometimes vanished from the camp, his followers venerated him.

At last he grew rich, and built a citadel in the fastness of the mountains. It stood upon a cliff and was rimmed with mighty walls. A thousand spears and a thousand spells guarded it. Within were white domes and white towers, a hundred fountains, and gardens that leaped up the mountain in roses and ran down it like children in the laughter of many waters. There Man sat at his ease and exchanged tales with his captains of their many wars. There he listened to the feet of his dancers as the pattering of rain, and meditated on their round limbs and smiling faces. And at last he grew tired of these things and, wrapping himself in Tarnung, vanished and was seen in that citadel no more.

Then he wandered in the steaming lands, where the trees grew taller than his towers and the men are shy and kill from the shadows with little poisoned arrows no longer than their forearms. There for a long while he wore the cloak Tarnung always, for no sword avails against such an arrow in the neck. The weight of the sword he had fetched from the high, hot lands oppressed him there, and the breath of the steaming lands rusted its blade, and so he cast it, one day, into a slow river where the black crocodiles swam and the river horses with amber eyes floated like logs or bellowed like thunder. But the magical sword Maser he kept.

And in the steaming lands he learned the ways of the great trees, of which each is an island, with its own dwellers thereon, and he learned the ways of the beasts of Zed, whose cleverness is so much less than the cleverness of men, and whose wisdom is so much more. There he tamed a panther with eyes like three emeralds, so that it followed him like a dog and killed for him like a hawk, and when he came upon a village of the men of the steaming lands he leaped from a high branch onto the head of their idol and smote the hut of their chief with the sword Maser and vanished from their sight. And when he returned after a year to that village, he saw that the old idol was destroyed and a new idol set up, with lightning in its hand and a panther at its feet.

Then he entered that village and blessed all the people and made the lap of that idol his throne. He rode an elephant with a bloodred tusk and two trunks; his war canoes walked up and down the river on a hundred legs; the heads of his drums were beaten with the white bones of chiefs; his wives were kept from the sun so their pale beauty would lure him to his hut by night and their fresh skins give him rest even in the steaming lands, and they were gorged with oil and meal until he lay upon them as upon pillows of silk. And so he would have remained had not the god Isid Iooo IoooE come to him in a dream of the night and commanded him to bestir himself, wandering and observing in the cold lands.

There he walked down a thousand muddy roads and kissed cool lips in a hundred rainy gardens. The people of the cold lands keep no slaves and have many laws, and their justice is the wonder of strangers, and so he found the bread of the cold lands hard and scant, and for a long time he cleaned boots for it, and for a long time dug ditches to drain their fields.

And each day the ship of Isid Iooo IoooE circled Zed, and when it had made several hundred such circles, Zed circled its lonely sun, and circled again, and yet again, so that Man's beard grew white, and the cunning that had won battles in the high, hot lands and burned the idol in the steaming lands was replaced with something better and less useful.

One day he plunged the blade of his shovel into the earth and turned his back to it. In a spinney he drew out Maser (which he had not drawn for so long that he feared its magic was no more than a dream he had had when young) and cut a sapling. With that for a staff he took to the roads again, and when its leaves withered—which they did but slowly in that wet, cold country—he cut another and another, so that he taught always beneath a green tree.

In the marketplace he told of honor, and how it is a higher law than any law.

At the crossroads he talked of freedom, the freedom of the wind and clouds, the freedom that loves all things and is without guilt.

Beside city gates he told stories of the forgotten cities that were and of the forgotten cities that might be, if only men would forget them.

Often the people of the cold lands sought to imprison him according to their laws, but he vanished from their sight. Often they mocked him, but he smiled at their mockery, which knew no law. Many among the youth of the cold lands heard him, and many feigned to follow his teachings, and a few did follow them and lived strange lives.

Then a night came when the first flakes of snow were falling, and on that night the god Isid Iooo IoooE drew him up as the puppeteer lifts his doll. A few friends were in the lee of a wood with him, and it seemed to them that there came a sudden flurry of snow spangled with colors and Man was gone.

But it seemed to him, as he stood once more in the presence of the god Isid

Iooo IoooE, that he had waked from a long dream; his hands had their strength again, his beard was black, and his eyes had regained their clarity, though not their cunning.

"Now tell me," Isid Iooo IoooE commanded him, "all that you have seen and done," and when Man had told him, he asked, "Which of these three peoples loved you the best, and why did you love them?"

Man thought for a time, drawing the cloak Tarnung about his shoulders, for it seemed to him cold in the belly of the ship of Isid Iooo IoooE. "The people of the high, hot lands are unjust," he said. "Yet I came to love them, for there is no falsity in them. They feast their friends and flay their foes and, trusting no one, never weep that they are betrayed.

"The people of the cold lands are just, and yet I came to love them also, though that was much harder.

"The people of the steaming lands are innocent of justice and injustice alike. They follow their hearts, and while I dwelt among them I followed mine and loved them best of all."

"You yet have much to learn, Man," said the god Isid Iooo IoooE. "For the people of the cold lands are much the nearest to me. Do you not understand that in time the steaming lands, and all of the Land of Zed, must fall to one of its great peoples or the other?"

Then while Man watched through his eyes, certain good men in the cold lands died, which men called lightning. Certain evil men died also, and men spoke of disease. Dreams came to women and fancies to children; rain and wind and sun were no longer what they had been; and when the children were grown, the people of the cold lands went down into the steaming lands and built houses there, and taking no slaves drove the people of the steaming lands behind certain fences and walls, where they sat in the dust until they died.

"In the high, hot lands," commented Man, "the people of the steaming lands would have suffered much. Many of them I had, toiling under the whip to build my walls. Yet they sang when they could, and ran when they could, and stole my food when they could not. And some of them grew fat on it."

And the god Isid Iooo IoooE answered, "It is better that a man should die than that he should be a slave."

"Even so," Man replied, "you yourself have said it." And drawing Maser he smote the god, and Isid Iooo IoooE perished in smoke and blue fire.

Whether Man perished also, who can say? It is long since Man was seen in the Land of Zed, but then he was ever wont to vanish when the mood took him. Of the lost citadel in the mountains, overgrown with roses, who shall say who guards it? Of the little poisoned arrows, slaying in the twilight, who shall say who sends them? Of the rain-washed roads, wandering among forgotten towns, who shall say whose tracks are there?

But it may be that all these things now are passed, for they are things of long ago, when the Universe was old and there were more gods.

## AFTERWORD

This is a story about which I cannot say anything of real substance. On its first publication, the word *maser* was changed by the proof-reader (I was told, at least, that it was by the proofreader) to *master*. Not all the time, only sometimes. The stories of other writers have suffered worse things, but when I read this one (or simply think about it) I can focus on nothing else. Most of you will already know what a maser is: a microwave amplifier.

Let us say you have this microwave, one that will scarcely hold a sixteen-inch frozen pizza. With a maser, you could make it a great big house-sized thing you might induce a proofreader to walk into. . . .

Oh, never mind!

# ON THE TRAIN

When I look out the window, the earth seems to have become liquid, rushing to flow over a falls that is always just behind the last car. Wherever that may be. The telephone poles reel like drunks, losing their footing. The mountains, white islands in the fluid landscape, track us for miles, the hills breaking to snow on their beaches.

The entire universe can be contained in three questions, of which the first two are: How long is the train? And from what station does it originate?

I do not remember boarding, although my mother, who was here in the compartment with us until a moment ago, told me she recalled it very well. I was helped on by a certain doctor, she said. I would go up and down the cars looking for him (and her), but one cannot thus look for a doctor without arousing the anxiety of the other passengers or exciting their suspicions. Certainly, however, I did not get on at the station of origin; my mother told me that she herself had already been riding for over thirty years.

The porter's name is Flip; he was once my dog, a smooth fox terrier. Now he makes our berths and brings coffee and knows more about the train than any of us. He can answer all the unimportant questions, although his answers are so polite it is hard to tell sometimes just what he means. My wife and I (all the children we helped aboard have gone to other cars) would like to make him sit with us. But he threatens to call his uncle, the Dawn Guard.

I have formed several conjectures concerning the length of the train. It is surely either very long or very short, since when it goes around a curve (which it seldom does) I cannot see the engine. Possibly it is infinite—but it may be of a closed as well as an open infinity. If the track were extended ever westward, forming a Great Circle, and all that track were filled with cars, would not the spinning earth rush past them endlessly? That is precisely what I see from the window. On the other hand, if straight trackage were laid (and most of it does seem to be straight) it would extend forever among the stars. I see that too. Perhaps I do not see the engine because the engine is behind us.

At every moment it seems that we are stopping, but we continue and even pick up speed. The mountains crowd closer, as if to ram us by night. I lie in my berth listening to the conductor (so called because he was struck by lightning once) come down the car checking our tickets in the dark.

∞

## AFTERWORD

Back before the deluge, Rosemary and I rode Amtrak to Seattle and back—northern route out, southern route back. Between meals, I busied myself by sitting high up in the observation car and writing a bunch of short-short stories. When I got home, I asked my agent to send them all to *The New Yorker*. To my pleased surprise, this one was accepted.

Flip was the ruffian clown who woke Little Nemo from his wonderful dreams, in one of the finest Sunday comics ever. My father gave Flip's name to the fox terrier we owned when I was very small: Flip's barking always woke my father up.

There was no reason for you to care, to be sure, but for both you readers who have stuck with this until now— The earliest memory I have of my mother is that of a lovely young woman bending over me as I lie abed on the seat of a railway car. Her eyes are blue. She wears a gray cloche; from under it peeps a stray lock of auburn hair. Would the year be 1934? I can't say for certain, but about that. Now I must stop, lest the afterword grow longer than the story.

# From the Desk of Gilmer C. Merton

Dear Miss Morgan:

No, you don't know me or anything about me—I got your name from Literary Marketplace. My own name is Gilmer C. Merton, and I'm a writer. I say that I am one, even though I haven't sold anything yet, because I know I am. I have written a sci-fi novel, of which I enclose the first chapter and an outline of the remainder (is that a dirty word?) of the book.

Please understand me, Miss Morgan: I have written the whole book, *and can send you complete ms. as soon as you ask for it. Will you represent me?*

Sincerely yours,
Gilmer C. Merton

Dear Mr. Merton:

Please send the rest of Star Shuttle. *Enclose $10.00 (no stamps) to cover postage and handling.*

Yours truly,
Georgia Morgan

Dear Miss Morgan:

Enclosed please find the remainder of my book, Star Shuttle, *and a Postal Money Order for ten dollars. I hope you enjoy it.*

You can have no idea how delighted I am that you are sufficiently interested in my book to wish to read the rest. I know something of your reputation now, having asked the Chief Assistant Librarian here in No. Velo City. It would be wonderful to have you for my agent.

Sincerely,
Gilmer C. Merton

Dear Mr. Merton,

I will definitely handle Star Shuttle. *When you sign and return the enclosed letter of agreement (I have already signed; please retain the* last *copy for your files), you will be a client of the GEORGIA MORGAN LITERARY*

AGENCY. Note that we do not handle short fiction, articles, or verse (Par. C.). I would, however, like to see any other book-length manuscripts, including non-fiction.

Cordially,
Georgia Morgan

P.S. Don't say sci-fi. That is an obscenity. Say SF.

Dear Miss Morgan:

Let me repeat again how much I appreciate your taking on my book. However, I wish you had told me where you intend to market it. Is that possible?

Your letter of agreement (top three copies) is enclosed, signed and dated as you asked. Let me repeat how happy I am to be your client.

Sincerely,
Gilmer C. Merton

Dear Gil,

I sent your Star Shuttle to the best editor I know, my great and good friend Saul Hearwell at Cheap Drugstore Paperbacks, Inc. Now I am happy to report that Saul offers an advance of $4300.00 against CDPI's standard contract. I discussed the advance with him over lunch at Elaine's (not to worry, Saul paid), but he says CDPI's present financial position, though not critical, is somewhat weak and he is not authorized to offer more than the standard advance. (Actually, that is four thou; I got him up three hundred.) I could be wrong, Gil, but with a first novel, I don't think you will get a better offer than this anyplace, market conditions being as they are. The "standard" contract is enclosed, as slightly altered by yrs. trly. (Note that I was able to hold on to 30 percent of video game rights.) I advise you to sign it and return all copies to me soonest.

Cordially,
Georgia

P.S. You will receive half the advance on signing.

Dear Georgia,

I have signed and dated all copies of the contract for my book. They are enclosed. Good job!

You will be happy to note that I have borrowed enough on my signature to trade in my old Underwood for a used word processor. (These are used words, ha, ha!) Interest is 18 percent, but there is no penalty for early payment, and when I get the $2,150 it will be easy enough to pay off the rest of the loan, and I understand that Hijo and several other horror-genre shockers were written on this machine before Steven E. Presley's untimely death. With the help of this superb *machine (as soon as I learn to run the damn thing) I hope to make much faster progress on a new book,* Galaxy Shuttle.

> Sincerely,
> Gil Merton

Dear Gil,

    *This is going to come as something of a shock to you, but I have just had a long phone conversation with Saul Hearwell, during which we discussed what Saul insists on referring to as "your problem." Meaning yours, Gil, not mine, though you are my problem too, of course, or rather your problems are my problems.*

    Star Shuttle *is bylined "Gilmer C. Merton," and Saul does not consider that catchy enough. Of course, I suggested "Gil Merton" right away. Saul feels that is an improvement, but not a big enough one. (Am I making myself clear?) Anyway, Saul would like to see you adopt a zippier pen name, something along the lines of Berry Longear or Oar Scottson Curd. Whatever you like, but please, not Robert A. anything. (Gil Donadil might be nice???) The choice is yours, to be sure, but let me know soonest so I can get back to Saul.*

> Cordially,
> Georgia

*P.S. I rather hate to bring up this delicate matter, Gil, but you will get $1835.00 and not the $2150.00 you mention. In other words, my commission will be taken out. And don't forget you'll have to pay taxes on the residue.*

Dear Georgia,

    *This is a wonderful contraption, but Steven Presley seems to have programmed it with some odd subroutines. I'll tell you in detail when I've figured out what all of them are.*

    *The new byline I've chosen is Gilray Gunn. What do you think of it? If you like it, please pass it along to Mr. Hearwell.*

    *I had assumed I paid you your commissions. Rereading our letter of agreement, I see that you receive all payments and deduct your part before passing mine on to me. I see the sense of that—it saves me from writing a check and so forth.*

> Sincerely,
> Gil Merton
> (Wolf Moon)

Dear Gil,

    *Good news! Saul likes your new byline, and I've already got a nibble from Honduras on* Star Shuttle. *Rejoice! When will I be seeing* Galaxy Shuttle?

> Cordially,
> Georgia

Dear Miss Morgan:

Thank you for your recent communication. I have altered the title of Galaxy Shuttle to Come, Dark Lust. It is to be bylined Wolf Moon, as I have indicated on the enclosed ms. See to it.

I require the half advance now due on Star Shuttle *immediately*. North Velo Light & Power Co. is threatening to shut off my service.

Wolf Moon
(Gilmer C. Merton)

Dear Gil,

Saul assures me you will get your money as soon as everything clears CDPI's Accounting Department. Have patience.

Now—the most stupendous news I've passed along to one of my "stable" in many a year! Saul was absolutely bowled over by Come, Dark Lust! He plans sym. hc., trade, and mass market editions. He's trying to get an advertising budget! He's talking an advance of $9,000, which is practically a signal that he's willing to go to $10,000.

Gil, I trust you're working on a sequel already (Come Again, Dark Lust???), but meanwhile do you have any short stories or whatever kicking around? Particularly anything along the lines of your fabulous CDL? I'd love to see them.

Fondly,
Georgia

Dear Miss Morgan:

I have legally changed my name to Wolf Moon. Gilmer C. Merton is dead. (See the enclosed clipping from the No. Velo City Morning Advertiser.) In the future, please address me as "Mr. Moon" or, in moments of extreme camaraderie, "Wolf."

I require the monies due me IMMEDIATELY.

Wolf Moon

Dear Wolf,

Saul assures me that your check is probably in the mail by this time.

The obit on Gilmer C. Merton was interesting, but didn't you have to give the paper some disinformation to get it printed? I hope you haven't got yourself into trouble.

The 10:00 news last night carried about a minute and a half on the mysterious goings-on around No. Velo City. Have you thought of looking into them? They would seem to be right up your alley, and it is entirely possible you might get a nonfiction book out of them as well as a new novel. (But that poor guy from the electric company—ugh!)

Since your name is now legally Wolf Moon, it would be well for us to execute a new agency agreement. I enclose it. All terms as before.

Very fondly,
Georgia

*Dear Georgia,*

*I was sorry to hear of the unfortunate accident that befell Mr. Hearwell's wife and children. Please extend my sympathy.*

*While you're doing it, you might mention my check, which has yet to arrive. If you could contrive to drop the words* disembodied claws *into your conversation, I believe you might find they work wonders.*

*Now a very small matter, Georgia—a whim of mine, if you will. (We writers are entitled to an occasional whim, after all, and as soon as you have complied with this one of mine I will Air Express you the ms. of my latest,* The Shrieking in the Nursery.*) I have found that I work best when everything surrounding a new book corresponds to the mood. I am returning all four copies of our new letter of agreement. Can I, dear Georgia, persuade you to send me a fresh set signed in your blood?*

*Very sincerely,*
*Wolf*

∞

## AFTERWORD

This is my editor's favorite. For the sake of such attorneys as he may employ, I desire to state now, and categorically, that there is no connection whatsoever between editor David G. Hartwell and "Saul Hearwell."

None!

My agent, who was still very much alive when this was written, was Virginia Kidd. "Georgia Morgan" is only a slight exaggeration. I have no idea whether Virginia liked this story, but I liked her a lot. I miss her terribly, and in that I have a whole bunch of company—including, I believe, David G. Hartwell.

# DEATH OF THE ISLAND DOCTOR

∞

This story took place in the same university I mentioned in the Introduction to *Gene Wolfe's Book of Days*.

At this university, there was once a retired professor, a Dr. Insula, who was a little cracked on the subject of islands, doubtless because of his name. This Dr. Insula had been out to pasture for so long that no one could remember anymore what department he had once headed. The Department of Literature said it had been History, and the Department of History said Literature. Dr. Insula himself said that in his time they had been the same department, but all the other professors knew that could not be true.

One crisp fall morning, this Dr. Insula came to the chancellor's office—to the immense surprise of the chancellor—and announced that he wished to teach a seminar. He was tired, he said, of rusticating; a small seminar that met once a week would be no trouble, and he felt that in return for the pension he had drawn for so many years he should do something to take a bit of the load off the younger men.

The chancellor was in a quandary, as you may well imagine. As a way of gaining time, he said, "Very good! Oh, yes, very good indeed, Doctor! Noble, if I may resort to that rather old-fashioned word, and fully in keeping with that noble spirit of self-sacrifice and—ah—noblesse oblige we have always sought to foster among our tenured faculty. And may I ask just what the subject of your seminar will be?"

"Islands," Dr. Insula announced firmly.

"Yes, of course. Certainly. Islands?"

"I may also decide to include isles, atolls, islets, holms, eyots, archipelagoes, and some of the larger reefs," Dr. Insula confided, as one friend to another. "It depends on how they come along, you know. But definitely not peninsulas."

"I see . . . ," said the chancellor. And he thought to himself, *If I refuse the poor*

*old boy, I'll hurt him dreadfully. But if I agree and list his seminar as Not for Credit,
no one will register and no harm will be done.*

Thus it was done, and for six years every catalog carried a listing for Dr. Insula's seminar on islands, without credit, and in six years no one registered for it.

Now as it happened, the registrar was a woman approaching retirement age,
and after registration, for twelve regular semesters and six summer semesters, Dr.
Insula came to her to ask whether anyone had registered for his seminar. And there
came a time, not in fall but rather in that dreary tag end of summer when it is ninety
degrees on the sidewalk and the stores have Halloween cards and the first subtly
threatening Christmas ornaments are on display, when she could bear it no longer.

She was bending over her desk making up the new catalog (which would be
that last one she would ever do), and though the air-conditioning was supposedly
set at seventy-eight, it was *at least* eighty-five in her office. A wisp of her own gray
hair kept falling over her eyes, and the buzz of the electric fan she had bought herself, with her own money, kept reminding her of her girlhood and of sleeping on
the screened porch in Atlanta when Mommy and Daddy took her to visit relatives.

And at this critical moment, the hundredth, perhaps, in a long line of critical
moments, she came to the section labeled "Miscellaneous" at the very end of the
catalog proper, just before the dishonest little biographies of the faculty. And
there was Dr. Insula's NO CREDIT seminar on islands.

A certain madness seized her. *Why, mistakes happen all the time,* she thought
to herself. *Why, only last year, the printer changed that lab of Dr. Ettelmann's to
Monday, Grunday, and Friday. Besides, NO CREDIT can't possibly be right. Who
would take a No-credit seminar on islands? Anyway, they really ought to run the air-
conditioning if they want us to work efficiently.*

Almost before she knew it, her pencil had made a short, sharp, vertical line in
the Credit Hours column, and she felt a great deal cooler.

So it was that *that year* when Dr. Insula came to inquire she was able to tell
him, with some satisfaction, that two students—a young man and a young
woman, as she said, judging from their names, as she said—had in fact enrolled in
his seminar.

And when the young man, and later the young woman, came to the Registrar's Office to ask just where the Friday afternoon seminar on islands was to be
held and one of her subregistrars (who naturally did not know) brought them to
see her, she was able to explain—twice and with almost equal satisfaction—
where it would be. For the good old custom of holding undergraduate seminars
in faculty living rooms had fallen so much out of use at the university that Dr. Insula himself and the old registrar were almost the only people who recalled it.

Thus it came to be, on a certain September afternoon when the leaves were just
beginning to change from green to brown and red-gold, that the young man and
the young woman walked up Dr. Insula's gritty and rather overgrown walk, and
up Dr. Insula's cracked stone steps, and across Dr. Insula's shadowy, creaking
porch, to knock at Dr. Insula's water-spotted oak door.

He opened it for them and showed them into a living room that might almost have been called a parlor, so full it was of the smell of dust, and mementos of times gone by, and stiff furniture, and old books. There he seated them in two of the stiff chairs and brought out coffee (which he called java) for the young man and himself, and tea for the young woman. "We used to call this Ceylon tea," he said. "Now it is Sri Lanka tea, I suppose. The Greeks called it Taprobane, and the Arabs Serendib."

The young man and woman nodded politely, not quite sure what he meant.

There was Scotch shortbread too, and he reminded them that Scotland is only the northern end of the island of Great Britain, and that Scotland itself embraces three famous island groups, the Shetlands, the Orkneys, and the Hebrides. He quoted Thomson to them:

> Or where the Northern Ocean, in vast whirls,
> Boils round the naked melancholy isles
> Of farthest Thule, and the Atlantic surge
> Pours in among the stormy Hebrides.

Then he asked the young man if he knew where Thule was.

"It's where Prince Valiant comes from in the comic strip, I think," the young man said. "But not a real place."

Dr. Insula shook his head. "It is Iceland." He turned to the young woman. "Prince Valiant is supposed to be a peer of Arthur's realm, I believe. You will recall that Arthur was interred on the island of Avalon. Can you tell me, please, where that is?"

"It is a mythical island west of Ireland," the young woman said, that being what they had taught her in school.

"No, it is in Somerset. It was there that his coffin was found, in 1191, inscribed: *Hic jacet Arthurus Rex, quondam Rex que futuris.* Avalon was also the last known resting place of the Holy Grail."

The young man said, "I don't think that's true history, Dr. Insula."

"Why it's not accepted history, I suppose. Tell me, do you know who wrote *True History?*"

"No one writes true history," the young man said, that being what they had taught him in school. "All history is subjective, reflecting the perceptions and unacknowledged prejudices of the historian." After his weak answer about Prince Valiant, he was quite proud of that one.

"Why, then my history is as good as accepted history. And since there really was a King Arthur—he is mentioned in contemporary chronicles—surely it's more than probable that he was buried in Somerset than in some nonexistent place? But *True History* was written by Lucian of Samosata."

He told them of Lucian's travels to Antioch, Greece, Italy, and Gaul, and this led him to speak of the ships of that time and the danger of storms and piracy, and the enchantment of the Greek isles. He told them of Apollo's birth on Delos; of

Patmos, where Saint John beheld the Apocalypse; and of Phraxos, where the sorcerer Conchis dwelt. He said, " 'To cleave that sea in the gentle autumnal season, murmuring the name of each islet, is to my mind the joy most apt to transport the heart of man to paradise.' " But because it did not rhyme, the young man and the young woman did not know that he was quoting a famous tale.

At last he said, "But why is it that people at all times and in all places have considered islands unique and uniquely magical? Can either of you tell me that?"

Both shook their heads.

"Very well then. One of you has a small boat, I believe."

"I do," the young man said. "It's an aluminum canoe—you probably saw it on top of my Toyota."

"Good. You would have no objection to taking your fellow student as a passenger? I have a homework assignment for both of you. You must go to a certain isle I shall tell you of, and when we next meet describe to me what you find magical there." And he told them how to go down certain roads to certain others until they came to one that was unpaved and had the river for its end, and how from that place they would see the island.

"When we meet again," he said, "I shall reveal to you the true locations of Atlantis, of High Brasail, and of Utopia." And he quoted these lines:

> Our fabled shores none ever reach,
> No mariner has found our beach,
> Scarcely our mirage is seen,
> And neighbouring waves of floating green,
> Yet still the oldest charts contain
> Some dotted outline of our main.

"Okay," the young man said, and he got up and went out.

Dr. Insula rose too, to show the young woman to the door, but he looked so ill that she asked if he were all right. "I am as all right as it is possible for an old man to be," he told her. "My dear, could you bear one last quotation?" And when she nodded, he whispered:

> The deep
> Moans round with many voices. Come, my friends,
> 'Tis not too late to seek a newer world.
> Push off, and sitting well in order smite
> The sounding furrows, for my purpose holds
> To sail beyond the sunset, and the baths
> Of all the western stars, until I die.
> It may be that the gulfs will wash us down;
> It may be we shall touch the Happy Isles,
> And see the great Achilles, whom we knew.

The young man and the young woman stopped at a delicatessen and bought sandwiches that the young woman paid for, she saying that because the young man was driving, her self-respect (she was careful not to say *honor*) demanded it. They also bought a six-pack of beer that the young man paid for, he saying that his own self-respect demanded it (he too was careful not to say *honor*) because she had paid for the sandwiches.

Then they followed the directions Dr. Insula had given them and so came to a sandy riverbank, where they lifted the aluminum canoe from the Toyota and set sail for the little pine-covered island a hundred yards or so downstream.

There they explored the whole place and threw stones into the water, and sat listening to the wind tell of old things among the boughs of the largest pine.

And when they had cooled the beer in the leaf-brown river, and eaten the sandwiches they had brought, they paddled back to the spot where they had parked the Toyota, debating how they could tell Dr. Insula he had been mistaken about the island when they came next week—how they could tell him there was no magic there.

But when the next week came (as the next week always does) and they stood on the shadowed, creaking porch and knocked at the water-spotted oak door, an old woman crossed the street to tell them it was no use to knock.

"He passed on a week ago yesterday," she said. "It was such a shame. He'd come out to talk to me that morning, and he was so happy because he was going to meet with his students the next day. He must have gone into his garage after that; that was where they found him."

"Sitting in his boat," the young woman said.

The old woman nodded. "Why, yes. I suppose you must have heard about it."

The young man and the young woman looked at each other then, and thanked her, and walked away. Afterward they talked about it sometimes and thought about it often, but it was not until much later (when it was time for the long, long vacation that stretches from the week before Christmas to the beginning of the new semester in January and they would have to separate for nearly a month) that they discovered Dr. Insula had not been mistaken about the island after all.

∽

### AFTERWORD

I love this story. In truth, I like all the stories in this book (although not all the stories I have written), but this is a special favorite. Not because it ended the cycle I began with "The Island of Doctor Death and Other Stories," but because it so resolutely refuses to be like other stories. It is its own wistful self, always, weeping as it smiles. I hope you love it, too.

# Redbeard

It doesn't matter how Howie and I became friends, except that our friendship was unusual. I'm one of those people who've moved into the area since . . . Since what? I don't know; someday I'll have to ask Howie. Since the end of the sixties or the Truman Administration or the Second World War. Since something.

Anyway, after Mara and I came with our little boy, John, we grew conscious of an older stratum. They are the people who were living here before. Howie is one of them; his grandparents are buried in the little family cemeteries that are or used to be attached to farms—all within twenty miles of my desk. Those people are still here, practically all of them, like the old trees that stand among the new houses.

By and large we don't mix much. We're only dimly aware of them, and perhaps they're only dimly aware of us. Our friends are new people too, and on Sunday mornings we cut the grass together. Their friends are the children of their parents' friends, and their own uncles and cousins; on Sunday mornings they go to the old clapboard churches.

Howie was the exception, as I said. We were driving down U.S. 27—or rather, Howie was driving and I was sitting beside him smoking a cigar and having a look around. I saw a gate that was falling down, with a light that was leaning way over, and beyond it just glimpsed, a big, old, tumbledown wooden house with young trees sprouting in the front yard. It must have had about ten acres of ground, but there was a boarded-up fried-chicken franchise on one side of it and a service station on the other.

"That's Redbeard's place," Howie told me.

I thought it was a family name, perhaps an anglicization of Barbarossa. I said, "It looks like a haunted house."

"It is," Howie said. "For me, anyway. I can't go in there."

We hit a chuckhole, and I looked over at him.

"I tried a couple times. Soon as I set my foot on that step, something says, 'This is as far as you go, buster,' and I turn around and head home."

After a while I asked him who Redbeard was.

"This used to be just a country road," Howie said. "They made it a Federal Highway back about the time I was born, and it got a lot of cars and trucks and stuff on it. Now the Interstate's come through, and it's going back to about what it was.

"Back before, a man name of Jackson used to live there. I don't think anybody thought he was much different, except he didn't get married till he was forty or so. But then, a lot of people around here used to do that. He married a girl named Sarah Sutter."

I nodded, just to show Howie I was listening.

"She was a whole lot younger than him, nineteen or twenty. But she loved him—that's what I always heard. Probably he was good to her, and so on. Gentle. You know?"

I said a lot of young women like that preferred older men.

"I guess. You know where Clinton is? Little place about fifteen miles over. There had been a certain amount of trouble around Clinton going on for years, and people were concerned about it. I don't believe I said this Jackson was from Clinton, but he was. His dad had run a store there and had a farm. The one brother got the farm and the next oldest the store. This Jackson, he just got some money, but it was enough for him to come here and buy that place. It was about a hundred acres then.

"Anyhow, they caught him over in Clinton. One of those chancy things. It was winter, and dark already, and there'd been a little accident where a car hit a school bus that still had quite a few kids riding home. Nobody was killed as far as I heard or even hurt bad, but a few must have had bloody noses and so forth, and you couldn't get by on the road. Just after the deputy's car got there this Jackson pulled up, and the deputy told him to load some of the kids in the back and take them to the doctor's.

"Jackson said he wouldn't, he had to get back home. The deputy told him not to be a damned fool. The kids were hurt and he'd have to go back to Clinton anyhow to get onto Mill Road, because it would be half the night before they got that bus moved.

"Jackson still wouldn't do it, and went to try and turn his pickup around. From the way he acted, the deputy figured there was something wrong. He shined his flash in the back, and there was something under a tarp there. When he saw that, he hollered for Jackson to stop and went over and jerked the tarp away. From what I hear, now he couldn't do that because of not having a warrant and if he did, Jackson would have got off. Back then, nobody had heard of such foolishness. He jerked that tarp away, and there was a girl underneath, and she was dead. I don't even know what her name was. Rosa or something like that, I guess. They were Italians that had come just a couple of years before." Howie didn't give *Ital-*

*ians* a long *I*, but there had been a trifling pause while he remembered not to. "Her dad had a little shoe place," he said. "The family was there for years after.

"Jackson was arrested, and they took him up to the county seat. I don't know if he told them anything or not. I think he didn't. His wife came up to see him, and then a day or so later the sheriff came to the house with a search warrant. He went all through it, and when he got to going through the cellars one of the doors was locked. He asked her for the key, but she said she didn't have it. He said he'd have to bust down the door, and asked her what was in there. She said she didn't know, and after a while it all came out—I mean, all as far as her understanding went.

"She told him that door had been shut ever since she and Jackson had been married. He'd told her he felt a man was entitled to some privacy, and that right there was his private place, and if she wanted a private place of her own she could have it, but to stay out of his. She'd taken one of the upstairs bedrooms and made it her sewing room.

"Nowadays they just make a basement and put everything on top, but these old houses have cellars with walls and rooms, just like upstairs. The reason is that they didn't have the steel beams we use to hold everything up, so they had to build masonry walls underneath; if you built a couple of these, why, you had four rooms. The foundations of all these old houses are stone."

I nodded again.

"This one room had a big, heavy door. The sheriff tried to knock it down, but he couldn't. Finally he had to telephone around and get a bunch of men to help him. They found three girls in there."

"Dead?" I asked Howie.

"That's right. I don't know what kind of shape they were in, but not very good, I guess. One had been gone over a year. That's what I heard."

As soon as I said it, I felt like a half-wit, but I was thinking of all the others, of John Gacy and Jack the Ripper and the dead black children of Atlanta, and I said, "Three? That was all he killed?"

"Four," Howie told me, "counting the Italian girl in the truck. Most people thought it was enough. Only there was some others missing too, you know, in various places around the state, so the sheriff and some deputies tore everything up looking for more bodies. Dug in the yard and out in the fields and so on."

"But they didn't find any more?"

"No, they didn't. Not then," Howie said. "Meantime, Jackson was in jail like I told you. He had kind of reddish hair, so the paper called him Redbeard. Because of Bluebeard, you know, and him not wanting his wife to look inside that cellar room. They called the house Redbeard's Castle.

"They did things a whole lot quicker in those times, and it wasn't much more than a month before he was tried. Naturally, his wife had to get up on the stand."

I said, "A wife can't be forced to testify against her husband."

"She wasn't testifying against him; she was testifying for him. What a good man he was, and all that. Who else would do it? Of course when she'd had her say, the district attorney got to go to work on her. You know how they do.

"He asked her about that room and she told him just about what I told you. Jackson, he said he wanted a place for himself and told her not to go in there. She said she hadn't even known the door was locked till the sheriff tried to open it. Then the district attorney said, 'Didn't you know he was asking for your help, that your husband was asking for your help, that the whole room there was a cry for help, and he wanted you to go in there and find those bodies so he wouldn't have to kill again?' "

Howie fell silent for a mile or two. I tossed the butt of my cigar out the window and sat wondering if I would hear any more about those old and only too commonplace murders.

When Howie began talking again, it was as though he had never stopped. "That was the first time anybody from around here had heard that kind of talk, I think. Up till then, I guess everybody thought if a man wanted to get caught he'd just go to the police and say he did it. I always felt sorry for her, because of that. She was—I don't know—like an owl in daylight. You know what I mean?"

I didn't, and I told him so.

"The way she'd been raised, a man meant what he said. Then too, the man was the boss. Today when they get married there isn't hardly a woman that promises to obey, but back then they all did it. If they'd asked the minister to leave that out, most likely he'd have told them he wouldn't perform the ceremony. Now the rules were all changed, only nobody'd told her that.

"I believe she took it pretty hard, and of course it didn't do any good, her getting on the stand or the district attorney talking like that to her either. The jury came back in about as quick as they'd gone out, and they said he was guilty, and the judge said sentencing would be next day. He was going to hang him, and everybody knew it. They hanged them back then."

"Sure," I said.

"That next morning his wife came to see him in the jail. I guess he knew she would, because he asked the old man that swept out to lend him a razor and so forth. Said he wanted to look good. He shaved and then he waited till he heard her step."

Howie paused to let me comment or ask a question. I thought I knew what was coming, and there didn't seem to be much point in saying anything.

"When he heard her coming, he cut his throat with the razor blade. The old man was with her, and he told the paper about it afterward. He said they came up in front of the cell and Jackson was standing there with blood all running down his shirt. He really was Redbeard for true then. After a little bit, his knees gave out and he fell down in a heap.

"His wife tried to sell the farm, but nobody wanted that house. She moved back with her folks, quit calling herself Sarah Jackson. She was a good-looking woman, and the land brought her some money. After a year or so she got married again and had a baby. Everybody forgot, I suppose you could say, except maybe for the families of the girls that had died. And the house, it's still standing back there. You just saw it yourself."

Howie pronounced the final words as though the story were over and he wanted to talk of something else, but I said, "You said there were more bodies found later."

"Just one. Some kids were playing in that old house. It's funny, isn't it, that kids would find it when the sheriff and all those deputies didn't."

"Where was it?"

"Upstairs. In her sewing room. You remember I told you how he'd said she could have a room to herself too? Of course, the sheriff had looked in there, but it hadn't been there when he looked. It was her, and she'd hung herself from a hook in the wall. Who do you think killed her?"

I glanced at him to see if he were serious. "I thought you said she killed herself?"

"That's what they would have said, back when she married Jackson. But who killed her now? Jackson—Redbeard—when he killed those other girls and cut his throat like that? Or was it when he loved her? Or that district attorney? Or the sheriff? Or the mothers and fathers and brothers and sisters of the girls Jackson got? Or her other husband, maybe some things he said to her? Or maybe it was just having her baby that killed her—baby blues, they call it. I've heard that too."

"Postnatal depression," I said. I shook my head. "I don't suppose it makes much difference now."

"It does to me," Howie said. "She was my mother." He pushed the lighter into the dashboard and lit a cigarette. "I thought I ought to tell you before somebody else does."

For a moment I supposed that we had left the highway and circled back along some secondary road. To our right was another ruined gate, another outdated house collapsing slowly among young trees.

## AFTERWORD

Long, long ago, when Rosemary and I were still a young couple with small children, we moved to a tiny town out in the country. If I remember right, the population was under three hundred. Everyone in town—except for us—knew everyone else. Half the time, they'd gone to kindergarten together. More than half the time, they were at least distantly related. Rosemary and I were outsiders, and very much so. It was much lonelier than an isolated house would have been, and lonelier too than any city apartment.

Often I drove past a big white house in which no one lived. Most of its windows were broken; one shutter hung from a single hinge. The yard was full of weeds. I never found out why the house had been abandoned or who had abandoned it, but it has come to haunt my fiction.

# The Boy Who Hooked the Sun

On the eighth day a boy cast his line into the sea. The sun of the eighth day was just rising, making a road of gold that ran from its own broad, blank face all the way to the wild coastline of Atlantis, where the boy sat upon a jutting emerald; the sun was much younger then and not nearly so wise to the ways of men as it is now. It took the bait.

The boy jerked his pole to set the hook, and grinned, and spit into the sea while he let the line run out. He was not such a boy as you or I have ever seen, for there was a touch of emerald in his hair and there were flakes of sun-gold in his eyes. His skin was sun browned, and his fingernails were small and short and a little dirty, so he was just such a boy as lives down the street from us both. Years ago the boy's father had sailed away to trade the shining stones of Atlantis for the wine and ram skins of the wild barbarians of Hellas, leaving the boy and his mother very poor.

All day the sun thrashed and rolled and leaped about. Sometimes it sounded, plunging all the Earth into night, and sometimes it leaped high into the sky, throwing up sprays of stars. Sometimes it feigned to be dead, and sometimes it tried to wrap his line around the moon to break it. And the boy let it tire itself, sometimes reeling in and sometimes letting out more line; but through it all he kept a tight grip on his pole.

The richest man in the village, the moneylender, who owned the house where the boy and his mother lived, came to him, saying, "You must cut your line, boy, and let the sun go. When it runs out, it brings winter and withers all the blossoms in my orchard. When you reel it in, it brings droughty August to dry all the canals that water my barley fields. Cut your line!"

But the boy only laughed at him and pelted him with the shining stones of Atlantis, and at last the richest man in the village went away.

Then the strongest man in the village, the smith, who could meet the charge of a wild ox and wrestle it to the ground, came to the boy, saying, "Cut your line, boy, or I'll break your neck," for the richest man had paid him to do it.

But the boy only laughed at him and pelted him with the shining stones of Atlantis, and when the strongest man in the village seized him by the neck, he seized the strongest man in return and threw him into the sea, for the power of the sun had run down the boy's line and entered into him.

Then the cleverest man in the village, the mayor, who could charm a rabbit into his kitchen—and many a terrified rabbit, and many a pheasant and partridge too, had fluttered and trembled there, when the door shut behind it and it saw the knives—came to the boy saying, "Cut your line, my boy, and come with me! Henceforth, you and I are to rule in Atlantis. I've been conferring with the mayors of all the other villages; we have decided to form an empire, and you—none other!—are to be our king."

But the boy only laughed at him and pelted him with the shining stones of Atlantis, saying, "Oh, really? A king. Who is to be emperor?" And after the cleverest man in the village had talked a great deal more, he went away.

Then the magic woman from the hills, the sorceress, who knew every future save her own, came to the boy, saying, "Little boy, you must cut your line. Sabaoth sweats and trembles in his shrine and will no longer accept my offerings; the feet of Sith, called by the ignorant Kronos son of Uranus, have broken; and the magic bird Tchataka has flown. The stars riot in the heavens, so that at one moment humankind is to rule them all, and at the next is to perish. Cut your line!"

But the boy only laughed at her and pelted her with the shining stones of Atlantis, with agates and alexanderites, moonstones and onyxes, rubies, sardonyxes, and sapphires, and at last the magic woman from the hills went away muttering.

Then the most foolish man in the village, the idiot, who sang songs without words to all the brooks and boasted of bedding the white birch on the hill, came to the boy and tried to say how frightened he was to see the sun fighting the line in the sky; though he could not find the words.

But the boy only smiled and let him touch the pole, and after a time he too went away.

And at last the boy's mother came, saying, "Remember all the fine stories I have told you through the years? Never have I told you the finest of all. Come now to the house the richest man in the village has given back to us. Put on your crown and tell your general to stand guard; take up the magic feather of the bird Tchataka, who opens its mouth to the sky and drinks wisdom with the dew. Then we shall dip the feather in the blood of a wild ox and write that story on white birch bark, you and I."

The boy asked, "What is that story, Mother?"

And his mother answered, "It is called 'The Boy Who Hooked the Sun.' Now cut your line and promise me you will never fish for the sun again, so long as we both shall live."

*Ah,* thought the boy, as he got out his little knife. *I love my mother, who is more beautiful than the white birch tree and always kind. But do not all the souls wear away at last as they circle on the Wheel? Then the time must come when I live and she does not, and when that time comes, surely I will bait my hook again with the shining stones of Uranus and we shall rule the stars. Or not.*

And so it is that the sun swims far from Earth sometimes, thinking of its sore mouth, and we have winter. But now, when the days are very short and we see the boy's line stretched across the sky and powdered with hoarfrost, the sun recalls Earth and her clever and foolish men and kind and magical women, and then it returns to us.

Or perhaps it is only—as some say—that it remembers the taste of the bait.

## AFTERWORD

Every so often I get optimistic and explain the best method of learning to write to students. I don't believe any of them has ever tried it, but I will explain it to you now. After all, you may be the exception. When I read about this method, it was attributed to Benjamin Franklin, who invented and discovered so much. Certainly I did not invent it.

But I did it, and it worked. That is more than can be said for most creative writing classes.

Find a very short story by a writer you admire. Read it over and over until you understand everything in it. Then read it over a lot more.

Here's the key part. You *must* do this. Put it away where you cannot get at it. You will have to find a way to do it that works for you. Mail the story to a friend and ask him to keep it for you, or whatever. I left the story I had studied in my desk on Friday. Having no weekend access to the building in which I worked, I could not get to it until Monday morning.

When you cannot see it again, write it yourself. You know who the characters are. You know what happens. You write it. Make it as good as you can.

Compare your story to the original, when you have access to the original again. Is your version longer? Shorter? Why? Read both versions out loud. There will be places where you had trouble. Now you can see how the author handled those problems.

If you want to learn to write fiction, and are among those rare people willing to work at it, you might want to use the little story you have just finished as one of your models. It's about the right length.

# PARKROADS—A REVIEW

～

One hardly knows what to say about *Parkroads*. Released in 1939 and 1984, it violates many of the canons of cinematography and must be considered a failure. Yet it is impossible to understand this remarkable film without an enlightened awareness of its many inexplicable experiments.

Strictly speaking, it is without opening credits. Instead the credits, such as they are, continue throughout all six (possibly seven) reels, spoken by the cast at pseudoappropriate moments. For example, as Tanya (or Daisy) reclines beside Belvedere Lake, her face concealed by an immense straw hat, she is heard to murmur, "Choreography by . . ." Jonquils are tossed by the wind, but there is no dancing per se.

*Parkroads* is neatly divided into alternating sequences, though in a few instances an episode of one type is followed immediately by another, quite different, episode from the same sequence. The later episodes—appearing generally in the first half of the film as it has been released in the U.S.—were produced in Brooklyn in the mid-1930s, presumably between Roosevelt's election and the dissolution of the NRA. They are set in Belgium (largely in Bruges) in the early years of the closing quarter of the present century.

The earlier episodes, in which each character explains or at least attempts to explain the plot, were completed in various parts of the Low Countries several years ago. They are laid in and around New York, and the effect of traffic simulated by putting cars, trucks, buses, and subway trains aboard canal boats is at times very pleasing. The plot (and unlike so many experimental films *Parkroads* has one and is almost too concerned with it) involves a Chinese family called Chin.

Or rather, it involves a Korean-Chinese family called Park, founded when a Chin daughter weds a Korean as the Chins pass through Korea while moving eastward to the West. A letter (possibly forged) received by another family in the Chins' native village in Hunan speaks of a paradisaical "Golden-Mountain-

Land." Chin Mai and Chin Liang resolve to undertake the trip, and the rest of the family—parents, three sisters, and a grandmother—accompanies them.

They travel to Wuhan, Nanjing, and eventually Peking (Beijing). While working as scullions in the famous Sick Duck, they encounter a wily junk captain who promises to transport them to Golden-Mountain-Land in return for one of the daughters. (There is an amusing scene in which the three vie in bad cooking.) His choice falls on Pear Blossom, whom he sells to a brothel.

The remainder of the family takes ship at Tsingtao and crosses the Yellow Sea. They disembark at Inchon, believing the junk will anchor there for several days; it sails without them.

One of the remaining sisters, Cloud Fairy, is betrothed to Park Lee, a Korean. With the aid she persuades him to provide, the other Chins move on, vaguely eastward, to P'ohang and perhaps eventually to Japan. Cloud Fairy lives out the remainder of her life in the Land of Morning Calm but bequeaths to her descendants a yearning irresistible and indefectible.

Drawn by their inherited memories, they reach California but fail to identify it as Golden-Mountain-Land (if indeed it is). They continue eastward, hitching rides with disappointed Okies returning to the Dust Bowl. In New York (these are the episodes recently completed in Belgium) they are befriended by a Turk who tells them that the world is circular, being in fact the crater of a quiescent cosmic volcano, Mount Kaf, which surrounds it upon all sides. The slopes of the crater, says the Turk, are doubtless Golden-Mountain-Land, but to reach them it is necessary to walk straight through the world, whose roads have the trick of bending human steps. Frank Park nods and soon vanishes. This bald stating of its theme is perhaps the weakest element in *Parkroads*.

As already indicated, *Parkroads* has been released in six reels; they are so staged that it is by no means easy to determine the order in which they are to be shown. There is, of course, a conventional indication on the film cans for the guidance of the projectionist, but this is almost certainly incorrect. The incidents in Hunan now given in flashback may have well been intended, at least at one time, as the opening of the picture. The sequence in the public gardens of Ghent during which Doris is asked why she has embraced decadence and answers, "Directed by Henry Miller" (or perhaps Müeller), was surely intended as the last, or next to last. Publicity releases from 1939 assert that if all the reels are projected in the correct order, it will be apparent the Parks have discovered that the village in Hunan that was the original home of the Chins was in fact Golden-Mountain-Land; in short, that the paradise described in the letter was merely that of nostalgia. One hopes not.

If so, it is a problem readily amenable to mathematical treatment. Any of the six reels could be chosen as the first. Five then remain for the second, yielding thirty combinations. Four remain for the third—one hundred and twenty combinations. Three remain for the fourth, two for the fifth, and only one for the last—a total of seven hundred and twenty showings, surely not an impossible number.

However, there are references to a missing seventh reel. If such a reel exists, the number of showings is substantially increased (to five thousand and forty), and the reel must first be found. But it is probable that the veiled hints in the old press releases only mean that when the six reels are projected in the correct order someone will be inspired to produce a seventh, in which the Parks' unwearied journeying returns them to the Far East.

In the brief space allowed me, I have been unable to comment on the performances of individual cast members, but it would be unjust to close without mentioning the late William Chang, who portrayed the captain of the junk. His scenes aboard seem initially grandiose. The vessel is too large, its mast impossibly tall, its rigging unnecessarily mysterious. Then we realize we are seeing it through the Chins' eyes. The Chins themselves appear small, shabby, and awkward, Chang a demigod; eventually we realize we are seeing him and them through the junk's eyes. *Distributed by Unconscious Artists, Inc. Rated R. Two and a half stars.*

∞

## AFTERWORD

This story first appeared in a university literary magazine. To the editor's intense delight, he received plaintive requests for months afterward. People—and particularly people who taught courses having to do with film—wanted to know where they could get it.

So would I.

# Game in the Pope's Head

*A sergeant was sent to the Pope's Head to investigate the case.*
—FROM THE *LONDON TIMES'* COVERAGE OF
THE MURDER OF ANNIE CHAPMAN,
SEPTEMBER 11, 1888

Bev got up to water her plant. Edgar said, "You're overwatering that. Look how yellow, the leaves are."

They were indeed. The plant had extended its long, limp limbs over the pictures and the sofa, and out through the broken window, but the weeping flukes of these astonishing terminations were sallow and jaundiced.

"It *needs* water." Bev dumped her glass into the flowerpot, got a fresh drink, and sat down again. "My play?" She turned up a card. "The next card is 'What motion picture used the greatest number of living actors, animal or human?' "

Edgar said, "I think I know. *Gandhi.* Half a million or so."

"Wrong. Debbie?"

"Hell, I don't know. *Close Encounters of the Third Kind.*"

"Wrong. Randy?"

It was a moment before he realized that she meant him. So that was his name: Randy. Yes, of course. He said, "Animal or human?"

"Right."

"Then it's animals, because they don't get paid." He tried to think of animal movies, Bert Lahr terrified of Toto, *Lassie Come Home.* "*The Birds?*"

"Close. It was *The Swarm,* and there were twenty-two million actors."

Edgar said, "Mostly bees."

"I suppose."

There was a bee, or perhaps a wasp, on the plant, nearly invisible against a yellow leaf. It did not appear to him to be exploring the surface in the usual beeish or waspish way, but rather to be listening, head raised, to their conversation. The room was bugged. He wanted to say, *This room is bugged*, but before he could, Bev announced, "Your move, I think, Ed."

Ed said, "Bishop's pawn to the bishop's four."

Debbie threw the dice and counted eight squares along the edge of the board. "Oh, good! Park Place, and I'll buy it." She handed him her money, and he gave her the deed.

Bev said, "Your turn."

He nodded, stuffed Debbie's money into his pocket, shuffled the cards, and read the top one.

> You are Randolph Carter.
> Three times you have dreamed
> of the marvelous city, Randolph Carter,
> and three times you have been snatched away
> from the high terrace above it.

Randolph Carter nodded again and put the card down. Debbie handed him a small pewter figure, a young man in old-fashioned clothes.

Bev asked, "'Where did the fictional American philosopher Thomas Olney teach?' Ed?"

"A *fictional* philosopher? Harvard, I suppose. Is it John Updike?"

"Wrong. Debbie?"

"Pass."

"Okay. Randy?"

"London."

Outside, a cloud covered the sun. The room grew darker as the light from the broken windows diminished.

Edgar said, "Good shot. Is he right, Bev?"

The bee, or wasp, rose from its leaf and buzzed around Edgar's bald head. He slapped at it, missing it by a fraction of an inch. "There's a fly in here!"

"Not now. I think it went out the window."

It had indeed been a fly, he saw, and not a bee or wasp at all—a bluebottle, no doubt gorged with carrion.

Bev said, "Kingsport, Massachusetts."

With an ivory hand, Edgar moved an ivory chessman. "Knight to the king's three."

Debbie tossed her dice onto the board. "Chance."

He picked up the card for her.

> You must descend the seven hundred steps
> to the Gate of Deeper Slumber.
> You may enter the Enchanted Wood

or claim the sword Sacnoth.

Which do you choose?

Debbie said, "I take the Enchanted Wood. That leaves you the sword, Randy."

Bev handed it to him. It was a falchion, he decided, curved and single edged. After testing the edge with his finger, he laid it in his lap. It was not nearly as large as a real sword—less than sixteen inches long, he decided, including the hardwood handle.

"Your turn, Randy."

He discovered that he disliked Bev nearly as much as Debbie, hated her bleached blond hair, her scrawny neck. Bev and her dying plant were twins, one vegetable, one inhuman. He had not known that before.

She said, "It's the wheel of Fortune," as though he were stupid. He flicked the spinner.

"Unlawful evil."

Bev said, "Right," and picked up a card. " 'What do the following have in common: Pogo the Clown, H. H. Holmes, and Saucy Jacky?' "

Edgar said, "That's an easy one. They're all pseudonyms of mass murderers."

"Right. 'For an extra point, name the murderers.' "

"Gacy, Mudgett, and . . . that's not fair. No one knows who the Ripper was."

But he did: just another guy, a guy like anybody else.

Debbie tossed her dice. "Whitechapel. I'll buy it. Give me the card, honey."

He picked up the deed and studied it. "Low rents."

Edgar chuckled. "And seldom paid."

"I know," Debbie told them, "but I want it, with lots of houses." He handed her the card, and she gave him the dice.

For a moment he rattled them in his hand, trying to imagine himself the little pewter man. It was no use; there was nothing of bright metal about him or his dark wool coat—only the edge of the knife. "Seven-come-eleven," he said, and threw.

"You got it," Debbie told him. "Seven. Shall I move it for you?"

"No," he said. He picked up the little pewter figure and walked past Holborn, the Temple (cavern-temple of Nasht and Kaman-Thah), and Lincolns Inn Fields, along Cornhill and Leadenhall streets to Aldgate High Street, and so at last to Whitechapel.

Bev said, "You saw him coming, Deb," but her voice was very far away, far above the the leaden (hall) clouds, filthy with coal smoke, that hung over the city. Wagons and hansom cabs rattled by. There was a public house at the corner of Brick Lane. He turned and went in.

The barmaid handed him his large gin. The barmaid had Debbie's dark hair,

Debbie's dark good looks. When he had paid her, she left the bar and took a seat at one of the tables. Two others sat there already, and there were cards and dice, money and drinks, before them. "Sit down," she said, and he sat.

The blonde turned over a card, the jack of spades. "What are the spades in a deck of cards?" she asked.

"Swords," he said. "From the Spanish word for a sword, *espada*. The jack of spades is really the jack of swords."

"Correct."

The other man said, "Knight to the White Chapel."

The door opened, letting in the evening with a wisp of fog, and the black knight. She was tall and slender and dressed like a cavalryman, in high boots and riding breeches. A pewter miniature of a knight's shield was pinned to her dark shirt.

The barmaid rattled the dice and threw.

"You're still alive," the black knight said. She strode to their table. Sergeant's chevrons had been sewn to the sleeves of the shirt. "This neighborhood is being evacuated, folks."

"Not by us," the other man said.

"By you now, sir. On my orders. As an officer of the law, I must order you to leave. There's a tank car derailed, leaking some kind of gas."

"That's fog," Randolph Carter told her. "Fog and smoke."

"Not *just* fog. I'm sorry, sir, but I must ask all of you to go. How long have you been here?"

"Sixteen years," the blond woman said. "The neighborhood was a lot nicer when we came."

"It's some sort of chemical weapon, like LSD."

He asked, "Don't you want to sit down?" He stood, offering her his chair.

"My shot must be wearing off. The shot was supposed to protect me. I'm Sergeant . . . Sergeant . . ."

The other man said, "Very few of us are protected by shots, Sergeant Chapman. Shots usually kill people, particularly soldiers."

Randolph Carter looked at her shirt. The name CHAPMAN was engraved on a stiff plastic plate there, the plate held out like a little shelf by the thrust of her left breast.

"Sergeant Anne Chapman of the United States Army. We think it's the plants, sir. All the psychoactive drugs we know about come from plants—opium, cocaine, heroin."

"You're the heroine," he told her gently. "Coming here like this to get us out."

"All of them chemicals the plants have stumbled across to protect us from insects, really. And now they've found something to protect the insects from us." She paused, staring at him. "That isn't right, is it?"

Again he asked, "Don't you want to sit down?"

"Gases from the comet. The comet's tail has wrapped all Earth in poisonous gases."

The blonde murmured, " 'What is the meaning of this name given Satan: *Beelzebub.*' "

A tiny voice from the ceiling answered.

"You, sir," the black knight said, "won't you come with me? We've got to get out of here."

"You can't get out of here," the other man told them.

Randolph Carter nodded to the knight. "I'll come with you, if you'll love me." He rose, pushing the sword up his coat sleeve, point first.

"Then come on." She took him by the arm and pulled him through the door.

A hansom cab rattled past.

"What is this place?" She put both hands to her forehead. "I'm dreaming, aren't I? This is a nightmare." There was a fly on her shoulder, a blowfly gorged with carrion. She brushed it off; it settled again, unwilling to fly through the night and the yellow fog. "No, I'm hallucinating."

He said, "I'd better take you to your room." The bricks were wet and slippery underfoot. As they turned a corner, and another, he told her what she could do for him when they reached her room. A dead bitch lay in the gutter. Despite the night and the chill of autumn, the corpse was crawling with flies.

Sickly yellow gaslight escaped from under a door. She tore herself from him and pushed it open. He came after her, his arms outstretched. "Is this where you live?"

The three players still sat at their table. They had been joined by a fourth, a new Randolph Carter. As the door flew wide the fourth player turned to look, but he had no face.

She whispered, "This is Hell, isn't it? I'm in Hell, for what I did. Because of what we did. We're all in Hell. I always thought it was just something the Church made up, something to keep you in line, you know what I mean, sir?"

She was not talking to him, but he nodded sympathetically.

"Just a game in the pope's head. But it's real, it's here, and here we are."

"I'd better take you to your room," he said again.

She shuddered. "In Hell you can't pray, isn't that right? But I can— Listen! I can pray! *Dear G—*"

He had wanted to wait, wanted to let her finish, but the sword, Sacnoth, would not wait. It entered her throat, more eager even than he, and emerged spent and swimming in scarlet blood.

The faceless Randolph Carter rose from the table. "Your seat, young man," he said through no mouth. "I'm merely the marker whom you have followed."

## AFTERWORD

There is a daydream, I believe, common to all of us who read mysteries. We are in a small group that is somehow isolated. A member of our group is murdered, and it is we who determine the identity of the killer.

In the course of a life that has now grown lengthy, I have known three people who have actually been murdered. In one case, an old schoolmate was shot by her third husband. In another, a wealthy young woman who often came into my father's café was murdered. Her husband was tried, acquitted, and subsequently murdered himself. The third was so fantastic that were I to describe it you would feel sure I was lying. There is a book about it: *Eros, Magic, and the Murder of Professor Culianu*. You will find my friend Jennifer Stevenson's name in the index; Jennifer introduced me to Ioan Culianu.

You see that I have excuses for my interest in murder, but if I had none I would be just as interested. At one time, I considered designing a board game based on serial murders; that game never really took shape, but this story came out of the idea.

# And When They Appear

Now Christmas is come,
Let us beat up the drum,
And call all our neighbors together,
And when they appear,
Let us make them such cheer,
As will keep out the wind and the weather.

—WASHINGTON IRVING

Concerned about Sherby, and himself as well, House sent forth both Kite and Mouse.

If you had seen Mouse, you would have seen nothing. That is to say, you would have told yourself, and quickly convinced yourself, that you had seen nothing, so swift did Mouse scurry over the snow. You were not present, but an owl saw Mouse and swooped down upon her, huge winged and silent as death, for owls are too wise ever to tell themselves that their eyes did not see what their eyes have seen. Its talons closed about Mouse, and a thin blade shot out. The blade was intended for fingers, but it worked well on talons. The owl shrieked, and flapped away upon wings that were silent still, leaving a claw-tipped fraction of itself bleeding on the snow.

Mouse squeaked (a sound too faint for human ears) as the blade retracted; this was the first time that it had been used since Mouse had been made, and the self-lubricating bearings it pivoted on were dry.

Kite soared higher than the owl ever had, so high that he saw Lonely Mountain whole. He saw the tracks of cars and people in the snow where a bridge crossed the Whitewater, and directed Mouse toward the great, domed doughnut that was the Jefferson house. That was how Mouse found Kieran Jefferson III (principal operating officer of the Beauharnais Group) dead next to his Christmas tree with his brand-new Chapuis express rifle still in his hands. Mouse told House about it right away.

"I have decided to have a Christmas party," House told Sherby. "I've thought the whole thing over, and decided it is the right thing to do."

"I'd like to see my mom and dad," Sherby told House. Not because it had anything to do with the party, but simply because the thought, filling his mind, had popped from his mouth as soon as he opened it. Sherby was still in his yellow pajamas, having worn them all day.

"And so you shall," House assured him, knowing full well that what it meant had nothing to do with what he meant.

"Not holos." Sherby could not read House's mind, but he had known House all his life; if he had been able to read House's mind, it would have made no difference.

Nor could House read Sherby's. *(The big steep steps down and down into the basement, the heavy door of the cold storage locker that Sherby could not open without House's help.)*

"You must write the invitations," House told Sherby. "I can't manage that. I think we should invite Santa Claus first of all. That will get things off to a fine start."

"I didn't see Santa Claus last night," Sherby objected. "I don't think he's real."

"You fell asleep," House explained gently, "and since he's very busy on Christmas Eve, and had dropped in without an invitation, he didn't awaken you. His busiest day is over now. He always relaxes on Christmas Day. He sleeps until dark, then eats a big dinner. He will be in a relaxed mood, and may very well come."

"All right." Enthusiasm comes easily at Sherby's age, and often arrives unbidden; Sherby's showed plainly on his face.

"You mustn't expect more presents," cautioned House, who had no more. "Santa gave away all the toys he had yesterday."

"That's okay," Sherby said. "I like real things better than toys anyway."

Then he went into the Learning Center, where House showed him how to make the letters, sometimes projecting hard ones (like $M$ and $Q$) right onto the drawboard where Sherby could trace them. Sherby wrote:

DEAR SANTA
PEOPLE MUST ASK YOU LOTS AND LOTS OF QUESTIONS MINE IS
WILL YOU COME TO OUR HOUSE ON LONELY MOUNTAIN FOR A PARTY
TONIGHT BRING THE ELFS IF YOU WANT TO

SHERBY

"That's a good one," House told him, "and while you were writing it I had another good idea. Let's invite all the rest of the Christmas people too. There are a great many of them, live toy soldiers, the Nutcracker, and countless others."

Sherby looked down sadly at the light pen, which felt very heavy in his fingers. "I don't want to write a whole bunch more of these," he said.

"You won't have to," House promised. "Only one."

So Sherby wrote:

ALL XMAS PEOPLE ESPCIALLY CHILDREN ARE INVITED TOO EVEN THE GRINCH

SHERBY

He had no sooner laid down the light pen than House's doorbell rang. Sherby ran to answer it, knowing that House was quite capable of doing it himself—and would too if the visitor were left standing outside for what House (who as a rule did not have a great deal of patience) considered an excessive length of time.

This visitor was not Santa Claus at all, and did not even look as though he might be much fun. He was an old man with granny glasses and wisps of white hair sticking out from under his tall beaver hat. But he wore a green greatcoat and a red cravat, and cried, "Hallo!" so cheerfully, and smiled with so many twinkles that Sherby got out of the way at once, saying, "Would you like to come in?"

"What's today, my fine fellow?" inquired the old man as he stepped into House, beating the snow from his greatcoat in blizzards. (It melted as it reached the floor, but left no puddles there.)

"Christmas," Sherby told him.

"Not Christmas Eve!" For a moment, the old man appeared quite frightened.

"No, Christmas Day. The night of it." House groaned as even the very best houses do on cold nights, and Sherby added tardily, "Sir."

"Ebenezer," said the old man, and offered Sherby his hand in the most friendly fashion possible.

"No, sir, my name's Sherby," Sherby told him. And was about to shut the door (since he was getting cold and House had not yet done it) when he caught sight of a man in foreign garments, wonderfully real and distinct to look at, with an ax in his belt, leading a little black donkey laden with wood up the moonlit drive.

"It's Ali Baba," the old man explained. "Dear old honest Ali Baba! He *did* come to see me one Christmas, my boy, just like this. Now it's your turn, and I've brought him to you, not only for his entertainment and yours, Sherby, but in order that you may know a great secret."

He twinkled more than ever when he said this, and Sherby, who liked secrets more than almost anything else, asked, "What is it?"

The old man crouched until their eyes were nearly at a level. "You think that I am House," the old man whispered. "And so I am."

"You're a holo," Sherby told him.

"Light projected upon air, Sherby?" The old man leaned closer. "Light's wondrous stuff, but it cannot speak. Or think."

"That's House," Sherby acknowledged.

"And that"—the old man pointed through the doorway and out into the moonlit night—"is Ali Baba. I brought him with me so that you could learn that there is a vagrant magic in Christmas still, after all these years. You have not as long to learn it as I had, perhaps." He straightened up. "May he bring his donkey in? I know it isn't regular, but the poor donkey would be uncommonly cold, I'm afraid, standing out all evening in the snow."

Ali Baba, who was close enough to overhear them by this time, grinned at Sherby in such a way as to guarantee that the donkey was housebroken.

"Okay," Sherby said, so Ali Baba brought his donkey in with him, and with the donkey, a little bare-headed man in sandals and a brown habit like a lady's dress, with a rope around his waist.

As they left the vestibule and went down the hall to the family room, Sherby tried to touch the little man's back, but his hand went right through like he knew it would.

A fat man in livery came in with a tray of drinks that Sherby could not drink, hors d'oeuvres that he could not eat, and a carrot for the donkey. Ali Baba had begun to unload it and build a big fire in the fireplace when the doorbell rang again.

This time it was twelve stout young men with clubs, and a thirteenth who wore a fox skin hanging down his back, with the fox's face for a cap, so that it looked as though the fox were peering over his head. All thirteen shouted: "Hail, Squire!" to Sherby; then they performed a dance to the rapping of their own clubs, coming together by sixes and striking their clubs together, while the fox (so Sherby thought of him) leaped and whirled among them.

When they were finished, the twelve with clubs ran past Sherby into House, each wishing him a merry Christmas. The fox seemed to have vanished, until Sherby closed the door and discovered that the fox was watching over his shoulder. "A glorious Yuletide to you, Young Squire," the fox said.

Sherby turned very quickly and backed away from him, and although he knew the fox was fake, the door that stopped him from backing farther was very solid indeed.

"I'm Loki," the fox told him, "the Norse personification of fire. I seek to steal the sun, and you've just seen me driven forth in order that the sun may return. I creep back in, however, as you also see. It's my nature—I am forever creeping back in. Will you not wish me Good Yule in return?"

"It's not Yule," Sherby said. "It's Christmas."

"Christmas for some, but Yule for all. *Yule* means 'tide,' and *tide* means 'time,' " the fox told him. "This is the time of winter solstice, when day begins to lengthen, and ancestral spirits must be placated. Did you know you had ancestral spirits?"

Sherby shook his head.

"We are they," the fox told him, and as the fox spoke, someone seemed to pound the door so violently that the blows shook House.

Two young men stood on House's porch, and five more were hauling an enormous stump across the snow. Six young women and three dogs followed them, and a seventh young woman rode the stump sidesaddle, one leg hooked about an upthrust root. She cried, "Faster! Faster!" when she saw Sherby standing in the doorway, and there was a great deal of laughter, barking, and shouting.

"House would like you to get to know all of us," the fox explained, "but Kite says there isn't time for more than a glimpse. Even so, you'll remember this Christmas as long as you live."

The seven young men pushed and pulled their Yule log into the vestibule, where the young woman dismounted. "Merriment all through the house," she told Sherby, "as long as the log burns. But you've got to save a brand to light the next one. Roast pig and peacock pie." She hurried away in the direction of the kitchen.

"The boar's for Frey," the fox whispered. "Frey rides a boar with golden bristles, a dwarfgift. When he left Asgard to dwell amongst men as Fridleef, King of Denmark, his folk served him a boar at Yule to show they knew him. The apple in its mouth was the sun he had brought back to them. Finding himself discovered, he mounted the roasted boar and rode back into the sky." The fox pointed through the open doorway. "Now look yonder, and see the type of your holly wreath."

There was a wheel of fire rolling down the mountain.

"House's holos can't reach that far," Sherby said, but the fox had vanished.

A young man came in with a spray of mistletoe, which he hung from the arch between the vestibule and the hall. "Do you see the white berries?" the young man asked. "Each time a girl gets kissed under the mistletoe, she's supposed to pull off one berry. When the last berry is gone, the mistletoe comes down."

*Everybody explains,* Sherby thought, *but nobody explains anything I want explained. House doesn't know.*

Sherby went out into the snow. It was cold, and tickled his bare feet in a very chilly way, but it was real, and he liked that about it. He walked clear around House and his five-car garage, until the ground fell away in icy rocks and he could look down into the shadowed valley of the Whitewater at the foot of Lonely Mountain. He could have seen the same things by looking out of the big picture window in the family room, but looking like this, with no glass between himself and the night and the cold, made it real.

He shivered, wishing that he had worn his blue bathrobe, and wiped his nose on his sleeve.

Down in the valley there was a little dot of red light where something was burning, and House was flying Kite over it, a speck of black against the bright stars. The fire was probably a bonfire or a campfire, Sherby decided, and there would be people around it cooking hot dogs and marshmallows. He shivered again; House might fix real food if Sherby asked. He looked up at the picture window, then went a little farther down the slope where he could see it better. It was dark, and there was no smoke rising from the chimney.

Climbing back up was harder than going down had been, and once he slipped and hurt his knee. When he got back to the front door, a small black and white horse with no one to ride him was coming up the drive. He stopped and turned his head to look at Sherby through one wide, frightened eye.

"Here, pony!" Sherby called. "Here, pony!"

The little horse took a hesitant step forward.

"Here, pony!" Sherby recalled the donkey's hors d'oeuvre and dashed into the vestibule, down the hall past the roaring family room, and into the kitchen.

The fat man in livery was there, talking to a plump woman in an apron as both put deviled oysters wrapped in bacon into little cups of paper lace. "Yes, Master Sherbourne," the fat man said, "what can we do for you?"

"I just wanted a carrot," Sherby told him. "A real one."

The big vegetable drawer rolled forward, and a neat white compartment was elevated twenty-six centimeters to display two fresh carrots. Sherby snatched one and sprinted back to the porch, certain that the little horse would have gone.

He had not, and he cocked his ears in a promising fashion when Sherby showed him the carrot.

"You will require a halter of some sort, I am afraid," a heavily accented voice behind Sherby said.

Sherby turned to find a very tall man wearing a very tall hat of starched gauze standing in House's front doorway.

"That is good, what you do now," the tall man said. "You do not look at him." The tall man fingered his small, round beard. "We men—even boys—there is *exousia* in the eyes. He is afraid of that, poor little fellow."

Sherby put his other hand in front of his eyes and peeped through his fingers. Sure enough, the little horse was closer now. "My bathrobe's got a long belt. Usually I step on it."

The tall man nodded sagely. "That might do. Go and get it, and I will watch him for you."

When Sherby returned, the tall man was standing beside the little horse's head. "You are very young yet," he told Sherby. "Can you tie a knot?"

"I think so," Sherby said.

"Then give him that carrot, and tie your belt about his head while he eats it."

Sherby was afraid of the little horse's big teeth at first, but the little horse took the carrot without biting him and munched away, seeming quite content to let Sherby tie the blue terry-cloth belt of his bathrobe around his neck, though it took three tries to get the knot right. "He smells like smoke," Sherby said. "I'm going to call him Smoky."

"His stable burned, poor little fellow, so it is a good name for him. My own is Saint Nicholas, now. It used to be Bishop Nicholas. I was Bishop of Myra, in Lycia; and though I am not Santa Claus, Santa Claus is me."

Sherby was looking at Smoky. "Do you think I can lead him?"

"I am sure you can, my son."

Sherby tugged at the blue terry-cloth belt, and the little horse backed away, his eyes wide, with Sherby stumbling and sliding after him. "I want him to come in," Sherby said. "My feet are cold."

"You are learning now what I learned as a parish priest," Saint Nicholas told him.

Sherby braced his feet and tugged again; this time the little horse seemed ready to bolt. "You said I could lead him!"

"I did, my son. And I do. You can lead him wherever you wish him to go. But you cannot pull him anywhere. He is eager to follow you, but he is a great deal stronger than you are."

"I want him to go in House!"

Saint Nicholas nodded patiently. "Yet you yourself were not going into House. You were faced away from him, matching your strength against his. Now you are facing in the correct direction. Hold your rope in one hand, as though you expected him to follow you. Walk toward me, and if he does not follow at once, jerk the rope, not too hard. Say *erchou*!"

Sherby tried it, making the word almost as guttural and rasping as Saint Nicholas had, and the little horse followed him readily, almost trotting.

When all three were in the vestibule and House had shut the big front door behind them, Sherby looked up at the tall, grave saint with new respect. "You know a lot about ponies."

"My charioteer knew much more," the saint told him, "but I know something about leading."

"Do you know if there are any other kids like me at the party?"

The saint, who had been solemn the whole time, smiled. His smile made Sherby like him very much. "There is one, at least, my son. He was speaking with Father Eddi when last I saw him. Perhaps Father Eddi can help you."

Sherby, still leading Smoky, had entered the family room before it occurred to him—much too late—that he ought to have asked Saint Nicholas what Father Eddi looked like. There were a great many people there, both men and ladies, and it seemed to Sherby that the men were all plenty old enough to be fathers, for many were older than his own father. He caught at the wide sleeve of a tall figure in black, but his fingers grasped nothing, and when the tall figure looked down at him it had the face of a skull and curling horns. Hastily Sherby turned away.

A small blond lady in a green dress that seemed (apart from its flaring collar of white petals) made of dark leaves appeared safer. "Please," Sherby said, recalling his manners after the scare he had gotten. "Do you know Father Eddi?"

The blond lady nodded and smiled, offering her hand. "I'm Christmas Rose. And you are . . . ?"

"Sherby."

She smiled again; she was lovely when she smiled, and hardly taller than he. "Yes, I know Father Eddi, Sherby. He is Saint Wilfred's chaplain, and he'd like this little horse of yours very much. Did my friend Knecht Rupprecht startle you?"

"Is he your friend?" Sherby considered. "I'd like him better if he wasn't so big."

"But he wouldn't frighten demons and bad children half so much if he were no bigger than I, Sherby. He must run through the streets, you see, on Advent Thursday, so that the demons will think that a demon worse than themselves holds the town. For a few coins he will dance in your fields, and frighten the demons from them too."

Quite suddenly, Knecht Rupprecht was bending over Sherby, the skeletal bone of his jaw swinging and snapping. "*Und den vor* Christmas, with Weihnachtsmann I come. You see here dese svitches?" He held a bundle of apple and cherry twigs under Sherby's nose. "You petter pe gud, Sherpy."

Surprising himself by his own boldness, Sherby passed his free hand through the bundle. "You're all just holos. House makes you."

He was sorry as soon as he did it, because Christmas Rose was so clearly disappointed in him. "It's true that what you see now are holograms, Sherby. But we are real, nonetheless. I am a real flower, and Knecht Rupprecht a real custom. You will learn more, believe me, if you treat us as real. And since Carker's Army is coming, you may not have much time in which to learn. Kite says they're at the McKays' already, and Mouse is going to see whether they left anyone alive."

"Will they come here?" Sherby asked.

"We have no way of knowing that, Sherby. Let's hope not."

Knecht Rupprecht said, "If dey do, I vill schare dem avay, Sherpy. I dry, und dot's a promise."

"I didn't like you at first," Sherby told him. "But really I like you better than anybody. You and Christmas Rose."

She made him a formal curtsy.

"Only I don't understand how you can scare them away if they're bad when you look like you're bad, too."

"Der same vay I schare der demons, Sherpy, und der pad *Kinder. Gut ist* nod schared of vot's *gut,* put pad's schared py vorse. See dese?"

He held out his switches again, and Sherby nodded.

"I tell you now a secret, put you must nod tell der pad *Kinder.* Vunce I gome vith dese to make der fruits grow. Id *ist* der dead manns, der dead animals vot does dat, zo I gome *vor dem.* Schtill I do, but der *Volk,* dey don' know."

Christmas Rose said, "We are comrades, Knecht Rupprecht and I, because of my other name. The botanists call me Black Hellebore. Not very pretty, is it?"

Sherby shook his head sympathetically.

"It's because my roots are black. See?" She lifted her skirt to show black snakeskin shoes and black panty hose. "Of course, I *am* poisonous, but I can't help it. I'm very pretty, I bloom in winter, and if you don't eat me, I'll never harm you."

"Did my mom and dad eat you?" Sherby asked.

"No, that was something else." Christmas Rose moved out of the way of a tall black man with a crown on his turban. "I could tell you its name, but that would convey no meaning to you. It's an industrial chemical; your father brought it home from one of his factories."

"They shouldn't have eaten any." A spasm of recollected sorrow crossed Sherby's face and was gone.

"Der mama nefer meaned it," Knecht Rupprecht told him kindly. "Do nod vorget dot, howefer old you lif."

"You should have stopped them!"

Smoky stirred uneasily at the rage behind Sherby's words.

"We couldn't," Christmas Rose told him; there was a catch in her voice that Sherby was too young yet to recognize. "We were not there, neither Knecht Rupprecht nor I."

"You could because you're House!"

"Who I say I am, I am." Red lights glowed in the eye sockets of Knecht Rupprecht's bleached skull. "Did I say I vas House?"

The fat man in livery, who had been passing with a tray of empty glasses, halted. "May I be of service, sir? I am House, the butler."

Christmas Rose said, "This little boy is looking for Father Eddi, House. If you happen to see him . . . ?"

"Of course, madame."

Sherby tried to grasp the skirt of House's blue-striped waistcoat, but no resistance met his fingers. "You should've stopped them! You know you should!"

"I could not, Master Sherbourne, as long as your father was alive. And as your mother was, ah"—the butler cleared his throat—"the first to leave us, I was helpless until your father's, hmm, demise. Had you not dawdled over your dinner, I should have been unable to preserve your life. As I did, Master Sherbourne." He returned his attention to Christmas Rose. "Father Eddi, madame. I shall endeavor to locate him, madame. There should be no great difficulty."

Sherby shouted, "You can make them go away! Make them all go away!" but the fat butler had already disappeared into the crowd.

As Sherby spoke, there was a stir on the other side of the big room. Knecht Rupprecht, who was tall enough to see over the heads of most of those present, announced, "Id ist der mama und der poppa, Sherpy. So priddy she ist lookin'!" He began to applaud, and everyone present except Sherby and Smoky joined in. Under the storm of sound, Sherby heard the *snick, snick, snick* of a hundred bolts shot home. A moment later the moonlit valley of the Whitewater slowly disappeared, blotted out by the descent of the picture window's security shutter.

A thin and reedy voice at his ear said, "A very merry Christmas to you, my son! You wished to speak with me?"

Sherby turned; it was the little man in sandals.

"I'm Father Eddi, my son. Are you Master Sherbourne? That big fellow in the striped waistcoat said you wished to speak with me, and I'll be glad to help if I can." When he saw Sherby's expression, Father Eddi's own face grew troubled. "You certainly look unhappy enough."

Sherby gulped, knowing that his mother and father, dead, were talking and laughing with their guests. "I— I sort of hoped some other kids would come."

"Some have," Father Eddi assured him. "Tiny Tim's over there with Mr. and Mrs. Cratchit, and Greg—the doctor's son, you know, who helped to make the pasteboard star—is about somewhere, and Louisa, the girl who felt sorry for the Little Guest." Father Eddi paused expectantly; when Sherby said nothing, he added, "I can introduce you to them, if you like."

"A man . . ." Sherby had forgotten the tall saint's name already. "A man said you were talking to some other kid. I thought that if I could find you, I could find him."

"So you can!" Father Eddi's smile was radiant. "Follow me. He's behind the tree at this very moment, I believe." He started away, then stopped so abruptly that Sherby and Smoky ran into him, burying their faces in his insubstantial, brown-clad back. "He's behind the tree, just as I told you. Every Christmas, he's behind the tree. Before it too, of course."

Christmas Rose called, "Good-bye, Sherby! Good luck!"

It was a most magnificent tree, as yellow and shiny as real gold, alive with lights and hung with ornaments that were like little toys, although Sherby was forbidden to play with them. Santa Clauses rode sleighs and airplanes and even spaceships, stepped into redbrick chimneys, swung gaily from the clappers of bells, and carried tiny trees of their own, mostly green. There were jumping jacks and jack-in-the-boxes, rag dolls and snowmen and tiny boys with drums, and lovely silver deer that might have been of almost any kind except reindeer. It smelled marvelous too; Sherby inhaled deeply.

A dark-eyed, rather swarthy boy with curling black hair stepped out from behind the tree. "Hello, Sherby," he said. "Were you looking for me?"

Sherby nodded. "You know my name."

"I was at your christening." The swarthy boy held out his hand. "I'm Yeshua bar-Yoseph. Welcome to my birthday party."

"This is my House." Sherby wiped his nose on his sleeve.

"I know," Yeshua said. "Thanks for letting us celebrate it here, Sherby."

Behind him, his mother exclaimed, "Oh, you've found the Baby Jesus!" She knelt next to Sherby, lifting the skirt of her beautiful gown so as not to kneel on it, and reached for the little blond ceramic doll in the miniature manger under the tree. Sherby knew she wanted to pick it up but couldn't because she was a holo and it was real.

"Never mind her," he told Yeshua.

"Oh, it's all right." Yeshua grinned, his teeth flashing in his dark face.

"Did you get real nice presents?" Sherby wanted to ask a favor, but he felt that it might be a good idea to talk a little more first and make friends.

"Lots. I haven't opened all of them yet."

Sherby nodded; he knew how that was. "What did you like the best?"

"My favorite present?"

Sherby nodded again.

"I'll tell you what mine was if you'll promise to tell me what yours was, after."

"Okay," Sherby said.

"Mine was what I said—you and your mother and father giving me this party," Yeshua told him. "It's really great, something I'll never forget. Now what was yours?"

Sherby patted the little horse's nose. "He is. I call him Smoky. I got a Distracto, and a copter that really flies and you can steer around, and a bunch of other stuff. But I like Smoky the best." He took a deep breath. "Will you do me a favor?"

"Sure."

"I want to go downstairs and open the big locker and . . . and—"

"Just look at them for a while," Yeshua supplemented.

"Uh-huh. An' I want you to come. I know you can't help work the door or anything, but I'd like you to come anyway. Okay?"

From no place and everyplace, all over the room, House said, "This is most unwise, Sherby."

Sherby ignored him. "Will you?"

Yeshua nodded, and Father Eddi said, "I'll go with you too, Sherby, if you don't mind."

Remembering the tall man with the tall hat, Sherby said, "That's good. Come on," and turned and hurried away, walking right through several people who failed to notice him and get out of his way, the little horse trotting after him, his hoofs loud upon the carpeted floor.

A wide door in the kitchen opened upon a flight of wooden steps. It was hard to persuade Smoky to go down them, but Sherby led to the best of his ability, saying, "*Erchou!*" half a dozen times, and praising Smoky each time he put a hoof onto a lower step. "Where's Yeshua?" he asked Father Eddi.

"Here with us." Father Eddi had been walking up and down the steps energetically to show Smoky how easily it could be done, and was rather out of breath.

"I don't see him."

"What you saw—the hologram—isn't here," Father Eddi explained.

"I'd like to see him."

"You don't think much of them." Father Eddi sat down on a step to wipe his forehead with the ragged hem of his brown habit. "So House did away with it. He's here just the same."

"Well, I'd like to see."

"Then you shouldn't have walked through the holograms upstairs, and should've wished your mother Merry Christmas."

"Are you a Christmas person? Like Knecht Rupprecht and Christmas Rose?" Sherby turned around to look back at Father Eddi, which surprised Smoky so much that he went down another step without urging.

"I certainly am."

"What makes you one?"

"One Christmas, I said a mass nobody came to except a donkey and an ox."

"Is that all?"

"I'm afraid it is." Father Eddi looked crestfallen. "I didn't put myself forward to House as a Christmas person, you understand, my son. But donkeys have been my friends ever since that night, so when you said that Ali Baba could bring in Kawi I came too, remembering my midnight service for the Saxons and hoping that I might be of some use here.

> The altar-lamps were lighted,—
> An old marsh-donkey came,
> Bold as a guest invited,
> And stared at the guttering flame.

"No doubt he forgot me and my service long ago, but I haven't forgotten him, my son—no more than you've forgotten your father and mother in the frozen-food locker down here. How did you get their bodies down these steps, anyway? You can't have carried them yourself."

"Mariah and Jeremy were here then. House had them do it. *Erchou!*" This last was for Smoky, who (gaining confidence as he neared the cellar floor) actually went down four more steps without further urging before he halted again.

"Then they went away and left you here with House? That wasn't very wise, I'm afraid."

"House made them," Sherby explained. "He's supposed to take care of me when there's nobody else to do it, and Mariah and Jeremy weren't supposed to take me anywhere unless my mom said it was okay. House wouldn't let them open the door as long as I was with them. They said they'd send somebody."

"Somebody else will get here sooner, I'm afraid," Father Eddi told him. "I will have some advice for you, if you can get the big stainless door open."

"You could ask House to open it for me. He can do that. You could pretend like you're doing it. You could put your hand on the handle and House would pull it and open the door and you could go inside and tell me to come in." It was a lot of talking for Sherby, and made him glad that Father Eddi was not much bigger than he was.

"He won't do it, my son," Father Eddi said gently. "He doesn't think it good for you to come down here and look at them. Neither do I. But if you get the freezer door open, I'll have some advice to offer, as I told you."

"*Erchou!*" Sherby said, and Smoky clattered down the last two steps to stand beside him. "Watch me."

He untied the blue terry-cloth bathrobe belt, then tied its ends together in a new knot, pulling hard to make sure it would hold. That done, he looped it around the handle of the big freezer door, and put the other loop over Smoky's head. Returning to the foot of the steps, he shouted, "*Erchou!*"

Smoky eyed him nervously.

"I think you'd better go back upstairs, my son," Father Eddi said.

"I was looking that time. That's not the right way to do it." Sherby started up the steps. "*Erchou!*"

Smoky pulled the big handle forward by perhaps half an inch.

"There's another carrot up there," Sherby said. "I *know* that'll work, only I want to try something else first. Watch me!"

He carried Mariah's empty scrub bucket to Smoky's side, inverted it, and mounted. "Now come on! *Erchou!*" Sherby kicked Smoky with his bare heels, and Smoky took a hesitant step or two forward.

The big stainless-steel door swung open.

"I'm going in to look at them," Sherby told Father Eddi. "You don't have to come in with me."

"I wish that I could."

Even to stand in front of the door was to enter a second winter, colder even than the snow and the night wind on Lonely Mountain.

Sherby stepped inside.

Father Eddi called, "I can't go any farther with you, my son. There are no hologram projectors in there."

"That's all right," Sherby told him. Sherby was looking at his mother. There was a fine powdering of ice crystals on her cheek, and one hand was lifted as if she had died gesturing. Telling his father not to eat what she had, Sherby decided. Only his father had meant to, and had done it anyway.

"It might be a good thing for you to take Smoky in with you and shut the door, my son."

Sherby shook his head, shivering. He was still looking at his mother, and absentmindedly stroking Smoky's nose.

"You can't be locked in. There's a push bar on the inside that makes the door very easy to open."

"I'm coming out in a minute," Sherby said. His father's face was twisted. Because he knew what was happening, Sherby thought. It had been wrong, wrong of his father particularly, to go away and leave him alone with House.

"You see, my son, Carker's Army is looting and burning all the homes along East Mountain Road, and they've left the McKays'. They will probably burn this house as well. If they do, that freezer is the part of House most likely to survive. If you snuggle up with Smoky, you might stay alive until they leave."

"No," Sherby said. He wanted his mother to pat his head the way she always had when she put him into bed, and thought of bending down and touching her hand with his head. He knew it would not be the same, but he did it anyway, then turned away, shivering worse than ever, and led Smoky out into the cellar again, where Father Eddi waited.

"This is your best chance, my son. You know that House can open this door. He'll open it for you when it's safe."

Sherby did not bother to reply. He pushed hard against the big door, swinging it shut.

"Are we going back upstairs? Santa Claus is about to appear. It will be the high point of the party."

"I don't care about Santa," Sherby declared.

Smoky, who had been so reluctant to go down the stairs, trotted up them quite readily. "House!" Sherby called when they were back in the kitchen. "House, say something! Answer me!"

"What is it, Sherby?" The big voice seemed to come from all around him, as it always had, but there was a tension in it that Sherby had never heard before.

"I want to see out front. Is it okay to open the front door?"

"No," House told him. "There is a screen in the study——"

"Not that. You let me open it before."

"They were not here then, Sherby. Now they are."

Sherby considered the problem. Behind him, Father Eddi said, "House would like to show you Santa Claus, and this may be the last chance you'll ever have to see him with a child's eyes. Won't you please go into the family room and look?"

House said, "I will make an agreement with you, Sherby. If you'll see Santa, I'll open the security shutter on one of the windows in the living room a little and let you look out there; I promise."

"All the way. And look for as long as I want."

House hesitated. Smoky stamped in the silence; faintly, Sherby could hear voices outside and the loud bangs of people pounding on things. At last House said, "All right."

There seemed to be fewer guests in the family room than Sherby remembered. Christmas Rose was talking to the tall, turbaned king and an older king with a long, white beard, but Knecht Rupprecht was nowhere to be seen. As Sherby and Smoky advanced toward the fireplace, in which the immense Yule log was blazing, Santa Claus stepped out of the fire, a fat little man no taller than Sherby himself, his red and white clothing all tarnished with soot and an enormous bundle of toys on his back.

"Look, my son!" Father Eddi exclaimed from behind Sherby. "There's Santa Claus! He came!"

Sherby nodded. A sort of aisle had opened between Santa Claus and himself. His mother was standing on Santa Claus's right, his father on his left, and an elf was peeping from between his father's legs. As Sherby came nearer, leading Smoky, Santa Claus roared with laughter. "Here I am again, Sherby! Second time today!"

"Are you really Santa Claus?" Sherby's voice wanted to shake. It was as if he had been crying.

"I certainly am!" Santa Claus laughed again, louder than ever: "*Ho, ho, ho, ho!*"

"Then you're nothing," Sherby told him. Sherby could not talk as loud as

Santa Claus did, but he talked as loud as he could. "You're a big nothing, and I never, never want to see you anymore. House! Are you listening to me, House?"

Sherby waited for House's reply, and all the guests were silent too. His mother and his father looked at each other, but neither spoke. Smoky nuzzled his hand.

"I'm the only one here, House! You've got to do what I tell you! You know you do!" Sherby looked for the butler in the crowd of guests, but could not find him. "Make them all go away. I mean it! No more promises. Make them all go away *right now*!"

He and Smoky stood alone in the big, dark, empty family room; the fireplace that had blazed an instant before was cold and dark.

Gradually the lights came up, so that by the time Sherby and Smoky had taken a few steps toward the door, the room was lit almost normally, though nowhere near as bright as it had been during the party.

"House, I'm hungry. I'm going to the study now, to look out. When I'm finished I want a bowl of Froot Loops. Get out the stuff."

House's big voice, coming from a dozen speakers in that part of the house, said, "There is no milk left, Sherby. I told you so at noon, remember?"

"What is there?"

House considered, and Sherby knew there was no point in interrupting.

"There are sardines and two slices of bread. You could make a sardine sand-wich?"

"Peanut butter?"

"Yes, a little."

"I'll have toast and peanut butter," Sherby decided. "Get out the peanut but-ter. Toast the bread and have it waiting for me when I'm through looking."

"I will, Sherby."

The hall was nearly dark, the study as black as pitch. House said, "If I turn on the lights, they will see you at once when I raise the security shutter, Sherby."

"Turn on the lights now so I can get over to the window," Sherby instructed him. "Then turn them off again. Then pull up the shutter."

His father's desk was still there, and the big computer console, its screen dark. Save for one large and equally dark window, books lined the walls—his grandfa-ther's law books, mostly; Sherby remembered his mother opening one for him to show him his grandfather's bookplate.

"I wish that you would go back to the frozen-food locker, Sherby. That would be the safest place for you and Smoky."

"What's that banging the front door?"

"A log."

The light above the desk dimmed, then winked out. Sherby flattened his nose against the chill, black thermopane of the window, and the security shutter glided smoothly up.

There were too many people to count outside, some of them so close they were nearly touching the glass. Among them were policemen and firemen, but no one paid any attention to them; when he had been looking out for perhaps half a minute, Sherby recognized one of the firemen as the fox. A man holding a big iron bar ran right through the fox toward the window, but two women stopped him and pulled him out of the way.

The window exploded inward.

Sherby found himself on the floor. The light was bright and the shutter closed again, and he lay in a litter of broken glass; his right hand was bleeding, and his head bleeding from somewhere up in his hair. He cried then for what felt to him like a very long time, listening to the *bang, bang, bang* from the big front door.

When he got up, he took off his pajama shirt, wiped the blood away with it, blew his nose in it, and let it fall to the floor. "Where's Smoky?" he asked.

"In the dining room, Sherby. He is all right."

"Is my toast ready?"

"It will be by the time that you reach the kitchen. I would not try to catch Smoky again right now, Sherby. The shots frightened him very much. He might hurt you."

"Okay," Sherby said.

Kneeling on a kitchen chair, he spread the last of the peanut butter on his toast. He found that he was no longer hungry, but he ate one piece anyway. Somebody banged on the security shutter of one of the kitchen windows and went away. Climbing the stairs to get to his bedroom, Sherby thought that he had seen Yeshua on the landing. Yeshua had smiled, his white teeth flashing. Then he was gone, and it seemed he had never been there at all. "Don't do that," Sherby told House.

House did not answer.

In his bedroom, Sherby slipped out of his pajama bottoms and pulled on underwear and long stockings, jeans, and his red sweater. He was not skillful at tying shoes, but that morning there had been green Wellingtons under the tree. Now, for the first time ever, he tugged them on; they were only a little bit too large, and they did not have laces to tie. His green knit cap kept the blood from trickling into his eyes.

"You are not to go out, Sherby."

"Yes, I am," Sherby announced firmly. "I'm going to get on Smoky and go someplace else." He paused, thinking. "Down the mountain." Smoky had been very unwilling to go down the cellar stairs, but Sherby felt pretty sure he would run faster down Lonely Mountain than up.

House said nothing more, but Sherby could hear people running and shouting downstairs. It sounded as if House was showing the party again, and Sherby told himself that if it sounded like the party it couldn't really be as bad as House had been pretending.

It was hard to decide which toys and books to take; in the end he settled on the yo-yo with the blinky lights in its side and the copter, telling himself that he could make the copter fly after him when he didn't want to carry it. He put on his big puffy down-filled coat, buttoned the easy buttons, slipped the yo-yo into one side pocket and the copter control into the other, and went out onto the landing again.

Knecht Rupprecht was there, standing at the head of the stairs—but a new Knecht Rupprecht, hideously transformed. Shreds of decaying flesh dangled from his skull face now, his eyes were spheres of fire, and he was taller than ever; in place of his bundle of switches he held a sword with a blade longer than Sherby and wider than Sherby's whole body.

People were clustered at the foot of the stairs staring up at him, arguing and urging each other forward. After a second or two, Sherby decided it might be better to go down the back stairs to the kitchen, but as he was about to turn away something very strange happened to Knecht Rupprecht: he vanished, reappeared, roared so wildly that Sherby took three steps backward, dimmed, and dropped his sword.

The lights went out.

Something knocked Sherby down, and something else stepped on his fingers. A flashlight beam danced on the ceiling before it too winked out.

Sherby tried to crawl on his hands and knees. Somebody tripped over him and said, "Shit! Oh, shit!"

Something was burning in the hall downstairs; from where he lay, Sherby could not see the flames, but he saw the red light of them and smelled smoke.

Thick, soft, warm arms scooped him up. "Little boy," the owner of the arms said in a voice like a girl's. "Little cute boy. Don't cry."

Outside the moon was up, and some of House's security shutters were lying on the snow-covered flower beds. Behind them, their windows glowed with orange light. Thick black smoke was coming through the shutters over his mother's and father's bedroom windows.

Smoky galloped through a milling crowd of people. One threw a bottle at him, and there were popping noises. Smoky stumbled and fell, tried to get up, and fell again. Someone hit him with a snowball, and someone else with a big stick.

"You want to hit him, little boy?" the man holding Sherby asked. Sherby could feel the man's whiskers scraping his ear. "You can hit him if you want to."

Sherby said nothing, but the man set him down anyway. "You can hit him if you want to," the man said again in his girl's voice. "Go ahead."

It would be better, Sherby thought, to do what they said. To be one. He got closer, not looking at the man behind him, stooped, and tried to scrape up enough of the trampled snow for a snowball. It stung his fingers and there wasn't enough, so he found a rock and threw that instead.

The fat man picked him up again. "I'm going to call you Chris," he told Sherby, " 'cause you're my Christmas present. You can call me Corporal Charlie, Chris." He was bigger than anybody Sherby had ever seen before, not as tall as Knecht Rupprecht but wider than Sherby's bed. "You come along with me, Chris. We'll go on back to my van. You got cut, didn't you?"

Sherby said, "Uh-huh."

"I'll put a little splash of iodine on that when we get back home. We—"

House's roof fell in with a crash as he spoke. A great cloud of swirling sparks rose into the sky, and Sherby said, "*Oooh!*"

"Yeah, that's somethin', ain't it? I seen it before. All these soldiers here are meaning to do some more, but you and me are going home." Corporal Charlie chuckled. "We'll take off our clothes and have some fun, Chris. Then we'll go to bed."

Corporal Charlie took up the whole front seat of the van, so Sherby rode in back with furniture and some dresses and a lot of other things. There was a thing there lying on some coats that Sherby recognized, and when he was sure that it was what he thought it was, he traded the copter control for it.

That night at Corporal Charlie's house, when Corporal Charlie was asleep and Sherby was supposed to be asleep on Corporal Charlie's smelly old sofa, Sherby got the thing he had found in the van out again. "Merry Christmas, Mouse," he said to the shiny round lens in front. "It's me, Sherby."

But Mouse was quiet, still, and cold.

Sherby put her under the sofa cushion.

Christmas was funny, Sherby thought, snuggling underneath the coats. Christmas was happy and sad, green and red, real and fake, all mixed together. "I don't like it," he muttered to himself, but as soon as he had said it, he knew it was not true. He wished—somehow—that he had been nicer to Santa Claus, even if Santa Claus was not real.

<hr>

### AFTERWORD

Do you know how M. R. James came to write all those great old ghost stories? He wrote one a year, no less and no more, to read to his family at Christmas. We associate ghost stories with Halloween now—see Neil Gaiman's marvelous "October in the Chair"—but ghosts at Christmas are far older. The three seen by Ebenezer Scrooge are not the beginning but almost the end of a lengthy tradition. If you were to return as a ghost, wouldn't you rather revisit your family at Christmas?

So I hope you noticed the ghosts, and that you noticed (as only a few readers do) that there is an anti-Santa, too. Poor Sherby rejects Santa Claus and gets someone much worse.

# BED AND BREAKFAST

∞

I know an old couple who live near Hell. They have a small farm, and to supplement the meager income it provides (and to use up its bounty of chickens, ducks, and geese, of beefsteak tomatoes, bull-nose peppers, and roastin' ears) open their spare bedrooms to paying guests. From time to time, I am one of those guests.

Dinner comes with the room if one arrives before five, and leftovers, of which there are generally enough to feed two or three more persons, will be cheerfully warmed up afterward—provided that one gets there before nine, at which hour the old woman goes to bed. After nine (and I arrived long after nine last week) guests are free to forage in the kitchen and prepare whatever they choose for themselves.

My own choices were modest: coleslaw, cold chicken, fresh bread, country butter, and buttermilk. I was just sitting down to this light repast when I heard the doorbell ring. I got up, thinking to answer it and save the old man the trouble, and heard his limping gait in the hallway. There was a murmur of voices, the old man's and someone else's; the second sounded like a deep-voiced woman's, so I remained standing.

Their conversation lasted longer than I had expected, and although I could not distinguish a single word, it seemed to me that the old man was saying, "No, no, no," and the woman proposing various alternatives.

At length he showed her into the kitchen, tall and tawny haired, with a figure rather too voluptuous to be categorized as athletic, and one of those interesting faces that one calls beautiful only after at least half an hour of study; I guessed her age near thirty. The old man introduced us with rustic courtesy, told her to make herself at home, and went back to his book.

"He's very kind, isn't he?" she said. Her name was Eira something.

I concurred, calling him a very good soul indeed.

"Are you going to eat all that?" She was looking hungrily at the chicken. I assured her I would have only a piece or two. (I never sleep well after a heavy meal.) She opened the refrigerator, found the milk, and poured herself a glass that she pressed against her cheek. "I haven't any money. I might as well tell you."

That was not my affair, and I said so.

"I don't. I saw the sign, and I thought there must be a lot of work to do around such a big house, washing windows and making beds, and I'd offer to do it for food and a place to sleep."

"He agreed?" I was rather surprised.

"No." She sat down and drank half her milk, seeming to pour it down her throat with no need of swallowing. "He said I could eat and stay in the empty room—they've got an empty room tonight—if nobody else comes. But if somebody does, I'll have to leave." She found a drumstick and nipped it with strong white teeth. "I'll pay them when I get the money, but naturally he didn't believe me. I don't blame him. How much is it?"

I told her, and she said it was very cheap.

"Yes," I said, "but you have to consider the situation. They're off the highway, with no way of letting people know they're here. They get a few people on their way to Hell, and a few demons going out on assignments or returning. Regulars, as they call them. Other than that"—I shrugged—"eccentrics like me and passersby like you."

"Did you say Hell?" She put down her chicken leg.

"Yes. Certainly."

"Is there a town around here called Hell?"

I shook my head. "It has been called a city, but it's a region, actually. The Infernal Empire. Hades. Gehenna, where their worm dieth not, and the fire is not quenched. You know."

She laughed, the delighted crow of a large, bored child who has been entertained at last.

I buttered a second slice of bread. The bread is always very good, but this seemed better than usual.

" 'Abandon hope, you who enter here.' Isn't that supposed to be the sign over the door?"

"More or less," I said. "Over the gate Dante used, at any rate. It wasn't this one, so the inscription here may be quite different, if there's an inscription at all."

"You haven't been there."

I shook my head. "Not yet."

"But you're going"—she laughed again, a deep, throaty, very feminine chuckle this time—"and it's not very far."

"Three miles, I'm told, by the old county road. A little less, two perhaps, if you were to cut across the fields, which almost no one does."

"I'm not going," she said.

"Oh, but you are. So am I. Do you know what they do in Heaven?"

"Fly around playing harps?"

"There's the Celestial Choir, which sings the praises of God throughout all eternity. Everyone else beholds His face."

"That's it?" She was skeptical but amused.

"That's it. It's fine for contemplative saints. They go there, and they love it. They're the only people suited to it, and it suits them. The unbaptized go to Limbo. All the rest of us go to Hell; and for a few, this is the last stop before they arrive."

I waited for her reply, but she had a mouthful of chicken. "There are quite a number of entrances, as the ancients knew. Dodona, Ephyra, Acheron, Averno, and so forth. Dante went in through the crater of Vesuvius, or so rumor had it; to the best of my memory, he never specified the place in his poem."

"You said demons stay here."

I nodded. "If it weren't for them, the old people would have to close, I imagine."

"But you're not a demon and neither am I. Isn't it pretty dangerous for us? You certainly don't look . . . I don't mean to be offensive—"

"I don't look courageous." I sighed. "Nor am I. Let me concede that at once, because we need to establish it from the very beginning. I'm innately cautious, and have been accused of cowardice more than once. But don't you understand that courage has nothing to do with appearances? You must watch a great deal of television; no one would say what you did who did not. Haven't you ever seen a real hero on the news? Someone who had done something extraordinarily brave? The last one I saw looked very much like the black woman on the pancake mix used to, yet she'd run into a burning tenement to rescue three children. Not her own children, I should add."

Eira got up and poured herself a second glass of milk. "I said I didn't want to hurt your feelings, and I meant it. Just to start with, I can't afford to tick off anybody just now—I need help. I'm sorry. I really am."

"I'm not offended. I'm simply telling you the truth, that you cannot judge by appearances. One of the bravest men I've known was short and plump and inclined to be careless, not to say slovenly, about clothes and shaving and so on. A friend said that you couldn't imagine anyone less military, and he was right. Yet that fat little man had served in combat with the navy and the marines, and with the Israeli Army."

"But isn't it dangerous? You said you weren't brave to come here."

"In the first place, one keeps one's guard up here. There are precautions, and I take them. In the second, they're not on duty, so to speak. If they were to commit murder or set the house on fire, the old people would realize immediately who had done it and shut down; so while they are here, they're on their good behavior."

"I see." She picked up another piece of chicken. "*Nice* demons."

"Not really. But the old man tells me that they usually overpay and are, well, businesslike in their dealings. Those are the best things about evil. It generally has ready money, and doesn't expect to be trusted. There's a third reason, as well. Do you want to hear it?"

"Sure."

"Here one can discern them, and rather easily for the most part. When you've identified a demon, his ability to harm you is vastly reduced. But past this farm, identification is far more difficult; the demons vanish in the surging tide of mortal humanity that we have been taught by them to call life, and one tends to relax somewhat. Yet scarcely a week goes by in which one does not encounter a demon unaware."

"All right, what about the people on their way to Hell? They're dead, aren't they?"

"Some are, and some aren't."

"What do you mean by that?"

"Exactly what I said. Some are and some are not. It can be difficult to tell. They aren't ghosts in the conventional sense, you understand, any more than they are corpses, but the people who have left the corpse and the ghost behind."

"Would you mind if I warmed up a couple of pieces of this, and toasted some of that bread? We could share it."

I shook my head. "Not in the least, but I'm practically finished."

She rose, and I wondered whether she realized just how graceful she was. "I've got a dead brother, my brother Eric."

I said that I was sorry to hear it.

"It was a long time ago, when I was a kid. He was four, I think, and he fell off the balcony. Mother always said he was an angel now, an angel up in Heaven. Do dead people really get to be angels if they're good?"

"I don't know; it's an interesting question. There's a suggestion in the Book of Tobit that the Archangel Raphael is actually an ancestor of Tobit's. *Angel* means 'messenger,' as you probably know, so if God were to employ one of the blest as a messenger, he or she could be regarded as an angel, I'd think."

"Devils are fallen angels, aren't they? I mean, if they exist." She dropped three pieces of chicken into a frying pan, hesitated, and added a fourth. "So if good people really get recycled as angels, shouldn't the bad ones get to be devils or demons?"

I admitted that it seemed plausible.

She lit the stove with a kitchen match, turning the burner higher than I would have. "You sound like you come here pretty often. You must talk to them at breakfast, or whenever. You ought to know."

"Since you don't believe me, wouldn't it be logical for you to believe my admission of ignorance?"

"No way!" She turned to face me, a forefinger upraised. "You've got to be consistent, and coming here and talking to lots of demons, you'd know."

I protested that information provided by demons could not be relied upon.

"But what do you think? What's your best guess? See, I want to find out if there's any hope for us. You said we're going to Hell, both of us, and that dude, the Italian—"

"Dante," I supplied.

"Dante says the sign over the door says don't hope. I went to a school like that for a couple years, come to think of it."

"Were they merely strict, or actually sadistic?"

"Mean. But the teachers lived better than we did—a lot better. If there's a chance of getting to be one yourself, we could always hope for that."

At that moment, we heard a knock at the front door, and her shoulders sagged. "There goes my free room. I guess I've got to be going. It was fun talking to you; it really was."

I suggested she finish her chicken first.

"Probably I should. I'll have to find another place to stay, though, and I'd like to get going before they throw me out. It's pretty late already." She hesitated. "Would you buy my wedding ring? I've got it right here." Her thumb and forefinger groped the watch pocket of her blue jeans.

I took a final bite of coleslaw and pushed back my plate. "It doesn't matter, actually, whether I want to buy your ring or not. I can't afford to. Someone in town might, perhaps."

A booming voice in the hallway drowned out the old man's; I knew that the new guest was a demon before I saw him or heard a single intelligible word.

She held up her ring, a white-gold band set with two small diamonds. "I had a job, but he never let me keep anything from it and I finally caught on—if I kept waiting till I had some money or someplace to go, I'd never get away. So I split, just walked away with nothing but the clothes I had on."

"Today?" I inquired.

"Yesterday. Last night I slept in a wrecked truck in a ditch. You probably don't believe that, but it's the truth. All night I was afraid somebody'd come to tow it away. There were furniture pads in the back, and I lay on a couple and pulled three more on top of me, and they were pretty warm."

"If you can sell your ring," I said, "there's a Holiday Inn in town. I should warn you that a great many demons stay there, just as you would expect."

The kitchen door opened. Following the old man was one of the largest I have ever seen, swag bellied and broad hipped; he must have stood at least six-foot-six.

"This's our kitchen," the old man told him.

"I know," the demon boomed. "I stopped off last year. Naturally you don't remember, Mr. Hopsack. But I remembered you and this wonderful place of yours. I'll scrounge around and make out all right."

The old man gave Eira a significant look and jerked his head toward the door, at which she nodded almost imperceptibly. I said, "She's going to stay with me, Len. There's plenty of room in the bed. You don't object, I trust?"

He did, of course, though he was much too diffident to say so; at last he managed, "Double's six dollars more."

I said, "Certainly," and handed him the money, at which the demon snickered. "Just don't you let Ma find out."

When the old man had gone, the demon fished business cards from his vest pocket; I did not trouble to read the one that he handed me, knowing that nothing on it would be true. Eira read hers aloud, however, with a good simulation of admiration. " 'J. Gunderson Foulweather, Broker, Commodities Sales.' "

The demon picked up her skillet and tossed her chicken a foot into the air, catching all four pieces with remarkable dexterity. "Soap, dope, rope, or hope. If it's sold in bulk, I'll buy it and give you the best price anywhere. If it's bought in bulk, I sell it cheaper than anybody in the nation. Pleasure to meet you."

I introduced myself, pretending not to see his hand, and added, "This is Eira Mumble."

"On your way to St. Louis? Lovely city! I know it well."

I shook my head.

She said, "But you're going somewhere—home to some city—in the morning aren't you? And you've got a car. There are cars parked outside. The black Plymouth?"

My vehicle is a gray Honda Civic, and I told her so.

"If I—you know."

"Stay in my room tonight."

"Will you give me a ride in the morning? Just a ride? Let me off downtown; that's all I ask."

I do not live in St. Louis and had not intended to go there, but I said I would.

She turned to the demon. "He says this's close to Hell and the souls of people going there stop off here, sometimes. Is that where you're going?"

His booming laugh shook the kitchen. "Not me! Davenport. Going to do a little business in feed corn if I can."

Eira looked at me as if to say, *There, you see?*

The demon popped the largest piece of chicken into his mouth like an hors d'oeuvre; I have never met one who did not prefer his food smoking hot. "He's giving you the straight scoop though, Eira. It is."

"How'd you do that?"

"Do what?"

"Talk around that chicken like that."

He grinned, which made him look like a portly crocodile. "Swallowed it, that's all. I'm hungry. I haven't eaten since lunch."

"Do you mind if I take the others? I was warming them up for myself, and there's more in the refrigerator."

He stood aside with a mock bow.

"You're in this together—this thing about Hell. You and him." Eira indicated me as she took the frying pan from the stove.

"We met before?" he boomed at me. I said that we had not, to the best of my memory.

"Devils—demons are what he calls them. He says there are probably demons sleeping here right now, up on the second floor."

I put in, "I implied that, I suppose. I did not state it."

"Very likely true," the demon boomed, adding, "I'm going to make coffee, if anybody wants some."

"And the . . . the damned. They're going to Hell, but they stop off here."

He gave me a searching glance. "I've been wondering about you, to tell the truth. You seem like the type."

I declared that I was alive for the time being.

"That's the best anybody can say."

"But the cars—" Eira began.

"Some drive; some fly." He had discovered slices of ham in the refrigerator, and he slapped them into the frying pan as though he were dealing blackjack. "I used to wonder what they did with all the cars down there."

"But you don't anymore." Eira was going along now once more willing to play what she thought (or wished me to believe she thought) a rather silly game. "So you found out. What is it?"

"Nope." He pulled out one of the wooden yellow-enameled kitchen chairs and sat down with such force I was surprised it did not break. "I quit wondering, that's all. I'll find out soon enough, or I won't. But in places this close—I guess there's others—you get four kinds of folks." He displayed thick fingers, each with a ring that looked as if it had cost a great deal more than Eira's. "There's guys that's still alive, like our friend here." He clenched one finger. "Then there's staff. You know what I mean?"

Eira looked puzzled. "Devils?"

"J. Gunderson Foulweather"—the demon jerked his thumb at his vest— "doesn't call anybody racial names unless they hurt him or his, especially when there's liable to be a few eating breakfast in the morning. Staff, okay? Free angels. Some of them are business contacts of mine. They told me about this place; that's why I came the first time."

He clenched a second finger and touched the third with the index finger of his free hand. "Then there's future inmates. You used a word J. Gunderson Foul-weather himself wouldn't say in the presence of a lady, but since you're the only lady here, no harm done. Colonists, okay?"

"Wait a minute." Eira looked from him to me. "You both claim they stop off here."

We nodded.

"On their way to Hell. So why do they go? Why don't they just go off," she hesitated, searching for the right word, and finished weakly, "back home or some-thing?"

The demon boomed, "You want to field this one?"

I shook my head. "Your information is superior to mine, I feel certain."

"Okay, a friend of mine was born and raised in Newark, New Jersey. You ever been to Newark?"

"No," Eira said.

"Some parts are pretty nice, but it's not, like, the hub of Creation, see? He went to France when he was twenty-two and stayed twenty years, doing jobs for American magazines around Paris. Learned to speak the language better than the natives. He's a photographer, a good one."

The demon's coffee had begun to perk. He glanced around at it, sniffed appreciatively, and turned back to us, still holding up his ring and little fingers. "Twenty years, then he goes back to Newark. J. Gunderson Foulweather doesn't stick his nose into other people's business, but I asked him the same thing you did me: how come? He said he felt like he belonged there."

Eira nodded slowly.

I said, "The staff, as you call them, might hasten the process, I imagine."

The demon appeared thoughtful. "Could be. Sometimes, anyhow." He touched the fourth and final finger. "All the first three's pretty common from what I hear. Only there's another kind you don't hardly ever see. The runaways."

Eira chewed and swallowed. "You mean people escape?"

"That's what I hear. Down at the bottom, Hell's pretty rough, you know? Higher up it's not so bad."

I put in, "That's what Dante reported too."

"You know him? Nice guy. I never been there myself, but that's what they say. Up at the top it's not so bad, sort of like one of those country-club jails for politicians. The guys up there could jump the fence and walk out. Only they don't, because they know they'd get caught and sent down where things aren't so nice. Only every so often somebody does. So you got them too, headed out. Anybody want coffee? I made plenty."

Long before he had reached his point, I had realized what it was; I found it difficult to speak, but managed to say that I was going up to bed and coffee would keep me awake.

"You, Eira?"

She shook her head. It was at that moment that I at last concluded that she was truly beautiful, not merely attractive in an unconventional way. "I've had all I want, really. You can have my toast for your ham."

I confess that I heaved a sigh of relief when the kitchen door swung shut behind us. As we mounted the steep, carpeted stairs, the house seemed so silent that I supposed for a moment that the demon had dematerialized, or whatever it is they do. He began to whistle a hymn in the kitchen, and I looked around sharply.

She said, "He scares you, doesn't he? He scares me too. I don't know why."

I did, or believed I did, though I forbore.

"You probably thought I was going to switch—spend the night with him instead of you—but I'd rather sleep outside in your car."

I said, "Thank you," or something of the kind, and Eira took my hand; it was the first physical intimacy of any sort between us.

When we reached the top of the stair, she said, "Maybe you'd like it if I waited out here in the hall till you get undressed? I won't run away."

I shook my head. "I told you I take precautions. As long as you're in my company, those precautions protect you as well to a considerable extent. Out here alone, you'd be completely vulnerable."

I unlocked the door of my room, opened it, and switched on the light. "Come in, please. There are things in here, enough protection to keep us both safe tonight, I believe. Just don't touch them. Don't touch anything you don't understand."

"You're keeping out demons?" She was no longer laughing, I noticed.

"Unwanted guests of every sort." I endeavored to sound confident, though I have had little proof of the effectiveness of those old spells. I shut and relocked the door behind us.

"I'm going to have to go out to wash up. I'd like to take a bath."

"The Hopsacks have only two rooms with private baths, but this is one of them." I pointed. "We're old friends, you see; their son and I went to Dartmouth together, and I reserved this room in advance."

"There's one other thing. Oh, God! I don't know how to say this without sounding like a jerk."

"Your period has begun."

"I'm on the pill. It's just that I'd like to rinse out my underwear and hang it up to dry overnight and I don't have a nightie. Would you turn off the lights in here when I'm ready to come out of the bathroom?"

"Certainly."

"If you want to look you can, but I'd rather you didn't. Maybe just that little lamp on the vanity?"

"No lights at all," I told her. "You divined very quickly that I am a man of no great courage. I wish that you exhibited equal penetration with respect to my probity. I lie only when forced to, and badly as a rule, and my word is as good as any man's. I will keep any agreement we make, whether expressed or implied, as long as you do."

"You probably want to use the bathroom too."

I told her that I would wait, and that I would undress in the bedroom while she bathed, and take my own bath afterward.

Of the many things, memories as well as speculations, that passed through my mind as I waited in our darkened bedroom for her to complete her ablutions, I shall say little here; perhaps I should say nothing. I shot the night bolt, switched off the light, and undressed. Reflecting that she might readily make away with my wallet and my watch while I bathed, I considered hiding them, but I felt certain that she would not, and to tell the truth my watch is of no great value and there was less than a hundred dollars in my wallet. Under these circumstances, it seemed wise to show I trusted her, and I resolved to do so.

In the morning I would drive her to the town in which I live or to St. Louis, as she preferred. I would give her my address and telephone number, with twenty dollars, perhaps, or even thirty. And I would tell her in a friendly fashion that if she could find no better place to stay she could stay with me whenever she chose, on tonight's terms. I speculated upon a relationship (casual and even promiscuous, if you like) that would not so much spring into being as grow by the accretion of familiarity and small kindnesses. At no time have I been the sort of man women prefer, and I am whole decades past the time in life in which love is found if it is found at all, overcautious and overintellectual, little known to the world and certainly not rich.

Yet I dreamed, alone in that dark, high-ceilinged bedroom. In men such as I, the foolish fancies of boyhood are superseded only by those of manhood, unsought visions less gaudy, perhaps, but more foolish still.

Even in these the demon's shadow fell between us; I felt certain then that she had escaped, and that he had come to take her back. I heard the flushing of the toilet, heard water run in the tub, and compelled myself to listen no more.

Though it was a cold night, the room we would share was warm. I went to the window most remote from the bathroom door, raised the shade, and stood for a time staring up at the frosty stars, then stretched myself quite naked upon the bed, thinking of many things.

I started when the bathroom door opened; I must have been half-asleep.

"I'm finished," Eira said. "You can go in now." Then, "Where are you?"

My own eyes were accommodated to the darkness, as hers were not. I could make her out, white and ghostly, in the starlight, and I thrilled at the sight. "I'm here," I told her, "on the bed. It's over this way." As I left the bed and she slipped beneath its sheet and quilt, our hands touched. I recall that moment more clearly than any of the rest.

Instructed by her lack of night vision (whether real or feigned), I pulled the dangling cord of the bathroom light before I toweled myself dry. When I opened the door, half-expecting to find her gone, I could see her almost as well as I had when she had emerged from the bathroom, lying upon her back, her hair a damp-darkened aureole about her head and her arms above the quilt. I circled the bed and slid in.

"Nice bath?" Then, "How do you want to do it?"

"Slowly," I said.

At which she giggled like a schoolgirl. "You're fun. You're not like him at all, are you?"

I hoped that I was not, as I told her.

"I know—do that again—who you are! You're Larry."

I was happy to hear it; I had tired of being myself a good many years ago.

"He was the smartest boy in school—in the high school that my husband and I graduated from. He was valedictorian, and president of the chess club and the debating team and all that. Oh, my!"

"Did you go out with him?" I was curious, I confess.

"Once or twice. No, three times. Times when there was something I wanted to go to—a dance or a game—and my husband couldn't take me, or wouldn't. So I went with Larry, dropping hints, you know, that I'd like to go, then saying okay when he asked. I never did this with him, though. Just with my husband, except that he wasn't my husband then. Could you sort of run your fingers inside my knees and down the backs of my legs?"

I complied. "It might be less awkward if you employed your husband's name. Use a false one if you like. Tom, Dick, or Harry would do, or even Mortimer."

"That wouldn't be him, and I don't want to say it. Aren't you going to ask if he beat me? I went to the battered women's shelter once, and they kept coming back to that. I think they wanted me to lie."

"You said that you left home yesterday, and I've seen your face. It isn't bruised."

"Now up here. He didn't. Oh, he knocked me down a couple times, but not lately. They're supposed to get drunk and beat you up."

I said that I had heard that before, though I had never understood it.

"You don't get mean when you're drunk."

"I talk too much and too loudly," I told her, "and I can't remember names, or the word I want to use. Eventually I grow ashamed and stop talking completely, and drinking as well."

"My husband used to be happy and rowdy—that was before we got married. After, it was sort of funny, because you could see him starting to get mad before he got the top off the first bottle. Isn't that funny?"

"No one can bottle emotions," I said. "We must bring them to the bottles ourselves."

"Kiss me."

We kissed. I had always thought it absurd to speak of someone enraptured by a kiss, yet I knew a happiness that I had not thought myself capable of.

"Larry was really smart, like you. Did I say that?"

I managed to nod.

"I want to lie on top of you. Just for a minute or so. Is that all right?"

I told her truthfully that I would adore it.

"You can put your hands anyplace you want, but hold me. That's good. That's nice. He was really smart, but he wasn't good at talking to people. Socially, you know? The stuff he cared about didn't matter to us, and the stuff we wanted to talk about didn't matter to him. But I let him kiss me in his dad's car, and I always danced the first and last numbers with him. Nobody cares about that now, but then they did, where we came from. Larry and my husband and I. I think if he'd kept on drinking—he'd have maybe four or five beers every night, at first—he'd have beaten me to death and that was why he stopped. But he used to threaten. Do you know what I mean?"

I said that I might guess, but with no great confidence.

"Like he'd pick up my big knife in the kitchen, and he'd say, 'I could stick this right through you—in half a minute it would all be over.' Or he'd talk about how you could choke somebody with a wire till she died, and while he did he'd be running the lamp cord through his fingers, back and forth. Do you like this?"

"Don't!" I said.

"I'm sorry; I thought you'd like it."

"I like it too much. Please don't. Not now."

"He'd talk about other men, how I was playing up to them. Sometimes it was men I hadn't even noticed. Like we'd go down to the pizza place, and when we got back he'd say, 'The big guy in the leather jacket—I saw you. He was eating it up, and you couldn't give him enough, could you? You just couldn't give him enough.'

"And I wouldn't have seen anybody in a leather jacket. I'd be trying to remember who this was. But when we were in school he was never jealous of Larry, because he knew Larry was just a handy man to me. I kind of liked him the way I kind of liked the little kid next door."

"You got him to help you with your homework," I said.

"Yes, I did. How'd you know?"

"A flash of insight. I have them occasionally."

"I'd get him to help before a big quiz too. When we were finishing up the semester, in Social Studies or whatever, I wouldn't have a clue about what she was going to ask on the test, but Larry always knew. He'd tell me half a dozen things, maybe, and five would be right there on the final. A flash of insight, like you said."

"Similar, perhaps."

"But the thing was . . . it was . . . was—"

She gulped and gasped so loudly that even I realized she was about to cry. I hugged her, perhaps the most percipient thing I have ever done.

"I wasn't going to tell you that, and I guess I'd better not or I'll bawl. I just wanted to say you're Larry, because my husband never minded him, not really, or anyhow not very much, and he'd kid around with him in those days, and sometimes Larry'd help him with his homework too."

"You're right," I told her, "I am Larry, and your name is Martha Williamson, although she was never half so beautiful as you are and I had nearly forgotten her."

"Have you cooled down enough?"

"No. Another five minutes, possibly."

"I hope you don't get the aches. Do you really think I'm beautiful?"

I said I did, and that I could not tell her properly how lovely she was, because she would be sure I lied.

"My face is too square."

"Absolutely not! Besides, you mean rectangular, surely. It's not too rectangular either. Any face less rectangular than yours is too square or too round."

"See? You are Larry."

"I know."

"This is what I was going to tell, if I hadn't gotten all weepy. Let me do it, and after that we'll . . . You know. Get together."

I nodded, and she must have sensed my nod in a movement of my shoulder, or perhaps a slight motion of the mattress. She was silent for what seemed to me half a minute, if not longer. "Kiss me; then I'll tell it."

I did.

"You remember what you said in the kitchen?"

"I said far too many things in the kitchen, I'm afraid. I tend to talk too much even when I'm sober. I'm sure I couldn't recall them all."

"It was before that awful man came in and took my room. I said the people going to Hell were dead, and you said some were and some weren't. That didn't make any sense to me till later when I thought about my husband. He was alive, but it was like something was getting a tighter hold on him all the time. Like Hell was reaching right out and grabbing him. He went on so about me looking at other men that I started really doing it. I'd see who was there, trying to figure out which one he'd say when we got home. Then he started bringing up ones that hadn't been there, people from school—this was after we were out of school and married, and I hadn't seen a lot of them in years."

I said, "I understand."

"He'd been on the football team and the softball team and run track and all that, and mostly it was those boys he'd talk about, but one time it was the shop teacher. I never even took shop."

I nodded again, I think.

"But never Larry, so Larry got to be special to me. Most of those boys, well, maybe they looked, but I never looked at them. But I'd really dated Larry, and he'd had his arms around me and even kissed me a couple times, and I danced with him. I could remember the cologne he used to wear, and that checkered wool blazer he had. After graduation most of the boys from our school got jobs with the coal company or in the tractor plant, but Larry won a scholarship to some big school, and after that I never saw him. It was like he'd gone there and died."

"It's better now," I said, and I took her hand, just as she had taken mine going upstairs.

She misunderstood, which may have been fortunate. "It is. It really is. Having you here like this makes it better." She used my name, but I am determined not to reveal it.

"Then after we'd been married about four years, I went in the drugstore, and Larry was there waiting for a prescription for his mother. We said hi, and shook hands, and talked about old times and how it was with us, and I got the stuff I'd come for and started to leave. When I got to the door, I thought Larry wouldn't be looking anymore, so I stopped and looked at him.

"He was still looking at me." She gulped. "You're smart. I bet you guessed, didn't you?"

"I would have been," I said. I doubt that she heard me.

"I'll never, ever, forget that look. He wanted me so bad, just so bad it was tearing him up. My husband starved a dog to death once. His name was Ranger, and he was a bluetick hound. They said he was a good coon dog, and I guess he was. My husband had helped this man with some work, so he gave him Ranger. But my husband used to pull on Ranger's ears till he'd yelp, and finally Ranger bit his hand. He just locked Ranger up after that and wouldn't feed him anymore. He'd go out in the yard and Ranger'd be in that cage hoping for him to feed him and knowing he wouldn't, and that was the way Larry looked at me in the drugstore. It brought it all back, about the dog two years before, and Larry, and lots of other things. But the thing was . . . thing was—"

I stroked her hand.

"He looked at me like that, and I saw it, and when I did I knew I was looking at him that very same way. That was when I decided, except that I thought I'd save up money, and write to Larry when I had enough, and see if he'd help me. Are you all right now?"

"No," I said, because at that moment I could have cut my own throat or thrown myself through the window.

"He never answered my letters, though. I talked to his mother, and he's married with two children. I like you better anyway."

Her fingers had resumed explorations. I said, "Now, if you're ready."

And we did. I felt heavy and clumsy, and it was over far too quickly, yet if I were given what no man actually is, the opportunity to experience a bit of his life a second time, I think I might well choose those moments.

"Did you like that?"

"Yes, very much indeed. Thank you."

"You're pretty old for another one, aren't you?"

"I don't know. Wait a few minutes and we'll see."

"We could try some other way. I like you better than Larry. Have I said that?"

I said she had not, and that she had made me wonderfully happy by saying it.

"He's married, but I never wrote him. I won't lie to you much more."

"In that case, may I ask you a question?"

"Sure."

"Or two? Perhaps three?"

"Go ahead."

"You indicated that you had gone to a school, a boarding school apparently, where you were treated badly. Was it near here?"

"I don't remember about that—I don't think I said it."

"We were talking about the inscription Dante reported. I believe it ended: *Lasciate ogni speranza, voi ch'entrate!* 'Leave all hope, you that enter!' "

"I said I wouldn't lie. It's not very far, but I can't give you the name of a town you'd know, or anything like that."

"My second—"

"Don't ask anything else about the school. I won't tell you."

"All right, I won't. Someone gave your husband a hunting dog. Did your husband hunt deer? Or quail, perhaps?"

"Sometimes. I think you're right. He'd rather have had a bird dog, but the man he helped didn't raise them."

I kissed her. "You're in danger, and I think that you must know how much. I'll help you all I can. I realize how very trite this will sound, but I would give my life to save you from going back to that school, if need be."

"Kiss me again." There was a new note in her voice, I thought, and it seemed to me that it was hope.

When we parted, she asked, "Are you going to drive me to St. Louis in the morning?"

"I'd gladly take you farther. To New York or Boston or even to San Francisco. It means 'Saint Francis,' you know."

"You think you could again?"

At her touch, I knew the answer was yes; so did she.

Afterward she asked, "What was your last question?" and I told her I had no last question.

"You said one question; then it was two, then three. So what was the last one?"

"You needn't answer."

"All right, I won't. What was it?"

"I was going to ask you in what year you and your husband graduated from high school."

"You don't mind?"

I sighed. "A hundred wise men have said in various ways that love transcends the power of death, and millions of fools have supposed that they meant nothing by it. At this late hour in my life I have learned what they meant. They meant that love transcends death. They are correct."

"Did you think that salesman was really a cop? I think you did. I did too, almost."

"No or yes, depending upon what you mean by *cop*. But we've already talked too much about these things."

"Would you rather I'd do this?"

"Yes," I said, and meant it with every fiber of my being. "I would a thousand times rather have you do that."

After some gentle teasing about my age and inadequacies (the sort of thing that women always do, in my experience, as anticipatory vengeance for the contempt with which they expect to be treated when the sexual act is complete), we slept. In the morning, Eira wore her wedding band to breakfast, where I introduced her to the old woman as my wife, to the old man's obvious relief. The demon sat opposite me at the table, wolfing down scrambled eggs, biscuits, and homemade sausage he did not require, and from time to time winking at me in an offensive manner that I did my best to tolerate.

Outside I spoke to him in private while Eira was upstairs searching our room for the hairbrush that I had been careful to leave behind.

"If you are here to reclaim her," I told him, "I am your debtor. Thank you for waiting until morning."

He grinned like the trap he was. "Have a nice night?"

"Very."

"Swell. You folks think we don't want you to have any fun. That's not the way it is at all." He strove to stifle his native malignancy as he said this, with the result that it showed so clearly I found it difficult not to cringe. "I do you a favor, maybe you'll do me one sometime. Right?"

"Perhaps," I hedged.

He laughed. I have heard many actors try to reproduce the hollowness and cruelty of that laugh, but not one has come close. "Isn't that what keeps you coming back here? Wanting favors? You know we don't give anything away."

"I hope to learn, and to make myself a better man."

"Touching. You and Dr. Frankenstein."

I forced myself to smile. "I owed you thanks, as I said, and I do thank you. Now I'll impose upon your good nature, if I may. Two weeks. You spoke of favors, of the possibility of accommodation. I would be greatly in your debt. I am already, as I acknowledge."

Grinning, he shook his head.

"One week, then. Today is Thursday. Let us have—let me have her until next Thursday."

"Afraid not, pal."

"Three days, then. I recognize that she belongs to you, but you'll have her for eternity, and she can't be an important prisoner."

"Inmate. *Inmate* sounds better." The demon laid his hand upon my shoulder, and I was horribly conscious of its weight and bone-crushing strength. "You think I let you jump her last night because I'm such a nice guy? You really believe that?"

"I was hoping that was the case, yes."

"Bright. Real bright. Just because I got here a little after she did, you think I was trailing her like that flea-bitten dog and I followed her here." He sniffed, and it was precisely the sniff of a hound on the scent. The hand that held my shoulder drew me to him until I stood with the almost insuperable weight of his entire arm on my shoulders. "Listen here. I don't have to track anybody. Wherever they are, I am. See?"

"I understand."

"If I'd been after her, I'd of had her away from you as soon as I saw her. Only she's not why I came here, she's not why I'm leaving, and if I was to grab her all it would do is get me in the soup with the big boys downstairs. I don't want you either."

"I'm gratified to hear it."

"Swell. If I was to give you a promise, my solemn word of dishonor, you wouldn't think that was worth shit-paper, would you."

"To the contrary." Although I was lying in his teeth, I persevered. "I know an angel's word is sacred, to him at least."

"Okay then. I don't want her. You wanted a couple of weeks, and I said no deal because I'm letting you have her forever, and vice versa. You don't know what *forever* means, whatever you think. But I do."

"Thank you, sir," I said, and I meant it from the bottom of my soul. "Thank you very, very much."

The demon grinned and took his arm from my shoulders. "I wouldn't mess around with you or her or a single thing the two of you are going to do together, see? Word of dishonor. The boys downstairs would skin me, because you're her assignment. So be happy." He slapped me on the back so hard that he nearly knocked me down.

Still grinning, he walked around the corner of someone's camper van. I followed as quickly as I could, but he had disappeared.

L ittle remains to tell. I drove Eira to St. Louis, as I had promised, and she left me with a quick kiss in the parking area of the Gateway Arch; we had stopped at a McDonald's for lunch on the way, and I had scribbled my address and telephone number on a paper napkin there and watched her tuck it into a pocket of the denim shirt she wore. Since then I have had a week in which to consider my adventure, as I said on the first page of this account.

In the beginning (especially Friday night), I hoped for a telephone call or a midnight summons from my doorbell. Neither came.

On Monday I went to the library, where I perused the back issues of newspapers; and this evening, thanks to a nephew at an advertising agency, I researched the matter further, viewing twenty-five- and thirty-year-old tapes of news broadcasts. The woman's name was not Eira, a name that means "snow," and the name of the husband she had slain with his own shotgun was not Tom, Dick, Harry, or even Mortimer, but I was sure I had found her. (Fairly sure, at least.) She took her own life in jail, awaiting trial.

She has been in Hell. That, I feel, is the single solid fact, the one thing on which I can rely. But did she escape? Or was she vomited forth?

All this has been brought to a head by the card I received today in the mail. It was posted on Monday from St. Louis, and has taken a disgraceful four days to make a journey that the most cautious driver can complete in a few hours. On its front, a tall, beautiful, and astonishingly busty woman is crowding a fearful little man. The caption reads: *I want to impress one thing on you.*

Inside the card: *My body.*

Beneath that is the scrawled name *Eira,* and a telephone number. Should I call her? Dare I?

Bear in mind (as I must constantly remind myself to) that nothing the demon said can be trusted. Neither can anything that she herself said. She would have had me take her for a living woman, if she could.

Has the demon devised an excruciating torment for us both?

Or for me alone?

The telephone is at my elbow as I write. Her card is on my desk. If I dial the number, will I be blundering into the snare, or will I have torn the snare to pieces?

Should I call her?

A final possibility remains, although I find it almost impossible to write of it. What if I am mad?

What if Foulweather the salesman merely played up to what he assumed was an elaborate joke? What if my last conversation with him (that is to say, with the demon) was a delusion? What if Eira is in fact the living woman that almost every man in the world would take her for, save I?

She cannot have much money and may well be staying for a few days with some chance acquaintance.

Am I insane? Deluded?

Tomorrow she may be gone. One dash three one four—

Should I call?

Perhaps I may be a man of courage after all, a man who has never truly understood his own character.

Will I call her? Do I dare?

## AFTERWORD

Because its demons are evil, this story is a favorite of Kathe Koja's.

I know how she feels. The first writer who presented Satan as a cheerful companion with supernatural powers was giving us an interesting novelty; that novelty has become the norm. Speaking not for Kathe but for myself alone, I have had it with little giants, chatty dragons, bumbling invaders, and their ilk. If you enjoyed this story, I hope you'll look into *The Knight*, a book that tries to return giants, dragons, and invaders to their roots—a book in which the knights who wage war on all three are hard-bitten fighting men.

# Petting Zoo

R oderick looked up at the sky. It was indeed blue, but almost cloudless. The air was hot and smelled of dust.

"Here, children. . . ." The teaching cyborg was pointedly not addressing him. "*Tyrannosaurus rex*. Rex was created by an inadequately socialized boy who employed six Build-a-Critter kits . . ."

Sixteen.

". . . which he duped on his father's Copystuff. With that quantity of Gro-Qik . . ."

It had taken a day over two weeks, two truckloads of pigs that he had charged to Mother's account, and various other things that had become vague. For the last week, he had let Rex go out at night to see what he could find, and people would—people were bound to—notice the missing cattle soon. Had probably noticed them already.

Rex had looked out through the barn window while he was mooring his airbike and said, "I'm tired of hiding all day."

And he himself had said . . .

"Let's go for a ride." One of the little girls had raised her hand.

From the other side of the token barrier that confined him, Rex himself spoke for the first time, saying, "You will, kid. She's not quite through yet." His voice was a sort of growling tenor now, clearly forced upward as high as he could make it so as to seem less threatening. Roderick pushed on his suit's AC and shivered a little.

It had been cool, that day. Cool, with a little breeze he had fought the whole way over, keeping his airbike below the treetops and following groundtrucks when he could, pulled along by their wake.

Cold in the old barn, then—cold, and dusty—dust motes dancing in the sunbeams that stabbed between its old, bent, and battered aluminum panels.

Rex had crouched as he had before, but he was bigger now, bigger than ever, and his smooth reptilian skin had felt like glass, like ice under which oiled muscles stirred like snakes. He had fallen, and Rex had picked him up in the arms that looked so tiny on Rex but were bigger and stronger than a big man's arms, saying, "That's what these are for," and set him on Rex's shoulders with his legs—*his* legs—trying to wrap around Rex's thick, throbbing neck . . .

Had opened the big doors from inside, had gone out almost crawling and stood up.

It had not been the height. He had been higher on his airbike almost every day. It had not been his swift, swaying progress above the treetops, treetops arrayed in red, gold, and green so that it seemed that he followed Rex's floating head over a lawn deep in fallen leaves.

It had been—

He shrugged the thought away. There were no adequate words. Power? You bought it at a drugstore, a shiny little disk that would run your house-bot for three or four more years or your drill forever. Mastery? It was what people had held over dogs while private ownership had still been legal.

Dogs had four fangs in front, and that was it, fangs so small they did not even look dangerous. Rex had a mouthful, every one as long as Roderick's arm, in a mouth that could have chewed up an aircar.

No, it had not been the height. He had ridden over woods—this wood among them—often. Had ridden higher than this, yet heard the rustling of the leaves below him, the sound of a brook, an invisible brook of air. It had been the noise.

That was not right either, but it was closer than the others. It had been the snapping of the limbs and the crashing of the trees falling, or at least that had been a lot of it, the sound of their progress, the shattering, splintering wood. In part, at least, it had been the noise.

"He did a great deal of damage," the teaching cyborg was saying, as her female attendant nodded confirmation. "Much worse, he terrified literally hundreds of persons. . . ."

Sitting on Rex's shoulders, he had been able to talk almost directly into Rex's ear. "Roar."

And Rex had roared to shake the earth.

"Keep on roaring."

And Rex had.

The red and white cattle Rex ate sometimes, so short legged they could scarcely move, had run away slowly only because they were too fat to run any faster, and one had gotten stepped on. People had run too, and Rex had kicked over a little prefab shed for the fun of it, and a tractor-bot. Had waded hip deep through the swamp without even slowing down, and had forded the river. There were fewer building restrictions on the north side of the river, and the people there had really run.

Had run except for one old man with a bushy mustache, who had only stood and stared pop-eyed, too old to run, Roderick thought, or maybe too scared. He had looked down at the old man and waved, and their eyes had met, and suddenly—just as if the top of the old man's head had popped up so Roderick could look around inside it—he had known what the old man was thinking.

Not guessed, known.

And the old man had been thinking that when he had been Roderick's age he had wanted to do exactly what Roderick was doing now. He had never been able to, and had never thought anybody would be. But somebody was; that kid up there in the polka-dot shirt was. So he, the old man, had been wrong about the whole world all his life. It was much more wonderful, this old world, than he, the old man, had ever supposed. So maybe there was hope after all. Some kind of a hope anyhow, in a world where things like this could go on, on a Monday right here in Libertyberg.

Before the old man could draw his breath to cheer, he had been gone, and there had been woods and cornfields. (Roderick's suit AC shuddered and quit.) And after lots of corn, some kind of a big factory. Rex had stepped on its fence, which sputtered and shot sparks without doing anything much, and then the aircar had started diving at them.

It had been red and fast, and Roderick remembered it as clearly as if he had seen it yesterday. It would dive, trying to hit Rex's head, and then the override would say, "My gosh, that's a great big dinosaur! You're trying to crash us into a great big dinosaur, you jerk!" The override would pull the aircar up and miss, and then it would give it back to the driver, and he would try the same thing all over.

Roderick had followed it with his eyes, especially after Rex started snapping at it, and the sky had been a wonderful cool blue with little white surgical-ball clouds strolling around in it. He had never seen a better sky—and he never would, because skies did not get any better than that one. After a while he had spotted the channel copter, flying around up there and taking his picture to run on everybody's threedeevid, and had made faces at it.

Another child, a scrubbed little girl with long, straight, privileged-looking yellow hair, had her hand up. "Did he kill a whole lot of people?"

The teaching cyborg interrupted her own lecture. "Certainly not, since there were no people in North America during the Upper Cretaceous. Human evolution did not begin—"

"This one." The scrubbed little girl pointed to Rex. "Did he?"

Rex shook his head.

"That was not the point at issue," the teaching cyborg explained. "Disruption is disrupting, and he and his maker disrupted. He disrupted, I should say, and his maker still more, since Rex would not have been in existence to disrupt had he not been made in violation of societal standards. No one of sensitivity would have done what he did. Someone of sensitivity would have realized at once that their construction of a large dinosaur, however muted in coloration—"

Rex interrupted her. "I'm purple. It's just that it's gotten sort of dull lookin' now that I'm older. Looky here." He bent and slapped at his water trough with his disproportionately small hands. Dust ran from his hide in dark streaks, leaving it a faded mulberry.

"You are not purple," the teaching cyborg admonished Rex, "and you should not say you are. I would describe that shade as a mauve." She spoke to her female attendant. "Do you think that they would mind very much if I were to start over? I've lost my place, I fear."

"You mustn't interrupt her," the female attendant cautioned the little girl. "Early-Tertiary-in-the-Upper-Eocene-was-the-Moeritherium-the-size-of-a-tuber-but-more-like-a-hippopotamus."

"Yum," Rex mumbled. "Yum-yum!"

A small boy waved his hand wildly. "What do you feed him?"

"Tofu, mostly. It's good for him." The teaching cyborg looked at Rex as she spoke, clearly displeased at his thriving upon tofu. "He eats an airtruckload of it every day. Also a great deal of soy protein and bean curd."

"I'd like to eat the hippos," Rex told the small boy. "We go right past them every time I take you kids for a ride, and wow! Do they ever look yummy!"

"He's only joking," the teaching cyborg told the children. She caught her female attendant's left arm and held it up to see her watch. "I have a great deal more to tell you, children, but I'll have to do it while we're taking our ride, or we'll fall behind schedule."

She and her female attendant opened the gate to Rex's compound and went in, preceded, accompanied, and followed by small girls and boys. While most of the children gathered around him, stroking his rough, thick hide with tentative fingers, the teaching cyborg and her female attendant wrestled a stepladder and a very large howdah of white pentastyrene Wicked wicker from behind Rex's sleeping shed. For five minutes or more they struggled to hook the howdah over his shoulders and fasten the Velcro cinch, obstructed by the well-intended assistance of four little boys.

Roderick joined them, lifted the howdah into place, and released and refastened the cinch, getting it tight enough that the howdah could not slip to one side.

"Thank you," the female attendant said. "Haven't I seen you here before?"

Roderick shook his head. "It's the first time I've ever come."

"Well, a lot of men do. I mean it's always just one man all by himself, but there's almost always one."

"He used to lie down so that we could put it on him," the teaching cyborg said severely, "and lie down again so that the children didn't have to use the ladder. Now he just sits."

"I'm too fat," Rex muttered. "It's all that good tofu I get."

One by one, the children climbed the ladder, the teaching cyborg's female attendant standing beside it to catch each if he or she fell, cautioning each to grasp the railings and urging each to belt himself or herself in once he or she had chosen a seat. The teaching cyborg and her female attendant boarded last of all, the teaching cyborg resumed her lecture, and Rex stood up with a groan and began yet again the slow walk around the zoo that he took a dozen times a day.

It had been a fall day, Roderick reminded himself, a fall day bright and clear, a more beautiful day than days ever were now. A stiff, bright wind had been blowing right through all the sunshine. He had worn jeans, a Peoria White Sox cap, and a polka-dot shirt, had kept his airbike low where the wind wasn't quite so strong, had climbed on Rex's shoulders and watched as Rex had taken down the bar that held the big doors shut. . . .

"Now," the teaching cyborg said, "are there any additional questions?" And Roderick looked up just in time to see the corner of the white Wicked wicker howdah vanish behind Rex's sleeping shed.

"Yes." He raised his hand. "What became of the boy?"

"The government assumed responsibility for his nurturing and upbringing," the teaching cyborg explained. "He received sensitivity training and reeducation in societal values and has become a responsible citizen."

When the teaching cyborg, her female attendant, and all the children had gone, Rex said, "You know, I always wondered what happened to you."

Roderick mopped his perspiring forehead. "You knew who I was all the time, huh?"

"Sure."

There was a silence. Far away, as if from another time or another world, children spoke in excited voices and a lion roared. "Nothing happened to me," Roderick said; it was clearly necessary to say something. "I grew up, that's all."

"Those reeducation machines, they really burn it into you. That's what I heard."

"No, I grew up. That's all."

"I see. Can I ask why you keep lookin' at me like that?"

"I was just thinking."

"Thinkin' what?"

"Nothing." With iron fists, stone shoulders, and steel-shod feet, words broke down the doors of his heart and forced their way into his mouth. "Your kind used to rule the Earth."

"Yeah." Rex nodded. He turned away, leaving Roderick his serpentine tail and wide, ridged back, both the color of a grape skin that has been chewed up and spit out into the dust. "Yeah," he mumbled. "You too."

AFTERWORD

I think I must have taken my mental picture of a boy riding a dinosaur from the *Calvin and Hobbes* Sunday strip. With it came another picture, one of that same boy grown to manhood staring at his caged dinosaur. Animals in zoos (we are told) believe that their bars protect them. We Americans have forged our own bars, built our own cage, and live in it more or less content as long as someone feeds us.

# THE TREE IS MY HAT

∞

**30** Jan. I saw a strange stranger on the beach this morning. I had been swimming in the little bay between here and the village; that may have had something to do with it, although I did not feel tired. Dived down and thought I saw a shark coming around the big staghorn coral. Got out fast. The whole swim cannot have been more than ten minutes. Ran out of the water and started walking.

There it is. I have begun this journal at last. (Thought I never would.) So let us return to all the things I ought to have put in and did not. I bought this the day after I came back from Africa.

No, the day I got out of the hospital—I remember now. I was wandering around, wondering when I would have another attack, and went into a little shop on Forty-second Street. There was a nice-looking woman in there, one of those good-looking black women, and I thought it might be nice to talk to her, so I had to buy something. I said, "I just got back from Africa."

She: "Really. How was it?"

Me: "Hot."

Anyway, I came out with this notebook and told myself I had not wasted my money because I would keep a journal, writing down my attacks, what I had been doing and eating, as instructed, but all I could think of was how she looked when she turned to go to the back of the shop. Her legs and how she held her head. Her hips.

After that I planned to write down everything I remember from Africa, and what we said if Mary returned my calls. Then it was going to be about this assignment.

**31** Jan. Setting up my new Mac. Who would think this place would have phones? But there are wires to Kololahi, and a dish. I can chat with people all over the world, for which the agency pays. (Talk about soft!) Nothing like this in Africa. Just the radio, and good luck with that.

I was full of enthusiasm. "A remote Pacific island chain." Wait. . . .

P.D.: "Baden, we're going to send you to the Takanga Group."

No doubt I looked blank.

"It's a remote Pacific island chain." She cleared her throat and seemed to have swallowed a bone. "It's not going to be like Africa, Bad. You'll be on your own out there."

Me: "I thought you were going to fire me."

P.D.: "No, no! We wouldn't do that."

"Permanent sick leave."

"No, no, no! But, Bad." She leaned across her desk and for a minute I was afraid she was going to squeeze my hand. "This will be rough. I'm not going to try to fool you."

Ha!

Cut to the chase. This is nothing. This is a bungalow with rotten boards in the floors that has been here since before the British pulled out, a mile from the village and less than half that from the beach, close enough that the Pacific smell is in all the rooms. The people are fat and happy, and my guess is not more than half are dumb. (Try and match that around Chicago.) Once or twice a year one gets yaws or some such, and Rev. Robbins gives him arsenic. *Which cures it.* Pooey!

There are fish in the ocean, plenty of them. Wild fruit in the jungle, and they know which you can eat. They plant yams and breadfruit, and if they need money or just want something, they dive for pearls and trade them when Jack's boat comes. Or do a big holiday boat trip to Kololahi.

There are coconuts too, which I forgot. They know how to open them. Or perhaps I am just not strong enough yet. (I look in the mirror, and ugh.) I used to weigh two hundred pounds.

"You skinny," the king says. "Ha, ha, ha!" He is really a good guy, I think. He has a primitive sense of humor, but there are worse things. He can take a jungle chopper (we said *upanga,* but they say *heletay*) and open a coconut like a pack of gum. I have coconuts and a *heletay,* but I might as well try to open them with a spoon.

I Feb. Nothing to report except a couple of wonderful swims. I did not swim at all for the first couple of weeks. There are sharks. I know they are really out there because I have seen them once or twice. According to what I was told, there are saltwater crocs too, up to fourteen feet long. I have never seen any of those and am skeptical, although I know they have them in Queensland. Every so often you hear about somebody who was killed by a shark, but that does not stop the people from swimming all the time, and I do not see why it should stop me. Good luck so far.

2 Feb. Saturday. I was supposed to write about the dwarf I saw on the beach that time, but I never got the nerve. Sometimes I used to see things in the hos-

pital. Afraid it may be coming back. I decided to take a walk on the beach. All right, did I get sunstroke?

Phooey.

He was just a little man, shorter even than Mary's father. He was too small for any adult in the village. He was certainly not a child, and was too pale to have been one of the islanders at all.

He cannot have been here long; he was whiter than I am.

Rev. Robbins will know—ask tomorrow.

**3** Feb. Hot and getting hotter. Jan. is the hottest month here, according to Rob Robbins. Well, I got here the first week in Jan. and it has never been this hot.

Got up early while it was still cool. Went down the beach to the village. (Stopped to have a look at the rocks where the dwarf disappeared.) Waited around for the service to begin but could not talk to Rob; he was rehearsing the choir—"Nearer, My God, to Thee."

Half the village came, and the service went on for almost two hours. When it was over I was able to get Rob alone. I said if he would drive us into Kololahi I would buy our Sunday dinner. (He has a Jeep.) He was nice, but no—too far and the bad roads. I told him I had personal troubles I wanted his advice on, and he said, "Why don't we go to your place, Baden, and have a talk? I'd invite you for lemonade, but they'd be after me every minute."

So we walked back. It was hotter than hell, and this time I tried not to look. I got cold Cokes out of my rusty little fridge, and we sat on the porch (Rob calls it the veranda) and fanned ourselves. He knew I felt bad about not being able to do anything for these people, and urged patience. My chance would come.

I said, "I've given up on that, Reverend."

(That was when he told me to call him Rob. His first name is Mervyn.) "Never give up, Baden. Never." He looked so serious I almost laughed.

"All right, I'll keep my eyes open, and maybe someday the Agency will send me someplace where I'm needed."

"Back to Uganda?"

I explained that the A.O.A.A. almost never sends anyone to the same area twice. "That wasn't really what I wanted to talk to you about. It's my personal life. Well, really two things, but that's one of them. I'd like to get back together with my ex-wife. You're going to advise me to forget it, because I'm here and she's in Chicago, but I can send e-mail, and I'd like to put the bitterness behind us."

"Were there children? Sorry, Baden. I didn't intend it to hurt."

I explained how Mary had wanted them and I had not, and he gave me some advice. I have not e-mailed yet, but I will tonight after I write it out here.

"You're afraid that you were hallucinating. Did you feel feverish?" He got out his thermometer and took my temperature, which was nearly normal. "Let's look at it logically, Baden. This island is a hundred miles long and about thirty miles at the widest point. There are eight villages I know of. The population of Kololahi is over twelve hundred."

I said I understood all that.

"Twice a week, the plane from Cairns brings new tourists."

"Who almost never go five miles from Kololahi."

"Almost never, Baden. Not never. You say it wasn't one of the villagers. All right, I accept that. Was it me?"

"Of course not."

"Then it was someone from outside the village, someone from another village, from Kololahi, or a tourist. Why shake your head?"

I told him.

"I doubt there's a leprosarium nearer than the Marshalls. Anyway, I don't know of one closer. Unless you saw something else, some other sign of the disease, I doubt that this little man you saw had leprosy. It's a lot more likely that you saw a tourist with pasty white skin greased with sun blocker. As for his disappearing, the explanation seems pretty obvious. He dived off the rocks into the bay."

"There wasn't anybody there. I looked."

"There wasn't anybody there you saw, you mean. He would have been up to his neck in water, and the sun was glaring on the water, wasn't it?"

"I suppose so."

"It must have been. The weather's been clear." Rob drained his Coke and pushed it away. "As for his not leaving footprints, stop playing Sherlock Holmes. That's harsh, I realize, but I say it for your own good. Footprints in soft sand are shapeless indentations at best."

"I could see mine."

"You knew where to look. Did you try to backtrack yourself? I thought not. May I ask a few questions? When you saw him, did you think he was real?"

"Yes, absolutely. Would you like another one? Or something to eat?"

"No, thanks. When was the last time you had an attack?"

"A bad one? About six weeks."

"How about a not-bad one?"

"Last night, but it didn't amount to much. Two hours of chills, and it went away."

"That must have been a relief. No, I see it wasn't. Baden, the next time you have an attack, severe or not, I want you to come and see me. Understand?"

I promised.

*This is Bad. I still love you. That's all I have to say, but I want to say it. I was wrong, and I know it. I hope you've forgiven me.* And sign off.

4 Feb. Saw him again last night, and he has pointed teeth. I was shaking under the netting, and he looked through the window and smiled. Told Rob, and said I read somewhere that cannibals used to file their teeth. I know these people

were cannibals three or four generations back, and I asked if they had done it. He thinks not but will ask the king.

*I* *have been very ill, Mary, but I feel better now. It is evening here, and I am going to* *bed. I love you. Good night, I love you.* Sign off.

5 Feb. Two men with spears came to take me to the king. I asked if I was under arrest, and they laughed. No *ha, ha, ha* from His Majesty this time, though. He was in the big house, but he came out and we went some distance among hardwoods the size of office buildings smothered in flowering vines, stopping in a circle of stones: the king, the men with spears, and an old man with a drum. The men with spears built a fire, and the drum made soft sounds like waves while the king made a speech or recited a poem, mocked all the while by invisible birds with eerie voices.

When the king was finished, he hung this piece of carved bone around my neck. While we were walking back to the village, he put his arm around me, which surprised me more than anything. He is bigger than a tackle in the NFL, and must weigh four hundred pounds. It felt like I was carrying a calf.

Horrible, *horrible* dreams! Swimming in boiling blood. Too scared to sleep anymore. Logged on and tried to find something on dreams and what they mean. Stumbled onto a witch in L.A.—her home page, then the lady herself. ("I'll get you and your little dog too!") Actually, she seemed nice.

Got out the carved-bone thing the king gave me. Old, and probably ought to be in a museum, but I suppose I had better wear it as long as I stay here, at least when I go out. Suppose I were to offend him? He might sit on me! Seems to be a fish with pictures scratched into both sides. More fish, man in a hat, etc. Cord through the eye. Wish I had a magnifying glass.

6 Feb. Still haven't gone back to bed, but my watch says Wednesday. Wrote a long e-mail, typing it in as it came to me. Told her where I am and what I'm doing, and begged her to respond. After that I went outside and swam naked in the moonlit sea. Tomorrow I want to look for the place where the king hung this fish charm on me. Back to bed.

Morning, and beautiful. Why has it taken me so long to see what a beautiful place this is? (Maybe my heart just got back from Africa.) Palms swaying forever in the trade winds, and people like heroic bronze statues. How small, how stunted and pale, we have to look to them!

Took a real swim to get the screaming out of my ears. Will I laugh in a year when I see that I said my midnight swim made me understand these people better? Maybe I will. But it did. They have been swimming in the moon like that for hundreds of years.

* * *

E-mail! God bless e-mail and whoever invented it! Just checked mine and found I had a message. Tried to guess who it might be. I wanted Mary, and was about certain it would be from the witch, from Annys. Read the name and it was *Julius R. Christmas*. Pops! Mary's Pops! Got up and ran around the room, so excited I could not read it. Now I have printed it out, and I am going to copy it here.

> *She went to Uganda looking for you, Bad. Coming back tomorrow, Kennedy, AA 47 from Heathrow. I'll tell her where you are. Watch out for those hula-hula girls.*

## SHE WENT TO UGANDA LOOKING FOR ME

7Feb. More dreams—little man with pointed teeth smiling through the window. I doubt that I should write it all down, but I knew (in the dream) that he hurt people, and he kept telling me he would not hurt me. Maybe the first time was a dream too. More screams.

Anyway, I talked to Rob again yesterday afternoon, although I had not planned on it. By the time I got back here I was too sick to do anything except lie on the bed. The worst since I left the hospital, I think.

Went looking for the place the king took me to. Did not want to start from the village, kids might have followed me, so I tried to circle and come at it from the other side. Found two old buildings, small and no roofs, and a bone that looked human. More about that later. Did not see any marks, but did not look for them either. It was black on one end like it had been in a fire, though.

Kept going about three hours and wore myself out. Tripped on a chunk of stone and stopped to wipe off the sweat, and *blam!* I was there! Found the ashes and where the king and I stood. Looked around wishing I had my camera, and there was Rob, sitting up on four stones that were still together and looking down at me. I said, "Hey, why didn't you say something?"

And he said, "I wanted to see what you would do." So he had been spying on me; I did not say it, but that was what it was.

I told him about going there with the king, and how he gave me a charm. I said I was sorry I had not worn it, but anytime he wanted a Coke I would show it to him.

"It doesn't matter. He knows you're sick, and I imagine he gave you something to heal you. It might even work, because God hears all sorts of prayers. That's not what they teach in the seminary, or even what it says in the Bible. But I've been out in the missions long enough to know. When somebody with good intentions talks to the God Who created him, he's heard. Pretty often the answer is yes. Why did you come back here?"

"I wanted to see it again, that's all. At first I thought it was just a circle of rocks; then when I thought about it, it seemed like it must have been more."

Rob kept quiet, so I explained that I had been thinking of Stonehenge. Stonehenge was a circle of big rocks, but the idea had been to look at the positions of certain stars and where the sun rose. But this could not be the same kind of thing, because of the trees. Stonehenge is out in the open on Salisbury Plain. I asked if it was some kind of a temple.

"It was a palace once, Baden." Rob cleared his throat. "If I tell you something about it in confidence, can you keep it to yourself?"

I promised.

"These are good people now. I want to make that clear. They seem a little childlike to us, as all primitives do. If we were primitives ourselves—and we were, Bad, not so long ago—they wouldn't. Can you imagine how they'd seem to us if they didn't seem a little childlike?"

I said, "I was thinking about that this morning before I left the bungalow."

Rob nodded. "Now I understand why you wanted to come back here. The Polynesians are scattered all over the South Pacific. Did you know that? Captain Cook, a British naval officer, was the first to explore the Pacific with any thoroughness, and he was absolutely astounded to find that after he'd sailed for weeks his interpreter could still talk to the natives. We know, for example, that Polynesians came down from Hawaii in sufficient numbers to conquer New Zealand. The historians hadn't admitted it the last time I looked, but it's a fact, recorded by the Maori themselves in their own history. The distance is about four thousand miles."

"Impressive."

"But you wonder what I'm getting at. I don't blame you. They're supposed to have come from Malaya originally. I won't go into all the reasons for thinking that they didn't, beyond saying that if it were the case they should be in New Guinea and Australia and they're not."

I asked where they had come from, and for a minute or two he just rubbed his chin; then he said, "I'm not going to tell you that either. You wouldn't believe me, so why waste breath on it? Think of a distant land, a mountainous country with buildings and monuments to rival Ancient Egypt's, and gods worse than any demon Cotton Mather could have imagined. The time . . ." He shrugged. "After Moses but before Christ."

"Babylon?"

He shook his head. "They developed a ruling class, and in time those rulers, their priests and warriors, became something like another race, bigger and stronger than the peasants they treated like slaves. They drenched the altars of their gods with blood, the blood of enemies when they could capture enough, and the blood of peasants when they couldn't. Their peasants rebelled and drove them from the mountains to the sea, and into the sea."

I think he was waiting for me to say something, but I kept quiet, thinking over what he had said and wondering if it was true.

"They sailed away in terror of the thing they had awakened in the hearts of the nation that had been their own. I doubt very much if there were more than a few thousand, and there may well have been fewer than a thousand. They learned seamanship, and learned it well. They had to. In the Ancient World they were the only people to rival the Phoenicians, and they surpassed even the Phoenicians."

I asked whether he believed all that, and he said, "It doesn't matter whether I believe it, because it's true."

He pointed to one of the stones. "I called them primitives, and they are. But they weren't always as primitive as they are now. This was a palace, and there are ruins like this all over Polynesia, great buildings of coral rock falling to pieces. A palace and thus a sacred place, because the king was holy, the gods' representative. That was why he brought you here."

Rob was going to leave, but I told him about the buildings I found earlier and he wanted to see them. "There is a temple too, Baden, although I've never been able to find it. When it was built, it must have been evil beyond our imagining. . . ." He grinned then, surprising the hell out of me. "You must get teased about your name."

"Ever since elementary school. It doesn't bother me." But the truth is it does, sometimes.

More later.

W ell, I have met the little man I saw on the beach, and to tell the truth (what's the sense of one of these if you are not going to tell the truth?), I like him. I am going to write about all that in a minute.

Rob and I looked for the buildings I had seen when I was looking for the palace but could not find them. Described them, but Rob did not think they were the temple he has been looking for since he came. "They know where it is. Certainly the older people do. Once in a while I catch little oblique references to it. Not jokes. They joke about the place you found, but not about that."

I asked what the place I had found had been.

"A Japanese camp. The Japanese were here during World War Two."

I had not known that.

"There were no battles. They built those buildings you found, presumably, and they dug caves in the hills from which to fight. I've found some of those myself. But the Americans and Australians simply bypassed this island, as they did many other islands. The Japanese soldiers remained here, stranded. There must have been about a company, originally."

"What happened to them?"

"Some surrendered. Some came out of the jungle to surrender and were killed. A few held out, twenty or twenty-five from what I've heard. They left their caves and went back to the camp they had built when they thought Japan would win and control the entire Pacific. That was what you found, I believe, and that's why I'd like to see it."

I said I could not understand how we could have missed it, and he said, "Look at this jungle, Baden. One of those buildings could be within ten feet of us."

After that we went on for another mile or two and came out on the beach. I did not know where we were, but Rob did. "This is where we separate. The village is that way, and your bungalow the other way, beyond the bay."

I had been thinking about the Japs, and asked if they were all dead, and he said they were. "They were older every year and fewer every year, and a time came when the rifles and machine guns that had kept the villages in terror no longer worked. And after that, a time when the people realized they didn't. They went to the Japanese camp one night with their spears and war clubs. They killed the remaining Japanese and ate them, and sometimes they make sly little jokes about it when they want to get my goat."

I was feeling rocky and knew I was in for a bad time, so I came back here. I was sick the rest of the afternoon and all night, chills, fever, headache, the works. I remember watching the little vase on the bureau get up and walk to the other side, and sit back down, and seeing an American in a baseball cap float in. He took off his cap and combed his hair in front of the mirror, and floated back out. It was a Cardinals cap.

Now about Hanga, the little man I see on the beach.

After I wrote all that about the palace, I wanted to ask Rob a couple of questions and tell him Mary was coming. All right, no one has actually said she was, and so far I have heard nothing from her directly, only the one e-mail from Pops. But she went to Africa, so why not here? I thanked Pops and told him where I am again. He knows how much I want to see her. If she comes, I am going to ask Rob to remarry us, if she will.

Started down the beach, and I saw him, but after half a minute or so he seemed to melt into the haze. I told myself I was still seeing things, and I was still sick, and I reminded myself that I promised to go by Rob's mission next time I felt bad. But when I got to the end of the bay, there he was, perfectly real, sitting in the shade of one of the young palms. I wanted to talk to him, so I said, "Okay if I sit down too? This sun's frying my brains."

He smiled (the pointed teeth are real) and said, "The tree is my hat."

I thought he just meant the shade, but after I sat he showed me, biting off a palm frond and peeling a strip from it, then showing me how to peel them and weave them into a rough sort of straw hat, with a high crown and a wide brim.

We talked a little, although he does not speak English as well as some of the others. He does not live in the village, and the people who do, do not like him although he likes them. They are afraid of him, he says, and give him things because they are. They prefer he stay away. "No village, no boat."

I said it must be lonely, but he only stared out to sea. I doubt that he knows the word.

He wanted to know about the charm the king gave me. I described it and asked if it brings good luck. He shook his head. "No *malhoi*." Picking up a single palm fiber, "This *malhoi*." Not knowing what *malhoi* meant, I was in no position to argue.

That is pretty much all, except that I told him to visit when he wants company and he told me I must eat fish to restore my health. (I have no idea who told him I am ill sometimes, but I never tried to keep it a secret.) Also that I would never have to fear an attack (I think that must have been what he meant) while he was with me.

His skin is rough and hard, much lighter in color than the skin of my forearm, but I have no idea whether that is a symptom or a birth defect. When I got up to leave, he stood too and came no higher than my chest. Poor little man.

One more thing. I had not intended to put it down, but after what Rob said maybe I should. When I had walked some distance toward the village, I turned back to wave to Hanga, and he was gone. I walked back, thinking that the shade of the palm had fooled me; he was not there. I went to the bay, thinking he was in the water as Rob suggested. It is a beautiful little cove, but Hanga was not there either. I am beginning to feel sympathy for the old mariners. These islands vanished when they approached.

At any rate, Rob says that *malhoi* means "strong." Since a palm fiber is not as strong as a cotton thread, there must be something wrong somewhere. (More likely, something I do not understand.) Maybe the word has more than one meaning.

*Hanga* means "shark," Rob says, but he does not know my friend Hanga. Nearly all the men are named for fish.

More e-mail, this time the witch. *There is danger hanging over you. I feel it and know some higher power guided you to me. Be careful. Stay away from places of worship; my tarot shows trouble for you there. Tell me about the fetish you mentioned.*

I doubt that I should, and that I will e-mail her again.

9 Feb. I guess I wore myself out on writing Thursday. I see I wrote nothing yesterday. To tell the truth, there was nothing to write about except my swim in Hanga's bay. And I cannot write about that in a way that makes sense. Beautiful beyond description. That is all I can say. To tell the truth, I am afraid to go back. Afraid I will be disappointed. No spot on earth, even under the sea, can be as lovely as I remember it. Colored coral, and the little sea animals that look like flowers, and schools of blue and red and orange fish like live jewels.

Today when I went to see Rob (all right, Annys warned me, but I think she is full of it) I said he probably likes to think God made this beautiful world so we could admire it, but if He had, He would have given us gills.

"Do I also think that He made the stars for us, Baden? All those flaming suns hundreds and thousands of light-years away? Did God create whole galaxies so that once or twice in our lives we might chance to look up and glimpse them?"

When he said that I had to wonder about people like me, who work for the Federal Government. Would we be driven out someday, like the people Rob talked about? A lot of us do not care any more about ordinary people than they did. I know P.D. does not.

A woman who had cut her hand came in about then. Rob talked to her in her own language while he treated her, and she talked a good deal more, chattering away. When she left I asked whether he had really understood everything she said. He said, "I did and I didn't. I knew all the words she used, if that's what you mean. How long have you been here now, Baden?"

I told him and he said, "About five weeks? That's perfect. I've been here about five years. I don't speak as well as they do. Sometimes I have to stop to think of the right word, and sometimes I can't think of it at all. But I understand when I hear them. It's not an elaborate language. Are you troubled by ghosts?"

I suppose I gawked.

"That was one of the things she said. The king has sent for a woman from another village to rid you of them, a sort of witch doctress, I imagine. Her name is Langitokoua."

I said the only ghost bothering me was my dead marriage's and I hoped to resuscitate it with his help.

He tried to look through me and may have succeeded; he has that kind of eyes. "You still don't know when Mary's coming?"

I shook my head.

"She'll want to rest a few days after her trip to Africa. I hope you're allowing for that."

"And she'll have to fly from Chicago to Los Angeles, from Los Angeles to Melbourne, and from there to Cairns, after which she'll have to wait for the next plane to Kololahi. Believe me, Rob, I've taken all that into consideration."

"Good. Has it occurred to you that your little friend Hanga might be a ghost? I mean, has it occurred to you since you spoke to him?"

Right then, I had that "what am I doing here" feeling I used to get in the bush. There I sat in that bright, flimsy little room with the medicine smell, and a jar of cotton balls at my elbow, and the noise of the surf coming in the window, about a thousand miles from anyplace that matters, and I could not remember the decisions I had made and the plans that had worked or not worked to get me there.

"Let me tell you a story, Baden. You don't have to believe it. The first year I was here, I had to go to town to see about some building supplies we were buying. As things fell out, there was a day there when I had nothing to do, and I decided to drive up to North Point. People had told me it was the most scenic part of the island, and I convinced myself I ought to see it. Have you ever been there?"

I had not even heard of it.

"The road only goes as far as the closest village. After that there's a footpath that takes two hours or so. It really is beautiful, rocks standing above the waves, and dramatic cliffs overlooking the ocean. I stayed there long enough to get the lovely, lonely feel of the place and make some sketches. Then I hiked back to the village where I'd left the Jeep and started to drive back to Kololahi. It was almost dark.

"I hadn't gone far when I saw a man from our village walking along the road. Back then I didn't know everybody, but I knew him. I stopped and we chatted for a minute. He said he was on his way to see his parents, and I thought they must live in the place I had just left. I told him to get into the Jeep, and drove back, and let him out. He thanked me over and over, and when I got out to look at one of the tires I was worried about, he hugged me and kissed my eyes. I've never forgotten that."

I said something stupid about how warmhearted the people here are.

"You're right, of course. But, Baden, when I got back, I learned that North Point is a haunted place. It's where the souls of the dead go to make their farewell to the land of the living. The man I'd picked up had been killed by a shark the day I left, four days before I gave him a ride."

I did not know what to say, and at last I blurted out, "They lied to you. They had to be lying."

"No doubt—or I'm lying to you. At any rate, I'd like you to bring your friend Hanga here to see me if you can."

I promised I would try to bring Rob to see Hanga, since Hanga will not go into the village.

Swimming in the little bay again. I never thought of myself as a strong swimmer, never even had much chance to swim, but have been swimming like a dolphin, diving underwater and swimming with my eyes open for what has got to be two or two and a half minutes, if not longer. Incredible! My God, wait till I show Mary!

You can buy scuba gear in Kololahi. I'll rent Rob's Jeep or pay one of the men to take me in his canoe.

11 Feb. I let this slide again, and need to catch up. Yesterday was very odd. So was Saturday.

After I went to bed (still full of Rob's ghost story and the new world underwater) and *crash!* Jumped up scared as hell, and my bureau had fallen on its face. Dry rot in the legs, apparently. A couple of drawers broke, and stuff scattered all over.

I propped it back up and started cleaning up the mess, and found a book I never saw before, *The Light Garden of the Angel King*, about traveling through Afghanistan. In front is somebody's name and a date, and *American Overseas Assistance Agency*. None of it registered right then.

But there it was, spelled out for me. And here is where he was, Larry Scribble.

He was an Agency man, had bought the book three years ago (when he was posted to Afghanistan, most likely) and brought it with him when he was sent here. I only use the top three drawers, and it had been in one of the others and got overlooked when somebody (who?) cleared out his things.

Why was he gone when I got here? He should have been here to brief me, and stayed for a week or so. No one has so much as mentioned his name, and there must be a reason for that.

Intended to go to services at the mission and bring the book, but was sick again. Hundred and nine. Took medicine and went to bed, too weak to move, and had this very strange dream. Somehow I knew somebody was in the house. (I suppose steps, although I cannot remember any.) Sat up, and there was Hanga smiling by my bed. "I knock. You not come."

I said, "I'm sorry. I've been sick." I felt fine. Got up and offered to get him a Coke or something to eat, but he wanted to see the charm. I said sure, and got it off the bureau.

He looked at it, grunting and tracing the little drawings on its sides with his forefinger. "No tie? You take loose?" He pointed to the knot.

I said there was no reason to, that it would go over my head without untying the cord.

"Want friend?" He pointed to himself, and it was pathetic. "Hanga friend? Bad friend?"

"Yes," I said. "Absolutely."

"Untie."

I said I would cut the cord if he wanted me to.

"Untie, please. Blood friend." (He took my arm then, repeating, "Blood friend!")

I said all right and began to pick at the knot, which was complex, and at that moment, I swear, I heard someone else in the bungalow, some third person who pounded on the walls. I believe I would have gone to see who it was then, but Hanga was still holding my arm. He has big hands on those short arms, with a lot of strength in them.

In a minute or two I got the cord loose and asked if he wanted it, and he said eagerly that he did. I gave it to him, and there was one of those changes you get in dreams. He straightened up, and was at least as tall as I am. Holding my arm, he cut it quickly and neatly with his teeth and licked the blood, and seemed to grow again. It was as if some sort of defilement had been wiped away. He looked intelligent and almost handsome.

Then he cut the skin of his own arm just like mine. He offered it to me, and I licked his blood like he had licked mine. For some reason I expected it to taste horrible, but it did not; it was as if I had gotten seawater in my mouth while I was swimming.

"We are blood friends now, Bad," Hanga told me. "I shall not harm you, and you must not harm me."

That was the end of the dream. The next thing I remember is lying in bed and smelling something sweet, while something tickled my ear. I thought the mosquito netting had come loose, and looked to see, and there was a woman with a flower in her hair lying beside me. I rolled over, and she, seeing that I was awake, embraced and kissed me.

She is Langitokoua, the woman Rob told me the king had sent for, but I call her Langi. She says she does not know how old she is, and is fibbing. Her size (she is about six feet tall, and must weigh a good 250) makes her look older than she is, I feel sure. Twenty-five, maybe. Or seventeen. I asked her about ghosts, and she said very matter-of-factly that there is one in the house, but he means no harm.

Pooey.

After that, naturally I asked her why the king wanted her to stay with me, and she solemnly explained that it is not good for a man to live by himself, that a man should have someone to cook and sweep, and take care of him when he is ill. That was my chance, and I went for it. I explained that I am expecting a woman from America soon, that American women are jealous, and that I would have to tell the American woman Langi was there to nurse me. Langi agreed without any fuss.

What else? Hanga's visit was a dream, and I know it, but it seems I was sleep-walking. (Perhaps I wandered around the bungalow delirious.) The charm was where I left it on the dresser, but the cord was gone. I found it under my bed and tried to put it back through the fish's eye, but it would not go.

E-mail from Annys: *The hounds of hell are loosed. For heaven's sake be careful. Benign influences rising, so have hope.* Crazy if you ask me.

E-mail from Pops: *How are you? We haven't heard from you. Have you found a place for Mary and the kids? She is on her way.*

What kids? Why, the old puritan!

Sent a long e-mail back saying I had been very ill but was better and there were several places where Mary could stay, including this bungalow, and I would leave the final choice to her. In fairness to Pops, he has no idea where or how I live, and may have imagined a rented room in Kololahi with a monkish cot. I should send another e-mail asking about her flight from Cairns; I doubt he knows, but it may be worth a try.

Almost midnight, and Langi is asleep. We sat on the beach to watch the sunset, drank rum-and-Coke and rum-and-coconut-milk when the Coke ran out, looked at the stars, talked, and made love. Talked some more, drank some more, and made love again.

There. I had to put that down. Now I have to figure out where I can hide this so Mary never sees it. I will not destroy it and I will not lie. (Nothing is worse than lying to yourself. *Nothing.* I ought to know.)

Something else in the was-it-a-dream category, but I do not think it was. I was lying on my back on the sand, looking up at the stars with Langi beside me asleep, and I saw a UFO. It was somewhere between me and the stars, sleek, dark, and torpedo shaped, but with a big fin on the back, like a rocket ship in an old comic. Circled over us two or three times, and was gone. Haunting, though.

It made me think. Those stars are like the islands here, only a million billion times bigger. Nobody really knows how many islands there are, and there are probably a few to this day that nobody has ever been on. At night they look up at the stars and the stars look down on them, and they tell each other, "They're coming!"

Langi's name means "sky sister," so I am not the only one who ever thought like that.

Found the temple!!! Even now I cannot believe it. Rob has been looking for it for five years, and I found it in six weeks. God, but I would love to tell him!

Which I cannot do. I gave Langi my word, so it is out of the question.

We went swimming in the little bay. I dived down, showing her corals and things that she has probably been seeing since she was old enough to walk, and she showed the temple to me. The roof is gone if it ever had one, and the walls are covered with coral and the sea creatures that look like flowers; you can hardly see it unless somebody shows you. But once you do it is all there, the long straight walls, the main entrance, the little rooms at the sides, everything. It is as if you were looking at the ruins of a cathedral, but they were decked in flowers and bunting for a fiesta. (I know that is not clear, but it is what it was like, the nearest I can come.) They built it on land, and the water rose, but it is still there. It looks hidden, not abandoned. Too old to see, and too big.

I will never forget this: how one minute it was just rocks and coral, and the next it was walls and altar, with a fifty-foot branched coral like a big tree growing right out of it. Then an enormous gray-white shark with eyes like a man's came out of the shadow of the coral tree to look at us, worse than a lion or a leopard. My God, was I ever scared!

When we were both back up on the rocks, Langi explained that the shark had not meant to harm us, that we would both be dead if he had. (I cannot argue with that.) Then we picked flowers, and she made wreaths out of them and threw them in the water and sang a song. Afterward she said it was all right for me to know, because we are us, but I must never tell other *mulis*. I promised faithfully that I would not.

She has gone to the village to buy groceries. I asked her whether they worshiped Rob's God in the temple underwater. (I had to say it like that for her to understand.) She laughed and said no, they worshiped the shark god so the sharks would not eat them. I have been thinking about that.

It seems to me that they must have brought other gods from the mountains where they lived, a couple of thousand years ago, and they settled here and built that temple to their old gods. Later, probably hundreds of years later, the sea came up and swallowed it. Those old gods went away, but they left the sharks to guard their house. Someday the water will go down again. The ice will grow thick and strong on Antarctica once more, the Pacific will recede, and those murderous old mountain gods will return. That is how it seems to me, and if it is true I am glad I will not be around to see it.

I do not believe in Rob's God, so logically I should not believe in them either. But I do. It is a new millennium, but we are still playing by the old rules. They are going to come to teach us the new ones, or that is what I am afraid of.

Valentine's Day. Mary passed away. That is how Mom would have said it, and I have to say it like that too. Print it. I cannot make these fingers print the other yet.

Can anybody read this?

Langi and I had presented her with a wreath of orchids, and she was wearing them. It was so fast, so crazy.

So much blood, and Mary and the kids screaming.

I had better backtrack or give this up altogether.

There was a boar hunt. I did not go, remembering how sick I had been after tramping through the jungle with Rob, but Langi and I went to the pig roast afterward. Boar hunting is the men's favorite pastime; she says it is the only thing that the men like better than dancing. They do not have dogs and do not use bows and arrows. It is all a matter of tracking, and the boars are killed with spears when they find them, which must be really dangerous. I got to talk to the king about this hunt, and he told me how they get the boar they want to a place where it cannot run away anymore. It turns then and defies them, and may charge; but if it does not, four or five men all throw their spears at once. It was the king's spear, he said, that pierced the heart of this boar.

Anyway, it was a grand feast with pineapples and native beer, and my rum, and lots of pork. It was nearly morning by the time we got back here, where Mary was asleep with Mark and Adam.

Which was a very good thing, since it gave us a chance to swim and otherwise freshen up. By the time they woke up, Langi had prepared a fruit tray for breakfast and woven the orchids, and I had picked them for her and made coffee. Little boys, in my experience, are generally cranky in the morning (could it be because we do not allow them coffee?), but Adam and Mark were sufficiently overwhelmed by the presence of a brown lady giant and a live skeleton that conversation was possible. They are fraternal twins, and I think they really are mine; certainly they look very much like I did at their age. The wind had begun to rise, but we thought nothing of it.

"Were you surprised to see me?" Mary was older than I remembered, and had the beginnings of a double chin.

"Delighted. But Pops told me you'd gone to Uganda and you were on your way here."

"To the end of the earth." (She smiled, and my heart leaped.) "I never realized the end would be as pretty as this."

I told her that in another generation the beach would be lined with condos.

"Then let's be glad that we're in this one." She turned to the boys. "You have to take in everything as long as we're here. You'll never get another chance like this."

I said, "Which will be a long time, I hope."

"You mean that you and . . . ?"

"Langitokoua." I shook my head. (Here it was, and all my lies had melted away.) "Was I ever honest with you, Mary?"

"Certainly. Often."

"I wasn't, and you know it. So do I. I've got no right to expect you to believe me now. But I'm going to tell you, and myself, God's own truth. It's in remission now. Langi and I were able to go to a banquet last night, and eat, and talk to people, and enjoy ourselves. But when it's bad, it's horrible. I'm too sick to do anything but shake and sweat and moan, and I see things that aren't there. I—"

Mary interrupted me, trying to be kind. "You don't look as sick as I expected."

"I know how I look. My mirror tells me every morning while I shave. I look like death in a microwave oven, and that's not very far from the truth. It's liable to kill me this year. If it doesn't, I'll probably get attacks on and off for the rest of my life, which is apt to be short."

There was a silence that Langi filled by asking whether the boys wanted some coconut milk. They said they did, and she got my *heletay* and showed them how to open a green coconut with one chop. Mary and I stopped talking to watch her, and that's when I heard the surf. It was the first time that the sound of waves hitting the beach had ever reached as far inland as my bungalow.

Mary said, "I rented a Range Rover at the airport." It was the tone she used when she had to bring up something she really did not want to bring up.

"I know. I saw it."

"It's fifty dollars a day, Bad, plus mileage. I won't be able to keep it long."

I said, "I understand."

"We tried to phone. I had hoped you would be well enough to come for us, or send someone."

I said I would have had to borrow Rob's Jeep if I had gotten her call.

"I wouldn't have known where you were, but we met a native, a very handsome man who says he knows you. He came along to show us the way." (At that point, the boys' expressions told me something was seriously wrong.) "He wouldn't take any money for it. Was I wrong to offer to pay him? He didn't seem angry."

"No," I said, and would have given anything to get the boys alone. But would it have been different if I had? When I read this, when I really get to where I can face it, the thing I will miss on was how fast it was—how fast the whole thing went. It cannot have been a hour between the time Mary woke up and the time Langi ran to the village to get Rob.

Mark lying there whiter than the sand. So thin and white, and looking just like me.

"He thought you were down on the beach, and wanted us to look for you there, but we were too tired," Mary said.

That is all for now, and in fact it is too much. I can barely read this left-handed printing, and my stump aches from holding down the book. I am going to go to bed, where I will cry, I know, and Langi will cuddle me like a kid.

Again tomorrow.

17 Feb. Hospital sent its plane for Mark, but no room for us. Doctor a lot more interested in my disease than my stump. "Dr. Robbins" did a fine job there, he said. We will catch the Cairns plane Monday.

I should catch up. But first: I am going to steal Rob's Jeep tomorrow. He will not lend it, does not think I can drive. It will be slow, but I know I can.

19 Feb. Parked on the tarmac, something wrong with one engine. Have I got up nerve enough to write about it now? We will see.

Mary was telling us about her guide, how good-looking, and all he told her about the islands, lots I had not known myself. As if she were surprised she had not seen him sooner, she pointed and said, "Here he is now."

There was nobody there. Or rather, there was nobody Langi and I or the boys could see. I talked to Adam (to my son Adam; I have to get used to that) when it was over, while Rob was working on Mark and Mary. I had a bunch of surgical gauze and had to hold it as tight as I could. There was no strength left in my hand.

Adam said Mary had stopped and the door opened and she made him get in back with Mark. *The door opened by itself*. That is the part he remembers most clearly, and the part of his story I will always remember too. After that Mary seemed to be talking all the time to somebody he and his brother could not see or hear.

She screamed, and there, for just an instant, was the shark. He was as big as a boat, and the wind was like a current in the ocean, blowing us down to the water. I really do not see how I can ever explain this.

No takeoff yet, so I have to try. It is easy to say what was not happening. What is hard is saying what was, because there are no words. The shark was not swimming in air. I know that is what it will sound like, but he was not. We were not under the water either. We could breathe and walk and run just as he could swim, although not nearly so fast, and even fight the current a little.

The worst thing of all was he came and went and came and went, so that it seemed almost that we were running or fighting him by flashes of lightning, and sometimes he was Hanga, taller than the king and smiling at me while he herded us.

No. The most worst thing was really that he was herding everybody but me. He drove them toward the beach the way a dog drives sheep, Mary, Langi, Adam, and Mark, and he would have let me escape. (I wonder sometimes why I did not. This was a new me, a me I doubt I will ever see again.)

His jaws were real, and sometimes I could hear them snap when I could not see him. I shouted, calling him by name, and I believe I shouted that he was breaking our agreement, that to hurt my wives and my sons was to hurt me. To give the devil his due, I do not think he understood. The old gods are very wise, as the king told me today; still, there are limits to their understanding.

I ran for the knife, the *heletay* Langi opened coconuts with. I thought of the boar, and by God I charged them. I must have been terrified. I do not remember, only slashing at something and someone huge that was and was not there, and in an instant was back again. The sting of the windblown sand, and then up to my arms in foaming water, and cutting and stabbing, and the hammerhead with my knife and my hand in his mouth.

We got them all out, Langi and I did. But Mark has lost his leg, and jaws three feet across had closed on Mary. That was Hanga himself, I feel sure.

Here is what I think. I think he could only make one of us see him at a time and that was why he flashed in and out. He is real. (God knows he is real!) Not really physical the way a stone is, but physical in other ways that I do not understand. Physical like and unlike light and radiation. He showed himself to each of us, each time for less than a second.

Mary wanted children, so she stopped the pill and did not tell me. That was what she told me when I drove Rob's Jeep out to North Point. I was afraid. Not so much afraid of Hanga (though there was that too) but afraid she would not be there. Then somebody said, "Banzai!" It was exactly as if he were sitting next to me in the Jeep, except that there was nobody there. I said, "Banzai," back, and I never heard him again, but after that I knew I would find her and I waited for her at the edge of the cliff.

She came back to me when the sun touched the Pacific, and the darker the night and the brighter the stars, the more real she was. Most of the time it was as if she were really in my arms. When the stars got dim and the first light showed in the east, she whispered, "I have to go," and walked over the edge, walking north with the sun to her right and getting dimmer and dimmer.

I got dressed again and drove back and it was finished. That was the last thing Mary ever said to me, spoken a couple of days after she died.

She was not going to get back together with me at all; then she heard how sick I was in Uganda, and she thought the disease might have changed me. (It has. What does it matter about people at the "end of the earth" if you cannot be good to your own people, most of all to your own family?)

Taking off.
     We are airborne at last. Oh, Mary! Mary starlight!

Langi and I will take Adam to his grandfather's, then come back and stay with Mark (Brisbane or Melbourne) until he is well enough to come home.

The stewardess is serving lunch, and for the first time since it happened, I think I may be able to eat more than a mouthful. One stewardess, twenty or thirty people, which is all this plane will hold. News of the shark attack is driving tourists off the island.

As you see, I can print better with my left hand. I should be able to write eventually. The back of my right hand itches, even though it is gone. I wish I could scratch it.

Here comes the food.

An engine has quit. Pilot says no danger.

He is out there, swimming beside the plane. I watched him for a minute or more until he disappeared into a thunderhead. "The tree is my hat." Oh, God.
     Oh my God!
     My blood brother.
     What can I do?

∞

### AFTERWORD

Some things you may have thought fantastic in this are simply true. There really were Japanese detachments left behind on various Pacific islands, marooned detachments that stayed right where they were until the local people turned on them and killed those left alive.

And there really are mysterious ruins on many South Pacific islands.

This story was done as a radio play by Lawrence Santoro, with Neil Gaiman playing Rev. Robbins. Gahan Wilson was our announcer—but when we closed our eyes it was Boris Karloff. There was weird music, and the whole production was far grander than I could have imagined. Thank you, Larry!

# Has Anybody Seen Junie Moon?

∞

The reason I am writing this is to find my manager. I think her name is really probably June Moon or something, but nobody calls her that. I call her Junie and just about everybody else calls her Ms. Moon. She is short and kind of fat, with a big, wide mouth that she smiles with a lot and brown hair. She is pretty too. Real pretty, and that is how you can be sure it is her if ever you see her. Because short fat ladies mostly do not look as good as Junie and nobody thinks, *Boy, I would really like to know her,* like I did that time in England when we went in the cave so she could talk to that crabby old man from Tulsa because Junie believes in dead people coming back and all that.

She made me believe it too. You would too if you had been with Junie like I have.

So I am looking for a Moon just like she is, only she is the Moon that I am looking for. The one she is looking for is the White Cow Moon. That is an Indian name and there is a story behind it just like you would think, only it is a pretty dumb story so I am going to save it for later. Besides, I do not think it is true. Indians are nice people except for a couple I used to know, but they have all these stories that they tell you and then they laugh inside.

I am from Texas, but Junie is from Oklahoma.

That is what started her off. She used to work for a big school they have there, whatever it says on that sweatshirt she wears sometimes. There was this cranky old man in Tulsa that knew lots of stuff, only he was like an Indian. He would tell people, this was when he was still pretty young I guess, and they would never believe him even if it was true.

I have that trouble too, but this cranky old man got real mad and did something about it. He changed his name to Roy T. Laffer and after that he would tell things so they would not believe him or understand, and then laugh inside. Junie never said what the *T.* stood for, but I think I know.

Do you know what it says on the tea boxes? The ones with the man with the cap on them? It says honest tea is the best policy. I know what that means, and I think that cranky old Roy T. Laffer knew it too.

He gave big boxes full of paper to the school Junie worked for, and Junie was the one that went through them and that was how she found out about White Cow Moon. He had a lot of stuff in there about it and Junie saw her name and read it even if his writing was worse even than mine. He had been there and taken pictures and she found those too. She showed me some.

It goes slow. Junie said that was the greatest secret in the world, so I guess it is. And there were pictures of a big old rock that Roy T. Laffer had brought back.

One picture that I saw had it sitting on a scale. The rock was so big you could not hardly see the scale, but then another picture showed the part with numbers and that big old rock was only about a quarter ounce. It was kind of a dirty white like this one cow that we used to have.

Maybe that was really why they call it that and not because a cow jumped over it like those Indians say. That would make a lot more sense, only I did not think of it till just now.

I ought to tell you things about me here so you understand, but first I want to tell more about Junie because I am looking for her, but I know where I am already, which is here in Florida at the Museum of the Strange and Occult. Only it is all big letters like this on our sign out front: THE MUSEUM OF THE STRANGE AND OCCULT ADMISSION $5.50, CHILDREN $2, CHILDREN IN ARMS FREE, SENIORS $3 OR $2 WITH ANOTHER PAID ADMISSION. The letters are gold.

Junie had been to college and everything and was a doctor of physic. When she got out, she thought she was the greatest since One Mug. That is what she says it means, only it is German. I do not remember the German words.

So she went to work at this big laboratory in Chicago where they do physic, only they had her answer the phone and empty the wastebaskets and she quit. Then she went back home to Oklahoma and that is why she was at the big school and was the one that went through Roy T. Laffer's papers. Mostly I do not much like Oklahoma people because they think they are better than Texas people, only Junie really is.

So if you see her or even just talk to somebody that has, you could come by and tell me, or write a letter or even just phone. I will be glad any way you do it. Dottie that works in our office here is putting this in her computer for me and printing it too, whenever I have got a page done. She says you could send e-mail too. That would be all right because Dottie would tell me. I would be very happy any way you did it. Dottie says www.Hercules@freaky.com.

My name is not really Hercules; that is just the name I work under. My name is really Sam, and that is what Junie calls me. If you know her and have talked to her and she said anything about Sam, that was me. If you want to be really formal it is Sam Jr. Only nobody calls me that. Most people I know call me Hercules. Not ever Herk. I do not like it.

Let me tell you how bad I want to find Junie. Sometimes there is a man in the tip that thinks he is stronger. I really like that when it happens because it is usually fun. I will do some things that I figure he can do too, like bending rebars and tearing up bottle caps. Then if I see the tip likes him, I will say something hard and let him win.

A week ago maybe there was this one big guy that thought he was really strong, so I did him like I said. I threw him the two-hundred-pound bell and he caught it, and when he threw it back to me I pretended like I could not catch it and let it fall when I had my legs out of the way and everybody was happy. Only yesterday he came back. He called me Herk and he said I was afraid to go up against him again. The tip was not with him then. So I said all right, and when he could not lift my five-hundred-pound iron I did it with one hand and gave it to him. And when he dropped it I picked him up by his belt and hung him on this high hook. I use for the pulley. I left him up there until everybody was gone too, and when I took him down he did not say a word. He just went away.

Well, I want Junie back so bad that if he was to tell me where she was I would let him win anytime he wanted.

I do not make a lot of money here. It is just five hundred a month and what I make selling my course, but they have got these trailers out back for Jojo and Baby Rita, who is a hundred times fatter than Junie or anybody. So I have one too and it is free. I eat a lot, but that is about all I spend much on. Some fishing gear, but I have got a real good reel and you do not need much else.

Well, you do, but it does not cost the world.

So I have a lot saved and I will give you half if you tell me where Junie Moon is and she is really there when I go look.

This is the way she got to be my manager. I was in England working at a fair that they had at this big castle where King Arthur was born and Junie was in the tip. So when it was over and they were supposed to go see Torchy, Junie would not go. The steerer said she had to, but she kept saying she wanted to talk to me and I could tell she was American like me. So after a while I said she probably knew that if she really wanted to talk to me all she had to do was meet me out back. So then she went.

When I went out back, which was where the toilets were, I did not expect to see her, not really, even if I had let her feel my arm, which is something I do sometimes. But there she was and this is what she said, with the little marks around it that you are supposed to use and all of that stuff. Dottie help me with this part.

"Hercules, I really need your help. I don't know whether I was really one of the daughters of King Thespius, but there were fifty of them so there's a pretty good chance of it. Will you help me?"

That was the first thing Junie ever said to me, and I remember it just like it was a couple days ago. Naturally I said I would.

"You will!?! Just like that????"

I said sure.

"I can pay you. I was going to say that. A hundred pounds right now, and another hundred pounds when I'm over the fence. I can pass it to you through the fence. Look." She opened her purse and showed me the money. "Is that enough?"

I explained how she did not have to.

"You'll be in danger. You might be arrested."

Junie looked really worried when she said that, and it made me feel wonderful, so I said that was okay. I had been arrested once already in England besides in America, and to tell the truth in England it was kind of fun, especially when they could not get their handcuffs to go around my wrists and then they got these plastic strap cuffs and put those on me and I broke six pairs. I like English people, only nothing they say makes any sense.

Junie said, "Back there, you threw an enormous barbell up in the air and caught it. How much did you say it weighed?"

I said, "Three hundred. That was my three-hundred-pound bell."

"And does it actually weigh three hundred pounds?"

I said sure.

"I weigh only a little more than half that. Could you throw me, oh, fifteen feet into the air?"

I knew I could, but I said I did not know because I wanted to get my hands on her.

"But you might? Do you really think you might be able to, Hercules?"

I sort of raised up my shoulders the way you do and let them drop.

"We—if you failed to throw me high enough I would get a severe electric shock." She looked scared.

I nodded really serious and said what we ought to do was try it first, right now. We would measure something that was fifteen feet, and then I would throw her up, and she could tell me if I got her up that high. So she pointed to the temporary wires they had strung up for the fair, and I wanted to know if those were the ones. She said no. They were not fifteen feet either. Ten or twelve maybe. But I said, "Okay, only do not reach out and grab them or you might get killed," and she said okay.

So I got my hands around her, which was what I had been wanting to do, and lifted her up and sort of weighed her a couple times, moving her up and down, you know how you do, and then I spun around like for the hammer throw, and I heaved her maybe ten feet higher than those wires, and caught her easy when she came down. It made her really scared too, and I was sorry for that, but I got down on my knees and hugged her and I said, "There, there, there," and pretty soon she stopped crying.

Then I said, "Was that high enough?" And she said it was.

She was still shaky after that, so we went back inside and she sat with me while I waited for the next tip. That was when she showed me the pictures that Roy T. Laffer had taken up on the White Cow Moon and the pictures of the rock that he had brought back, a great big rock that did not hardly weigh anything. "He let a little boy take it to school for a science show," Junie told me, "and afterward the science teacher threw it out. Mr. Laffer went to the school and tried to reclaim it the following day, but apparently it had been blown out of the Dumpster."

I promised her I would keep an eye out for it.

"Thank you. But the point is its lightness. Do you know why the moon doesn't fall into the Earth, Hercules?"

I said that if I was going to throw her around she ought to call me Sam, and she promised she would. Then she asked me again about the moon and I said, "Sure, I know that one. The moon beams hold it up."

Junie did not laugh. "Really, Sam, it does. It falls exactly as a bullet falls to Earth."

She went and got a broom to show me, holding it level. "Suppose that this were a rifle. If I pulled the trigger, the bullet would fly out of the barrel at a speed of three thousand feet per second or so."

I said okay.

"Now say that you were to drop that weight over there at the very same moment that the rifle fired. Your weight would hit the ground at the same moment that the rifle bullet did." She waited for me to argue with her, but I said okay again.

"Even though the bullet was flying along horizontally, it was also falling. What's more, it was falling at virtually the same rate that your weight did. I'm sure you must know about artificial satellites, Sam."

I said I did, because I felt like I could remember about them if I had a little more time, and besides, I had the feeling Junie would tell me anyhow.

"They orbit the Earth just as the moon does. So why doesn't the bullet orbit it too?"

I said it probably hit a fence post or something.

She looked at me and sort of sucked on her lips, and looked again. "That may be a much better answer than you can possibly be aware of. But no. It doesn't orbit Earth because it isn't going fast enough. A sidereal month is about twenty-seven days, and the moon is two hundred and forty thousand miles away, on average. So if its orbit were circular—that isn't quite true, but I'm trying to make this as simple as I can—the moon would be traveling at about three thousand, five hundred feet a second. Not much faster than our rifle bullet, in other words."

I could see she wanted me to nod, so I did.

"The moon can travel that slowly." "Slowly" is what she said. Junie is always saying crazy stuff like that. "Because it's so far away. It would have to fall two hundred and forty thousand miles before it could hit the Earth. But the bullet has to fall only about three feet. Another way of putting it is that the closer a satellite is, the faster it must move if it is to stay in orbit."

I said that the bullet would have to go really fast, and Junie nodded. "It would have to go so fast that the curve of the Earth was falling away from it as rapidly as the bullet itself was falling toward the Earth. That's what an orbit is, that combination of vertical and horizontal motions."

Right then I do not think I was too clear on which one was which, but I nodded again.

Then Junie's voice got sort of trembly. "Now suppose that you were to make a telephone call to your wife back in America," is what she said. So I explained I did not have one, and after that she sounded a lot better.

"Well, if you were to call your family, your mother and father, your call would go through a communications satellite that circles the Earth once a day, so that it seems to us that it is always in the same place. It can do that because it's a good deal lower and going a great deal faster."

Then she got out a pen and a little notepad and showed me how fast the bullet would have to go to stay in orbit just whizzing around the world over and over until it hit something. I do not remember how you do it, or what the answer was except that it was about a jillion. Junie said anything like that would make a terrible bang all the time if it was in our air instead of up in space where stuff like that is supposed to be. Well, about then is when the tip came in for the last show. I did my act and Junie sat in the front row smiling and cheering and clapping and I felt really swell.

So after it was all over we went to Merlin's cave under the big castle and down by the water, and that was when Junie told me how King Arthur was born there, and I told her how I was putting up at the King Arthur, which was a pub with rooms upstairs. I said they were nice people there and it was clean and cheap, which is what I want anywhere, and the landlord's name was Arthur too, just like the pub's. Only after a while when we had gone a long ways down the little path and got almost to the water I started to sort of hint around about why are we going way down here, Junie, with just that little flashlight you got out of your purse?

Maybe I ought not say this right here, but it is the truth. It was scary down there. A big person like I am is not supposed to be scared and I know that. But way up on the rocks where the fair was the lights kept on going out and you could see the fair was just sort of like paint the old walls of that big castle. It was like somebody had gone to where my dad was buried and painted all over his stone with flowers and clowns and puppies and kitties and all that kind of thing. Only now the paint was flaking away and you could see what was underneath and he had run out with his gun when the feds broke our front door and they killed him.

Here is what I think it was down there and what was so scary about it. King Arthur had been born there and there had been knights and stuff afterward that he was the head of. And they had been big strong people like me on big strong horses and they had gone around wearing armor and with swords and for a while had made the bad guys pay, and everybody had loved them so much that they still remembered all about them after a hundred years. There was a Lancelot room in the pub where I was staying and a Galahad room, and I was in the Gawain room. And Arthur told me how those men had all been this king's knights and he said I was the jolly old green giant.

Only it was all over and done with now. It was dead and gone like my dad. King Arthur was dead and his knights were too, and the bad guys were the head of everything and had been for a long, long time. We were the paint, even Junie was paint, and now the paint was getting dull the way paint does, with cracks all over it and falling off. And I thought this was not just where that king was born; this was where he died too. And I knew that it was true the way I meant it.

Well, there was a big wire fence there with a sign about the electricity, only it was not any fifteen feet high. I could have reached up to the top of it. Ten feet, maybe, or not even that.

"Can you pick me up and throw me over?" Junie said.

It was crazy, she would have come down on rocks, so I said I could, only she would have to tell why she wanted me to so much or I would not do it.

She took my hand then, and it felt wonderful. "People come back, Sam. They come back from death. I know scientists aren't supposed to say things like that, but it's true. They do."

That made me feel even better because it meant I would see my dad again even if we would not have our farm that the feds took anymore.

"Do you remember that I said I might have been one of the fifty daughters of Thespius three thousand years ago? I don't know if that's really true, or even whether there was a real King Thespius who had fifty daughters. Perhaps there was, and perhaps I was one of them—I'd like to think so. But this really was Merlin's cave and Roy T. Laffer was Merlin in an earlier life. There were unmistakable indications in his papers. I know it with as much certainty as I know Kepler's Laws."

That got me trying to remember who Kepler was, because I did not think Junie had told anything about him up to then. Or after either. Anyway, I did not say much.

"I've tried to contact Laffer in his house in Tulsa, Sam. I tried for days at a time, but he wasn't there. I think he may be here. This is terribly important to me, and you said you'd help me. Now will you throw me over?"

I shook my head, but it was really dark down there and maybe Junie did not see it. I said I was not going to be on the other side to catch her and throw her back, so how was she going to get out? She said when they opened in the morning. I said she would get arrested and she said she did not care. It seemed to me that there were too many getting arrested when she said that, so I twisted on the lock, thinking to break the shackle. It was a pretty good lock and I broke the hasp instead. Then I threw the lock in the ocean and Junie and I went inside like she wanted. That was how she found out where White Cow Moon was and how to get on it too, if she wanted to.

It was about two o'clock in the morning when we came out, I think. I went back to the King Arthur's and went to bed, and next day Junie moved in down the hall. Hers was the Lancelot room. After that she was my manager, which I told everybody and showed her off. She helped me write my course then, and got this shop in Falmouth to print it up for us.

Then when the fair was over she got us tickets home, and on the airplane we got to talking about the moon. I started it and it was a bad mistake, but we did not know it for a couple of days. Junie had been talking about taking pictures and I said, "How can you if it goes so fast?"

"It doesn't, Sam." She took my hand and I liked that a lot. "It circles the Earth quite slowly, so slowly that to an observer on Earth it hardly seems to move at all, which was one of the things Roy T. Laffer confided to me."

I said I never had seen him, only the lady with the baby and the old man with the stick.

"That was him, Sam. He told me then, and it was implied in his papers anyway. Do you remember the rock?"

I said there had been lots of rocks, which was true because it had been a cave in the rocks.

"I mean the White Cow Moon rock in the picture, the one he lent to the science fair."

I said, "It didn't hardly weigh anything."

"Yes." Junie was sort of whispering then. "It had very little weight, yet it was hard to move. You had to pull and pull, even though it felt so light when you held it. Do you understand what that means, Sam?"

"Somebody might have glued it down?"

"No. It means that it had a great deal of mass, but very little weight. I'm sure you haven't heard of antimatter—matter in which the protons are replaced by antiprotons, the electrons by positrons, and so on?"

I said no.

"It's only theoretical so far. But current theory says that although antimatter would possess mass just as ordinary matter does, it would be repelled, by the gravitational field of ordinary matter. It would fall up, in other words."

By the time she got to the part about falling up Junie was talking to herself mostly, only I could still hear her. "Our theory says a collision between matter and antimatter should result in a nuclear explosion, but either the theory's mistaken or there's some natural means of circumventing it. Because the White Cow Moon rock was composed of nearly equal parts matter and antimatter. It had to be! The result was rock with a great deal of mass but very little weight, and that's what allows the White Cow Moon to orbit so slowly.

"Listen to me, Sam." She made me turn in my airplane seat till I was looking at her, and I broke the arm a little. "We physicists say that all matter falls at the same rate, which is basically a convenient lie, true only in a hard vacuum. If that barbell you throw around were balsa wood, it wouldn't fall nearly as fast as your iron one, because it would be falling in air. In the same way, a satellite with great mass but little weight can orbit slowly and quietly through Earth's atmosphere, falling toward the surface only as fast as the surface falls away from it."

"Wouldn't it hit a mountain or something, Junie?"

"No, because any mountain that rose in its path would be chipped away as it rose. As light as the White Cow Moon must be, its mass has got to be enormous. Not knowing its orbit—not yet—we can't know what mountain ranges it may cross, but when we do we'll find it goes through passes. They are passes because it goes through them."

Junie got real quiet for a while after she said that, and now I wish she had stayed quiet. Then she said, "Just think what we could do, Sam, if we could manufacture metals like that rock. Launch vehicles that would reach escape velocity from Earth using less thrust than that of an ordinary launch vehicle on the moon."

That was the main trouble, I think. Junie saying that was. The other may have hurt us some too, but that did for sure.

We were flying to Tulsa. I guess I should have written about that before. Anyway, when we got there Junie got us a bunch of rooms like an apartment in a really nice hotel. We were going to have to wait for my bells to come back on a boat, so Junie said we could look for the White Cow Moon while we were waiting and she would line me up some good dates to play when my stuff got there. We were sitting around having Diet Cokes out of the little icebox in the kitchen when the feds knocked on the door.

Junie said, "Let me," and went, and that was how they could push in. But they would have if it had been me anyway because they had guns. I would have had to let them just like Junie.

The one in the blue suit said, "Ms. Moon?" and Junie said yes. Then he said, "We're from the government, and we've come to help you and Mr. Moon."

My name never was Moon, but we both changed ours after that anyway. She was Junie Manoe and I was Sam Manoe. Junie picked Manoe to go with *JM* on her bags. But that was not until after the feds went away.

What they had said was we had to forget about the moon or we would get in a lot of trouble. Junie said we did not care about the moon, we had nothing to do with the moon, what we were doing mainly was getting ready to write a biography about a certain old man named Roy T. Laffer.

The man in the blue suit said, "Good, keep it that way." The man in the black suit never did say anything, but you could see he was hoping to shoot us. I tried to ask Junie some questions after they went away, but she would not talk because she was pretty sure they were listening, or somebody was.

When we were living in the house she explained about that, and said probably somebody on the plane had told on us, or else the feds listened to everything anybody said on planes. I said we were lucky they had not shot us, and told her about my dad, and that was when she said it was too dangerous for me. She never would tell me exactly where the White Cow Moon was after that, and it traveled around anyway, she said. But she got me a really good job in a gym there. I helped train people and showed them how to do things, and even got on TV doing ads for the gym with some other men and some ladies.

Only I knew that while I was working at the gym Junie was going out in her car looking for the White Cow Moon, and at night I would write down the mileage when she was in the living room reading. I figured she would find the White Cow Moon and go there at least a couple of times and maybe three or four and then the mileage would always be the same. And that was how it worked out. I thought that was pretty smart of me, but I was not going to tell Junie how smart I had been until I found it myself and she could not say it was too dangerous.

I looked in her desk for moon rocks too, but I never found any, so that is why I do not think Junie had been up there on the White Cow Moon yet.

Well, for three days in a row it was just about 125 on the mileage. It was 123 one time, and 124 and then 126. So that was how I knew 63 miles from Tulsa. That day after work I went out and bought the biggest bike at the big Ridin' th' Wild Wind store. It is a Harley and better for me than a car because my head does not scrape. It is nearly big enough.

Only that night Junie did not come home. I thought she had gone up on the White Cow Moon, so I quit my job at the gym and went looking for her for about a month.

A lot of things happened while I was looking for her on my bike. Like I went into this one beer joint and started asking people if they had seen Junie or her car either. This one man that had a bike too started yelling at me and would not let me talk to anybody else. I had been very polite and he never would say why he was mad. He kept saying, "I guess you think you are tough." So finally I picked him up. I think he must have weighed about three hundred pounds because he felt about like my bell when I threw him up and banged him on the ceiling. When I let him down he hit me a couple of times with a chain he had and I decided probably he was a fed and that made me mad. I put my foot on him while I broke his chain into five or six pieces, and every time I broke off a new piece I would drop it on his face. Then I picked him up again and threw him through the window.

Then I went outside and let him pick himself up and threw him up onto the roof. That was fifteen feet easy and I felt pretty proud for it even if it did take three tries. I still do.

After that, two men that had come out to watch told me how they had seen a brown Ford like Junie's out on this one ranch and how to get there. I went and it was more than sixty-three miles to go and Junie's brown Ford was not there. But when I went back to our house in Tulsa it was sixty-eight. A lot else happened for about two weeks, and then I went back to that ranch and lifted my bike over their fence real careful and rode out to where those men had said and sat there thinking about Junie and things that she had said to me, and how she had felt that time I threw her higher than the wires back in England. And it got late and you could see the moon, and I remembered how she had said the feds were building a place for missiles on the other side where nobody could reach it or even see it and that was why they were mad at us. It is supposed to be to shoot at other countries like England, but it is really to shoot at us in case we do anything the feds do not like.

About then a man on a horse came by and said did I want anything. I told him about the car, and he said there used to be a brown car like that parked out there, only a tow truck cut the fence and took it away. I wanted to know whose truck it had been, but he did not know.

So that is about all I have got to say. Sometimes I dream about how while I was talking to the man on the horse a little white moon sort of like a cloud came by, only when I turned my head to look it was already gone. I do not think that really happened or the little woman with the baby and the old man with the stick in the cave either. I think it is all just dreams, but maybe it did.

What I really think is that the feds have got Junie. If they do, all they have got to do is let her go and I will not be mad anymore after that. I promise. But if they will not do it and I find out for sure they have got her, there is going to be a fight. So if you see her or even talk to anybody that has, it would be good if you told me. Please.

I am not the only one that does not like the feds. A lot of other people do not like them either. I know that they are a whole lot smarter than I am, and how good at telling lies and fooling people they are. I am not like that. I am more like Roy T. Laffer, because sometimes I cannot even get people to believe the truth.

But you can believe this, because it is true. I have never in my whole life had a fight with a smart person or even seen anybody else have one either. That is because when the fight starts the smart people are not there anymore. They have gone off someplace else, and when it is over they come back and tell you how much they did in the fight, only it is all lies. Now they have big important gangs with suits and guns. They are a lot bigger than just me, but they are not bigger than everybody and if all of us get mad at once maybe we will bring the whole thing crashing down.

After that I would look through the pieces and find Junie, or if I did not find her I would go up on the White Cow Moon myself like Roy T. Laffer did and find her up there.

∞

### AFTERWORD

One of life's principal lessons is that intelligence is a minor virtue. The cardinal virtues are prudence, justice, temperance, and fortitude. Sam is not bright; no doubt you are, and if you are you could probably swindle him without much difficulty. But would it be prudent?

You will probably not need to be told that Roy T. Laffer is a thinly fictionalized Raphael Aloysius Lafferty. His byline was R. A. Lafferty, and we called him Ray in consequence. I didn't know him well, and I know of no one who did. He was enormously learned and terribly shy, and drank too much when he had to appear in public. Other than that, I suggest you consult *Faces of Science Fiction*, if you can find a copy. There is a fine photograph of him there, with a few paragraphs of autobiography. He is a great writer who remains undiscovered.

# A Cabin on the Coast

It might have been a child's drawing of a ship. He blinked, and blinked again. There were masts and sails, surely. One stack, perhaps another. If the ship were really there at all. He went back to his father's beach cottage, climbed the five wooden steps, wiped his feet on the coco mat.

Lissy was still in bed, but awake, sitting up now. It must have been the squeaking of the steps, he thought. Aloud he said, "Sleep good?"

He crossed the room and kissed her. She caressed him and said, "You shouldn't go swimming without a suit, dear wonderful swimmer. How was the Pacific?"

"Peaceful. Cold. It's too early for people to be up, and there's nobody within a mile of here anyway."

"Get into bed then. How about the fish?"

"Salt water makes the sheets sticky. The fish have seen them before." He went to the corner, where a showerhead poked from the wall. The beach cottage—Lissy called it a cabin—had running water of the sometimes and rusty variety.

"They might bite 'em off. Sharks, you know. Little ones."

"Castrating woman." The shower coughed, doused him with icy spray, coughed again.

"You look worried."

"No."

"Is it your dad?"

He shook his head, then thrust it under the spray, fingers combing his dark, curly hair.

"You think he'll come out here? Today?"

He withdrew, considering. "If he's back from Washington, and he knows we're here."

"But he couldn't know, could he?"

He turned off the shower and grabbed a towel, already damp and a trifle sandy. "I don't see how."

"Only he might guess." Lissy was no longer smiling. "Where else could we go? Hey, what did we do with my underwear?"

"Your place. Your folks'. Any motel."

She swung long, golden legs out of bed, still holding the sheet across her lap. Her breasts were nearly perfect hemispheres, except for the tender protrusions of their pink nipples. He decided he had never seen breasts like that. He sat down on the bed beside her. "I love you very much," he said. "You know that?"

It made her smile again. "Does that mean you're coming back to bed?"

"If you want me to."

"I want a swimming lesson. What will people say if I tell them I came here and didn't go swimming?"

He grinned at her. "That it's that time of the month."

"You know what you are? You're filthy!" She pushed him. "Absolutely filthy! I'm going to bite your ears off." Tangled in the sheet, they fell off the bed together. "There they are!"

"There what are?"

"My bra and stuff. We must have kicked them under the bed. Where are our bags?"

"Still in the trunk. I never carried them in."

"Would you get mine? My swimsuit's in it."

"Sure," he said.

"And put on some pants!"

"My suit's in my bag too." He found his trousers and got the keys to the Triumph. Outside the sun was higher, the chill of the fall morning nearly gone. He looked for the ship and saw it. Then it winked out like a star.

That evening they made a fire of driftwood and roasted the big, greasy Italian sausages he had brought from town, making giant hot dogs by clamping them in French bread. He had brought red supermarket wine too; they chilled it in the Pacific. "I never ate this much in my life," Lissy said.

"You haven't eaten anything yet."

"I know, but just looking at this sandwich would make me full if I wasn't so hungry." She bit off the end. "Cuff tough woof."

"What?"

"Castrating woman. That's what you called me this morning, Tim. Now *this* is a castrating woman."

"Don't talk with your mouth full."

"You sound like my mother. Give me some wine. You're hogging it."

He handed the bottle over. "It isn't bad, if you don't object to a complete lack of character."

"I sleep with you, don't I?"

"I have character; it's just all rotten."

"You said you wanted to get married."

"Let's go. You can finish that thing in the car."

"You drank half the bottle. You're too high to drive."

"Bullshoot."

Lissy giggled. "You just said 'bullshoot.' Now *that's* character!"

He stood up. "Come on; let's go. It's only five hundred miles to Reno. We can get married there in the morning."

"You're serious, aren't you?"

"If you are."

"Sit down."

"You were testing me," he said. "That's not fair, now is it?"

"You've been so worried all day. I wanted to see if it was about me—if you thought you'd made a terrible mistake."

"We've made a mistake," he said. "I was trying to fix it just now."

"You think your dad is going to make it rough for you—"

"Us."

"—for us because it might hurt him in the next election."

He shook his head. "Not that. All right, maybe partly that. But he means it too. You don't understand him."

"I've got a father myself."

"Not like mine. Ryan was almost grown-up before he left Ireland. Taught by nuns and all that. Besides, I've got six older brothers and two sisters. You're the oldest kid. Ryan's probably at least fifteen years older than your folks."

"Is that really his name? Ryan Neal?"

"His full name is Timothy Ryan Neal, the same as mine. I'm Timothy Junior. He used Ryan when he went into politics because there was another Tim Neal around then, and we've always called me Tim to get away from the 'Junior.'"

"I'm going to call him Tim again, like the nuns must have when he was young. Big Tim. You're Little Tim."

"Okay with me. I don't know if Big Tim is going to like it."

Something was moving, it seemed, out where the sun had set. Something darker against the dark horizon.

"What made you Junior anyway? Usually it's the oldest boy."

"He didn't want it, and would never let Mother do it. But she wanted to, and I was born during the Democratic convention that year."

"He had to go, of course."

"Yeah, he had to go, Lissy. If you don't understand that, you don't understand politics at all. They hoped I'd hold off for a few days, and what the hell, Mother'd had eight with no problems. Anyway, he was used to it—he was the youngest of seven boys himself. So she got to call me what she wanted."

"But then she died." The words sounded thin and lonely against the pounding of the surf.

"Not because of that."

Lissy upended the wine bottle; he saw her throat pulse three times. "Will I die because of that, Little Tim?"

"I don't think so." He tried to think of something gracious and comforting. "If we decide we want children, that's the risk I have to take."

"*You* have to take? Bullshoot."

"That both of us have to take. Do you think it was easy for Ryan, raising nine kids by himself?"

"You love him, don't you?"

"Sure I love him. He's my father."

"And now you think you might be ruining things for him. For my sake."

"That's not why I want us to be married, Lissy."

She was staring into the flames; he was not certain she had even heard him. "Well, now I know why his pictures look so grim. So gaunt."

He stood up again. "If you're through eating . . ."

"You want to go back to the cabin? You can screw me right here on the beach—there's nobody here but us."

"I didn't mean that."

"Then why go in there and look at the walls? Out here we've got the fire and the ocean. The moon ought to be up pretty soon."

"It would be warmer."

"With just that dinky little kerosene stove? I'd rather sit here by the fire. In a minute I'm going to send you off to get me some more wood. You can run up to the cabin and get a shirt too if you want to."

"I'm okay."

"Traditional roles. Big Tim must have told you all about them. The woman has the babies and keeps the home fires burning. You're not going to end up looking like him though, are you, Little Tim?"

"I suppose so. He used to look just like me."

"Really?"

He nodded. "He had his picture taken just after he got into politics. He was running for ward committeeman, and he had a poster made. We've still got the picture, and it looks like me with a high collar and a funny hat."

"She knew, didn't she?" Lissy said. For a moment he did not understand what she meant. "Now go and get some more wood. Only don't wear yourself out, because when you come back we're going to take care of that little thing that's bothering you, and we're going to spend the night on the beach."

When he came back she was asleep, but he woke her carrying her up to the beach cottage.

Next morning he woke up alone. He got up and showered and shaved, supposing that she had taken the car into town to get something for breakfast. He had filled the coffeepot and put it on before he looked out the shore-side window and saw the Triumph still waiting near the road.

There was nothing to be alarmed about, of course. She had awakened before he had and gone out for an early dip. He had done the same thing himself the morning before. The little patches of green cloth that were her bathing suit were hanging over the back of a rickety chair, but then they were still damp from last night. Who would want to put on a damp, clammy suit? She had gone in naked, just as he had.

He looked out the other window, wanting to see her splashing in the surf, waiting for him. The ship was there, closer now, rolling like a derelict. No smoke came from its clumsy funnel and no sails were set, but dark banners hung from its rigging. Then there was no ship, only wheeling gulls and the empty ocean. He called her name, but no one answered.

He put on his trunks and a jacket and went outside. A wind had smoothed the sand. The tide had come, obliterating their fire, reclaiming the driftwood he had gathered.

For two hours he walked up and down the beach, calling, telling himself there was nothing wrong. When he forced himself not to think of Lissy dead, he could only think of the headlines, the ninety seconds of ten o'clock news, how Ryan would look, how Pat—all his brothers—would look at him. And when he turned his mind from that, Lissy was dead again, her pale hair snarled with kelp as she rolled in the surf, green crabs feeding from her arms.

He got into the Triumph and drove to town. In the little brick station he sat beside the desk of a fat cop and told his story.

The fat cop said, "Kid, I can see why you want us to keep it quiet."

Tim said nothing. There was a paperweight on the desk—a baseball of white glass.

"You probably think we're out to get you, but we're not. Tomorrow we'll put out a missing persons report, but we don't have to say anything about you or the senator in it, and we won't."

"Tomorrow?"

"We got to wait twenty-four hours, in case she should show up. That's the law. But kid—" The fat cop glanced at his notes.

"Tim."

"Right. Tim. She ain't going to show up. You got to get yourself used to that."

"She could be . . ." Without wanting to, he let it trail away.

"Where? You think she snuck off and went home? She could walk out to the road and hitch, but you say her stuff's still there. Kidnapped? Nobody could have pulled her out of bed without waking you up. Did you kill her?"

"No!" Tears he could not hold back were streaming down his cheeks.

"Right. I've talked to you and I don't think you did. But you're the only one that could have. If her body washes up, we'll have to look into that."

Tim's hands tightened on the wooden arms of the chair. The fat cop pushed a box of tissues across the desk.

"Unless it washes up, though, it's just a missing person, okay? But she's dead, kid, and you're going to have to get used to it. Let me tell you what happened." He cleared his throat.

"She got up while you were still asleep, probably about when it started to get light. She did just what you thought she did—went out for a nice refreshing swim before you woke up. She went out too far, and probably she got a cramp. The ocean's cold as hell now. Maybe she yelled, but if she did she was too far out, and the waves covered it up. People think drowners holler like fire sirens, but they don't—they don't have that much air. Sometimes they don't make any noise at all."

Tim stared at the gleaming paperweight.

"The current here runs along the coast—you probably know that. Nobody ought to go swimming without somebody else around, but sometimes it seems like everybody does it. We lose a dozen or so a year. In maybe four or five cases we find them. That's all."

The beach cottage looked abandoned when he returned. He parked the Triumph and went inside and found the stove still burning, his coffee perked to tar. He took the pot outside, dumped the coffee, scrubbed the pot with beach sand, and rinsed it with salt water. The ship, which had been invisible through the window of the cottage, was almost plain when he stood waist deep. He heaved the coffeepot back to shore and swam out some distance, but when he straightened up in the water, the ship was gone.

Back inside he made fresh coffee and packed Lissy's things in her suitcase. When that was done, he drove into town again. Ryan was still in Washington, but Tim told his secretary where he was. "Just in case anybody reports me missing," he said.

She laughed. "It must be pretty cold for swimming."

"I like it," he told her. "I want to have at least one more long swim."

"All right, Tim. When he calls, I'll let him know. Have a good time."

"Wish me luck," he said, and hung up. He got a hamburger and more coffee at a Jack in the Box and went back to the cottage and walked a long way along the beach.

He had intended to sleep that night, but he did not. From time to time he got up and looked out the window at the ship, sometimes visible by moonlight, sometimes only a dark presence in the lower night sky. When the first light of dawn came, he put on his trunks and went into the water.

For a mile or more, as well as he could estimate the distance, he could not see it. Then it was abruptly close, the long oars like the legs of a water spider, the funnel belching sparks against the still-dim sky, sparks that seemed to become new stars.

He swam faster then, knowing that if the ship vanished he would turn back and save himself, knowing too that if it only retreated before him, retreated forever, he would drown. It disappeared behind a cobalt wave, reappeared. He sprinted and grasped at the sea-slick shaft of an oar, and it was like touching a living being. Quite suddenly he stood on the deck, with no memory of how he came there.

Bare feet pattered on the planks, but he saw no crew. A dark flag lettered with strange script flapped aft, and some vague recollection of a tour of a naval ship with his father years before made him touch his forehead. There was a sound that might have been laughter or many other things. The captain's cabin would be aft too, he thought. He went there, bracing himself against the wild roll, and found a door.

Inside, something black crouched upon a dais. "I've come for Lissy," Tim said.

There was no reply, but a question hung in the air. He answered it almost without intending to. "I'm Timothy Ryan Neal, and I've come for Lissy. Give her back to me."

A light, it seemed, dissolved the blackness. Cross-legged on the dais, a slender man in tweeds sucked at a long clay pipe. "It's Irish, are ye?" he asked.

"American," Tim said.

"With such a name? I don't believe ye. Where's yer feathers?"

"I want her back," Tim said again.

"An' if ye don't get her?"

"Then I'll tear this ship apart. You'll have to kill me or take me too."

"Spoken like a true son of the ould sod," said the man in tweeds. He scratched a kitchen match on the sole of his boot and lit his pipe. "Sit down, will ye? I don't fancy lookin' up like that. It hurts me neck. Sit down, and 'tis possible we can strike an agreement."

"This is crazy," Tim said. "The whole thing is crazy."

"It is that," the man in tweeds replied. "An' there's much, much more comin'. Ye'd best brace for it, Tim me lad. Now sit down."

There was a stout wooden chair behind Tim where the door had been. He sat. "Are you about to tell me you're a leprechaun? I warn you, I won't believe it."

"Me? One o' them scamperin', thievin', cobblin' little misers? I'd shoot meself. Me name's Daniel O'Donoghue, King o' Connaught. Do ye believe that, now?"

"No," Tim said.

"What would ye believe then?"

"That this is—some way, somehow—what people call a saucer. That you and your crew are from a planet of another sun."

Daniel laughed. "'Tis a close encounter you're havin', is it? Would ye like to see me as a tiny green man wi' horns like a snail's? I can do that too."

"Don't bother."

"All right, I won't, though 'tis a good shape. A man can take it and be whatever he wants, one o' the People o' Peace or a bit o' a man from Mars. I've used it for both, and there's nothin' better."

"You took Lissy," Tim said.

"And how would ye be knowin' that?"

"I thought she'd drowned."

"Did ye now?"

"And that this ship—or whatever it is—was just a sign, an omen. I talked to a policeman and he as good as told me, but I didn't really think about what he said until last night, when I was trying to sleep."

"Is it a dream yer havin'? Did ye ever think on that?"

"If it's a dream, it's still real," Tim said doggedly. "And anyway, I saw your ship when I was awake, yesterday and the day before."

"Or yer dreamin' now ye did. But go on wi' it."

"He said Lissy couldn't have been abducted because I was in the same bed, and that she'd gone out for a swim in the morning and drowned. But she could have been abducted, if she had gone out for the swim first. If someone had come for her with a boat. And she wouldn't have drowned, because she didn't swim good enough to drown. She was afraid of the water. We went in yesterday, and even with me there, she would hardly go in over her knees. So it was you."

"Yer right, ye know," Daniel said. He formed a little steeple of his fingers. " 'Twas us."

Tim was recalling stories that had been read to him when he was a child. "Fairies steal babies, don't they? And brides. Is that why you do it? So we'll think that's who you are?"

"Bless ye, 'tis true," Daniel told him. " 'Tis the Fair Folk we are. The jinn o' the desert too, and the saucer riders ye say ye credit, and forty score more. Would ye be likin' to see me wi' me goatskin breeches and me panpipe?" He chuckled. "Have ye never wondered why we're so much alike the world over? Or thought that we don't always know just which shape's the best for a place, so the naiads and the dryads might as well be the ladies o' the Deeny Shee? Do ye know what the folk o' the Barb'ry Coast call the hell that's under their sea?"

Tim shook his head.

"Why, 'tis Domdaniel. I wonder why that is, now. Tim, ye say ye want this girl."

"That's right."

"An' ye say there'll be trouble and plenty for us if ye don't have her. But let me tell ye now that if ye don't get her, wi' our blessin' to boot, ye'll drown—hold your tongue, can't ye, for 'tis worse than that. If ye don't get her wi' our blessin', 'twill be seen that ye were drownin' now. Do ye take me meaning?"

"I think so. Close enough."

"Ah, that's good, that is. Now here's me offer. Do ye remember how things stood before we took her?"

"Of course."

"They'll stand so again, if ye but do what I tell ye. 'Tis yerself that will remember, Tim Neal, but she'll remember nothin'. An' the truth of it is, there'll be nothin' to remember, for it'll all be gone, every stick of it. This policeman ye spoke wi', for instance. Ye've me word that ye will not have done it."

"What do I have to do?" Tim asked.

"Service. Serve us. Do whatever we ask of ye. We'd sooner have a broth of a girl like yer Lissy than a great hulk of a lad like yerself, but then too, we'd sooner be havin' one that's willin', for the unwillin' girls are everywhere—I don't doubt but ye've seen it yerself. A hundred years, that's all we ask of ye. 'Tis short enough, like Doyle's wife. Will ye do it?"

"And everything will be the same, at the end, as it was before you took Lissy?"

"Not everythin', I didn't say that. Ye'll remember, don't ye remember me sayin' so? But for her and all the country round, why 'twill be the same."

"All right," Tim said. "I'll do it."

"'Tis a brave lad ye are. Now I'll tell ye what I'll do. I said a hundred years, to which ye agreed—"

Tim nodded.

"—but I'll have no unwillin' hands about me boat, nor no ungrateful ones neither. I'll make it twenty. How's that? Sure and I couldn't say fairer, could I?"

Daniel's figure was beginning to waver and fade; the image of the dark mass Tim had seen first hung about it like a cloud.

"Lay yerself on yer belly, for I must put me foot upon yer head. Then the deal's done."

The salt ocean was in his mouth and his eyes. His lungs burst for breath. He revolved in the blue chasm of water, tried to swim, at last exploded gasping into the air.

The king had said he would remember, but the years were fading already. Drudging, dancing, buying, spying, prying, waylaying, and betraying when he walked in the world of men. Serving something that he had never wholly understood. Sailing foggy seas that were sometimes of this earth. Floating among the constellations. The years and the slaps and the kicks were all fading, and with them (and he rejoiced in it) the days when he had begged.

He lifted an arm, trying to regain his old stroke, and found that he was very tired. Perhaps he had never really rested in all those years. Certainly, he could not recall resting. Where was he? He paddled listlessly, not knowing if he was swimming away from land, if he was in the center of an ocean. A wave elevated him, a long, slow swell of blue under the gray sky. A glory—the rising or perhaps the setting sun—shone to his right. He swam toward it, caught sight of a low coast.

He crawled onto the sand and lay there for a time, his back struck by drops of spray like rain. Near his eyes, the beach seemed nearly black. There were bits of charcoal, fragments of half-burned wood. He raised his head, pushing away the earth, and saw an empty bottle of greenish glass nearly buried in the wet sand.

When he was able at last to rise, his limbs were stiff and cold. The dawnlight had become daylight, but there was no warmth in it. The beach cottage stood only about a hundred yards away, one window golden with sunshine that had entered from the other side, the walls in shadow. The red Triumph gleamed beside the road.

At the top of a small dune he turned and looked back out to sea. A black freighter with a red and white stack was visible a mile or two out, but it was only a freighter. For a moment he felt a kind of regret, a longing for a part of his life that he had hated but that was now gone forever. *I will never be able to tell her what happened,* he thought. And then, *Yes I will, if only I let her think I'm just making it up.* And then, *No wonder so many people tell so many stories. Good-bye to all that.*

The steps creaked under his weight, and he wiped the sand from his feet on the coco mat. Lissy was in bed. When she heard the door open she sat up, then drew up the sheet to cover her breasts.

"Big Tim," she said. "You did come. Tim and I were hoping you would."

When he did not answer, she added, "He's out having a swim, I think. He should be around in a minute."

And when he still said nothing. "We're—Tim and I—we're going to be married."

❧

## Author's Note

I had intended to end this collection with "Has Anybody Seen Junie Moon?" Vaughne Hansen and Chris Cohen, who market my work from the Virginia Kidd Agency, insisted on my including this.

Which gives me a fine opportunity to explain. You may wonder who selected these stories. Except for this one, I did, choosing my best work to the best of my poor ability. You have every right to disagree, but don't tell me if you do; it won't accomplish a thing. Tell Tor Books instead. Name your favorite, and demand that it be included in a second volume.

If enough of you do that, there will be one—chosen by you.